TS 8-6-12

CIRCULATE AS IS

The Blue and Distant Hills

JUDITH SAXTON

The Blue
and
Distant Hills

St. Martin's Press
New York

Library of Congress Cataloging-in-Publication Data

Saxton, Judith.
The blue and distant hills / Judith Saxton.
p.   cm.
ISBN 0-312-10944-X
1. Inheritance and succession—England—Shropshire—
History—20th century—Fiction. 2. Man-woman
relationships—England—Shropshire—Fiction. 3. Young
women—England—Shropshire—Fiction. 4. Orphans—
England—Shropshire—Fiction. 5. Shropshire (England)—
Fiction. I. Title.
PR6069.A97B58   1994
823'.914—dc20   94-1928   CIP

First published in Great Britain by William Heinemann.

First U.S. Edition: May 1994
10 9 8 7 6 5 4 3 2 1

For Linda,
Terry and Jocelyn Wood,
with lots of love

Acknowledgements

I should like to thank everyone in the Clun area
of south Shropshire who helped me with snippets
about life there in the 1940s, and Marina Thomas
and the staff of the Wrexham Branch Library,
who did their usual magnificent job
of chasing essential books for me.

The Blue and Distant Hills

Prologue

Autumn 1941

She had been picking grapes all day, stopping when the others did, eagerly devouring a slab of bread and a handful of olives, drinking the thin first pressing mixed with water, because at twelve years old one is still considered more child than woman, even in Italy.

She glanced down at herself; her fingers and the palms of her hands were dyed purple, there were streaks of juice down the front of her smock and she had to keep on wiping off the sweat which trickled down her face, so she knew her face must be dirty too.

It was a good job her father couldn't see her now; she smiled to herself at the thought. She remembered the neat suburban house, the pretty garden, the school she attended daily and how hot under the collar her father got over the uniform – it had to be just right because otherwise, he said, the teachers would say he wasn't a good father to her.

He wanted to be a good father – and he was, she thought. She had never known her mother but Daddy made up for the lack. Before they came to Italy he had been teaching her to play tennis; she smiled to herself, remembering that day on the local grass courts, her father patiently throwing a ball across the net until she could hit it back to him hard and low.

She picked another bunch of grapes, then put some into her mouth. So sweet, so juicy ... Daddy loved grapes, there was often a bunch on the sideboard. He sang a song about grapes, too ... about Marguerita treading grapes. She began to hum it under her breath.

From higher up the hillside, someone called her name. She

looked up, shading her face with her hand. It was her aunt, coming down the terraces, her step quick, confident.

'Yes? What is it?'

She spoke in English, her mind still with her father so that it seemed natural to use her native tongue, but even as she did so she saw the grey-clad figure of a German foot-soldier walking down the road, his gun on his arm, his eyes searching the pickers.

She went cold. Fear almost stopped her breath. Next to her, old Arturo continued placidly to pick but he made a sign, plain as words. 'Calm down, pick, ignore him!'

She obeyed, trembling. What a fool she had been! After spending so much time pretending she was just another peasant she would go and forget herself with a German soldier only fifty feet from her. I'll never do it again, she promised the fates, keeping her head down and picking feverishly. I'll never think of home again, I'll put it right out of my head; Daddy will understand, he'll know it's the sensible thing to do.

The soldier had stopped. Someone handed him a bunch of grapes; he took them, grinned, congratulated them on the crop in bad Italian, then continued down the hill.

She tried to relax but the trembling continued. Next time she might not be so lucky. So there must never be a next time. She was not English, she had no father waiting for her, she was the daughter of an Italian peasant who could neither read nor write, she wanted only to work on the land, eat, sleep sound at night.

She did not speak English again for five years.

One

1947

It was a bitter January day and as Questa came up the steps from the underground station in Piccadilly Circus, it started to snow. The flakes, large and lazy, drifted down, landing on heads, shoulders, skin, on the dirty pavements, on window ledges and on vehicles as they drove past, windscreen wipers beginning to creak into action. Passing Londoners, all in a hurry, all self-absorbed, glanced skywards with looks of disgust, then turned up their coat collars and hurried on their way.

Snow! Questa thought. Had it snowed when she had lived here, long ago? She had a vague memory of snow, lying like a white blanket across a suburban garden, of her father shovelling it clear, pushing it into white mountains until he was red-faced, sweating, helping her to make the biggest snowball in the world … or was that just a dream, dreamed to help her to remember England when she was far away? Had the reality been very different – a churned-up mess, grey and slushy, which had skidded under their feet as they walked, hand in hand, back from the shops? Like this London snow was now, on pavement and roadside?

It was the saddest thing, she thought, from the shelter of a doorway where she could watch the flakes whirling past, how memories let you down, tricked you. She had been ten in 1939 when they had left England for a few weeks to stay with her mother's family in the delicious warmth and sunshine of north-ern Italy – and now she was seventeen, a woman, and back here for the first time for seven years. She had hoarded her memories of England, taking them out in her darkest moments, examining them, re-living them. But they had grown vague and pale beside

3

the unpleasant reality of wartime Italy and now, when the memories could have comforted, helped even, they were unreliable. A sort of mixture of fairy-stories she had been told, her father's memories of his own childhood and the dim reality which she could sometimes snatch from her mind's hotchpotch of recollection.

And what had hurt most was her realisation, one day, that she could no longer see her beloved father's face in her mind's eye. She knew he was fair-haired and blue-eyed, she knew he had loved her as much as she loved him, and there it stopped. His face, his figure, and their life together had slid into oblivion whilst she struggled to remain alive, and there seemed nothing she could do to bring it back.

She remembered stories, though, particularly stories of Daddy's childhood when he had spent his holidays staying with an uncle, in the country. Because in Italy she had lived in the country too, though rarely under one roof for very long. But she had worked on the land, and whilst doing the dullest, hardest, most repetitive farm work, she had derived much comfort from remembering Daddy's stories of helping on the farm, fishing, watching the oats being harvested, the cows being milked, the barley cut, whilst his uncle's gardener hoed between the rows of vegetables in the kitchen garden and told the small Charles Adamson how his father – Questa's grandfather – had learned all his horticultural skills in this very spot.

The first ten years of her own childhood had been spent in a small semi-detached house just outside Slough. Her mother had died before she was two and Questa could not remember her any more clearly than she could remember Daddy, but she remembered Mrs Harris who cleaned and cooked for them five days a week, still, after seven years or more, seeing in her mind's eye the round, bright blue eyes, the small, pursed mouth, the mole on Mrs Harris's rather receding chin. Yet almost everything else had gone in the peculiar, selective fog which had cut Questa off from her past almost as thoroughly as her Italian relatives had urged, all in the cause of fooling the Germans, convincing them that she was just another Italian village brat and as such would not interest them.

Life before the war must have been hard on her father, particularly at weekends, when Mrs Harris was off duty and he would have had to rely on Questa to help, she thought, and wondered what use a child of her age could possibly have been. She had podded peas, she had a clear recollection of sitting on a chair in the sun, with a pan beside her and a quantity of peapods lying in her pink cotton lap. Or had that happened in Italy? Only she did not recall ever owning a pink cotton skirt whilst in Italy; she had been dressed as cheaply and unobtrusively as possible by old Aunt Vittorina, with whom she had lived when the family had smuggled her away from Rome and down to southern Italy after the Germans came. In the terrible years which followed she had succeeded in forgetting so much of that earlier English life that now, when she was free to let her mind roam back, it refused to go. It simply cut out in mid-recollection, leaving her frustrated and tearful. With enormous effort, she could just about bring her own pre-war bedroom to mind – pink walls, white paintwork, a patchwork quilt on the bed, teddy sitting on the windowsill – but the rest of the house was a blur.

'Excuse *me*; we've not all got time to 'ang arahnd gettin' in people's way … shove over!'

A pert, sharp-faced girl pushed her needlessly to one side and went through the door in front of which Questa had been hovering. Questa flinched away; she could not bear to be touched, especially in anger, and English, which had once been her first language, still sounded strange to her, almost foreign. But the girl's attitude, and the push, spoke as strongly as words and Questa felt the blood rush to her cheeks. She shrank back against the window pane beside her; was it forbidden to stand in doorways then, to keep out of the snow? Her coat was thin and shabby, short in the sleeve, too tight across the chest. Her shoes were cheap, cardboardy things with large brass buckles which were already becoming detached. She moved to the front of the doorway and peered doubtfully out. She could no longer see the traffic clearly though she could hear the muffled roar, and the passers-by, pale-faced and grim, were coated in snow, no longer bothering to try to knock it off themselves but concentrating, instead, on getting out of it as fast as possible.

5

Questa sighed and turned up her own coat collar. She picked up her brown paper bag, trying not to notice that it was already beginning to disintegrate where the wet had penetrated. Alan Patterson, her father's best friend as well as his solicitor, had spent nearly a year after the war searching for her without success; she had gone to ground too well, had ended up reluctant to reveal even her own name in case she brought trouble upon herself. She had written to her father of course, giving her address as that of a kindly disposed official, and Alan had written back, explaining that her father had been killed and that she could rely on him, as Charles's executor, to do his best for her. At first she had not been able to believe her father was gone; the pain of acknowledging that she had no one of her own, no refuge to fly to, was too great. But gradually, as the weeks and months passed, she was forced to acknowledge that it was true. Had he been alive her father would have searched till he found her, she knew it. He had loved her so, protected her from everything bad ... she knew from the few letters he had managed to get smuggled into Italy before events overtook them that he was half-mad with worry over their enforced separation.

'I'll come for you,' he had written. 'Darling, take great care of yourself, do as the family tell you, and remember that as soon as it's humanly possible I'll be there.'

In the course of the war she had made her way from Rome in the north right down to the toe of Italy in the south. When it ended she had made her way back to Rome, but even in the relative quiet of peacetime it had taken a good while. Her mother's family were scattered, and asking questions was a dangerous thing to do; besides, it was pointless. They would be no keener to see her now than they had been during the war. It was in Rome that she had contacted Alan and eventually received his letter telling her of her father's death. She had been stunned as well as bereft, and for a long time her attempts to convince someone that she was English and should be repatriated were half-hearted. What was the point? Without her father England held no charms. Yet she knew she could not stay in Italy; she was a stranger here, now the conflict had ended, with no sort of standing. She would have to go back to Britain.

So she had written to Alan again, not knowing what else to do, and he had answered immediately, with a letter full of warmth and friendship. She had desperately needed that warmth, that friendship. He explained that he could not come for her, instead she must come to him. He had spent eight long months in Italy trying to find her, now he must remain with his firm or there would be no firm to remain with. Accordingly, he enclosed money for her journey and instructions on how to find his office in London – it was down a small side-street not far from the Piccadilly Circus underground. He had offered to meet her train but, even with her fare, getting out of Italy had been a major task for a skinny, underfed girl who spoke Italian like a native and could only lisp uncertain, half-remembered English. What was more, her looks were against her. She had her mother's large, dark eyes and dark hair and her skin was deeply tanned after years of working out of doors in all weathers. Displaced children were many and it had taken her the best part of a year to find someone who believed she really was Questa Adamson, someone who could get her the documentation necessary to leave the country.

At that point she had sent Alan a postcard, telling him she was on her way. No doubt he would have met her if she could have told him which train, which ship, she would arrive on, but the dignity of such foreknowledge was denied her. She waited and waited, being told one thing one day and something entirely different the next, and finally found herself on a ship bound for Southampton with a morose woman called Rosie Ellis in nominal charge of her, which meant Rosie had taken her into the dining saloon on their first day out and had pointedly ignored her for the rest of the voyage whilst flirting heavily with every man on the ship. When they docked Mrs Ellis had put her on a train, told her, in Italian fortunately, to get out when she reached the terminus and make her way to Piccadilly Circus, and abandoned her.

Alan had told her which exit from the underground to use, then he had said she must turn right. She had been very confused in the warmth and brightness of the tube station by all the people and noise, but she thought she had done as he advised.

Fortunately she had only to follow the instructions and keep her head, it was not necessary to speak to anyone. And now, since the snow was clearly not going to stop but would probably get worse, she might as well move.

She stepped on to the wet pavement. To her alarm it seemed to be getting darker – street lamps were glowing through the thickening flakes and the sky overhead was threatening. She quickened her pace; she had no desire to be caught out by darkness as well as snow – she must reach Mr Patterson's offices before night fell.

It was hard to see the street names, but her eye-sight was excellent and she spotted Tyler Street at last and made for it. Down here, first right, right again and …

Above a fruiterer's, he had said. She glanced doubtfully into the window of the small shop; some cabbages. Were cabbages fruit? But there, on a narrow, black-painted door, was a small brass plate: *Clark, Patterson & Clark, Solicitors, Commissioners for Oaths.*

She pushed tentatively at the door and it gave beneath her hand. Behind it, a flight of dusty wooden stairs led up and out of sight. Gingerly she mounted them. At the top was a tiny, square landing, as dirty and deserted as the stairs. There were three doors leading off it, one to the left, one to the right, one straight before her. The one to the left said 'Enquiries', the one straight ahead said, unkindly, 'Private' and the one to the right said 'Please knock and wait'.

It is usually easier to do as you are told; Questa knocked timidly and waited. No one came. Nothing stirred. She could hear street noises vaguely and other noises, tapping, clicking, but no voice booming at her to enter, or even to go away.

She waited another minute or so, then turned to 'Enquiries'. So far as she could remember, enquire was a questioning sort of word and since she was here to ask questions … She took hold of the handle and opened the door. It led into a small, square room where an elderly woman rattled away on a typewriter and a youngish man in a sleeveless Fair Isle pullover sat apparently counting a pile of papers. The room was dark and crowded with big metal filing cabinets, documents, shelves of dull-looking

8

books and several ugly office chairs. There was a window with a tired houseplant leaning against the dirty glass, whilst beside the plant on the narrow windowsill stood a collection of chipped cups and saucers. The young man had a pencil behind his ear and what looked like a red rubber thimble on one finger, and he was flicking the sheets over at a tremendous rate, muttering to himself as he did so.

'Seventy-eight, seventy-nine ... Can I 'elp you, duck?'

He gave her a tight little grin as he spoke and Questa could tell he thought her younger than she really was. The English expected a woman to look like one and not like a skinny boy, she concluded. She had chopped off her hair because, cropped short, it attracted fewer small, unpleasant visitors. But this, of course, would not occur to the English, who had not had to fight in the fields and woods, or to suffer starvation or enemy aliens in their homes; one must remember that. Though the faces in the streets were tired and cross, their plain, dull clothing was of good quality and people looked fed, if not well fed.

'I want to see Signor Patterson,' Questa said carefully. She had rehearsed this over and over. 'I am Questa Adamson.'

The elderly typist looked up. Her eyebrows rose towards her hairline but then she smiled and stood up, giving the young man a quick, reproachful shake of the head.

'Good afternoon, Miss Adamson, we've been expecting you. I trust you had a good journey?'

'Umm ... good,' Questa confirmed. 'Quite good. Umm ...'

Her English had suddenly fled as though it truly wished to embarrass her, but even as she felt the hot blood rise to her cheeks the woman was moving across the room and taking what looked like an elderly telephone down from the wall. She jiggled something on the rest, then turned and smiled at Questa again, as though no more words were necessary, and spoke into the receiver.

'Mr Patterson? Miss Adamson has arrived. Yes, sir. Right away, sir.'

She put the receiver down and turned to Questa.

'Mr Patterson says I'm to take you through right away,' she said. 'Mr Bancroft, perhaps you would like to put the kettle on?'

'Sure, Miss Emms,' the young man said. 'D'you take sugar, miss?'

'Do you take sugar *Miss Adamson*,' Miss Emms said rather reproachfully. 'It's all right, put the sugar in a bowl on the tray, then Miss Adamson can help herself.'

Conditions in Italy were chaotic; sugar was available on the black market, but Questa had not seen a whole bowlful of it for a long time. She knew that rationing was still in force in England because she had been issued with a temporary ration card, but a bowl full of sugar? Had she misunderstood? It seemed very likely.

But Miss Emms had opened the office door and was waiting, so Questa, clutching her sodden paper carrier, obediently followed her out of the room. Miss Emms tapped briskly, not on the door marked 'Please knock and wait', but on the door marked 'Private', and a voice bade her enter.

She stood in the doorway, holding the door for Questa, beckoning her inside with a slight but unmistakable jerk of the head.

'Miss Adamson, this is Mr Patterson,' she said, very formally. And then Questa was inside the room and the door was closing softly behind her.

Alan Patterson put the telephone down and gazed expectantly at the closed door, ready to spring to his feet as soon as it opened. He had awaited this moment with a good deal of curiosity. What would she be like, the child of his best friend, the man who had fought beside him, been killed beside him? Charles Adamson was fair-haired, blue-eyed, a humorous man with an easy-going, affectionate nature. He had died bravely, as he had lived, driving his jeep up to a food store in the desert in an endeavour to obtain extra supplies for his men, not knowing it had been booby-trapped until the mines exploded under him.

Alan had been lucky to escape with his own life, would not have escaped had Charles not dropped him off to hide behind an ancient building half buried in sand, insisting that he go on to the store alone.

'You can join me as soon as I tell you the coast's clear,' he had said. 'No point in both of us running into trouble.'

But he had not expected the booby-traps, he had thought that

German forces might be loading up and they might walk straight into them, because it was a German dump.

Charles had not died at once, either. Alan had rushed across the sand and tried to pull his friend clear of the burning jeep, but it was too late. Alan had only long enough to grin, to say 'I told you so, Pat!' and then his face had changed, as though he suddenly knew, and he had mumbled, 'Find Questa for me when this lot's over,' and had died in Alan's arms.

The child had meant a lot to Charles, though he was in some ways a careless parent, Alan thought. His passion for archaeology, for quite literally digging up the past, had sometimes caused him to be casual about leaving the child in the charge of others. He had certainly loved his beautiful, intelligent Italian wife, had been heartbroken for several months after her death. But he had concentrated, during that time, on his daughter, and right from the start the small girl had adored him, with the sort of uncritical devotion only a child can give. And though Alan might have been privately uneasy over of some of Charles's actions, as the executor of his friend's will he acknowledged that his friend had done his best to protect Questa and to give her the sort of life that he and Fortunata would have wanted for their daughter.

Most of it had been wasted, though, since she did not go to the English boarding school which Charles had put her name down for, and because he had put his money into War Bonds, God alone knew when the young woman – for she was no longer a child – would be able to draw them.

But there was Eagles Court; that would be an incentive, he hoped, to stay in England.

The door opened. Miss Emms stood there, pulling a very odd sort of face; a warning face, he supposed vaguely. Why should she warn him? What could she be trying to say?

He looked past her – and immediately knew. A creature with savagely cropped black hair and the enormous, starting eyes of a terrified deer stood in the doorway. She could have been a boy of twelve, so thin and straight was she, and the travel-stained coat, the shoes on her bare feet, did nothing to lessen that first impression. He had hoped for – perhaps expected – either Charles's fairness and charm or Fortunata's striking beauty, but this poor little scrap had neither. She was just a frightened kid, gawky and sallow, standing there staring at him, her mouth drooping as though she expected him to shout. Was this, could this be, the offspring of handsome blond Charles and striking Fortunata? But despite appearances he knew she was no impostor. She had gone into the embassy in Rome and showed them the tiny, thin gold bangle which he had given her as a christening present, the only thing she had managed to keep, she explained, from 'before'. Now, as she raised a hand nervously to her mouth, he saw the gold of it shining on her skinny wrist.

Secretly he was upset and shocked by her looks and attitude, the way she stood there, forcing herself not to turn and run, but he was far too experienced to make the mistake of letting her know it. He was on his feet in one smooth movement, a hand held out, a welcoming smile on his face.

'My dear Miss Adamson – or may I call you Questa? I feel as though I've known you for a long time, although this is our first meeting since you were a toddler. But your father and I were such old friends ... at school, then university, then in the Army together ... let me take your coat.'

He spoke slowly and with care, realising that English no longer came easily to her. She responded with a guarded and uncertain smile but she made no attempt to shake his hand; indeed, she did quite the opposite, thrusting her own small fists deep into her coat pockets so that he was forced to change the gesture into a sort of foolish salute. But she inclined her head in a way at once queenly and submissive, before beginning to unfasten her coat.

'Hello, Mr Patterson; it is very nice to meet you,' she said with brittle formality. 'Outside, it snows.'

'Indeed it does; what a dreary welcome home, Questa.' She was such a child, he considered, that even though she was seventeen she was unlikely to object to his using her first name. He continued to speak, but this time in his own slow, careful Italian: 'I am sorry it is snowing on your very first day in England; I mean to take you out to dinner before booking you into a hotel but your coat does not look very warm. Never mind, we will travel by taxi. I may call you by your first name, may I? And you must call me Alan, like your father did.'

12

This time her smile was warmer and her eyes lit with interest. With considerable dismay, Alan realised that she had probably not understood anything he had said to her in English. What a handicap! And how on earth would she manage in the days ahead? But she was talking jerkily, her hands flickering as she spoke, her eyes fixed on his face. Suddenly he saw a fleeting resemblance to Fortunata, though her present starveling state made it hard to reconcile her looks with Fortunata's remembered poise and beauty.

'Oh, you speak Italian! As for the snow, what does it matter that there is a little snow, a little cold? But it matters that I seem to have forgotten my English ... it is so embarrassing ... I am so sorry.'

Alan shook his head, pulling a rueful face. 'My grasp of Italian is far from perfect,' he admitted. 'I'm afraid I'm rusty, though when I was searching for you I spoke it almost daily. We will both improve, no doubt.'

'And my English is rusty also,' she agreed sadly. She continued in her rapid, lilting Italian, 'I've not spoken it, you see, for many years. It is strange to hear it all around me.'

'It must be,' Alan said. 'But you're young, you'll learn fast. Look, my dear, we have a lot to discuss but you're later than I expected so I suggest we talk over a meal. I'll ring the general office and get Bancroft to find us a taxi ...'

She looked disappointed. She stared down at the floor for a moment, then looked up at him and spoke in English.

'But there is a bowl of sugar ... it is for me, the lady said ...'

'Miss Emms? Oh lord, I asked for tea when you arrived but I hadn't realised you'd be so late. Look, I'll tell her to forget the tea for today and we can ...'

A knock on the door interrupted him. He opened it and Miss Emms, carrying a loaded tea-tray, came into the room. She smiled warmly at Questa.

'Here we are, Miss Adamson, a nice cup of tea,' she said cheerfully. 'D'you want Mr Bancroft to get a taxi, sir, whilst you drink it? Because it's getting on for five o'clock and the wretched things are like gold dust once the rush hour starts.'

'Order it now, then. We'll put plenty of milk in and be down in two shakes.' He turned to Questa. 'Can you drink your tea quickly, my dear? I don't want to keep the taxi waiting.'

She nodded. He thought she had understood the gist of his remark even though he had spoken in English.

'Good. Thank you, Miss Emms.'

Questa looked at him, then at the tea-tray, then at the cup of tea he had just poured. She picked up the spoon, dug it into the sugar and transferred a heaped spoonful to her cup. She did this twice, then held out the spoon to Alan.

'You would like? It is right you take?'

'Thank you, but I don't take sugar. I see you do!'

'Oh yes, when I can, thank you very much,' Questa said. She gave him another of her small, tight smiles, then picked up the sugar bowl and carefully transferred it to the top of her soggy paper carrier. She had taken a month's sugar ration, Alan saw, in a way he had not actually anticipated. But it would not do to laugh or say he had not meant it quite that literally. Instead, he drank his tea, watching her over the rim.

She sat sedately on the chair, the saucer in one hand and the cup in the other. She drank quickly, neatly; he could see the smooth movements in her throat as the tea went down, then she put the empty cup on the saucer and the saucer on the tray. She wiped the back of her hand across her mouth, then stood up.

'I'm ready,' she announced. 'You did say drink quick?'

'Well done! Yes, I did. Umm ... shall I ask Miss Emms if she can find a paper bag for the sugar?'

'Oh, I'm so sorry, of course the bowl is hers; I did not think,' Questa said, looking stricken. She took the sugar bowl out of her bag and stood it on the desk, giving it a wistful glance as she did so. 'A ... a bag, did you say?'

'Yes. Wait a moment, perhaps ...'

Alan found a document envelope and poured the sugar carefully into it, then sealed it down and handed it to his guest. She took it hesitantly, watching his face as she did so. Had he let his amusement appear? But after that one long look she seemed satisfied, buttoned her thin coat and opened his office door. She went on to the small landing and leaned over the banister to look down the stairs. 'What a long way down it is! Oh, there's someone ...'

One moment she was leaning over the banister, the next she had flown back into his office. She was white-faced, terrified. He felt his own heart speed up; what had she seen? Someone she knew, or thought she knew?

'What's the matter, Questa?' he said, trying to make his voice matter of fact, though her reaction had shaken him. 'Who's out there? I expect it's only young Bancroft.'

'No.' She shook her head, her voice lowered to a whisper. She was trembling, her hands gripped into white-knuckled fists. 'A man I do not know, a man in uniform.'

Alan went to the banister and leaned over.

'Shan't be a tick,' he called down. 'Wait for us in the cab, would you?'

Returning to the office, he glanced uneasily at his guest. He wanted to take her arm, to pat her hand, but knew he must not. He decided it was best to ignore her trembling but nevertheless he gave her a reassuring smile as he walked beside her to the stairs.

'It's all right,' he said soothingly. 'It's just the taxi driver; they wear heavy greatcoats and peaked caps sometimes ... it's none too warm driving a hansom cab in this sort of weather.'

'Oh.' She stopped on the top step, considering him doubtfully. 'Not a policeman? Not a soldier?'

'No. Neither, I promise you. Just a man who drives a taxi. Come along, Questa, I'm hungry and I expect you are, too.'

She nodded. He could almost see the tension draining out of her as they began to descend the stairs.

'Yes, I am hungry. Is it far to this restaurant?'

He had been going to take her to a smart place in the West End but now, on the spur of the moment, he revised his plans. He hated to think how she would react to a uniformed commission-aire, and the waiters with their noses in the air and their restaurant French would probably confuse her even more than she was confused already.

'It will take us half an hour in the cab,' he said. 'But I think you'll like it. It's a little Italian restaurant called La Bardigiana, and it's quite near the hotel where you'll spend the night. We have a great deal to discuss: your father did not leave you much money but there are other things which have led to certain complications ... but I'll leave business until tomorrow morning. This evening you must have a good, hot meal and then a nice long night's sleep. Tomorrow will be plenty soon enough to discuss what you would like to do. I'll come to your hotel at nine and we'll have our chat in their lounge.'

In the taxi, Questa kept giving him surreptitious glances out of the corner of her eye whenever he was not actually looking at her. She had heard a lot about Alan Patterson from her father, but long, oh so long ago. Daddy's best friend. They had been at the same boarding school though their friendship had not developed until they were in their teens. Once in those early days though, Alan's parents had gone abroad and Charles Adamson had invited him to his Uncle Joshua's house for the summer holidays. That, of course, was before his uncle had decided he was too old to cope with boys.

Perhaps it was after that holiday that they had grown close, going to Cambridge together, where one had studied law – that was Alan – and the other physics – her father, of course. They had joined the army together as well and their friendship made it all bearable, allowed them to joke about the bad times. Her father trusted Alan totally, had written and said as much when he had realised there was no way of getting her out until the war was over.

'Al and I will come and fetch you as soon as hostilities allow,' he had written, sending the letter by heaven knew what circuitous route through neutral countries. 'You'll love Alan, darling; he's the best friend a fellow could possibly have. If anything happens to me – which it won't – you can rely on Alan Patterson completely.'

She did not know quite what she expected of her father's best friend, but this gangling, bespectacled man was not it. She had been surprised by the bowler hat until she remembered her father had always worn one to work, and although she could not remember a thick tweed coat and a briefcase, she was sure that

Charles had also owned such things. But her father had been young and handsome, a hero-figure for a small girl. He had wanted her happiness above everything: she could remember vaguely going bird-watching, wading in ponds with a fishing net and an empty jam-jar, examining their catch of caddis flies, larvae, water nymphs, toadlings, whilst someone – her father, surely – had told her all about their strange and secret lives.

Because he was a widower and therefore as good as a bachelor, he had been much in demand for bridge parties, tea parties, country house parties, yet his social life had come second to Questa, she had never had any doubt of that. He had probably gone away sometimes, for he had a demanding job with one of the largest petroleum companies in the country and a great many friends, but neither was as vital to him as keeping his daughter happy and amused and making sure that, just as he was the most important person in her life, she was the most important person in his.

He had talked about his friend Patterson often and the fog which had dulled so many of Questa's recollections had never crept over talk of Alan Patterson. She could no longer hear her father's voice extolling Alan, but she could remember pretty well what he had said, she thought. Alan was good at all the things her father was good at, he excelled at cricket, tennis, rugger. He was a solicitor, 'a legal eagle', her father assured her. He had always impressed upon her that if for some reason he was not around and she needed help, Alan was the fellow to ask. She could not remember Alan; they must have met quite frequently when she was small, but later Alan had taken up a partnership in Glasgow. It was only after his elder brother's death that he had come down to London to work with his father's old firm.

Questa glanced sideways at him again. He had a thin, serious face and the pallid skin of a man not often out of doors. He looked strained. He had taken his bowler hat off when they got into the taxi and leaned back with a sigh of relief; she thought his head must have ached with the band pressing into his brow. Now she could see that behind the horn-rimmed glasses his eyes were dark and tired-looking and that there were deep frown lines on his forehead. She had noticed, when he walked out to the taxi, that he dragged one foot a trifle and because he was so tall he stooped a bit, but somehow that made him seem more human. He seemed pleasant enough, her father had loved him, yet there was something ... she shrugged internally, knowing that she was suspicious of people now, found it difficult to trust anyone. But he was not at all as she had imagined, he looked older, she knew he was ... her thoughts stopped short. Eight years ago her father had been thirty-five. Had he lived he would have been forty-three. He might even have begun to stoop or to need glasses.

As though he knew what she had been thinking, Alan Patterson turned to her.

'I must have been quite a surprise to you, Questa, since when Charles and I knew each other I didn't wear glasses and hadn't lost much hair,' he said cheerfully. 'But since I've not seen you since you were a toddler with a fat little face and fat little legs, you were a surprise to me too. Now we've met we'll soon get to know each other. Not much further to go, either, though the snow's held us up a bit I'm afraid. Fortunately, my house is quite near the hotel I've chosen for you, so I can reach you easily tomorrow on foot, but I daresay we shan't be able to get much actual work done. I'll get someone to deal with your ration card and so on though.'

Questa murmured something appropriate and turned her attention to the view outside. What she could see of it, that was. Great buildings, half-hidden by the fast-falling flakes, people scurrying past, cars, their headlights fighting a losing battle against the snow, creeping along, hooting at pedestrians who ploughed across the road in front of them. A strange scene, but somehow almost familiar.

'Did it snow when you lived here?' Alan said, once more seeming to divine her thoughts. 'I really can't remember, so much has happened in between.'

'I'm not sure,' Questa murmured. 'I get muddled. We had snow in northern Italy, of course ... sometimes I think I remember things, but often I remember wrong, or I remember my father's stories, not real events. It is strange when you can't tell one from the other.'

Alan patted her arm. She had to steel herself not to flinch, not to move away from him. He would notice such a movement in the close confines of the taxi and he meant nothing but kindness, but she could not bear to be touched.

'I'm sure it is,' he said. 'Did Charles ever tell you ...?'

The story was a loved one, familiar. But as Alan's voice murmured on, the tale reminded her so vividly of her father that it was like a knife twisting in her breast. The tears would not be denied but she sat proudly upright, ignoring them, letting them build and spill, not deigning to acknowledge them by wiping them away.

'And we careered down that hill, three of us on one very small tea-tray,' Alan was saying. 'It was midnight, the moon was just a slip of a thing in the black, frosty sky, and the snow had a crust on it because it had frozen again, so the tray made a lovely whooshing sound as it carried us down that hill. We were ghost-hunting, so we wanted to arrive silently, you see ... but alas for the best-laid plans, the tray hit a fir tree and we were all tipped out on to the snow. Someone's boot caught my nose a terrible blow, Charles slammed into the tree with one shoulder, and Grace landed in a drift and nearly suffocated, or so she claimed. We made so much noise that any self-respecting ghost would have gone long since.'

'Yes, my father told me. That was at Eagles Court, the house he loved,' Questa said stiffly. 'He laughed about it very much. There were many things which made him laugh.'

'True,' Alan said, nodding. 'We all laughed a lot, always. Even when ...'

He stopped short. Questa continued to stare blindly out of the window, but the tears were drying on her cheeks, she would be safe to turn towards him presently.

'Yes?'

'Yes, we laughed a lot,' he said with a sort of determined finality. Questa knew he had been going to say something more but had decided against it. 'Ah, we've arrived. Turn up your coat collar, my dear, run for that doorway – the one with the scarlet canopy, see it? – and wait for me inside whilst I settle with the driver.'

Questa slid out of her seat, grasping her carrier bag. She did not want to go into the restaurant alone but in the event she was saved from what would have been an ordeal by her paper carrier, which simply disintegrated when she climbed out of the taxi. A soiled dress, some underwear and the envelope of sugar fell on to the slush and she scrabbled on the pavement, picking them up, standing with them in her hands, wondering what to do next.

Alan paid off the driver and turned to her. 'Dear me, I was afraid that might happen,' he said. 'The trouble is, I've only my briefcase and ... oh, you weren't carrying much; pop that stuff in here.'

He held the briefcase invitingly open. As she stuffed her few possessions inside, Questa saw that it was empty save for some papers. How strange, to carry a large and quite heavy case around with you almost empty! But it was like the bowler hat, she supposed. It told everyone that you were on your way to or from work, so if they stopped you and questioned you ...

Alan closed the briefcase and accompanied her across the pavement and into the slight shelter of the red canopy, only right now it was so snow-laden that it could have been any colour. He opened the glass panelled door and immediately a wave of warmth, of delicious odours, of pinky-gold light, flooded on to the pavement, enveloping Alan and Questa as they stood in the doorway.

'Here we are,' Alan said cheerfully. 'Let me help you off with your coat.'

She did not particularly want to take her coat off, not even in this new and delicious warmth, but she meekly surrendered it and saw it carried away by a small, swarthy man with greying black hair and an olive complexion. She was wearing a black dress, a horrible, much altered garment which had once belonged to Aunt Vittorina and so was at least three sizes too large. And Questa, who cared nothing for her appearance, was suddenly conscious of the big safety-pin acting instead of a button on the waistband and the white of the tacking cotton showing through on the bodice where she had tried to make it a better fit. She rubbed her arms with her hands, remembering that one sleeve was longer than the other and that both had the nibbled look of wear.

But Alan rose to the occasion. 'I see your dress is more suitable for Italy than for snow,' he said. 'Never mind, this will keep you warm.'

He had taken off his tweed overcoat and now he laid around her shoulders the scarf he had been wearing. Questa glanced down at herself. It was *the scarf*, after all these years – and she had recognised it at once! She drew it around her and disposed it elegantly, as though it were an evening wrap and not a navy, maroon and gold scarf; then she smiled timidly at her companion.

'My father had one – it's your school scarf, isn't it?'

He touched her elbow. Just a feather of a touch, but it said more, Questa thought, than words. Her father had worn his scarf often, in the winter he had wrapped it round his neck and gone out to dig the drive clear. The sight and feel of the scarf had brought memory flooding back, she could remember it now, every detail, it was no dream, it was a fact, it had happened!

'Signore, signorina ... here is a quiet corner table ... the menu ... would the signorina like a drink before her meal?'

Alan smiled at her as the waiter pushed her chair in and fussed around her, then he leaned forward across the starched white tablecloth.

'Would you like a drink, Questa? Or a fruit juice?'

'I heard ... I understood,' Questa said. 'I don't know anything about English drinks. Only lemonade and orange squash, from when I was small.'

'This is an Italian restaurant,' the waiter reminded her. She had spoken in Italian and he followed suit. 'What would you like, signorina? We cannot, alas, squeeze you fresh oranges, but the tinned stuff is quite good.'

'Orange juice is nice,' Questa nodded. She looked around her. Several of the other tables were occupied but no one seemed to be eating. Ah, yes ... someone had some bread ... the water rose to her mouth as she saw it. Food! Nice though orange juice would be, bread would be nicer. She was always hungry and today she had eaten nothing.

As though he could read her thoughts the waiter leaned over and took a round wicker basket off the next table. He put it down between them. It contained a number of delicious-looking bread rolls and, in the middle, a small glass dish of what looked very like butter.

Questa looked at the bread, at her host, at the waiter. Alan held the basket out to her. She took a roll and bit into it ... it was glorious, fresh and soft yet with a crisp crust.

'Have some butter,' Alan said. But it was too late. The roll was gone. She felt ashamed because his bread was still on his side plate, but he picked up the basket and held it out again, smiling. The waiter had left them, so she took another roll and, this time, put it carefully down on her plate. She watched as Alan put a pat of butter on the side of his plate, broke his roll, buttered it, bit, buttered, bit, buttered ... and followed suit. The trouble was, she was so hungry! By the time Alan had eaten his roll she had devoured the other five and was glancing hopefully around. The smell of food was unbelievable; where had the waiter gone? What happened next?

The waiter came back with more bread rolls and her orange juice. He smiled at her and put the basket down. Then he fetched more butter – this time it was in little rolls, dewed with water. But, though he took a roll himself and nodded to her to take one too, Alan told the waiter they would not need the basketful and said that they would order now, please.

It was a wonderful meal. They had minestrone soup, thick and good, with more of the little bread rolls. Then they had spaghetti in a wonderful sauce with a delicious green vegetable which she did not recognise. They had a beautiful pudding, all air and lightness, the waiter told her it was made with wine and sugar and eggs, and then they had cheese and biscuits and coffee ... real coffee, not the sort you made with earth and acorns.

Questa ate and ate. They did not talk at all, or at least Questa did not, though Alan kept up a flow of little remarks. He asked her a couple of questions at first, then stopped because he must have realised she could not talk and eat, and eating, naturally, was the important thing at mealtimes.

After the cheese and biscuits and the coffee her stomach was so full it actually hurt – she touched it tentatively with her fingertips and it was tight, like a drum or a hardboiled egg. Alan asked her if she would mind if he smoked ... she said she did not mind and wondered what he would have done had she answered differently … and he had a little glass of something which smelt hot and interesting. She would have liked a tiny taste, or even a chance to sniff at the glass, but he did not offer and she was far too conscious of her obligation to him for the wonderful meal to ask any more favours. Instead, she found herself drifting into a pleasant daze in which there were bright lights, laughter, and people dancing past her whilst colours flashed and buzzed in her head.

Someone was shaking her. Very gently but persistently. She opened her eyes and there was Alan, with a cigar smouldering in the ashtray on the table in front of them, smiling down at her and saying that he had not realised how exhausted she must be, and perhaps it would be best if he took her to her hotel now?

She felt foolish, even a little afraid, but everyone was so nice about it. The waiter told her she must come again, the chef would make her something special because she came from his own country – and from the south, which was even better, for didn't we all know that those from the north of Italy were … a gesture, as of extreme hauteur, a hand, fluttering upwards. The man at the next table said she had only done what he always wanted to do after one of Benigno's marvellous meals, and Alan said it was all his fault and the waiter was fetching them a taxi, so if she would just like to stand up, he would help her on with her coat.

'But the hotel is very near,' Questa reminded him, and he smiled and reminded her that it was still snowing, that her coat was thin and her shoes thinner, and that he himself might as well ride back to his flat in a taxi since otherwise he would get soaked.

Still dazed with food and warmth, she allowed herself to be bundled into the taxi and driven a short way, then Alan helped her out, hurried her across a wide pavement, past a large man in maroon and gold braid and into the hotel, which seemed very large and very bright and very impersonal to Questa.

'Don't go,' she whispered when she saw the man in uniform, but Alan said he was just a servant who wanted to take her things up to her room. She did not understand all the following conversation, but gathered that the man was puzzled because she had no suitcase. Alan told several lies here – she admired him for it –

and said that her luggage would be following; it had been lost in Southampton docks, so she would buy some things in the morning, when the shops were open. Then he went to the desk and there were a lot of forms and she signed some and Alan signed some and then, at last, she was led into a little creaking lift-cage which took her slowly upwards until they reached the third floor. The man in uniform carried Alan's briefcase – how absurd, it scarcely weighed anything, why had Alan allowed him to take it, or was it that the man could not function without carrying *something*? – and when they reached the room he put the briefcase down and Alan fumbled in his pocket and money clinked, changed hands.

The uniformed one stood back and Alan said he would leave the briefcase with her and would see her at nine o'clock in the morning, in the lounge. Then he and the uniformed one exchanged a few low-voiced remarks and Alan said that he would see her in the dining room, since he had decided to have breakfast at the hotel next day.

'Sleep well, my dear,' he said in the doorway.

Then they left.

Questa looked around the room. It was nice. A square of pink carpet, a basin in one corner with two taps – she went over and experimented and one really did have hot water inside it – pink curtains at the window, already pulled across to shut out the night, a small chair and a dressing table and mirror. The bed was best of all, though. It had sheets and blankets, two pillows, a pretty coverlet and a table beside it. She went over to the curtains and pulled one back a little. Outside the dark seemed to press against the panes and she could see the big flakes still chasing each other to earth. What was more, as she stood there, she could feel warmth. It was a radiator, hot to the touch.

She would have liked a wash in hot water, but decided she was simply too tired, she could not keep her eyes open another minute. Accordingly she threw her coat and Alan's school scarf across the chair, kicked off her buckled shoes and pulled the black dress over her head, then got straight into bed, as she was.

The bed was cold but she was so warm herself, so full of food, that in a matter of moments she was comfortable. She curled round, one hand under the pillow, the other rubbing hypnotically against the edge of blanket pulled close to her chin. She intended to re-live her day, from the moment she left the ship until now, but too much had happened, too many thoughts and feelings jostled in her tired brain. In a matter of moments she was fast asleep.

The breakfast meeting went well. Questa, with her cropped hair washed and brushed and her thin face shining with soap and water, was alert and wide awake. Her black dress looked even shabbier in the strong morning light, and her painful thinness could not be disguised, but she was sitting at the table tucking into her breakfast with gusto when Alan came into the dining room. She had before her a boiled egg and a pile of bread and butter, a coffee pot, a jar of marmalade and an empty cereal dish. He slipped into the seat opposite hers and smiled a good morning.

During the night he had thought long and hard about this poor waif, and had decided that he would feel happier if she could see a doctor. It could not be normal for a young woman of seventeen, going on eighteen, to look just like a very young, unformed boy. I'll send her to Rachel Barnes; she's a doctor now and she was a good friend of ours before the war, he decided at last. Rachel would make sure Questa wasn't suffering from some awful wasting disease and then she could tell Alan what best to do with his protégée.

'Good morning,' Questa said politely. 'I *remembered* porridge; isn't it delicious?'

'And you charmed an egg out of them, I see,' Alan said approvingly. 'To say nothing of all that bread and butter.'

'They gave me an egg,' Questa admitted. 'I woke up very hungry. I had two bowls of porridge first.'

'The waiter approached the table. He looked disapprovingly at Alan.

'Miss, is this gentleman ...'

'It's all right,' Alan said quickly, guessing what was to follow. 'I'm Miss Adamson's solicitor, we're having a meeting over breakfast so if you would just bring me coffee and toast ...'

25

'You can have some of my bread and butter,' Questa said gloomily.

'It's all right, miss,' the waiter said. He sounded fatherly. 'I'll fetch the gentleman a breakfast of his own with plenty of bread and butter. It won't take but a minute.'

'Ah, good,' Questa said, digging her spoon into her egg. She sliced the bread into fingers, then looked around them. The hotel was mainly used by business people so at nine-thirty they were alone in the dining room. Apparently comforted by this, she began to dip the fingers of bread and butter into the yolk of her egg. 'I think here comes your breakfast.'

Alan had a round of bread and butter, but since the coffee was hot and strong and the toast crisp, he had no grumbles over the food. He did not make the mistake of trying to talk to Questa whilst she ate – he had seen the error of his ways the previous evening – but as soon as she had crunched down her last piece of toast and leaned back in her chair he poured them both another cup of coffee, cleared his throat and began.

'Now Questa, I didn't want to go into too much detail when I wrote, but your father's house was hit by one of the V2 flying bombs three years ago, and totally destroyed. The house was rented, but the furniture would have been yours ... I am sorry to be the bearer of such bad news but clearly you will need to know where you stand financially. However, there was a little money which your father had put aside, though he bought War Bonds with most of his savings and I don't know when it will be possible to redeem them. Still, he had some money in the Post Office which you will have in a few weeks, when we've cut through the legal tangles.'

'I see.'

'It isn't very much money, but there is something, despite the loss of the house and contents.'

They were speaking Italian. Questa nodded, her eyes on his face.

'I see. So there is nowhere for me to live, then.'

'Her voice was low, resigned. Alan wanted to hug her, reassure her. Had she been ten years younger – or ten years older, probably – he would have done just that; as it was he could only smile and try to put all his sympathy into his expression. He had noted her quick withdrawal the previous day from anything resembling physical contact and had supposed, vaguely, that it must have something to do with her experiences in Italy. He found himself reluctant to enquire what these had been, and no doubt Questa would be equally reluctant to talk about them, for a while at any rate.

'Nowhere in London, anyway. But did your father ever speak of a house called Eagles Court, in Shropshire?'

Her eyes brightened and she nodded vigorously, with more animation than she had yet shown. 'Yes, he did. It was the family home for many years, it belonged to his Uncle Joshua. My great-uncle. Daddy spent all his school holidays there, didn't he? He took you there – that was where you and he went ghost-hunting in the snow.'

'That's right. I went only once, whilst my parents were abroad, but Charlie spent most of his time there when he wasn't in school. His parents were in the diplomatic service and though he did go abroad he much preferred Eagles Court. Unfortunately the year he was sixteen there was a row of some sort ... Anyway, your father didn't go near the place again for several years. Uncle Joshua never asked him, you see, and so Charles couldn't go. It must have been like being shut out of Eden for Charles, but Joshua never married so he had no heirs to leave the place to, and underneath it all I believe he was very fond of your father. What's more, there's an entail; that means the property has to stay in the family.'

Questa frowned. 'I understand that; to hurt one's family and leave property away from them would be very wrong,' she said. 'Would great-uncle let me live there with him, is that what you are trying to say? I could be very useful, I know a great deal about living in the country.'

'Unfortunately, Questa, your great-uncle died more than three years ago. He had willed Eagles Court to your father and your father, in his turn, willed everything he possessed to you. Fortunately, there is no law which says the distaff side of the family may not inherit, but anyway so far as we know there are no male heirs extant.'

She blinked. He had spoken in Italian but even so it was a bit of a mouthful, he supposed ruefully. She had probably understood only one word in ten. But he underrated her. After a thoughtful pause, she said:

'Legally a woman may inherit, even if she's under age, as I am? But since there are no male heirs, I suppose the law has little choice. Does that mean I *do* have somewhere to live, then?'

'Well, let us say you are the owner of a considerable property, though whether it's in a fit state for anyone to live there ... The army took it over during the war, you see, and many of the properties they requisitioned needed a great deal of work when they left. They went from Eagles Court in 1945, two years ago, and so far as I know no one's set foot in it since. I ought to have visited it on your behalf but having spent so long in Italy searching for you, I've not dared to leave the business again to go down to Shropshire.'

Questa's dark eyes were glowing and there was a faint flush of colour in her cheeks. Alan saw again a glimpse of Fortunata and thought that the child might one day be beautiful, but then it was gone and she looked down at the cloth, her mouth drooping.

'But how can I get to Shropshire? I must get a job, find some way to support myself.'

'There's enough money in your father's savings account to keep you for a while,' Alan said guardedly. He did not want to start delving too deeply into Charles's financial affairs at this stage. Explaining about War Bonds would not be easy, for a start, since the government, which had happily borrowed the money, seemed far less inclined to pay it back. 'Your great-uncle's estate will pay out for things like hotel bills. You are the heiress, after all, and must be able to take your time deciding what to do with your inheritance.' He paused again, eyeing her thoughtfully. She was intelligent, but without a good grasp of the language she would be at a tremendous disadvantage with estate agents, servants and so on.

'Whilst you can't sell, you can most certainly rent or lease the property to an interested landowner, say. However, work may be needed in it before such a thing is possible so I suggest we wait until we've seen the property for ourselves. And since there's very little point in either of us going down to Eagles Court whilst this snow lasts, and you will need to improve your grasp of the language before you can ask the right questions of the right people, I suggest you move into a cheap room in a guest-house perhaps, rather than a hotel, and concentrate on polishing up your English for a week or two. And I'm going to take you along to an old friend of your father's, Doctor Rachel Barnes. She has consulting rooms in Harley Street, she's a charming woman, you'll like her. She'll be able to confirm that you are in good health and tell us how to make sure you stay fit. You are very thin, Questa, and the weather here is different from that of Italy. Dr Barnes will help you regain your normal weight as soon as possible. I suggest that you visit her weekly for a month or two and then in say, March, we can talk again.'

'A lady doctor! Well, I know I'm thin and I cough a lot, but I don't think I'm ill. She is a friend of yours? And of my father, also?' At his nod she smiled. 'Very well, I will go to her consulting rooms. And who will help me to re-learn English, then? You?'

He laughed, shaking his head. 'No, I'll send you to a language school. It's a bit like sending you to see Dr Barnes; I can see you're too thin but I don't know what to do to make you fat and jolly, and I can hear that your English isn't quite right, but I can't tell you how to speak it properly again. The language school are the experts, they'll have you talking – and understanding – English in a very short time. The snow can't last for ever either, so by the time you can speak English properly you'll be fatter and fitter and we'll be able to set off for Eagles Court.'

'I see,' she said. She looked lost and scared. Alan thought remorsefully that this was all too much for anyone to take in, but she had to come to terms with it herself. He could only help her to a certain extent.

'I think the first thing the doctor will say is that I need warmer clothes for this climate. Are there shops? Will there be some money for a jersey, perhaps?'

'Yes, I'm sure the doctor will insist that you are properly clothed. There are a great many shops which cater for youngsters, though you'll need clothing coupons ... I can take you up West on a Saturday, when I'm not working ... no, I've a better idea.

Look, you spend a quiet day here, I'll arrange for them to serve you some lunch and I'll join you at dinner. I think I know someone who might be able to help you with clothes and so on. Not Dr Barnes, she's a busy woman, but my secretary, Miss Emms – you met her yesterday.'

'Thank you,' Questa said dully. Alan felt very sorry for her. Dragged from one culture to another, from one country to another, dumped in a small hotel on the outskirts of the city, told to amuse herself … and with the cold so bitter, the snow so thick, that even now, glancing out of the window, he could not see across the pavement. But she was a survivor, she would survive this too; in a day or so, when the snow cleared, she would get the visit to the doctor over, begin her lessons and make friends, start to enjoy life.

Two

It snowed for a month. Train services were disrupted, roads blocked, the tram points froze so that the trams were stranded all over the place like great, useless whales, and food, scarce ever since the war, suddenly became almost unobtainable. London was full of unemployed, and the electricity had to be cut off because it was being drained by people desperate for warmth, so yet more shops and offices closed.

It grew worse, not better. Street lighting went off, the underground could no longer function. And the cold! It seemed to freeze one's very blood, it was impossible to get warm; meals – when you got them – were nearly always eaten cold. For Questa, who had come lately from Italian sunshine, it was a severe test of purpose. But she soldiered on because now that she knew about Eagles Court, she had a goal ahead. She went daily to the language school, did her best to keep cheerful and hardly ever grumbled. And despite her secret fears, she liked Dr Rachel Barnes and got on well with her.

The first visit was a bit daunting, however. Dr Barnes had her consulting rooms in a big, old-fashioned Victorian mansion with three steps up to the front door and a wide, marbled hall which patients had to cross to reach the receptionist. The receptionist was a dragon in her sixties with white hair set stiff as a board, blue-painted eyelids and a basilisk stare. When Questa got to know her better she realised that a certain fierce efficiency was necessary to deal with the rich patients of the half-dozen doctors who shared the premises, but on that first day she was overawed and jumped every time the older woman spoke.

Alan went with Questa on that first visit and she was glad of his company, though she did her best not to show it. She talked very little but sat in a black leather armchair and pretended to read a glossy magazine so old that the pages were falling apart, whilst her heart beat a tattoo so loud that she could scarcely hear when Alan spoke, and her insides alternately screwed up tight or wobbled like a jelly.

'Miss Adamson, please, for Dr Barnes.'

The nurse was all in white with scarlet lips and clumping black lace-up shoes. She told Questa to follow her and led her across the big hall, up a flight of linoleumed stairs and through a white-painted door into a pleasant room with a faded blue carpet and matching curtains, a couch with a couple of hand-crocheted blankets thrown down on it, and a massive mahogany desk, behind which sat a dark-haired woman with a sweet smile and a serene expression.

'Miss Adamson ... may I call you Questa? You and I have met before, though you won't remember; your father brought you to see me when you'd had measles rather badly. You were four or five, quite small. My dear, I'm so very sorry about your father, Charles and I were good friends, but I'm glad that you've come home! Alan told me you've had a pretty grim time ... now you won't want to go into that, but just sit down there and we'll get to know each other. How long have you been in England? And how old are you? I ought to know, but I'm afraid I've forgotten. Presently I'll weigh you and measure you and take a look at you but, as I said, let's talk first.'

She talked of many things, discussed Questa's childhood attack of measles, laughed as she recalled a dinner party at the Adamson house when the small Questa had toddled downstairs in the middle of it, demanding that she, too, should have chicken. But as she talked her shrewd eyes were taking Questa in from top to toe and she interspersed her gentle chit-chat with some searching questions. Since she spoke no Italian they were forced to converse in English, but already Questa could understand almost everything said to her and was beginning to remember whole chunks of the language which she had thought totally forgotten.

'Now I'll take a look at you,' Dr Barnes said at last. 'Would you like to go behind the screen, my dear, and take your clothes off? Then lie on the bed and pull the blanket over you. Call me when you're ready.'

Questa began to shake. She just sat in the chair and shook and stared at the doctor as a bird stares at a snake. Dr Barnes made a small sound of distress and jumped to her feet. She came around the desk and took both Questa's hands in hers, so gently and with such care that for once Questa did not snatch her hands away. The doctor knelt so that they could look into each other's eyes, her gaze so full of compassion and understanding that Questa's fears began to subside. Close to, like this, without the desk between them, she saw that Dr Barnes was quite young and pretty, with a soft, motherly bosom beneath her white coat, and she felt her trembling begin to subside as her confidence in this woman grew.

'Oh my dear child, I'm so sorry! What can I say to you? I would not hurt you for the world, but in order to measure the extent of your debilitation I have to examine you. Don't be afraid … shall I bring my nurse in? Usually I would send for her, but I thought it might be easier if it was just the two of us.'

'I'm sorry. Yes, I'll undress.'

Questa got jerkily to her feet and went behind the screen. She removed the black dress, the woollen vest, knickers and thick grey socks which Miss Emms had acquired for her, and the gaping cardboardy shoes. She climbed on to the couch and looked miserably at her clawlike feet and emaciated, blue-white legs, at the pathetic wisp of pubic hair at the base of her stomach and the way her hip bones protruded. She did not look at her hands, she knew too well what she would see. And even if you did not count her hands she knew other people did not look like she did, so thin and bony and unhealthy. But Dr Barnes was kind, she would understand …

'I'm ready,' she said in a small, shaky voice. 'I'm ready, Dr Barnes.'

'Mr Patterson, if you would come through for a minute? Miss Adamson has gone with nurse to get weighed and measured and to have some vitamins dispensed.'

The receptionist smiled kindly at Alan, who decided she must be nicer than she looked and smiled back. But it was with considerable apprehension that he went into Rachel Barnes's surgery and closed the door behind him. Rachel, writing something on a sheet of paper, looked up, smiled, then capped her pen and laid it down on her blotter.

'Ah, Alan. Well, thank God Charles can't see her now – or Fortunata, for that matter. Poor kid!'

'I know ... but is she as ill as she looks, Ray? She told you she was going to be eighteen in June? That's a matter of months away.'

'She told me. And don't look so worried, Alan, because considering what happened to her, she's remarkably fit. Half-starved, of course, and goodness knows what sort of resistance to disease she has because of it, but the cough is just that, nothing more. Although she's got some patches of dry skin and has been suffering from a variety of minor ills – boils at one stage, then constant head colds, then mouth ulcers – I think with the proper diet and less anxiety, she'll soon pull round.'

'But she's seventeen, Ray, and she hasn't got any ...' Alan's hands made vague motions at his chest ... 'no bust,' he concluded. 'No hips, either. She's just like a couple of boards clapped together.'

'Alan, there's a lot you don't know about women! During the war women living like soldiers or like animals stopped menstruating because they weren't well-nourished, because pregnancy would have killed them. It doesn't matter why womanhood hasn't happened to Questa, what matters is that it hasn't, not yet. She didn't even start her periods when she would normally have done because normality had left her life. She was too busy keeping alive to go through all that puberty business and now her body simply wants time to adjust, plus good food, fresh air and a life-style which isn't fraught with fear and danger. She has been much abused, and part of the defence she has put up has been memory loss and a reluctance to have anything to do with other people. She's scarred, probably mentally worse than physically, but she can recover completely – will, with the right treatment. All she needs is time and the chance to mend, and a simple, uncomplicated life-style plus decent food and eight hours' sleep a night. And no worries, if that's possible. Can you understand that?'

'Yes, I think so. She doesn't like to be touched, and she said something about not being able to remember her pre-war life too well; that all underlines what you've said. I'm her guardian in a way since I'm Charles's executor, but that doesn't mean I can be with her twenty-four hours a day, so I'll have to think how best to guide her. Are you saying that she is, to all intents and purposes, a twelve-year-old, who will reach her proper age some time soon, but until then must be treated as a child?'

Dr Barnes shook her head very decidedly. 'No indeed, Questa would be rightly insulted if you treated her as a child because apart from anything else a twelve-year-old couldn't have had her experiences, her degree of suffering. No, she's only got the physical appearance of a twelve-year-old. Mentally, she's probably older than either of us.'

'Older than ...'

Rachel Barnes laughed. 'Sorry, I'm making things worse, not better. She has seen things and suffered things which we can't imagine, never having lived under enemy occupation. She was taken by the Germans at some stage – she won't tell you about it, she wouldn't tell me – but leave that, for the moment. What you want to know is, will she recover, become a normal young woman of seventeen or so? Well, the answer's yes. She's a tough cookie, to borrow a phrase from our American cousins. It's my belief she'll come through, but she's got a rough road to tread and she's the only one who can tread it; all you can do is give her all the support you can. I'm putting her on a course of vitamins, codliver oil, Radio Malt, orange juice, things like that, and I'll keep my eye on her for a few weeks. Where's she living?'

'In a bed-sit. Alone, I'm afraid. I have a spare room, but she shies away from any sort of closeness, so the bed-sit seemed the answer. Should I try to get her into a hostel or something?'

Dr Barnes shook her head, frowning. 'Not unless she wants it. Let her do what she wants as much as you can, Alan. She's been pushed around too much, she needs to be able to make her own decisions. It's as important for her to be independent and happy as it is to have flesh on her bones; in fact she won't begin to gain weight until she's happy.'

'And ... and the other things, Ray? The young woman things?'

35

Rachel Barnes laughed. 'Oh Alan, don't be afraid to use the right words: menstruation and puberty, you mean! They'll both come, in time. As I said, what she needs most is time, and understanding. Love, too. Love works most miracles, you know. And don't try to force her confidence, because there are things best forgotten and her mind will work that miracle, too, given the opportunity. Incidentally, as you remarked, she can't remember much about her life pre-war; don't be tempted to fill in the details or tell her about it. For some reason her mind has cut off that part of her life; she thinks it will come back and so do I, but I also think she cut it off because she wasn't able to cope with it. So, no matter how you're tempted, don't go giving her little clues, odds and ends of information. Let her mind decide when it's ready to know what went on in the thirties, because by then she'll be able to cope with it.'

'You mean don't tell her about Charles? Or about the sort of life she lived, the things she did? But I should have thought that would have helped her a lot!'

Dr Barnes shook her head. 'No, in fact, quite the reverse. There are things – we both know what they were – which are best forgotten about those years, but in my experience once you start memory stirring it isn't just the pretty things that come back, it's the whole can of worms. Leave her. Let her make her own discoveries, her own revelations. That way she'll come to terms with what she had and with what she's got in its place. Now don't forget, I want to see her once a week for a month and at the end of that time I'll have a much better idea how she's progressing.'

She held out a slim, well-manicured hand. 'Good luck, Alan! She's a nice child; she'll be even nicer as she begins to regain her full health.'

Questa attended her language classes, went once a week to see Dr Barnes to be weighed, measured and assessed, and soldiered on despite the increasingly difficult conditions in an austerity Britain labouring under the worst winter in living memory. She found it easier than most to keep cheerful because of Eagles Court. Alan had dangled it like a carrot before a donkey – her father's beloved home, the place he had most wanted to be.

Whilst it was there, the winter's chill could never swamp her hopeful optimism that better times were just around the corner. But she had dreadful nightmares, and woke in the icy pre-dawn blackness with her heart hammering and sweat channelling down her body, terrified of Them. Even when she woke, she was slow to realise that it was just a dream, that They were not still on her trail.

She could not talk about the nightmares, partly because they made her feel so guilty. She had lived whilst others died, she had somehow managed to eat whilst others starved. She had fallen into German hands but she had lived to tell the tale whilst others, not so desperate, or so quick, or just not so plain lucky, had died hideously.

Even now, in the coldest, blackest winter Britain had known, she knew herself to be fortunate. In Italy they might not have this terrible cold, but hunger would be their constant companion. Bad people would be pushing back into power, stamping on the poor in their struggle to reach the top of the heap. Everything was disorganised, they were still an occupied country. She had had no papers, no credibility; without doubt she would have starved.

Here, the people were used to hardship and rationing. They moaned and grumbled but everyone had something, no one had nothing. You heard no tales of children eating earth or women killed for possessing a bag of turnips.

By mid-February, Questa only popped in to see Dr Barnes for a chat and a quick weigh. She was much better, her cough had disappeared, her painful boils were things of the past, her mouth was clear of the peppering of tiny, agonising ulcers. Even her skin improved, though she did not put on a great deal of weight. Dr Barnes had explained about menstruation, had said that she would find physical changes taking place as she grew stronger and more confident, but as yet she was still just Questa. Having talked to one or two of the girls at the language school, further-more, she was not that keen on menstruation. It sounded painful and a nuisance; Questa thought she could get on very well without it. But she examined her armpits anxiously for some sign that the fluff there was about to turn into what the magazines described as 'unsightly under-arm hair'. When it came, she decided, she would magic it all away with one of the preparations extolled by those same magazines. But as yet her armpits remained clear of anything but pale, wispy fluff.

March came. It came in like a lion and would go out, Questa thought, like an even hungrier one. She was right, though not quite in the way she had meant. In mid-March the Great Freeze thawed and all over the country, from the Bristol Channel to the Wash, the melting ice swelled the rivers and broke their banks. Questa paddled to the shops, for she was becoming a seasoned bed-sit dweller, and queued for dried potato because there were no fresh ones and stood in line for meat, a tiny square of cheese, a few ounces of flour or rice.

The nightmares came almost every night but no one heard her sobs and gradually, as the weeks went on, the dreams came less often and were, for that reason, easier to bear.

Yet for all this the past still haunted her. She was afraid to be alone but in crowds she had attacks of what she thought of as 'the ice terrors', because she would quite literally freeze where she stood, unable to move an inch, consumed by fear; then as suddenly as it had come the feeling would go and she would slowly unclench her fists, lower her chin, feel the sweat break out on her brow. She hated lifts because they were like prisons, and low-ceilinged rooms, underground places, because they reminded her of the Gestapo headquarters where they had taken her for interrogation. She sometimes thought she recognised a face in a crowd and once fainted clean away, so terrified was she. But when she came round she said she had slipped on the icy pavement, and got away with it.

She never spoke of such things to Alan; why should she? They were her personal cross, as her father's death was a personal cross. Inside her head she mourned constantly for her father, the one man in whom she'd had complete trust. She was afraid and ill-at-ease with other men, even Alan. She acknowledged that Alan missed Charles Adamson, mourned him too, in his way, but only she could miss him, mourn him, as the most important person in her life, the person who could have made her into a trusting, affectionate girl again. Alan could not do that; she doubted that anyone could.

In April the floods eased. Questa's English was now excellent, she had found with every day that passed that it came back stronger and more positively, and because she worked so hard her vocabulary was soon better than most. What was more, she was beginning to feel at ease with girls her own age and was getting used to the city. But her most ardent desire was still to go to Eagles Court, which her father had talked of with a wistful longing he was quite unable to disguise. The house might be run-down, but the land over which the young Charles Adamson had played would be unchanged. She would see with her own eyes the woods, the meadows, the mere and the river, the blue and distant hills. They would still be there to be cherished and enjoyed. To be remembered, if only secondhand. Her inheritance.

'We'll go down there in my old bus as soon as the weather's reasonable,' Alan promised. 'But don't expect too much, Questa. It probably won't be fit to live in, and anyway, my advice is to rent it out and live on the proceeds. You like London, don't you? Surely you'll be happier here? Look, I'll introduce you to a – a friend of mine. She's been talking about starting up a little business in a country town, only she needs a partner and some financial help. Perhaps you could get together.'

'A friend? Who is this? Someone my father knew, also?'

They were in Alan's office, Questa perched on the edge of her seat, trying to hide her excitement at the thought of seeing Eagles Court – owning it – whilst Alan leaned back in his swivel-chair, fingers steepled, regarding her. Had he not noticed that April was half over and the weather was beginning to seem springlike even to Questa's prejudiced eyes? How could he talk of businesses and country towns when he had given her momentous news? All she wanted from him right now was the exact date of their departure for Shropshire! But if Alan's friend was a friend of her father's, at least she would listen to the proposal with what patience she could muster.

'Someone …? Oh! well, yes, he did know Grace. But she's a bit younger than us, seems closer to your generation really. You'll like her. Tell you what, why don't we invite her to come down to the Court with us when we go? Then you'll get a woman's eye view of the place as well as hearing what I think.'

'If you like,' Questa said. 'If that means we may go sooner to the Court then bring her, certainly.'

She told herself that she did not mind who accompanied them if it meant that Alan would actually plan a visit instead of putting her off all the time, but it seemed as though Alan's delaying tactics were over at last. A week later, when she answered a knock at the door of her room, there stood Alan, with a woman beside him.

'Ah, Questa, may we come in? This is Grace Syrett, the friend I told you about. Grace, this is Questa Adamson, Charles's daughter.'

Questa murmured politely whilst taking in the older woman's appearance. Grace was tall, almost statuesque, with blonde hair in a pageboy style and lazy blue eyes. She wore a tweed coat in a misty azure shade and elegant, high-heeled black shoes. Her skin was rich and creamy with a dimple next to her mouth which came and went, and when she smiled she showed very white and even teeth.

'Hello, Questa. Nice to meet you at last – Alan often talks about you; I believe we're vaguely related.'

She had a slow, drawling voice, but the eyes which swept Questa from head to foot were shrewd. Questa decided she did not trust this beautiful lady and hoped that foolish, easily led Alan had not been taken in by her. But Grace was a guest in Questa's house, even if the house was only one room. So she thanked her stars that it was tidy and led her visitors over to the gas fire and the two upright chairs beside it.

'Do sit down,' she said politely. 'I'll put the kettle on, then join you.'

There were only two chairs and though she could have boiled the kettle on her primus stove she could not have offered tea since she had no milk, and no tea-leaves, either. Fortunately however, Alan shook his head.

'We won't put you to any trouble, I've just brought Grace round so the two of you can get acquainted,' he said. 'I'll buy you both tea and cakes at Fuller's Tearooms, but I can't stay with you. I'm off to book three rooms at the hostelry nearest Eagles Court, if that's all right, Questa?'

Questa swallowed nervously. It was what she wanted most in the world. Not even the unasked for and unwanted company of this elegant lady could spoil that.

'Yes, thank you,' she said earnestly. 'I'll get my coat.'

It was only a short walk to the tearooms and once there, settled at a window table in the late afternoon sunshine with some highly coloured cakes between them, she decided she had better make friends with this Grace Syrett person, otherwise Alan might make yet more excuses to stop them from visiting Eagles Court. She told herself to be grateful that Grace was a woman; she might not like her very much, but women did not arouse in her the same fear and unease that their male counterparts did. Women, by and large, had been good to her in Italy, whereas men ...

'Have a cake,' she said as cordially as she could. 'And explain to me how you know Alan. And my father, of course. Did I know you when I was in England before?'

'You were too young to remember me, but I knew you,' Grace drawled. 'I came to the house quite often to see Fortunata, your mother, and you were usually somewhere about. In fact when she was rushed into hospital with meningitis your father got in touch with me and you stayed with me for a couple of days. You must have been about sixteen months then, I imagine.'

'You knew *me*? And my mother?' Questa gasped, all animosity temporarily forgotten. This was wonderful – she longed to ask about her mother, wished ardently that she had been more curious as a child, not so afraid of hurting her father by talking about Fortunata. 'I know so little about my mother – was she *very* beautiful? Was I a nice baby?'

Grace laughed and her expression, which Questa had considered to be cool to the point of unfriendliness, softened a little.

'You were nice enough, as babies go,' she said. 'And your mother was very striking. Dark, like you. I'd known Charles for years and I must say I wondered why he married Nata at first; but when I got to know her you could see the attraction. She was lively and clever, and so slim and quick-moving! She made me feel big and dull.'

'Oh,' Questa said inadequately. 'I'm sure she didn't mean to do any such thing. You are so very fair, perhaps ...'

41

'Yes, that was the strangest thing of all. Charles had always preferred fair women, so when he wrote to say he was married I expected ... well, not your mother, at any rate.'

'Did you like her?' Questa said after a short pause. She helped herself to the least bilious-looking cake and sipped her tea.

Grace considered this, her own cup poised.

'Like her? Yes, I liked her well enough. She had very few friends in England, you understand, Charles was busy earning a living for his new family, so when he introduced us she was glad of a friendly face. We played tennis together in the summer and when I got a boyfriend we made up foursomes, had dinner out once or twice. But she died after only a couple of years of marriage, so I didn't have long to know her.'

Questa nodded. Despite her words, she felt that Grace had not, in fact, liked Fortunata very much and was prepared to pass on her mild dislike from mother to daughter. I shall never like this beautiful, cold woman, Questa thought. But I only have to be nice to her until we get to Eagles Court; then, since I don't intend to return to London, we need never meet again.

This thought gave her increasing satisfaction as they ate their tea and waited for Alan to return. Questa knew that it was unnatural for a girl of her age to want only her own company, to long to be alone, but that was how she was. Her experiences in Italy had filled her with a great distrust of humanity, it was only in her own company that she felt safe, could act completely naturally. She thought she might come to terms with other women one of these days, but men ... ah, you were best far away from them. And though Grace seemed pleasant enough, behind the polite façade, Questa was sure, lurked animosity towards herself. But why? She knew me only as a small child, Questa reminded herself reasonably. A child that young cannot, surely, give offence to an adult? But the question was an academic one and would probably never be answered, so she ate her cake and when Alan returned for them and accompanied Questa back to her room, he was able to tell her that he had booked them into The Passing Soldier for three nights, from the first of May.

'Why can we not go at once?' Questa said immediately.

'Because Grace can't get away until then,' Alan said patiently.

'Poor Questa! But you've waited so long, another fortnight is nothing surely?'

It was, but it would have been ungrateful to say so. And the time will pass, Questa told herself after Alan had left, walking across her ugly, dark little room and peering out of the window. Far below, she could see Grace's blonde head looking almost luminous in the street lights, then she noticed that Alan's hand was on her arm and she tightened her lips. Fool! But men were always fools about women, and at least she would be away from it all soon. Besides, she should be grateful that there were women like Grace on whom men could practise all their nasty wiles. How odd it was, she mused, that she, who hated and feared men, could still not like to see her father's friend taken in by a beautiful, bad woman.

Not that she *knew* Grace was bad; she just sensed a hardness, a coldness, which seemed at variance with the older woman's lovely face. And anyway, it won't matter one way or the other once we get to the Court, Questa reminded herself. I know they have to come, and I have to make Alan see that it really is my place, as it was once my father's, but then they'll go and I'll be alone there. Where Daddy was. In a way he'll still be there, her thoughts continued. You do stay somewhere if you've been happy there, or I believe you do. I'll look at the things he looked at and live in the house he loved so much, and somehow I'll become the girl he wanted me to be. I'll clean and tidy, I'll do the garden and see to the fields, and my reward will be – ordinariness. I'll be ordinary, there. Not afraid of men, not haunted by nightmares, not even thinking about what happened in Italy. I'll be the real Questa Adamson, the one Daddy knew.

As for London and her life there, she would not miss it in the slightest. Let Alan and Grace have London, and each other; they were welcome to both.

Appersley village was even smaller than Questa had imagined: a tiny shop which sold just about everything and had a post office in one corner, a blacksmith's forge which doubled as a garage with one solitary petrol pump, a grey church nestling beside a mere, and the pub, The Passing Soldier, opposite the village green.

43

It had taken them all day to get here, though. Questa sat in happy solitude in the back of the car, which was an old soft-top Mercedes, and admired the passing scene whilst Alan and Grace chatted or fell silent. At one stage it occurred to Questa that they were arguing, but she was not sufficiently interested to try to make out what they were saying and besides, though the car purred along quietly enough, the wind of its passage made what was being said between the front seat passengers almost inaudible.

They left early in the morning and drove solidly for a couple of hours, through scenery which was first houses and streets with the occasional patch of green as a churchyard or school playing-field whizzed past. Then it grew more rural, and after a while Alan turned off the main road into a quiet country lane. He drove a short way along it until the lane humped itself up to climb over a railway line. Beside the bridge was a gateway with sufficient room to park the car. Alan manoeuvred into the gateway off the road and then cut the engine and turned to smile at Questa.

'Breakfast time!' he said cheerfully. 'Ready for it? Get out the flask and the sandwiches would you, old girl?'

He was addressing Grace, so presumably any argument had been of short duration. Grace, digging about in her grey and white striped holdall, did not comment.

'Here, marmalade sandwiches,' she said presently, handing Questa a small packet wrapped in greaseproof paper. 'Want some coffee?'

The flask was produced and three enamel mugs filled. Questa took her share and ate and drank, enjoying the scent of the coffee – though it was only Camp – and the warmth of the sun as a cat would, physically, without examining any deeper feelings.

'Apple?' Alan said when the sandwiches were all gone and the paper neatly folded for the next picnic. 'I can eat whilst I drive.'

They ate wrinkled pippins and Alan taught them how to sing parts, *Row, row, row the boat, gently down the stream* ... and because the day had been such fun Questa sat there smiling to herself and felt the friendly buffeting of the wind and smelled the sweet scents of grass and trees and was fiercely glad she was alive and, for a moment, dismissed guilt and fear as a giant irrelevance, a nothing on such a day.

44

They had lunch in a pub, eating bread and cheese, pickled onions and salad followed by flaky almond tarts. They sat by the river and drank cool bitter beer, then drove on towards the sinking sun and Alan slowed the car once more.

'Nearly there,' he said. 'Chuck us the map, Questa; it's down the side of your seat.'

He unfolded it with one hand and spread it across the steering wheel and examined it without stopping, though Grace said rather tartly that this was a stupid thing to do; Questa thought it was a good trick.

'First left, then left again,' Alan said presently, as they reached the village. 'There's the inn – do you want to go up to the Court now, Questa, or shall we leave it until tomorrow morning?'

Questa was about to answer when Grace interrupted. 'We told them we'd be arriving at six, and it's ten to the hour now,' she observed. 'Better leave the house till tomorrow.'

Arguing would have been undignified and probably useless and, besides, Questa suddenly realised that she was not over-keen to see Eagles Court for the first time when she was tired and tense – not with Grace looking on, anyhow.

'Yes, tomorrow,' she said, and Alan, who had slowed before the low, stonebuilt inn with its crinkly red tiles and the sign depicting a fierce-looking Napoleonic soldier in a red coat, turned the car into the entrance at the side, drove across a cobbled yard, and parked outside what appeared to be the back door.

'I'll bring the cases,' he said. 'You two had better go and explain who we are and so on.'

Grace swept in and Questa tagged behind, looking curiously about her. The inn was clearly very old: the ceiling was striped with low, blackened beams, the walls bulged unevenly and the windows were small, not so much for views as for security, Questa felt sure. Yet the place was cosy, welcoming, and the fat landlady who asked them to sign the visitors' book and took them to their rooms was welcoming too.

'I thought as 'ow you two ladies wouldn't mind sharin',' she said as she creaked ponderously before them up the steep and narrow stairs. 'We don't 'ave many single rooms and that's a fact, but you're in our best double, and you've got a bed each, a twin.

It's our Mr Paulett, you see – he's a reg'lar, comes in for a long weekend once a month. I didn't realise this was 'is weekend when I booked you in, but being as 'ow you're both ladies ...'

Questa waited for Grace to object, to point out that Alan had booked three singles, but although Grace sighed rather deeply she said nothing and was fulsome in her praises when they saw the room.

'It couldn't be nicer, Mrs Watson,' she said warmly. 'What a lovely view as well ... what a big pond!'

Mrs Watson chuckled indulgently. 'I can see you aren't from round yur,' she said. 'That's the mere, Appersley Mere, same's the village. A bit bigger'n a pond, that is ... you can row a mile or more, should you choose.'

'Well, mere or pond, it's an enchanting view,' Grace said. She sat down on the wide window seat and smiled up at the landlady, the dimple much in evidence. 'What time do you serve dinner, Mrs Watson?'

'Well, if half past six would suit?'

'Marvellous,' Grace said at once. 'Just time for a hot wash and a change of clothing. And where do we eat?'

'Dining room's through the bar. You'll 'ave your breakfast there too. What time do you want that?'

'Nine o'clock will be plenty soon enough,' Grace decided. 'We won't want to be up too early, we've had a long journey.'

Questa cleared her throat. This woman, too, was behaving as though Questa was a child, not consulting her at all.

'Mrs Watson, can you see Eagles Court from here? Which direction is it in?'

Mrs Watson smiled but shook her head. 'No, dearie, it's all of two mile to Eagles Court, and not much to see there now, either. Very run-down, it is. The army 'ad it, you know, and left it in a bad way, or so my son Sam tells me. The Rimmers can't cope no more – well, they'm old – so it goes from bad to worse. You interested in the 'ouse? There's plenty better around 'ere.'

'We're going to see it in the morning,' Grace said easily before Questa could answer. 'It used to be a fine old house, I understand.'

'Oh ah, that'ud be before the war,' Mrs Watson said. 'I didn't

46

know it were for sale, truth to tell – now I wonder if old Mr Atherton knows? He was talkin' of buyin' it off the old feller before he died, but my Sam did say it couldn't be sold … only to family, suffin' like that.' She patted the nearest bed, neatly made up with a checked counterpane and pillows and sheets of icy whiteness. 'Well, I better get down or your dinner won't be cooked! Take your time, now.'

'There's a bathroom along the corridor,' Grace said as the landlady left the room. 'I'll go and get a wash. Are you going to change out of that skirt?'

'No,' Questa said baldly. Just who did Grace Syrett think she was?

'Oh! Well, I'm going to put on something fresh.' Grace rummaged in her small suitcase and produced a spongebag. 'See you later.'

She left. Questa chose the bed she thought she would prefer, then turned the covers down, rooted through her bag and got out her cotton nightie, placing it prominently on the pillow. Then she went over to the window.

Grace was right about the view, she thought, if nothing else. In the last slanting rays of the sun the water of the mere was red and gold, the church with its tile-capped tower gilded around the edges. Far out on the water someone came into view, rowing a small boat. The ripples of his going spread, shattering the placid surface of the mere, casting a long blue shadow across the red and gold. From a nearby tree, clad in the pale green of fresh leaves, a wood pigeon cooed and someone, somewhere, rang a bicycle bell, its silvery tinkle sounding almost intrusive in the evening calm.

Questa leaned her forehead against the glass and wondered rather desperately when they would go to see Eagles Court. It would not be dark for a couple of hours yet, why shouldn't they just take a peep tonight? She would ask Alan over dinner, she decided, turning back into the room again. And until then she would jolly well go out and explore the village; she saw no reason why she should hang about here, waiting for Grace.

'More coffee, Questa? No? I expect you're tired, so I think we

47

should all have an early night. Grace said you'd gone off whilst she had a bath; what did you find? Not Eagles Court, of course, that's two miles or more off. Did you see High Elms Farm? It's rather a nice mixed farm, or was in my time. And there's the church – those strange-looking fortified churches can be found all over south Shropshire and nowhere else, so far as I can make out. Did you see Lilac Cottage, where Grace stayed when she was small? Charles and I went to tea there once and played Snap with Grace and her aunt, and thought Grace was a boring kid and best avoided.'

Alan laughed but Questa turned her head away. He had been trying to draw her out all evening, with little success. Questa had explored the village, put her head around the door of the village shop, talked to the blacksmith, asked the farmer if she might go into his shippon and see the cows being milked. She found that she was not nearly so nervous of people who seemed kindly disposed towards her in a placid, countryish sort of way, so different from people in the city, who seemed to resent anyone they did not personally know. So despite her shyness she had rather enjoyed herself, but once back at The Passing Soldier, her grievances had surfaced once more. This was *her* expedition, *her* house, yet Alan deferred to Grace over everything. She did not want Alan's undivided attention, but neither, she discovered, did she enjoy feeling an unwanted third, when in fact it was Grace who had forced her company upon them.

'I don't know whether I saw Lilac Cottage or not. And I saw *a* farm,' Questa said sulkily. 'What time shall we have breakfast?'

She knew that Grace had ordered it for nine o'clock but she was still hopeful that Alan would overrule her and insist that they ate earlier.

'Oh, I don't know; eight?' Alan said. Questa was beginning to say that sounded fine when Grace cut across her, sounding bored.

'Oh, but eight is far too early for a weekend; Mrs Watson would find nine easier, I'm sure. Besides, I've already told her nine, so I think we should let it stand at that.'

'Oh yes, of course, nine will be grand,' Alan said heartily. He shot a quick look at Questa. Was it an apologetic look or just a warning one? Questa was not sure, but she was sure that Alan was trying to say something to her. 'Well, bed now, eh, Questa? Grace and I will just have a last drink in the bar ...'

'I'm going for a walk,' Questa said firmly. She was not a child and would not be packed off to bed by anyone! 'I like a breath of fresh air before I turn in.'

Her father always used to say that. Questa, who happened to be looking at Grace as she spoke, noticed that something very like pain flashed across the older woman's face and was as swiftly gone. Had she imagined it? Why should it hurt Grace to hear Questa use one of her father's expressions, anyway? With an inward shrug, Questa got up from the table and headed for the front door. Alan must have followed her though, for in the hall a hand caught hold of her arm in a light grip.

'Questa, wait a moment, I'd like a word ...'

At the touch, Questa felt a wave of revulsion crash over her, cold and bitter as salt water. She jerked away, pressing herself against the front door, fumbling for the latch. Her heart was beating overtime and she knew her skin was sickly pale.

'Don't! Ah, don't!'

Alan looked stunned, embarrassed. Questa, seeing the look, tried to prise herself away from the door, tried to look rueful and not just plain terrified.

'Sorry, you startled me. Do you want something?'

'Yes, I saw I'd startled you. I just wanted a word, my dear ...'

The dining-room door into the hall opened. Grace was framed in the doorway. She looked straight at Alan, but Questa was aware that Grace's glance had included her own frightened figure.

'Alan, my love, are we going to have a little drinkie once the child has gone to ... oh! Good night, Questa.'

'Good night,' Questa said breathlessly, but annoyance surged in her, swamping her stupid fears. To Alan, still hovering uncertainly, she added in a hissing whisper, 'Go along, the boss wants you!'

It made him smile, albeit sheepishly. He opened his mouth to respond, then hesitated. Questa, lifting the latch, thought for a moment that he would accompany her into the evening, perhaps walk with her towards the farm, talking. But then he raised his brows, shrugged, gave a sort of shiver, and went meekly towards the bar and Grace.

Tightlipped, Questa stepped out into the village street. Let them stew, the pair of them! She had every intention of going to Eagles Court right now, whether they liked it or not. If they missed her and worried, then that was their concern, not hers. With a resolute step and her head held high, Questa turned into the shop. She would get directions and leave at once.

It was every step of two miles, if not more, but a lady working in her garden gave her precise instructions and a passing farmhand showed her a short cut and after about forty minutes of fast walking Questa found what she sought: two stone pillars each topped by a round stone ball, each ball bearing a large bird with a curved beak and cruel-looking talons.

Eagles Court at last! Dusk had fallen as she walked, which was a nuisance, and the drive was long and dark, the trees overhanging it turning it into a rather gloomy tunnel. But the tunnel ended in a wide sweep of weedy gravel and a larger sweep of long, hay-coloured grass and beside the gravel was the house, at last. Questa stood still for a moment, just staring. The house was big! It was difficult to make out details in the tricky moonlight, for the sun had gone down and the moon come up long since, but she could see a great many windows, some reflecting the moonlight, others seeming blank and dark, and there was a climbing plant of some description, perhaps a rose, growing up over the pillared portico. She could smell wafts of its perfume as she stood, framed by the tree-girt drive, and stared towards the house.

What should she do now, though? Retreat? She had done as she meant to do, she had seen Eagles Court. Now, surely, she could turn back with honour, return to the inn, and tell Alan and Grace tomorrow that she had stolen a march on them, had already seen the house.

But it would scarcely impress either of them to learn that she had just stood outside for a few minutes. Better go and peer through a window, try a door. Alan had keys, but if what Mrs Watson said was true, there should be some other means of access to an old house which was in a state of considerable disrepair.

She crossed the weedy gravel, scarcely making a sound on the thick mat of chickweed and ground elder, then climbed the steps and put a hand on the front door. It was warm beneath her fingers, the wood rough, the paint blistered. And as she stood there, she felt the silence grow and grow, until it seemed as though the house, the grounds, even the distant road, were holding their breath, begging her to listen, not to knock or make a noise but to listen. And then she might hear something wonderful, something she longed to hear.

There was a knocker on the door in the shape of an eagle with spread wings, it looked like brass, but she could not have knocked now to save her life. It was as if the house itself was begging for silence, advising her not to ruin this moment. Besides, she knew no one was within, yet if she knocked, if she shattered this silence …

Far off, a trumpet sounded. Its long, silvery note wavered on for a moment, then died. Abruptly, with the breaking of the silence, Questa's legs seemed to give under her and she sat down on the step, leaning against the warm wood of the door, facing outwards. She felt neither afraid nor lonely, just very interested in her surroundings. She saw the silvered expanse of grass and the wood, the trees clustered so thickly that she could scarcely see between them, save for what looked like a glimpse of distant water – or could it be the road she had walked along earlier, as she made her way from the village?

Staring at the trees, she thought she saw a movement. Someone was there, yes, she could make out a column of marching men through the trees. Of course, a trumpet was a military instrument, the men she could dimly see must be soldiers from some barracks nearby, marching home after a long day's training.

Questa got to her feet. The road was nearer than she had thought; she should be able to get back to the village quicker than she had come if she went through that wood.

She crossed the gravel, then the grass, and plunged into the trees. She could see no marching men now, but faintly, on the night breeze, she could hear the scuffle and thud of their feet as they made their way along the white, moonlit road through the wood, and she could hear their voices too, as they softly sang.

51

Ah, the road is long to my true love's side,
Yet still I must journey on,
Though my back is sore where my harness chafes,
And the spring in my step is gone.
For the love of a girl who is sweet and true,
Is the prize that I ne'er can take,
Whilst I'm far from home let her dream of me,
For I'd lay down my life for her sake.

The tune was wistful, a lament in a minor key, and as it gradually faded Questa became aware of a deep sense of sadness and loss. They had gone, and she had never really seen them. What a strange song they had sung, she had never heard it before ... but then why should she have heard it? She knew very few English songs and had had little to do with soldiers, save to keep out of their way to the best of her ability.

She turned back to the house, walked through the trees, then remembered that she had meant to return to the village by the short cut, the road through the wood. She glanced over her shoulder, then stopped and stared hard. Two minutes ago, it could scarcely be more, she had stood amongst these very trees and looked out of them on to a stretch of road. She had glimpsed marching men, she had heard their song.

But now the trees clustered close, and though she went back into the wood and searched, she saw nothing resembling a road.

She hunted for ten minutes, maybe more, then left the wood and walked back to stare hard at the house. Was she dreaming? She must have been dreaming. She put her hand out to the door, intending to give it a hard push, then abruptly changed her mind. She lowered her hand and walked away until she could see the whole frontage of the house, then spoke to its blank façade.

'What *is* going on? I'll find out, even though I shan't come in, yet. I'll be back in the morning, though – with reinforcements.'

The house, not surprisingly, stared blankly back at her, indifferent to her threats. And suddenly the humour of the situation struck Questa – talking to a house as though it might heed her, not liking to knock in case she disturbed ... what? Why, nothing, because there was nothing to disturb, the place was obviously deserted.

Annoyed with herself, she marched back to the house, raised the eagle knocker, and lowered it with all her strength. The resultant crash sounded horribly loud in the night hush and suddenly Questa was sure someone was listening. She was aware of the held breath, the cocked head, and then someone was actually coming, moving towards the door!

She fled. Not exactly from fear, but as a naughty child, knocking on doors on April Fool's day out of devilment, will run. She tore down the drive, giggling, breathless, and hurled herself between the great stone gateposts and into the little country road. She ran for half a mile, not glancing back, still not afraid because even in the darkness she had thought the house her refuge, but then she slowed and stopped, sauntering along, hearing the night sounds of a country which had long been strange to her – a mouse skittering in dead leaves, a bird, disturbed from its perch and cheeping, rustling. Somewhere she could hear the cluck and chuckle of moving water and, as she neared the village, the creak of a gate, a soft voice calling a cat indoors, a horse cropping grass, stopping at the sound of her footsteps, blowing softly through its nostrils as it raised its head to stare.

She reached The Passing Soldier; the front door was unlocked, fortunately, though the bar was dark and deserted. She stole up the stairs, across the landing, into their room. It was in darkness, Grace a humped shape in the bed, the one Questa had chosen, of course, the nicest one, against the wall. Still, it would be easier to climb unnoticed into the nearer bed.

She heaved her jersey over her head and unbuttoned her skirt. Grace had pulled the curtains, but imperfectly, so that a long ray of moonlight shone across the bed, illumining Questa's night-dress, tossed carelessly down in a crumpled heap. Questa picked it up and pulled it over her head. She drew back the covers and climbed into bed, then snuggled down. She smiled to herself as Grace, whose breathing had been quite heavy enough to count as snoring, suddenly gave a snort and a whistling sigh. So much for her regarding Questa as a child – she had not even noticed that Questa was still out at bedtime!

'And where do you think you've been?'

The voice, cold and condemnatory, definitely came from the

other bed. Questa, who had almost jumped out of her skin, said nothing. Horrible woman, who did she think she was, talking to someone like that? She would pretend to be asleep, which must have been what Grace had been doing just now, or how else could she have noticed Questa's arrival?

'Oh, yes, I heard all about it – what a fool I've been! I believed you when you said you loved me, I drank in every word because it was what I wanted to believe, so when Millie told me ...'

She's talking in her sleep, Questa thought wonderingly. She wasn't talking to me at all! Now what do I do? Ought you to wake someone up when they're talking in their sleep, or ignore it?

'And fancy choosing *her*,' Grace's voice continued sadly. 'How could you, when you knew how I felt? She'll never love you like I do, it just isn't possible. Oh Cain, don't leave me, don't, don't!'

And then, to Questa's horror, Grace began to sob.

There was only one thing to be done.

Questa sat up in bed, leaned over the side, and picked up her bag. Then she swung it hard against the wall. The crash was satisfyingly loud.

In the other bed, Grace stirred and mumbled something.

Questa ran her fingers over the brass bars at the head of the bed, then banged the bag against the wall once more.

Grace snorted and her breathing became lighter; she might not have woken, but whatever dream had troubled her sleep had probably gone. Nevertheless, Questa waited until she began to snore again before lying down once more and pulling the covers up over her ears. If she does start talking, I won't hear it, she told herself sternly.

Nevertheless she lay tense in the darkness, dreading the resumption of Grace's weird, one-sided conversation, but as Grace snored on, she began to relax. And presently, slept.

Questa's last thought before falling asleep was that she must be up first the next morning, but in the event she woke late, to find Grace's bed empty. Half relieved and half annoyed with herself, she turned over and stared towards the window. It was a bright morning, she could see a long slit of blue sky through the gap in the curtains and, judging from the sounds floating up from the pub downstairs, it was by no means early.

There was no clock in the room and Questa was just wondering whether to get out of bed and start dressing hurriedly when she heard the church clock begin to chime. She counted eight strokes and relaxed. She was not particularly late, not late at all in fact. Grace, for some reason, was early. And since it was sunny, she had probably woken Alan and taken him for a wander round the village. They would not, surely, go to the Court without her.

The threat of such action got her out of bed faster than a flying kick would have done. They would not – *dare* not – go to her home without her, would they? She scrambled into her clothes, rehearsing what she would say if she found they had visited the Court, splashed cold water in the general direction of her face and ran down the stairs. Mrs Watson, laying the fire in the public bar, looked up as she hurried down into the hall.

'Well, who's in a rush then?' she said placidly. 'Want your friends? They've gone for a stroll; won't be long. Tell 'em breakfast in ten minutes, that'll put skates under 'em.'

'Which way did they go?' Questa said. 'I overslept.'

Mrs Watson shrugged. 'Don't know, but whichever way you go you're bound to see 'em.' she observed. 'You're only five minutes or so behind 'em.'

'Thanks,' Questa said.

She hurried out of the inn and into a fresh and pleasant morning. Dappled sunshine fell through the leaves of the trees surrounding the churchyard and a little breeze ruffled the smoothness of the mere. A cock crowed incessantly and from the nearby farm came the lowing of cows as they were brought out of the milking shed. Someone shouted at a child, a car gave a harsh preliminary cough before clattering into life, and of course every bird in creation, or so it seemed, was singing its tiny heart out.

In the village street, Questa paused for a moment. Which way, which way? But then, glancing towards the mere, she saw two familiar figures. Here they were, strolling as Mrs Watson said, Grace with her hand tucked into Alan's arm. Questa turned towards them, feeling positively weak with relief. They had not visited the Court, or even thought of it, probably. They were coming from the wrong direction and, anyway, Alan would not do such a thing. He was a kind man, he had been good to her – if only she was not so untrusting, so constantly suspicious!

'Morning, Questa,' Alan said as soon as they were near enough. 'Did you have a good night?'

'Yes, thank you,' Questa said. 'You're about awfully early; I thought you said nine o'clock breakfast?'

'It will be nine o'clock by the time we get back,' Grace said.

This morning she was wearing a cream-coloured shirt and a caramel-brown skirt. Her thick, pale hair was tied back from her face and held in position by a flat tortoiseshell slide and she wore soft brown brogues on her feet. She looked casual and country-ish, Questa thought, yet just right, really smart. How well Grace dressed, considering that austerity was the order of the day. Well, it paid to be old, because that meant you had clothes left over from before the war, Questa thought sourly, glancing down at her own grey skirt and shabby blue blouse.

'Mrs Watson says breakfast in ten minutes,' was all she actually said, however, 'so you'd better come back now.'

Grace pulled a face.

'We said nine, Alan.' She consulted a small gold watch on her wrist. 'It isn't even half past eight. I don't see why we should have to hurry ourselves.'

'We shan't,' Alan pointed out mildly. 'We're on the way back.'

Grace heaved an exaggerated sigh. 'Oh, all right. I'm quite hungry, actually.' She turned to Questa, who had fallen into step beside them. 'And where were you last night?'

'I went for a walk,' Questa said guardedly. She had not in-tended to deceive anyone, but now she realised that if she said she had been to the Court Grace might make it an excuse not to hurry over breakfast. And anyway, last night had been strange – had she really been to the Court or had she dreamed it? It was all so odd: the big house brooding at the top of the long drive, the soldiers marching on their white road and singing that sad song, the listening silence ... no, she would not say where she had been.

'Well, I know *that*,' Grace said scornfully. 'You were gone long enough, though. I fell asleep before you got back. Where did you walk to?'

'Oh, just round and about the village,' Questa said. 'Was I late? I don't have a watch so I can't tell.'

'If Grace was asleep, she can't really complain because you were late,' Alan pointed out. 'We must get you a watch, Questa, when we get back to town. No matter what you decide to do you'll need to know the time.'

'Not in the country,' Grace said. 'That damned church clock woke me at midnight, bonging away.'

'I thought you said you were asleep when I got back,' Questa said. 'I was back before midnight.'

'And I thought you said you didn't know what time you got in,' Grace pointed out. 'Either you did or you didn't.'

'I was in bed when the clock struck midnight,' Questa said with what patience she could muster. How the wretched woman found fault! 'I know because I lay and counted the strokes. By the way, who's Cain?'

There was a moment of total silence, then Alan and Grace both spoke at once.

'Cain? That chap in the Bible?'

'What on earth are you talking about now?'

Questa shrugged. She felt ashamed to have asked the question because, when all was said and done, to listen to someone talking in their sleep is bad enough, but to make use of any information thus overheard is, in an odd way, tantamount to spying.

'Oh, someone mentioned Cain and I didn't know what they meant. I wonder what's for breakfast?'

Over porridge and scrambled eggs, Questa eyed the two sitting on the other side of the table and did quite a lot of wondering. They seemed calm enough now, but there had been that odd silence after she had asked her question. Still, she was probably imagining it. And she need not wonder about Cain any more; whatever Grace had said had probably been just the mad ramblings of a dream, but she was still very puzzled over her own night-time experience.

Had it really happened? Part of her was sure it had, part thought it could not have been real. I couldn't have gone up there all by myself and run most of the way home, I must have dreamed it, Questa thought one moment. The next, she remembered the blistered paint on the front door and the song the soldiers had sung, and was sure it had happened.

Three

Seen in company, and in the bright light of a sunny May morning, Eagles Court was still pretty impressive, though thankfully nowhere near as huge as it had seemed the previous night. By daylight Questa saw it was a rambling house built in warm Cotswold stone and roofed with russet tiles. Tall, twisted chimneys poked rosy-red fingers at the blue sky and the climbing plant which Questa had thought a rose proved to be something which looked like clumps of pale blue grapes.

'It's wisteria,' Alan said when she asked. 'It must be very old indeed to have reached the tiles – look at the thickness of the stem! Smells nice, doesn't it?'

Questa, agreeing, glanced appreciatively at a lilac tree to her right and a laburnum nearby, already dripping its gold on to the ground beneath. There were good things here, she could see them with her own eyes, it was not all bad news. But being a practical girl she saw, too, the dilapidation which had been hidden by the kindly mantle of darkness; broken windows, shutters hanging by one hinge, peeling paint and a faulty gutter, since over the right-hand windows tell-tale streaks of green showed where water had overflowed or run from a broken trough. Looking upward, she saw that the house had been built at the foot of a gentle hill – protection, no doubt, from the prevailing wind – and glancing behind her, that the tangled grasses had once been a lawn, for she could still see rose bushes, half-strangled and leggy with age and lack of pruning, struggling up in what must once have been flower beds.

There was no doubt about it, the place must have been splendid, once. They had approached it along the tunnel-like drive – Grace had said contemptuously that it was more like a neglected track than a drive – under some sort of flowering tree.

Alan told her they were rhododendrons and Questa agreed the purple flowers were beautiful, though privately she thought the trees gaunt and depressing. But they were cultivated trees, not wild ones, and must have cost someone a pretty penny once.

Alan had slowed so that they might look at the house, now he drew the car to a gentle halt on the weedy gravel sweep. Without comment, he got out, crossed to the front door and unlocked it, with some difficulty, for the lock was stiff and rusty. Then he swung the heavy door open and gestured Questa forward.

'It's your house; you go first,' he said gently, and Questa, without demur, moved past him and into the hall. The long awaited moment had arrived, she was entering her home at last!

The first thing Questa noticed was the leaves; piled up in the corners, they swirled lazily as the opening door let the wind into the hall, then fluttered back into comparative stillness as Alan hastily swung the big door shut. It was not usual to find leaves in such quantities on a marble floor, for the black and white tiles looked like marble to her and the sweep of the staircase was so beautiful that one did not notice the stained and battered wood, the fact that an elegant banister had been ruined by the application of what looked like mud, and the tattered state of what had once been fine wallpaper.

'There's a smell,' Grace said.

Questa sniffed. Grace was right, but it scarcely seemed important beside the feelings which were attacking her, beating round her head like bat wings ... times past, the feelings said, times past ... and all yours, Questa Adamson, all yours.

'It's probably damp,' Grace continued. 'Oh dear God, look at that!'

She had pushed open a door and was surveying the corridor beyond with open distaste. Questa, following her gaze, saw that the linoleum-covered floor was filthy, thick with mud, pigeon droppings and worse. The panelling was daubed with green and brown paint, the light fittings were smashed, and the tall doors leading off were without handles, their panels cracked and scrawled over, and even the brass scratch plates were missing.

Alan, peering past the girls, shook his head. 'No, I don't think it is damp – the smell,' he said. 'It's just years of neglect and probably mice and ...'

Grace screamed affectedly. 'Mice? My God, and beetles, you name it, it's lived here. Need we go on?'

'No, we needn't,' Alan said. 'Go and sit in the car, Grace. Or you can walk back to the village. Questa and I have a job to do.'

It made Questa's day. She had to repress a smile, and waited hopefully for her enemy – for she saw Grace as very much her enemy – to retreat in confusion. But Grace was made of sterner stuff. She stared at Alan for a moment, then flung her arms round him and buried her face in his shoulder.

'Alan, I didn't mean ... it's just that I'm scared of mice and I don't much like beetles. I'll be good, really I will. Tell me what you want me to do and I'll do it.'

Questa waited for Alan to say something sensible, like go away, or shut up, but instead he said, in a mollified voice, 'I knew you wouldn't let me down, Gracie. Just come round with us and make useful suggestions. We can all see how bad it is, what we want to know is how to improve it so that Questa can rent it out.'

So the three of them did a tour. Questa walked reverently; every floor she trod had known her father's feet, every room she peeped into, he had known and loved. She could almost feel his presence, his love of the place, and knew without a shadow of a doubt that this was for her, that she could be happy here, would love it as he had.

The main rooms were beautifully proportioned, dry, and almost empty. Neglect seemed endemic; a small rosewood piano in a big room with french windows leading on to what had once been a rose terrace was thick with dust and covered with rings made by cups and plates. When Alan opened it and touched a key softly no sound emerged, only a faint bumping. Investigation showed that several keys were out of commission for no reason that was immediately obvious.

But wherever she looked, Questa was aware that her father's eyes had rested, and she knew that this, if anywhere, was where he would have chosen to spend the rest of his days but for the accident of war. He had loved it, and so did she, despite the state of it. It was like a beautiful, neglected child and she was here to see that it remained beautiful, but was neglected no longer.

The kitchen was dreadful, yet at least it was furnished after a fashion. A huge, blackened cooking range with the fire-front open and the bars thick with white ash took up the end wall, with a big Welsh dresser facing it. There were four blue-and-white banded mugs hanging on the dresser and some odd plates untidily stacked at one end. Neither mugs nor plates, Questa saw, were dusty, which meant that someone had been here quite recently.

There were four wheel-backed wooden chairs, the seats polished with use though the backs were thick with dust, a big table made of pine, a matching bench along one wall and a rack holding pans ranging from enormous to tiny. An airing rack, lopsided but intact, hung from the ceiling and there were several pictures on the walls, though the subjects were impossible to identify through the filth. Everything in the room was dirty save for the china and chair seats, but the pans were so layered that it was impossible to tell if they were copper, enamel or cast-iron.

Grace took one off the wall and pulled a face.

'Look at that, it's been put away unwashed,' she said disgustedly. 'There's custard or something caked all round the sides!'

'It's a good quality pan though,' Alan said, taking it from her and hefting it thoughtfully in one hand. 'I like heavy pans – it's copper, I imagine. I remember Charles saying the stuff here was all good, though it was old then, and that was years ago.' He hung the pan back on the wall and headed for the kitchen door. 'No time for conjecture, though; I wouldn't be surprised if we found some of Joshua's decent stuff locked away in the attics. The authorities usually told owners to do that when they requisitioned a place.'

They trooped up to the attics, glancing in a bedroom or two on the way. One was filled with rusting iron bedsteads, clearly army issue, and rotting flock mattresses. Another, with the window open, had been inhabited by pigeons, several of whom took off with startled cries and swooped out into the spring sunshine where they skulked about, peering crossly through the window as Questa tried to pull it down.

'Didn't Joshua have any money?' Questa asked timidly as they climbed the attic stairs. Even to her prejudiced eye this house needed a small fortune spending on it to get it respectable once more. 'Or did he leave it to someone else?'

'He didn't bank it, that's for sure,' Alan told her. 'I'm inclined to believe there was money; we'll take a look if we find a desk or a safe or anything. I remember Charles telling me the furniture was antique, though, and that some of the pictures were worth a bit. Don't say that door's locked! Now that is a good sign – let me try my keys.'

He tried three from the bunch before striking lucky. He opened the door, but they could not get into the room for furniture. Tallboys, wardrobes, beds, dressing-tables, they were all here, stacked up tidily, layered in velvet dust.

'We'll have to go through it room by room,' Alan said tiredly. 'My God, there's so much work! It'll take weeks ... we'll have to pay someone, and keep an eye on them, too.'

'You could have a sort of foreman; it'ud pay you in the end, because she won't be able to let in this condition,' Grace said. She turned and smiled at Questa. 'Sorry, I shouldn't have said she, I meant Questa wouldn't be able to let.'

'I'll do the work,' Questa said. 'I'm the one who'll benefit so it's fair that I should do the work.'

'You?' Alan turned to stare, then smiled. 'My dear child, you couldn't possibly , you'd need an army of experienced cleaners and the muscle power it would take to get this lot down to the ground floor. No, it's out of the question, I'm afraid. We'll have to contact a firm, I suppose. I knew it could be bad, but I had no idea just how bad.'

'I'll do it,' Questa said again, knowing she sounded mulish but not caring. She was surprised when Grace suddenly spoke up.

'She isn't a child, Alan, for all she looks so young, and she's worked hard enough over the years, you told me so yourself. Why shouldn't she at least help with the work if that's what she wants? Even if she only stays in the house and keeps an eye on things it would save the estate money.'

'And I want to do it. I'm not going back to London to stew in a dirty bed-sit whilst I learn to type,' Questa said defensively. 'I like it here, it's my home and I'm staying.'

She turned on her heel and clattered down the attic stairs, then down the elegant swoop of the main staircase and into the hall. The other two followed her, Grace looking amused, Alan worried.

'Well, of course, if you're determined,' Alan began, then took her arm and led her into the big reception room to the right of the front door. 'But just take a look, my dear, and see if you wouldn't rather change your mind.'

They entered the room. It was big and empty, the walls daubed with dark paint, the floor splattered with what looked like chicken dirt. But it overlooked the front garden and Questa took a cursory glance round her and then headed for the window. She sat down on the wide window seat, head turned to look out. She could hear Alan arguing and Grace saying that Questa was seventeen and old enough to be useful, that this was, after all, her home ... but suddenly it no longer seemed to matter. Staring out at the brilliant green and gold of the woods beyond the lawn, she could just make out something, or was it someone? She could see a figure under the trees, standing quite still facing the house. Was that an arm, stretched out ... the glint of a smile ...? She wanted to end this stupid argument so that she could go and see for herself who stood there, staring towards the house.

'And then there's the language,' Alan was saying with a sort of mulish desperation. 'She talks as though she's never had five years of not using English, but just suppose she was lost for an important word, how would she get on then? And she'd be so alone. I don't think Charles would have dreamed of allowing such a thing, he would have relied on me to stop her. If she comes back to London I'll make a real effort, bring her down at least once a month and stay for a couple of days ...'

'I want to stay here,' Questa said without turning, though she knew Alan was addressing Grace. 'I'll be all right, really I will.'

Staring harder, she saw that the figure had been a trick of the light and shade; no one stood there, watching the house. There had never been anyone, so why did she feel so flat suddenly, so disappointed?

'That's all very well, Questa, but it isn't a question of your enjoyment exactly, it's whether …'

They all heard it at the same moment: a shuffling, wheezing sort of noise, coming from the other side of the door. Questa swung around from her fruitless staring at the uninhabited wood, Grace turned towards the sound, Alan crossed the room in a couple of strides and flung the door open.

A bent old woman stood there. She was thin as a stick and brown as one too, but her dark eyes were lively and she grinned at them, showing teeth so perfect that they had to be false.

'Arternoon,' she said composedly. 'I'm that sorry I din't hear you knock, but I were down in the kitchen garden. If only we can git on top of them weeds we'm going to have a crop of taters no one would sneeze at. And broad beans, too – the flowers smell powerful lovely when the sun's on 'em.'

'Who …? What …?' Alan stammered.

The old woman held out a gnarled hand.

'How d'you do?' She gave a little bob which might have been a curtsey. 'Ellen Rimmer, sir. Alfie and meself live in the coachman's flat, have done ever since the army moved in. Mr Joshua liked it that way and the army didn't mind, so long as we kept the garden cultivated and minded our own business.'

'Oh, how d'you do, Mrs Rimmer. I'm Alan Patterson, my firm is handing the legal business concerning Eagles Court, this is Mrs Syrett, and the young lady is Charles Adamson's daughter, Questa. I don't know if you ever met Mr Charles Adamson …'

'What, young Master Charles? To be sure I did! You an' all, sir, though you don't remember I, do you? Old Ellen as lived in the end cottage of the row down by the lake, with old Mr Rimmer, who used to chase you off of 'is 'ayricks. Why, when the pair of you came fishin' …'

'Mrs Rimmer, how could I have forgotten!' Alan held out a hand. 'Nice to see you again after all these years. I don't suppose you remember Mrs Syrett – she was Grace Caldicott then of course? She used to stay with her Aunt Prue in Lilac Cottage in the village. She came over a couple of times when I was staying here.'

'Can't say as I recall, sir. But I were that fond of Master Charles

... knew him as well as me own lad and a right young limb he was, if you don't mind me saying so, sir. And how *is* Master Charles? He's not been near nor by since he and Mr Joshua fell out, but I daresay you know all about that.'

'Charles was killed in the desert campaign,' Alan said. 'I'm most awfully sorry, Mrs Rimmer, that no one told you. But Charles's daughter Questa here has inherited the estate, so we're having a look around. I'm sorry I didn't let you know, but the truth is I don't believe you're even on the estate books any more, I certainly didn't realise you were still living here.'

'Yes, we are; caretakers we'm described as, or was, at any rate. But we int on a pay-roll, seeing as 'ow Alfie works for Mr Atherton at the Hall. We only lives here, see, and does the garden, like. Well, I'm real sorry to hear about Mr Charles, sir, I wondered why he'd been neither near nor by since the master's death. And you'm 'is daughter,' Mrs Rimmer added thoughtfully, hobbling over to Questa and staring up into her face. 'You don't favour Master Charles much, miss, so I daresay you're like your ma. Well, well, Master Charles's little girl in this old 'ouse and me not here to offer you so much as a cup of tea! You must come along to my place and I'll put that right, and introduce you to Alfie and all, when he gets 'ome.'

'That's very kind of you, Mrs Rimmer, but we're due back at The Passing Soldier for dinner in less than an hour ...' Alan began, only to be ruthlessly interrupted.

'I'll come with you,' Questa said eagerly. 'I'd love to see your flat, and meet Alfie. Is he your husband, Mrs Rimmer?'

She felt as though she had known Mrs Rimmer all her life, and did not anticipate any dread over meeting Alfie Rimmer either. Eagles Court is already making me better, she thought exultantly.

'Bless you no, lovie; Rimmer passed on a good ten year back. No, Alfie's my boy, just a young'un not yet fifty, only a lad you might say.' She chuckled again, her bright eyes twinkling up at Questa. 'So the old feller left the place to young Charlie, just like we thought, only he's passed on, so it's come to you! And you'm goin' to get the old place together, eh? Put it back in order?'

66

'That's right,' Questa said, falling into step beside the old woman as she hobbled back towards the kitchen. 'But we'll need some money to hire help. I wonder if you could tell me, Mrs Rimmer, where old Mr Joshua kept his valuables?'

She could almost feel Alan's astonished eyes on her back, see Grace's shrug. They had never known her natural with people, of course, but Mrs Rimmer was family, as good as.

'Valuables? He was as cunning as an old magpie, that I do know. He had money, but we reckon, Alfie an' me, that he hid it all away under floorboards and in old clocks an' that, and then couldn't lay 'ands on it in time when the army come.' She shook her head regretfully. 'Things bein' what they are they devils probably made off with it two year ago, when they left.'

'I do hope not,' Questa said fervently. 'Was it Alfie who helped old Mr Joshua to take the furniture up to the attics? That must have been a very long job!'

'Took 'em three days. Young Bert Rimmer, me nephew, 'elped, an' Alfie acourse, and so did John and James Fryer, that's the blacksmith and 'is son.' Mrs Rimmer sighed gustily. 'John were killed in forty-two, got a lump of shrapnel through the 'ead when he was firewatching, but James is still about. Not that 'e could help you much,' she added, 'seeing as 'ow he's simple an' always 'as been. Still, if there's money hid, a young thing like you will find it; bound to, stands to reason.'

They were in the kitchen now, and heading for the back door into the yard. Questa was close on the old woman's heels, aware that Alan and Grace were following. She hoped that she was not causing them embarrassment, then shrugged inwardly. What did it matter, after all? What was important was getting the house back into shape and that meant any money which might be hidden must be found, and it seemed likely that the Rimmers might aid in her search. Besides, if she was going to live here – and she was determined to do so – the Rimmers would be her near neighbours and it would be nice to be friends.

Mrs Rimmer led them across the yard, which was mossy and cobbled and as neglected as the house, and into what had once been a working stable. Hay was still heaped in musty piles and on the walls hung rosettes, bridles, strange farm implements.

Questa would have liked to linger and look but Mrs Rimmer showed no signs of stopping. Instead she went across the stable and began to mount a flight of dusty stairs in one corner. At the top of them a wooden door with a small brass knocker in the shape of a horse's head guarded Mrs Rimmer's domain. She opened the door and led them straight into a small, crowded living room, looking rather surprised when Questa was closely followed by Alan and Grace.

'Oh, so you decided to come along after all! Well, come in, come in, the more the merrier,' she said with great hospitality. 'I'll just set the kettle on the fire and then we can have a nice cuppa. Now what did I do with them biscuits? Sit yourselves down, do; I don't stand on ceremony ... no room for it up here.'

She chuckled at her own joke, then indicated two creaking basketwork chairs with brightly crocheted cushions and a pouffe with a hand-embroidered picture of a camel cantering across a desert. Questa took the pouffe and glanced around her. Several rag rugs, clearly made by Mrs Rimmer, lay on the polished floorboards and the dresser standing against the wall was filled with odds and ends of fine china. The fire was an open one, so the kettle, blackened by constant use, sat on top of the coals to boil, though there was a hob in the grate on which it could sit and sing whilst not in use.

Grace and Alan sat in the basketwork chairs and Questa watched as Mrs Rimmer bustled round making the tea, bringing a jug of milk over to the teapot from its place in what looked like a small rabbit hutch under her makeshift sink. Necessity had clearly made Mrs Rimmer clever; a blue washing-up bowl stood on a low table, an enamel jug of water stood beneath it and a dipper was balanced on top of the jug. On the wall above the table hung some highly polished nails and from each nail depended a pan, ranging from small to medium, each one polished until it was like a little mirror. When Mrs Rimmer opened the rabbit hutch to put the milk back, Questa saw a tiny square of butter, some cold meat and half a loaf of bread. Clearly, the wire mesh kept flies at bay so the hutch acted as a pantry, much as the washing-up bowl was used as a sink.

Mrs Rimmer finished making the tea, took a pretty floral plate off the dresser, opened a blue tin with a picture of Trafalgar Square on the lid and set out some biscuits.

'Here we are, my dears. Made 'em meself this morning. Hazelnut cookies I calls 'em. Alfie picked the nuts last backend and I grind 'em up and grate 'em down, then I uses the 'oney from the 'ives to sweeten 'em ... a bit of oatmeal, some milk, an hour in me bake-oven, and they're ready.' She smiled at Questa. 'Why don't you pour the tea, my love, while I fetches another chair through?'

'I'll fetch the chair,' Alan said, getting to his feet. 'We mustn't stop, though; as I said we're due back in the village quite soon.'

'I'd like to see the rest of the flat,' Questa said, getting to her feet. 'It's very cosy, Mrs Rimmer. Just big enough for the two of you, I should think.'

'Seeing as 'ow you owns it, you might as well come round and see what's what,' Mrs Rimmer said cheerfully. 'Twon't take long, that you can guess.' She led the way, Questa following.

There wasn't much more to it, Questa soon saw. A bedroom with a twanging brass bedstead and a curtain to hide Mrs Rimmer's meagre wardrobe, and a tiny slip of a room with a truckle bed for Alfie and a small square table on which rested Mrs Rimmer's sewing machine.

'It suits us,' Mrs Rimmer said when Questa commented timidly on the size. 'Better'n a caravan, I can tell you.' It seemed a strange comparison to Questa, but she just agreed and then said, not entirely ingenuously, that no doubt the Rimmers could make use of such storage space as the court itself offered, seeing as how it was empty.

'No need, with all the outbuildings much nearer to 'and,' Mrs Rimmer pointed out. 'Our bicycles are in the tackroom, along with my cleaning things, and there's a proper shed for gardenin' tools. What else should we need?'

'So you bicycle down to the village, do you?' Questa said, trying not to sound too surprised. 'And that's all you need, I suppose,' she added. She felt it would scarcely be tactful to ask where they bathed or what they used for a lavatory – besides, she was not sure she would much like the answer! 'Mrs Rimmer, if I move back into the big house, will you give me a hand to get a room or two decent? Mr Patterson thinks I'd be silly to try to live here myself, but it's all I've got left of my father, in a way. He loved it so much, you know.'

'Course I'll give you an 'and, my love,' Mrs Rimmer said at once. 'So will Alfie. We'll see you right, don't you fret. I was mortal fond of Mr Charles though to tell you the truth, I don't 'member much about Mr Patterson. He was never 'ere of right, you might say, jest a visitor 'e was, that one summer. Never come again that I can recall, and after the disagreement, nor did Master Charles, more's the pity.'

'Thanks, Mrs Rimmer. And now we'd better go back to the others.'

Returning to the kitchen, Questa had a cup of tea thrust into her hand by a Grace clearly impatient to be off.

'Come along, Questa, we mustn't keep Mrs Rimmer talking to us when she's probably got to get her son's tea,' she said. 'Those biscuits are absolutely delicious, Mrs Rimmer; you must give me the recipe some time.'

They drank their tea, ate their biscuits and then stood up to go. Having thanked the old woman for her hospitality, Alan suddenly turned back just as they were about to descend the stairs. 'Mrs Rimmer, forgive me for asking, but I imagine the arrangement is that you don't pay any rent but keep an eye on the house? And so no money changes hands? Have I got it right?'

'More or less. 'Cept as I said, we does the garden and now that the army's gone, we uses what we grows.'

Alan, who had seen the state of the garden, looked sceptical, but Questa said suddenly, 'Which garden? We've only seen the garden at the front of the house.'

Mrs Rimmer sniffed. 'Call that a garden? More like an 'ayfield if you ask me! The kitchen garden's what I mean, acourse. Want to tek a quick look?'

'We really don't have time ...' Grace began, but was overruled once more by Alan.

'Nonsense; five minutes won't hurt,' he said briskly. 'Lead on, Mrs Rimmer.'

Across the walled yard, the wall itself abutting on to the steeply sloping hill, and to their right Mrs Rimmer led them. There was a small, green painted door in the wall which she flung open, then gestured them past her.

'There it is; all our own work,' she said proudly. 'Wish we could'a done more, but with Alfie at the Hall most days this is all we can manage.'

Questa, Alan and Grace stared. The walled garden was very large and only about a quarter, if that, was cultivated, but that quarter was magnificent. Fruit trees were trained against the bricks, borders divided into small squares in which herbs flourished, and there were long rows of vegetables of every description and at every stage of development. Questa stared, fascinated, as Mrs Rimmer pointed out young carrots, turnips, broad beans, peas, embryo sprouts and summer cabbage. It was so similar yet so different – cultivation carried out to make the best possible use of the land available, as on a peasant's holding in southern Italy, yet with few of the familiar crops her Aunt Vittorina had grown.

'Celeriac, broccoli, radishes, cos lettuce, cucumbers under frames …' Mrs Rimmer chanted. 'We'm bringin' on some tomato plants an' all, in th'old glass'ouse. Oh ah, that sees us through do that.'

'I've never dreamed a garden could be so lovely – it's wonderful,' Questa breathed. 'Could you teach me about English gardens? It would be such a help if I could get the rest of this garden under cultivation – why, I could grow all my own food and sell stuff, too!'

'I could tell you what to do, that's for sure,' Mrs Rimmer said, in the same breath that Alan objected, 'but you won't be here for long enough, my dear.'

Questa turned away from the garden. 'Let's go back to the inn now,' she said to Alan. 'I can see we've rather a lot to discuss.' She added, to Mrs Rimmer as the other two walked ahead of them, 'I'll see you soon, Mrs Rimmer.'

There was a row, of course. Alan honestly believed that he was *in loco parentis* to Questa and should therefore stop her doing anything so foolish as moving into the Court in its present state. It cost Questa dear to talk back to him, to fight her corner, but because she felt sure it was what her father would have wanted she was bold, insistent. And rather to her surprise her determination was not held against her by Grace, who took her side and said she thought Questa was sensible to want to do the job herself.

'She's got a right to try, Alan,' Grace pointed out, 'and she isn't a child, she's a young woman. When I was seventeen I was still at school, but Questa's been earning her own living for years. You have no right to step in and try to stop her doing what she feels she must – and anyway, you won't succeed, you know. She'll go ahead with or without your permission.'

It was true, too, and Alan must have realised it. So the next morning saw Questa, bag in hand, setting out from The Passing Soldier, to walk to Eagles Court. She had scorned asking Alan for a lift because she knew he did not approve and she had no desire to ask and be refused.

She was wrong. It was a dull, grey day, overcast and with light rain falling at intervals, and Questa was trudging through a shower when a car drew to a halt beside her.

Alan got out, took her bag and threw it in the back, then indicated the passenger seat. 'Get in, my dear,' he said. 'Look, I don't like it, but I can take defeat like a gent, I trust! Grace says if you want to come back to London you only have to telephone and I can come down right away, and I suppose she's right. The only thing is, are you going to rent it out when you've got it straight? Grace thinks you will, but I'm not so sure.'

Questa got into the passenger seat and then smiled across at Alan as he slid behind the wheel.

'Grace is wrong; I'm going to try to live here,' she said. 'I'm sorry, Alan, I know you think I'm ignoring your advice, but I can't help it. I'm happy here, it's my place, I can almost see my father, feel his presence. Can you understand?'

'I understand very well, in fact. Look, Questa, ever since we arrived I've been trying to get you on your own to say how sorry I am that you and Grace don't seem to have taken to each other. I shouldn't have brought her, it was your trip, after all, but she wanted to come so much and I thought it might be easier for you with another woman along.'

'I can't understand why she wanted to come,' Questa admitted.

'She doesn't like the country much, does she?'

'No, I see what you mean, and that's the odd part. You'll have gathered that when we were ... oh, fifteen, sixteen, something like that, she was rather wished on us by her aunt. She was ten or so and a nice kid, loved the country and was eager for company because it was lonely shut up in that cottage all day with her old aunt. I remembered how bright and perky she was, how she enjoyed all the things we liked – but people change. And as a kid she had a real crush on Charles which I think turned into genuine liking as they got older. Indeed, when your father married, she befriended Fortunata and was very sweet to her – I'm sure Nata, a stranger alone in a strange land, valued her friendship. Charles was very grateful to Grace for that, in fact when Nata died I wondered ... but I shouldn't have brought her and I'm sorry if it's made you more determined to stay on here, so that you don't even have to share the journey back to London with us.'

Questa laughed. 'I'm not so silly,' she said. 'It's a pity that Grace and I can't be friends, but at least she's seen my point of view over Eagles Court – she understands why I want to stay.'

'Perhaps,' Alan said cautiously. 'You know she married?'

'Yes. Someone called Simon, wasn't it?'

'That's right; Simon Syrett. Well they had a little boy, Dickie, and she's been saying for ages that she would like to take him into the country to live, so I thought that if you decided to rent the Court and got a decent sum from it, then you and she might like to buy property in a country town somewhere and start up a little business, a shop, perhaps. If you chose somewhere like Bath then I could keep an eye on both of you, make sure you weren't cheated or overworked, yet you could enjoy country living. If the two of you had got on perhaps it might have been possible ... don't shake your head, if circumstances had been different ...'

'It wouldn't have made any difference,' Questa assured him. 'It's the Court itself that I want ... need. It was my father's home for much of his life and I want it to be my home, not someone else's, I want to bring it back to life again. He would have, if things had been different.'

'Yes, well, don't forget, I'm at the end of a phone if you want me. The army left the telephone in, though it's been disconnected, so my present to you is going to be reconnection as soon as that can be arranged. And in the meantime if you need me just go to the box at the end of the drive, or send Alfie with a message. I'll come, no matter how busy I may be.'

'It's very kind of you,' Questa said. The car was crawling up the tunnel drive now, and suddenly it came out into the light again. Low cloud and the drizzle made it less light than usual, but still, this was home. Questa smiled at the house and felt sure it smiled back. It could see the good times coming as surely as she could. She would get Alan to send the better antiques to auction to pay for the repairs, work like stink, sell garden produce, find out how best to use the land ...

'I'm not being kind; I believe it's what your father would have wanted,' Alan said bluntly. He stopped the car opposite the front door. 'You'll be all right? You won't hesitate to get in touch if you need us? Don't forget, we'll be at The Passing Soldier until about ten tomorrow morning, if you change your mind.'

'I won't. But thanks.' Questa got out of the car, slinging her bag on to one shoulder. 'Anyway, you know I'll get in touch when we've sorted the furniture out a bit.'

'Yes, of course. Good luck, then.'

Questa stood on the front steps and watched him drive away. When he had gone she looked across the long, rain-flattened grass towards the dripping woods. She looked in the hope of ... what? Seeing the man she thought she had seen for a moment yesterday? Or the column of marching troops, the white dusty road, the magical moonlight? But one had been imagination, the other a dream. Hadn't it?

She walked around the side of the house, through a gateway – the gate had long since crumbled to dust – and into the cobbled yard. She dumped her bag outside the back door, then went across to the stable, intending to go up to the Rimmers' flat. Mrs Rimmer would be up there, wouldn't she? It was raining and dull, a pretty horrible day, surely she would be indoors?

But she knew, really, where she would find Ellen Rimmer. And sure enough, there she was, in the kitchen garden, digging in the wet and heavy loam. She looked up when she heard the door in the wall open and beamed at Questa.

'Mornin'. Need any 'elp?'

'No thanks, it's all right. I'm going to sort out some bedding and get a fire started in the small parlour. That's where I'll live for a time, anyway. Is there any dry wood though, Mrs Rimmer? I shan't be able to start a fire with this wet stuff.'

'Alfie brought some in last night, night afore,' Mrs Rimmer said. 'In the kitchen, on the stove. We lit it yesterday; burned all right. And 'e brought a mattress down, and a few blankets They're all in the kitchen, keepin' aired.'

'Mrs Rimmer, you're marvellous – but how did you know I'd come back?' Questa asked. 'We were still arguing about it when we left you.'

'Best call me Ellen; everyone else does,' the old woman said. 'As for knowing – you're an Adamson, ain't you? Course you'd come back.'

And with that she began digging again, leaving Questa to return, starry-eyed, to the kitchen, where sure enough she found dry wood, dry bedding and a kettle, cleaned and filled. With a great sense of adventure, Questa went through into the small parlour and began to lay the fire.

'She's going to have to learn a lesson, that young lady,' Alan said positively, when Mrs Watson asked whether 'miss' would be all right up there alone. 'She's a nice enough child, but it's a lonely, weird experience to spend the night alone in an empty house. She'll come running tomorrow morning, just you wait and see; then we'll take her home with us and arrange things properly.'

'They say the Court's haunted,' Mrs Watson ventured. 'I'd never sleep up there alone, not if you paid me an 'undred pounds.'

Grace, sitting on a bar stool sipping a gin, pulled a face.

'Haunted? Well, if she's whitehaired by morning I suppose you'll blame me, Alan! But I don't think she'll just give up, I think she'll stick it. She's quite a lot like Nata, you know. Iron

75

fist in velvet glove and all that. Besides, she's got Mrs Rimmer.'

Behind the bar, Mrs Watson made a sound which, in someone less ladylike, might have counted as a snort.

'Her! A fat lot of good that old gypsy would be if there was trouble! Bring it on the young'un more like, with 'er strange ways. You didn't oughter 'ave left miss with old Ellen, beggin' your pardon, sir.'

'She seemed sensible enough,' Alan said doubtfully. 'She's made a marvellous garden up there and she must be seventy if she's a day.'

'Eighty-two,' Mrs Watson said authoritatively. 'As for gardenin', well she would be good at it, like. Keeps her out in the open, not under a roof. She's a gyppo sir, sure's I'm standin' here.'

Mr Watson, a meek, balding little man with a harassed expression, came out from the back, a cloth and glass in his hand. He continued to polish whilst he spoke, clearly rather in awe of his plump, determined wife.

'You can't say Ellen's a gypsy when she's lived under a roof and been a good wife to Rimmer and a good mother to Alfie for more'n fifty years,' he protested mildly. 'She was a gypsy, or so we've been told, but that was years ago, before she settled.'

'Once a gypsy always a gypsy,' Mrs Watson said flatly. 'Alfie's all right, but then he's only half gyppo. Ellen's strange; I always say them vegetables she grows are too fine by half.'

'Magic, Mrs Watson?' Grace said derisively. 'Surely you don't believe in magic?'

'No, course not. Only there's ways ... Alfie once told Mr Watson that a 'tater planted at full moon would grow bigger'n a 'tater planted at the wane. And 'twas true, for 'un tried it.'

'Country magic,' Alan said. 'Anyway, she won't harm Questa; she'll be glad of the company, poor old girl. Someone else about the place all day, someone young.'

'Well, sir, so long as you're sure ... will you go up and fetch her first thing, then?'

'She'll be back here, probably in the middle of the night; would you mind not locking up, Mrs Watson, just in case?' Alan said.

'I wonder if I ought to drive round now, just take a look at her? Poor kid!'

'Oh no, I wouldn't,' Grace said at once. 'You underestimate her, Alan. You always underestimate women. She'll stay there all night, if only to show you. Though you may be right about her coming back in the morning.'

But she didn't really believe it, and looking at Alan, she thought he didn't believe it either.

Questa ate with Ellen and Alfie, at their invitation, though good manners rather than hunger brought her to their door at six o'clock. The truth was, she burned with impatience to be alone in her home, to watch the light fade from the grey sky, to see darkness come.

It had been dark that first night, when she had seen – or thought she had seen – the troops through the trees, and whether she had dreamed it or not, she had not dreamed the almost mystical oneness she had felt with the house, the past. She almost believed that, if she had stayed a little longer when she had heard that rustling step on the other side of the door, she might have met her father face to face, a little boy again. Why else should she so long to take up residence at the Court?

Yet he had not lived here after he was fifteen or sixteen, he had been unwise enough to argue or quarrel with Uncle Joshua and had been cast out of Eden, sent back to London. He had liked Cambridge and his job with the oil company and the semi-detached house near Slough well enough, but she knew he had longed, wistfully, to be allowed back again, into the ancient home of his family, which by a cruel twist of fate was now hers. If only he'd not been so brave, so unselfish! If only he'd let Alan drive up to the desert cache … Alan had neither chick nor child, if he had been killed…

Questa's thoughts stopped short. She was shocked at herself. Her father would not have wanted to live at Alan's expense, any more than Alan had wanted to live at her father's expense. It was just one of those things: fate, destiny, call it what you will. And now she was here and must comfort herself with the thought that this, of all places, was where he would want her to be.

So she went up to Ellen's flat and met Alfie, who proved to be a shortish, sturdy, black-haired man with eyes just like his mother's and a broad, friendly grin. He held out his hand to her, and Questa had steeled herself to take the calloused palm, then was glad she had. She, who so feared and dreaded touch, felt reliability and humour emanating from him; there was no hint in his handshake of anything but honesty and friendship. Yet she did not know why this should be when Alan, who meant her nothing but good, had seemed such a threat. Is it the Court, she wondered, taking her seat at the kitchen table and watching Ellen produce from the bake-oven potatoes in their jackets and golden-crusted Cornish pasties. Or is it that I'm getting better at last, being strong, forgetting the bad times?

'Will one 'tater do you, lovie?' Ellen enquired. 'You need feedin' up, from what I've heard.'

'One will be very nice,' Questa said. 'I'm not used to eating a lot. Everyone in England seems to eat so much!'

'When we can get it,' Alfie remarked, spearing a second potato on his fork and splitting it open to cool down the floury centre. 'We'm lucky 'ere. What with Mam's garden and the 'ens and ducks – well we eats better'n most.'

'You are a very good cook, Ellen,' Questa said, having tasted the Cornish pasty almost unbelievingly. It tasted ... pre-war, she decided, spearing a piece of potato on her fork. 'What is the meat in the pastie?'

'Oh, bit o' this, bit o' that,' Ellen said unhelpfully. 'Like it, do you?'

'It's lovely,' Questa said. 'Perhaps, when you have time, you might teach me to cook, also, as well as to grow plants and vegetables?'

Ellen chuckled. 'I might at that, lovie. Stewed apple an' custard for afters, so save room!'

Politeness dictated that Questa remained at Ellen's flat whilst they ate and cleared the meal, then she and Ellen washed up whilst Alfie read the newspaper.

Clattering the dishes, Ellen turned to fix her with a shrewd, bright eye. 'Sure you'll be awright over there, gal?' she asked.

'Sure you'll sleep, alone in the 'ouse? Though there's none there to 'arm an Adamson, that I'll guarantee.'

'I may not sleep awfully well, because I don't always,' Questa said honestly. 'But it won't be because I'm afraid of being alone in the house. I – I have nightmares, sometimes.'

'Oh ah? Alfie, lad, go to me dressing-table an' bring the piller you'll find there.'

'It's all right, I've got a pillow, and some blankets, too,' Questa said quickly. 'Alan would only let me stay if I had proper bedding.'

Ellen chuckled, shaking her head. 'This ain't no ordinary piller,' she said as Alfie came back into the room with a small, squashy little pillow in one hand. The pillowcase was rough and coarse, but it was clean. 'Smell of it – go on.'

'It smells nice,' Questa said, sniffing the rich, herby smell. 'What is it?'

'It's a yurb piller. This one's full o' wild thyme,' Ellen said impressively. 'You won't 'ave nightmares sleepin' on that piller; allus sure of a good night's sleep an' sweet dreams if you goes to your rest wi' one of me thyme pillers under your 'ead. Try it!'

'Thanks,' Questa said. She tucked the small pillow under her arm and looked hopefully out of the window. When would it be polite to say she had best get back and settle down for the night?

But Ellen was equal to everything. She nodded to herself, apparently pleased that Questa had accepted the pillow without demur, and then said that perhaps Alfie would like to see miss back to the house since she would want to settle in, like, before it grew totally dark.

'You've a coupla candles,' she said. 'But you'll be tired; I reckon you'll be asleep before ten.'

'Perhaps. But I don't want my fire to go out,' Questa said, suddenly anxious. Although May was steadily advancing it was still very cold at night and she had no desire to wake up freezing in the small hours. 'There's no need for you to come over, Alfie – it's not far!'

But in the event, both Alfie and Ellen accompanied her since Ellen said she wanted to make sure that Questa was snug. They let themselves in through the back door and went up the corridor and into the small parlour. It was a pleasant little room with a bay window and an old-fashioned cast-iron fireplace, the fire glowing redly still. Questa had brought a basketwork chair through from the kitchen, Alfie had provided the mattress and a couple of blankets, and now Ellen handed over a small tin filled with her homemade biscuits.

'Make yourself a cuppa tomorrer and have a nibble of these,' she advised. 'Then come and 'ave some breakfast with us. You'll be hungry again by then, I daresay.'

Questa thanked her but could not quite hide her eagerness for them to leave so that she might settle down. Ellen and Alfie bade her goodnight, told her to sleep well, and left. To be sure Ellen turned back at the last moment, but it was only to say, 'You use the piller; sweet dreams, lovie,' before disappearing down the corridor in her son's wake.

There were no curtains at the windows. The room faced the side of the property where the rose terrace was, but the cloud cover was thick and the view all greys. A slight wind had got up and now and again rain gusted against the panes. Questa made up the fire and boiled the kettle. Then she made herself a cup of cocoa and ate one of her biscuits, though she was not at all hungry. But it was nice to have her first meal at the Court, even though some might have argued that a biscuit and a cup of cocoa scarcely constituted a meal. Once the biscuit had gone and her cocoa was half drunk, Questa undressed, put on her nightgown and blew out the candle. Immediately, to her pleasure, the garden seemed closer, more intimate. She could see the trees, their branches moving at the wind's behest, and as she snuggled down beneath her blankets she saw that the clouds, too, were moving faster across the sky. Perhaps, presently, the clouds would part and allow the moon to shine through.

Just before she settled down she reached for the thyme pillow and regarded it thoughtfully. A pillow could not possibly keep nightmares at bay – or could it? Certainly it smelled very sweet, with a wild, out-of-doors smell. She could lie with her head on the pillow and imagine herself anywhere, on some gentle hillside, in a wood, by a stream ...

But it had been a long day and she was tired. Perhaps she was being silly, giving credence to an old woman's superstition, but she did not want to offend Ellen by not using the pillow. She snuggled it under her cheek, enjoying the rustling of the contents, feeling safer than she had felt for many years.

Presently, she slept.

Four

The dream started gently, as it always did. There was the lovely valley, the surrounding hills carpeted with vines, the long shadows stealing across the landscape as the sun set in a welter of crimson and gold. Questa was strolling quietly along with the little stream on her right, deep in the cleft it had spent maybe a thousand, two thousand years, cutting for itself. She could hear it, and now and again caught a glimpse of tumbling water, but for the most part it was just a presence, out of sight but known to be there.

The village was no more than half a mile away. A cluster of small white houses perched halfway up a steep hill. A walled village, which had basked all day in the sun and would gather in on itself as night drew on, as the rosy afterglow turned blue with dusk.

Soon the track upon which she trod turned away from the valley and began to climb. There were fig trees growing on the rough cliff face; as she walked she reached a long wall, crumbling, ancient, whose pale stones were the home of sinister little scorpions and lazy lizards who slid neatly out of the cracks to bask in the dying sun. The tops of fig trees growing further down the mountain reached over the wall; their purple fruit with its rough cat's-tongue skin could have been picked as she walked but there had been a drought. She knew the fruit would be small and hard, not worth gathering.

Questa strolled on through the warm evening air. She knew the path well, every bend, every view of the valley below. She came this way often, though not usually alone. Usually she would be with a crowd of other villagers who had been working the fields at the foot of the hill. She was beneath the outer wall of the village when her skin prickled a warning. What was it? Had she heard a sound? Noticed a smell? Something was not as usual, not quite as it should have been. She ignored the wall to her left but leaned over the crumbling wall to her right, reaching for a fig. She could not quite touch it, which was as well since she was playing for time, listening with every fibre of her being, trying to discover what was wrong, different.

Above in the village a woman called a child, a cat miaowed plaintively. As she listened, she began to hear the little sounds of a community whose long, hard day was drawing to a close. Buckets clanked – there was only one well and the women would be bringing in the water for the night – and a hoe tinkled as its owner dragged it up the last metre or so of stony path. A low voice sang ... she froze, the hairs on the back of her neck prickling erect. The voice was singing a familiar tune, a haunting lilt about a little shepherdess ... but the words were wrong!

'Go back, go back, go back, child, there's danger here, there's danger here, go back, go back, go back, child, there's danger, danger, here!'

Questa reached the fig, pulled it off its twig, then turned away, her thumb pressing through the roughness of the outer skin, revealing the sweet darkness of the inner fruit. She turned down the track again, as though she had only strolled up to pick the fig, knowing now that her instincts had not been wrong. The song was meant for her – They were in the village, waiting. If she strolled casually down the steep track and then ran very fast she might yet escape.

But she heard footsteps behind her, heavy army boots grating on the cobbles, and she ran. She had to run, she could not afford to let Them catch her. As she ran she saw the darkness of night creeping across the sky, the stars beginning to prick out, yet she ran on, reaching the fields and copses at the foot of the hill, doubling back on herself, dodging, hoping that this time, this time ... and behind her, relentlessly, the thud of footsteps, the harsh sound of their voices as they called one to another, the rush of small stones and gravel scattered before them.

They caught her. They held her, fingers biting into flesh, thrusting their rough, hateful faces close to hers. She knew what they would do; her body cringed away from the prospect, her bones began to ache, and suddenly, from somewhere, a new knowledge came, a knowledge which had never been hers in The Dream before. She stared at them as they began to question her, waiting for the moment, feeling strong, defiant.

'You're English! Someone told us – bloody Wops, supposed to be our allies, but they've hidden a spy. They'll suffer for it, but not the way you'll suffer! You'll be taken to Rome, tortured, hanged in front of the Vatican, but right now ... give me your hands!'

'You're not real!' Questa shouted, staring at the ring of evil faces. 'You're just shadows ... this is only a dream, you can't hurt me, I've got my thyme pillow, you can't hurt anyone, Nazi pigs!'

She wrenched herself free from her tormentors and hit the nearest face with all her force. The man squealed like a pig, his eyes got bigger and bigger whilst the rest of him began to dwindle to a moaning heap, the others backed away, got smaller and smaller ...

She woke.

She was lying in her bed in the small parlour. Beneath her cheek the thyme pillow rustled as she moved. Outside she could hear the fresh, buffeting wind in the treetops and above her head the stars shone. She turned her eyes to the window and saw the wind hurrying the tiny streamers of cloud across the sky so that they flickered across the moon's bland, blue and silver face. A branch creaked somewhere, and an owl gave one of those banshee shrieks which can bring your heart into your mouth for a moment.

But not Questa's. She was filled with happiness and the most tremendous elation. The dream was just that – a dream! She had conquered it, seen it for what it was, it need never frighten her again. Was it really the thyme pillow, or this place, or just that sufficient time had elapsed for her to conquer her fears? But it was the pillow, she was sure, helped by the Court. It had been her father's home once and now it was hers, and as her father had never let harm come to her whilst he was able to prevent it, the house would keep her safe now, in his absence.

The owl shrieked again. Questa got out of bed and went to the window. She saw the bird's dark shape float across the terrace and shuddered momentarily for small creatures crouched in the hedge, the froglet, the scurrying mouse frozen into terror by the harsh cry and the soundless shadow. She had once been as they, but now she was free, as free as they would be when daylight came.

She stood, nose pressed to the glass, and marvelled at her feelings. The windy night was wild and the woods would be wild too, not tame the way they were in daylight. As a boy, her father had gone out into the grounds in darkness or in light, he had loved the place so, and now she would do the same. She had conquered The Dream, now she would conquer the night.

Her dressing gown lay at the foot of the bed. Questa moved away from the window and put the gown on. There were biscuits in the kitchen, and the means of making a drink. She did not think she would sleep for a bit, she was too excited, too euphoric at the ending of The Dream. I'll make a hot drink and have some biscuits she thought vaguely. Then, if I feel like it, I'll go out for a moment into that wonderful windy darkness.

She went into the kitchen, all black and silver in the moonlight. The tin of biscuits was there, and the kettle, the cocoa. The room was warm still and smelled of food long past, but she went straight to the back door, fumbled it open and stepped into the yard. She crossed the cobbles, giving a quick glance up at the coachman's flat, but the curtains were pulled across and if Mrs Rimmer was awake there was no sign of it. She hesitated by the door into the kitchen garden but she knew, really, that it was the woods that drew her. She needed in some way to be a part of this night and not just an observer. So she went under the arch and across the gravel, skirting the old flower beds, heading for the woods she had seen and walked in that other night.

The long grass smelled of English summers, and there was a lovely scent as she moved under the trees. Was it cypresses which smelled so sweet? She remembered warm Italian nights when puffs of perfume had accompanied the cicadas' song, the faint cry of a sleepy nightbird, the bark of a distant dog echoing off the nearest hill. I'm a night creature, she told herself, crossing the grass and reaching the trees. It's easier to hide and run in the dark ... but that was yesterday and that's over. Now

I must learn to love the night for its beauty and strangeness, not for what it can hide.

She entered the wood and immediately wished she had put shoes on. Beech mast was prickly and her feet had lost the hardness they had gained in wartime Italy. But after wandering for a while, admiring the great trees in the moon-dappled shadows, she sat down under a tree, on a big beech root, and leaned against the smooth trunk. She was gazing around her, completely, totally happy, when she realised that she was really very tired and rather cold and that The Dream had exhausted her as it always did. How silly she would look if she fell asleep under the trees, and besides, she did not have her thyme pillow, she might have another nightmare. She stumbled to her feet and made her way out of the wood. All around her was the sort of breathless beauty she had dreamed of whilst in Italy, but she was too tired to take much notice. She stumbled into the kitchen, across it and into the small parlour. Her makeshift bed looked unbelievably inviting – especially the little pillow.

She lay down, her eyelids drooping, closing. For a moment she could hear her own breathing steadying, growing deeper. Then she slept.

She woke because something was tickling her nose. She realised she must have slept for a long time, because she could feel the sun's warmth on her skin, see the pinky gold of it through her eyelids. The tiny itchy feeling moved across the tip of her nose and danced across one cheek. Perhaps it was a butterfly ... or a large spider!

Her eyes shot open and one hand flailed at her face. She felt nothing, but nearby someone gave an ill-concealed snort of amusement. She turned her head out of the direct glare of the sun and saw a figure squatting a couple of feet away from her; a man, dark-browed, with a long stem of grass in one hand. The grass seeds bobbed as he stood up and frowned down at her.

'So you're awake at last! I spoke to you but you just went on sleeping, so ...' he gestured with the stem of grass. 'What are you doing here?'

He barked the question rather than asked it, with the black brows drawing together in a scowl as he looked down at her.

'Me?' Questa, still confused by sleep, frowned back at him. 'What are *you* doing here? Who are you? Don't you know these woods are private?'

He had been looking down at her almost aggressively, but at her words his face relaxed and he grinned. He had curly black hair, dark eyes narrowed at this moment into amused slits, and tanned skin. He was wearing a sort of smock shirt with rolled-up sleeves so that she could see his muscular arms and what looked like leather breeches which came just below his knees, and he had sandals with leather laces which criss-crossed his calves. Questa might have thought him a real country bumpkin, but there was something about him, an air of authority perhaps, which overrode his garments.

'So they are; they're my woods,' he said harshly, though his tone softened on the next words. 'Are you by any chance a neighbour? I thought you must be a servant from the villa, since I don't know them all yet, not having been here long. But servants don't usually upbraid their master ... Come on, lady; who are *you*?'

'I'm – I'm from n-next door,' Questa stammered, suddenly doubtful. She got to her feet, fighting a strong urge to run. She was on someone else's land, trespassing in fact. She had no idea what penalties, if any, this man could extract from her but he was powerfully built and clearly a force to be reckoned with. 'I-I'm sorry, I didn't know ...'

She looked up timidly into the dark face above her own and saw that the man was smiling, holding out a hand in the universal gesture of friendship.

Timidly, feeling that she had been wrong-footed and must not now add insult to injury by pretending not to see the hand, Questa put her own small paw into it and felt it gently clasped and then immediately released.

'My neighbour! I've been wondering when I should meet those of my neighbours who live close enough to visit, and I start off by browbeating you. We'd better start again. We must introduce ourselves as neighbours should; I am Marcus Augustae, son of

Tiberius, who is lately dead. I have marched with the legions ever since I came to my full strength and was up north, holding a fort in border country for the emperor, when my father died. So I was sent here, with the governor's blessing, to take up my inheritance.'

He said it beautifully, unselfconsciously, but it was still a bit like a poem he had learned by heart. Questa frowned, puzzled. It was not an ordinary way to introduce oneself!

'My home is behind you ... there.'

He gestured and for the first time Questa realised they were on the edge of the wood, where the grass grew lush, and followed his pointing finger. There was the house, snoozing in the sunshine.

It was definitely not Eagles Court. She could see the smoothness of lawn and a huge sand and gravel sweep; small, serious cypress trees lined the sweep, and beyond them was the house. Long and low, with narrow windows and whitewashed, timber-framed walls, it was roofed with large, bronze-coloured tiles and a good deal of the frontage was smothered in some sort of climbing plant. It was considerably newer and more modern than Questa's own home, just as the grounds were a great deal tidier and more functional.

'And you, lady? What is your name?'

'Oh,' Questa said feebly. How well he said his piece; it made her own explanation sound rather ordinary. 'I'm Questa, daughter of Charles Adamson and his wife Fortunata. My parents are both dead, so I'm living at Eagles Court and trying to make it into a proper home, farm the land and so on.' She gestured to the beautiful house which was Marcus's home. 'Your place is lovely, very well kept and modern-looking. Mine is falling apart really, so I have a lot to do just to make it habitable, and of course the land needs a lot of work. I don't know a great deal about agriculture but I intend to learn. We'll get it right in the end.'

'I, too, have a great deal to learn,' Marcus agreed. 'Come, I'll show you some of what I've done, though mainly it is the work of my servants.' He put a hand gently beneath her elbow and steered her across the rough grass and on to the smoothness of the shaven lawn, and Questa, who hated to be touched, found an odd sort of comradeship in the feel of his fingers on her skin. 'I did tell you I was lately arrived? You see, in our family the eldest son farms the land and the younger enters the army, so since I was my father's second son I've never taken much interest in the estate. In fact, it is more complicated even than that, since I was brought up in Gaul, on the estate of my uncle, but then my elder brother was killed ... with estates in border country such as this there is always the threat of danger ... and my father died, and so I am here whether I will or no, to do my best for future generations.'

Questa laughed; she couldn't help it, he sounded so gloomy at the thought of future generations.

'I expect you'll learn to love it,' she said. 'I want to be a good farmer very much and I have good ... good servants to help me. Besides, there are worse fates – fresh air, sunshine, lots of food which you grow yourself. And I suppose since you mentioned future generations you intend to marry, raise a family?'

'Aye, but that's for old men, not for those young enough to march under the eagle!' He scowled, the thick brows knitting into a bar across his broad, tanned forehead, and Questa noticed a scar on his brow, slanting from left to right, still with the slight puckering which showed it had not been there long. 'How I kick against the pricks, Questa! It's good that I've met you, good that we've talked. I wouldn't say I have servant trouble, exactly, but the women weep and the men go pale when I give orders. They cannot understand how I feel, they've been bred to the land. I am a good few years older than you, but I have just as much to learn of farming, and of how to deal with servants. We'll learn together, share our trials. What about it?'

Questa looked up at him. They were halfway across the lawned part of his garden and now he stopped to look down at her, his expression serious, questioning. He was not as old as she had at first thought, she realised, probably no more than in his early twenties. He had a narrow, strong face, a humorous mouth, eyes which could laugh or frown. Oddly enough, the scar did not detract from the attraction she felt for him; she thought he had a strong and beautiful face. She knew, suddenly, that this was a man for whom she could feel great respect as well as great liking, a man to honour.

'Yes! I'd like to get your advice from time to time, talk things over. You're right, s-servants aren't quite the same. Though I do wonder ...'

She felt a traitor to Ellen even saying the word servant, but could not think of another word to describe the older woman, not without going into more detail than she wished at any rate.

'What do you wonder? Go on, never be afraid to tell me when I'm wrong.'

'Well, you say the women weep, and you did shout at me, you know, when you woke me up. And you say you've been a soldier – perhaps you frighten them.'

He looked astonished, then sighed. 'I'm gentle as a lamb. You should hear me when I urge my men into battle! But you could be right ... I'll try to ask and not order, perhaps. And now let's seal our bargain of mutual help.'

He took hold of her hands and drew her close, until their bodies were almost touching. Then he kissed her forehead; she felt his lips, warm and soft as a moth, touch her skin, then he held her back from him, and he was smiling down at her as though he had known her for years. She saw that he had a dangerous face, the face of a man of action, and understood for a fleeting moment what it would mean to him to give up the army, the excitement, and settle down far from civilisation on his family's estate, to work, not for his emperor and his country, but for a future generation which, as yet, meant nothing to him.

'We've sealed our bargain with a kiss, Questa, daughter of Adamson. Now look before you, up there!'

She followed his pointing finger with her eyes. Above his house reared a hill, and now that she looked closely she could see that it swarmed with men and with donkey carts, some men piling soil into the carts whilst others led the laden donkeys away.

'What, the hill do you mean? What's happening? It's rather steep for cultivation, isn't it?'

'Aye. Which is why we're terracing it. See the fellows with the big hoes? And the stone-gatherers? They'll have the work done in another week to ten days and then what do you think I should grow there?'

'Oh, vines, I suppose. When I was in Rome ...'

90

She had spoken thoughtlessly, instinctively, and he cut across the sentence in the same spirit, his dark face lightening.

'You are recently from home? Though why I should think of Rome as my home when I've never been there, nor my father before me, I can't explain. In truth I'm as British as my steward, but the family think of themselves as Roman. We're more like citizens of the world I suppose. I spent my childhood in Gaul, my adult working life until now wherever Rome needed the legions … but tell me about your Roman vines, for you're right, I do intend to plant a vineyard on that hill.'

'There isn't much to tell, except that whilst I was in Italy I spent time … years … on many small farms and holdings where grapes were grown. Naturally I helped to cultivate them so I do know a little about it. But can one grow grapes here? Isn't it too cold?'

He shook his head pensively, then suddenly grinned.

'You sound like all the old women now toiling resentfully on that hill, terracing it for my young vines! By Jupiter, I told them, why should it be any colder in Britain than Gaul? Come to that, when I came to Britain across the sea, from my uncle's estate, I saw vines growing down south. They were planted on gentle hills facing seawards, but I see no reason why they shouldn't flourish here too. That hill faces south, gets the best of whatever sun there is … and won't it be good to see the vine leaves turn from young green to old gold, and the grapes form, ripen, split with goodness? We pay good money for foreign muck, why not make our own?'

'Our own muck?'

He laughed again, then caught hold of her shoulders and gave her a quick, comradely hug. His arms were hard, his chest harder, yet Questa felt no fear, no repugnance, only pleasure that this man was so easy with her that she, in her turn, could be easy with him.

'Wicked one! Our own good wine, I should have said. Now tell me, when were your vines planted? At leaf-fall?'

'Yes, I think it was autumn. Certainly, when the grapes were picked and trodden, that was the time for pruning and manuring the crop, digging the stuff into the soil, putting straw down around the roots if they grew in an exposed spot.'

He nodded thoughtfully. 'Aye, straw around the roots is a good idea, I'll do that. I've sent for the vines, they should be here any day. You must come over when we plant them. In which direction is your home?'

Questa looked all round her. She shook her head. The low sun was in her eyes and somehow she could not remember which way she had come. Indeed, she must have walked a long way, probably in her sleep, since she could see no sign of Eagles Court nor of the mere. Good lord, she must have come from behind the range of hills she could see when she looked back, rising above the woods; she must have walked miles and miles!

She pointed to the blue and distant hills.

'I come from … there, somewhere. I'd better go back or I'll – I'll lose my way.'

She expected him to pooh-pooh what seemed like a feeble excuse, but he nodded, serious. He touched her arm and they turned back, towards the woods.

'Aye, it doesn't do to be out after dark in border country. Where are your dogs? Did you ride over or come on foot?'

'I have no dogs, not yet. Why?'

He frowned, looking anxious now. 'But you should always have a dog or two with you when you leave your estate! And if you've come far you should come on a pony, or with a companion … look, I'll take you home, I can't let you go alone.'

Questa shook her head, suddenly uneasy. She felt like an impostor, yet she was no such thing; she really did not know quite where she had come from. Nor where she was going, for that matter. But she knew she must be alone, that to get back she would have to return to the woods. She glanced back at the house, then nodded in that direction.

'It's not very far. Marcus, did you say you had a dog? Is it that fawn hound dog coming round the corner of the house now?'

He looked. There was such a dog, a lean, fast-looking animal which stared across at them and, when Marcus whistled, came bounding towards them, long tail swinging in ecstatic welcome.

'Aye, that's Abacus. Here, boy, come and meet my friend Questa.'

His back was to her and the woods were not too far to reach without running. She walked casually away; in the shelter of the trees she risked a quick glance back. He was fussing the dog, producing something from his pocket, the dog was taking it, eating, licking Marcus's fingers …

She walked determinedly into the trees. How strange it was; the day had been far from over seconds earlier, when she was with Marcus, yet now it looked dark ahead, almost as though a storm were approaching.

She sat down against the trunk of a big old beech and leaned forward, resting her head on her arms. She closed her eyes. Behind the lids confused pictures chased each other; Marcus and the dog, the people working on the hill behind the house, a pair of piercing dark eyes under heavy brows, with pleasure in their depths because he had met someone of his own kind, someone with whom he had something in common … Without realising what was happening, her thoughts slid into dreams.

She awoke. She was curled up in her bed and outside the window of the small parlour the moon shone down through the trees and the wind raised its voice and tossed the branches about so that the moonlight coming through the window was splintered into spears and patches and pools of silver as it fell on the floor.

Questa looked around her. No tall, dark, dangerous Marcus, no beautiful Roman villa, no dogs barking in the distance. She struggled to sit up. She felt stiff and sleepy and rather foolish. She had simply been dreaming, but what a very weird dream – and it had taken no time at all, the moon was still high in the sky, the wind still moaned through the trees, yet she had travelled a long way in her dream, met a friend, seen his lovely home, talked about …

She frowned. Something niggled at her mind, something almost remembered but not quite. Then she got it; he had called her *lady*. He had known at once that she was a woman, and had treated her as such, even when he thought her just a servant. Yet here people continually mistook her for a boy. It had been nice to find oneself accepted as a woman, she decided.

And they had talked about grapes. So far as she knew grapes were never grown in Britain, yet in the not too distant past she had known quite a lot about viticulture; probably she still did …

when you had toiled on the land you didn't just forget the precious lessons you learned. But wasn't it odd, to dream about growing grapes so vividly? Only, dreams being what they were, perhaps she had been in Italy in her dream? Had Marcus said he lived in England? But she could not really remember.

She was halfway to sleep again when it occurred to her that Marcus had said they grew grapes down south. She didn't know precisely where he had meant but she was suddenly sure he had been talking about England. That hill, though – it had slumbered full in the afternoon sun, there had been trees on it at intervals, which would give shade to the pickers, and the terracing had been going on apace. There was no reason why Marcus shouldn't grow grapes, even if she could not. And who was to say that she could not, anyway? She knew about viticulture, she had enjoyed working the vines, next time she saw Marcus she would ask him how the vines were flourishing in this cooler, damper British climate.

She was drifting on the very borders of sleep when it came to her; there was a very good reason why Marcus would never grow grapes on his hill and that was because he was just a dream, and dream men, no matter how nice they may be or how determined, very rarely grow successful vines.

It was odd, though. He had seemed so *real*. Questa shrugged the blankets up over her ears and decided to try to will herself back into the dream, and this time she would stay for a bit, meet his dogs, see how he ran things.

But when she slept it was dreamlessly and soundly, until morning.

'Miss Questa, where d'you want this put?'

Ellen's nephew Bert, cap on the back of his head, face shiny with effort, addressed Questa as she crossed the hall below him. Bert and his son Patrick were lugging an enormous piece of furniture down the stairs, a sort of combined cupboard and bench, which Questa fancied in the kitchen. It would be useful both as an extra seat and to keep their waterproofs in, and what was more, she was learning from experience. People were willing to pay satisfactorily large sums for old, well-polished piecrust tables, nice old chairs with interestingly carved legs and arms, desks and dressing-tables and bureaux. But the really old stuff, the really big stuff, simply wasn't worth selling. Which did not mean, however, that it was not worth using in the house.

Now she smiled as the two men manoeuvred the colossal piece of furniture down the last few stairs, and she pointed down the passageway which led to the back of the house.

'In the kitchen, please Bert. On the wall between the back door and the window, it should just fit. Is Ellen still busy in the garden? If so I'll make a pot of tea for us all. I think we've earned it.'

They had. Every time a piece of furniture was sold in London, here in Shropshire a fresh plan swung into action. A second-hand tractor was Questa's proudest possession and Patrick's time – at present he worked three hours a day for her and six for a dairy farmer up Smethwick way – was her next biggest expenditure. Cleaning the house was still going on, as were repairs. Ellen said Questa would still be unblocking gutters and clearing nests out of chimneys in ten years, and though this might have depressed some people it made Questa happy, because it meant that Ellen, at least, could see that she would still be here in ten years' time.

And she was busy! From dawn until dusk she worked, either on the house or the kitchen garden. She was not afraid of hard physical work, liked it in fact, and already she had a large part of the kitchen garden under cultivation, and had plans for the rest. The wild old orchard which pressed up against the rosy bricks of the kitchen garden wall, as though anxious to share in the calm shelter on its further side, had been discounted by the Rimmers, too busy to cope with the extra work load, but Questa had gone poking round there and learned to use a scythe to keep the grass down.

'It needs pruning; some of the trees have never been touched,' she told Alfie and Ellen that night over high tea. 'But there will still be a decent crop – what happened to last year's?'

'Put some in apple loft, give some to Snorkie, left the rest to rot,' Alfie said. 'Snorkie likes 'em, but they does all come ripe at once and windfalls go rotten too quick.'

'The cider people pay quite well for windfalls,' Questa said. 'I asked, in the village. And I want a pig of my own ... will Snorkie have babies?'

'Her's a boar,' Alfie said rather confusingly. 'Last year we 'ad Rosie as well, she were a sow. But we sold 'er to Athertons.' He chuckled. 'Now they pays us to let Snorkie 'ave 'is way with 'er. Less fag, like.'

'Less money, too,' Ellen pointed out. 'But the work were gettin' us down, I do admit.'

'I should have thought Snorkie was more trouble than any mere sow could be,' Questa observed. Snorkie was large, vicious with strangers and sometimes forgot his enormous weight and pinned visitors to his sty against the wall or the gate. His greed was notorious; food put in his trough disappeared noisily down the hatch in seconds, and Snorkie turned his piggy eyes to heaven and demanded more. But Alfie loved him, spent hours oiling his coarse, flaky skin, tickling him behind the ears, throwing buckets of water over him when it was warm and then scrubbing him with the yard broom, whilst Snorkie, his white lashes half down over his bright little eyes, dreamed of sows and fighting and huge banquets of rotting apples, acorns and pigmeal.

'Oh ah; but Alfie do love 'er,' Ellen said sagely. 'An' Snorkie love Alf; 'twouldn't be the same without them two together.'

'Athertons 'ave piglets though,' Alfie said after a short silence during which, presumably, he mused on the love between pig and man. 'Want me to git a couple, 'stead of the servin' fee?'

'Oh, yes please!' Questa said at once. 'I bet they make up into fine pigs – Snorkie's babies, I mean.'

'Best you'll ever buy,' Alfie said, sounding like a proud father. 'Get two gilts, then un can go to Snorkie; you'll 'ave a pig-farm 'fore you knows it.'

But right now Alfie was at Athertons working, Ellen was picking soft fruit for bottling, Mary Drew from the village was washing walls, ceiling and floor in the big front room, and Questa, still pigless, ought to be making the tea for elevens.

She went through into the kitchen. It looked good, she considered, even though the seat-cupboard was askew – Bert was not too good on placing furniture artistically – and the windows needed cleaning. Outside, June sunshine poured down, a blessing to those who had been facing up to the worst the British weather could throw at them until this last week. The fire was smouldering a bit so she gave it a poke, then put the kettle on the hob. In the long pantry she found a tin with oatcakes and got them out, then she walked over to the window and gazed out at the sunny yard.

The dream of Marcus and his vines – if it was a dream – still haunted her. She had hoped to dream it again, but she had not done so. She really wondered, what was more, if it *had* been a dream. She must have neighbours, after all, it stood to reason. Why should she not have met one of them, then, and got muddled somehow? She had asked, carefully, about the Athertons. Yes, there was a son but the old man was very much alive ... an old devil in some ways, Alfie said. Just one son? she asked, and was told that there had been an older boy but he had been killed in the war, which left the younger one in charge.

Questa wanted to meet them. Naturally. They were her neighbours, and the memory of Marcus stayed with her. She could see his face more clearly in her mind's eye than she could see the faces of those friends and relatives she had left behind in Italy. More clearly, now that she thought about it, than she could visualise Alan or Grace. If he really was an Atherton then the sooner she went over there and met them the better. She was beginning to think that, good though her life here was beginning to be, it lacked something, lacking Marcus. And no one could feel like that about a man in a dream, could they? So she must find him if he was to be found and if that meant bearding the Athertons in their den, bearded they should be.

Behind her, the kettle began to sing and splutter. Questa made the tea, poured it into the cups, went to the kitchen door and hollered for Mary, Bert and Patrick, then let herself out into the yard. She crossed it, pushed open the little green door and addressed Ellen's back, humped over the strawberries she was picking.

'Ellen, elevenses!'

Presently, sitting round the table, she asked about the Athertons. 'Should I go and see them? Would it be polite? I've been here a month now, after all, I know most people in the village, but not them.'

'Might not do ... or then again, it might,' Mary volunteered. 'Old man Atherton wanted to buy your land, when Joshua had it. Reckons it was 'is, way back. He's a nice enough feller though – but the young 'un ... no one cares much for 'im.'

'Oh!' Questa said, rather dismayed. 'What's he like?'

But no one really seemed to know. Bert said he was known to be mean with a poor feller tryin' to catch a few rabbits – the young'un, that was – and Mary said he'd tried to stop the kids fishin' the stream up near the house, though all they'd got were flour bags on canes. Weren't likely to get a whale in one of they!

'Still, best to be neighbourly,' Ellen said suddenly. She had listened to the general opinions without giving her own until now. 'The young'un's strange to it, like, same's you are, me dear. Give 'un a chance, see 'ow 'e seems.'

'Why not? I'll go after tea,' Questa decided. Excitement bubbled up in her at the prospect of finding out something about Marcus. She had asked Ellen and the others, casually, but they had been unable to shed any light on the matter. 'Can I take them some strawberries, Ellen?'

'Course you can. Happen that'll soften 'em,' Ellen said. 'Pick 'em just afore you go, so's they'm sweet wi' the sunshine.'

It was lovely to be outside, picking strawberries and putting them carefully into a long straw basket lined with cabbage leaves. Questa chose each strawberry for its redness and size and soon had a respectable pile. Then she went indoors, leaving the fruit on the kitchen table, and washed her face and hands, dried them on one of the towels recently rescued from the attic – linen of good quality had been discovered in a series of chests – brushed her hair hard, noting that it was growing nicely and now waved appealingly over her ears, and set off down the stairs. Wouldn't it be grand if she walked right into Marcus, and he saw her in her decent skirt, with her hair newly washed and brushed ... Not that he'd care, he liked her for herself, she was sure he was indifferent to appearances.

There was no one in the hall to tell her she looked all right, but Ellen was still in the kitchen, pottering about clearing away their high tea. She usually made the meal there, the three of them ate together, then she and Alfie returned to the coachman's flat whilst Questa settled into whatever tasks she had set herself for the evening.

But today she suspected that the task would be rather more of a strain than most. If she had known that she would meet only Marcus it would have been different, but she still found meeting people she did not know an ordeal and, try though she might, she found shaking hands a hateful business. With one's hands enveloped by another's, one was so painfully vulnerable to ... to ... Questa's mind snapped shut, darkly. Don't think, don't think! Besides, she could not help hoping that by meeting the Athertons she might get a clue as to how to meet up with Marcus again. The more she thought about that meeting the more sure she became that it had happened, had not been a dream. Dreams weren't like that, you didn't think about them again once day had dawned. It stood to reason that, in her miserable and nervous state after the nightmare, she had wandered outside, gone to sleep somewhere, woken, met Marcus.

But that wouldn't do, because she'd woken in bed. All right, she told herself recklessly, you've met him before, some time, and forgotten until now, because you dreamed of him. And since you want to meet him again you'd best get on to Atherton Hall and even if you don't meet him there you can start up some sort of a social life, then you're absolutely bound to meet him, it stands to reason.

Because there was a strong possibility that Marcus might not be the young 'un' who had put backs up so thoroughly in the village. Even so, it seemed worthwhile going ahead with her plan. Besides, he could not possibly be as unpleasant as everyone seemed to think. Why, she might even like him; he might be as friendly towards her as Marcus had been.

Furthermore, it was a lovely evening. Sunshine, low and golden, slanted through the trees as she made her way down the long drive. She knew the way, thanks to Ellen, though she did think that if she made a habit of visiting the Athertons she would not go again by road. It seemed silly when Atherton land marched with Adamson land the way it did.

But this was a formal visit, so Questa turned left outside the gates, walked for a mile or so along the dusty road, crossed a hump-backed bridge and looked down wistfully on the shallow river with the big, pale-coloured stones and the weed, thick as mermaid tresses, and the willows and alders arching over the water. How beautifully cool it looked, and she had walked a long way already ... there would be no harm in paddling in the shallows for a moment, just to cool her feet, would there?

To think, in this instance, was to act. Questa hopped nimbly up on the parapet of the bridge and dropped down on to the sloping bank, climbed down to water level, shed her shoes, hung the basket of strawberries on a low branch, and waded into the water.

It was wonderfully cool and soothing. The stones were big and flat, delightful to walk on, and the weed was mainly in midstream and best avoided anyway since it was sure to be slippery. Questa discovered that the river was full of life: tiny fish no bigger than her little finger, water snails on the stems of the rushes by the bank, a thousand oddities which, she knew, she would once have been able to name. It brought happy memories back with such a rush that she had to swallow a big lump in her throat and her eyes filled with tears. Oh, if only, if only! Daddy would have rolled up his trousers and paddled with her, pointing out the dragonfly skimming the reeds, the brown trout in a deep pool, the tiny wren watching her antics from the shelter of a nearby elder. She had changed her working trousers for a skirt rather reluctantly, but now she was glad because she could tuck the skirt into her knicker elastic and go much deeper than trousers would have allowed.

She had waded far upstream and the light was going from the sky when she suddenly remembered her visit and her strawberries. She turned and made for the bank, then began to run along it, anxious now, all her pleasure in the river gone. It would be too late to go calling, she would look rude, a complete idiot – whatever had got into her to behave so badly, to forget her duty?

She found the tree where she had stashed the basket of berries and was reaching up to get them down when a voice spoke behind her.

'Stay quite still; don't move a muscle. I've got a gun trained right in the middle of your back.'

The voice was speaking in English, otherwise it might have come straight out of her nightmare. At once, the little fingers on both Questa's hands began to throb and her stomach turned to water. It had happened, what she had always dreaded. They had found her, come for her, now they would kill her!

Her hands were on the basket; behind her, she could *feel* his nearness as a chill on her skin, a creeping certainty that he was getting closer. It was dim under the willows, and quiet save for the murmur of the wind and the chuckle and slap of moving water. But her ears, finely tuned by terror, could hear his every movement. His breathing, fast and husky. The slight sounds his clothing made as he shifted from foot to foot.

'Now, let's have a look at ...'

He moved as he spoke, but Questa moved faster. She grabbed the basket, swung it round and brought it crashing into the man's face.

He was not expecting it. He staggered back, cursing. She knew he was cursing by the ugly, hateful way he spoke, though the words were all strange to her. She saw that he was of medium height, brown-haired, with a thin, straight nose and almost black eyes. Then she was running, terror lending wings to her feet.

'Here, lad ... by God, it's a girl ... stop! Hang on! Here ...'

She was halfway up the bank and heading for the stone bridge when splinters of stone spattered on her. He had fired, missed, hit the bridge. She must escape, she must get away or he would undoubtedly kill her! She made one last desperate effort, gained the parapet of the bridge, felt something sharp hit her leg, wobbled and fell.

She rolled down the bank and was immediately grabbed. She closed her eyes, feigning death, unconsciousness, anything to put him off his guard. But he kept hold of her and suddenly water deluged her, making her gasp, turn her head.

'So you aren't unconscious! Open your eyes or I'll ...'

She opened them. He was crouching over her, pale-faced save for where a long, sluggishly bleeding scratch traced the basket's

101

recent path. Despite her fear, Questa felt a tiny stirring of satisfaction. That would teach him that she was not quite helpless.

'Look ... I didn't realise. I thought you were poaching. But you're trespassing anyway, you had no right in the river. Sit up!'

She sat up, realising as she did so that this was no Gestapo agent pursuing her, no killer on her trail. It was simply the hateful young Mr Atherton, who had wanted to stop her paddling in his wretched river and had threatened her with a gun, grabbed hold of her, fired after her ...

'It wouldn't have hurt you, it's only shot, I was after rabbits,' he said gruffly, seeing her glance stray to the gun at his side. 'Where did you steal those strawberries from? I'll get you for that, even if I can't prove you were poaching.'

Questa pushed the hair back from her face. He seemed to take fright at the gesture, as though it meant she was about to run, and grabbed her again, his fingers closing, with spiteful force, over the soft flesh of her upper arm. Questa gave a hoarse little grunt and tore herself out of his grasp, shuddering with revulsion. She had been afraid but now, suddenly, she was very angry. This was England and this man, damn his eyes, was her neighbour! She stared at him with all the hatred and contempt she could muster.

'You! Who do you think you are to talk to me like that? I was taking some strawberries to my neighbour, Mr Atherton, when you jump on me, frighten me, fire at me ... Do you really think you can get away with such behaviour?'

He made a rude, derisive noise through pursed lips. He sprayed her with spit as he did so and despite herself, Questa flinched.

'Your neighbour, indeed! I know everyone for miles around, everyone the old man knows, anyway. You're just some little servant girl from the village.'

'I'm Questa Adamson, of Eagles Court,' Questa said flatly. 'And you are young Atherton. They said in the village that you were a bully and a braggart, a thoroughly nasty piece of work.'

'I'm Atherton and this is Atherton land ...'

Questa shook herself and stood up. She felt stiff and swimmy and now that she was on her feet she simply longed to run and run and run, to escape from him completely, to get home and wash his hateful, creeping touch from her person, but suddenly she knew she must not let herself down before this smug and hateful young man. And to think she had thought of his family in the same breath as Marcus! She knew now, quite certainly, that there could be no connection.

'You've said it all before. If your father wants to prosecute me for paddling in the river, then he can do his worst. As for you, don't you dare try to stop me, because I'm going home now.'

'Just a minute! You aren't just walking off like that, young woman, we've got things to discuss!'

Questa ignored him, walking steadily on into the woods. She was shoeless, basketless, but she could not possibly turn back, not now. She would not run, she would not give him that satisfaction, but dusk was deepening and if she intended to get home before darkness actually fell she must step out. Damn him, damn him, she would *not* go round by the road, even though crossing the fields meant she was trespassing and he might try once more to stop her.

Behind her, she heard his heavy tread. But the hedge through which Questa slid, slim and pliable herself as one of the hazel wands she pressed to one side, proved too much of an obstacle. He shouted something, an obscenity she suspected, then walked along the hedge, clearly searching for a gap. Presumably he found none for presently she heard him retreat, crashing through the undergrowth around the river, half-blinded by temper and the increasing dark.

Questa trudged on, her bare feet making light work of meadow grass and only slightly harder work of crops. She had been so busy in the house and kitchen garden that she had not had time to explore her own grounds, and despite the frail curl of silver in the sky which was the new moon she began to look curiously about her as she went.

There was a stream; she thought it must be on her land since the nettles and thistles here – she winced – were rampant, and presently she came upon a bend of the river, also seemingly on her land. She could see the outline of the woods dark against the sky and climbed over some chestnut palings rather than try to find the gate by what light there was, made her way through the trees and saw the comforting bulk of Eagles Court snuggled against its hill before her.

She limped towards it, suddenly smitten by a terrible loneliness. Such a short time ago, it seemed, she had courted loneliness, longed for it, plotted to be left to herself. But things had changed. Without fully realising it, she had begun to enjoy company: Ellen's, the men's. She had felt safe when she was with them. And with Marcus she had felt best of all. How badly she wanted him – needed him! Her own company was no longer enough.

Happily on her own this evening, she had been frightened, attacked, bruised. Now she felt loneliness as a painful thing, a thing to be avoided. Because she had been alone she had lost her shoes, her basket, even the strawberries picked with such care. And now she was going home, to wash her wounds and put herself to bed, because no one was interested in Questa Adamson. Not now that there was no Daddy to look after her.

But all that will change when I find Marcus again, Questa told herself as she trudged through the trees. He can't just be a dream, you don't make friends in dreams and I like him better than anyone else I've ever met. I like him as much as I hate young Atherton. And I'll find him again, because I'm determined to do so. And in the meantime, that young Atherton had better watch out, because I won't be bullied and knocked about again; I'll kill him first!

The fire was still glowing in the kitchen, so she riddled it and got it roaring, then heated water for washing. Whilst the kettle boiled she lit the lamp, then cut herself a hunk of bread and spread honey thinly over it. When that was no more than a memory, she had a hot drink and began to wash.

She was filthy and every bit as bruised and battered as she had imagined. But she did her best to make herself clean and tidy, brushed her hair and made the fire up for the night, piling ashes on top to damp the flames. She turned out the lamp and made her way through into the small parlour. There was no sense in sleeping upstairs when the parlour was so nice and cosy and the bedrooms all so large and bare, and anyway she liked sleeping down here. It made it easier to reach the kitchen when she couldn't sleep – not that she suffered from sleeplessness much, not now. She was usually so tired she slept exhaustedly as soon as her head touched the pillow.

Tonight would surely be no exception. She was tired and unhappy, bruised and sore. She snuggled down therefore, and waited for sleep to come.

Five

She woke under a tree. It was evening, the sky that palest of pale greens which sometimes follows a glorious sunset. She looked around her, aware of a feeling of pleasant anticipation; a friend was near, she could feel it.

He came round the great trunk of the tree, saw her and stopped short, with a muttered exclamation. He looked pleased to see her, as pleased as she felt to see him.

'By Jupiter, you startled me! I've looked for you over and over since that first time, but you didn't come. I've been busy of course, as you have, but even so ... it's a long time to wait, many months ... and then this evening as I was checking the vines I got such a strong feeling, like a voice talking in my head. She's in the wood, it said, that girl of yours is in the wood; why don't you go and look for her? So I did, and here you are. Now don't run off this time, come up and see the vines. There are grapes already, though of course the bunches are small at this time of the year. Come with me, let me show you!'

He held out his hands and caught hers, pulling her to her feet. Questa could have shouted with delight. She had needed a friend, she wanted to tell him ... but she could not remember what she wanted to tell him and anyway it didn't seem to matter. What mattered was going with him to see his grapes and perhaps visiting his house. Nice, ordinary neighbours did things like that.

He led her over the lawn and across the great sweep of sand and gravel, past formal garden beds and to the left of the house and round into an inner courtyard which she had not seen on her last visit. It was a bigger house than she had realised from the front, built around the square courtyard, the many outbuildings thatched though the house itself was tiled. People were everywhere; they smiled or saluted Marcus, then continued with their work. Dogs sniffed, straggled, trotted at heel. A donkey pulled a basketwork cart carrying rushes, plodding, head lowered, through the side entrance. Marcus drew her through the people, nodding, not stopping, and out under another arch. Here the hill reared, terraced now and edged with vines. They climbed, hand in hand, from terrace to terrace, up a flight of broad concrete steps. Halfway up he stopped, pulling her to a halt as well. His chest scarcely heaved with the climb but Questa panted like a dog, a hand to her ribs.

'You must be fit! What a pace you set, Marcus, it nearly killed me!'

'Sorry. But look!'

He made a broad, sweeping gesture with his arm, encompassing the whole of the terraced hillside.

'Well, what do you think of them? They've had more than a year's growth, we spread muck last autumn. What d'you think?'

Questa did not answer at once; she sensed he was wanting a considered reply. She walked a little way along the row as she had seen the wise old peasants doing. She brushed the bloom off a tiny bunch, tested the firmness of the grapes, felt the leaves, smooth and dark with summer, slid her fingers delicately along the wood. The vine was healthy, the grapes would be good if the weather stayed fair.

She said as much.

'That's fair enough. I'm glad you approve; you do approve, I take it?'

'Yes. I envy you, Marcus. Some day I'll grow grapes on my estate, I swear it to you.'

He laughed, throwing back his head so that she could see the strong, tanned column of his throat.

'So you swear it, do you? But we had a severe winter, we even had snow, and it lay. Yet they lived. What do you say to that? Did you think it could happen – that they would survive a hard winter? We had frosts, of course, though not after February. I dreaded the cold weather, but we survived, or they did, rather. Viticulture is being encouraged because of the price of wine from

Gaul, but there's little official advice available to would-be growers such as myself. Very few estate owners can be bothered, I suspect, what with local labour being dead against anything they don't understand and the problem of harsh winters. I wonder if there is any means of combating frost that local people do know, but don't associate with grapes?'

Questa frowned. 'Let me think. We had bad winters in Rome but the grapes seemed to survive, and down south, where I got most of my experience, it was very much warmer. We had to spray against mildew, prune properly, dig in rotted horse-muck … but Ellen was saying the other day … oh, let me think!'

She sat down on a step of the hillside and Marcus sat down beside her. His eyes slid lazily over his estate; the crops, the beasts, the spread of the farm and its outbuildings below him. There were people crossing and recrossing the courtyard still, and men in the fields. It was easy to see that Marcus employed a great many people; Questa just wished she could do the same. But wages were expensive and she was still cautious with her money. Watching his brooding profile now, however, Questa's mind went back to Ellen, who was so wise in the ways of growing things. A few days ago, in the kitchen garden, Ellen had been telling her how she had collected a number of muslin curtains, and when the wireless forecast an unexpected late frost one May she had spread her curtains over the currant bushes and saved the crop.

'Mind, I could smell there were a frost comin',' she had assured Questa. 'I'd a known even without that wireless. Oh ah, a few light curtains 'a saved a crop more'n once.'

She had gone on to explain that it was not the winter frosts which killed off a crop, because in winter a tree would be bare, its buds tightly clenched against the cold. The damage came when spring lured the buds into unfurling, the young fruit into forming. Then a late frost would nip the buds and blight the young fruit beyond redemption.

After some thought Questa turned to Marcus.

'Look, it's only late frosts which kill a crop. Locally, they cover one or two precious bushes with muslin, or I've heard tell you can water the frost off before the sun comes up. I did tell you to straw the roots, I suppose you could build up the straw a bit, even scatter it over the branches of one or two more advanced vines. But for an entire crop spread across a wide hillside, like this one, all you can do is pray.'

He nodded, accepting what she said as naturally as though she were a dozen years older than he and infinitely more experienced. It was one of his charms, Questa guessed, that he could take advice when it was offered, either from the men who worked for him or from a relative stranger like herself.

'I'm saying nothing against the power of prayer, but I'll get my people to rise early if we have a May frost next year. For now they'll be safe enough, so it looks as though we'll be gathering a crop in a few weeks. As for manuring, that will be done as it was last year, when the leaves have fallen and the crop is gathered. What about libations? Do you favour them?'

Was that another word for pruning, or nipping out? Ellen was full of such talk, she would ask her. In the meantime, play safe.

'Sometimes yes, sometimes no,' she said. 'Let's look at the rest of the vines, shall we?'

They walked solemnly along the rows and Questa took the bunches in her hands gently so as not to spoil the bloom, then advised Marcus to nip out the tinier bunches so that the plant could use more energy on the ones remaining.

'You'll get a better shape and fuller fruit, and though it should by rights have been done earlier it won't hurt the crop,' she explained. 'What will you do next?'

'Pick 'em, press 'em, drink 'em,' Marcus said. 'Maybe sell them to others, or at least sell the wine. As I said, the imported stuff is expensive, so this crop represents quite a saving. Shall we go down, now? I've started up another sort of farming which might interest you … hey, hold up!'

Questa, turning, had slipped on the edge of the terrace and Marcus grabbed her sleeve, pulling the full whiteness away from her arm. Automatically glancing down at herself Questa saw beneath the thin white material, the swell of small, pointed breasts. She was still staring at them, fascinated, wondering that such a physical change could come about so quickly when Marcus jerked her to a halt. With her sleeve pulled up to the elbow, Marcus's eyes were fixed on her arm and its purple and blue bruises and abrasions.

'Who's beaten you? Who has dared?' He sounded angry, as though at a personal affront. 'How did this happen? You are no slave and no man should beat a child hard enough to mark her!'

'I'm not a child, Marcus. I was careless; I fell off the coping of a bridge, bounced down the river bank ... it hurt, but it was my own fault.'

She spoke precisely, like the child he had just called her, suddenly determined not to admit what had really happened. He stroked a hand down the side of her face and she winced when his fingers touched the long graze down her cheek. He shook his head at her, grinning.

'You aren't a child, but what other young woman climbs bridges and then falls off them? Be more careful, little one, it is a short step between a few bruises and a broken skull. Act like the mistress of your house.'

Questa nodded. 'You're right, I'll do as you say.'

'Good. And now I'll show you where I mean to have the grapes trodden, the barrels that await them and the carts the donkeys will pull.'

They had reached the bottom of the hill. Questa stopped short, shaking her head.

'I can't come with you now, it's getting late again. I must get home before dark.'

'I'll walk part of the way with you. Wait here whilst I fetch Abacus; he's my favourite hound. You'll like him.'

He disappeared under the arch into the courtyard she could still see dimly through the gathering dusk.

Questa set off at once for the woods. She had the feeling that she had overstayed her welcome, though she could not have said why. So she ran lightly across the sandy gravel and into the trees, dodging the tall trunks, padding along in her light sandals. Sandals? She had no sandals! She stopped short, her heart thudding, and bent to examine her footwear ...

... And woke. The sun was shining, the window in the small parlour was half open and somewhere a cock shouted that it was a lovely morning and hadn't everyone better get up? Questa pushed back the covers. She was trembling and glanced curiously down at herself in her cotton nightie. The feminine curves which had so delighted her in the dream were no more, but the bruises on her arms stood out blackly in the sunlight.

'I'd like to give that young feller a good clout round the lug,' Ellen said for the tenth time that morning. 'How dare 'e set about you like that, lovie! I've a good mind to go straight over there an' see what the old feller says. Wait till I sees our Alfie, that's all!'

'I don't see what harm I was doing, paddling in the river,' Questa said, also for about the tenth time. 'He shot at me, he could have killed me. But I shan't go round there now. They can be thankful I didn't go to the police. I mean, how can you get to Atherton Hall if you're trespassing when you set foot on his land?'

'Young brute,' Ellen muttered. 'What you want for them bruises is a nice bit o' steak ... not that I sin a bit o' steak these past eight, nine year. But one of me lotions will work wonders I shouldn't be surprised. Sit there a moment, lovie, whiles I get ...'

She bustled out of the kitchen. Questa, still clad in her night-gown and sitting on a cushion to spare her skinny, bruised rear the discomfort of a wooden chair, leaned back and thought about a hot bath. It would be lovely, and now that the fire had been made up, it was not an impossibility either. The truth was she was horribly stiff after her experience of the previous evening and worried over the loss of her shoes. Shoes were expensive, not only in money but in coupons. She could not afford to say goodbye to those good, practical brogues. And then there was the basket. Ellen had made light of its loss, saying they would doubtless get it back in the next day or so, but Questa had seen her using it time after time now that the soft fruit were in season and guessed that Ellen wanted it back more badly than she would admit.

When her friend came back into the kitchen with a black bottle full of evil-looking liquid, therefore, she asked again, 'How is one meant to reach the hall then, Ellen, without trespassing?'

Ellen, pouring black, tarlike stuff out of the bottle on to what looked suspiciously like a faded duster, snorted. 'Trespass! No such thing as trespass, not *as* such. They've gotta prove you was doin' somethin' 'urtful to the land, stealin' or chasin' sheep or some such. Why, lovie?'

'Because I want my shoes back, and our basket,' Questa admitted unhappily. 'I need those shoes, Ellen, they're the only sensible ones I've got. I wish I'd thought when I was with Marcus, we could have gone over there together and ...

She stopped short. Ellen, dabbing sticky black stuff on her bruises, cocked a bright eye.

'What's that, lovie? 'Oo's Marcus, then?'

'No one. How stupid, Ellen. Only I've dreamed about him twice, and somehow he seems so *real*; but he isn't, of course. He's just someone I dreamed.'

Ellen nodded and continued to dab. The stuff was really soothing, Questa discovered, as bruise after bruise eased under its touch.

'So you dream 'im, do you?' Ellen said conversationally after a few moments. 'Well, that's nat'ral enough, stuck 'ere be yourself most of the time. Young things need company, and who's to say the feller ain't sent? 'Sides, dreams is strange things ... There's a book in the library, I read it once when I were younger, it tells about Egypt, them pharaohs and that. Tells about true dreams, too.'

'Sent? Who'd send him? And true dreams? What does that mean?'

Ellen pushed the cork into her bottle and leaned against the table, surveying her handiwork.

'True dreams? Oh, they'm more like visions, almost 'appenings you could say. Seems the old pharaohs 'ad the power to dream true, to go through time or space in their dreams and find out what were really 'appening, like.'

'That sounds like a fairy-story,' Questa observed. 'That stuff in your bottle's wonderful though, Ellen. I feel ever so much better.'

'Oh ah, that's good stuff,' Ellen agreed. 'Now I knows you'll 'ave been thinkin' about an 'ot bath, but leave that till tonight.

That there stuff needs an hour or three afore you get the full benefit. Feel like a bite of breakfast now?'

Earlier, Questa had not been hungry, but now she discovered she was starving. She said as much and Ellen cut thick slices off the loaf and toasted them in front of the fire, then spread one with honey and the other with Marmite. Questa ate both, drank the tea which accompanied them, and announced herself fit for a day's gardening.

'Well, you're young. 'Twon't 'urt,' Ellen decided. 'Start off there, any road.'

They started off. Questa rather liked digging, mulching, seeing the weedy ground grow rich and dark. Later they would pick strawberries, later still she and Ellen would make jam. She examined the apples in the orchard each day, and was more than ever convinced that the crop would be good. Ellen advised her to thin the tiny green fruitlets out so she had done so, albeit reluctantly, and now awaited the results of her labour with watering mouth. She realised now that her advice to Marcus about his grapes had been precisely the advice she had been so reluctant to accept over her apples, but giving advice was much more fun than taking it, she concluded. Besides, not only did she enjoy eating and preserving apples, she needed the money a good crop would bring. She intended to send only windfalls to market, for cider, especially since she would be a pig-owner when autumn came. She was not deterred by the paperwork which owning a pig apparently brought in its wake; Ellen said Alfie would help her to fill in the forms and so would Mr George, the village policeman.

'There's good pork an' bacon for us if you 'ave a fattener,' Ellen said rather wistfully, but Questa was not sure she could bring herself to eat a pig she had personally nurtured. She thought she could have enjoyed a Snorkie-steak – the previous day she had taken a bowl of scraps out to the pig and had received a nasty nip as Snorkie, unconvinced that the bowl was empty, had tried to wrest it from her grasp.

'I'll think about it,' she said now. 'Is pig manure good for the land, Ellen?'

'That's purty good,' Ellen said, forking something which

smelled pretty nasty into the trench Questa had dug. 'But not as good as 'orse muck, to my mind. A nice bit of 'orse muck, well strawed, breaks up the soil somethin' wonderful. 'Tis easier to 'andle than pigs, bein' not so loose, like.'

'We used any manure in Italy,' Questa said dreamily, resting on her spade. 'Goats, cows, pigs – people's, too. And we got pretty good crops, if we were left alone.'

'Oh ah? Different ways, different ways,' Ellen muttered, forking away. 'Any muck's better'n none, I reckons. But I stand by 'orse as bein' the best of 'em all.'

'I mean to get a horse,' Questa said, reaching the end of her row and leaning on her spade for a moment whilst perspiration trickled down her face. 'I can't ride a bicycle but anyone can ride a horse.'

'Anyone?' Ellen snorted, then cackled. 'Young fool! Still an' all, anyone can *learn*, that I will grant you.'

Questa, who had seen peasants riding side-saddle on donkeys for years and had ridden so herself, looked sceptical, but forbore from further comment. She realised that Ellen knew an awful lot and would pass on information only when she was ready to do so. Perhaps English horses, being larger than the skinny, undersized donkeys of southern Italy, were a trifle more spirited.

'Well, I'll learn, then,' she said equably. 'But a horse could pull a cart and that would help us with spreading our muck, wouldn't it, Ellen? I mean it's all right in the kitchen garden, but when we get whole fields under cultivation it'll be a different matter.'

'Oh ah,' Ellen agreed. 'You'll want to go to the autumn 'orse fair at Craven Arms, then.'

'Do I? Why?'

'Cos they'm cheaper there. An' better, if you've got someone what knows a bit about 'orseflesh to 'and.'

'Craven Arms isn't far! Do you mean Alfie when you say someone who knows about horses? If so, do you think he'd...'

'Alfie!' Ellen's snort was unmistakably disgust this time. 'What does 'e know about 'orseflesh? Eh?'

'Oh! Did you mean yourself, Ellen?'

Ellen hurled another forkful of muck into the trench and pressed a hand into the middle of her back. 'Well, I din't mean Constable George,' she said. 'I been brought up alonger 'orses. Eh, but me back's twingin' me.'

'Poor Ellen! But would you come with me then? Please? We could go on the bus, make a day of it.'

'I wouldn't mind,' Ellen said in a grudging tone belied by the sparkle in her eyes. 'Yiss, that 'ud be a rare thing, a day out. We might get some 'ens, an all. Mebbe chicks, too.'

'Oh, they sell all sorts, then. But how can we get the things we buy home?'

'Carrier,' Ellen said briefly. 'Unless we buys a cart as well as the 'orse. If we did that we could bring anything else we fancies back.'

'That's marvellous. When is the fair? And should we take some fruit to sell?'

After some consideration Ellen vetoed the fruit selling because of the difficulties of carrying their wares, but said she would discover the exact date of the fair since Questa was so keen to know. It seemed to Questa that if they did not know the date then they were unlikely to pick up many – indeed, any – bargains, but she knew better than to voice this feeling to Ellen. The old woman was shrewd and intelligent, but Questa knew that reading and writing were a great labour for her and, though the seasons were all in her head, actual dates were vague.

'But readin's important, so I med sure Alfie got book learnin',' she had told Questa when they discussed education. 'You learn all you can, gal, or you'll live to regret it.'

'And this afternoon we've got a cleaning party,' Questa remembered as the two of them leaned their tools against the wall to go in for their lunch-break. 'We're getting the stuff down out of the attic at a good rate now, Ellen. Mr Patterson is coming down some time, he *will* be surprised! What's more, we should have some more stuff to send away; I was up there the other afternoon, just browsing, and I came across the most beautiful gilded mirror. There are cupids and horses with wings on their backs and lions and all sorts. I should think we'll get lots of money for it when it goes to the sale.'

Ellen chuckled.

'Don't go sellin' the lot and regrettin' it later,' she advised. 'When you moves up into the bedrooms you'll be glad of a nice mirror.'

Questa snorted. 'What for? To show me, as if I didn't know, that I'm plain as a pikestaff? No, I'd sooner have the money, thanks very much.'

Ellen looked consideringly across at her. 'You in't as bad as you was,' she stated. 'An' you'll be better yet. That hair of yourn is rare pretty now it's a bit longer.'

'I wish it was fair, like my father's,' Questa said wistfully. 'He had lovely hair.'

'So did your mam,' Ellen said sharply. 'Come along, I want to put the soup on.'

She went through the doorway, stomping off towards the kitchen. Questa ran after her.

'Ellen, I didn't know you knew my mother! What was she like? When did you see her? I don't have a photo of either of them, not even of Daddy ... Would you say my mother was pretty?'

Ellen crossed the kitchen and dived into the pantry. She came out with a bowl of soup which she tipped into a large pan.

'Get some bread, gal, it makes it more of a meal,' she advised. 'I met your mam when Charlie tried to make up wi' old Joshua. The old feller wasn't one for the wimmin, so bringin' your ma wasn't a good idea. Charlie left 'er with me for an hour, but even so ...' she sighed, staring into the soup as though she could see pictures in its murky depths. 'Oh well, that's all a long time ago,' she ended.

'But Ellen, you never said if she was pretty! Grace said she was, but then...'

'Grace! She's a one to talk, when ... yes, your ma was a very pretty woman. Not unlike yourself, lovie. And now let's get this pan over the 'eat afore I drops dead wi' 'unger!'

For the rest of the day Questa worried, on and off, about the shoes and the basket. Ellen's calm acceptance of the fact that someone in a dream seemed real was comforting, but it did not

116

solve the problem of her lost possessions. When Alfie came home Ellen mentioned that young Atherton had knocked Questa over, and who did he think he was, but Alfie only repeated that 'Everyone knows 'e's a mean bugger,' and left it at that.

By bedtime, she had decided to forget her property. The truth was, the very thought of returning to the river filled her with a sort of cold horror; her little fingers ached so badly that they kept her awake, lying there nursing them and wishing, how she wished, that Marcus were real and could have supported her against young Atherton.

She fell asleep at last, but woke when an owl shrieked. The brilliant day had been followed by a clear night; through the window she could see the moon. She looked around her; why had she woken? She was sure, suddenly, that Marcus, who meant well by her, seemed fond of her, would protect her if she sallied forth. Questa sat up, confidence surging through her veins. She had been foolish and weak, but now everything had changed. She felt wide awake and tinglingly alive and knew that she could go and search for her things with impunity. That detestable young man would be tucked up in his bed but, if he wasn't, her friend would keep her safe. Unreasonably perhaps, but positively, she felt that Marcus was telling her to go, telling her that he'd deal with young Atherton if he tried to touch her again.

A nod was as good as a wink on such a night. Questa jumped out of bed, dressed, and set off.

The night was warm. She moved confidently through fields and sloping meadows, waded across the bend in the river, and all the time she felt as though a strong, protective friend walked alongside. In this manner she soon found herself on Atherton land again. She slid through the tiny gap in the hedge and felt no fear, nothing but a calm certainty that all would be well. She found the bridge and easily located the willow in which she had hidden her strawberries. The basket lay nearby, the last of the fruit withering in the bottom. She picked it up, located her shoes in a clump of reeds, shoved them on her bare feet and turned to survey the moon-silvered river and the magic curve of the bridge, black against the mirroring water.

117

Beside her, invisible, was the spirit of her friend.

'Thank you, Marcus,' she said softly. 'I'm going home now.'

She returned to her bed without incident, feeling strong and triumphant. She was no coward, to weep for her lost possessions and do nothing, she had braved the night and the possibility of another beating and brought back her spoils. There was no shame in being comforted by the invisible support of a friend, after all.

She slid into bed, feeling such a sense of achievement and triumph that she could have laughed out loud, and closed her eyes, secure in the knowledge that she had done what she intended. Whether or not Marcus had supported her just now, in dreams he could come to her as a physical presence, and be thanked for the support he gave her, however obliquely.

She slept at once, easily, deeply, her cheek nestling into the thyme pillow.

But she did not dream.

It was a brilliant summer. The only disadvantage to the long hot days was that they were accompanied by drought, but after the terrible winter, most English people simply revelled in the sunshine and put the drought to the back of their minds. The drought made a lot of extra work of course; Questa, Ellen and Alfie carted water nightly to the kitchen garden, but it was worth it to see their vegetables flourishing, even though bedtime got later and later and Questa swore her arms were producing muscles better than most men's.

Another disadvantage, if you could call it that, was she simply stopped dreaming, or if she dreamed she had no recollection of it when she awoke. She was glad not to dream about the war, but she missed Marcus sorely and tried a good many times to get herself into the right frame of mind so that he would come to her. But there was so much work, and life was deeply satisfying. As the days and weeks passed Questa thought about Marcus often, about his lovely home, his clean, well-tilled fields, his new vineyard. But it became less easy to see his face in her mind's eye, easier to tell herself that a dream was just that, a dream. And though at first his absence was a nagging ache at the back of her mind, she gradually grew reconciled to her loss.

So working hard, sleeping soundly, Questa began to believe Ellen when she told her she was looking better too. Her skin glowed with health, she put some weight on, her figure burgeoned. She explored the estate and found that she owned a good deal of land, most of which had been badly neglected of late years: a water-meadow, rushy and overgrown, the steep hill which rose behind the house, thistle-ridden and stony, fields which had once grown good crops now thick with briars and rank grass. She knew enough to make haste slowly, but even so with every month that passed the land deteriorated a little more. She wished she could have asked Marcus how he managed … then examined anew the money available and the work that needed doing and became depressed.

Some people might have been glad that they simply had a roof over their heads and food in the kitchen garden, but Questa felt that the estate was a sacred trust. To see a cleared field grow weedy once more mattered to her, distressed her. She planned how to deal with them, field by field, meadow by meadow. Even the woods, which were so green and pleasant, could do with judicious thinning, and the lake was choked with reeds and lilies, the fish safe beneath a carpet of water plants run amok. But planned was one thing; putting such plans into action was quite another.

Soon they would need workers and something for them to work with too, but as yet she could not pay well enough. Atherton Hall was taking men on; their fields were yielding well, Alfie said. And shortly after her experience with young Atherton, he had been served out, though no one knew by whom.

'Beaten black an' blue,' Alfie said with satisfaction at teatime when he came home with the news. 'Over some woman, I daresay; nasty young brute. The old man give 'un several rare looks, that 'e did. It wouldn't surprise me if there's trouble brewin' there. Wish the old man 'ud get Mr Martin back.'

But despite the hated hand of young Atherton, men wanted to work at the Hall, to use the new machinery which the old man was buying, to earn the overtime being paid for producing the food the country so desperately needed.

Questa saw young Atherton a couple of times, once across a ploughed field, once in the village when she was going into the shop and he was coming out. She thought she saw bruises and hoped he was limping but they studiously ignored each other on both occasions, though Questa knew her cheeks flushed at the sight of him and thought that he looked uncomfortable, too. But she did not attempt to call at Atherton Hall, and to all intents and purposes the Atherton family might not have known she was living not much more than a mile from their home. It's their place to come over and welcome me, she told herself once, when she remembered her earlier resolution to become friendly with her neighbours. But they did not come to her and she could not go to them, not after the way young Atherton had treated her, so most of the time she put the whole business out of her mind and thought of pleasanter things.

Things like how to improve her property in ways which would not cost too much nor need too much manpower. She fretted for Marcus as though he really existed, so sure was she that he could advise on her many and various problems. And indeed, she thought that he *did* exist; it was just that she could not find him, not in the everyday world she usually inhabited.

Ellen was wonderful, but she had only worked the garden, never the fields. She knew about horses but very little about cows. Alfie knew about pigs but very little about chickens or ducks. If only I'd thought to ask Marcus this, or that... Questa mourned a dozen times a day, but whatever the key was to her dreams, she seemed to have lost it. So she soldiered on alone and saved every penny to buy some labouring hours when the autumn ploughing started.

By the end of August she had enough money for part-time workers. Questa did not intend to woo Alfie back to the Court, particularly since he was earning good money where he was, but she secured the services of Bert and Patrick and was well pleased. Patrick was a marvel with the tractor; his father swore it would sit up and beg for his son, and, despite its age and certain difficulties in starting of a morning, the autumn ploughing would be done before winter set in.

Ellen and Questa began to get quite excited about the horse fair as October got nearer. They had found a tea-chest crammed with papers which turned out to be shares, some of them what Alan called 'negotiable', and he began selling them, a few at a time, whenever the market was right. Questa, knowing nothing of shares, would have sold them all at once and bought a dairy herd, but Alan told her it would be foolish and insisted that the shares be sold as they rose, not as they fell. And Questa and Ellen were earning too, not much but enough, from the sale of fresh vegetables and such fruit as they could spare. The money was meticulously divided, but Ellen insisted that two-thirds should go to Questa and one third to herself and Alfie.

'We all depend on Eagles Court, gal,' she declared. 'If you goes under, we all does, and that wouldn't do at all. Spend the money on the 'ouse an' grounds an' we'll all benefit.'

Questa wondered aloud whether it was right to sell fruit and vegetables, but Ellen reassured her on this as on so many other matters.

'We shan't go 'ungry this winter, no matter who else do,' Ellen said with grim satisfaction, regarding the shining array of bottles and jars on the shelves in what she called the still-room. 'There's enough in 'ere to last us till next backend. If you can get us a heifer or two, lovie, we'll be self-sufficient, justabout.'

'I'll get the cow at the fair,' Questa said. It was her standard answer, now, to requests for stock. 'You said yourself, Ellen ...'

'Oh ah, turn me words agin me,' Ellen grumbled. 'Not but what it's true; we'll see some decent heifers there.'

Then, one fine morning in early October, with just enough of a nip in the air to make one realise that summer was not going to last for ever, that autumn would soon be here, the unexpected occurred.

Questa was picking runner beans. She was standing on a small stool the better to reach the topmost crop and dropping the beans into a large shoulder-bag which Ellen had made out of an old sheet, and she was singing the song which seemed to come to her over the wireless every time she turned it on.

The shore was kissed,
By sea and mist,
Tenderly;
I can't forget,
How two hearts met,
Breathlessly.

Ellen was in the kitchen salting the beans down for the winter, Alfie was at work over at Atherton Hall, Mary and her daughter Flo were lovingly cleaning and polishing a collection of Jacobean silver which Questa, looking at the intricacies of it, thought she could very well manage without. Peace, the peace of work being satisfactorily done, seemed to wash in waves over her as she balanced on her stool and reached into the jungle of leaf and stem. All around her the afternoon hummed with birdsong, and above her the perfect blue arch of the sky seemed near enough to touch.

The peace was shattered by a voice.

'Questa, what *are* you doing? Good God, girl, I can hardly see you for foliage; you'll be covered in beetles and spiders!'

Questa turned and peered.

Grace stood there, holding a small boy by the hand.

It was a shock. Not a surprise, a shock. Grace, furthermore, looked wonderful. She was tanned to an even shade of brown, her hair gilded by the sun to a shade between silver and gold, and she was wearing a full-skirted blue cotton dress which exactly matched her eyes. The little boy – sturdy, fair, grave – seemed quite at home in the kitchen where Questa led them, looking around with that mixture of interest and indifference which only a child can produce. Questa thought him an attractive little boy – when he suddenly grinned he reminded her of someone – but he was Grace's offspring and therefore slightly suspect.

'Ellen ... Mrs Rimmer, we've got visitors! It's Mrs Syrett, I don't know if you remember her, and her little boy.'

Ellen turned from chopping beans and laying them in serried ranks on the scrubbed table to give Grace a brief, chilly glance.

'Oh aye,' she said shortly, 'I'll put the kettle on.'

'Thank you,' Questa said. 'Do sit down, Grace. By the way, how did you get here?'

'Alan brought us. He's down in the village, booking a room at the local pub. Oh, I almost forgot, this is my son Dickie. Dickie darling, this is Questa, she's vaguely related to us, and that's Mrs Rimmer, who works for her.'

Questa smiled at the boy, who smiled back, then held out a hand.

'How do you do, Questa?' He turned to Ellen. 'How do you do, Mrs Rimmer?'

Ellen turned towards him and, for a moment, froze. The knife was poised over the beans, the old lady's eyes were fixed on the child's politely smiling face. Then, abruptly, she relaxed, and turned back to her task.

'How d'you do, young man,' she said.

'Nice to meet you, Dick,' Questa said in her turn, feeling like a language lesson. 'I didn't know we were related.'

'Only vaguely,' Grace said quickly. She sounded defensive. 'Can I help you with that tea, Ellen?'

'I'll manage,' Ellen said. She clattered cups.

'Grace, why are you here?' Questa asked. It sounded rude, but there was no help for it. She was entitled to know, after all. 'Did Alan bring you for the ride or what?'

'Well no, not exactly. In fact I've been evicted, and when Alan said he was coming down for a weekend I thought I might come along as well. God knows, properties down here can't possibly be as expensive as they are in London, and I thought perhaps I could afford something ... I suppose you aren't considering letting rooms?'

It was said lightly, yet Questa sensed a deadly earnestness behind the almost joking words.

'No,' she said flatly. 'You might get something in the village, I suppose, but you'd be better off, surely, in a town? I thought you wanted to start a shop?'

'Oh, that ... no, all I want is a roof over our heads, Dickie's and mine. I'd be quite willing to help out, of course. I'd housekeep and so on. Alan suggested that it might be fun for you and I to run this place together.'

'I have Ellen and her son,' Questa said. 'Besides, the house isn't important, not really. It's the land that matters most.'

'Really, Questa, you wouldn't let this lovely old place go to rack and ruin, surely? Why, if you let it you could get ...'

'I'm not going to let it,' Questa said. She watched as Ellen poured three cups of tea, then filled the last cup with milk for the child. 'Besides, it'll be months, no years, before it's straight. And I'm not letting it go to rack and ruin, I'm just taking it slowly, that's all.'

'Here,' Ellen said. She slapped a cup of tea down in front of Grace, then pushed the milk over to Dickie. Questa leaned forward and helped herself to a cup and then Ellen took the last cup with her to the far end of the long table and continued to chop beans. The rest of the conversation was punctuated by sharp thuds as the knife hit the wood.

'Then I don't see why you can't take a couple of boarders, especially if we work our passage,' Grace said. 'Go on, Questa, you won't regret it.'

'No, I shan't, but you would if I was silly enough to do it,' Questa said. 'Dickie's too young to work his passage as you call it, and you don't like me much, Grace, you know you don't. Why should I have you here when I know very well you despise me?'

There was a shocked silence. Questa stole a glance at Grace across the cool, shadowy kitchen and saw her mouth and eyes rounded. It was clear that the older woman was not used to such plain speaking. Questa deliberately let the silence stretch and stretch before breaking it.

'Now let's talk about something pleasanter, shall we? Why has Alan come down? He's only been twice before, and both times it was to pick up some antiques I was selling.'

'I think he said he wanted to see what you'd got left, if anything,' Grace said sulkily. 'Whether you let the Court or live in it, there's no point in furnishing it with rubbish, which is all you'll have left at the rate you've been selling the stuff.'

'Did Alan say that?'

Grace shrugged, then turned to her son, who was sipping milk and watching the face of whichever adult was speaking.

'Why don't you go and play in the garden, darling? There used to be a swing in the old orchard, right up at the far end, near the ruined greenhouse.'

Questa waited until the child had drained his milk and clattered out of the back door, then she turned once more to Grace.

'You seem to know a lot about the place for someone who's only been here a couple of times,' she said pleasantly. 'You let me think it was all new to you, Grace, that first time.'

Grace looked warily across the table at her, then shot a quick sideways glance at Ellen, still chopping beans.

'I came here as a child, probably several times. I was fond of old Joshua in my way. But that was a long time ago. I couldn't remember anything about it, except I was surprised it wasn't bigger.'

'But you remembered the swing and the ruined greenhouse.'

'Yes, but I remembered them from last time. I believe I wandered in the orchard when you and Alan were busy in the house. Look, Questa, I know you don't like me, but won't you think about it? For Dickie's sake as much as mine.'

'It wouldn't work,' Questa said, shaking her head. 'People think I must be lonely here, but I'm not. I like it. I've got Ellen all day, and Bertie and Patrick work outside and would come at once if I needed them, and I enjoy being alone in the evenings. Besides, I expect Dickie would get very bored and I'm absolutely positive you would.'

'Oh, what rubbish. Kids love country houses,' Grace cried. 'Dickie would be in his element! And I'd do my best to fit in, really I would. Why don't you think about it? We're here for a couple of nights, after all.'

Questa glanced at Ellen. The old woman was putting her soul into her chopping, her mouth set tight like a rat-trap and her eyes fixed on the beans as though she was enjoying beheading each one. I don't believe Ellen likes her any more than I do, Questa thought, and it gave her courage to be firm.

'I can think about it for a week but I shan't change my mind,' she said. 'Some things can't work, and us sharing a house is one of them. Just ask Alan what he thinks.'

'Alan is all in favour. He thinks you need someone older to keep you company – no offence, Ellen – and introduce you to

125

the county. I hear you've not met the Athertons yet, for instance.'

'I've met the son,' Questa said shortly.

'Oh, have you? It's years since I've seen him, but he was rather a nice boy, I thought.'

'He's changed then,' Questa muttered. She drained her teacup and got to her feet. 'Do excuse me, Grace, but I've got an awful lot to do. Feel free to take a look around, but I must get that bean row stripped before dark.'

'I'll give you a hand,' Grace said, putting her teacup down. 'I'll pick the lower ones whilst you stand on the stool and do the top ones.'

They went out together into an afternoon which had suddenly lost its peace. Questa climbed back on her stool and began to pick; from below, Grace kept up a barrage of comment and small talk, none of which interested Questa in the slightest. Indeed, she found it exhausting trying to hear what was being said in order to reply intelligently, and in the end she simply fell silent and worked grimly on, longing for the moment when Grace would take herself off.

Dickie wandered back, complained that the swing was too high for him to reach and wandered off again. After an hour Grace stood back and looked up at Questa through the leaves, still industriously picking away.

'I don't know how you *can*,' she said crossly. 'I'm scratched and dirty and my arms ache. I'll take these in to Ellen and see if I can give her a hand with the processing.'

Ha! Questa thought to herself, shoving a handful of furry, clinging beans into her makeshift carrier, so Grace could help out, could she? Why, she's decorative, not useful; let her find herself a man to take care of her, she's not going to hang on my sleeve.

When her carrier was full she lingered, reluctant to return to the kitchen, but she could not stay there all night, hiding from Grace, so she went indoors and tipped her beans on to the table. Ellen looked up and smiled.

'Finished, 'ave you? Thought you'd stay out there all night, sooner than face madam again!'

126

'Where is she?' Questa demanded, looking furtively round the large shadowy room. 'She said she'd come in and help you when she found how scratchy the beans are.'

'Oh, Mr Patterson arrived and carried 'er off. Said to tell you 'e'd be back in an hour to take you to The Passing Soldier for dinner. Said to put your best bib and tucker on.'

'I don't want to go,' Questa said immediately. 'Why should I go and be pestered?'

Ellen put a finger to the side of her nose and looked knowing.

'You go, lovie,' she advised. 'Best get it sorted. 'Sides, who's to say Mr Patterson's goin' to try to persuade you? If 'e's fool enough to be sweet on 'er, which I do believe 'e is, then why should he encourage 'er to come down 'ere to live, when it means they'll be miles apart? And then you've more stuff to sell – can't afford to fall out with your man of business!'

Questa agreed that this was fair comment, had a good wash in cold water in the sink, and went through to the small parlour. By now it was almost respectable, with a wardrobe, a dressing-table, a chair and a bit of carpet as well as the single bed. She opened the wardrobe, got out a clean print dress and put it on, then added a pair of lightweight sandals which the vicar's wife had put into the jumble sale, and a necklace she had found with a great many other bits of trashy-looking jewellery pushed into the back drawer of an old chest. The necklace was old and heavy, but its yellowish metal looked good against the tan of her neck and it gave her confidence, made her feel dressed up.

When she was ready she went into the kitchen. There was no sign of the beans, but Ellen and Alfie sat at the table, eating shepherd's pie, summer cabbage and mashed potatoes. Questa posed like one of the model girls in Ellen's knitting magazine.

'Well? Do I look all right to go out to dinner?'

'You're a picture,' Alfie said. 'Smashing necklace; careful it don't pull you face down into your soup!'

Questa giggled. 'It is a bit heavy,' she admitted. 'Ellen, what do you think?'

'You look grand,' Ellen said. 'Go you off, lovie, I hear a car coming over the gravel. Pop up and tell us 'ow you got on when you get home; you won't be late, I daresay.'

'Your hearing's very sharp,' Questa said. 'I can't hear ... oh, yes, *now* I can. See you later then!'

She trotted out of the back door and under the arch. The car was just coming to a halt and, to her relief, Alan was alone. He saw her and waved, then leaned across and opened the passenger door.

'Hop in,' he said. 'Nice to see you, Questa. How are you?'

'I'm very well,' Questa said. She settled herself in her seat, then turned to her companion. 'Why did you send her, Alan?'

'Send her? I don't know what you mean.'

'Yes, you do,' Questa said impatiently. 'You know very well. You sent Grace round to the Court this afternoon, to see whether she and her son might move in with me. She said you thought it was a good idea, that you felt I needed an older woman to keep an eye on me.'

Silence. Questa stole a glance at Alan and saw that the colour in his cheeks had deepened. He took a deep breath, sighed, then shook his head gently, never taking his eyes off the road.

'Well? Is it true or isn't it?'

Alan sighed again, then slowed the car as the end of the drive approached. 'I did think it might be an answer, yes. Just a temporary one, of course. Grace has a little money, I thought it might help if she paid you for a room and brought the boy, but I guessed you wouldn't like it. I'm not a particularly sensitive man but the antagonism which radiated from you when you first met Grace seemed too strong to have evaporated in the course of a few months.'

'From *me*? It wasn't me, it was her! She was rude, she kept having digs at me ... I would have liked her if I could, but she wouldn't let me!'

Questa's indignation made her voice shrill, but Alan, easing the car slowly from the drive on to the road, shook his head. 'No, my dear, from you. The antagonism was all on one side; Grace wanted to befriend you but you just wouldn't have it. I suppose she thought, if she brought the boy, that you might soften towards them. But this obviously isn't the case. I'm sorry.'

'Alan, that just isn't *true*. Don't you remember telling me you were sorry that we hadn't got on? You said you shouldn't have brought her, but she wanted to come, and I said if she wanted to come she had a funny way of showing it. Don't you *remember*?'

'That was before I understood how hard Grace had tried, and how difficult you had been. I'm sorry, Questa my dear, because I know you've been through a great deal, but you seemed to dislike Grace from the start and her kindness to you, her offers of help, made no real difference. Even Dickie ... I take it you took against him, too?'

The unfairness of the remark almost took Questa's breath away, and she was about to answer hotly when commonsense came to her rescue. The man speaking was, she supposed, a man deeply in love with and therefore completely under the spell of an unscrupulous and untruthful woman. Unfortunately, however, she was in no position to tell him how she felt about his lady-friend, since Alan was her legal adviser, sold her furniture, her stocks and shares, got her the best possible deals and generally helped to keep her precarious little ship afloat. If she antagonised him, maybe he would still work for her, but he was only human and would probably not do everything in his power to help her.

A soft answer was said to turn away wrath. Questa took a deep breath, swallowed a desire to shake Alan until he saw reason, and spoke thoughtfully.

'I'm sorry Grace feels I disliked her. It isn't true. But clearly we each got a false impression of the other. And anyway, Alan, even if we could become bosom friends I couldn't share the house with her. Not now, not yet. There is so much to do, indoors and out, and though Grace assures me she can housekeep with the best – and I'm sure she's speaking the truth – you can't have two women in one kitchen. Ellen Rimmer has lived at the Court all her life, she's a marvellous gardener and an exceptionally good cook. I simply could not manage without her and having seen Grace picking beans, I don't believe she would ever take kindly to horticultural work, she's far too delicate.'

Thinking of Grace's excellent physique, she wondered if she had gone too far, but a besotted man believes what he wants to believe. Grace, to Alan, was indeed delicate.

'I see what you mean. Yes, I do understand. It would not do to try to persuade Mrs Rimmer to step down for Grace and, as you say, she couldn't possibly do what amounts to farm work, not Grace. But you don't feel you could let a couple of rooms to her and the boy? Just for a few weeks? I'm sure she'd soon realise that the country wasn't ideal and would come back to town.'

'I thought she couldn't afford to live in London,' Questa said rather tartly. It seemed to her that Grace was not the only one who manoeuvred the truth to suit herself. 'No, I think Grace had better see if she can find somewhere else. Why not Shrewsbury? She might find work there, to keep her occupied whilst Dickie's in school.'

'She says Dickie needs country air,' Alan explained. 'Otherwise I'm sure she'd have tried harder to find a flat in London. Poor love, she'd made her house into a little palace ... but there you are, that's landlords for you.'

'Alan, what's wrong with your place?' Questa asked, highly daring. 'I mean, you could let her have a couple of rooms, couldn't you? The two of you are old friends, and ...'

'She's not interested in marriage, if that's what you mean. Says it's too soon, that she needs time to find herself,' Alan said morosely. 'I understand, of course, but once she's stuck out in the country I'll never see her. At least if she were here I'd have an excuse to visit every couple of weeks, but if she goes anywhere else I daresay I'll never clap eyes on her again.'

'Many thanks for the compliment,' Questa said drily. 'So I, too, have my uses – as a means of your seeing Grace! Alan, you are ... you are very much in love.'

She had intended to say besotted, but remembered, almost too late, that she was trying to build bridges not break them down.

'She's a beautiful woman,' Alan said. 'She has everything; a delightful nature, a good sense of humour, a lot of charm. She loves children and animals, she enjoys country living, she's a real homemaker. But I'm a pretty dull sort of chap, so I suppose it was a bit much to expect her to return my feelings. You won't say anything, Questa? I've had to pretend I've taken my dismissal in good part and want us to remain friends, whereas I can't help hoping ... but I daresay it will come to nothing.'

'Nonsense,' Questa said bracingly. 'She needs time, that's all. Just get her settled in a nice little house somewhere and before you know it she'll be inviting you round and suggesting the three of you go out together. Why, you can bring her down here at weekends now and then, if you like – once the house is straight, I'll even put you up!'

The car was purring down the village street now. Alan laughed, leaned across and tried to take her hand, only she snatched it out of the way in time, pretending that she needed to blow her nose.

'Questa, you've given me hope! Well, we must forget our troubles this evening and enjoy ourselves, and tomorrow perhaps we can have a chat about the stock you intend to buy. The Jacobean silver will realise a great deal of money, I imagine you know that.'

'No, I didn't, but I'm glad. I wonder what Mrs Watson has cooked for us?' Questa said as the car drew up outside the inn. 'I'm terribly hungry – we usually have our tea at six.'

'I've never known you turn down food,' Alan said. 'Dickie had tea earlier, so he'll be in bed; it'll be just the three of us so let's hope we shall all get to know one another better.'

Six

Strangely enough, and despite all the odds, the evening at The Passing Soldier was a success. Grace went out of her way to be nice to Questa, deferring to her when farming and horticulture was discussed; she teased Alan about his passion for cars and the way he kept his little house, and she talked about Dickie just as any proud mother would. After two hours, during which they ate lentil and carrot soup, Mrs Watson's steak and kidney pie and an apple snow which melted in the mouth, all of them seemed in good charity with one another.

But Questa, though she enjoyed herself, was not fooled for one instant into believing that she and Grace could share a house. Grace was intent on using her, and if that meant being pleasant then Grace would be pleasant – until she was firmly established. Once she got her feet under the table, Questa was sure, the older woman would return to her true self, and peace would fly out of the window.

However, she extended her invitation to Grace to come down for a weekend as soon as the house was straight and Grace, who had had more than her share of the two bottles of wine Alan had ordered, said with a giggle that a weekend would have to do.

'It's Dickie I care about,' she mumbled. 'He's precious. Did you like him, Questa? Did Ellen like him? Wha' did she think of my baby?'

'He seems a nice little chap,' Questa said cautiously. 'I'm sure Ellen liked him, too. Only to have a child in the house ...'

'He'd be no trouble, I'd see to that. However, if you're going to refuse us shelter then suppose we'll have to make do with a weekend now and then, to keep an eye on things,' Grace said, and gazed with drunken suggestiveness at Alan, who turned pink and looked imploringly at Questa as if to say that Grace could not help being tipsy and wasn't she the prettiest drunk Questa had ever seen? And indeed, with her lovely face flushed and her ladylike sharpness gone for the duration, Grace was extremely pretty and very charming and Questa could almost see how Alan had come to be so taken in by her. For she clung grimly to her theory that Grace did nothing without calculation and that included some of her seemingly meaningless conversation when in her cups.

When Alan stood up, after coffee and liqueurs, to say that he would run Questa home, Grace stood up too and said she would go with them.

'But my dear, you can't leave Dickie,' Alan protested. 'You should be in bed, getting your beauty sleep. Don't worry, I can see Questa home in no time.'

'Dickie will be fine; he's asleep, anyway,' Grace insisted. 'I want to come with you, Alan sweetie.' She lolled on his shoulder, then turned and winked at Questa with much fluttering of her long, light-brown lashes. 'Ish'nt Alan a sweetie, Ques? You think he's a sweetie too, don't you, and awfully handsome, don't you?'

'Of course,' Questa said. It was an embarrassing question since Questa thought Alan kind but exceedingly plain. However, little white lies are essential if life is to run smoothly. 'You go up to bed, Grace, you can't leave your son alone for too long.'

Grace was inclined to argue but Alan settled the point by telling her to go up to her room to fetch her coat. Whilst she thumped her way up the stairs, he and Questa shot through the back, climbed into the car and made their getaway.

'She'll probably fall asleep on the bed and not remember to come down,' Alan said guiltily as he turned the car into the village street. 'Poor love, she's been under so much strain lately, that's why the wine went to her head the way it did.'

'She drank quite a lot of it,' Questa observed. 'I bet she sleeps well tonight.'

'She won't be the only one,' Alan said. 'I'm worn out, and you must be the same. What time shall we come up to the Court in the morning?'

With an inward sigh for the plural, Questa resigned herself to a business discussion with four people instead of two.

'Oh, come at ten,' she said. 'I'll make coffee and biscuits and if the weather's as nice as it was today then Dickie can play in the garden. Perhaps Grace might like to mend the swing for him, since he was complaining that it was broken.'

'I'll do it, when we've had our talk,' Alan said. He drove for a while in silence, his eyes fixed on the moonlit ribbon of road ahead, then he shot a glance at her. 'You are all right, aren't you, Questa? Mrs Watson said she thought things hadn't always been easy for you – there was some trouble with the Athertons, she said – but you seem happy and self-sufficient.'

'I'm fine,' Questa said. The car swung into the drive and raced up the dark tunnel. Alan was clearly eager to get back to his girlfriend before she passed out on the floor or made a fool of herself in some way. 'Don't worry about me, please. I'm enjoying every minute, really.'

The car stopped with a scattering of gravel. Alan jumped out and opened the passenger door, then hesitated, looking uneasily at the dark bulk of the house behind them.

'I ought to come in with you. Are you sure you'll be all right? Only Grace was a little the worse for wear, and I feel I ought to get back as soon as possible.'

'I'm fine,' Questa said again. 'The Court looks after me. See you in the morning, Alan.'

She stood and watched as the car turned and re-entered the drive, then made her way slowly round to the stableyard. The light was still on in the coachman's flat; she went up the stairs but before she reached the door, Ellen came down towards her, carefully carrying a steaming jug.

'I've made you some cocoa,' she announced. 'And a tot of me elderberry wine to 'elp you sleep. I daresay you've 'ad quite an evening!'

'I'll take them; you go back upstairs,' Questa said, but Ellen insisted on accompanying her into the kitchen where she poured the drink into a mug, got down the biscuit tin, and said that Questa should lie in next day and she, Ellen, would bring her a bite of toast in bed.

'Why are you spoiling me?' Questa said, taking a drink. 'Ooh, this is lovely, Ellen, sweet and milky.'

'Because that feller don't 'preciate you,' Ellen said. 'Is that Miz Syrett movin' in 'ere?'

'No, not if I can help it,' Questa assured her. 'Why, Ellen? Would you like her to come?'

Ellen cackled. 'That I would not! Fancy piece!' she said obscurely. 'But I gotta 'ave a think, mebbe tek a look at the cards. We want to do what's right, you an' me. Sleep well now, lovie. See you in the marnin'.'

Questa, however, did not sleep well. Despite her show of firmness, she could see that, should Alan insist, she would have little option but to give Grace a place beneath her roof. And when she came to think about it, she was being pretty unreasonable; why should Grace and Dickie not live with them, even if they did nothing to help? They would do nothing to hinder, she thought. Ellen did not like Grace, so there would be two of them to see that the other woman did no harm.

Then there was Ellen's enigmatic rejoinder when Questa had asked her outright if she wanted Grace to live in the house. No she did not, then they wanted to do what was right, and something about cards. And that vague relationship? She really should have asked Alan what Grace was getting at. But she hadn't, and she realised she needed to know all sorts of things which, as yet, were hidden from her.

She fell asleep in the early hours of the morning and dreamed horribly, in a way she had not dreamed since she came to the Court.

She was back in the terrifying cellars of the big house, where they had dragged her. The big man had hold of both her wrists; despite knowing it was a dream, for that at least was on her side, she also knew what would happen, had happened.

The big man ran his hands down hers, then gripped both her little fingers.

'Tell us! I must have names!'

'I don't know anything,' the young thing who was Questa Adamson moaned softly. 'Please, don't, I swear ...'

She heard the crack as he bent the little finger on her left hand until it snapped, screamed and screamed, heard the little finger on her right hand go, screamed, screamed ...

And woke sweat-soaked in her bed, cramp turning her fingers into claws which hurt right up her arm; hurt nearly as much as her broken fingers had hurt that night five years ago.

She sat up. Her heart was beating so loudly that it seemed like a physical presence in the room, a drum being beaten by her side. She was breathing very fast and shallowly, panting really, and the pain in her hands was echoed in her ribs.

Unthinking, she held out a hand. Her throat was raw with screaming, and around her the house was silent as though listening.

'Marcus! They hurt me, they hurt me! Marcus, I'm afraid. Why did you leave me? I need you so much!'

Just talking to him brought her a measure of comfort. She sensed his nearness at once, knew he was reminding her that it was only a dream, that there were other, good dreams. That he had not gone for ever, would be back when the time was ripe.

Oh, the sweet relief of his presence, the strength of him, pouring into her frightened mind, soothing, reassuring! Questa sat in the moonlight and mopped her brow with the top sheet, then lay down again. What a horrible dream, but it was only a dream. Totally unconscious of any discrepancy in her thoughts she lay down again, soothed and calm.

And noticed that the thyme pillow had slipped from under her head during the nightmare, and now lay on the floor. Or had it slipped out earlier, whilst she tossed and turned and worried over Grace and Dickie Syrett? Was that why she'd had the nightmare? And it was true that she fell asleep within seconds of her head touching the thyme pillow, and slept soundly until morning.

At breakfast, when Questa was debating whether to have her boiled egg now or to eat it for lunch, Ellen dropped her bombshell.

'I bin thinkin',' she announced portentously, 'about that woman an' the little lad.'

'So've I,' Questa acknowledged through a mouthful of

136

porridge. 'I had nightmares, Ellen. I haven't had nightmares for ages until last night.'

'Oh ah.'

'It's that Grace,' Questa said, glowering. 'There's something about her ... it worries me.'

'Ah.' It was agreement, Questa knew. 'But what about the little lad, eh? What about 'im? Do 'e count for nothin'?'

'Well, I don't really know him, so I suppose I don't care all that much,' Questa said frankly, finishing her porridge and pushing the dish away with a satisfied sigh. 'That was lovely, Ellen. Can I have some toast now?'

'Course you can. That lad.'

'What about him?' Questa asked, surprised. Dickie had been the last of her worries. From her own experience she knew that children are happiest with the people they love, whether those people live in a castle or a suburban house with almost no garden. 'He'll be happy wherever he is you know, Ellen.'

'Oh ah, mebbe. But 'e should be here, wi' us. Wish us could 'ave un wi'out that Grace,' she added in a grumbling voice. 'But if we can't ...'

'She doesn't like me,' Questa muttered, her heart sinking. 'She won't help, Ellen, she'll just criticise and carry tales.'

'I'll soon put a stop to *that*,' Ellen said. 'Don't worry, lovie, they'll settle in well enough. An' that Mr Patterson will likely come weekends, take 'em off of our 'ands.'

She hobbled across the kitchen and handed Questa a slice of toast. Questa, spreading honey, realised with not a little dismay that the question of whether or not to have Grace and Dickie to live with them had been settled, and not in the way she would have wished. Yet, when she thought about it, where was the harm? Grace would be busy with the boy, she didn't like work so was unlikely to interfere with what Questa and Ellen were trying to do, and the house was large. She and Ellen could clean two of the bedrooms – not the best ones, Questa decided on the spur of the moment, but two at the back – and they need see very little of Grace or the boy.

On the good side, it would salve Questa's conscience, which had been uneasy ever since she had remembered the housing

137

situation – the papers were full of it – and the fact that she was living in what was almost a mansion, alone. If the war had still been on they would have billeted evacuees on me, she told herself now, munching toast. When she went down to the shop to buy their weekly rations, old Mrs Pibble, who ran it with the lethargic aid of her daughter Janet, told her lots of stories about the evacuees and their various devilments. So I could have been worse off, she concluded; I could have had people who weren't just no help but were a downright nuisance to share the Court.

She still felt, though, that Ellen had in some mysterious way found her wanting. Why else would she agree to the presence of a woman she disliked? It was all very well to say it was for the sake of the boy, but she hadn't taken much notice of him the previous day, had she, apart from giving him a long, cold look?

'More toast, lovie?'

'No thanks,' Questa said absently. She was thinking that she could easily go against Ellen's expressed wishes, that Ellen would never even know. She could walk down to the village now, go to The Passing Soldier and tell Alan that she would think about it and needed a week in which to do so. Then she could tell Ellen that Grace had changed her mind, didn't fancy the country after all, and she would be in the clear.

But you wouldn't sleep at nights, her conscience reminded her smugly. Or you might even start those dreadful nightmares off again; how would you like that? And her bent, deformed little fingers began to ache.

'Ellen, what about our visit to the horse fair? Can we still go?'

She had not meant to say that but somehow it was reassuring to hear Ellen say that they would carry on just as usual with their lives and if Madam didn't like it then she would soon be told what she could do.

'We'll 'ave their rations, too,' Ellen said. 'Meks it easier to manage. Don't know why, but it's so. I've found it easier wi' three books than wi' two, and that's God's truth.'

'Oh, well … perhaps Grace will have changed her mind, though. Perhaps she'll change it when I show her which room she can have,' Questa said, thinking of the little back bedroom with pigeon droppings all over the floor and the hole in the ceiling through which all sorts of things might come. 'She can jolly well clean it out herself, for a start. And anyway, I bet she doesn't stay long, not once it gets cold and snowy.'

'Mebbe. I'll give the room a go-over, though,' Ellen said. 'She'll want one what's with a bath ... 'ow about the yaller room?'

The yellow room was one of Questa's favourites. It had the prettiest wallpaper: Chinese style, with willow trees and rising suns and delicate arched bridges all over it, and the dark cream paintwork made it look cheerful and sunny on the coldest day.

'Oh, no! Well, I suppose it's near the bathroom,' Questa admitted. 'Where will Dickie go, then?'

'In the dressin' room. Bath's on the right, dressin' room on the left,' Ellen explained. 'I'll get Mary up. Tell Mr Patterson it'll cost 'er, though.'

'Oh, all right,' Questa said, bowing to the inevitable. 'When will you do it? Today?'

'Today, with the rest of the beans to get salted down? Nah, next week some time,' Ellen said. 'They can go back to London and come down agin next weekend. She's got stuff to bring, no doubt.'

'Trunks and trunks of clothes and stuff to put on her face I expect,' Questa said gloomily. 'What about her furniture, though?' With vague thoughts of Grace being able to claim permanent occupancy if she allowed her to bring her own stuff, she added sharply, 'She can't bring it here, I don't want it, I won't let her! We'll bring stuff in – she'll have to throw her things away, and perhaps she won't like that.'

Ellen cackled. 'We'll see,' was all she said, however. 'They comin' up this marnin'?'

'Yes; Alan wants to have a look at the rest of the furniture. I said I'd have coffee and biscuits for them at about ten.'

'I'll do it; you tek 'em up to the rooms,' Ellen said. 'Until then, we'll strip the beans rows.'

After they had all drunk coffee and Alan had told Questa how he was progressing with the sale of Uncle Joshua's effects, Questa took Grace up to see the rooms she had offered them.

Grace professed delight, admired the bathroom – huge marble

139

handbasin, enormous bath with lions' feet perched on a pedestal, mahogany lavatory seat with a porcelain bowl which announced it was 'The Efficient Flusher' – said that Dickie's room was so nice for a small boy, and then went downstairs again. Alan suggested that she might take Dickie around the gardens, then jerked his head at Questa and strolled out of the room. He went as far as the small parlour, pushed open the door and walked in, gesturing Questa to follow.

'I know it's your room, my dear, but it's probably the only place Grace won't simply walk into without waiting for an invitation,' he said with remarkable forthrightness, considering how he felt about Grace. 'And I want a quiet word. But first, I must tell you how much I appreciate your having Grace and the boy. I'm delighted, though very surprised. Last night you didn't seem very keen to have them under your roof.'

'Last night I was being selfish,' Questa said. 'But I got to thinking, and I remembered how people all pulled together during the war, and what they've been saying on the wireless about homelessness in London, and I felt ashamed to keep this big house all to myself. And then I had a word with Ellen, and she agreed that we'd manage very well, even if ...'

'If what? Oh, I suppose you mean if Grace didn't do much outside, and couldn't help without being thought interfering in the house,' Alan said. 'But I'll come down most weekends and I'll do any heavy work you need done, of course.'

'And you'll take Grace and Dickie out of our hair,' Questa said sunnily. 'Yes, Ellen said that, too. So we're going to try very hard to fit in, all of us, and if it doesn't work ...'

'If it doesn't work I'll take her back to London and try to find her a small flat, or a couple of rooms,' Alan said jubilantly. 'Thanks, Questa. We both appreciate it. Grace will pay rent, of course.' He named a sum which sounded like a fortune to Questa.

'That seems fair,' she said judiciously. 'Now tell me, if you don't mind, just what Grace meant when she said she'd been evicted?'

'Oh, the landlord put her rent up, almost doubled it in fact, and because accommodation is so hard to find she no sooner said she couldn't afford it than he let to someone else. She called a taxi and came straight around to my house, then asked if I'd bring her down here. I must say it did seem a good idea, which, as we now see, it was.' He looked pleased with himself. 'So all's well that ends well,' he finished.

'Probably,' Questa said cautiously. 'And that reminds me, Alan. Who was Dickie's father?'

'Well, I never knew him, to tell you the truth. Apparently Grace met some fellow by the name of Simon Syrett, I think he was a Hurricane pilot in the Air Force; he proposed, she accepted, and then before Dickie was even born, Simon was shot down over Germany. She thought a lot of him, naturally, which is why she hasn't married again.'

'Why she hasn't married again yet,' Questa said thoughtfully.

Alan smiled. 'Yes, yet,' he agreed. 'I'm full of hope, my dear, especially now that I'll be seeing her each weekend.'

The day of the Fair dawned at last. Questa, who had begun to think it would never come, woke early. It was one of those marvellous mornings when the dew spangles the grass, spiders' webs are jewelled by it, and in the sloping upland meadows white mushrooms with pink undersides can be picked by the basketful.

Hopping out of bed, Questa washed in cold water, threw on her most practical clothing, and headed for the kitchen. It was empty still, and grey with early morning, for the small parlour faced east and caught the rising sun whereas the kitchen faced west and saw the sun as it slid down the sky in the evening.

From long habit Questa riddled the fire, tipped the ash into a bucket, pulled the kettle over the flame and then took the bucket's handle to carry it out to add to the cinder path she and Ellen were making in the kitchen garden. Cinders were cheaper than gravel and since they had to get rid of them somehow a path seemed a good idea.

It was going to be a nice day, Questa decided as she pushed open the little green door and entered the garden. Because of the walls the sun would not rise here for another hour or more, but a pale blue sky arched overhead and there were wreaths of mist still hovering over the beds.

On her way back she glanced at the stable, just as Ellen emerged. Ellen, she saw, was in her best. She wore a long black coat, a violet velvet hat and black shoes and she carried a pair of black woollen gloves, a walking stick and a navy-blue handbag. She also looked rather grim.

'Ellen? You *do* look nice! We're going to have a lovely day, I think. I put the kettle on.'

Ellen sniffed, then nodded reluctantly. 'Aye, the weather's not so bad,' she conceded. 'Dampish, but it'll get out nice later. Me leg's playin' me up, though.'

Questa had heard Alfie saying that his mother's leg was more useful to her than a whole hospital full of doctors, since it always allowed her to do the things she enjoyed, but came on awful bad whenever something unpleasant threatened. Since she knew that Ellen was dying to go to the Fair, however, Questa made sympathetic noises but did not suggest that Ellen might be too poorly to accompany her. And indeed Ellen crossed the stable-yard in a lively manner, hopped into the kitchen and immediately began assembling toast, honey, margarine and porridge oats.

'Can we stop for breakfast?' Questa asked rather apprehensively. Dickie and Grace had not moved in as soon as she and Ellen had imagined they would, but even so they had been living at the Court now for two weeks, and although Grace was probably doing her best to be helpful and to keep out of the way, Questa still found her intrusive. She would give her opinion when Questa and Ellen were discussing how best to use the land they had managed to get ploughed, or whether asparagus was worth growing since it needed a good deal of manuring and was really intended for the luxury market. Grace would put her oar in and never seemed put out when they pointedly ignored her or continued to talk over her more foolish twitterings.

'Ha! Tes not yet sun up, lovie; she won't stir for a coupla hours,' Ellen said, knowing instinctively what Questa was thinking. 'Sides, 'eaven knows what time we'll git 'ome tonight. Better get us a breakfast.'

'We're having lunch out,' Questa reminded her. 'You said it was good business to go to the pub for lunch, as well as being quite cheap on Fair day. Still, I wouldn't mind some porridge and toast.'

'You mek the toast,' Ellen commanded. 'It'll be ready quick enough. The coach is pickin' us up at the end of the drive at eight. It ain't eight yet, is it?'

'No, we've got half an hour, but we'd better get a move on,' Questa said, holding the toasting fork as close to the fire as she dared and closing her eyes against the heat.

Halfway through their makeshift meal the kitchen door opened. Questa stiffened, convinced that Grace would wander in with some remark about being woken by their voices, but it was Dickie, looking like a baby owl, all eyes and sleep-ruffled plumage. He blinked across at them, then wandered over to the table.

'Is it time to get up?' he said. 'Can I have toast, too?'

'Course you can, Dickie,' Questa said. 'Want some honey?'

Ellen made a sort of cooing noise, then ladled porridge on to a plate. 'Let un cool, boy,' she said. 'I'll spare some milk for you.'

'Thanks, Ellen,' Dickie said. He sat at the table and poured a thin stream of honey over the porridge, then started to eat. 'Where are you going?' he asked presently, the worst of his hunger obviously sated. 'You've got a hat on, Ellen! I didn't know you wore a hat.'

'We're going out on business,' Questa said rather repressively. She had noticed that Ellen, though often taciturn, was apt to spoil Dickie. 'We'll be home this evening though.'

'Can I come?'

'Well, my dear, 'tes for those who're buyin' stock really,' Ellen began, but Questa cut in at once.

'No, Dickie, of course you can't come, your mother would be very worried. Now eat up your porridge and go back to bed, there's a good boy. It's far too early for you to be up.'

Dickie obeyed her but she noticed him eyeing her broodingly and felt guilty. He was a nice kid, open and friendly, he could scarcely help it if Grace was his mother, she should not hold it against him. But the Fair was far too important to her to saddle herself with a small boy to entertain, and Ellen, she felt, should have appreciated that. She said as much when Dickie had gone off again and she and Ellen were getting ready to go.

'I expect you think I'm hard on Dickie, Ellen, but I don't mean to be. It's just that he is Grace's responsibility and I've got enough on my hands with the house and all the things we need today. I couldn't keep an eye on him as well. I'm surprised you nearly said we'd take him, to tell you the truth.'

'I didn't,' Ellen said, heading for the back door. 'Come along, lovie, we dunna want to be late for the coach. As for Dickie, he's best stayin' at the Court.'

The two of them hurried down the drive, between the dark rhododendrons, the flowers just a memory now, and the autumn-tinted oaks and beeches which made up most of the woodland here. If you looked into the trees you could see wreaths of mist curled around the trunks, and when they got into the coach, which was already half-full of villagers who greeted them cheerfully, they were able to see that the mist still hung above the river and coiled about the steaming fleeces of the sheep and the smooth hides of the cattle standing on the low-lying water-meadows.

'It's gonna be a fine day,' someone shouted from the front of the coach. 'A fine day for buyin' up 'alf Shropshire!'

'We'm getting an 'orse,' Ellen remarked. 'A quiet mare with plenty a' muscle. And mebbe a cart.'

'Oh ah?' someone else said. 'No better place for 'orses than the Fair. I'm after pigs, meself. And calves.'

'How will you get them home?' Questa asked curiously.

'Drover,' a farmer near the front of the coach called over his shoulder. 'You'll get a feller willing to bring 'em for a few shillin'. These days they put 'em on a train if it's too far, but usually they drive 'em along the road. Takes a few hours, but 'tes good value. Beast don't get too tired, an' they graze as they comes.'

'Well, I never knew that,' Questa said to Ellen. 'Could we use a drover, do you suppose?'

'Nah, not for a coupla heifers an' a little mare,' Ellen said. 'Well, we could if we put 'em in with someone else's herd, supposin' someone from the village buys a herd, acourse. But we'm best keep independent.'

Questa had been into Craven Arms before, but never on Fair day. The big beast market was usually busy, but today the livestock were taking up double the room and the horses were parading round a big meadow not usually opened for beasts. Looking round her and listening to the burring Shropshire accents, Questa decided that every farmer in the county was present and a good few from farther afield too, either buying, selling or simply enjoying a day out.

'The sheep are lovely,' she said longingly to Ellen, hanging over a pen full of broad-backed black-faced sheep. 'Wouldn't I like a dozen or so of these! Some of our fields, the hilly ones, need sheep on them.'

'Oh ah, but we'm after heifers,' Ellen reminded her. 'Come an' tek a look at the 'ens!'

'Oh, just a couple of sheep, then,' Questa begged as they pushed through the people towards the poultry, stacked higher than their heads in cages which might have been clean to start with but which smelt pretty strong now. 'Gosh, Ellen – goats!'

'Keep your mind on what you wanted when you set out, not what you've eyed since,' Ellen grumbled. 'An' keep 'old of your purse; this place is famed for pickpockets.'

Questa leaned over the pen containing the goats, and the distinctive smell of them brought a particular night in the mountains in Italy rushing back into her mind. She had forgotten all about it, her mind dismissing much that was good along with the bad, apparently, but now it was there, clear as clear. The cramped hovel, with elderly people and children sleeping on every available space and with the family's goats herded into a lean-to, and snow on the ground outside, whilst a wicked wind moaned round the walls and penetrated every chink. Questa had arrived at the house, gone in and offered to work in exchange for a night's shelter. They knew she wasn't local, of course, knew she would be on the run from something or someone, but they took her in anyway.

'You'd best sleep with the goats,' the woman of the house advised her. 'It's warm, and no one will look for you there. Don't come out till we tell you it's safe.'

The goats had smelled pretty strong, but your nose got used to it in the end, and they were so wonderfully warm! They lay down as close as they could get, accepting Questa's presence, curled up amongst them on the dirty straw, as the most natural thing in the world. And they chewed the cud, whickered their odd hiccuping calls, and chewed the cud again. And Questa, for the first time for a week, slept feeling safe, feeling that the goats not only meant her no harm but would connive with her hosts to hide her from prying eyes.

But right now Ellen was tugging at her arm, trying to get her to move on.

'Oh, Ellen, a goat would eat any old grass and thistles, they seem to thrive on bad countryside, they'd do a lot to get the worst of the weeds eaten, and anyway, what's one little goat? Why, their milk is so rich and good you wouldn't believe ... goats' cheese is famous in Italy and ...'

'Leave off, lovie, an' foller me,' Ellen commanded grimly. 'Well I never did, an' you thought Dickie would be a nuisance!'

Despite Ellen's strictures, by the end of the day Questa had bought rather more stock than she had intended. A nanny goat with an evil yellow eye and a kid at heel and two nice little heifers, both in calf, or so the seller swore. Ellen had put her gnarled old hands to the heifers' bellies and agreed that there did seem to be a young'un within, so that was probably all right, but she was less enthusiastic about the purchase of ten ewes, all marked by the ram and therefore, in theory at least, in lamb.

'I don't know anythin' about sheep,' she declared. 'God knows how you'll rear 'em.'

But Questa pointed out that Ellen was fond of telling her that she knew nothing about cattle or pigs either, so they might as well learn together, and that stopped Ellen's grumbles for a good half-hour.

She agreed with buying a dozen fluffy yellow chicks in a cardboard box with holes in the lid and a dozen in-lay pullets in a crate, especially after they had bought a gypsy's piebald pony and the small, homemade cart it had been pulling. The pony had thick little legs ('sturdy', Ellen said approvingly), wide-set, dark brown eyes ('trustable', Ellen insisted), and well-muscled shoulders and flanks ('strengthy', said the horse-woman knowingly). All in all, it seemed a willing little beast and made no objection when the pullets and chicks were thrust into the cart.

'I'll look for a drover to bring the sheep,' Questa said, after a neighbour had offered to put the heifers on a lorry and drop them off at the Court later that evening. 'Someone our way must have bought sheep, surely?'

'Mr Atherton have,' the friendly farmer who had talked to them on the coach told her. 'He've got most of the flock. You ask him, Miss, he won't mind obligin' you.'

'Oh, but I couldn't ...' Questa was beginning, when Ellen dug her firmly in the ribs.

'Thank 'ee,' she said gruffly, 'we'll 'ave a word with 'un.'

'I really couldn't ...' Questa began again as soon as the farmer had wandered off, but Ellen shook her head reprovingly.

'Don't carry on so, lovie. 'Tes old Atherton he's talkin' of. Don't you listen to no gossip when you'm down the village? The young feller's took off, 'ad words wi' the old feller and upped sticks. He've gone abroad they say. The old 'un's managin' for hisself for a while.'

'Oh. Only I don't know old Mr Atherton ... Questa began, only to be firmly put in her place.

'Soon put that right. There 'e is! Come on.'

Mr Atherton turned out to be a lively-looking man in his sixties, with very dark eyes which contrasted oddly with thick, silver-white hair, thick black brows and a straight, shrewd glance. He was of medium height and build and wore an elderly tweed jacket, worn corduroy breeches and ancient wellington boots. When they approached he was standing still, leaning on a walking stick and apparently admiring a number of calves being brought out of one of the pens.

'Oh, Mr Atherton, sir, this yur's Miss Questa Adamson of Eagles Court, she were wonderin'...'

Ellen's introduction brought the man's dark gaze round to Questa. He looked at her for a moment, then smiled. He had a craggy, brooding sort of face but the smile lit it, made him, for a fleeting second, almost handsome.

'Miss Adamson – how very nice to meet you at last! Randolph Atherton – how can I help you?'

He made as if to put out his hand, then turned it into a sort of half-salute, which was as well since both Questa's hands were pushed hard into the pockets of her dufflecoat.

'Oh, um ... I bought some sheep ...' Questa stammered. How

147

rude he must think her, yet she could not shake hands, she could not let a man …

'And you'd like them to travel back to Appersley with mine? It will be a pleasure. I'll get my man to drop them off tomorrow, since they might as well spend tonight at my place.' Abruptly, he turned his head and whistled. A tan and white border collie trotted up to him and pressed herself against his knee. He fondled her ears, then looked across at Questa.

'If you're going to keep sheep you ought to think about having a dog, you know. Kipper here has a litter which I'll be happy to show you, if you'll come round to the Hall? Any day would do – how about Tuesday? After all, we are neighbours. I should have called before, but getting about isn't easy for me – I can't drive myself at present – and Alfie said you'd probably come calling before too long.'

'I'm – I'm sorry,' Questa stammered. 'I did start out once, b-but …'

'Think nothing of it!' He waved a stick dismissively. 'See you on Tuesday, then? Goodbye for now, Miss Adamson.'

He moved slowly away and Questa realised that he was crippled, could walk only with a peculiar, swaying gait, aided by two sticks.

'Ellen, why didn't you tell me he couldn't walk?' she hissed as soon as he was out of earshot. 'Poor man, I'd have gone despite his horrible son if I'd known.'

'Didn't think; everyone do know 'e's a cripple, reckon I thought you knowed an' all. He were injured in a huntin' accident before the war – ridin' like a fool, acourse. Ah well, you knows now.' Ellen paused. 'I reckon 'e's lonely now the lad's left 'im,' she observed. 'Be glad to 'elp with advice an' that, if you'd ask 'un.'

'I will ask,' Questa said. 'He seems nice. Not a bit like young Mr Atherton.'

'No. Knows a lot about sheep does Mr Atherton. The pups will be good'uns, an' all. You could do wuss than tek a look.'

'Right; I'll go round on Tuesday,' Questa said. 'Thanks for introducing me, Ellen. I'm glad we've met up at last.'

'Questa, can I help you to feed the goat? And the sheepses?'

'Sheep, Dickie. One sheep is a sheep, and ten sheep are ten sheep. And I don't have to feed them yet, there's lots of lovely grass, they're eating that.'

Dickie was at the kitchen table, eating porridge, whilst Questa washed up. She had already done a number of jobs around the place and was about to have her own breakfast which Ellen was cooking over the fire.

'One sheep is one sheep and ten sheep are ten sheep,' Dickie said thoughtfully. 'One pig is one pig and ten pig are ten pig?'

'*No*, you idiot, two pigs are two pigs. It's only sheep who don't have an extra ... oh, eat your porridge!'

'I am,' Dickie said placidly. 'School after Christmas; are you glad?'

'Yes,' Questa said grumpily, drying her arms and turning away from the sink. 'Wish it was tomorrow.'

She was watching Dickie and saw the colour come up into his face. Immediately she was sorry she had been so abrupt. Poor kid, he wasn't too bad at all really, he was a lot of fun in some ways, especially if you could forget Grace was his mother.

'Look, Dickie, I didn't mean that. Why don't you come out with me later in the day? I'm going over to see Mr Atherton. He's the gentleman who brought the sheep home for us.'

'Oh, yes,' Dickie said happily. He screwed himself around in his seat to face Ellen, cooking bacon behind him. 'Can I, Ellen?'

'Your mum's takin' you into town to buy your school cap an' that,' Ellen reminded him. 'She isn't goin' to be thrilled, exactly, if you go orf out wi' Questa.'

'I'll go shopping another day,' Dickie said. 'I've nearly finished, Questa; shall I get my coat?'

'I haven't started, though,' Questa said. She fetched a plate off the dresser, cut herself a chunk of bread, and held the plate out to Ellen, who slid a fried egg on to the bread and flanked it with two thin pink curls of bacon. 'Perhaps you'd better ask Mummy first.'

'No! She'll want me to go shopping. If we just go out quick ...'

'Dickie, darling, where's my cup of tea? Did you forget? Oh well, I'm down now, no point in bringing one up, I'll just sit here and drink it and pretend I'm still cuddled down.' Grace walked into the room in the pale blue silk housecoat she favoured in the mornings, rumpled her son's hair and took her place at the table. 'Any porridge going begging, Ellen?'

'You said you din't like it; said it were bad for your figure,' Ellen observed grimly. 'Sides, there ain't none left.'

'Oh, in that case ... put me some toast on, would you?'

Alan had brought an electric toaster down the last time he came. Unfortunately, whoever had made the toaster had done so with thin slices of bread in mind and no one could slice Ellen's homemade loaves that thin, or not until they were too stale to bother with, anyway. Ellen grunted.

'Here,' Questa said. 'Have the loaf. Ellen's a bit pushed.'

'Good God, I thought Ellen came over here each morning to make everyone breakfast, not just you, Questa,' Grace murmured cattily. She took the loaf, picked up the knife, then eyed the bread with what she no doubt considered to be a pretty air of indecision. 'Dear me, where should one start? It looks like a mountain range!'

'Jest cut it,' Ellen advised. 'If you want toast, that is.'

Grace heaved a huge, martyred sigh and began to cut. Questa, with her mouth full of bacon, reached for her cup of tea. She watched Dickie who was watching Grace and felt sorry for him. Poor sprog, she'd seen mice watch cats with less anxiety. But he would have to ask, she could not be a party to keeping Dickie from his parent!

Questa was a quick eater. She finished her food, drained her mug, then got to her feet.

'I'm just going to put a clean shirt on, then I'll be off.'

'Right,' Ellen said.

Dickie got to his feet and went and leaned against his mother's blue silk thigh.

'Mummy, I was talking to Questa just now and ...'

Questa went into the small parlour, stripped off the smock she wore to work in, found a clean shirt and put that on instead, checked that her beloved trousers were respectable – they were, fairly – and ran a comb through her hair. Convinced she now looked just as she ought to go visiting she returned to the kitchen.

You could have cut the atmosphere with a knife. Dickie looked as though he had been crying, Grace was deathly white with patches of scarlet on both cheeks, Ellen, cutting bread, was doing so with an efficiency and viciousness which made Questa suspect that her old friend was pretending she was cutting something quite other.

'Well, I'm off. Anyone coming?'

Dickie gave an enormous sniff. 'Can't,' he said mournfully. 'Got to go shoppin'.'

'I've had my say,' Ellen muttered. 'You knows what I thinks.'

'And I've had *my* say,' Grace said, her tone very bright and brittle. 'Dickie does as his *mother* tells him. Anyone else's opinion is immaterial. Is that clear?'

This time, no one answered. Dickie stared at the table, but Questa saw a tear trickle down his cheek. Ellen continued to cut bread. Grace, still with cheeks like a dutch doll, smiled artificially round her.

'It is? Come along then, Dickie, you can smarten yourself up a bit whilst I get ready.'

She left, dragging her reluctant son and closing the kitchen door far too forcefully behind her.

'And what was all that about?' Questa asked, picking up an abandoned piece of toast and spreading honey on it. 'Grace was in a state.'

Ellen sniffed. 'She should'a let 'im go with you, lovie,' she said. 'How'll 'e ever learn, else?'

'Oh well, there's other times,' Questa said. 'I'm going to try riding Scamper this afternoon; Dickie can have a go after me, he'll be home again by then. He'll probably be better at it, too.'

They had named the pony Scamper because of her fast trot and the perkiness in her step. Ellen, who wanted to call the pony Beauty, thought it a foolish name and said so, but Dickie approved.

'Aye, he'll be back be then,' Ellen agreed. 'And that woman, too.' She made the sort of angry hiss which Questa was beginning to associate with Grace's name; one thing was sure, though Questa was being sensible and doing her best to get along with Grace, Ellen had given up all pretence. She disliked Grace, let it show, seemed unrepentant. What was more, she had a soft spot for Dickie, let that show, and was equally unrepentant about it.

'Well, if you remember, it was you ...' Questa began, then stopped to give Ellen a quick squeeze. 'Sorry, that was horrid of me. And I do think Dickie loves it here and would rather be with us than anywhere else.'

'True,' Ellen said. 'Get along wi' you, then. Give Mr Atherton my regards.'

'Okay. Bye, Ellen. I'll be back by lunchtime.'

Questa enjoyed a walk in the early sunshine, and took advantage of the fact that she had a legitimate reason not to be working to go and peep at her goats in their prickly, nettly pasture, and her pony, grazing happily on a sloping water-meadow.

She had got up very early, before the sun had risen, but she could see that already it was gilding the distant hills, bringing their humped shapes into prominence. Looking at them almost idly, she was suddenly struck by an odd thought; where had she seen that particular series of shapes before? Not just here, every morning when she looked up, but somewhere else ... Or was it that strange thing, *déjà vu*, which made you think you had been somewhere you could never recall visiting?

But hills are hills, no matter how blue and misty, no matter how beautiful. Questa, who had known the Appenines well, wondered if there was some resemblance between them and the Welsh hills, then dismissed the matter from her mind. Experience told her that, when it no longer bothered her, the answer would hop into her head.

But right now she had an errand, so she would take the short-cut. Through the narrowest part of the wood, across a meadow, over the river – shoes in her hand, feet and legs wet – over another meadow, a field of golden stubble, and she was on strange territory, though she had walked this way once or twice after she knew young Atherton had definitely gone.

But never before had she walked along beside the crumbling stone wall until she reached the white, five-barred gate. Never before had she swung it open, walked through, crunched across clean, weed-free gravel and up to a side door sheltered by a small glass porch.

The porch had no outer door, but she stood in its shelter and looked around her. Shelves lined it, with comfortable family things on them. A pipe-rack with two pipes, a handful of clothes pegs, a tray of seedlings, a number of small pots, each one containing a geranium cutting. Under one shelf there was a pile of old magazines, mostly *Picture Posts*, and under another a box full of what looked like peat. As Questa stood there a cat came coolly around the corner into the porch and stood looking up at her out of large, amber eyes. After a long scrutiny it miaowed once, commandingly. It was telling her to ring the bell, dammit, since both of them wanted to get inside. Smiling, Questa found the bell and pressed it. Far off, she heard it tinkle.

'All right, cat?' she said. 'Someone will come quite soon, I expect.'

She did not hear approaching footsteps but suddenly the door shot open. For a startled moment she saw no one, then she realised that Mr Atherton, seated in a wheelchair, had whizzed up and opened the door for her on soundless wheels.

'Come in, come in,' he said pleasantly. 'Oh hello, Monty; you can come in too, old feller.'

Monty was the cat, Questa guessed. He was a handsome tom, ginger all over save for white paw-tips, and as soon as he was in he climbed on to Mr Atherton's lap and began to purr like a small motorbike.

'Thanks, Mr Atherton,' Questa said. 'Shall I close the door?'

'Might as well. Sheep all right?'

'Fine, I think. I don't know much about sheep but I've put them in a nice big meadow where the grass isn't all thistles. I hope they'll be all right. Alfie says we'll have to buy feed for the winter, though.'

'Aye, supplements. That's right,' Mr Atherton agreed. 'Any sign of scrapey or scab?'

'I wouldn't know what to look for,' Questa said. 'I'm hoping you'll be able to tell me a thing or two; Ellen says you know a lot about stock.'

'Well, I've been farming a while,' Mr Atherton agreed. 'The Athertons have been here as long as if not longer than the Adamsons. We're both from ancient, landowning families, m'dear, and that's not a bad thing, not a bad thing at all. Now let me show you Kipper's sons and daughters. They're out in the stables so I'll need my sticks.'

'Can't you use the chair?' Questa asked timidly. 'I imagine you can get along faster in that than most people with two legs!'

He grinned, nodding. 'Aye, it's fast and convenient, but it's a devil on kerbs and up and down steps – useless, in fact. Come on, through to the back.'

He set the wheelchair in motion and, as she had guessed, Questa had her work cut out to keep up. As they hurried through the house she got a vague impression of lovely furniture, richly coloured carpets, a lot of dark panelling and a great many oil paintings. But her host, clearly used to his own house, glanced neither right nor left but simply kept moving.

'Kitchen door next on the right,' he said as they made their way down a long, dark corridor. 'Can you open up for me?'

Questa stepped ahead of him, opened the door, and the three of them – Mr Atherton, Monty and Questa – entered the room.

It was a very big kitchen, beautifully kept, with gleaming work surfaces, lots of cupboards and a huge fireplace in which a wood fire burned brightly. Questa saw a modern electric cooker, two fridges, rows of shining saucepans, more rows of kitchen utensils – and the biggest, fattest woman she had ever seen.

'Ah, Mrs Clovelly, meet my new neighbour, Miss Questa Adamson,' Mr Atherton said. 'Mrs Clovelly is my housekeeper, and very good at her job she is, so don't try to poach her away from me, please! Questa's come to see Kipper's pups, Mrs C., and to pick my brains on how best to take care of sheep. We'll take a look at the pups first, but then I think we might be ready to try some of your delicious fruit cake and a cup of coffee, if you could manage that? We'll have it in my study, please.'

'Certainly, Mr Atherton. I'll get Daphne to bring it through,' Mrs Clovelly said placidly. To Questa she added kindly, 'Nice to meet you, miss. The pups are grand and Kipper's a marvellous mother to 'em. See you presently, then.'

Whilst the woman was talking, Mr Atherton had managed to get himself up out of the wheelchair and balanced on his two sticks. Without being asked this time, Questa opened the back door and her host swung himself across the kitchen floor, over the lintel and down a step on to the paved yard. He crossed it equally quickly with his curious, lop-sided gait, then used a stick to push open one of the stable half-doors. He turned and smiled at Questa.

'Take a look! Then, if you want to, we'll go inside.'

Questa took a look and her expression must have spoken louder than words, for Mr Atherton opened the door and ushered her in, and Questa immediately leaned over the wooden fencing which had been constructed across the front of a straw-filled loose-box, the better to contain the puppies gambolling about inside it.

'One, two, three ... gracious, there are seven,' she declared with shining eyes. 'They're the loveliest little dogs ... how old are they, sir?'

'Eight weeks. Old enough to leave Kipper, and don't think she'll be sorry because they're wearing her out, poor old lady. Nice, aren't they? Look at those markings.'

'Yes, oh look at him!' A tiny pup pranced across the box, stared up at Questa and barked, with a great display of white pin-teeth and pink tongue. 'Oh, he's so pretty!'

'He's a bitch,' Mr Atherton said. 'But I do agree with you, I think she's the prettiest, too. And probably the one biting the other one's tail – see him, the dark brown one? – is the cleverest.'

'And you are the fattest, you adorable thing,' Questa said, picking up a plump white pup with a brown patch over one eye. 'And that one's the biggest ... oh, look at her, she must be the tiniest ... I wish I could have them all!'

'In fact, I was only half-serious when I suggested you might need a dog,' Mr Atherton admitted. 'These are working animals, very intelligent and strong, and they need work, they shouldn't be pets. Unless you intend to build up your flock quite fast you won't have work for a dog like these for a number of years, maybe not at all.'

'Oh! But I may well have a lot of sheep,' Questa said, deciding on the spur of the moment that sheep-farming would be fun, and profitable too. And she did want a puppy! 'Besides, it would guard the house, wouldn't it? And keep an eye on Dickie, who lives with us at Eagles Court. And fetch the cows in for milking, when they have milk, and do all manner of useful things.'

'We-ell, I tell you what, since you're a neighbour I'll let you have the runt, and if she makes up into a nice, intelligent animal, you must mate her with Speck, my best dog, and I'll take the pick of the litter instead of a stud fee.'

'The runt?'

'That's the tiny one; she may not come to much, but she'll have a lovely nature, they all will, and she'll be a good worker even though she may never be strong. How's that for an offer?'

'Oh, the little one! I love her best' Questa said. 'How much will she cost me?'

'She won't cost you a penny, that's what I was trying to explain. I'll take the pick of her litter when she has one, that will be payment enough.'

'Oh. That sounds very generous,' Questa said doubtfully. 'Are you sure, sir? She's so sweet, I'm sure you could sell her for a lot of money.'

'Perhaps I could ... and please stop calling me sir, I much prefer Ran, which is what my wife used to call me. After all, though there is a considerable discrepancy in our ages, we are neighbours! When my son comes back ... have you met my son?'

'Yes, I think so,' Questa murmured. All of a sudden the puppies seemed less attractive. 'Is he coming back? I thought he had moved away.'

'He did, but he's agreed to come back. I've been very patient, because I know all young men need to sow a few wild oats, live dangerously, but he'll be back within a twelve-month, I daresay. He's not such a bad lad, but you'll know that if you met him when he was home last. Now will you take your puppy now or in a week or so?'

'Can she come now?' Questa said. 'Dickie is lonely, we're a long way from the village and his mother doesn't encourage him to play with other children. I think the pup will be doubly welcome.'

'Yes, of course. Pick her up. Kipper won't mind. As I said she's getting rather fed up with them. What'll you call her?'

'Roma,' Questa said without knowing why she had said it. 'Yes, Roma.'

'Nice. Puts her in the same general area as you: two Italian names,' Mr Atherton observed. 'On second thoughts, perhaps you'd better leave her with her brothers and sisters until you're ready to go home; Mrs Clovelly and Daphne might not be best pleased if she puddled in the study.'

'I don't blame them,' Questa said, replacing the puppy reluctantly in the loose-box. 'But my place is such a mess still that it will scarcely matter. Do puppies take long to house-train? In Italy they were always kept outside, so it didn't arise.'

'Yours won't take long,' Mr Atherton said positively. 'All Kipper's pups are bright as buttons, they'll learn anything you're capable of teaching. Within reason, of course. Now that we've settled the puppy, come in and have that coffee and then, if you're agreeable, we'll just walk across to Ladies Meadow and take a look at the flock.'

The coffee was delicious, the cake more so, and Questa found herself very much at ease with this man whose son had treated her so badly. Indeed, she thought him delightful, and when he told her he remembered her father she settled down happily for a good gossip.

'Tell me about him, please,' she said. 'I'd be most grateful.'

'You miss him, don't you?' And, at her nod, 'I can't take his place of course, no one could, but I've always wanted a daughter ... if I can be of some small help to you ... you'll let me do my best for you?'

Alan had said much the same thing and been gently but definitely repulsed. Ran, however, was not offering because he felt he had to do so, he was offering from the heart. Questa sensed it and accepted in the same spirit.

'I will, I'll be glad of your help. And now tell me about my father.'

They had taken their coffee into the small drawing room, a pleasant place with comfortable, elderly furniture, a faded carpet garlanded with roses and french windows leading out to a private piece of garden, completely hedged about with a small-leafed, close-growing shrub.

'Right, here we go, then. Charles was rather a serious little boy, but like all boys he could kick up a row now and then. When he was young, under fourteen I suppose, Joshua was patient enough with him but as Charles grew up they tended to argue. Oddly enough, the thing they both had in common, a tremendous interest in archaeology and ancient history, was the thing that had them at each other's throats most. Charles had a number of theories about archaeological digs and what certain artefacts had been used for and so on, and these theories were, apparently, anathema to Joshua, so they argued constantly – not always amicably either, I'm afraid.

'There was a big argument when Charles was about fourteen, which got so personal that Joshua refused to have the boy back at the Court for some years, but when Charles got into Cambridge Joshua apparently decided to forgive him and the visits started all over again.

'Unfortunately by then Charles had done quite a lot of home-work on estate management and he started to criticise Joshua for the way he neglected the Court, the run-down fields and so on, and began to read up on modern farming methods which he urged Joshua to put into practice. Joshua, who had never cared for that side of things, grew bitter once more and began to want to bend Charles to his will, see him dance to his tune.

'I think the genuine, deep-rooted difference between Charles and Joshua was that Joshua was a scholar and all he wanted were his books on ancient civilisations, a decent fire, good food, and peace. Your father, my dear, was a much more practical charac-ter. Once he was old enough he would go off on archaeological digs at the drop of a hat and Joshua, whilst approving of the principle, didn't approve of Charles coming back to the Court and laying down the law, telling him that the pottery he revered as Roman ware was actually much later, or that his coin collection contained some notable fakes.'

'Do you know, I had no idea my father was interested in the Romans?' Questa said. 'How odd that I shouldn't have known!'

'Didn't you know? It was the reason he took you to Italy with him, in thirty-nine, or so I understood. But of course I might be mistaken.'

'I – I thought we went to visit my mother's relatives,' Questa said uneasily. 'I know we were with my aunt and uncle when Daddy was called back to England on urgent business, anyway. Daddy wanted me to go home with him, but the aunts begged him to let me stay, and he agreed, and by the time he wanted to come back it was too late. I never saw him again.'

'Yes, I remember; it must have been dreadful for you both. Come to think of it, someone told me that Charles was investigating some finds up in the hills to the north of the city, so I suppose it was only sensible to kill two birds with one stone and see his late wife's relatives at the same time.'

'I see,' Questa said. 'I wonder where Uncle Joshua made his finds of Roman pottery and coins, Ran? Was it near here? I suppose it's even possible that there might have been a Roman settlement at Eagles Court, or the Hall, for that matter. Why, hundreds of years ago there might have been a villa where the Court is today!'

'It would have been nearer two thousand years ago,' Ran said. 'The Roman conquest of Britain started very soon after Christ's time on earth. It's a fact that the Romans mined for lead around here, so it follows they lived here, too. The road that runs through the village is part of Watling Street, and Charles said that in his opinion there must have been something, perhaps a villa or a military camp of some sort, where the Court is today because of the lie of the land. He would have loved to dig, but apparently Joshua got very annoyed when he suggested it – said he knew more about the Romans in Britain than Charles ever would and that he would have excavated had he believed there was any possibility of making any discoveries.'

'I don't see why Daddy couldn't have dug, though,' Questa said. 'If he was proved right even Uncle Joshua would have been pleased, and of course if Daddy was wrong his uncle could have crowed like anything!'

'Well, between ourselves, Charles did dig, and he did find bits and pieces. Some he managed to spirit away, but the rest Joshua froze on to, vowing they were not what Charles thought they were. You'll probably find various odds and ends as you go through the attics.'

159

'Good. I'd like to prove they were what my father thought they were. But, Ran, tell me more about Daddy when he was your friend.'

'Well, he would have been delighted in the interest you're taking in the old place, and the way you're working to put it all in order,' Ran said thoughtfully. 'One thing I do remember, he always wanted Joshua to try to grow vines on the hill behind the house. He said it had been terraced once and could be terraced again, but I never knew whether he was serious or just trying to goad old Joshua.'

Questa gasped. 'Now that *is* extraordinary, because I asked Ellen if vines had ever been grown there, and she said it wasn't terracing, it was sheep-paths. I wish I could grow vines; that would please Daddy, and it would please me because I do know quite a bit about viticulture.'

'You'd be taking one hell of a chance, the weather being what it is ,' Ran said, frowning thoughtfully. 'I'd keep it in the back of my mind for later, when you've got the rest of the place sorted, if I were you. Now, I was supposed to be telling you about Charles, not so much as a boy, because I didn't see much of him then, but later, when we became friends.'

'Sorry,' Questa said. 'It just intrigued me to discover that he had an interest which I knew nothing about. But then I've forgotten so much ... Go on, tell me how you came to know my father well, and be his friend.'

'Well, when he was about twenty Charles took to coming over here to talk about my horses – I bred horses before the war, mostly Hanoverians and one or two other breeds – and since he rode well and my young stock always needed exercise and extra schooling, we got a good deal of mutual benefit from our friendship. Charles was still fascinated by the Roman conquest of Britain, but his interests were, well, widening. My son wasn't very old, three or four I suppose, and my wife welcomed Charles gladly – she was a keen horse-rider herself – so I flattered myself that we had a good relationship going, one which made up to Charles for the constant arguments and antagonism he got from Joshua. And Charles was a real find, make no mistake about it, he could ride anything on four legs. He was magic with horses, even my stud stallion took to him, and Gulliver didn't take to many.' He gave Questa a long, quizzical look. 'I wonder if you ride?'

'No, but I'm going to learn,' Questa said at once. 'We bought a fat little pony ... do you still have horses here?'

'Oh yes, quite a few. I don't ride them, of course, but I still breed, and they've produced some fine foals. Gulliver is old now, getting towards his quarter-century, but he's still a magnificent animal. You must come over and see him when you've the time to spare. Once, it would have grieved me to think that I had no one to exercise the old fellow; my son still rides him when he's at home, but mostly Gulliver dreams in his pasture and takes only the gentlest exercise – like me, alas.'

'It must have been wonderful for Daddy to have all that riding,' Questa said. 'Did Uncle Joshua mind?'

'I don't think so, but I wouldn't really know. Our paths seldom crossed,' Ran admitted. 'After the final, crashing row, when Charles stopped coming for good, I wanted to get in touch, to suggest he came here instead, but Joshua was furious when I asked for the boy's address. Refused point-blank to give it. I waited, hoping Charles would come round or contact me in some way, but he never did. End of story, I'm afraid.'

'I wonder what the row was about?' Questa said, standing up and going over to hold the door open so that Mr Atherton, and his sticks, could swing through into the hallway. 'It was very sad for my father though; he loved the Court so much.'

'Yes, it was. But at least he was growing up by then, with other interests, his work, friends ... Now young lady, don't keep me here chattering when I ought to be taking you to see my sheep.'

'And the horses? Shall we see the horses, too?' Together, they went out of the room, across the hall and through the side door. 'When I told Ellen anyone could ride a horse she laughed. Is it hard?'

Ran laughed too, swinging along on his sticks, scarcely faltering when they came to uneven ground or a smallish step.

'It isn't easy,' he told her. 'Want me to teach you?'

'Oh, could you? I would be so grateful. Scamper is quite a small pony, though, and rather fat. She doesn't look much, I can't imagine her throwing anyone, but Ellen's pleased with her.'

'And if anyone knows horseflesh, it's your Ellen,' Ran said, rather to Questa's surprise. 'She's a mine of information, though some of her ideas are a bit old-fashioned. None the worse for that, though, I daresay. But I'll teach you to ride on a quiet little mare, it'll be easier than bringing your pony over here each time. Now if you look to your left, through those trees ... see that hillside?'

Questa squinted through the trees, already beginning to shed their burden of red and yellow leaves. 'Yes, just about.'

'That's Gloaming Hill, where we keep the horses, though they'll come down at night-time during the winter months. Can you see Gulliver? He's the biggest brown blob, over to your right, almost at the summit.'

'I *think* I see him,' Questa said. 'But there are several ... three, or is it four?'

'Ten, actually. I daresay some are hidden by the trees, or by a dip in the ground. I'm afraid it's a bit far for me to take you over there now, but are you on the telephone? If so, I'll ring next time I bring them down and you can see them in the stables.' He had paused whilst they looked at the horses, now he swung into motion once more.

'We haven't had the telephone connected up again yet,' Questa said. 'Apparently there's a long waiting list. They said it could be months.'

'Oh, did they? Well, I'll have a word. After all, a girl your age, living by herself, needs a telephone far more than some of these city gents who only come into the country at weekends.'

'I'm not really living by myself now, though,' Questa said rather sadly. 'A friend of Mr Patterson's – he is my father's executor – has moved in with me. Her name's Grace Syrett. She's got the little boy I talked about – Dickie.'

'Oh? Ah yes, I remember someone saying ... tall, fair woman? Expects everyone to jump when she says so?'

Questa laughed at this frank opinion and Ran Atherton laughed too, his eyes twinkling.

'I'm quoting village gossip,' he admitted. 'Daphne lives on the council estate, she's married to Pete Bullock, my cowman, but the village is crawling with their relatives and what she actually said was, *She'm a lazy one, that Mrs Syrett; everyone say so, even 'er what run the post office, an' she should know, bein' as 'ow she'm so idle 'erself.'*

'Yes. Well, I keep trying to like her, but it's uphill work. Dickie's nice though, and Ellen says we should put up with Grace for his sake. Oh, I know, when you bring the horses in, if you tell Alfie ...'

'Of course, local telegraph is much quicker than a mere telephone,' Ran agreed. 'Now, what do you think of them?'

They had reached Ladies Meadow and there were the sheep, dotted about in small groups, placidly feeding on the still-green grass.

'They look ... like sheep,' Questa confessed. 'I can't tell a good one from a bad one, I'm afraid. So how I'm going to manage mine ...'

'You'll manage. You should, because this is hill country and we rear a lot of sheep. Now if you'll just go over there and catch me a fat ewe, we'll have a lesson. I can't show you disease on my sheep, or I hope I can't, but I can tell you where to look and what to look for. Off with you. I should have brought Kipper, she'd have done it better than either of us, but lacking her, sneak up behind one.'

'I'll do my best,' Questa said. She swung herself over the gate and set off across the meadow at a determined trot, conscious of tremendous elation. It was beginning! She had a friendly neighbour, she would be a farmer in the end!

'Ellen? I'm awfully sorry I wasn't back for lunch but Mr Atherton asked me to stay ... isn't he *nice*? Then he showed me his shearing shed and his sheep-dip and I had a lesson in how to recognise various illnesses – sheep ones, of course – and he's going to teach me to ride on the nicest little chestnut mare ... and look what he's given me!'

Ellen was in the kitchen garden, clearing a bed. As Questa walked through the doorway she stopped work, put a hand to the small of her back, then came across the newly dug earth.

'Reckon I've done enough for one day,' she observed. 'What you got, then?'

'A puppy. Isn't she sweet, Ellen? She'll help me with the sheep

163

when she's older, but I thought it would be nice for Dickie – he's lonely, poor kid. What do you think?'

'Bit small,' Ellen said, looking critically at the brown and white, wriggling bundle in Questa's arms. 'Still, it'll do, I daresay. The boy's bound to like it, seein' as 'ow ...' She stopped short.

'Seeing as how what? Did they go shopping? I looked into the kitchen but it was empty, so I came out here. Are they still out? I can't wait to see Dickie's face when he sees Roma.'

'Oh ah,' Ellen said. 'They'm back, but Madam's in a nasty sorta mood, if you asks me.'

'Oh. Well, perhaps when she sees the puppy ...'

'Tek 'im in now,' Ellen advised. 'She'll be wantin' 'er tea, when she sees it's all ready she'll probably be sweet as pie.'

'Yes, good idea,' Questa agreed. 'You won't be far behind me, will you?'

'Not far; run along now, do. I'll jest tidy up 'ere, then I'll come in an' dish up.'

Seven

Questa and the puppy went quietly into the kitchen. The room was empty but the table was laid for a meal; from the oven came a pleasant savoury smell, whilst a pan of potatoes bubbled away over the fire. Questa rummaged in the pantry, emerging with a cardboard box. She found an old piece of sheet for the bottom of the box and put the puppy into it, but Roma would not settle. She climbed straight out, her small, blunt face turning this way and that. She's searching for her brothers and sisters, poor little thing, Questa decided. Never mind, she can come and sit on my bed whilst I brush my hair.

Roma not only sat on her bed, she also puddled on it, squatting there with an anxious expression as though already unsure that this was correct procedure.

'No, that's naughty!' Questa scolded, but what was the point? Puppies are babies, she reminded herself, and babies need nappies for ever such a long time. No use scolding, I must just put her out of doors whenever she wants to go, and even when she doesn't. Not that she could keep her out of doors, if she was to befriend Dickie, because Dickie was nearly always indoors. Grace hated the outdoors so Dickie must hate it too, and the fact that he did not, that he loved to play outside as most children do, was something Grace simply ignored – or denied, if it was put to her.

Already, Questa had severe doubts about Grace's love for her son; if she really did love him, it seemed a very selfish sort of emotion. Grace vowed that everything she did was for Dickie, but she gave him so little freedom, so little of her time. He was supposed to stick around in case she needed him, to be quiet because she hated noise, and to do as she asked immediately, because she could not bear having to ask twice. Other than that

165

the poor child might do as he pleased... only Grace said she never felt safe when he was out of sight, which severely limited his activities.

But if he has Roma, then I can remind Grace that she needs exercise, and offer to walk with them, Questa planned, brushing her hair vigorously. The puppy sat watching her, then squeaked a tiny, shrill bark. Questa put down the brush, bent over, plucked the puppy off the floor and set off for the kitchen once more. She thought she had heard someone descending the stairs and, sure enough, Dickie was standing on a stool and washing his hands at the sink whilst Grace drained the potatoes.

'Dickie, look what I've got!'

Dickie looked round. He had been crying; his eyes were pink and puffy, but his expression brightened the moment he saw the puppy.

'Questa! Oh, a little dog! Mummy, look what Questa's got!'

'I thought we needed a dog,' Questa said rather stiltedly, because Grace was staring at her. 'She'll be company for you, Dickie, then Mummy won't worry when you go out and play in the garden. Her name's Roma – do you want to hold her?'

Speechless, Dickie held out his arms and Questa was putting the pup into them when Grace intervened.

'Questa, we're about to have a meal, I will *not* have animals in the room where food is being served and, what's more, you're encouraging Dickie to touch it when he's just going to have his tea. Put it outside this minute, Dickie.'

Questa felt rage roar through her until she could actually feel it pounding in her ears. How *dare* Grace try to tell her what she might and might not do in her own home! How dare she command Dickie to put the puppy outside, as though Roma were a bit of rubbish to be thrown out into the yard? Where were the older woman's normal human instincts at the sight of something small and helpless? Why, where they always were: non-existent. All she was interested in was what's in it for me? Nothing. Can you eat it? No. Then get rid of it!

'Dickie, you mustn't put Roma outside because she's only a baby. Here, if Mummy's afraid your hands will get dirty, you'd better give her back to me.'

166

Dickie was a biddable child. He was, after all, only five years old. But at her words he set his lips and turned on his mother.

'No! Questa gave her to me; you can't make me put her down!'

'Grace, please, he's only a little boy, all children love ...'

Grace pounced on her son like a cat on a mouse. She shook him, then tore the puppy from his grasp. The puppy yipped, and Questa hurled herself across the room, pushed Grace hard, and took the puppy from her. She was shaking, so was the puppy, Dickie was in tears – only Grace looked calm. She seemed to be almost enjoying the fracas, Questa thought wonderingly.

'Dickie is *my* son; if I say he is not to have a puppy, not to handle the dirty little thing, then ...'

No one had been aware of the back door opening until Ellen spoke. Yet her words brought instant calm and wiped the triumph off Grace's smug, lovely face.

'What's this? Your son is 'e, Mrs Syrett? But not *jest* your son, ho no, someone else 'ad an 'and in 'is mekin', that I *do* recall. Sons don't allus favour their mothers, do they, Mrs Syrett? Now what was you saying'?'

Questa had felt that Grace regarded Ellen with a sort of uneasy respect, now she was sure of it. Grace actually fell back a step, for she had been about to attack her son again, and brushed the hair back from her face with a casual hand before returning to her task of draining the potatoes as though nothing much had happened at all.

'Oh, I suppose if I'm to share your house then I can't be too fussy, but really, Questa, animals in the kitchen! Dickie, sit down, then we can all have our tea.'

They all sat down. It was an uneasy meal, but at the end of it, when Dickie got up, Questa said, 'Coming to take Roma for a walk, Dickie? Just a short little walk, she's got short little legs, but I think we ought to give her a chance to do a puddle or two.'

'Umm ...' Dickie said, looking at his mother from under his brows.

'Yes, Dickie, you may go,' Grace said easily. 'But if you touch the puppy, remember to wash your hands afterwards. Puppies are covered in germs.'

'Rubbish,' Ellen said testily. 'We're all covered in germs, come

167

to that – you too, Mrs Syrett. Now, Dickie, I'm a-goin' to mek you up an earth-box an' a bed-box for Roma, 'cos you'll want 'er to sleep in your room, won't you?'

Grace looked daggers at Ellen but, to Questa's real surprise, said nothing.

'Oh, Ellen,' Dickie breathed. 'What's the earth-box for?'

'For the pup to do 'er little widdles in,' Ellen said. 'Off with you both. Give 'er a good run.'

Outside, Dickie tucked a hand into Questa's.

'Isn't Ellen *brave*?' he said. 'Can I really have Roma in my room, Ques?'

Questa, who had hoped to be the one with whom the puppy slept, looked down at his small, serious face and nodded.

'Yes, of course you can. You'll have to feed her and everything, so that she knows you're her master. Tomorrow we'll walk down to the village and buy a tiny collar and lead ...'

'Oh, oh!' Dickie said. 'Oh, Ques, I do love her so much!'

They walked the little pup round the yard a few times, watched her produce several puddles and a tiny curl of excrement, then took her back indoors. Dickie trotted off to bed with the boxes and his new possession and Questa and Ellen sat in the lamplit kitchen and mended socks, a task at which Questa was pretty poor, though Ellen was no great shakes herself, having long ago given up darning as such in favour of an activity known as cobbling.

They did not talk much, save about sheep and their ailments. Questa knew that Ellen would not answer the question she was dying to ask – what hold do you have over Grace? – and she was anxious to pass on all her recently acquired knowledge about sheep so that, between them, Ellen and she would have a good idea when a sheep ailed.

In fact, it was not until she was in bed and preparing to snuggle down that it occurred to Questa that she had handed over her dog, the only dog she was ever likely to own, to a small boy who, until today, she would have said she did not particularly like. But he's worse off than me, she thought with some surprise. At least I had Daddy until I was ten. Poor Dickie's only got Grace and she isn't nice at all. And he's completely in her power, really.

168

Or was. But Ellen knows something; she can keep Grace down a bit.

And I do like the kid. I like him very much.

She turned over and pressed her face into the cool pillow. Dear little Roma, she thought, I wonder if she's gone to sleep yet? She was tempted to get up and find out, but it would be awful if she woke Dickie, or walked right into Grace. Better leave it and ask Dickie tactfully, in the morning, whether he had been disturbed by the puppy.

And presently, with the warm knowledge that she had been kind to someone less fortunate than herself, Questa fell asleep.

She slept deeply, as one occasionally does, until the small hours. Then she woke. She lay on her back, staring up at the ceiling and wondering what had woken her, if anything, and whether to simply turn over and go back to sleep again.

But it had been an odd sort of day. Grace had shown herself in her true colours, Questa had allowed her natural feelings for Dickie to rise to the surface, and she had made a new friend in Ran Atherton.

What was more, in the quiet night-time hush, she thought once more about her dream, and Marcus. She wanted to know how his grapes were doing, whether he had harvested a crop from them yet. After all, if she was to grow grapes for her father's sake – and for her own – it might be helpful to see how her friend's vines flourished. And then there were all the people he employed – what sort of wages did he pay, would he advise her to get more workers or simply use the ones she had in a different manner? His house looked nice, too. He had invited her inside; why had she never gone? She had thought she would, next time ... then there had been no next time. But tonight, she was suddenly sure ...

Obeying an instinct which called on no logic for its existence, Questa turned over, cuddled down and waited. She could feel sleep creeping over her, insidious, desirable. Soon she slid willingly into its embrace.

She awoke to sun, shining golden through her lids, dappled with the blue of shadows. She opened her eyes quickly, gladly, sure she was in the wood, knowing Marcus was near ... only she wasn't. She was sitting on the terraced hillside, with the vines above, below and all round her, and looking across to the blue and distant hills, as she had looked once before.

But this time, she recognised them.

They were her Welsh hills, the very same hills she had stared at from Eagles Court as the sun rose the previous day. Had she ever really believed that Marcus lived in a house a short way from Eagles Court? Had she been avoiding the fact that it was – had to be – Eagles Court? But she had not, then, sat on this very spot and looked outwards, towards the hills. This time, she knew she could not possibly be mistaken. The line of hills she faced were without the shadow of a doubt the Welsh hills she was already growing to love. So the house below, which so strongly resembled a Roman villa, was just that, but not a modern house, not one of the villas she had seen as she made her way from Sorrento up to the city of Rome. The villa below her came from an earlier time, when such homes had been scattered the length and breadth of England.

And now she faced what she had known, in her heart, for a couple of days if not longer. Marcus was not a neighbour, or not in the usual sense of the word. He was a neighbour in time, if you liked; she was dreaming of the past. The house she looked down on was an earlier Eagles Court, built, as her home was, to get the maximum shelter from the hill, with a thickly wooded slope before it to keep off the worst of the winds, and the hill, with its lines of vines, keeping the villa's back secure.

She looked outwards; from here, yesterday, she had seen her meadows and woods and a part of Appersley Mere, shining in the early sun. Now she could see meadows and forest, the glint of the river and a sizeable man-made pond. The pond would be for irrigation when they had a dry summer, she realised. Were her woods all that was left of the great forest which stretched from the boundaries of Marcus's estate to the Welsh hills? Had the mere really grown from a Roman irrigation pond? But she supposed it must have, for over a mighty stretch of time changes had to take place.

A small stone bounced down the hillside past her and

cannoned off the nearest vine. She looked up. Marcus was coming down towards her, jumping from terrace to terrace. He looked excited.

'Hail, Questa! I've looked for you for months, but I know I mustn't reproach you or you'll stay away even longer next time. What d'you think? It's coming on well, isn't it? Have you planted your own vines yet? We've had good wine from last year's crop and we'll have a good pressing this autumn, so folk who said it was a freak crop or a freak year will have to think again. Come down with me and I'll show you where we tread the grapes and where we store them, and don't say you're too busy because it's quite early yet.'

'Well, I will, only I wanted to ask you whether you rear sheep ...' Questa began, just as he reached her. He sat down beside her. He was breathing hard and a trickle of sweat ran down the side of his tanned face. He smelt of clean young male and of straw and something else too, something sharp and pungent, something familiar, yet ...

'Sheep? We rear them in a small way, but I've begun to breed horses, little neighbour, and that is something which *can* be said to bring in money! We need sheep, pigs, cattle for our own use, but the horses I can sell as far away as Verulanium, and for good money too. Everyone needs horses, of course, but an army pays better than most.'

Horses! Of course, that was the familiar scent, she loved grooming Scamper and breathing in the sharp, evocative smell which emanated from the pony.

'You sell horses to the *army*?'

'Of course. I know what you're thinking, that the Roman soldier marches and does not ride, but a great many officers ride into battle, and all the hauling of siege weapons, the carrying of food and equipment, is done by horses. Want to see 'em? I've got a sizeable herd down in Ladies Mead, though next summer I'm going to take some of 'em up into hill country. Someone will have to stay with them – well-armed – because the theft of horses and cattle seems to be one thing the native British do well, but if I'm to build up my herd then I need more grazing land.'

171

'Ladies Mead? Down by the river? I thought that was where ...'
He turned, staring at her.

'That's where what?'

'I thought you k-kept sheep there,' Questa stammered. 'I s-saw you had built a pond – for irrigation?'

'Aye, and for watering the herds. If the river runs low we can take from the pond for the villa, too.'

'I see. What animals do you have on Gloaming Hill, then?'

He considered, counting on his fingers. 'On Gloaming? Let me see, we've half-a-dozen chesnut geldings which have been bought by Andreus Cattalus, probably for chariot racing. I'm over-wintering them for him. And a couple of ponies from the hills of Wales. Tough little stallions, both of 'em, so I'm putting them to a couple of fine-boned Arabian mares to try to breed for speed and stamina. It's fascinating, you know, what you can do with selective breeding.'

'And the vines? How are they doing? But they've not over-wintered again since I saw you last, of course, so ...'

He stared at her, a frown-line between his brows. 'Yes they have! It must be almost twelve months since you were here last. I asked all over for you and someone said you must be the girl from the farm up in the hills ... wild country. I almost sought you out, but there's no sense in courting danger – they don't like us Romans much up there, do they? – so I waited. I knew you'd come back, though I didn't know you'd take so long about it! And here you are, but don't leave it so long again, will you! I've missed you, I swear by all the gods.'

'I missed you, too,' Questa admitted. 'I'm not sure I can get here whenever I want, though. It's quite – tricky – sometimes.'

The dark brows lifted. 'Is it? I don't see why, considering you've a reputation as a wild one. They say you're the daughter of an important man whose death left her alone, but that you're by no means helpless! That you're used to getting your own way and you run an estate as big as this one with only an old woman and a simpleton to help you! Seriously, are you from the hills?'

Questa found she did not know quite how to reply.

'I probably am,' she said cautiously. 'It sounds a bit like me. Can we go and look at your horses now?'

He stood up and held out his hands. This time she held out her own and let him pull her to her feet. His hands were warm and hard, a worker's hands. She could feel the callouses on his palms, the remains of a blister where perhaps a rein had chafed. When he had her on her feet he put his arm round her waist. It was a gesture at once comradely and yet more than that. She felt she should flinch back, but she did not feel threatened by him, she felt ... honoured. He liked her, he was not ashamed to show it, and she liked him. She trusted him, yet by his own admission he had been a soldier, he had probably killed men. But he would not torture anyone, she told herself as they jumped from step to step. He would not hurt a defenceless girl; I'm safe with Marcus.

'Down the hill ... don't bring my terraces down with you, girl, steer clear of the edges and pick up your feet as my sergeant used to say when I was a raw recruit! When we reach the horses I'll show you how to mount without a block. D'you ride?'

'No, but I'm going to learn,' Questa said. 'A neighbour is going to teach me.'

'I'll teach you,' Marcus said. To Questa's amusement, at the mention of a neighbour he had ruffled up like a fighting cock, even his dark hair seeming to stand on end. 'One of the mares is in foal; it quietens them down, you can have your first lesson on her in five minutes. Bareback mind, but you won't care about that.'

Remembering that she was supposed to be the spoilt, wild daughter of a rich man living on a hill farm, Questa said boldly that she would not mind at all. Marcus's arm tightened round her for a minute, then he let her go. For the first time in her life, Questa felt two quite different sensations. One was a lovely warm glow in the pit of her stomach, a glow which said, *you enjoyed that.* The other was disappointment that Marcus had let her go, had not continued to cuddle her.

'There they are – like 'em?'

There was no hiding the pride in his voice, the confident expectation of approval. And indeed he was right to be proud, for the horses grazing contentedly in the wide meadow were magnificent. Tall, well-muscled war-horses, great lumbering cart-horses with backsides like huge, round chestnuts, ponies sleek and smooth and strong, lean race-horses. They were all here, and all, to Questa's eyes at least, as near perfection as it was possible to get.

'They're grand,' she gasped. 'Can I really have a go on one? I'm sure it'll be easy enough once I start.'

Marcus grinned wickedly.

'Indeed you can. I'll catch one for you.'

The next two hours were hectic. Marcus gave Questa a leg up and the lesson began.

'Grip with your knees,' Marcus urged breathlessly. 'Rest your hands lightly on her withers and grip like hell with your knees. Pretend you're cracking walnuts with your kneecaps ... squeeze Hades out of her, girl!'

It was easier said than done, though. Without stirrups to rest her feet in, without a saddle or a bridle, she slipped and lurched. And then, after an agonising hour, she suddenly got it; for a moment she was not just bumping up and down and grabbing and slipping, laughing, crying, she was actually riding! She rose and fell in easy rhythm the way she had seen others do and Marcus, running alongside, gave a shout of triumph.

'There, you can do it! Come off then, enough's enough! Stand!'

The horse stopped abruptly and Marcus caught Questa as she went on going. He held her close to his breast for a moment, then let her slide down until her feet were on the ground.

Then he kissed her.

Questa had wondered about kissing, but always with that slight shudder of revulsion which any physical closeness to another human being brought. But this was different. She melted against Marcus, offering her mouth willingly, eager for this intimacy which, with anyone else, would have repelled her. He moved his tongue against her lips and her mouth opened for him, quickly, sweetly, whilst their bodies pressed close, comforting and being comforted.

After a little he held her back from him. His dark eyes were glowing, his mouth was half-smiling.

'I was hungry, and you fed me. I was thirsty, and you gave me to drink. I was lonely and you comforted me. And the strange thing is, I didn't realise how lonely I was till this minute.'

'Nor I,' Questa whispered. 'Nor I.'

She woke in bed, conscious of muscles aching and of a strange stiffness in her legs, but her heart sang. There were two of them now, two against the world! Marcus loved her and she loved him, what did it matter if they could only meet in a dream, what did it matter if ...

He's a Roman and you're English and he's been dead and gone for nearly two thousand years, a mean little voice in her head reminded her. There cannot possibly be love between you, you've fallen in love with an idea, a nothingness, a dream.

You don't know that, Questa told the little voice. No one can really explain about time, or about dreams. Or about feelings, come to that. He kissed me, didn't he? I can still feel his hard hands at my waist, straining me close, his mouth, moving on mine ...

Imagination is a wonderful thing, especially when it occurs in an untried spinster-girl, the voice jeered. Kisses, what do you know of 'em? How can you judge them, knowing nothing? The only man ever lucky enough to touch you broke both your ...

'No!' Questa said the word aloud, crashing it out, shooting upright in bed, sweat standing on her brow, her heart pounding. 'No! You won't spoil it, you shan't!'

There was no answer; the house around her was silent, the night outside the window dark and still. Questa sat there for a few moments, daring the voice to speak again, then lay down ... and slept.

Questa woke early and lay still for a moment, wondering why she was so happy. It certainly wasn't the weather! Outside, rain dashed against the panes and the wind gusted fretfully, so that one moment she could see the branches of the nearest trees lashing wildly and the next, momentarily, they would be still. And inside, as she discovered as soon as she got out of bed, winter had definitely arrived. The chill of an old house which had not been properly heated for years seeped into her bones. She flew through to the kitchen to riddle the fire but it had gone out, so, dismissing hopeful thoughts of a hot wash, she had a quick sluice-down in the sink, huddled her warmest clothes on and set about cleaning and re-laying the kitchen stove.

But throughout all these trials, she was conscious of an enormous, unconditional happiness. She was cold – so what? The house was cold – well, she would soon warm it up. They had planned to pick the last of the apples today, and the windfalls had to be bagged up in the course of the next few days or they would begin to rot. But I can pick apples in the rain and gather windfalls through the stormiest weather, Questa thought sunnily, getting the loaf out of the bread-bin and hacking off a large, uneven slice. I can do anything, because I'm not alone any more.

She felt sure she would never be miserable again, and this resolve was tested during the course of the day that followed. Roma made puddles all over the kitchen because she didn't like the rainy yard. Dickie shouted at his mother for shouting at the puppy, and Grace, not at all in her usual style, burst into tears and fled the room.

Questa, leaving Ellen and Dickie staring wide-eyed, followed her.

'Grace, what on earth's the matter? This isn't like you!'

'You're all against me,' Grace sobbed, leaning on the banister, for she had fled up the stairs and was halfway to her room before Questa caught her up. 'I'm so miserable. Everyone hates me, even my own little boy.'

Questa hesitated; this was perhaps not quite the moment to point out to Grace that if people hated her, it was at least ninety-eight per cent her own doing. Yet it was undoubtedly an opportunity to try to make Grace see her son's point of view.

'Dickie doesn't hate you,' she said reasonably. 'He just hates what you seem to be trying to do to him. Grace, you were a kid once – you played outside with your friends, mucked around with cousins, went to school, even. Dickie's five and he's lonely.'

'He's got me! I love to be with him, I ...'

'You love him to be with you,' Questa corrected. 'That's a rather different thing. You don't want to kneel in the dust and make mud-pies, or catch tiddlers in a flour-bag and put them into a jam-jar, or ...'

'Dickie doesn't want to do things like that either – or he didn't, until we came here,' Grace moaned. 'He's changed; you're turning him into someone quite different. I want my baby back!'

'But no one stays a baby for ever,' Questa said. 'You didn't, Grace, so why should Dickie? He's a really nice little chap and this puppy could be the making of him – if you'll let it. But if you stop him playing with other kids or make him give Roma up I don't think he'll ever forgive you. You have to let go, Grace, otherwise one of these days you'll look round and he'll be gone.'

'Gone? But he's only a little boy … he's all I've got …'

'Nonsense,' Questa said briskly. 'You could have Alan tomorrow if you wanted him, and probably lots of other men, too. You like Alan, don't you?

'He's very nice,' Grace said, rather sulkily. She dabbed at her eyes with the full sleeve of her apricot woollen two-piece. 'But you don't necessarily want to marry someone just because they're nice. The truth is, Questa, that I'm still in love … no matter that he's dead. And it isn't *fair* that he died before … well, before we'd had a chance to learn about each other, to tell each other things. Besides, if I did marry anyone else, even Alan … oh, I don't know why I'm telling you all this, I'm sure. It's not as if we like each other very much. You said it yourself, you said we didn't get on.'

'But perhaps we could, Grace, if you were a bit easier on people. Not just on me, I don't really matter, but on Dickie and Ellen. Even on Alan, because you do give him the runaround, don't you?'

Grace sniffed and combed her hair back from her face with her fingers, then she stared, long and hard, at Questa.

'I don't understand you; you're really happy,' she said. 'And what have you got? A big house which is a mess, a lot of muddy fields, four sheep and a couple of cows. You've no friends, no future … why, even this place …'

'I do have friends,' Questa said quietly. 'Ellen's my friend, and Dickie. And Ran Atherton's my friend, too. He's going to teach me to ride the pony we bought from the fair.'

'He's an old man, a cripple,' Grace said, as though this was the biggest bar to friendship ever known. 'How can a girl of your age pretend she wants to be friends with an old cripple?'

The words were offensive but the tone, for once, was not. Grace was honestly curious, honestly interested. Questa, swallowing annoyance over the words, answered the tone instead.

'He's not yet seventy, so Ellen says, and though he does have to use sticks or a wheelchair, he can get around pretty well. And he's lively and interesting – he breeds horses, did you know that, just like ...'

'Just like who? Don't say you're going to start breeding horses, now?'

'Just like an Italian friend of mine does,' Questa said, visited by inspiration.

'Oh, really? Well, given that you find him good company, I suppose you can enjoy his friendship, but that doesn't help *me* much, does it!'

'Everyone has to find their own friends,' Questa said gently. 'You just don't try very hard, Grace.'

'I don't try? But how can I, stuck out here, miles from any sort of civilisation? I can't drive and we don't have a car anyway, and even though I've been thinking, sometimes, about going back to London, how will I live? I can't afford even a tiny flat, not really, and anyway the country air's good for Dickie ...' her voice faded away. 'Why are you looking at me like that? What have I said?'

'Well, you said the country air was good for Dickie, I remember you saying it before, yet you won't let him go out in it! It doesn't seem to hang together somehow, Grace.'

Tears welled up again in Grace's large blue eyes, making them look even larger. Her full lower lip trembled. 'Oh Questa, I'm so *unhappy*,' she declared in broken tones. 'But I'll try to be better, really I will, if you'll try not to hate me!'

'We'll all work harder at being friends,' Questa said, not bothering to deny that there had been bad feeling. 'Let's start by all of us taking Roma for her morning walk.'

But though Grace returned to the kitchen and kissed Dickie and smiled in a watery way at Ellen, she took one look out of the back door and decided she would pass on the walk.

'There's no sense all of us getting soaked to the skin,' she pointed out. 'You two go; I'll give the big bedroom in the front a real turn-out. I'll enjoy that and it will be a help, because you keep saying that when Alan comes down next he must stay at the Court.'

She left, humming a tune beneath her breath.

Ellen, who had not been party to the outpourings on the stairs, looked surprised, but continued stolidly to eat her porridge.

'That thing drowns the lad,' she said, when Questa began to wrap Dickie in a waterproof cape at least seven sizes too big, 'But why don't you tek a look in the little room under the eaves, by the back staircase? There's a cupboard in there full of stuff.'

Questa ran up the back stairs and came down, round-eyed, with a yellow sou'wester and matching cape made, it seemed, for a child of Dickie's size.

'Fancy that!' she said, adjusting the hat on Dickie's round yellow head. 'You look like a lifeboatman, old Dickie!'

'He look like his dad,' Ellen muttered. 'The spittin' image.'

'Does he?' Questa stared at Dickie's fair, smiling face. 'I didn't know you'd met Mr Syrett, Ellen.'

'Hmm. There's a lot of things you don't know,' was the gruff response. 'And why are you so bright-eyed an' bushy-tailed when the rain's bouncin' roof-high and the wind's likely to fetch off every apple in that there orchard?'

'Because I'm happy by nature,' Questa said aggravatingly. 'I could hug you, Ellen – in fact I will!'

Ellen cackled, but hugged her astonishingly hard in return, and when Questa stood back, smiling, she saw that the old woman had tears in her eyes and her little brown nutcracker face was working convulsively.

'Hey, Ellen, did I hurt you? What's up?'

'Well, gal, I never thought you'd give I a hug, like that. You've kep' your distance. Your dad was one to hug.'

'It wasn't that I didn't want to hug you,' Questa said. Plucking up all her courage she held out her hands. 'It's my little fingers; they – they got hurt and I'm afraid of knocking them. I don't like to get close to anyone really.'

Very slowly, Ellen's little brown paws reached out and took Questa's hands. She held them gently, close to her face, and stared at the bent, deformed little fingers.

'Eh, lass,' she breathed. 'Who done that to you?'

'The Nazis. It doesn't matter, Ellen, it was a long time ago. But they still hurt.'

'Ah. They would. But I've got a salve ... I'll fetch it whiles you an' the boy tek the dog a-walkin'.'

'It's a bit late for salve,' Questa said gently, 'but thanks all the same.'

'Aye, perhaps you'm right. Only this salve will 'elp, I think you'll find.' She let go of Questa's hands and stepped back. 'Go on, off with the pair of you. Some of us 'ave got work to do!'

Picking apples in the rain isn't everyone's favourite pastime, but nothing could detract from Questa's happiness. For three solid days she climbed the dripping trees and picked the cold, wet fruit, and was happy. Grace was being reasonable, letting Dickie behave naturally instead of like a plaster saint, Ran Atherton was her friend and would teach her to ride when the weather improved, and at the back of her mind was the nicest thing of all.

She had Marcus; no, even better than that, they had each other. And though she could not dream of him whenever she wished, at least she did so fairly often. But in her heart she feared the chanciness of her dreams, the fact that she had sometimes gone for many weeks without once being able to dream of him. Suppose one night she went to bed and found the trick had gone, and she was stuck in the nineteen-forties, with no hope of seeing Marcus again?

But at the moment, tomorrow could take care of itself; never did a person live so thoroughly for today, even if today was really yesterday. Questa did her various tasks: picked apples, bottled them, stored them, sent sacks of windfalls off to make cider, and every few nights she would fall asleep and find herself dreaming of her friend.

Marcus was always there, always waiting, with servants all about who drew back, smiled, stared. She knew they were saying she was the master's fancy, the wild girl from the hills, and she and Marcus touched hands and exchanged long sweet glances.

Some of the servants were slaves, Marcus told her. So far as she could see, this meant that they worked hard and were not paid for their work, but in every other way they were as well treated and as highly regarded as his senior servants. Marcus said that his villa did not have an ergastulum, a place of correction for slaves, because he valued his servants, tied or free, and punished them when occasion demanded by the withdrawal of privileges for a short time.

'That way, we're all satisfied,' he said, and Questa, besotted enough to agree with every word he said, smiled and took one of his broad, brown hands in both of hers and dropped a kiss on the palm.

'Oh, my love, my dear love,' Marcus murmured, his fingers tracing circles in the palm of her hand, 'don't tease me; come to the woods with me!'

She laughed, as she always did, and said that one day ... and then they went and examined the vines, or took chunks of apple to his favourite horses, or rode around the meadows and winding lanes.

He wanted to make love, he would cuddle and kiss and grow hot and bothered, as indeed Questa did, but when she stopped him short, when she said enough, he always sighed and let her go, moved a little apart. He never sulked or reproached her either, which she knew from conversations with girls at the language school was often the way men behaved when baulked of the natural ending to their games.

'You won't leave me?' he would ask anxiously, from time to time. 'When winter comes, when I'm old and grey ... you won't leave me?'

And she always promised she would not, because leaving him was out of the question, unthinkable.

At home, Eagles Court settled into winter, drew in on itself. The long, dark evenings were here, Christmas preparations began. There was no spare money to spend on rare black-market goods, but the woods were full of ivy and holly berries starred the dark and prickly ilex trees. In the orchard great swags of mistletoe could be seen on the upper branches, and the small field which Patrick had proudly ploughed and watched his father sow with potatoes was planted out again with brussels sprouts and the potato crop stored away for winter in two long clamps.

Dickie was taken each day to the small village school, whence

181

he returned with various objects hidden in his tiny satchel. Woolly balls made by winding wool round two cardboard milk-bottle tops, decorative streamers made from brightly painted strips of newspaper, a tiny cushion stuffed with cut-up lisle stockings and covered with someone's old party dress.

'Make do and mend,' Ellen cried, fishing in the bin for a dress which Grace had thrown away, considering it both outmoded and faded. She turned it into aprons for them all and Grace refrained from making acid comments more than once or twice a day about people who took without asking.

It was common knowledge that Sir Stafford Cripps would eat shredded carrot, apples and walnuts for his Christmas dinner, someone said on the wireless; why didn't everyone follow this excellent example? We are constantly reminded that it is economic planning which will bring the country through, said the speaker, and that means it's not so much who has the biggest slice of cake which matters; what matters is to create a bigger cake, so that larger slices may be enjoyed by all.

Questa found most of this puzzling, but she did understand that some people would only have vegetables for their Christmas dinner. She, however, saw no need to be one of them. She, Dickie and Roma went over and visited Ran Atherton just before Christmas, to issue a seasonal invitation.

'We've got Ellen, Alfie, Grace, Dickie and me for Christmas dinner, and heaps and heaps of sprouts and potatoes and things like that,' she said as they sat in the small drawing room, beside a roaring log fire. Roma was stretched out in front of it, small pink belly uppermost, dreaming of chasing rabbits and eating cream cake – at least Questa guessed she was dreaming of something she liked by her twitching paws and drooling mouth – whilst Dickie sat by her, staring curiously at Ran, who stared equally curiously back.

'That sounds delightful,' their host said courteously. 'Do you have a Christmas pudding, I wonder?'

'Yes, certainly. I can't remember Christmas pudding, but Ellen assures me I'll like it, even though hers is an economy one without a great deal of dried fruit. But what I wondered was ...'

She paused, suddenly anxious not to give offence.

'Go on, what you wondered was ...'

'Well, we wondered if you'd like to come over to us for Christmas dinner? We can't kill one of my hens, I can't spare one, but Alfie says he's sure of a rabbit.'

'I'll bring a chicken,' Ran said, grinning at her. 'And a leg of pork. That'll be my contribution to the feast. What do you say to that, eh?'

'Oh! Ellen said ... I mean, that would be wonderful,' Questa said quickly. 'We'll have our dinner at midday. Come round for a drink first. Alan says we'll have sherry and port, only port is for after dinner, he says.'

'Oh, so you've discovered Josh's secret cellar, have you?' Ran said. He leaned forward and clouted one of the logs with the poker, causing it to flare up in a shower of sparks. 'He used to boast about it, but I never saw it myself; thought it was just wishful thinking, to tell you the truth.'

'Secret cellar? I don't think we've discovered anything but emptiness down there,' Questa said. She could not bring herself to go down into the cellars; they brought back, by their mere smell, the horrors of her incarceration in Gestapo headquarters.

'Probably the army drank it,' Ran said gloomily. 'Still, I'll accept your kind invitation happily, dear, particularly since it means that I shan't be here alone on Christmas Day. Mrs Clovelly and Daphne are going to relatives just for twenty-four hours, though they'll be back for Boxing Day.' He turned to Dickie. 'Do you want to take Roma through to see her mother, old boy? She's in the kitchen, with Mrs C. I daresay they'll find you and Roma something nice.'

When the child had gone Ran looked thoughtfully across at Questa, sitting curled up on the chair opposite. They were good friends now, Ran having much admired Questa's ability to stick in the saddle, which he thought remarkable for one so inexperienced. Since explaining was impossible, Questa had accepted the compliment gracefully; she could scarcely confess to lessons from an ex-centurion, after all!

'Questa, my dear, whose child is that? He reminds me forcibly of a lad I knew, once.'

'Grace Syrett's, the woman I told you about.'

'Yes, I realised … but who was the father?'

'Simon Syrett.'

He thought, frowning into the fire.

'Hmm. Do I know him?'

'I suppose it must be Simon who's a relative,' Questa said suddenly, having given the matter some thought. 'How odd. When Grace said that Dickie and I were vaguely related, I thought she meant *she* was some sort of long-lost cousin. Can it be that Simon was related to the Adamsons? Perhaps you met Simon as a youngster. Most of the family seem to have congregated down here at one time or another.'

'Yes, that must be it,' Ran agreed, but his frown did not clear. 'Well, shall we join Dickie and Roma in the kitchen? Mrs Clovelly would be sorely put out if you didn't offer her the compliments of the season and try her economy mincepies!'

Eight

Christmas Day seemed to be approaching at a gallop, far too fast for Questa's liking. She still had things to do on Christmas Eve, though by teatime all her important tasks were done, all her presents wrapped. Alan, who had said he would try to get down some time on Christmas Day, had not yet been in touch. He had rushed down to see them a couple of weeks before, full of gloomy prognostications that he would be too busy to get down at Christmas and would spend the holiday slaving over his books, but Questa thought he would turn up, though possibly not until dinner was over.

Grace, however, was more doubtful. She was in a strange mood over Alan, though much easier with everyone else. One minute she decided she liked him, the next that he was just a hanger-on and a nuisance. Sometimes she said it wouldn't be Christmas without him, at other times she said they would have far more fun if he stayed away. Questa did not know what to make of her, but was relieved that Grace's earlier antagonism towards her and Ellen seemed to have dissipated, for the time being at any rate.

Christmas Eve had dawned cold and wild and continued so all day. By evening it was bitter, the wild kitten Dickie had found starving in an outhouse refused to leave the warmth of the kitchen and Questa took extra rations to Scamper, the piebald pony, and dragged Nanny and Nonny, the goat and her kid, in from their thistly pasture to share Scamper's warm stable, though not her loose-box. Questa knew only too well that, given the opportunity, Nanny and Nonny would eat not only all the hay she had left for Scamper but her straw bedding as well.

As the evening progressed it grew steadily colder. Alfie and

Patrick had spent the previous two days, with Scamper between the shafts of the small cart, bringing in any fallen trees they could lay their hands on. By Christmas Eve all the wood had been sawed and chopped into respectable logs and this meant that no matter how it rained, snowed or stormed, Questa and Grace would not have to venture farther than the woodshed to have the makings of a fire.

'We'll keep the fires in if we possibly can,' Questa said when she went out to fetch more logs and found it was snowing quite hard, and lying, too. 'The last thing I want to do on Christmas morning is have to light every fire in the place.'

'We'll need the fire in the big drawing room, since we've got guests,' Grace said. 'I thought we'd take that lovely walnut table through, and use the old silver. And there's the most beautiful lace cloth, it's like a spider's web it's so fine. We could use that, too.'

'Why not? And don't nag Dickie if he spills food on it, because it'll wash. I say, have you wrapped all your presents yet?'

'Not quite, but nearly. Questa, why don't we all move down into the small parlour tonight? The snow will make the house awfully cold, and we could light the fire in there and be snug. Dickie will wake at the crack of dawn I expect, to open his stocking. It would be much more fun if we were all in the same room.'

'We can't lug all the beds downstairs,' Questa pointed out. 'Tell you what, you've got plenty of space in your room, we'll wheel Dickie's little bed in there, and I'll bring in one of those cots, and we'll all spend the night in your room. We'd better light the fire straight away, though, in case the chimney's blocked or something.'

'Lovely,' Grace said. 'Where's Dickie? Supper's ready, and he'll want to take Roma out, snow or no snow. What's more he'll be tickled pink to find us all sleeping in the same room, it'll be as good as an extra Christmas present.'

'He's upstairs, wrapping parcels,' Questa said. 'If you fetch him down I'll dish up. It's shepherd's pie, with one of Ellen's fruit jellies for afters. He loves them both.'

'All right; shan't be a tick,' Grace said, and set off up the stairs.

Questa, left alone, pottered about laying the table, fetching down a fresh bottle of Ellen's pickled onions, and contemplating her lot.

Things were going well, she decided, getting the blue pottery plates from the dresser and sliding them into the oven to warm. Ever since the showdown with Grace over the puppy, the older woman had been downright human, almost good fun. She still made sharp remarks sometimes, but she laughed at herself too, and really did seem to have taken Questa's remarks about Dickie to heart. The little boy was allowed to bring school friends home, to stay out to tea, even to play around the sheds whilst Questa rubbed Scamper down, fed the stock or cleaned tack.

Questa was now taking lessons in milking the cows from Alfie, who pretended he could not understand why Blossom and Daisy would let him draw off a gallon of milk but objected to poor Questa's taking a pint. So Questa, who had milked goats in Italy but never cows, took lessons and kept her expertise in goat milking a dark secret. She much preferred feeding the calves with a hand inside the bucket of warmed milk and water, but she was determined to master milking the cows before winter was out.

Nanny was a real horror to milk, so Questa cravenly let Alfie do that particular chore. Nanny seemed to have set her mind on producing milk only for Nonny, and despite her relatively small size proved to Alfie that she was a far tougher proposition than the most determined cow. When Alfie crouched on the stable floor and caught hold of her dugs she kicked, bleated, backed, rushed forward and, if all else failed, bit any part of him within reach.

Ellen fared best, but even she usually only got a cup of milk before Nanny jerked free and began to beat up anyone within reach.

'I've gotta keep on if I want to mek goats' cheese,' she said crossly, when Alfie suggested that they should just give up and send Nanny to market when spring came. ''Sides, if Nonny sees 'er gettin' away wi' murder, like this, 'ow d'you think she'll milk when her turn comes?'

But now, perhaps because it was Christmas, the milk of human kindness – if not of an irritable she-goat – had made Questa get the goats under a roof and once Nanny had realised that this was not in order to purloin her milk she seemed almost grateful, rubbing her head quite affectionately against Questa's knee and failing to charge when Questa was half out of the stable door.

Blossom's calf was a heifer, Daisy's a little bull calf. They had weaned both the calves on to the bucket now, and it meant that Questa needed to be able to milk since Alfie was not always available and Ellen sometimes simply too busy with other things. What was more they used a lot of milk, and Ellen made tiny amounts of the most delicious butter and cheese, but it was hard work and it would probably be more efficient to sell the milk to what Ellen called 'this noofangled milk marketin' board', and make do with margarine and their cheese ration, as others did.

The kettle boiled and Questa warmed the pot, then made the tea and stood the pot on the side of the stove. She wondered what Marcus did for Christmas, whether he kept the festival; probably not. He talked about gods in the plural and there had been a sharp, unpleasant spat between them over the sacrificing of goats, but it had not affected their friendship, which simply grew stronger and deeper with each meeting. But at the moment she was in no position to ask him about Christmas, since she'd not had her dream for a while. Ellen had remarked that her interest in the place seemed to be waning, that she was in a world of her own half the time, and she had pulled herself up, frightened at the implied criticism. She could not spend all her time mooning over Marcus, whilst Eagles Court slid back into disrepair. Whatever the outcome, she must work on her estate and put her personal feelings aside.

Marcus never reproached her for the times she did not come to him, but she thought he enjoyed her presence more for its rarity and, certainly, when she went from the bitter chill of the Shropshire winter to the blue and sunny skies of Marcus's time, she revelled in it as others revelled in foreign travel to strange, exotic places.

She had finished laying the table and was bringing the jelly through from the cold of the outer scullery when someone knocked on the back door. Questa stood the jelly down and stared at the door, rather surprised. Country ways were already her ways, and most country people just walked in. Indeed, in clement weather the back door was permanently open since Roma needed to be able to get out quickly when she had to. But now Questa opened it, expecting to find either Ellen or Alfie on the step, perhaps smitten by awkwardness in case either she or Grace was present-wrapping on the kitchen table.

It was Alan. He wore his school scarf around his neck, a thick coat, and wellington boots on his feet. He had snow on his hair and two enormous bags of parcels hung from each hand. He must have knocked with his *nose*, it certainly looks red enough, Questa thought irrepressibly, as she ushered him hospitably inside.

'Alan! How lovely that you've managed to get here after all, and a day earlier than we expected you, as well. Goodness, you are laden ... and wet! Where have you come from – you didn't walk up from the village, did you?'

Alan dropped the bags in front of the fire, and shivered. He began to take his coat off slowly, with pauses. Questa thought he looked ill as well as tired and took the coat from him, then pressed him into a chair.

'Sit down, do. I'll drape your coat over the clothes rack, it'll be dry in a moment in the warmth of the fire. I'll call Grace down presently – the meal's nearly ready, you timed your arrival well.'

'Sorry; no, I didn't walk, I put the car in the cart-shed and just came across the yard. I haven't booked in to The Passing Soldier because you did say that you'd have a room ready for tomorrow and I thought, hoped ...'

'We've already made up your bed in the spare room,' Questa said, crossing her fingers fervently behind her back. 'But as it happens to be snowing and cold, Grace, Dickie and I are all moving into her room, so you'd be a lot warmer down in the small parlour. I'll light the fire there in a tick and then you can go to bed in a nice warm room.'

'Thanks,' Alan said thickly. 'I do hope I'm not going to be a nuisance, but I feel dreadful, hot and feverish and yet chilly all over.'

'Sounds like 'flu,' Questa said. 'Oh dear, I hope it's just a cold, Alan, or it will ruin your Christmas.'

'It can't be much,' Alan said, leaning forward and holding out thin hands to the blaze. 'I worked like the devil to clear my desk, mind, just so I could take a few days off with a clear conscience. Oh, I'm sure I'll be fine after a decent night's sleep.'

Presently, with the food on the table, Questa called the others and Grace and Dickie came trooping in, both pink-faced from heaving furniture about upstairs. Dickie greeted Alan politely but almost absentmindedly, then ran out into the yard and banged the old gong vigorously to tell Ellen and her son that the meal was on the table. He came in again, snow dusting his fair hair, and announced that he was the hungriest person in the world, and could he have his food right now, please, without waiting, because he had so much to do before bedtime?

Alan would have come to the table with the others, but Questa shook her head warningly at Grace and Grace, after a quick glance, said that Alan might as well eat near the fire since he was obviously still very cold. Rather to Questa's surprise, Alan raised no demur but sat in his chair with a tray on his lap, taking very little part in the animated conversation amongst the others. But he ate most of the food on his plate, had some fruit jelly and then, when Grace asked him if he would not be more comfortable in bed, agreed that he was very tired and perhaps an early night ...

Alfie took him off to the small parlour and helped him to undress, though Alan said he would manage very well. When Alfie came back and announced that Alan seemed to have settled, Grace went and put her head round the door and then returned, looking a little disturbed, to tell them that Alan was already sleeping deeply.

'Do 'im good,' Ellen said, clattering plates into the washing-up water. 'Works too 'ard, doesn't rest even when 'e's 'ere.'

'Oh well, we'll make sure he rests over Christmas,' Questa said. 'He can have breakfast in bed tomorrow; we'll let him lie in.'

The evening was spent enjoyably, singing carols around the ·fire, with the wireless as accompaniment. Ellen brought out a bag of chestnuts and they roasted them, shrieking when the nuts popped in the flames and fishing their chosen delicacy out of the ashes with many squeaks and much flourishing of the toasting fork and the poker. At nine o'clock, however, Ellen and Alfie made for their flat and Questa said she thought Roma ought to go out, now, so that Dickie, visibly wilting, could make his way to bed.

'I'm not tired,' Dickie said in a voice which was perilously close to a whine. 'I needn't go to bed, need I, Mummy? It's nearly Christmas Day!'

'We're all going to bed,' Grace said at once. 'Go up and fetch our night things, Dickie darling, then we can undress down here in the warm.'

'Why? Has the fire upstairs gone out?' Questa said. 'I thought I made it up pretty well, too.'

'Oh, is it lit already?' Grace looked gratified. 'Was the chimney all right? It didn't smoke or anything?'

'It's fine. I laid it earlier, lit it just after supper, and now we can go upstairs and change in front of it.' Questa grabbed Dickie and lifted him up above her head. 'Won't it be fun to open our stockings in the morning, all squeezed into one bed?'

'I want to go to bed *now*,' Dickie commanded, eyes shining. 'I forgetted that we were all in Mummy's room. Come on, Mummy, race you up the stairs!'

But Grace said she would make hot drinks and take one through to poor Alan, with some aspirin, and Questa and Dickie might take Roma out and check that all was secure for the night.

Trust Grace to find herself a nice cosy job being a ministering angel indoors whilst someone else trudges through the snow, Questa thought resignedly as she took her dufflecoat off the back door and jammed her arms into the sleeves. Still, she loved her stock, so she should be glad to see that they were all right before finally locking up and going to bed. And Dickie was great company, he usually held the torch so that she could check the doors, and always chattered away nineteen to the dozen as they did their rounds.

Tonight, however, the snow made the torch almost unnecessary. Roma was fascinated by the intriguing white stuff which melted when she tried to eat it and made her paws interestingly cold. She yipped when Dickie threw a snowball at her, skidded when she dashed across the yard, jumped up and snapped at the falling flakes until she was dizzy. Then, as they approached the stable, Questa remembered the old fable that on Christmas Eve all the animals kneel and worship the baby born in just such a stable as theirs, long ago. She told Dickie about it and they crept up to the stable and opened the door with the greatest caution, though all they saw was Scamper stolidly munching hay and turning to gaze at them from great, dark eyes, whilst Nanny and Nonny, cuddled up together in their straw, scarcely bothered to open their yellow slit-eyes and clearly did not intend to rise, either to their knees or to their usual positions.

'I spec' we just missed it,' Dickie said when Roma had done two yellow puddles in the snow and seemed quite keen to return to the warm kitchen. 'I've a feeling they're kneeling right this minute, Ques – shall we go back and look?'

Foreseeing a night spent traipsing up and down between their room and the stable, Questa said hastily that the animals only prayed once, and since Dickie was sure he had almost caught them in the act, they would not have another chance to view the phenomenon until the following year. Though he sighed, Dickie was too excited over the thought of what was to come to argue, and the two of them raced Roma back to the kitchen, took off their snowy coats, hung them on the back of the door, rubbed Roma's soft baby fur until it was dry, and then raided the biscuit tin.

'Snow makes me very hungry,' Dickie observed, taking a ginger nut. 'Where's my cocoa?'

'Mummy probably made it and took it up,' Questa was beginning, when the kitchen door opened and Grace appeared.

'I took Alan a hot drink,' she said, 'but he was still fast asleep and looking quite comfortable so I didn't disturb him. He looks a lot better now, he's not nearly so flushed.'

'He'll probably be his normal self in the morning,' Questa replied. 'Did you make us a hot drink, Grace?'

'I'll do it now,' Grace said hastily. She was definitely improving, Questa thought as Grace pulled the kettle over the fire again. Once she would have simply said, 'No', and walked away from it; at least now she was beginning to realise that one reaps what one sows!

'Can I have another biscuit?' Dickie said, a grubby paw hovering over the tin. 'Just one? A little one?'

'Oh, it's nearly Christmas, let him have another,' Questa said when Grace began to say that one biscuit was plenty for a small boy. 'It's silly, really, that we stuff ourselves to the eyebrows one day a year ... he might not have room for another biscuit tomorrow.'

'Well, a digestive or a marie, then,' Grace said. 'But not anything too rich; we don't want nightmares, do we?'

Questa winked at Dickie, who took a shortbread finger and hastily bit a piece out of it.

'No, of course not,' she said soothingly. 'Come on then, Dickie, let's put Blot into her box ... oh, she's done it herself ... and get Roma up to her room. She's had a long day, poor little mite.'

'I'll carry her,' Dickie said, grasping Roma around her fat little tummy and hefting her in his arms. 'Coo, she's getting awful fat!'

Together, the small procession trooped up the stairs, Grace leading. They went into the larger of the two bedrooms and found it warm and welcoming, with the fire blazing up the chimney and a basket of logs, brought up earlier by Questa, standing by.

'When we're ready to put the lamp out I'll damp the fire down until morning,' Questa said. 'Where's your stocking, Dickie?'

'On the foot of the bed, where Mummy said to put it,' Dickie said, his voice trembling with excitement. 'How will Father Christmas get down that chimney though, with the fire burning up?'

'He won't. He'll come down the chimney in your room, that's why we've left him a note, explaining,' Questa said glibly. 'Just get into bed, Dickie, and drink your drink there. Mummy and I will sit by the fire until you're asleep.'

They had already hidden a full stocking down Grace's bed, ready to switch the pair once Dickie slept, but it seemed as though Dickie would never drop off. Every time they got stealthily to their feet to tiptoe over to him, he sat up, eyes huge in his small, exhausted face.

'Is it daytime?' he demanded over and over in a voice slurred by tiredness. 'Has he been yet?'

Finally Grace and Questa got into bed, thinking that with the lamp out and the fire damped down, Dickie would soon relax. And so it proved. Minutes later Grace switched the empty stocking for the full one, got into bed and was soon sleeping soundly, or at least she snored now and then, which Questa took to be a sign.

It wasn't long after that when Questa, too, succumbed, and the moon, emerging for a moment between the dark snow-clouds, shone down on three sleepers, all cosy in their beds.

Questa did not know what woke her, she simply became abruptly awake. The room was in darkness still, but when she turned her head cautiously on the pillow she could just make out a lighter strip where the curtains did not quite meet, and the dull red glow from the banked down fire.

For a moment she was disorientated because she did not immediately remember that she had changed her bedroom and was no longer in the small parlour. Surely the window should be to her left, the fire to her right, and not vice versa? And why was the fire lit? She no longer lit it now that the house was at least partially aired. And then, as a shadow moved across the fire, she remembered. She wasn't in her usual room.

She would have closed her eyes again, tried to go back to sleep, but someone was moving about the room, she could hear the creak of a board, the soft shush of footsteps. Was it Dickie, on his way down to the stable to catch the animals at their prayers? Or Grace, forgetting that the stocking had already been placed on Dickie's bed? Or Alan, perhaps, coming quietly upstairs to win his fair lady by climbing into her bed, not realising that she was sleeping in what was virtually a dormitory?

Questa turned over as naturally as she could, and looked out from between her lashes. It was Grace, walking about the room in her long white nightie, looking strange and rather frightening. She was clutching something in one hand, holding it like a weapon, and hissing gently between her teeth as she came. When she turned in Questa's direction, Questa saw that her eyes were turned up in her head so that only a line of glistening white showed. She looked blind, but not at all helpless; she looked threatening, dangerous.

She went past Questa's bed, reached the window, tugged at the curtain. Her movement let a little more light into the room, yet it was plain that she needed no light, she was sleepwalking. And the object in her hand, far from being a weapon, proved to be two of the fluffy woollen balls which Dickie had made at school, with the aid of milk-bottle tops.

'Cain, Cain!' She moaned the words softly, beneath her breath, but Questa could hear her clearly even above the thumping of her own heart, the sudden speeding up of her own breathing. This was awful, whatever was Grace doing?

'I thought I could do it, I thought I could, but now I'm not so sure. She isn't what I thought – she's a poor, lost soul, like me. A poor damned soul. I'm empty, since you've gone. Empty, empty. Ah, if only I knew whether I should do it ... but I'm not sure any more. It was better to hate – to love again only hurts. Dickie ... he's you ... my little boy ...'

Her voice trailed off into vague, meaningless mutterings. Questa lay very still, staring fixedly at the hand which held the woollen pom-poms. Now and then it clenched, lifted, then fell aimlessly. But she had little doubt that whatever Grace was dreaming, she believed she had a weapon in her right hand and not her son's pom-poms.

'What'll I do, Cain? Tell me what I should do?'

There was so much pain in Grace's voice that it gave Questa courage. She sat up in bed, cleared her throat, and spoke in a voice as like Alan's as she could manage.

'Go back to bed, my dear. Go back to bed and sleep. Tomorrow's another day, Christmas Day. Sleep now. Sleep. Sleep.'

And it was extraordinary how Grace reacted to a simple instruction. She laid the pom-poms carefully on the mantelpiece,

195

leaning across the fireguard in order to do so as though well aware that the fire was still in, turned round and went straight to her bed. She climbed into it, pulled the blankets over her shoulders, and within two minutes was sleeping soundly.

Which was more than Questa could do. She lay sleepless for a long time, trying to fathom out what Grace had been up to. She had talked about Cain again ... said she thought she could do something, but was no longer sure ... hate was better than love, because love hurt ...

For God's sake, Questa, forget it and go to sleep, she ordered herself after an hour of fruitless wondering. You knew ages ago that Grace talks in her sleep, now you know she walks, as well. And people talk rubbish in their sleep, everyone knows *that*, so only an idiot would try to make sense of such mad ramblings. But Grace had mentioned Cain the previous time, too. And she had sounded so unhappy! Questa, who knew better than most what bitter agonies of fear can be experienced by a nightmare sufferer, decided that she would get out of bed and wake Grace at once if it happened again. And perhaps tomorrow I ought to tell her what she said, she thought uneasily. Only ... it was still awfully like spying, and what good could it possibly do? Grace would have no more idea than Questa why she'd said the things she did – unless it brought the memory of her nightmares back, and she certainly wouldn't thank Questa for that!

So all in all, it seemed both kinder and more sensible simply to forget the incident had ever happened. With Grace's snores sounding comfortingly in her ears and her own sheer exhaustion getting the better of her, Questa fell asleep.

She woke next morning when something landed on her tummy with a thump and a shrill, excited voice shrieked, 'He's been, he's been!'

Opening her eyes, she saw Dickie's face not a foot from her own and hanging between them a brown lisle stocking bulging with tiny parcels.

'Father Christmas, he's been, Ques! You've got a stockin' too, an' so's Mummy. Can we open 'em now? Do wake up proper, Ques!'

'I am awake, more or less,' Questa said, blinking. 'What time is it?' A glance at the curtains showed that they had been ripped back to reveal a cloudy grey sky and scudding flakes. 'Oh Dickie, love, do get off my tummy ... where's Roma?'

'She's here ... and I can't tell the clock,' Dickie said breathlessly. 'Mummy's still asleep, I tried to wake her but she just pulled the covers over her face. Can I start my stocking, please?'

'Yes, of course you can. Here, climb into my bed whilst I get the fire going,' Questa said. 'Darling, can you start opening by yourself for a moment? Because Roma ... oh dear, too late!'

Roma, with a look of deep guilt on her small face, was squatting as near to the door as she could get.

'Sop it up with my grey jumper, it needs washing,' Dickie said cheerfully. 'Come back to bed, Ques, I want to open my stocking.'

'Yes, all right old boy. I'll just wake Mummy though,' Questa said, quite looking forward to giving Grace a good shake. Who had lain awake for hours and hours, listening to Grace snoring away? And who had been scared out of her wits to find Grace looming over her and talking rubbish in her sleep? It had been Questa, yet now it was Questa being woken betimes whilst Grace snored with the blankets around her ears.

But she had barely bent over the bed and put a hand on Grace's shoulder when the other woman woke. She stirred, moaned, made eating motions with her mouth and said pathetically, 'Oh, I'm dying for a cup of tea! Is it *really* getting up time? Where's Dickie, then?'

'I'm here, Mummy,' Dickie said. 'Wake up! I'm going to start my stocking!'

'Grace, if you'll just sit up and watch Dickie for a moment I'll go and get you a cup of tea and let Roma out and bring up a bowl of water and a floor cloth to clean up her pee,' Questa said resignedly. 'If you're going back to sleep, though, you can whistle for tea.'

Grace's fair face and yellow, sleep-rumpled hair emerged from the covers. She blinked, yawned, then smiled at Questa.

'Fair's fair, I suppose,' she remarked. 'Come into my bed, Dickie, and start your stocking. Ques won't be long.'

Dickie needed no second bidding. He leaped from bed to bed like an energetic little kangaroo and began to rip the paper off his first present. As she made her way along the corridor and down the stairs, Questa could hear his delighted exclamations and Grace's murmured replies.

I wouldn't mind a child, she thought, and was surprised at herself. What nonsense! She did not want a husband, far less a brat in his image! No, what she wanted was … but she was not sure what she wanted, that was the trouble. She longed for Marcus, that went without saying. But apart from Eagles Court and a living wage from it, which she believed she was in a fair way to getting, she still had no particular aim in mind.

Right now the kitchen fire needed riddling, the ashes needed carrying out, the curtains were unpulled and there was a faint smell of yesterday's supper. Questa tied her dressing gown cord more tightly round her middle, exchanged her old slippers for wellington boots, and flung open the back door.

Snow blew in. The cobbled yard was just a blanket of snow, the flakes falling slowly now though, spiralling down to lie, light as feathers, on walls, doorsills, tree branches. Beside her, Roma gave a little yip and charged out, skidding to a halt on her bottom six feet from the door. The wild kitten poked a white nose with a black blot on it – hence his name – out into the cold, thought about it and decided that decency demanded a quick foray. He stalked outside, dug a tiny pit in the cold whiteness, performed with his back to the watcher, then covered it over and stalked back indoors, all with a tremendous dignity which belied his small size and extreme youth. Cats have stronger bladders than dogs and think more highly of privacy, Questa concluded, as Roma stained the snow yellow and then wandered unconcernedly back towards her.

Having seen the dog and cat return to the kitchen, Questa sallied forth herself. Or rather she ran at top speed over to the stable, burst in and slammed the door behind her. Scamper stared, the goats, mother and child, stared too. Three pairs of eyes, all suggesting that breakfast would not be a bad idea, fixed themselves hopefully on this sudden but welcome visitor.

Obedient to their wordless request, Questa climbed up to the hayloft and threw a bale down which she divided between the animals. Then she waded through the drifting snow to the old barn with more hay for the sheep still awaiting their lambs. Ellen and Alfie would milk the cows today and the pigs would be fed later; until then they were snug enough in their sty. Later she would do her rounds, but now her duty was clear; she had fed the stabled animals, now she must get Grace her tea so that their day could begin.

And it was a happy day, because for once they were all in complete accord: Christmas is a time for children, this was Dickie's first Christmas at Eagles Court, and all of them – Ellen, Alfie, Alan, Grace and Questa – were determined to make the day memorable.

They started with a cooked breakfast; porridge first, then bacon, egg and fried potato, then thick slices of toast with Ellen's precious butter sparingly spread. Alan came in for breakfast in his dressing gown and slippers and actually looked a little better. Grace made him sit by the fire though, and waited on him in a manner which could have been considered quite affectionate, except that she sighed rather a lot and rolled her eyes to the ceiling once or twice in a meaningful manner.

After breakfast Dickie gave out his presents, which were all lovingly made by himself. Cards, oddly shaped and vividly crayoned, pom-poms in different colours – when she saw them, Questa remembered Grace's sleepwalking and felt a momentary unease – calendars with cut-out pictures, and a collection of household articles such as jam-jars and sauce-bottles, washed out and decorated with more cut-outs and deemed to be flower vases or useful containers.

There were effusive thanks, of course, and cries of well-simulated surprise (the women had seen Dickie purloining empty jam-jars and chopping pictures out of newspapers and magazines for weeks). Ellen was honestly delighted with her smudged calendar and Alfie gave Dickie a hug and a bag of broken chocolate in exchange for a jam-jar with a picture of a screwdriver on the front, 'to keep your tools in,' Dickie explained seriously.

'In the old days, we had presents around the tree in the afternoon,' Grace told Questa, as the three women worked to serve dinner. 'I know we've got a tree, and I know we talked about having dinner in the drawing room, but even with the fire lit it's awfully cold, and we don't have an awful lot of presents to unwrap, so shall we have dinner in here, where it's warm, and undo our presents after the pudding?'

Questa agreed. The kitchen was warm and pleasant, the leg of pork and the chicken were both roasting away in the oven, awaiting the arrival of the man who had sent them over the previous day as his promised gift. She was looking forward to Ran Atherton's arrival, but even so she felt separated, almost detached, from the preparations and pleasures around her. This was her first English Christmas without her father and suddenly she found she was suffering her loss all over again, feeling lonely, missing him.

Alan must have guessed how she felt for he called her through into the drawing room to talk about which wine they should serve with the meal, and when she appeared smiled encouragingly at her.

'Questa, it's Christmas, one of the unhappiest times of year for anyone suffering a bereavement, because at such a time it's impossible not to remember those other, happier times, when the person you've lost was still with you. I've had longer than you to get used to the idea that Charles isn't going to walk through that door, but it still hurts, I still wish he was around. So don't feel totally isolated, will you? Your father was much loved and is much missed. Take comfort from that and try not to grieve too much.'

'I shouldn't mind so much, because Dickie can't remember his father at all and that must be worse, really,' Questa said, staring fixedly out of the window at the deepening snow outside. 'Only it doesn't work like that because what you never have you never miss. And Daddy talked about snow so much and the games you and he and the others played.'

'I know, chick, I know. And though Grace doesn't say much, she misses Dickie's father a lot more than she lets on.'

'I know.' Questa swung round from the window. 'Alan, she talks in her sleep, walks too. Last night it was quite frightening and I'd really made up my mind to sleep in another room tonight,

200

but perhaps it would be kinder to stay with her, wake her? I think she has ... awfully sad dreams.'

Alan nodded. 'Yes, sad dreams are almost worse than frightening ones. Well, you must do as you think best of course, but perhaps, just for a few more nights, you might like to stay together? After I leave, Grace might think it odd if you continued to sleep upstairs but right now, with the cold so intense, it's simply common sense to share a warmed room. You're awfully lucky to have so much wood, incidentally. Families who depend on coal for their heating are having a bad time.'

'We're lucky in all sorts of ways,' Questa said. 'In our neighbour, for instance. Wait till you meet Mr Atherton. You'll like him.'

'I think I knew him once,' Alan said. 'He was a grand bloke, if it was the same one. He bred horses; Charles was a marvellous rider and though I wasn't anywhere near as good I went over a couple of times and Ran Atherton found me something quiet to ride. Oh yes, I do know your new friend.'

And when Ran Atherton arrived he was in the best of tempers and obviously intended to enjoy his day. He was introduced all round, said he remembered Alan, and gave Dickie a book about dogs illustrated by Cecil Alden.

'I loved it when I was a boy, and my son loved it, too,' he said as Dickie became absorbed in the lively pictures. 'It isn't new, I doubt if you could get a copy today, but I thought Dickie, being a dog-owner, might enjoy looking at it.'

They were still in the kitchen. The fire in the drawing room was lit, the room was beginning to lose its chill, but Alan, still looking tired to death, had decreed that it would not be habitable until early evening so, with some relief, they had remained in the cosy cave of the kitchen.

Ran sat in one chair and Alan in the other, and they talked animatedly about world and local affairs whilst Grace and Questa prepared the midday meal in all its glory. Questa, listening, heard swine fever, the desert campaign, the Cold War and foot and mouth disease discussed with all the interest and intelligence possible, and it occurred to her that it must be doing Ran good to talk to another man who, if not of his generation, was at least

201

nearer to it than his son was. And his son had been gone since the summer, so even that companionship had been denied him.

By the time they dished up the two men had found that they agreed on a great many things and had to be persuaded to leave their chairs and their chat and come and sit at the table like everyone else, and Dickie, one rather grimy forefinger tracing the adventures of the dogs in his book, had to be reminded that if he did not ring the gong soon the Rimmers would have a cold dinner. Restored to the real world, Dickie ran into the back yard and banged his gong, bringing a flushed Alfie and a grinning Ellen into the kitchen in a rush and the two cooks, with their table fully manned at last, were able to relax. Questa had refused to allow either Ellen or Alfie to help, saying that Christmas dinner would be just about the only meal since her arrival that Ellen had not masterminded; fortunately everything went well, even the gravy agreeing to remain lump-free, hot and tasty.

'That was delicious,' Alan said when nuts and apples replaced Ellen's economy pudding, and Questa brought round coffee in beautiful little shell cups, pink outside, white within, and gilded round the rims. 'It was positively pre-war, wasn't it, Ran?'

'I don't know how you did it, girls,' Ran said. 'Sheer genius, not only in the cooking, but in the acquiring. That chicken was prime!'

'Well, it was,' Questa said. 'If it hadn't been for you, it would have been a pretty boring meal … though we'd have done our best without it.'

'I'd 'a managed a rabbit,' Alfie said, grinning. 'Or th'old fox mighta got 'is teeth into one of them wild geese you're so fond of, Mr Atherton!'

You could tell how nice Ran was by the way Alfie treated him, Questa thought to herself, as Ran told Alfie what he would do to any fox, two- or four-legged, who harmed his precious geese. The birds were overwintering on the mere and Ran, armed with binoculars, was keeping a proprietorial eye on them.

There were not many labourers who could sit down to Christmas dinner at the same table as their employer and feel completely at home, Questa concluded. And not every employer would find it so easy to mix with his men as Ran clearly did.

After the meal was over it was time to listen to the king's speech on the wireless. Dickie nudged Questa at one point – Alan and Ran were both asleep, sitting as though listening intently, but with closed eyes and breathing rather too stertorous for mere attention.

'Are they *sleepin'*, Ques?' he said incredulously. 'It isn't bedtime, is it?'

Assuring him that it was merely the result of eating a large meal and sitting in a warm room, Questa nevertheless glanced across at the window. Dickie, she thought, could be forgiven for assuming that night had come. The overcast sky, pregnant with more snow, made it look almost like night out there and the contrast between the bright, firelit kitchen and the black and white of the snow scene outside was startling.

The king's speech finished and Grace tiptoed across and turned the wireless off, but instead of allowing the two men to continue to doze, the sudden silence seemed to rouse them to a realisation of their whereabouts. Ran snorted, sighed and opened his eyes; opposite him, Alan followed suit. Like Tweedledum and Tweedledee, Questa thought, and suppressed a giggle. Whatever was the matter with her? The next thing you knew she would say that the darkness outside was due to the wings of an enormous crow, come to Get Them!

'Sorry, I dropped off for a moment or two there,' Ran said, grinning at Dickie, who smiled sweetly back. 'Well, old chap, want to play a game?'

Dickie was delighted at the thought, and the rest of the afternoon was spent playing a variety of games suitable for a five-year-old, a crippled man nearing seventy and another suffering from a heavy head cold. Grace and Questa washed up, Ellen knitted and Alfie joined in the games until it was time for the milking, when he went off, whistling, to the cowshed.

'They've been in all day,' Questa said when Ran asked where Blossom and Daisy had spent Christmas. 'Alfie said no point in putting them out with no chance to graze. The sheep are in too, and Scamper. Tell me, Ran, do you use Shire's cattle-cake? And what about feeding turnips? Only Ellen says they make the milk taste.'

A lively agricultural discussion began and, rather to Questa's surprise, Alan proved quite knowledgeable on a number of subjects such as scrapy in sheep and the fat content of a gallon of milk. When she showed her surprise, Alan grinned faintly.

'The truth is no one could spend time with your father and not pick up a certain amount of knowledge,' he said. 'Not when we were younger, of course, then he had other interests, but at Cambridge he decided to learn all about farming. He didn't get the chance to do much practical work, but though he was a very good engineer his heart wasn't in it. He hankered after a farm … perhaps that's why you're so keen, dear.'

Questa nodded dumbly. She knew so little about her father, really. She had managed to forget all about his interest in Roman Britain, she could not remember him ever expressing an interest in farming … In fact she was beginning to suspect uneasily that the father she thought she remembered had never really existed. Or perhaps it was more that she had known him as a child knows its parent but never as one adult knows another. Alan and he had been on the same wavelength, they had known each other in a way that she, so far behind them in years, could never have done.

Thinking back, she realised that she had no memories, even partial, misty ones, of her father as either miserable or lonely, but he must, at times, have been both those things. Bringing up a daughter alone, for she was sure he had spent all his free time with her, must sometimes have been a thankless task. In the nature of things there must have been occasions when he was less than happy, when he longed for someone to share the sorrows as well as the joys of his suddenly circumscribed life. Why had he not sought out some pretty, good-natured woman to become his second wife? It would, surely, have been a natural thing to do, especially when you considered how good looking her father had been.

But she would never know the answer to that one, not now. Perhaps he had thought he would wait until his daughter was a little older, perhaps he never met anyone he liked enough, possibly his memories of Fortunata were so perfect that anyone else fell short. Still, she had a lot to be thankful for; Charles had been hers and hers alone.

'Questa?' It was Grace, coming across the room towards her. She patted Questa's shoulder. 'Don't be sad, come and help me instead. I'm just going to move everyone through into the drawing room, so if you'll lay the tea-trolley with cups and plates I'll make some sandwiches.'

There was an outcry from the men who said they could not possibly eat another thing, but Grace bullied them into the drawing room, with help from Ellen, and presently the laden trolley was pushed through and everyone discovered that they did have room left for egg sandwiches, buttered scones and a slice of Christmas cake.

After tea Questa went out to check on the stock as was her custom, and Ran went with her, leaning heavily on his sticks. Alan was pulled back by Grace when he tried to join them. 'You're not taking that cold out into that cold!' she adjured him sharply, and it seemed to Questa that he turned back into the house willingly enough. Dickie, coated and hatted, accompanied them though, and listened as Ran admired Daisy and Blossom, told Questa to be mean to Nanny and to tie her head up tight to a stake before attempting to milk her and to separate the goat from her kid as she had done with the cows and their calves.

'Isn't it cruel?' Questa asked rather timidly, to be told firmly that one farmed for profit, not for the animal's convenience, and sometimes, furthermore, it was necessary to be cruel to be kind.

'Oh. Right,' Questa said. Alfie had said something similar but it seemed hard on Nanny; the cows had each other for company but Nanny had no one. 'Come and look at your piglets now.'

The Athertons had sold her two piglets and they had done well under Alfie's expert care. Fat, pink, complacent, they grinned up at Ran and Questa from their sty, rootling contentedly around for anything extra to eat, squealing with excitement when Dickie threw them a couple of handfuls of cattle-cake.

'Nice,' Ran said. 'But Alfie's my pig-man, they should be nice. He's not that knowledgeable about cattle, my dear, but I'm sure he's told you that.'

'Yes, he has. We're learning together, Ellen says. And she knows lots about horses, so Scamper's all right. But I do worry about the sheep. You're the only person I know who farms sheep, Marcus has some but ...'

'Marcus?'

'Oh, he's a friend in Italy,' Questa said glibly. 'He has some sheep but he isn't particularly interested in them, though he shears them for wool of course, and slaughters in the autumn, for meat. Horses are his passion. He breeds them. He's got some beauties, one of them's pure white, she's a mare, she's his favourite mount – when I'm good enough ...'

'When did you see him last? Is he farming here?' Ran asked. They were leaning on the pig-sty gate, gazing at the grunting gilts within. 'You sound as though you've seen the mare at least fairly recently.'

'Oh! Oh well, no, but we write ... exchange letters,' Questa said in some confusion. 'When I'm good enough I'm – I'm going to buy myself a mare just like her; that's what I was going to say.'

'She'll be difficult to keep clean if she's a grey,' Ran observed. 'Still, I daresay Scamper needs a fair bit of grooming. How is your riding coming along?'

'Haven't had much practice lately,' Questa muttered. She could feel the hot blood flaming in her cheeks. How stupid she had been, she had nearly given herself away to Ran, and she did want him to consider her a sensible person, to whom he could sell stock and give advice! 'You mustn't ride a horse when the ground's hard, must you?'

'No, it's not advisable; who told you that? Not your friend Marcus, surely?'

Questa turned large, enquiring eyes on him, wondering uneasily why he had put it like that, but he soon set her mind at rest.

'I don't suppose they have frost and snow much in Italy, that's what I meant,' he said, smiling at her. 'And now we'd better get back to the house; I don't know about you but I'm getting quite chilly.'

They returned to the house, Questa somewhat subdued. Grace

and Alan both looked rather flushed when they entered the kitchen. Questa hoped that Grace was not about to catch Alan's cold, then forgot about it as they began to set the table for the simple supper they had planned.

The rest of the evening passed uneventfully. After they had washed up they played card games with Dickie until it was time for bed, and then Alfie drove Ran home in Alan's car, because once again Grace said she would rather Alan stayed indoors.

'Going to come with us and make sure we don't end up in a snowdrift?' Ran said, so Questa got her dufflecoat and climbed into the back seat and they skidded and squeaked over the snow, with Alfie, who drove the tractor at the Hall and also drove the long, dark red Lagonda when Ran wanted to go out, managing the car very skilfully considering the conditions.

'There's sacks in the back and a spade, in case,' Alan had said when handing Alfie the keys. 'Chains, too, though you probably won't need 'em since you'll be driving on fresh snow.'

When they reached the Hall there was a light on in the kitchen.

'Someone's home,' Questa observed, hopping out and going round to the passenger door with Ran's sticks. 'Is it Mrs C, or Daphne?'

'Not likely. It's probably Barnaby, my foreman,' Ran said. 'Go off, the pair of you. I'll be fine.'

But Alfie saw him in and then returned to the car. He got in, started the engine and circled the yard carefully, then pointed the bonnet in the direction of the Court.

'Who was it?' Questa said curiously. 'In the house, I mean.' She had seen a tall silhouette, nothing more, moving across the lighted window for a moment, and had thought it was a man.

'The son,' Alfie said shortly. 'Surprise visit. Only 'ere for a coupla days.'

'Oh! I thought he was in Canada.'

'Oh ah, so 'e was. On 'is way to Australia now, 'e said. The old man sent 'im off to study farmin', said it would mek a man of 'im. At least it stopped 'em flyin' at each other's throats. But I reckon there's times Mr Atherton wishes 'e'd never done it, stuck 'ere farmin' a big place like this alone.'

'Ye—es. So he'll be coming back, one day?'

Alfie shot her a curious look.

'Oh ah, bound to be. Tes 'is 'eritage, you might say.'

'So it is,' Questa agreed and said no more for the remainder of the journey.

Nine

Questa slept the sleep of the truly tired on Christmas night, and assumed that Grace had done the same since she was not disturbed by either walking or talking. She woke on Boxing Day with that indefinable sensation of disappointment which sometimes follows an exciting event. Then she remembered that Christmas Day might be over – well, it was – but all that really meant was that spring was a day nearer, and also that if the snow was still on the ground, she would have a chance to do many of the things her father had talked about with such enthusiasm. Sledging, skating, snowballing ... she could remember playing with her father in the snow in their little back garden, but their activities had been restricted by her youth and their city environment. Now, at last, she was in a position to experience the thrills he had so graphically described. And, what was more, an air of holiday would prevail whilst Alan was with them, and he had promised to stay at least until the twenty-eighth, so if he felt better today he might be persuaded to take them romping in the snow.

Accordingly she got up, intending to go downstairs without waking either of the others. She plucked Roma's warm, sleepy body out of the nest she had made for herself in her box and kissed her on the nose, then tucked her, wriggling, under one arm. Better get her outside as soon as possible or there would be more puddles. Before she left the room, however, she glanced at the two sleepers. Grace was sleeping with uncharacteristic abandon, sprawling on her face, hair everywhere, a fist in her mouth, but Dickie lay tidily on his back with his head turned sideways, sleeping like the little angel he most certainly was not.

Seeing him like that, in repose, eyes closed, Questa was pricked by a recollection of someone, somewhere ... only she could not quite remember who, or indeed where, and turned away with a sigh. How annoying it was, to have eighteen years of your life spread out behind you, yet to know that over the first ten of those years, and over a good few of the subsequent five, were huge patches of blankness, as though wreaths of mist had formed over happenings which should have been ice-clear.

She was tiptoeing down the stairs when another thought struck her. She had been so busy and so happily employed lately that she had not once dreamed of Marcus. It wasn't because she didn't want to see him, precisely, it was because she did not think, in her heart, that she would be able to span the distance between them. She had to want, very badly, to see Marcus, to be able to dream of him. But she did not think the length of time between each dream was terribly important; Marcus wouldn't run away. He was there for her as she was there for him.

Reassured on that point, she opened the kitchen door and was halfway into the room before she saw the figure in the armchair. It made her jump, gave her quite a shock, but then she realised it was Alan, wearing his greatcoat with a blanket wrapped round him. He was sipping something in a glass and looked up as she entered, giving her an uncertain smile. He was very flushed.

'Oh, Questa, I came for some more aspirin; to tell you the truth I don't feel so good.'

Questa crossed the room and very gently felt his forehead. He was burning hot and his hair was wet with sweat. He shivered when she touched him, almost cringing away from her hand.

'Sorry – that hurt, I ache,' he mumbled. 'My head's thumping and I'm freezing cold. The fire's right down in the parlour.'

'I'll get you a hot bottle,' Questa said. She opened the back door, slipped the puppy out into the snow, and returned to the stove. The kettle, filled ready for tea, soon began to sing so Questa got a rubber hot-water bottle from the scullery, filled it and went through with it to the parlour. Alan was right about the fire, so she poked it, made a wigwam of dry logs above it and then returned to the kitchen. Roma was whining at the back door so she let the puppy back in and then turned to Alan.

'Bed,' she said firmly. 'Your bottle's in, I've made up your fire, and now I'm going to get you a hot drink. And after that, Alan, you'll just have to stay in bed until we can get the doctor. You can't go on like this, you know.'

'I'm all right, really,' the sufferer said hoarsely. 'I'll give you a hand once I'm a bit warmer.'

'Bed.'

'But it's not fair, Questa, leaving you and Grace with all the work. I'll be fine ...'

'Bed!'

'Oh dear! But I suppose you're right.'

Alan stood up, swayed, and almost collapsed. Questa sprang forward and put an arm round his waist, then began to lead him gently towards the small parlour. Alan tried to manage alone, but had to lean on her.

'Sorry, chick, but my legs keep giving way. I'll soon get my strength back, though, if I have an hour or two in bed.'

'Or a day or two,' Questa said breathlessly, almost carrying him across the hall. 'You've got 'flu, Alan. There's a lot of it about.'

They reached the bedroom and Alan thumped down on to the bed so hard that Questa winced for the springs.

'My God, that took it out of me more than I'd have believed possible,' he gasped. His high colour had fled, leaving him alarmingly pale. 'Thanks, Questa. I appreciate your helping, especially as you don't much like touching people.'

Questa felt her own cheeks warm. No one had ever put it into words before, but she should have realised it was obvious. Not that there was any particular reason to feel ashamed – she could not help her aversion. Besides, now that she thought about it, she realised she was improving. She often held Dickie's hand, she had shaken Grace awake, she had even hugged Ellen ... yes, she must be getting better.

She said as much to Alan as she helped him out of his dressing gown and back into bed.

'So you see I don't mind nearly as much as I did,' she ended, tucking him firmly in. 'I'm beginning to forget the horrible things that happened to me, and with every day that passes I seem to think about it less.'

'Good. The trouble is, Questa, you look perfectly all right, so

211

people don't make allowances. Whereas someone like Ran, well, you can see there's something wrong.'

'There is something wrong; his poor legs,' Questa pointed out. 'With me, it's more in my mind.'

'Grace said you had a broken finger.'

'*Grace* said? But I've said nothing to her, I know I haven't!'

'Perhaps not; hasn't it occurred to you that Grace isn't the only one who talks in her sleep? Don't look so shocked, dear, she told me she heard you cry out in your sleep one night and say your finger was broken, and next morning she glanced at your hand and saw one of your fingers had been … hurt. Questa, you must believe me when I tell you that Grace is trying very hard to understand you, just as you're trying to understand her. If people everywhere understood each other, you know, there wouldn't be any wars.'

'I didn't know I talked in my sleep,' Questa said humbly. 'Anyway, I've not had that dream for ages, not since I moved in here, so you see I am beginning to forget the dreadful things that happened, or if not to forget exactly, at least I've pushed them to the back of my mind. Only I do wish, Alan, that I could remember more about what happened before the war. It's as though because I dared not think about it whilst I was in Italy my mind deliberately wiped it all out. And now that it's safe to look back, there's nothing left to look back on.'

'I didn't realise you'd forgotten to that extent, but I'm sure it will all come back in its own good time,' Alan said. He was leaning back against his pillows, dreamily eyeing the fire as it began to crackle into life once more. 'In fact, Dr Barnes said it would come back, and that it was better that you should remember for yourself than that we should try to help you. But I tell you what, chick, I'll look out some old photographs; they may remind you of the past.'

'Do you have photos with Daddy in? And my mother? Oh, Alan, I'd give an awful lot to see them, particularly my father, because I do remember him a bit. And it would be lovely to see pictures of Fortunata, though I can't remember her at all I don't think.'

'You weren't even two when she died,' Alan said. His voice

was slowing, slurring. Questa could see he was on the very brink of sleep. 'Ask Gracie if she's got photographs; she and Nata were very friendly at one time, they used to play tennis together.'

'I'll ask, but you go to sleep,' Questa said. 'I'll pop in later, Alan, to see if you want anything.'

She crept out of the room, but doubted if Alan had heard her last words. As she gently closed the door behind her he gave a small, bubbling snore.

Questa's diagnosis proved correct. Alan had influenza and was very ill for a week, and even at the end of that time he could not leave the house but sat in the kitchen languidly writing letters or working on the books for Eagles Court. Questa, knowing nothing of economics, had not dreamed of setting down her outgoings – there were few incomings as yet – but she sat patiently by Alan's side during that second snowy week and learned double-entry book-keeping and how to run a small but efficient filing system.

Ran came over almost every evening now, to play chess with Alan and talk to him about various things. Alfie ran him round in the Lagonda and then took him home again and walked back across the fields. Questa guessed that Alfie was paid to do it, but she was sure he would have done it free, and welcome. There was no doubt Alfie was fond of Ran Atherton and considered any help he might give to be a perk of the job rather than a chore, since it gave him the opportunity of being in Ran's company and discussing the various problems of pig-farming.

When Alan tired of chess and talk and needed to rest, Ran took the opportunity to explain to Questa the intricacies of form-filling demanded by the Ministry of Agriculture and the need to remember an inspection might take place with only a few hours' notice. Because she intended to increase her stock, he lectured her on permits, on the attitude of ministry officials who would grant or refuse licences, on her need, one day, of a good foreman or manager.

'I'll help you to find someone suitable,' he said. 'Once the place is up and running you'll need more professional help than either Ellen or Grace can give … and I do know most of the up-and-coming farmers' sons hereabouts. The sad fact is that when a man

213

farming on a small scale has more than one son they have to move away from home. It's all this wretched mechanisation – it's no longer economic to employ too many farm workers.'

'I'd appreciate that, when the time comes,' Questa said earnestly. 'You're such a help, Ran. Somehow you make things easy to understand, even quite complicated things. I'm beginning to understand all the stupid paperwork, though I still don't think it's necessary.'

In the autumn she had wondered what Ellen was on about when she talked about a bee-sugar permit and worried that it might not arrive in time to feed the bees up for winter, but now she knew. If you got the permit you were allowed to buy the extra sugar the bees needed to make honey; if you didn't get the permit your bees would starve. No wonder Ellen had been anxious, and had sworn old-fashioned oaths against the ministry man who had not 'got movin' on me papers', as she put it.

'I'll lend you some books,' Ran said. Questa, who still had some difficulty with reading, thanked him with little enthusiasm, but when the books arrived she was fascinated. There were books by both men and women, all of whom were farming up and down the country and tackling the problems she would tackle, some of them with no more experience than she and in even harsher conditions. One man had lived for three long years in a big old barn with no fire, no running water, no sanitation. He had actually farmed the land under these conditions winter and summer; it made Eagles Court appear the height of luxury, Questa's thistly pastures Elysian fields! But best of all, the books Ran lent her were written amusingly and interestingly, so that even though reading was hard work for her, Questa was reluctant to put them down and sometimes read far into the night.

Alan was with them three weeks, and in that time Questa's knowledge of farming increased tenfold. She planned the sheep dip she would build, or rather cause to be built, the following summer for use in the autumn, and the lovely modern homes she would make – they were far too good to call sties – for the offspring of her fat gilts when they were put to the boar. She also thought about ridding the outbuildings of rats, but not very hard or very often. Taking life was still something she preferred to leave to others; instead she had brought down from the attic some large tin trunks and put her cattle-cake and feed-corn in them, but in her heart she knew that if she intended to expand the only sensible answer would be to get rid of the rats.

The snow continued to fall, and to lie, and very soon Questa's first task each morning, after seeing to the fires and putting the dog and cat out, was to dig a pathway through the latest fall, across the yard to the stable, then to the pigsties, then to the barn. Usually, red-cheeked and perspiring, she was met halfway by Alfie, digging his way out, and the two of them would exchange grins and remarks on the depth the new snow had reached, before labouring on.

It was not all work, though. Despite Alan's inability to go out with them, he was full of advice for would-be sledgers, would-be skaters. Ellen found some old skates and when the ice on the mere was thick enough Questa and Grace went outside and had a go, with no particular success. Questa was bold but spent most of her time sitting on her bottom and laughing, and Grace was timid and tottered round clutching at anything which looked strong enough to bear her weight. Since that included Dickie, who promptly fell as well, she tried skating only once.

Sledging, though, was another thing altogether. Armed with a tray each, they got Alfie to take them to Hazel Hill, so called because of the number of hazel trees growing at the foot of it. Alfie went with them happily enough and showed them where the local kids, when he was a lad, had brought their sledges and trays. It was, he said, fast but flat, and thus ensured the sledgers a long, exciting run. It proved to be a smooth, steep meadow, ending in a stream around which grew a number of hazel trees, stumpy alders and willows.

'Won't we cannon into the trees and get killed?' Grace asked anxiously. Clearly her days of careering merrily down hillsides perched on a tiny tray were long past, if they had ever existed. 'What if we go straight into the stream?'

'Tes iced over, so you won't drown,' Alfie said. 'What 'arm can come to you, Miss Grace? Questa an' me, we'll pick up the bits iffen you crash.'

'Oh, that *is* a consolation,' Grace said sarcastically. 'Ques, you

215

can jolly well go first – no, Dickie, you aren't to get on that tray until a grownup has gone down the hill.'

So Questa got on her tray and promptly disappeared down the hill like a bullet from a gun. Her bloodcurdling shrieks made Grace gasp and Dickie giggle, and presently they saw the great arc of loose snow, which was about all they could see of her, slew round just before the trees and there was Questa, pink-faced, shiny-eyed, toiling up the slope once more and shouting that it was: 'The best thing I've ever done. I'm having another go at once!'

They spent two hours on the hill. Dickie was so light that his speed was frightening even to Questa, but Dickie was delighted with it and much preferred his solitary hurtle to a staider journey down on the tray with either Questa or his mother.

'I wish we could go ghost-hunting on a sledge in the snow,' he said later that afternoon as they sat round the fire eating hot buttered toast. 'Like you did, Mummy, when you were a girl.'

Questa looked up. For the first time she realised that the story which she had heard from two different sources definitely did include Grace as a participant.

But right now, there was Grace, buttering toast, and Alan, eating it, and she really couldn't see a reason for anyone not admitting to anything as simple as a childhood friendship. She opened her mouth to say so, then caught Dickie's eye. Dickie was munching toast and smiling away, slipping bits to Roma every now and then, and it seemed silly to break the good atmosphere with questions which might annoy, if not embarrass. Instead, she remembered something else. Though she knew her father and Alan had been ghost-hunting, it had not before occurred to her to ask just what ghost they hoped to uncover.

She said as much now, but casually. 'Isn't it odd, my father told me that story when I was little too, Dickie. Grace, I never asked – what ghost was supposed to haunt the Court? Or did you make it up?'

Grace, holding a toasting fork with a round of bread out to the flames, winced as it caught for a moment and blew violently on the singed bread.

'Which ghost? Well, apparently when Uncle Josh was a kid,

he had an elder sister and she always swore she met a ghost one day, walking down by the mere. Wasn't that what we were after, Al?'

'Was it? Do you know, I've forgotten. But I always fancied it was a Lady of Shalott-type figure, all flowing draperies and long, loose hair. Or that other one, what was it?' Alan closed his eyes and concentrated, then snapped his eyes open and smiled triumphantly. *I met a lady in the meads, full beautiful, a faery's child.'*

'Isn't that Keats? *La Belle Dame sans Merci*?' Grace enquired. 'We did it at school, which is why I remember it. But surely she was a rather sinister woman, wasn't she? Not the type you want to meet on an icy, moonlit night!'

'True. And we were scared of seeing a ghost, but somehow we all thought it would be a friendly ghost ... don't know how you can have two feelings like that at the same time, but I think we did. Why, chick? Have you met a lady in the meads?'

Questa shook her head, holding her own bread out to the fire on a common or garden fork and getting far too hot as a result.

'No; I'd run a mile!' She looked around her. What harm in a simple question, after all? 'Alan, I have been meaning to ask you whether Grace was the same Grace who ...'

Ellen was making potato cakes on the table behind them. Whilst Questa was still fumbling for words which would elicit the answer she wanted there was an almighty crash behind her. Startled, she spun round, the toast falling unregarded into the ashes.

'Good God, Ellen, are you all right?'

'Oh, oh, me best yaller bowl! Oh look at it, me best bowl in a thousand pieces! Oh, where'll I iver git another like it, eh? That aint done me 'tater cakes much good, either.'

Ellen, face creased with distress, poked about amongst the disaster on the kitchen floor as though hoping to salvage something. Questa got up and went to the broom cupboard.

'Poor Ellen, but that lot's had it, I fear. I'll clean up whilst you chuck the bits in the bin. The mixture's so muddled up with broken china that not even the pigs can eat it. But we've lots of potatoes, I'll start peeling now and you can make some more cakes later. They weren't for supper, were they?'

'Why wuz I so careless?' Ellen mourned. 'Ole fool, I am ... ruined good food ... even the pigs can't 'ave it.'

'It doesn't matter, Ellen, I'll get you another big bowl,' Grace put in. 'My stuff's in store, but I had at least one bowl just like that and with only Dickie and me to cook for, I doubt if I've used it more than once or twice. You're welcome to it. Tell you what, couldn't you fetch it out of store for me, Alan, when you're back in London?'

'Willingly,' Alan said. 'Here, Questa, your toast is spoiled; have my piece. I've eaten more than I should already.'

Questa, with the coal shovel laden with broken china and potato cake, said he might as well eat it himself since she would take this lot straight out to the midden. And by the time she got back the conversation had turned to what other things Alan should rescue from the storage place and how useful certain sophisticated items of kitchenware would be to Ellen. Later, when she was thinking of asking once more why Grace had led her to believe that she had only known Charles Adamson slightly, Ellen gave her a poke, pulled a face, and beckoned her through to the scullery, where she was washing up.

'Don't say nothin', lovie,' she hissed. 'I'll tell you what you needs to know tomorrer, when we'm milkin'.'

'I don't see why it's all so secret,' Questa mumbled crossly. 'If Grace came here when she was a girl, why doesn't she talk about it?'

'I said I'll tell you tomorrer,' Ellen repeated. 'You'll see why, then.'

It was warmer in the cowshed than it was in the yard but, even so, Questa wore her thickest clothing and huddled as close to Daisy's brown flank as she could get. In the next stall, Ellen milked with long, steady pulls, the milk sizzling into the tin bucket. Questa sighed to herself, took the long pink teats between her fingers, and began to pull and gently squeeze as Alfie had taught her. The milk came, in short bursts at first and then, at last, in long, steady streams, hissing against the bucket's side.

'You're right, Ellen, Daisy *is* easier,' she called when she could feel the flow beginning to slacken. 'The bucket's brimming! Gosh, wait till I tell Ran!'

'That's right, lovie. Tomorrer you can 'ave a go at Blossom. Thing is, now you've got your confidence, it'll give 'er confidence, too. Likely she'll let down 'er milk an' no trouble.'

'I hope so.' Questa moved her bucket out of harm's way – she had already been taught a hard lesson when Blossom kicked out, catching the half-full bucket a resounding blow and sending the hard-won milk all over the cowshed floor – and went round to see how Ellen was doing. 'Yours is nearly full, too, and you started a lot later than I did. But you're an old hand at it and I'm still learning.'

'That's right,' Ellen agreed. She hissed the last short bursts into the bucket, then smoothed a gnarled hand down over Blossom's rich tan hide. 'You're a good gal for ole Ellen, that you are.'

'Shall I pour mine into the churn?' Questa asked. 'Then your lot can go straight into the scullery. You'll want yours for butter and cheese, won't you?'

'Oh ah, likely I will. I'll tek mine indoors now and ...'

'Hey, hang on! What about explaining? Ellen, you promised you would, and I haven't said a word to anyone. You can tell me now – Dickie's still not dressed and Grace is seeing to him and Alan ... well, he'll still be in bed I daresay. Why did you break that yellow bowl and spoil all the potato cakes?'

Ellen stood her bucket of milk down and grinned.

'Saw through me, didjer? No one else did, I reckon, an' it stopped you askin' awkward questions of the wrong people. Well, lovie, no one wanted you to know, but to my way of thinkin' you was bound to find out sooner or later.'

'Find out what? Ellen, tell me!'

'I am, aren't I? Don't be so impatient. That Grace was engaged, with a ring an' everything, to your dad. Charles promised to marry 'er, then 'e met your mum. See?'

'Wha – at? Not really, Ellen? But that was an awful thing to do! An engagement means that two people intend to marry, doesn't it? I just can't believe it, because Daddy was such a kind man. What happened?'

'Well ... look, lovie, come up to my place. You aren't a-goin'
to like what I tell you an' that's the truth, so it'll be easier if no
one don't go walkin' in on us.'

Without a word, Questa followed Ellen up to the flat and sank
down in the chair opposite Ellen's own by the fire. Ellen sighed
and looked into the flames for a moment, then reached out with
the poker and began, absently, to mend the fire. She added an
extra log, pulled the kettle over the flame and then faced Questa
squarely.

'It waren't so bad as it sounds, so mind you hear me out, young
leddy. Now Mr Joshua, your dad's uncle, had no time for
children. But 'e was mortal fond of Grace. And acourse, 'e didn't
'ave no direct heir.'

'Got you,' Questa said when the silence began to stretch. 'But
the property is entailed, isn't it? It *has* to go to an Adamson. So
Joshua couldn't have left the place to Grace.'

'Right. But your daddy, 'e didn't know that.'

'He didn't? I wonder why not?'

'Because 'im and the old feller 'ad a row, and though Joshua
still kept in touch, paid your daddy an allowance and so on, 'e
didn't intend to tell 'im the place would be 'is one day, because
'e was a grudging ole bugger, and who else was there who knew
and could tell, eh? No one. In fact, Joshua behaved real bad, from
what I've 'eard. So there was your daddy, shut out of the place
'e loved best in the world ... but young Grace Caldicott, she were
still 'ere from time to time, visiting 'er Aunt Prue, coming up to
the Court to see the old man. So your daddy come down to stay
at The Passing Soldier when 'e could and did 'is best to 'eal the
breach 'tween 'imself and his uncle. And Grace was always
around. She'd been in love with Mr Charles since she were a
nipper, see? Next thing we knew, they was engaged.'

'So my father thought he loved her,' Questa murmured.

Ellen nodded slowly. 'Aye, that's about it. Mr Joshua was real
pleased and welcomed your dad back to Eagles Court. Mr Charles
lived for this place, mek no mistake, lovie. The Adamson blood
ran in 'is veins an' the urge to own land and do right by it ran
'longside it. And Grace was rare pretty in them days ...'

'She is still,' Questa contributed. 'Beautiful, really.'

'Aye, per'aps. But she were pretty an' your dad didn't know many gals. Fair enough, they got engaged.'

'Then I suppose he met my mother, and really fell in love. But where did he meet her, and how? I never asked, I just took it for granted that they met in London, I suppose.'

'No, it weren't London; in fact it musta bin bitter to the old feller, because it were all 'is own fault. Joshua 'ad a notion to grow vines up on the 'ill at the back, said if they'd been grown there long ago, like your dad believed, 'e didn't see no reason why they shouldn't flourish again. So Mr Charles went off to Italy to study vines an' bein' a cantankerous old bugger I've no doubt Mr Joshua thought if the vines died 'e could blame young Charles an' if they throve 'e could tek the credit.'

Ellen leaned forward and poked the fire, and Questa held out her chilly hands to the resultant blaze.

'Horrible old man,' she said. 'I'm glad I didn't have to contend with him when I came home.'

'Aye, 'e wouldn't 'ave 'elped,' Ellen agreed. 'But don't interrupt me story, lovie, let me get it straight.'

'Sorry; go on, then.'

'Well, old Joshua probably weren't all that keen on a couple of lovebirds about the place, either, so off goes Charlie to Italy to find out all 'e could about growin' vines. And 'e met your mother an' wrote back it were love at first sight.

'I reckon your dad wrote to Grace, too, but Joshua 'ad been hoist on 'is own petard and that made 'im fit to kill. He wrote back to young Charlie makin' it clear 'e wouldn't be forgiven, said 'e didn't want to set eyes on 'im ever again.

'Your dad were a nice lad, lovie, but 'e 'ad 'is share of the Adamson temper. Told Joshua where to git off, 'e did, then 'e bought an 'ouse in London or somewhere sim'lar an' got spliced. I reckon it upset Grace, though. She'd done nothin' 'cept to fall in love with a man who couldn't love 'er. So you might say if it 'adn't been for Joshua's fancy to grow vines, lovie, you'd 'ave growed up in Eagles Court, wi' Grace as your mum.'

'Gosh,' Questa said inadequately. 'That's the saddest story, Ellen, but I'm so grateful to you for telling me. If I'd known I'd have been nicer to Grace, really I would, because I'd have understood why she resented me and was so horrid sometimes. And I've just thought of something else; when my father died, Grace must have thought she'd get the house. Oh Ellen, *poor* Grace!'

'Aye. She's related to th' Adamsons somewhere along the line, and there ain't no other relatives, so she may 'ave wondered about 'er chances. What she didn't think was that you'd turn up. You'd disappeared into Italy like a raindrop in a puddle, I reckon no one thought you was alive, dearie. So seein' as 'ow 'er great-grandma 'ad been an Adamson an' 'uman nature being what it is, she must ha' wondered.'

'Gosh,' Questa said again, but thoughtfully this time. 'No wonder she hates me!'

Ellen looked surprised. 'She don't 'ate you, lovie; not no more, any'ow. But she's not 'appy. Your dad broke more than the engagement, you know. She din't trust men no more after that, not for a long while.'

'But she got married,' Questa said. 'Simon thingummy, the pilot.'

'Mebbe she did, but gettin' married don't mean much, you can git married just to show someone you ain't wearin' the willow. An' it didn't last long, that particular marriage, not long enough to bring 'er confidence back. But anyway, if you ask me, she's still achin' for your daddy.'

Questa sighed. 'Thanks for telling me, Ellen,' she said soberly. 'What a muddle it is, though! Don't we hurt each other, us people? I can't imagine anything worse than loving someone, believing they love you back, and then discovering that they don't, after all.'

'Very true; yet it 'appens all the time,' Ellen said. 'So now you know, d'you feel 'appier?'

'Yes, in a way. And I'll be more careful what I say,' Questa admitted. 'Do you think Grace may marry Alan though, Ellen? He is very nice and he'd take great care of her, and of Dickie.'

She was looking at Ellen as she spoke and saw, to her surprise, a shuttered look of extreme obstinacy close down over Ellen's normally lively nutcracker face.

'Leave well alone, lovie,' was all she said, however. 'Dickie don't need no one he ain't got already.' And then, before Questa could answer, she got to her feet and took the steaming kettle off the fire. 'A nice 'ot cuppa an' then we'll start work agin,' she announced. 'Get me a coupla mugs, there's a good gal!'

Questa had been as disturbed by Ellen's story as Ellen expected her to be, and was naturally distressed over what her father had done to Grace, but after some thought she absolved him from blame in the matter. She knew very well that falling in love was not something you could choose about; either it happened or it did not, and if it did, you were helpless in the grip of this strange and yet comfortable emotion. But what particularly intrigued her were the vines which Joshua had intended to plant and her father's trip to Italy to learn about them.

How very strange life was! In her dreams Marcus grew vines on that slope, and he grew them successfully, what was more. From somewhere, or someone, Daddy had begun to believe that others had grown vines on the hill in the past, and had wanted to emulate them. And she, from the very beginning, had thought the hill looked as though it was terraced for vines, even after Ellen had told her that it had been sheep-paths and nothing more.

But there was nothing she could do with this new knowledge, not yet. She was certain, now, that her father would have planted vines had he been given the opportunity, would have planted them now, had he lived. So she would do it for him, with love, and she would make wine and sell it and everyone would say how sensible she was, to use the knowledge, culled in wartime Italy, to beautify and use her ancestral land.

However, the time for planting vines was not yet, and the day Alan left for London once more, Grace went down with the 'flu. Heavy-eyed, thick-voiced, she staggered down to the kitchen to see him off, assuring him that she had overslept and was just a bit hoarse as a result and would be fine in an hour. But once the car had gone chugging down the still snowy lane, she burst into tears, told Questa she was sick to death of Eagles Court and wanted a bit of life for a change, and collapsed on to a chair.

'I'll get the doctor,' Questa said wearily, going to the back door for her coat. 'No point in your sitting there, Grace. Go back to bed.'

Questa had quite enjoyed Alan's convalescence, particularly the last week, when he had been almost well and able to keep Grace occupied. The two of them had gone up to the attics in search of saleable stuff and had cleaned and prepared for auction a number of smallish items. Now, Questa was glad she had not accompanied them, not if being together had caused Grace to catch the wretched 'flu. She just hoped Dickie would not fall victim too.

The doctor came, looking harassed, and said that the strain of influenza at present sweeping the country was very infectious and unpleasant. He gave Grace cough medicine, an inhalant, tablets for the discomfort – she had a terrible headache and a wheezy chest – and rather more good advice than she wanted.

'You'll have to have Dickie in your room,' she said mournfully when Questa took her a glass of hot lemon and honey after Dr Speed had left. 'The doctor doesn't want him to catch it; he says kids take it hard, much worse than adults, and it can kill old people, too.'

'I hope Ran will be all right,' Questa said anxiously. 'It's bad enough being crippled in the legs without adding 'flu to your lot.'

'I wish I hadn't got so close to Alan,' Grace said tearfully later, whilst she was sitting up in bed with a towel over her head, inhaling Friar's Balsam floating in a bowl of boiling water. 'He wasn't as ill as this … oh, and now he's gone happily off to London and doesn't even know I'm ill.'

'How close did you get?' Questa asked. It was an innocent question, asked solely because she, too, had been nursing Alan, but Grace chose to see it as criticism.

'What do you mean? Oh, you're so horrid to me, Questa Adamson, I can't think why I stay in this godforsaken hole! As for Alan Patterson, if you want him you're welcome!'

'He's old,' Questa said thoughtlessly. 'He doesn't want me, he wants …'

'He is *not* old!' Grace flung back the towel the better to glare at Questa. Her face was red and running with perspiration, her nose glowed, her eyes were suffused from hanging her head down. She looked thoroughly unattractive and spiteful which, it soon turned out, was just how she felt. 'I know you're an ugly little thing, so men won't want you, but you're rich – that ought to bring your plenty of chances!'

Questa kept her temper, not without difficulty.

'I know I'm ugly, but it's not something I can help, and you didn't have to remark on it,' she said in a tight little voice. 'But I am *not* rich, if I was I'd do no end of things here.'

Grace blew her nose violently and hung her head over the basin once more.

'I didn't mean it, in fact you're getting prettier day by day,' she said, her voice muffled by the steam and the towel. 'It's just that I feel so ill, and Dr Speed said I wasn't to go down to the kitchen until I'm free from infection, nor to see Dickie. I'm really miserable, Questa. I wish I were dead!'

'You will be if you say horrible things,' Questa told her. 'Don't look on the black side, Grace, you're strong, you'll soon pull round. As for Dickie, we'll take good care of him, you know that. And if you do as Dr Speed says, you'll probably be out and about in a week, two at the most. Look at Alan, he's older than you, but it only took three weeks for him to be fit for work again.'

'He's not all that much older than me,' the muffled voice said. 'Do you know how old I am?'

'No.'

'Oh. Good,' Grace said ungraciously. 'Well, I'm a lot younger than Alan, anyway.'

Despite herself, Questa giggled. Two such contradictory remarks simply meant that the 'flu was talking and not Grace. She would be better once she got over the first five days or so, and once her temperature went down. Even Alan, the most eventempered of men, had been scratchy and quick to take offence that first week.

'Well, that's good to know,' she said tactfully. 'You've inhaled enough, Grace, I bet your chest is clearer now. I'll take the basin and the towel away and bring you up a hot drink, then you can take your tablets and have a rest.'

Grace mumbled something but relinquished the basin and towel and when Questa put her head around the door an hour later, she was fast asleep.

Dickie did not get the 'flu and nor did Ran. Despite nursing everyone else, Questa did not get it either. And Grace, clearly as strong as she looked, was up and about after a fortnight.

She was actually in the kitchen, making a pot of tea for breakfast when Questa came hurriedly in from the cowshed, where she had been milking. She had a bucket of milk in one hand, an old sack round her shoulders, for it was raining softly but persistently, and a worried look on her face.

'Grace, take the milk, will you, and put it in the larder. Ellen hasn't put in an appearance yet … I do hope she isn't ill.'

But she didn't think for one moment that Ellen, the tough old bird, was anything but fighting fit. Nevertheless she climbed the stairs in the stable with some apprehension. Ellen was over eighty, if she had fallen …

No one answered her knock so she walked in. The fire in the kitchen was out and Alfie's breakfast dishes were still on the table. Alfie generally had breakfast at home, though Ellen always came over to the house for hers. Indeed, she usually cooked breakfast for everyone, it being her boast that no one could make rations go round like she could.

'Ellen?' Questa said. Her voice seemed to echo hollowly round the small room. 'Ellen, are you all right?'

She thought she heard a faint answering hail so went through into the bedroom. Ellen lay in the big brass bedstead, her tiny wrinkled face rosy, her bright eyes heavy with fever.

'Oh, Ellen, you've got the 'flu! Here, don't move, I'll run back to the house and fetch the tablets the doctor gave Grace and the rest of her medicine. I'll call him when we've had breakfast and he can come and take a look at you and tell us what you need. Oh, poor Ellen … does Alfie know you're ill?'

'No. Got 'is breakfuss an' then come back to bed,' Ellen said in a hoarse voice. 'There's a posset in the back cupboard be'ind the meat safe … if you could warm it through …'

The posset looked like dark red syrup and smelt pleasantly of roses. Questa warmed it through, served it in Ellen's best pink cup, made Ellen a hot bottle – it was a stone one, but she said it stayed hot longer than a rubber one and insisted that it be put at her feet – and then hurried back to the house. Grace was making porridge.

226

'Is she all right? Oh Questa, what's happened?'

'She's got 'flu, I guess,' Questa said. 'Give me a plateful of that stuff, Grace, and then I'd better bike into the village. Thank heaven the snow's gone, at least I can bike all right. I'll get Dr Speed to come up later. Old people take it bad, he said.'

'I can't think of Ellen as old, though,' Grace observed, spooning porridge into a dish. 'If you're going into the village, can you take Dickie with you? It'll save me a journey.'

Ever since the snow had cleared Grace had been riding one of the bikes into the village, with Dickie perched on the saddle. She left him at school and rode home, then did the return journey in the afternoon and picked him up again. It was quite useful, since it meant that she could do odd bits of shopping and was sometimes in the shop when something difficult to obtain – lemons, fresh onions, real coffee – was delivered.

'Yes, of course I'll take him,' Questa said readily. 'Unless you'd like to call on Dr Speed instead of me? Only with Ellen laid up I'll have to do her work as well as my own.'

'Yes, of course, I forgot,' Grace said resignedly. 'Pity though – I'll get soaked this morning and I washed my hair last night.'

It was no use believing that Grace would ever learn to be totally unselfish, Questa supposed now, rapidly eating porridge. She was still lazy, preferring watching to working, but she was good in the house, cleaning and dusting quite cheerfully and even cooking from time to time, though Ellen liked to do the cooking whenever possible.

'I makes an ounce do an 'alf pound job,' she was fond of remarking. 'You young'uns think times is 'ard; you doesn't know the 'alf of it!'

'You'll go, then?' Questa said, walking across and putting her porridge bowl into the washing-up water. 'Do get Dr Speed to call, don't let him just give her medicine. She is old, Grace, and she looks really ill; she's like a furnace, too, though she's shivering. I think we ought to bring her over to the house, that bedroom of hers is unheated and we can't do anything about it, there's no chimney or anything.'

'Mrs Pibble has a paraffin stove in the shop; it smells a bit but it does keep the place warm,' Grace volunteered. 'Didn't Ran say something about having one spare, over Christmas? I'm sure he did, you know.'

'Yes, he did,' Questa admitted. 'But nursing her from here is going to be so awkward. Everyone else has slept in the small parlour whilst they've been ill and we've managed. I can't see how we can see to her properly up there. What about nights, for instance?'

'Can't Alfie do nights? I agree we'll have to keep an eye on her during the day ...'

'Keep an eye! It's plain you didn't notice how often I was in and out of your room when you had it,' Questa said with only passing bitterness. 'Grace, Ellen and I kept your bottles hot, cooled your skin with tepid water when your temperature was at its worst, steamed you with Friar's Balsam every three hours when your chest was tight, gave you tablets, spooned that pink cough stuff into you, helped you on to the chamber pot ...'

'All right, all right, you were very good – marvellous, in fact. Both of you, Ellen too. So we'll have her in the small parlour, but how on earth are we going to get her there?'

It was quite a facer. The yard was flooded with rain, the rain showed no sign of stopping, and although Ellen was small and light, neither girl fancied trying to carry her down the stable-loft stairs.

'I'll fetch Alfie,' Questa said decidedly. 'Look, you go off to the village with Dickie and get the doctor, I'll finish the milking and go straight round to Atherton Hall and explain we need Alfie for an hour.'

'Right,' Grace said. Dickie wandered into the room with his hair on end and no shoes on his feet. 'Darling, whatever are you doing? Why aren't you dressed? When I left you you'd got everything on but your shoes and that was half an hour ago.'

'I can't get 'em on,' Dickie growled, flourishing his small brown walking shoes. 'My feets have growed in the night.'

'Oh Dickie,' Grace exclaimed, taking the shoes from him. 'You got those shoes soaking wet yesterday ... did you put them in front of the fire last night?'

'Yes; you said to do it.'

'Yes, but not for long, they must have been there for *hours*. Oh

Ques, they've shrunk and the leather's gone hard as nails, whatever shall I do?'

'Rub 'em with dripping and pray,' Questa recommended. 'I'm off to the cowshed. See you tonight, old Dickie.'

It was a devilish day by any standards. Not only did it rain continually – 'February fill-dyke', Ellen said sourly as Alfie carried her blanket-wrapped body across the yard – but everything that could go wrong did. Questa milked Nanny successfully, then remembered that she did not have the foggiest idea how to make goats' milk cheese. Whilst she was standing staring at Nanny and trying to remember at least the first steps, Nonny pranced up, knocked the bucket flying and butted Questa hard in the rear. Questa fell on the earth floor and skinned both knees, then tried to chase Nonny and fell again, this time doing both the bucket and herself considerable damage.

'I hate bloody goats,' she stormed, dripping milk all over the kitchen floor and dumping the dented bucket crossly in the sink. 'I'll sell the pair of them when spring comes ... if it ever does.'

'Why wait till spring?' Grace said mildly, bringing a cloth over and beginning to mop Questa's coat. 'Why not do it next week?'

Questa giggled and began to strain the remaining milk.

Grace said she would make some soup for lunch; Ellen's bread had been baked the day before, fortunately. The soup would have been nice, only it caught whilst Grace was trying her hand at a meat and onion pie, and although no one could call Ellen fussy she simply could not drink the soup.

'I casn't swaller,' she said wearily, when Questa tried to persuade her to take a little more. 'Don't pester I, lovie.'

Rebuked, Questa took the soup away and tried an onion boiled in milk, Alfie's suggestion. Like all the 'flu sufferers, Ellen slept a lot but when she woke she did manage to drink a little of the milk, though she waved away the onion saying that her throat had closed on her.

Dr Speed, harassed, weary, took a look down her throat and hummed a bit, then told Questa, in the kitchen, that Ellen had a very nasty throat with what might prove to be a quinsy one side.

'Give her lots of drinks, see she takes the tablets and the cough medicine, and when she's stronger, she can inhale the Balsam,' he instructed. 'Don't let her poison herself with those remedies she's got lining her kitchen, stick to what I've given you, with as much nourishment as she can get down.'

'They aren't poisonous, really,' Questa said timidly. The doctor was an official of sorts and as such, frightened her a bit. 'Some of them are really good; her lotion helped my bruises and my broken fingers, too.'

Dr Speed shrugged. 'All I can do is advise,' he said briefly. 'I'll come again in a week if she's no better.'

Questa sat up with Ellen for three nights, alarmed by the old woman's weakness, the way her flesh had fallen away so that her tiny face looked like a death's head, yellow against the white of the pillow. But on the fourth night Grace said she would stay up since she refused to allow Questa to kill herself, and Questa went up the stairs and collapsed into bed.

She slept deeply for a couple of hours, then woke. She sat up, staring out into the darkness. Where was she? What was happening? Shouldn't she be downstairs, looking after Ellen?

Then, of course, she remembered. She was in Grace's room and in Grace's bed, with Dickie in the room next door, no doubt sleeping soundly with Roma cuddled up close to him. They all knew that as soon as the light was switched off Roma jumped out of her box and nipped on to the bed, but provided she was not on the bed when they went in to wake Dickie next morning, nothing would be said. What was the point, after all, Ellen had remarked, in forcing the child to lie to save his friend?

Reassured, Questa lay down again. Outside, the wind moaned around the eaves of the house and now and then rain beat on the windowpanes. It was the sort of night when just being indoors was nice. But tonight, though she was terribly tired, she just could not sleep. As she lay there, her thoughts began to take charge, to prod at her conscience, her interest even, forcing her to think about a number of things she would far rather forget.

Daddy had behaved badly to Grace, though it was scarcely his fault that he had fallen in love with someone else. Because of it, Grace had disliked Questa for a long time, though now she accepted Questa as the person she was and not the person she had imagined her to be. After all, Questa had had nothing to do with her father's behaviour ...

How she wished she could just fall asleep and dream of Marcus. She wondered what he did when the snow was on the ground, whether he wore his leather leggings, his sturdy boots, the sheepskin cloak with the wool on the inside which he had told her about. Dreaming of Marcus was relaxing and instructive, too, she told herself drowsily; she could ask him about his vines.

She had always loved his vines, and now she thought that one day, when she had the leisure and the money to experiment, she too would have a go. She played with the idea of putting them behind glass, because surely the summers must have been hotter in Roman times, winters less severe? How else, she thought, could Marcus possibly have succeeded as well as he appeared to have done? But her father had cared nothing for weather or position or anything else, so far as she could see, he had simply wanted to see vines on that hill, and though he would never have his wish and had quite possibly forgotten all about vines once he fell in love with Fortunata, she could make it all come true if she asked Marcus the right questions and took his advice. Of course, it would mean using that expertise she had acquired in Italy and had done her best to forget. Pruning, feeding, spraying against mildew, thinning out, cutting back ... oh, it would be fun to grow vines, to make wine, to see the faces of the sturdy Shropshire farmers when she told them what she intended to do!

Excited by the prospect, she decided to go down to the library, which was a musty little room at the back of the house jam-packed with damp-spotted and out-of-date volumes, and see whether she could find anything on viticulture. Reading up on grape-growing might well get her off to sleep if nothing else.

Questa got out of bed and put on her dressing gown. She left her borrowed bedroom and padded down the stairs, hesitating when she reached the bottom. She had to cross the hall, then pass the kitchen. She had to walk right the way down a long, unlighted corridor, find the book she sought, if it existed of course, and then sneak back the way she had come. And it would be terribly cold downstairs judging from the wind which howled round the house and the rain which spattered her bedroom window.

She reached the hallway without incident however, carefully missing the creaking stair three from the bottom. She was tiptoeing past the small parlour when she noticed a line of light under the door.

Uncertain, she hovered, staring at it. Was Grace awake in there, alert and listening? Might the sound of Questa's padding footsteps send her into a panic, or worse, make her rush out into the storm to raise the alarm that they had burglars? Suppose, on the other hand, that Grace had fallen asleep and Ellen needed something, heard her footsteps, imagined that help was at hand ...

Questa sighed and walked quietly towards the small parlour. She opened the door very, very gently, just a crack. Grace was sitting up in the makeshift bed, reading. She was wearing her glasses. Questa knew Grace owned a pair of glasses but had never seen her wear them; they made her look quite different, sober, industrious, thoughtful, all the things Grace normally was not. But she looked up when the door opened and snatched the glasses off, peering towards the door, and Questa wondered how often she had interpreted what she now knew to be a short-sighted stare as a scowl or a withering glance. People, she thought, not for the first time; people are downright odd!

'Questa? Is that you?'

Grace's whisper sounded scared; how extremely vain she must be, to remove the glasses which would have allowed her to see, without peering, just who it was opening the door. Questa slid into the room and gave Grace a smile.

'Yes, it's me. I couldn't sleep so I came down for a hot drink and thought you might like one. Cocoa?'

Grace got carefully out of bed and drew Questa into the hall.

'Take a couple of aspirin with your hot drink, then you'll sleep like a baby,' she advised. 'You're over-tired, that's what it is. Sometimes sheer tiredness actually stops you from sleeping, you need something to knock you out. I've been longing for a drink for ages, but Ellen kept moaning in her sleep and muttering about the hens and her precious garden, so I didn't dare leave her.

However, she seems to have gone off at last, so I'll come and talk to you whilst you make us both some cocoa. I don't think she'll wake for a bit, but she's a lot worse than either Alan or I were. I keep telling myself what a tough old bird she is, but you can't help worrying.'

'She is a dear, isn't she? I don't know how we'd manage without her,' Questa said, spooning cocoa powder into two mugs. 'But if she's anything like you and Alan, she should begin to get better any day now.'

'And then we'll both be able to get some sleep,' Grace said, going to the larder for the jug of milk. She came back with the milk and a small bottle. 'Aspirins. Take them and sleep soundly.'

Questa took the aspirin and the cocoa back upstairs with her and Grace was absolutely right. After half the drink and two aspirin tablets she fell asleep and slept deeply and dreamlessly until morning.

Ten

Slowly, as time passed, Ellen began to recover. First she sat up in bed and sipped tea or warm milk when it was offered, then she ate a spoonful or two of soft food such as boiled onions – her favourite – or sweetened apple pulp. Her bright humour and common sense had never deserted her, but her voice regained its sharpness and she began to fret to go into the kitchen, to help out as she put it.

'Dr Speed said you weren't to do *anything* until he gave the word,' Questa reminded her. 'You've had us so worried, Ellen! Alfie's been frantic. He doesn't like our cooking the way he likes yours.'

'Ha! And what about me cows? Who's bin milkin' em, eh?'

'Me. I'm getting quite good, Alfie says. And Grace has been a brick, really she has, plugging away at the cooking and cleaning. And when you're up and about we aren't going to let you work so hard again, we hadn't realised … you aren't a spring chicken any more, Ellen, you must take things easier.'

'What about me goats' milk cheese, then? And me butter?'

'We tried,' Questa admitted. 'And we failed. You'll have to give us lessons in case you're ever ill again.'

Ellen grinned her familiar, nutcracker grin. 'Case I dies on you next time, you means! Well, well, best to be sensible. I'll give the pair of you lessons in dairy work soon's I'm up and about agin.'

'Lovely. I'm teaching poor Grace to milk the cows, though she absolutely hates it. I don't know if she'll ever be any good – she doesn't like the *feel*, she says. It gives her the jitters.'

Ellen snorted. 'Jitters! I'll give 'er jitters when I gets on me feet again! Still an' all, you've managed a treat, the pair of you. No quarrels? No fights?'

234

Questa thought back. She was sitting on the edge of Ellen's bed in the small parlour, with the afternoon sunshine warm on her face. Although it was only March there were already signs of spring in the garden. The snowdrops were over but crocuses were everywhere, forsythia blossom starred the branches – Dickie called it the scrambled egg tree – and the big viburnum bushes were spangled with balls of sweet-smelling pink and white blossom.

'Quarrels? Not many, anyway. Grace and I fell out once over who was to bike into the village to post letters, then Dickie and Grace had words when he wanted to go to school in his blazer and Grace thought he'd catch a chill and made him wear his winter overcoat, then Alfie told me off for feeding the pigs green potatoes, said it 'ud give them bellyache ... No, we've not argued overmuch.'

'What about Alan? I don't remember seein' 'im.'

'No, because when he did come, and he's only come once, he stayed in the village. Grace was afraid he might get re-infected so she told him to stay away, and I felt we'd enough on our hands without adding another visitor to our load.' She patted Ellen's small claw where it lay on the coverlet. 'You've been awfully ill,' she said gently. 'Iller than you realise, perhaps. But thank God you're better, now. We need you so much, Ellen.'

Ellen cackled again. 'Well, it's good to be needed when you're past eighty,' she said cheerfully. 'But you'd best get used to managin' on your own, lovie, for one of these days you're going to 'ave to see me off.'

'But not for years, I hope,' Questa said. 'You're a tough old bird, Ellen. Alfie said so a dozen times whilst you were ill and he was right. You pulled round.'

'Oh aye. But I daresay it's left me weaker'n I was. Now 'ow about a nice piece of buttered toast, eh, with some of me honey on? Me throat still likes honey.'

'I'll get it,' Questa said at once. 'Dr Speed's coming tomorrow some time, to say whether you're fit enough to get up. So eat as much as you can, then you'll be strong enough to totter into the kitchen for tea, perhaps.'

Sure enough, next day Ellen got up and had tea in the kitchen and the following day announced that she was going back to the coachman's flat over the stable.

'I wants me own place and Alfie wants 'is mum,' she said bluntly, when the girls begged her to stay a little longer, until she had her full strength. 'Bless you, lovies, you've been wonderful, but I wants me own little flat now I'm gettin' better.'

So when Alfie got home from work that night he found Ellen installed in her own kitchen with the fire burning brightly, a meal on the table, and Questa just delivering a bunch of daffodil buds which, she assured Ellen, would be in bloom in twenty-four hours once they got in the warm.

'Keep an eye on your mum though, Alfie,' she said quietly to him when he saw her out on to the loft stairs. 'She's not as strong as she thinks she is, Dr Speed said she must rest and start acting her age instead of taking everything on her own shoulders. We can do the meals – we've been doing them for five weeks – so she can concentrate on you and your place, and there's nothing much to do in the garden, or if there is, one of us will do it. Make her rest; we want her with us for years yet.'

'Tain't easy to mek Mum rest, or do anything she don't fancy,' Alfie said doubtfully. 'But I'll do me best, you know that. I'm mortal fond of the old bird.'

Crossing the yard again on her way back to the house, Questa suddenly wanted to see how the kitchen garden was looking. She pushed open the green door and viewed the neat beds, the little box hedges, the rich and crumbly earth, with considerable satisfaction. It would soon be time to start work in earnest here once more, and this year she meant to do most of the work herself because Ellen must not be allowed to dig and plant and sow. A little gentle weeding perhaps, on a warm afternoon, but not the kind of market-gardening Ellen had taken for granted for years.

As she emerged from the garden, Questa suddenly realised that, for the first time since winter set in and everyone got the 'flu, she was free to please herself. Tied neither by having to nurse people nor by the bitter weather, she was free to go for a walk in the grounds, wander in the woods, stroll by the mere. She could climb the hill behind the house and look at the terraces and decide how she would plant her vines, and choose the spot where she would have her sheep-dip. She could start looking round for a handyman to build her new pigsties and with her lambs all born – two sets of twins and all the rest big, healthy lambs – she could get Patrick to fence in another field for them. Soon she would visit Ran – she had not seen him since Ellen's illness – and ask his advice on when to begin enlarging her flock. She could pick flowers, clip hedges, mow grass.

Spring is wonderful, Questa thought contentedly, strolling across the yard. Soon I'll begin to see the results of all our hard work.

It was strange to sit down to table without either Ellen or Alfie, even stranger to see the small parlour as it should be and not littered with medicines, inhalants and all the paraphernalia of sickness. Questa had not lit the fire, there seemed little point in her having a warmed bedroom when she was used to a cold one, but she had made up the bed with clean sheets. Her dressing gown hung behind the door, her slippers were pushed under the chair, her candle stood on the washstand.

'You'll have to move upstairs one of these days,' Grace said, but she said it in a friendly sort of way, not critically, as she would have done once. 'Ellen was saying the other day that when Joshua's mother was alive she used the small parlour as her private sitting room. She did her sewing there, and arranged flowers and wrote in her day-book and sent for cook when the meals needed planning.'

'Well, for the time being it's my private sleeping room,' Questa said. 'You're probably right, I'll need to move upstairs one day. But not now, not yet.'

Dickie had followed them into the parlour and now he looked contentedly round him.

'It's a nice room. Questa can see the garden,' he observed. 'At night, when I wake up, I can see the moon and the tops of the trees, but Questa can see the garden and the flower beds.'

'Not when the curtains are drawn, sweetheart,' Grace said. 'And nor should you be able to see things … I always draw your curtains when I put you to bed.'

'If I wake up there's sometimes a little gap,' Dickie said. 'The moon puts a finger through and wakes my eyes up and then the rest of me wakes. I like it. And if it feels exciting and if I'm very awake I get out of bed and go and look out of the window and see the shadow-people on the lawn.'

'Shadow-people? Dickie, darling, what an imagination you've got! Do the shadows look like people, then?'

Dickie thought that one out, then clearly decided to humour his mother.

'Some shadows *are* people; my shadow is,' he said. 'Who's going to hear me read tonight?'

Dickie read a small piece from his *Radiant Reader* each evening, and whoever heard him read, then had to read him a story from the book of the moment. At present it was *The Just So Stories* and since Questa was halfway through the story of 'How the Elephant Got his Trunk' and enjoying it very much, with vague memories of having had it read to her when she was about Dickie's age, she volunteered for the job. Dickie read a passage about a but-ter-cup fai-ry, then Questa took the Elephant's Child on his journey to the great, grey-green, greasy Limpopo river whilst Dickie listened, absorbed, and let a skin form on the top of his milk.

When the story was finished she went upstairs with Dickie, who held his nose most of the way and shouted 'Led go, you're hurtig be!' at frequent intervals. She tucked him up in his small bed, left his nightlight on, for Grace was not only an enlightened parent, she also rather disliked the dark herself, and bade him good night.

'Don't draw the curtains *too* well,' Dickie mumbled round his thumb when she walked across the room towards the window. 'I like a little crack for the moon to show through.'

'All right.' Questa peered through the curtains, her nose almost resting on the glass. 'But there's no moon tonight, chick. It looks like rain again.'

She left the room and joined Grace in the kitchen for their

usual evening of small household tasks, talk and planning. Grace had gradually become interested in the reclamation of Eagles Court so that occasionally she would come up with a good idea which saved time, or money, or just effort. And the fact that there were two of them trying to make a go of it made it more fun as well as more rewarding.

On this particular evening they pored over Questa's plan of the kitchen garden. Whilst Ellen had been crossly convalescing, Questa had drawn up the plan, and in the end Ellen had got truly interested in it, seeing not just Questa's cockeyed attempts at drawing rows of strawberries or cabbages, but the reality which would one day result from such a plan.

She had made a great many suggestions and Questa intended to put most of them into practice. Questa had discussed with Ran how she should reclaim the fields and meadows: make haste slowly was Ran's favourite motto, but Ellen was quite the opposite. She wanted everything done at once and, since her illness, Questa had understood why. Ellen wanted to leave them reasonably self-sufficient when she had to go. Ideas that she must have nurtured hopelessly for years – peaches and apricot trees fanned out against a south wall, a thicket of raspberries and loganberries instead of her own demure couple of rows, asparagus beds piled with Scamper's contribution to the muck-heap – came tumbling out, and Questa could see the sense in all of them.

'The only thing lacking all those years was the money to buy the necessary stock and the labour,' Questa told Grace. 'Ellen's a born market-gardener, she understands the soil, the weather, the plants, everything. But there were only so many hours in her days, and she simply didn't have the cash to buy either stock or a labourer's time. We can, you know. Ellen says that even if we can't afford Bert full-time, we could use him for enough hours so that with what he makes up from his other job he's quite comfortable. And he won't mind, you know, if he spends quite a lot of his time in the garden and not doing farm work. All farm labourers can dig and mulch and weed. I reckon she's right and it will save Ellen. Plus he's happy to bring the cows in for milking each morning, and deal with the flock. So I think we ought to give it a try, don't you? Especially as we aren't ever going to keep sheep in a really big way.'

'Oh, are we going to sell the lambs, then?' Grace said in a disappointed voice. 'Dickie will be upset, he loves the little new ones, and I thought you liked them, too.'

'Good Lord, we'll keep the lambs, and buy more, next backend,' Questa said at once. 'But I don't want a huge flock; if we keep it down to say thirty ewes, that should do us. Ellen says Bertie can cope with a flock of that size and keep up with the gardening so long as he has casual labour to help him. Which is probably us,' she added with a chuckle.

So now, poring over their plan, they decided that they would go quite mad and ask Mary, who still came up from the village from time to time, to come up daily for a while to help Ellen with the housework and to do bits and pieces of cooking.

'If she helps Ellen with the meals and the housework, that would release both of us for the garden,' Questa planned busily. 'Don't worry, Grace, you'll like it once you get started. Not digging,' she added hastily, seeing the look of dismay on the older woman's face. 'Just hoeing and sowing, the sort of gardening you can do without getting your hands dirty.'

She crossed her fingers behind her back as she spoke, but Grace took the remark at face value and smiled gratefully.

'Oh, I wouldn't mind that ... not when it's sunny,' she said. 'And I enjoy feeding the hens and the pigs and I'm getting used to milking. When Alan comes down next he won't recognise me!'

'He said he'd spend Easter with us,' Questa said thoughtfully. 'I wonder how he'll shape with a spade?'

Grace laughed. 'Poor Alan! I don't know, but I can tell from your expression that I'm going to find out!'

Grace took off her spectacles – she had taken to wearing them in front of Questa – and went over to the Aga, where she made cocoa.

'See you in the morning,' she said, tucking her specs into her pocket and picking up her latest reading matter, a seed catalogue from Suttons. 'I'm going to make that violet bed Ellen told us about; with so much austerity around I should think people will be glad to buy scented violets next year.'

'I think you're right, which is why we're going to go in for asparagus beds and peaches,' Questa agreed, picking up her hot drink. 'Goodnight, Grace.'

She had not mentioned the fact that she intended to grow vines to anyone, not even to Ellen. She wanted to be sure that they had a chance before she said anything, and she could not tell until she saw Marcus again whether the wine from his latest treading had been good enough to sell as well as to drink at home, or whether he had decided to give up the idea.

Questa opened her eyes and was immediately aware that something was different. She usually found herself in the woods or the fields but – she blinked round her – she was halfway up the terraced hillside, amidst the vines.

And she was not alone. She was in the middle of a crowd, or so it seemed at first glance. All around her, figures were stooping over the vines, figures with big woven baskets already half filled with grapes. They were picking! It looked as though the vines were a success.

Beside her lay a big shallow basket. Hastily, Questa picked it up and bent over the nearest vine. The grapes were bursting with ripeness, they were a beautiful deep red colour overlaid with bluish bloom, and the swags were heavy, the vine leaves already tinted with autumn. She began to pick, glancing at the girl picking beside her. She was a lovely thing: slim, golden-haired, wearing a simple fawn-coloured tunic caught up on one shoulder with a big metal brooch. She was tanned to fawny-gold herself, bare-legged and bare-armed, and presently she turned and smiled at Questa.

'They're picking well, aren't they? We've had a good summer, of course, but even so, the wine should be delicious.'

'Yes, it's easy picking,' Questa agreed. She felt very odd; everyone but Marcus had always seemed unimportant, though she had exchanged vague greetings and the odd remark with a good few of the outdoor workers, now. 'Your basket is nearly full.'

'Aye, it is. I'll take it down presently and empty it into the cart. How's yours?'

'Oh, nearly empty. I've only just arrived,' Questa said.

The golden-haired girl chuckled. 'At a good time – they're about to bring the wineskin round.'

Questa followed her pointing finger and there, sure enough, was a tall figure with a wineskin in one hand: Marcus, looking more handsome and self-confident than ever. His companion, a shorter, darker man, carried a quantity of roughly made pottery mugs in a basket similar to the one Questa held.

The men reached her row, came along it. Marcus hefted the wineskin and poured into a mug, pointing out brusquely that the man holding the mug had missed grapes on the lower branches, then turned to the golden girl, beginning to smile, starting to speak ... and then his eyes moved along the row and he saw Questa.

He stopped short. Questa, too, stopped picking as their eyes locked.

'Questa! It's been a long time!'

'Yes, I know. We're planting vines in this year ... your grapes look good, Marcus, and pick easily.' It all came out in a rush whilst her eyes told a different story, a story of wanting him, missing him. She could read the same story in Marcus's dark eyes, narrowed against the brilliant light of the sunny September afternoon.

'We're doing quite well.' He said it with an indifference which barely masked his pride, his triumph. 'Men who laughed will laugh no longer ... the weight of the grapes, Questa! More than I dreamed to reap in their third year. The soil's just right, chalky, light, but with a certain something which lends a sweetness to each grape ... taste!'

He picked a fat grape, held it to her lips. She opened her mouth and felt his fingers touch her, felt heat and a strange longing stir within her, then the grapeskin burst and the juice flowed and she was laughing, astonished at the piquancy of the fruit, the generosity of the juice.

She spat the pips into her hand and thrust them into her pocket, then smiled up at him.

'Wonderful, Marcus. I hope I taste the wine one day.'

He looked along the row of vines, calculating. 'Oh yes, in a few months, a year perhaps. The servants will drink the *mezz vin* this year, of course, but we'll not start on it for another year, probably, and even then it'll be rough. The following year it will smooth down and the year after that it will begin to grow in richness and flavour. You must visit me then, dear Questa, and you may drink your fill. But come, we need to talk.'

He held out his hand. She put her basket down and took his fingers unhesitatingly. She, too, wanted to be alone with him and not out on this busy, colourful hillside with what seemed like a hundred pairs of eyes curiously watching their every move.

They went down the hill together, past the girls and the women, the young men and the old, all picking the abundant grapes and laying them carefully in the woven baskets. Below, a donkey stood patiently in the shade of a tree, waiting for the next load. Flies buzzed around the cart, settling on the patches of purple where the last lot of grapes had rested.

'Everyone's picking today; do you want to see the horses?'

'I'd love to.' Questa said.

They strolled on together, their heads close, not needing to talk.

'Here, take my hand,' Marcus said presently. 'This bridge isn't safe.'

She put her hand in his; it felt right there. The bridge they were crossing was no more than a couple of stout planks over an irrigation ditch. Furthermore, it was steady as a rock. Presently, as though he could no longer stop himself, he put his arm round her, pulled her close and drew her to a halt under some trees.

'Oh, Questa, I missed you.'

'And I missed you.'

'Mm, hmm. But not so much that you needed to see me, is that right? Things are better for you?'

Questa thought about it, gazing into his strong, beautiful face.

'Yes, things are better. And they're better for you, too, aren't they?'

She did not know how she knew this, she just knew it

suddenly. He looked so calm and self-confident, so much the man. Not at all like the centurion who had come into his inheritance and found himself divorced from the life of action he knew and loved, pushed into trying to make a success of agriculture when he neither knew nor cared about the land. This was a different man from that scowling soldier who resented the dependence of others, the abrupt abandonment of his life with the legions. Marcus knew what he was doing now, and he loved it. Loved the land, the people, his stock, and was determined to make it work for him.

But now he inclined his head, acknowledging the truth of her remark. 'Yes, it's beginning to come together. Even the workers – the girl you were picking with, for one – are on my side now, working for me and not against me.'

'She's pretty,' Questa said. It gave her a curious pang to speak the words. She saw herself suddenly, in her mind's eye – scrawny and thin, her dark hair badly cut, her skimpy cotton nightie with the torn hem ...

She looked down at herself. She was wearing a simple tunic garment in white, with a big gold brooch at the shoulder. She turned her attention back to Marcus, letting her weight lean slightly against him, tilting her chin the better to see his face.

'Yes, I suppose she is pretty, for a British-born slave,' Marcus said in an offhand tone which didn't fool Questa for one moment. He was a virile young man, he would have noticed the girl's body if not her looks. But perhaps – *perhaps* – he was too busy to take much notice of the servants. 'She's got nice hair, I grant you,' he added casually.

He has noticed; I wish I was beautiful too, Questa found herself thinking wistfully; she who had never cared tuppence one way or the other about her looks.

'Questa, I knew you'd come back, but why so long? Another twelve months, a full season, have passed since you were last here. Are things bad up in the hills?'

Questa shrugged. 'Things are good. Perhaps that's the trouble, Marcus. As you said, when I'm busy and happy I suppose I don't need you in quite the same way ... only that isn't true, it isn't!'

She flung both her arms round his waist and hugged him tight. 'I need you so badly, yet I can't come to you whenever I want. Oh, I wish I could explain!'

He cradled her in his arms, a hand stroking the length of her hair and continuing down her back, making her tingle with desire, love, all the sweeter emotions.

'You don't have to. Just come to me whenever you can and don't ever forget me, don't ever leave me.' He moved her so that he could look down into her face. 'I've never felt this way about a girl before. You aren't just important to me, Questa, you are essential. How this can be, when we see each other so seldom, I don't know, I only know it's so. Without you, I would not know such a deep, satisfying pleasure when I look around me at all this. Without you, it would mean nothing.'

His gesture included the vines on the hill, the woodland and pasture, the pond, even the horses grazing along the hedge, so close she could hear the snort of their breathing, the tearing tug as they crunched grass.

'I'm the same, yet you've never seen my estate,' Questa said. 'It's having someone else, someone who understands and cares, I suppose. But there's more to it than that; it's as if we were made for each other, Marcus. I do wish we could be together properly, for always.'

'We can. One day we will. One day you'll lie in my arms between silken sheets and we'll love one another and make a child together. When I have a son ...' he took her in his arms again, holding her tight against him. 'When *you* have a son, Questa, daughter of the hills, I hope that he may look a little like me!'

'I don't know much about sons, but the woman who shares my house has a boy. I like him very much. Yes, perhaps I would like sons ...' she drew away from him, smiling wickedly into his face. '... especially if they looked like you, dearest Marcus.'

He put his arm round her waist, squeezing her, then they set off towards the horse-meadow, walking awkwardly because of the difference in their heights but enjoying the closeness.

'You've not met my brother Gaius – a dreadful child, be glad he's three days' ride away, at Wroxeter, learning the martial arts

245

I learned at his age.' He chuckled. 'It'll put his nose out of joint when I marry; not that he'll care, he's made for the legions as I was … but the sun's already lower in the sky; I know you can't stay, you must get back home before dusk, but you'll come again? Soon, dear Questa? We'll take my horse and the little mare you learned to ride on and go up into the hills, with food and wine to make us a meal whilst the weather is fine. Thus it is that a man and a woman grow closer, learn each other.'

'I'll try,' Questa said, her breath quickening. She knew what would happen if they took a picnic up into the hills, miles from anyone. Did she want it to happen? How could she tell? She had never known any man other than Marcus and so far their intimacy had gone no further than kissing and some delicious cuddling. But it was not in her hands. If she could come, she would.

'Try hard,' he commanded. 'You don't want me to be forced to come and fetch you? Then try hard to come to me, Questa, daughter of Adamson!'

She laughed.

'Oh Marcus, I do love you! And I will try to come back soon.'

Home again, waking in the small parlour with the sun fighting its way through the curtains and falling warm across her face, Questa asked herself how she could feel so intensely in a dream. She wanted to be with Marcus, but she also wanted to be here, at Eagles Court. She was growing easier with Grace and fonder of her with every day that passed, though she knew that, in a sense, Grace was using her. And sometimes she felt sure that her dreams of Marcus had a meaning, a message, which she could not as yet interpret.

She also felt that falling in love had not been part of the plan, if it was a plan.

Love is strong though, stronger even than the tug of the land, the sweetness of friendship and shared rewards. She had only to remember the way Marcus's hands felt when they ran, hard and possessively, down the line of her back, the leashed strength of his body against hers, the way his mouth had gently persuaded her own, and she knew that she could not bear to think of life without him.

The question of why she continually dreamed of Marcus was still unsolved; she was not sure she even wanted to solve it. She was happy in her two worlds. She knew very little of what it meant for a man and woman to make a baby, but she had sat up night after night with her ewes to help the lambs into the world and she had taken Rosemary and Marjoram, the two sows, over to the hall and watched as the big, tusked boar served them. And when Marcus touched her and feelings she did not understand arrowed through her ... ah, but she loved him! Whatever he wanted to do was all right with her.

She lay for a little longer, wondering, worrying, but then her thoughts turned to other things, to the horses, the vines, to the promise of a day out with Marcus, in the hills.

Over the next few weeks it was impossible not to notice how distracted Questa was, how quick to anger, how unlike her usual self. Grace and Ellen exchanged puzzled looks and Grace grew defensive and began to work very hard without being nagged to do so.

There seemed to be no reason for it. The sun shone, the lambs gambolled in their lush meadow and the sows and their piglets, the hens and their chicks, improved daily and began to show the results of good feeding and careful husbandry. The calves grew sturdy and their voices deepened and they ate and ate and rushed to the gate whenever they saw a human being with a bucket.

Ellen was still taking things gently, but Questa had spoken to Bert and Mary from the village and both had agreed to work up at Eagles Court, though Bert had to give a fortnight's notice to the builder who was employing him as a labourer at present. And best of all, perhaps, the kitchen garden was flourishing, and Grace and Questa, between them, were keeping up with the work.

So why was Questa so unhappy? It was because she had been totally unsuccessful in her attempts to dream of Marcus, that was why. She went to bed early one night, late the next. She tried the thyme pillow despite her secret doubts of its efficacy. When she woke, having been nowhere at all, she got out of bed and padded round her property, but as soon as she got outside she knew that it was not going to be any good. She had always known that her dreams of Marcus were not entirely a matter of her will to see him again. Perhaps the need had to be twofold, perhaps Marcus had to want her as badly as she wanted him, she didn't know. All she knew was that planning to see him was useless; she might as well forget it and wait for fate to intervene, which it seemed remarkably reluctant to do.

And perhaps because her whole being now yearned for Marcus, she found she could no longer be content with things as they were. She went through each day in a daze, not of unhappiness precisely, but of what was almost indifference. Marcus dominated her thoughts, her feelings, everything. She *wanted* him, needed him, so why could she not go to him?

Ellen, on her feet again, though still shaky, waited a while and then took Grace to one side for a conference.

Questa, she said, was acting like a lovesick dairy-maid, and did Grace have any idea who ...? But Grace, of course, could only shrug.

'There's nobody, Ellen – you must know that quite as well as me! Alan's the only eligible male who comes anywhere near us, and he's a bit long in the tooth for Questa. As for younger men, well, so far as we're concerned they don't exist. No, whatever the trouble is, it isn't man-trouble. I wonder if she got the 'flu after all, but it didn't come out the way it did with the rest of us? She's pale, tired, depressed – I wouldn't be at all surprised if she were ill. She isn't sleeping well, I do know that, yet the other day she fell asleep in the middle of the afternoon, sitting on the kitchen doorstep taking her wellies off! Now I ask you, is that a natural way to behave if you're fit?'

Ellen sniffed but forbore to remind Grace that Questa walked miles, rode Scamper, dug in the garden and milked the cows, all without any signs of the distress which a sick person might have been expected to show. She decided, however, to tackle Questa direct. She waited until the two of them were alone in the scullery making cheese and continued placidly giving Questa instructions for a while and chatting idly of this and that. It seemed to her important to get Questa relaxed before she asked any pertinent questions.

'Now come along, lovie, give the 'andle a good old turn ... that's right, that's about it ... then give it a rest. And whiles we wait, you can tell me what's mekin' you go round like all the troubles in the world is on your shoulders ... no, 'tes worse'n that, 'tes as if you wouldn't care if the old world stopped spinnin', lovie.'

'I didn't know I was behaving like that, but now you mention it, I don't much care about things right now. Not even the garden. Well, it isn't that I don't care, it's just that it doesn't seem as important as it once was.'

'And Dickie? Grace? Your life at Eagles Court? Ain't that important, lovie?'

Questa sighed and gave her a sidelong look.

'Ellen, I used to have this dream and now I can't. If only I could have the dream again then I'd be all right, but something's gone wrong and I'm stuck here with no dreams. It's making me so unhappy!'

The last words were almost a wail. Ellen reached out a little brown paw and patted Questa's arm consolingly.

'A dream, eh? One of them dreams we talked about once?'

'A true dream! Yes, sort of. Oh Ellen, is there a way back?'

'Mebbe, lovie. How d'you fancy tekin' a picnic into the 'ills over there?' Ellen waved vaguely towards the familiar humped shapes of the Welsh hills.

Questa stared. 'What makes you ask that, Ellen?'

'Because you've 'ad that thyme piller a whiles, lovie. Best to use the yurb when it's new-growed. Only I ain't got no fresh wild thyme by me and it grows in abundance in the 'ills.'

'Oh, Ellen!' Ellen was pleased to see the girl's entire face light up, her cheeks flush with delicate, rose-petal pink. 'Oh Ellen, when can we go?'

'Tomorrer, if it's fine,' Ellen promised recklessly. 'We'll get Mr Atherton to come too, so's 'e can bring 'is car – Alfie'll drive as 'tes a Sunday. I'll pack a nice tea and we'll mek a day of it.'

'Oh, Ellen,' Questa said, 'you are so good!'

All her listlessness, all her indifference, had fled. Her cure, Ellen told herself, was as good as accomplished.

Eleven

'But why, Questa? Why traipse all that way when we could perfectly well have a picnic in the orchard? Why not wait till next week, when Alan's down? I don't understand you, really I don't.'

'Because we need a break, that's why,' Questa snapped at last, facing Grace angrily across the kitchen table. 'Anyway, you should be glad that Ran said he'd let Alfie drive us rather than complaining all the time.' She was cutting sandwiches and boiling eggs and washing watercress all at once, or trying to, whilst Grace moaned because her quiet Sunday was being interrupted by a picnic, when she had planned all sorts of interesting diversions such as washing her hair, giving herself a manicure and a pedicure, and putting a frill on to the hem of a summer dress to make it as New Look as possible.

Dickie, on the other hand, was on fire with excitement. Jumping from foot to foot, ordering Roma to sit, stand, roll over and die for the king until the poor dog was dizzy; demanding to be allowed to take his swimsuit one moment and a pair of skates the next, he was clearly going to enjoy his day whatever anyone said.

'We could have gone to the sea,' Grace said accusingly, 'Now that would have been fun – why don't we save the petrol this weekend and go to the sea next?'

Dickie stopped jumping and stood very still, staring at his mother. Like most children, he knew now was important, tomorrow might never come. But Questa leaned over and ruffled his hair before continuing to cut the loaf.

'Don't worry, Rickie-Dickie, we're going today, not next week. Mind you, if Alan wants to take us to the sea next week that would be very nice. Not that he will; he comes down here to relax, he's always telling us so.'

'Well, I think ...' Grace began, but her words were interrupted by Ellen stomping into the kitchen with a large basket covered with a tea-towel in one hand. She dumped it on the middle of the table, not heeding Questa's sandwich-making activities.

There y'are,' she declared, folding back the tea-towel to reveal a quantity of food and two dark brown bottles. 'One 'arvest cake, one 'unter's pie, one gallon of cider. That'll keep us goin' for a bit. Ha'nt you done them sandwiches yet?'

'Not yet,' Questa said. 'Grace is putting me off, moaning about next weekend.'

'*Next* weekend? Ain't this weekend enough for 'er?'

'Mummy wants to go next weekend instead of today,' Dickie said impatiently. 'But we're going today, *now*, aren't we, Ellen? Alfie's picking us up in twenty minutes, you said. It's a pity Uncle Ran can't come, but he's reading the lesson in church, and he's asked the vicar to lunch afterwards, he said. So you'll sit in the front seat, Ellen, by Alfie, and Mummy, Ques and me will squeeze into the back seat – squeeze, squeeze – with Roma on our laps. And Roma's going to be ever such a good girl, because if she's bad she'll have to walk home, Questa said,' he added warningly, stroking Roma's silky, pricked ears. 'And if she chews Uncle Ran's nice car she'll get a smack.'

'I 'opes you can all fit in the back,' Ellen mused, looking pointedly at the mound of food on the table. 'I thought I said I'd bring the grub.'

'Grub?' Dickie said. 'What's grub?'

'It's another word for food,' Questa told him. 'Ellen, for the millionth time, the doctor said you weren't to overdo it, you were gardening all of yesterday, and last thing you should have done is set to and cook. But thanks, and it looks delicious.'

Ellen grunted and Questa finished the last sandwich and turned to Grace.

'Pack them in greaseproof, there's a dear, whilst I go and change. It's so nice and warm I thought I'd wear my summer frock.'

Grace sighed but started to pack the sandwiches neatly and Questa shot out of the room and into the small parlour. Truth to tell, she was so excited and happy that she could, she thought, have flown to those blue and distant hills without having to borrow Ran's car at all.

Soon there was a pip-pip on a horn and everyone piled out of the kitchen, across the yard and into the Lagonda.

Alfie turned to grin at them and then jumped out and opened the front passenger door and the back one as well.

'Hop in, Ma, sit up wi' me, like Lady Muck,' he said. 'Come along, young ladies and gent, in wi' you.'

It was a comfortable car and the red leather upholstery smelt of polish and sunshine. Dickie sat between Questa and Grace at first, but Questa swopped with him because he couldn't see out, and willingly suffered Roma's rear paws dancing up and down on her knee as the dog strove to push her pointed black nose out through the half-open window. The weather was still lovely, the breeze of their going blew Questa's hair straight out behind her and made Grace exclaim with annoyance more than once as it blew across her face. But Dickie's excitement was infectious, as were Questa's high spirits. Presently Alfie began to sing and before they knew it they had all joined in, belting out songs at the tops of their voices, laughing, chattering, begging Alfie to slow down when a particularly beautiful area came into view.

'We want the open spaces above the tree-line,' Ellen ordered her son. 'Tek us as near as you can, lad.'

'The day is young,' Alfie said dramatically, then spoiled it by adding, 'You're goin' to 'ave to walk, Ma; I can't tek the car beyond the road.'

'Oh well, never mind. Find us somewhere nice to picnic,' Questa said. 'Anyway, we none of us mind walking.'

'I hadn't planned a route march,' Grace said sourly. She was still cross because the day she had intended to spend on beautification had somehow turned into an outing, Questa realised. 'If you're walking far you can leave me with Ellen. And Dickie's legs are too short for long distances.'

'Don't nag, Grace,' Questa said. 'Oh, look at that stream!'

'You can go further up than this yur, lad,' Ellen said however, when Alfie went to draw up by the water. 'Tek this lane ... I seem to 'member it come out 'igh... we'll look down on Eagles Court I reckon.'

They found their ideal picnic spot up the lane, just as Ellen had remembered. After about a mile the lane petered out, but a footpath continued under ancient oak trees with mossy, gnarled trunks, and there was a stream, sweet green grass and a bank covered in primroses.

'It's beautiful,' Questa gasped as they unloaded the car. 'Oh, the air is like wine!'

It was. Cool and sweet was the air beneath the fresh-leafed trees, with the faint scent of primroses wafted to them by the breeze. They set out their food and Dickie took off his shoes and socks. The tiny stream was crystal clear and tinkled along between mossy banks rich with hart's tongue fern, violets, wood anemones and kingcups. Even Grace seemed to relax as, one by one, they spread the car rugs on the grass and sat down. Ellen looked around her contentedly.

'Good's a sannytorium,' she said, rather strangely, Questa thought. 'I wouldn't mind a month of this.'

'Nor me,' agreed Alfie. 'Ma, you knows a thing or two.'

'Oh ah. Pass us the cider.'

Questa had packed Bakelite mugs and plates. Despite their contentment with their surroundings, they were all hungry – perhaps the air really did have something to do with it – and as soon as the baskets were unpacked everyone fell to and ate heartily, even Ellen, whose appetite had not fully recovered after her illness.

'Now we'll 'ave a nap,' Ellen announced. 'Nothing like a spot of shut-eye after a good blow-out. Dickie, go an' tek a look at the stream, see if you can find any fishes.'

Dickie, nothing loath, set out at once, and though Grace murmured that he must be careful not to drown it was hard to see how even the smallest child could accomplish such a feat in water no more than a few inches deep.

'He ought to learn to swim,' Questa remarked lazily. Oh, the warmth of the sun, the coolness of the breeze, the sweet freshness of the air up here in the hills! 'You said ages ago that he should, Grace. Why not teach him now, in that dear little stream?'

'I can just see me trying to give him lessons in six inches of water! Still, I daresay he'll be all right. Oh, but I'm so sleepy.'

'Me too,' Questa agreed. She opened her eyes and peered at the tiny flowers no more than an inch from her nose. 'What's that nice smell? Does it come from these little purple flowers?'

'Nay; them's violets. The smell comes from the wild thyme,' Alfie said, sitting up on his elbow for a moment and then collapsing bonelessly on his back. 'You're lyin' on a patch of it, gal. Eh, but I've not et so much since Christmas!'

'Mmm,' Questa said drowsily. 'I'm going to have forty winks.'

She remembered her father saying that; odd how little bits and pieces came back now and then, a remark, an expression, the way Daddy liked to settle back in his chair after Sunday lunch and have those forty winks that he regarded so highly.

Daddy. Just for a moment his face came clear in her mind, the blunt nose, the blue eyes narrowed against the smoke from his pipe, the way a wing of fair hair would flop across his broad forehead ... But then it had gone and another face superimposed itself upon her memory. Aunt Leonida, whom everyone had told her was the very image of her mother, Fortunata.

It's all coming back, Questa thought drowsily. Behind her aunt, in her mind's eye, was the first farmhouse where Aunt Leo had taken her, thinking it safer than Rome. She could see Maria, the farmer's wife, standing in the doorway of the wine cellar, supervising the treaders, making them step first into a bucket of cold water and wash their feet, then watching them closely as they stepped up into the long wooden trough already laden with grapes. Questa had done her share of the treading, of course, and Aunt Leo. Thinking about it really brought it back; the strange, slippery feel of the grapes underfoot, the juice squirting between your toes, the stickiness which you had to wash off before you went out of the cellar. And Aunt Leo squeaking because she hated the feel of the pips and the sweetness of the grape juice which came out through the spigot and could be drunk by those who had toiled long and hard at the treading.

I was happy, then, still believing that Daddy would come for me, still seeing the war as more adventurous than sinister, Questa reminded herself. That first farm, with Aunt Leo to keep me company, was more fun than most things, and there had been other children of her own age, Rena and Paolo. As well as working hard, they had done more childish things: they had sung rude songs, played around by the well when they were sent to carry home buckets of water, nicked bunches of grapes or a couple of ripe tomatoes to eat as they sat on the crumbling old wall in the sunshine, waiting for something to happen.

But then something had. Aunt Leo had gone shopping in Fidenza, the nearest big town. Questa had gone too, with a list of necessities for Maria. Planes appeared in the sky, children screamed, people fled. Questa and Leo ran. Leo fell. Questa, panic-stricken, had run on, out of the open street into a covered market, seeing her aunt lying still, then struggling into a sitting position, rolling over the better to get up ...

She knew what was coming, tried to block it ... failed. She saw again the arcaded square, the colourful stalls of the weekly market, the well, pigeons strutting.

Then the colossal explosion, the pile of rubble which once had been a smart shop, and Aunt Leo's face, quiet, as though in sleep, the long dark lashes lying still on the sallow cheeks.

'She's dead, my child,' a black-robed priest said. 'Your mother? No? Ah, your aunt, I see. I knew you were related, the resemblance is striking. Well, you'd best go home and tell your parents; there's nothing you can do here.'

And now, remembering Aunt Leo for the first time for many years, Questa saw that peaceful dead face, the black hair shining through the dust even then settling on it. Aunt Leo was pretty, but once I looked sufficiently like her to cause a man to think us mother and daughter, Questa thought. Oh, I *did* love Aunt Leo – I'm glad I've remembered her again; now I can remember her with love and thank her in my head for all those many kindnesses. And mourn her in my heart.

Remembering Aunt Leo was like suddenly finding a long-lost relative; she felt warm and loved, no longer quite so alone in the world. Questa sniffed at the delicate, herby smell of the wild thyme, yawned, sighed, and fell asleep.

She woke simply, with the sunshine still on her face, the cool breeze still caressing her. Even the smell of thyme and the faint scent of primroses was still there, yet she was sure, she *knew*, that she was not in her own time. It had happened! After all her strivings to dream again it had happened when she least expected it, when she was relaxed and calm. She was in the dream and Marcus must be near.

She opened her eyes. She was lying on a soft patch of grass on a little ridge, high on a hillside. She could hear no voices, see no one, yet she was sure that people were not far off. She rolled over and sat up, staring with great care all around her. Nothing. No one. She was up very high, far higher than she had climbed with the family. She stood up and looked across, and saw what she searched for.

Marcus's villa. Looking calm and serene in the sunshine, it lay there, across the valley, for all the world like a model of a little Roman villa set down in rolling countryside for her amusement.

She had been right then; this was the dream and presently she would find Marcus. She began to climb, thinking that she would get the best view from higher up. The hill was steep and very soon she came out of the trees and on to what looked like a heather moor. There were gorse bushes growing amidst the heather, and rocks pushed their granite noses out of the ground-cover. A bird of prey flew overhead, eyes fixed, wings at the hover. Somewhere a mouse squeaked and the bee-hum filled her head.

She walked on dreamily, downhill now in the gentle spring sunshine; she had almost reached the foot of the hill when she saw a movement through the trees to her right. She stopped, squinting against the play of sunshine and shadow. *Was* that movement or just a trick of the light? She could just make out, through the silvery treetrunks of a copse of birches, a small glade, sun-kissed, grass-grown. She entered the trees and knew that Marcus was near. She went quietly, though, with care. She would surprise him, for a change, see what he thought of her woodcraft. She reached the edge of the birch copse and peered through into the tiny glade.

He lounged on the grass, as beautiful as she remembered him; one hand was behind his head, the other ...

She stayed where she was for one long minute, as though turned to stone. The other hand lay on the smooth, flat belly of the golden-haired girl who had talked to Questa in the vineyard. She was naked. And even as she watched, Questa saw that strong and sensitive hand, the hand that belonged to the only man she felt she had truly loved in her entire life, move caressingly down across the girl's sweet, sun-kissed flesh.

She could not move, not even then. But she could close her eyes. Indeed, they closed of their own accord, in pain and revulsion, and she screwed her lids up tight, tight, and wished herself away from here, anywhere but here, in the darkest nightmare of her life, anywhere where she would not have to watch the man she adored making love to another woman.

She woke with a start to find herself lying on the thyme-scented grass, with Grace nearby and Alfie sitting up and advising Dickie, in a low voice, to paddle along a bit, to where it was deeper and his jam-jar might catch a tiddler perhaps, or at least a tadpole.

She felt nothing; no pain, no anguish. That would come later. Right now she just felt numb.

Afterwards, Questa did not know how she got through the rest of that picnic. Yet get through it she did, moving in a daze, responding to questions and suggestions only after what seemed like a perceptible pause during which she re-aligned her thoughts to whatever had been said.

And nobody noticed, though she felt that Ellen understood. It was difficult to explain in what way she was supporting Questa because she neither said nor did anything unusual, but her steady, commonsensical strength was like a strong breakwater, keeping back the tide of disillusion and despair which beat against it, wanting to roll in and swamp Questa for ever.

They even picked the thyme. Why not? I never really believed the pillow brought the dreams and anyway I needn't use it, Questa told herself drearily, obediently filling the bag Ellen had given her. She tried to eat and was astonished by the sheer impossibility of something she had always taken for granted. No saliva would come into her mouth, she could not swallow the bread or the cake or even the fruit, though she drank several mugs of tea.

After tea they paddled and walked to the top of the ridge and looked down on Eagles Court, small below them, nestling against its hill.

'Let's go home, now,' Grace said. 'Dickie must be tired and you look all-in, Questa.'

There was concern in her voice but Questa could not respond to it.

'I am,' she said flatly. 'I'll go to bed early, I think, after I've seen to the animals.'

But what did the animals matter, for God's sake? What did anything matter? She sat between Ellen and Dickie in the car and when Ellen pressed Questa's head on to her shoulder she pretended to fall asleep. Instead she sat there, willing herself to think of something, anything other than Marcus, whilst around her the others talked, joked, said again what a perfect day it had been, how they must do it more often.

'Learning to relax is almost as important as learning to work,' Grace said at one point. 'When Alan comes down we really should try to have a day at the seaside ... oh, I do like to be beside the seaside!'

As if on cue, Ellen's thin soprano and Alfie's bass roar joined in, with Grace catching up belatedly on what it seemed she had said by accident:

> Oh I *do* like to be beside the seaside,
> Oh I do like to be beside the sea.

Questa's head raised itself slowly off Ellen's thin and bony shoulder. She remembered the song! When she had been very young her father had sung it to her and later she had joined in as they made their way to the station, to the train which would take them to the seaside. At least once every year and sometimes twice they had caught a train at Liverpool Street station and gone miles and miles through beautiful, flat, watery countryside until they finally reached their destination: a small terraced house in Cromer where a fat fisherman's wife let her two front bedrooms to visitors and made them strange but delicious food – brown shrimps with bread and butter, crab and salad, hollow biscuits and cheese, samphire in a pot in the middle of the table, eaten cold as a garnish or hot on tiny pieces of crisp buttered toast. She could remember the woman's name, Mrs Carter, and see again the bedroom with the wide window-seat overlooking the narrow cobbled street below. She could even visualise the pictures on the walls: an amateurish oil painting of the lifeboat being launched in a gale, a print of a fat Victorian girl cradling a lapful of kittens and a black-paper silhouette of a pretty lady with a retroussé nose and ringlets. The lady was Mrs Carter's great-grandmother and was much admired, she told Questa, by all her summer visitors. It had given the small Questa a lovely, warm feeling of fellowship to know that, when she reluctantly left Mrs Carter's front single at the end of her fortnight's holiday, another little girl would move in and put her teddy on the wide windowsill and her bucket and spade in the curtained alcove. She would lay her pyjamas on the clean pink counterpane and then stand with her nose inches from the silhouette, loving that dainty profile, those prodigious curls.

> Oh I do like to stroll
> Along the prom, prom, prom,
> While the brass bands play
> Tiddley om pom pom!

Another voice joining in this time, a small, uncertain voice. Her voice! She remembered the words; just for a moment she could see her father's fair face, the way he looked when his mouth opened to sing and he tried to smile at the same time. Oh, it was coming back, it was all coming back! She remembered Mr Carter, coming in from fishing still reeking of his catch, his jersey covered in fish-scales and a couple of crabs or a gurnet – odd, angry-looking fish – held casually in one huge, spadelike hand.

'Hello there, littl'un,' he would roar, red-faced and loud-voiced from years of facing into and shouting against the strong winds of the east coast. 'You gonna lead the singin' when you've et your tea? Thass one of these hare fellers tonight ...' waving a crab or a gurnet under her nose, 'which d'you fancy, hey? Best speak out, do you'll git neither!'

And after tea, when she and friends she had met came in from the beach, Mrs Carter would take her knitting and her old upright chair on to her front step so she could chat with the neighbours or any passer-by who took her fancy, and Mr Carter would sit out of doors too, and sing seashanties with great verve and at great length, urging his neighbours between songs to 'Give us a toon, bor, doon't mek me do all the wark!'

She could see her skinny, scratched, sandy legs, crossed under her, as she settled between the two of them. Close by the front door would be Mr Carter's catch in a huge wooden barrel, sea-fresh still and sometimes sluggishly moving, which he would sell to holidaymakers or townsfolk as they passed by on their way to or from the beach. Questa would shell peas, or top and tail gooseberries, anything to be useful, and enjoy the slow, broad Norfolk dialect of the Carters and their friends, the sharper speech of Londoners and city dwellers, the envious glances of small day-trippers, trailing wearily up from the beach to the waiting charabancs, envying her the right to sit there and shell peas, knowing she would wake up here tomorrow morning with a day of sand and sea ahead, whilst they, at home once more, woke to the dull routine of an inland town or city.

All that, from a song! All those memories, fugitive for so long, suddenly back, hurting yet comforting. She would remember it all one of these days; there would be no blank patches, no drifting, infuriating fog.

The car stopped. Everyone scratched, stretched, yawned and said how much they wanted a nice hot cup of tea. Dickie was asleep on Questa's lap, having succumbed during the singing. He was tenderly lifted out by Alfie and suddenly Questa was two people at once: herself, watching, and Dickie. She could remember being lifted out of a car, drowsy, half awake, skin hot from sun and dry from the salt water. She must have been very young indeed, for she could even smell a sort of milky smell, feel someone's soft woolly jumper against one cheek, the comfort of familiar arms. It was all there, waiting for her, that rich, forgotten past. All she had to do, it seemed, was to let her mind take its time and it would remember everything.

And Marcus?

261

Making her way into the kitchen, she gave a mental shrug. She would learn to live without him, in the world she was beginning to love so much. That was the sensible, grownup thing to do.

'Want some cocoa, lovie? That's my girl, git you to bed an' I'll bring it in to you.'

Ellen's little brown face was drawn with fatigue though; the day had taken it out of her, Questa saw. So she forced herself back to the present, to the kitchen, cluttered with the detritus of their picnic, the stove clinking and settling, and Dickie, barely awake, sitting in the big armchair with his knees drawn up, waiting for his hotwater bottle, for the nights were chilly still.

'Thanks, Ellen, but I'll make some cocoa and bring it up to you for a change! Go on, off with you. I was tired but I slept in the car and now I'm fine. The kettle's on – I'll give you ten minutes to get to bed!'

Ellen chuckled and shook her head.

'What a girl you are, lovie! Well then, I'm off. See you presently.'

With Grace carrying Dickie off to bed, Questa had the kitchen to herself. She looked round it, slowly and deliberately. She loved the place! All right, so she had loved the Marcus of her dreams more – the pain stirred in her breast – but she had lost him, so she had better make the most of what she had left. And that wasn't so bad! She and Grace were getting on much better, the place was beginning to show that, with hard work, it could flourish and repay them for their efforts.

Then there was Ellen, who understood so much. And Ran, who spared no effort to see she did right by the land. And Alfie, coddling her pigs in his own time, since his working life was spent at the Hall. And Alan, beavering away in London to find Uncle Joshua's money and sell anything which might benefit her. And last but by no means least, Dickie, the little boy who would grow up here, as her father had grown up, and who was already fond of her, and loved the Court. So why was she aching? Why did she feel so alone?

She made the hot drinks, put some biscuits on the tray and carried it across the yard, up the stairs and into the coachman's flat. Alfie grinned at her.

'Nice work,' he said cheerfully. 'Mum's in bed; you trot through wi' that whiles I mend the fire.'

Ellen accepted her drink, leaning back against her pillows in the creaking brass bedstead.

'Thanks, lovie,' she said. 'We'll 'ave that piller ready for you by this time tomorrer.'

'Thanks,' Questa said politely. 'Now go to sleep, Ellen. Tomorrow is another day.'

Ellen's eyebrows shot up. 'So? What med you say that, lovie?'

Questa smiled. 'I don't know. I expect it was one of the things Daddy used to say to me, if I wasn't too pleased with things. Look, today has been tiring and it's not that long since you were ill; why don't you lie in tomorrow and I'll bring you your breakfast in bed?'

'I'll be up and about as usual,' Ellen said, but she said it absently, her eyes fixed on Questa's face. 'What's the matter, lovie?'

'Nothing that a good night's sleep won't cure. But I've grown up a lot today,' Questa said. 'See you in the morning, Ellen.'

She left. Behind her, she sensed Ellen's troubled gaze, but what could she do or say? There were no comfortable words, not yet at any rate. She had to come to terms with losing her lover before she had even had him ... just as Grace had, all those years ago. But knowing that Grace had suffered this same pain did nothing to lessen Questa's very real distress. Marcus was the only person with whom she had shared her inmost feelings and secret desires. He had proved unfaithful, unworthy, so now she turned in on herself, wanting to find a cure for love rejected, not a fellow-sufferer.

When she lay in her bed and saw, through the window, the new moon shining, she began to think a little more kindly of Marcus. He had begged her to go back and she hadn't been able to, and since Marcus was only human, he had needs, as a man, which she could not fully understand. So she should think of his liaison with the other girl not as a love-affair but as a physical necessity, necessary because Questa had let him down.

She examined the argument from all angles, and could find no serious fault in it. If a nice young man came along and wanted

263

to marry me what would I do? Questa asked herself, staring at the ceiling above her head. But it was unanswerable, because she knew no other men, wanted no other. She could not imagine anything apart from shyness and a painful self-consciousness coming from any other liaison; she knew she was plain and unlovable, so any man other than Marcus who tried to make love to her would be doing so for the wrong reasons; for her land, her meagre possessions. And besides, if a man touched her ... she remembered the cellar and shuddered away from even the thought. The pain and humiliation she had suffered that night could scar her for ever, if she let it. She would never, *never* want to marry, never want a man's body near hers!

Yet Marcus had been different. He had been almost a part of her, someone who cared deeply yet loved her too well to force attentions on her which could only be unwelcome. He had waited until his attentions were not only welcome to Questa but actively desired. He must have known that her resistance was crumbling because he was a man who had known women. She did not know how she knew this; she just knew it. Yet for all his experience, he had been as gentle and tender with her as though he knew, in his own body, her shrinking, could understand her fears and dreads.

She turned her face into her pillow on the thought, and wept. There could be no other, not for her. Just Marcus Augustae, son of Tiberius, who had been her lover only in her dreams.

Apparently the night's rest had done Ellen good, for next morning when Questa came into the kitchen for breakfast, feeling as though she had not closed her eyes all night, there was Ellen, presiding over a large saucepan full of porridge and another, smaller one of boiled eggs.

She looked up as Questa came in, then said without preamble: 'Alfie wants an 'and wi' the pigs. I give 'im 'is breakfast earlier but 'e ain't gone to work yet. Says one of the sows needs a dose of summat ... you go on, I'll save your grub.'

'Oh! Yes, all right, but what about the milking? Is Grace about yet?'

'I woke 'er,' Ellen said with a certain satisfaction. 'She'll see to it if you'm still busy. Get a move on, lovie, Alfie ought to 'a bin at the 'all ten minute ago.'

Questa hurried out, snatching a slice of bread as she went. Alfie was so marvellous with pigs, he could recognise the signs of trouble before they had begun to do damage, so whatever was wrong with her gilts would soon be treated. And it wouldn't take long to dose a pig, so she'd be able to give Grace a hand with the milking. Best to keep busy, she thought grimly, slipping inside the piggery. That way you didn't have too much time to think useless, painful thoughts.

Left alone in the kitchen, Ellen dished up the porridge and carried the eggs over to the table, slipping each one into its cup and then transferring them to the oven where they would stay warm until the others came down.

She wanted to talk to Grace, had been meaning to do so ever since that nasty attack of 'flu, but somehow the chance had just never arisen. Questa and Grace were often together, Dickie hung around, Ran came over or Alan was spending the day ... but she must do it before Grace went off on the holiday she planned, otherwise something might go wrong and if that happened she, Ellen, would never forgive herself.

Dickie clattered down the stairs whilst Grace was only just crossing from her room to the bathroom overhead. Ellen heard the pad of her feet and then the sound of the bathroom door closing. She smiled at Dickie. He wore dungarees and a checked shirt today, and had a big smile on his face.

'Ellen! It's sunny ... I'm going over to Uncle Ran's, he's going to let me try the fat pony today!'

'Yes, lovie, and he wants you there early,' Ellen said mendaciously. 'You can git a lift wi' Alfie, he's over in the piggery wi' Questa. Gobble that egg, now, don't keep 'im waitin'.'

She did not mention the porridge; Dickie played games with his porridge. There were the marsh warriors who used the milk-paths, whilst the bog people followed the honey trails... it could take that boy a year an' a day to get a bowl o' porridge down 'im, Ellen reminded herself.

'Oh, goody!' Dickie, bless him, picked up his egg, wrapped a slice of bread round it, and headed for the back door. 'See you for lunch, Ellen!'

'Aye, unless Mrs Wozzname offers you to stay,' Ellen called back. 'We shan't worry, we'll guess if you ain't 'ere by noon.'

Presently, Grace came downstairs. She was wearing pale blue cotton trousers and a matching shirt and she was barefoot. Even to Ellen's prejudiced eyes – Ellen thought blondes cold – she looked very lovely with her ash-blonde hair tied back with a blue chiffon scarf and her face innocent of make-up and shining with soap and water.

'Morning, Ellen, where's Dickie?'

'Mornin'. Grace, I bin meanin' to 'ave a few words. Seems now's as good a time as any.'

Grace, who had taken her bowl over to the stove and was ladling a very small portion of porridge into it, immediately looked wary. And well you might, my lady, Ellen thought, not dissatisfied. Mebbe you've fooled Questa, and that lummock Alan in 'is pinstripe suit, but you ain't fooled old Ellen, not for one moment you ain't.

'What on earth can you want to talk to me about, Ellen? But carry on; I daresay I can eat and listen.'

She sat down at the table. Ellen ladled herself out a bowl of porridge and sat down opposite her.

'You must 'a noticed Questa ain't too comfortable, right now,' she started. 'She's workin' 'ard and enjoyin' life, but there's suffin' missin', and she knows it.'

'What?' Grace said baldly. 'D'you mean a man, Ellen? Because if so, you're way out. What you've never had you never miss, and Questa's never so much as looked at a bloke. But I, on the other hand, know what a woman's life could be like, and I do miss it.'

Ellen nodded slowly, spooning in porridge.

'That's very open of you. And that's what I want to say – from the look o' things, you're a-goin' to 'ave to choose.'

Grace waited whilst the silence stretched, trying to force Ellen to enlarge on what she had said. Finally her nerve broke and she spoke.

'Choose? I don't know what you mean.'

266

'Oh ah, you've more'n a notion. Alan's doin' all right, ain't 'e? Nice little 'ome, nice little business, an' you know 'e'll likely pop the question, you know 'ow 'e feels about you.'

'Oh, I *see*! You mean I'll have to choose whether to marry Alan and lose my independence or stay here, with Questa. Yes, that's fair enough, I shall have to make that decision if Alan does ask me to marry him. But it's very much my choice, Ellen, and since Alan hasn't actually asked me yet ...'

Ellen simply shook her head; slowly, sadly, definitely. She waited until Grace's words petered out before she spoke.

'No, me dear, that ain't what I meant. I meant you'll 'ave to choose between stakin' a claim for the lad or keepin' your mouth shut an' marryin' Alan. Because you know you can't do both, don't you? And there's no denyin' Alan wouldn't like it if 'e knew why you'd come down 'ere, would 'e? A straightforward sorta bloke, Alan, if a bit doolally-dally an' lah-di-dah. Because you've deceived 'im, there's no two ways about that.'

'I don't know what you mean! How could I possibly stake a claim for Dickie, and to what?' Grace shook her head and glared, but her eyes were shifty and her lower lip trembled. 'If you're trying to upset me, Ellen, you've succeeded. I don't want any more breakfast, I'll go straight out and get on with the milking.'

She would have got up, but Ellen's brown claw shot across the space between them and clamped down on Grace's wrist. She said, softly, 'Sit down!' and fixed her eyes on Grace's with all the power at her command in them.

Grace sat back. Her face was flushed and her eyes darted about as though seeking a way of escape, but she made no further move.

'Look, me dear, I'm sorry for you in some ways, but it's greed got you into this mess an' you've got to give up one or t'other, either your 'opes for the lad, or your 'opes of marriage. What'll it be? Eh? Because I tell you straight, the day you marries Alan without renouncin' any claim to this place, I tells what I knows.'

Grace leaned forward. 'What *do* you know, Ellen? You may guess, but what proof have you?'

'The proof's in your little lad's face, me dear. And gettin' stronger every day. That Questa, she's a good gal, if she knew,

I'm not sayin' she'd step down, but she'd make things right for the lad, see 'e got a share, like. On'y you wouldn't be content wi' that, I'm thinkin'. You'd want it all.'

It was Grace's turn now to shake her head.

'No, Ellen, not any more. That was why I came at first, to let her do the work and then tell her … but I couldn't do it, not now. I'm fond of Questa and so's Dickie. Besides, although what you say is true – Dickie is the spitting image of Charles at his age, I've got photos to prove it – I don't even have a marriage certificate any more. The registry office was flattened, Charles's house was bombed, it was just luck that I wasn't there at the time.'

'Any witnesses?'

'No one either of us knew, just two people off the street, a soldier and a cleaner I think it was. We kept it quiet, you see, because Charles wanted to tell Questa himself. I thought she was dead, I just humoured him by pretending I thought she'd come back. When she turned up last year I was devastated, at first. And the will, Ellen – he never changed the will, he left everything to her, not so much as a postcard came to me.'

'The will would've bin made long afore you come back into 'is life,' Ellen said softly. The expression on Grace's face was almost frightening in its bitterness. 'Charles 'ad 'is faults, that I do 'ave to say, but we won't go into that, eh? You knows better'n ever I could what they was. Howsomever, 'e din't 'ave a mean bone in 'is body, 'e would 'a give you money, anything. He'd 'ave provided for you, if 'e could.'

'Yes, I hope he would. And he never knew about Dickie, because he was killed before I could tell him. Oh, Ellen, what a mess it is! And I can't tell Alan, he'd be … upset. So I do see what you mean when you say I've got to choose. I like Alan enormously, but I don't know about living with him, what that would be like. You see, Charles wasn't with me for very long and Simon – yes, I did marry Simon Syrett – got himself killed six weeks after the wedding, so that wasn't much help.'

Ellen tutted, but her grip on Grace's wrist relaxed.

'Got himself killed, me dear; that's no way to speak of the feller! If 'e'd 'ad 'is way 'e'd be 'ere today, like as not.'

268

'Yes, I suppose I was being a bit unfair, but I only married Simon so that there'd be someone for me when the baby was born. He was nice-looking but I didn't know him all that well ... oh Ellen, what am I to do?'

'Foller your 'eart,' Ellen said with uncharacteristic sentimentality. 'What does your 'eart say, me dear?'

'My heart withered and died the day I got the telegram saying Charles was dead,' Grace said. Slow tears filled her eyes and trickled down her cheeks. She had never looked lovelier, or more forlorn. 'There's nothing there any more, Ellen, except a desire to be safe, with enough money to be comfortable and good prospects ahead for Dickie.'

'Aye, I can understand that. And what did you plan to do, me dear, when you fust come to Eagles Court?'

Grace shrugged and her evasive look reappeared.

'Oh, watch for an opportunity to push Questa over a cliff, so that I could tell everyone that Dickie was the real heir, and the authorities would have had to help me to prove it instead of hindering me at every turn. Only then there was so much hard work to do, and I didn't understand any of it, so I thought I'd let Questa get the place straight and then push her over a cliff. Only I got to like her, and I knew Charles would never have forgiven me if I'd hurt her, and anyway I wouldn't *really* have pushed her over a cliff, not in real life. And now, of course, there's Alan.'

'So? What'll you do? Come clean? Or forgit who fathered the boy?'

'I still don't know what to do for the best,' Grace said distractedly, literally wringing her hands. 'Don't bully me, Ellen! I'm awfully fond of Alan, but I love this place and so does Dickie. And as you say, I can't have both. But we're going off for this holiday, we may even go over to Ireland so that Alan can show me where his family came from originally, and surely, in two weeks or more, I'll make up my mind?'

'Oh ah,' Ellen said. 'Well don't forgit, me dear. You can't 'ave it both ways – I'll see to that.'

'I know you think it's silly, you've said so a dozen times ... no, forty or fifty times! But it's something I badly want to do, to see the hill hung with vines, like ... like in Italy.'

'Heaven knows, I never interfere with what you're trying to do at the Court,' Grace said untruthfully, 'but this is just a waste of time and effort – money, too. It'll cost the earth to get the vines brought in from France or somewhere, you know it will.'

The two girls were in the kitchen garden picking blackcurrants, and something in the way the bunches hung, or their blackness, or the smell of ripe fruit, had started Questa thinking about her grapevines again; and, unfortunately, talking about them too. She had dosed the pigs with Alfie's help, milked the cows, gone over to Ran's place and admired Dickie's bumping progress on the fat pony, and now Grace, who had been quite placid of late, had suddenly decided to be actively against Questa's plans for a vineyard which, naturally, had made Questa even more determined.

'I don't know what it will cost,' she said now. 'But I won't start by planting out the whole hill, I'm not that stupid. I'll get to work on the terracing first and when it's dug over and manured I'll put in a score or so of plants ...'

'Just digging up there will be next to impossible, because it's so steep,' Grace pointed out. 'Patrick won't be able to get the tractor up there, you know, so it'll have to be dug the old-fashioned way, with a spade. You'll end up doing it yourself, and you do too much already.'

'If I don't mind, why should you?' Questa said. 'Anyway, I shan't plant the vines until November and October's quite a quiet month.'

'Quiet?' Grace snorted her disbelief. 'What about picking the apples and pears? And the ordinary ploughing? And top-dressing the grass or whatever it is you were talking about the other day? And you promised to help Ran with his wheat.'

'Oh, that! He's got a combine harvester, I want to find out how it works, but he'll cut a good deal earlier than October, I can tell you!'

'Hmm. What does Ellen say?'

'Ellen knows nothing whatsoever about grapes or vines,'

Questa said, not without satisfaction. 'She doesn't pretend to either. But I spent a lot of the war cultivating vines so for once I do know what I'm talking about. And if they grew here once ...'

Grace had been bending over, picking. She stopped short on the words and shot a deeply suspicious glance at Questa. Her face, red from stooping, grew redder.

'What do you mean, *grew here once*? It's the first I've heard of it!'

'Ellen told me that Daddy had thought about growing grapes and ...'

Grace stood up straight. She looked very angry, but there was another look there too, which did not quite add up. She looked as though she was being angry to hide another feeling; pleasure?

'Ellen told you? Just what did she tell you? About what your father did to me, I hope. I suppose dear Ellen found out somehow that he'd been sent to Italy to learn about vines, whilst his fiancée – me, Questa – waited at home. Only he met Fortunata somewhere and decided to dump me. A simple, straightforward decision no doubt. I wasn't very old, either ... about your age, dear, and it came hard, to know I'd been dumped for some ... well, I didn't know Nata then so I thought for some greasy little wop.'

'I'm sorry, Grace, but Daddy fell head over heels in love and once that happens I don't think people are responsible for their actions. I'm sure he didn't meant to hurt you, it was just ...'

'It was just that I'm not lovable, is that what you're trying to say? I just wasn't good enough? Well, as it happens that simply isn't true, because ...'

She stopped short. The smirk was barely hidden this time and suddenly Questa felt creepy, as though Grace were deliberately telling her only a part of something and had some hidden motive for doing so which she, Questa, would not like.

'Of course it isn't true that you aren't lovable; Simon married you because he loved you,' Questa said bracingly. 'But haven't you noticed, Grace, that love is most awfully powerful? It won't go away just because someone's not there any more.'

271

Without realising it, her voice had dropped a tone, gone flat. Grace stared at her and then sighed.

'Whatever is the matter with me today? I know more about loving than you'll ever know, and for once I don't mean it nastily. Unrequited love is a burden which can sour a person, only mine wasn't unrequited, not in the end it wasn't. Oh God, what on earth am I doing, talking to you like this? Just don't plant vines, eh? For me, Ques.'

'All right,' Questa said slowly and with considerable reluctance. 'If it's going to upset you I'll leave it for this year.'

Grace nodded and turned back to the blackcurrant bush. 'Thanks. It's silly, I suppose, but it does rather bring it all back. Perhaps in a year or two ...'

The two girls continued with their work of stripping the bushes and soon Ellen called them in for tea. Dickie had arrived home from school full of talk about end-of-term parties and plans for the summer holidays stretching ahead. He always rushed to find Roma and the two of them made their way across the yard, Roma looking harassed. Dickie was training her to do various things and they found it both absorbing and exhausting, especially when Roma could not or would not understand Dickie's instructions. If Dickie kept cool and spoke softly, all went well, but if he lost his temper, Roma would cower in a corner and they would both be unhappy.

Now, they all trooped into the kitchen, dirty and hot, took it in turns to wash, then sat down at the table to eat Ellen's homemade oatcakes and to drink several cups of weak tea.

Grace seemed to have forgotten her earlier unhappiness and was her usual self, chatting to Ellen and Questa and asking Dickie about his day and Roma's training programme, but every now and then Questa surprised a certain look in the older woman's eyes which, try though she might, she could not interpret. She kept shooting glances at Ellen too, which were half placatory, half annoyed. It was odd, Questa thought now, how the mere mention of vines had changed Grace from her normal self to the catty, edgy woman Questa had so disliked when she first met her. Now that she thought about it, it had been many months since they had argued like that.

But perhaps it was understandable; Grace had been badly treated, the mention of vines had reminded her of what had happened, it was only natural that she should have turned on Questa, whose father had been the guilty party and whose talk had sparked her memories of the event.

After tea Ellen went into the dairy with the two younger women and watched them using the separator and the churn. The goats were older and more placid, which meant that their white butter and cheese was often on the table. The Min of Ag, which was so fussy about other products, seemed content to let the goats' milk be used on the farm, though they were still very restricted in other ways, and form-filling and keeping on the right side of the ministry's many and various laws was a constant headache.

'You'm improvin', the pair of you,' Ellen said when they had finished processing for the day. 'I'm off now. I'm mekin' some socks for Alfie out of them old bits of wool you two found up.' She cackled. 'Wait till 'e sees 'em – every colour of the rainbow they be!'

'Alan's coming down tomorrow,' Grace said as Ellen set off across the yard. 'And the 'phone's being connected. I can't wait … imagine, being in touch with the outside world again!'

'Imagine the bills! You mustn't use the phone you know, unless you put money in the box,' Questa said for the dozenth time. She was very worried about owing money, so Alan had suggested a box into which each caller would put not just the pennies owed on the call, but a penny extra each time, towards the rental charge. 'Still, it will be useful for ordering animal feed and so on. And we'll be able to get in touch with Ran whenever one of the beasts is ill; or the vet, of course.'

'Ran's cheaper,' Grace said, stating the obvious. 'He knows a lot, too. And he doesn't mind giving advice, thank goodness.'

'True. Grace, are you and Dickie going to let Alan take you away for a couple of weeks? Don't think I'm anxious to get rid of you, because I'm not, you work hard and I'll miss you, but I would like to know.'

'Why don't you come?' Grace asked. 'Alan wouldn't mind and it would be company for me.'

'Ha! As if you need my company when you've got Alan's! But I couldn't, you know that. Someone's got to be here to keep an eye on things.'

'Yes, I suppose ...' Grace turned and tucked her hand into Questa's arm. She gave a little squeeze, then released her. 'Sometimes I'm a bitch to you, Ques,' she said. 'But you do work hard, and ... oh well, it wasn't your fault what happened over those damned vines. If you're dead set on planting them I'll have to grin and bear it. I might even end up getting sozzled on the product.'

'Thanks, Grace, it does mean a lot to me to have a go with grapevines, and I hope you *will* get sozzled on the wine,' Questa said joyfully. 'As for blaming me, it's odd you should say that because I used to feel that way about Dickie.'

They had been walking back across the yard. Grace stopped for a second, stared at Questa, then walked on.

'How did you feel about Dickie?'

'Well, when you were being particularly cross I used to tell Dickie to leave me alone and go and play somewhere else, pester someone else. Only really I was simply getting my own back on Dickie because he was your son, which was as unfair as you nagging me because of what Daddy ...'

'Yes, I see what you mean. The sins of the fathers, sort of thing. And you definitely won't come to the seaside with us – if we go, that is?'

'I definitely won't. I've got far too much to do here.'

Grace nodded and they went into the kitchen together. Dickie, sitting at the table playing with a magnetic fishing set, looked up hopefully as they entered.

'Goody! Who's going to play with me? Mummy, Uncle Al's coming tomorrow – are we going to the seaside? Are we? Can Ques come? What about Ellen? I'll have to take Roma, she's never seen the sea; will we learn her to swim, Mummy? Can I swim? Will you learn me as well?'

'Shut up, sonny Jim, or I'll send you to bed,' Grace threatened with a laugh in her voice. 'I don't know how we stand you, Ques and I. As for Ellen ...'

'Ellen spoils me rotten,' Dickie said with satisfaction. 'I heard you telling Uncle Ran that she'd ruin me with in-dul ... can't remember what.'

'Indulgence, I expect,' Questa said. 'Move over, Dickie, and give me one of those little rods. I bet I get more fish than either of you in one minute flat!'

Twelve

Questa had expected to enjoy the fortnight's peace and quiet whilst Grace, Dickie and Alan disported themselves at Colwyn Bay, but instead, and much to her surprise, she missed them.

As requested by Dickie they had taken Roma too, and the little dog's habit of trotting close at Questa's heels when Dickie was not around meant that Questa was constantly turning round to address a remark to someone who wasn't there. Even Ellen, who should have revelled in the time she could now spend pottering round the garden and kitchen, because with help outside and Mary Drew to clean three days a week there was less to do, admitted she was lost without the Syretts.

'Never thought I'd miss that Grace, but she ain't altogether bad,' she said grudgingly, when Grace and Dickie had been gone a couple of days. 'We've improved her, lovie, that's what we done, an' now she's gone and bobbled off to the seaside, daft crittur.'

'It's only a fortnight,' Questa comforted her. 'Not even that, now. And you must admit it's quiet.'

'Aye, quiet enough,' Ellen said broodingly. 'I've a good mind to get Alfie's young 'oman over for a week or two. 'Twould do us all good to 'ave some young company.'

'Alfie's young lady? I didn't know he had one!'

'Oh ah. Kathleen, 'er name is. She's a traveller, acourse. Still, be the time me message caught up with 'em, Mrs Syrett an' the lad 'ud be back.'

'Probably,' Questa said. 'So Alfie's got a girlfriend; he's a dark horse!'

Ellen cackled. 'What'ud 'e do when I passes on, wi'out a woman to see to things?' she said mockingly. 'A woman can manage wi'out a feller, but a feller can't manage wi'out a woman, you mark my words.'

'Well, ask her to come anyway,' Questa said. 'I'd like to meet her. So would Grace, I expect.'

'Nah, I'll give it a month or two yet,' Ellen said. 'We're all shakin' down quite well, don't want to do nothin' to change that.'

They were in the kitchen. Ellen sighed and picked up Dickie's gazooka from the table. Grace, a fond mother, had still made sure that Dickie and the gazooka were parted for their holiday. Many a time, since he had started playing the thing, Ellen had cursed him and his instrument, but now, it seemed, she thought more highly of the little pipe. At any rate, she picked it up and played a lugubrious tune on it, then laid it down again almost reluctantly.

'Niver did I think I'd want to 'ear the lad tootlin' on that 'orrible thing,' she said. 'But I wouldn't mind, not even if it were 'Twinkle, twinkle'. In fact when 'e come back, 'e's welcome to play old 'arry if he wants.'

'When I was little we played comb and paper,' Questa said, then widened her eyes and grinned at Ellen. 'Did you hear what I said? That's another thing I've remembered without really trying!'

'It'll come, di'n't I tell you?' Ellen demanded. 'Give it time, lovie, an' it'll all come back. Now what've you an' Mary made for our teas?'

Questa went into the pantry, smiling to herself. Ellen had maintained she could manage perfectly well as she had always managed, and now that Mary was up at the Court so often she was apt to tell Questa privately that it was a waste of money, but in fact she rather enjoyed having food cooked for her, and often had a rest after lunch, sitting on a bench in the kitchen garden and snoozing with her mouth open in whatever sunshine there was.

'There's a beef pie and a small apple crumble,' Questa called now, opening the wire safe where Mary usually left any cooking she'd had time to do for them. 'And there's a pan of peeled potatoes and some cleaned cabbage on the draining board; better get them over the fire.'

Alfie came in whilst they were serving up and ate his usual hearty tea, telling them about his day as he did so.

'Saw old 'arris this marnin'; asked after the piglets 'e did. Says as 'ow 'e's lookin' for a nice sow or two to give 'im a start wi' pigs.'

'Who's Harris?' Questa asked. 'Does he keep pigs already? I don't want mine to go to someone who's ignorant and might not treat 'em right.'

'At least 'e ain't lookin' for fatteners,' Ellen pointed out grumpily. 'Gawd knows it's 'ard enough findin' people who want to breed; if old 'arris wants breedin' stock jest be thankful. Them pigs'll get out of control if you 'as your way.'

'Ellen, we've only got seventeen, plus the breeding sows. But I reckon you're right, the pigs will have to be sold on, even if ... oh, but they are so sweet!'

'Don't give me that,' Ellen said irascibly. 'Sweet ain't the point; you want to mek the place pay, doncher? A workin' farm rears beasts for slaughter, just remember it. I like a nice rasher wi' me eggs.'

Questa sighed and agreed that she would sell the pigs to Mr Harris or anyone else who wanted to buy them and left it at that. Later, when Ellen and Alfie had gone home, she prepared for bed and slid between the sheets wondering rather drearily what she would do for the next couple of weeks.

Ellen was not the only one; Questa, too, missed Grace and Dickie more than she had imagined she would. But even that's a sign that I'm coming to terms with things, she told herself reassuringly, turning restlessly over in bed. Missing friends is a great deal more sensible than missing your dreams, so I'll think about what they'll be doing and keep my mind occupied with pleasant plans.

So she thought about Dickie's first trip to the seaside, Grace and Alan holding hands beneath the moon, Punch and Judy shows and the theatre on the pier, until her hard day caught up with her, and she slept.

Despite having had a full and tiring day, however, Questa had a restless night. She woke in the early hours, went along to the kitchen and made herself a cup of tea, and when it was finished she closed the front of the Aga once more and went back to bed, but not to sleep. Somehow, there were too many things to think

278

about, there was too much on her mind. She wondered what would happen if she tried to run a farm without producing any animals intended for slaughter; she thought about trying her hand at horses, like Ran and ... like Ran had once done. She intended to keep her flock for their fleece, but she would have to sell lambs on eventually and she could not guarantee that beasts sold in such a fashion would not be slaughtered for meat.

Everyone ate meat. Everyone, except a few cranks who called themselves vegetarians, tucked into beef pie, roast mutton, chicken supreme or smoked bacon. Questa was shamefully fond of a nice pork chop and she enjoyed bacon and egg, yet she loved her pigs. There was no logic in it.

Her thoughts slowed, as thoughts do when sleep hovers, and she awoke to broad daylight and the nasty feeling that she had overslept. She sat up muzzily; her eyes felt gummy and heavy-lidded and she peered uncertainly at the clock by her bed, but it had stopped so she got up anyway, feeling cross with herself. There was plenty to do at the best of times, but with Grace away she needed every moment of her day.

She flicked the curtains wide and morning sunshine streamed into the room; it was going to be another hot day, Questa thought, trying to hurry into her clothes with fingers that were all thumbs. So much to do, only herself to do it, and breakfast waiting to be eaten; she wouldn't bother to wash today, if she just ran a comb through her hair she would do until later.

She hurried into the kitchen, casting a self-conscious eye at the clock. Oh curses, it was really late, Ellen would have gone long since. Why on earth hadn't she woken Questa up, though? It wasn't like Ellen!

The kitchen was empty, the curtains still drawn across, the fire slumbrous. Questa swished back curtains, threw open windows, riddled the Aga and set the kettle over the flame. She opened the back door, though there were no animals to let out this morning and, on impulse, hurried across the yard, through the stable and up the stairs. She knocked on the flat door, then opened it.

The room was deserted. Alfie's breakfast plates were stacked on the draining board, the loaf and the butter still stood on the table. Heartbeat quickening, Questa crossed the kitchen and went into the tiny hall. She knocked on Ellen's bedroom door and heard a faint call from the further side. She opened it and went in.

Ellen was sitting on the bed, pushing her feet into slippers. Her hair was a tangled mess and her cheeks were very red. She jumped when the door opened, then grinned across at Questa.

'Overslept I did, lovie, for the first time for Gawd knows 'ow many years! Me 'ead feels all stuffy and peculiar; I reckons I got one of them 'ead colds you youngsters talk about. Still, I'll come straight over and get on. Oh lor, 'as Mary arrived yet?'

'Not yet, it's not that late,' Questa said thankfully. 'As for you, Ellen, just stay in bed, will you? A chill can be nasty, especially in mid-summer. I can manage all right for a few days, so you concentrate on getting well, there's a dear.'

She spoke cheerfully, but in truth her heart sank; Ellen always boasted that she had never caught a cold in her life, had never ailed until the 'flu. Did this mean that the infection really had weakened her natural resistance?

Ellen sighed. 'I don't deny it might be sensible ... oh, go on wi' you, jest this once, then.'

'Give me twenty minutes to make your breakfast,' Questa said. 'Have you had a cuppa?'

'No. Slept right through Alfie's breakfast, so I reckon 'e got 'is own. I wouldn't mind some tea to wet me whistle though.'

'I'll bring you a cup right away, your kettle's on the hob,' Questa promised. 'Two ticks, Ellen.'

She took the tea through, told Ellen off briskly for not yet getting back between the covers, and set off, this time for her own kitchen. There, she assembled the makings of breakfast, made up a tray, and started cooking.

It took her a little longer than she had intended because the telephone rang. It was Grace, saying that they were moving on today, deeper into Wales.

'Alan wants to take us over to Ireland, on the Holyhead boat,' she said. 'It might mean we're away a few days longer, but you and Ellen can cope, can't you?'

'Of course,' Questa said crisply. 'Have a good time and don't worry about us. How's it been so far? We've had awfully good weather, so I suppose you have, too.'

'Oh, lovely,' Grace said. 'We've been swimming every day and Dickie says to tell you he can do a dog paddle, he just copied Roma, he says. We're all brown as berries and eating far too much. Alan says are you sure you can manage if we go on to Ireland for a week?'

'Certain sure. Just enjoy yourselves,' Questa said. 'I'll give your love to everyone. 'Bye, Grace.'

She put the phone down and returned to her task of making the tray look nice for Ellen by adding a few sweet-smelling pinks arranged as tastefully as she could manage in a tiny crystal vase. Now all she needed was the food. She put porridge in a blue pottery dish on the tray, then added a round of toast with a pat of butter beside it and a large dab of marmalade. Two eggs, a rasher and some fried tomatoes completed the food, covered with one of the heavy silver tureen lids which Ellen had not allowed her to sell, saying they were family heirlooms and someone else might appreciate them one day, even if she did not.

Coffee in the cup, a spoonful of mustard by the rasher ... and now I'm ready, Questa told herself. She lifted the tray, which was heavy, and set off across the yard.

It really was a grand day! A cockerel crowed loudly nearby, then came strutting around the side of the house. Spotting her and obviously feeling more than usually daring, he made a beeline for her, wings half up, tail fanned and beak making aggressive darting movements in the vicinity of her bare calves. Questa was wearing bedroom slippers and not boots but she kicked out anyway and the cockerel squawked, then came back to the attack, but more as a matter of form than from a conviction that he could send her packing. Questa stopped and readjusted the tray.

'Stupid bird,' she called after him. 'Go and take care of your hens and leave bigger people alone!'

She opened the stable door and, eyes fixed on the door above her, went to mount the stairs. She took a step up, or rather tried to do so, but her foot caught on something. She gasped and looked down, tried to recover and knew she could not do so even as the tray slipped from her grasp and she lurched forward and fell, landing on something soft, something which groaned as her

281

knees dug into it, so that she rolled instinctively to her right, smack into the debris of Ellen's breakfast.

It was Ellen, lying in a motionless huddle at the foot of the stairs, face ashen now, the flush quite gone.

Somehow Questa scrambled to her feet and leaned over the injured woman. She was still breathing – oh, thank God, thank God – but she looked odd, awkward. One leg ... Questa swallowed, putting a trembling hand to her rounding mouth; one leg was bent right up her back. She was badly hurt, her breathing was hoarse, shallow.

'Ellen? Don't try to move, my love, just lie there. I'm going to get help ... don't try to move!'

The sensible, logical part of her mind knew that Ellen was unconscious and would not be able to move even if she could hear, but the other part, a loving, foolish part, was concerned to give Ellen what comfort she could.

She flew out of the stable and into the house. Mary was there, still in the headscarf and jacket which she wore to cycle to work. She was undoing the headscarf though and turned to stare, eyes round with surprise, as Questa burst in.

'Morning, dear ... whatever's the matter?'

'It's Ellen, she's had an accident, she's lying at the foot of the stable stairs and it looks as though she's broken her leg,' Questa gabbled. 'Can you ring the doctor, Mary? And tell him it's dreadfully urgent; get him to send an ambulance. She's breathing funny.'

'Right,' Mary said, not wasting words. 'Then I'll ring the Hall and ask if Alfie can come home, shall I?'

'Please. Oh, Mary, you are good. I'll just get a blanket and make a hot bottle because I read somewhere that shock kills more people after a fall than anything, and can you bring over a cup of hot, sweet tea when you've made the phone calls?'

'Yes, of course. The kettle's boiled.'

Mary hurried out and Questa made the bottle, lugged a blanket off her bed and set off across the stableyard once more. Ellen was still huddled at the foot of the stairs but now, when Questa knelt down beside her, she opened her eyes. They stared blankly around her for a moment, then fixed on Questa's face.

'Questa? Oh, lovie, I feels mortal queer!'

'I've sent for the ambulance,' Questa said hurriedly. 'What happened, Ellen? How did you fall?'

The lids drooped over the round, brown eyes for a moment.

'Dunno. I can't feel me legs.'

'They're still there, Ellen,' Questa said, trying for a lighter touch. She spread the blanket tenderly over the little form and arranged the bottle so that Ellen could hug it, but Ellen's arms did not move. 'Here ... can you feel the hot bottle?'

Ellen sighed. 'Am I in bed? I feels a bit warmer.'

'No, you aren't in bed exactly, but if I got you a pillow you'd be more comfortable. Shan't be a moment.'

Questa stepped over Ellen, ran up the stairs, snatched a pillow off Ellen's bed and returned to her patient.

'Here ... let me lift your head.'

But Ellen, who had said she couldn't feel her legs, gave a strange, hoarse shriek when Questa tried to move her head.

'That 'urt mortal bad,' she muttered. 'Me back nigh tore in two.'

'Right. Then if you can't raise your head without pain we'd better leave you just as you are,' Questa said with what cheerfulness she could muster. 'The doctor's coming, and the ambulance.'

Ellen's eyelids, which had drooped shut once more, shot open.

'Ambulance? I ain't a-goin' to 'orspital! You wouldn't let them tek me to 'orspital, lovie? If I'm a-goin' to die it'll be from 'ere, not in some strange, cold 'orspital bed. 'Sides, if I move I'll break into bits.'

'They'll move you properly, in a way that won't hurt,' Questa said, her own voice breaking. 'Oh dearest Ellen, you aren't going to die, not from a little fall! You'll soon mend, I'm sure you will.'

'Can't shake me 'ead,' Ellen muttered. 'I feels mortal bad. Me body's goin' numb. Got to talk to you, lovie.'

'Talk away, but don't tire yourself,' Questa said, sitting down on the floor by the old woman's head and taking her hand in a gentle clasp. 'If you want to sleep, Ellen, you just sleep.'

'Sleep? Why should I want to sleep? Nah, there's plenty time for that. You know that photy you keeps in your room, the one with young Charles on?'

'Which one? The one Alan found of my parents on their wedding day? Or the little snap of Daddy in his uniform? Shall I go and fetch them both?'

'Fetch 'em? Whatever for? No, lovie, I jest want to know if you've ever wondered over the likeness.'

'Likeness? I'm sorry, Ellen, I don't think I know what you mean.'

'Oh lovie, 'aven't you noticed, not even with them photys? Why, young Dickie's got the look of your daddy, plain as plain. I 'member 'ow young Charlie looked when 'e first come 'ere … He was the spit of young Dickie. Didn't you ever wonder why I wanted the lad to stay wi' us? That was why; because I reckoned 'e was your daddy's get.'

Questa stared. Ellen must be rambling, she thought. What on earth did she mean – your Daddy's get? It didn't make sense, did it? But perhaps she should humour the old woman.

'Dickie's very fair and Daddy was too, I can remember that much,' she said slowly. 'I expect Simon was fair, too, and he was related, as well. Yes, that must be it. Now I don't think you should talk any more, Ellen. You'll say something you don't mean and wear yourself out as well.'

Ellen closed her eyes, then opened them again.

'I knows what I means,' she said. To Questa's distress her voice was slurring, thickening. 'Will you listen to me, lovie, while I can still say what I means?'

There was a world of pleading in her tone. Ashamed, Questa nodded and rubbed the thin old fingers gently with her own warm, young ones.

'Sorry, Ellen, of course I'll listen. Go ahead.'

'Dickie's young Charlie's son. I don't know why Grace didn't come straight out with it, why she let you think the lad were that Simon's kid, but the truth's in 'is face, lovie, for them with eyes to see. If Alan 'asn't noticed it's acos 'e don't want to, but I noticed an' I reckon Ran Atherton 'ad 'is suspicions. Why, there's a photy up in me flat of my Alfie wi' Charlie when 'e was around seven … they could be the same lad, lovie. That means Dickie's your brother, good as.'

'My brother! Oh, Ellen, I'd love Dickie to be my brother, but why on earth didn't Grace tell me, if it's true?'

Ellen took a deep, gurgling breath. There was something in her throat; she cleared it a couple of times, but when she spoke her voice was still hoarse.

'Wanted you to do the work, I reckons,' she got out at last. 'For the boy ... mek the place right for the boy, see? She ... still ... don't ... understand ... about ... the ... entail.'

'You mean she thinks Dickie might inherit instead of me?' It was a deeply unwelcome thought. That Grace, who had appeared to befriend her, might have been doing it all for her own sake, would be a most painful treachery. 'Is it true? Might the Court be his?'

Ellen closed her eyes again and strained to fill her chest with air. Every time she took a shallow breath, it seemed to Questa, she lost it in a long sigh, but at last she managed another short sentence.

'Were he born in wedlock?'

'Ellen, she was married to Simon Syrett, so if you're right and Dickie is my brother, then he can't have been born in wedlock! I mean, it just isn't possible to marry two men at the same time, is it?'

'See marriage lines?'

The words were so faint, so slurred, that Questa scarcely caught them. She leaned closer, clasping Ellen's hand convulsively. What did it matter if Dickie inherited the Court and she just worked on it, for God's sake? What mattered was Ellen ... please God, she prayed fervently, let her live, let her live!

'Ellen, please, I'll sort it out, I swear it, if only you'll rest now, give yourself a chance.'

Ellen sighed. 'Good girl. Promise?'

'I promise. Now let's just sit here quietly, shall we, and wait for the ambulance? It won't be long.'

'Awright. Alfie?'

'He's coming. Just lie quiet, Ellen, and rest.'

Alfie arrived simultaneously with the doctor. He was very pale and for the first time Questa thought he looked his age. He knelt

285

on the floor beside his mother and bent down until his ear was against those pale lips. No one save Alfie could hear what she murmured now, but he looked at the doctor and shook his head slowly.

'No 'ospital,' he said. 'No 'ospital, Dr Speed.'

'No point,' Dr Speed whispered back. 'She's right, Alfie, no point.'

The ambulancemen were turned back before they had got across the stableyard.

'We can't move her,' the doctor said quietly to Questa as they stood in the stableyard after dismissing the ambulancemen. 'I've given her quite a stiff injection though, against the pain. Bring more blankets, there's a good girl, and have you got a little, flattish pillow or cushion? I'd like to get something under her head, but she won't last long, I'm afraid. I'm sorry, my dear, but it's best that you know. She does.'

'She can have my thyme pillow,' Questa said. 'It's small and flat; she made it for me.'

They wrapped Ellen in blankets with bottles at her feet, behind her knees, and against her stomach. She smiled at them a couple of times, but Questa thought it was just an automatic reaction to their care and the love which hovered almost palpably over her. She did not know at whom she smiled or for what reason. The doctor slid the thyme pillow under her head and she sighed, then sniffed.

'Ah, *that's* more like,' she said dreamily. 'That's more like!'

At midnight, Alfie told Questa to go back to the house and get some sleep.

'It's my place to be by 'er,' he said. 'We'll call you if we needs you.'

Questa went and lay down; she may even have slept briefly. At two a.m. she swung her feet out of bed and padded through into the kitchen. It was a warm, summery night, the stars enormous in the dark sky. She went across to the stable block, opened the door quietly ... and stared, dumb with disbelief.

There was no sign of Alfie, or of Ellen. There was no bedding, nothing to indicate that an old woman had lain there, dying, only a couple of hours earlier. Had it all been a dreadful nightmare, then?

Questa turned away from the stable and was halfway across the yard once more when she heard a low, sobbing moan coming from nearby. It froze her blood, brought the hair prickling erect on her scalp. Someone was hurt ... my God, suppose Ellen had wandered ...

She looked around wildly; the door to the kitchen garden was open. She crossed the intervening space in a bound, then stopped short in the doorway.

Ellen lay, straight and small, on the blankets. Her hands were crossed on her flat breast and her eyes were closed, demure as a dead pigeon. Alfie, leaning over his mother, was crying un-ashamedly; Questa could see his tear-wet face, hear the deep, racking sobs.

'Alfie? Is ... is she ... ?'

'Gone,' Alfie said. 'But in the open, like she wanted. Not under a roof. I carried 'er, like she said. Never made a sound, brave old soul, not so much as a sound.'

Questa looked down on Ellen, and saw that her friend had already fled. The small, brown face was severe, grim almost, the dark eyes, so full of life and humour, had sparkled up at her for the last time.

'Oh, Alfie, what'll we do without her?' she whispered at last. 'What'll we do?'

There was no means of contacting Grace or Alan, but Questa did not want to do so. They had been fond of Ellen, but not in the way she and Alfie were, and Dickie was too young to cope with the sudden death of someone he loved. So Questa went to Ran.

'She was an excellent wife to Rimmer and a marvellous mother to Alfie, a positive tower of strength to you all, as I know,' Ran said. 'And there were others ... you'll find they'll all come to pay their respects now she's gone. And don't worry, Questa, Alfie's already spoken to me. I'll see to all the arrangements when the uninvited guests arrive.'

And arrive they did, in droves, in legions: Gypsies. Men, women and dirty, brown-faced children, they came up the long drive, spoke to Alfie, took one last long look at Ellen, and withdrew. But they did not leave. They waited for the funeral.

'Will she be buried in the churchyard?' Questa asked, but Alfie said no, gypsies did not bury their dead, they burned them; it was cleaner and more final for a travelling people who had no claims to even six foot of earth. Questa had horrible visions of Alfie lighting a huge funeral pyre, but Alfie assured her that his mother's body would be taken to the nearest crematorium.

'Twenty year ago it 'ud have been the pyre,' he admitted. 'We'd 'a burnt the 'van she died in too, which is why we allus try to get out from under a roof when our times comes. But now us'll burn 'er clothing and personal things, and when she's gone, 'er ashes will be scattered to the four winds.'

'How did they know, the people out there?' Questa asked. 'Did Ellen send for your young woman, Alfie? But even if she did, who told the others? Where have they all come from? More seem to arrive every day.'

'Mam didn't 'ave time to send for anyone; they just knowed,' Alfie said, shrugging. 'She were good to them in the war; what she 'ad, she'd share. She were allus like that.'

Questa nodded; it was a good epitaph, even if it would only be written on the wind.

Questa missed Ellen almost unbearably at every turn that first week. She saw her everywhere, in the kitchen garden, the fields and meadows, the stables and outbuildings. She mourned her, too. Alfie was white-faced, old. He did his work around the yard, saw to the pigs, went off to the Hall each day, but you could see his heart wasn't in it.

And oddly enough, Ellen's last words, which had been mysterious enough, scarcely crossed Questa's mind. She saw the photograph and Ellen was right, the little boy in the picture might indeed have been Dickie Syrett. But it didn't seem to matter whose child Dickie was, and if Grace really had deceived her that was pretty horrid but the world would scarcely stop turning. People, Questa acknowledged sadly, deceived other people all the time; all you could do was act honestly yourself and bring up your own children to know right from wrong, good from bad.

Not that she would ever have children. Unacknowledged, her grief for lost love seeped through even into her grief for Ellen. But at least her loss in the real world had helped to make her forget her loss in her dream world – indeed, the loss of that other world. And very soon Grace, Dickie and Alan would be back and although they would all miss Ellen horribly, their lives would eventually take on an even tenor once more. Ellen had prepared them, unobtrusively but thoroughly, to manage without her. Both women could now milk a cow, make butter and cheese and deal with most household tasks. Questa was becoming more sensible about her stock and had agreed to sell her piglets and even some of the male lambs when autumn came. The workload seemed horribly heavy without Ellen's cackling laugh and oft-repeated old wives' tales, but Questa soldiered on, managing somehow.

Then Alfie brought her the thyme pillow.

'She wanted you to 'ave it back,' he said gruffly, pressing the small thing into Questa's hands.

Questa could feel the dried thyme through the cotton cover, smell it, strong and sweet.

'Thanks, Alfie.'

'She wouldn't let me take it into the kitchen garden with 'er,' Alfie said gently. 'She din't die on it, lovie.'

'It wouldn't worry me if she had; she was a good woman,' Questa said. 'Oh, Alfie, how I miss her!'

'Aye, you ain't the only one,' Alfie said gruffly. 'I'm goin' to send word for my Kathleen though, now the old girl's gone.'

'Oh yes, your young woman. Do you know until a few days before Ellen died, I didn't know you had anyone in mind?' Questa said. 'She told me then, almost as though she knew her time was near. I'm glad for you, Alfie, I hope the two of you will be very happy!'

'She's a decent sorta gal,' Alfie said, much embarrassed. 'Reckon she'll suit me well enough. Do you 'member Sara Swingler?'

Questa and Ellen had once met Sara in the village. She was a gypsy, dark haired, sly-eyed, with a bold hip-thrusting walk and a way of glancing at men which set Questa's teeth on edge. With considerable foreboding, Questa admitted she remembered Sara Swingler.

'Well, my gal's 'er darter, they calls 'er Kat. Got red 'air, but I can put up wi' that.'

Questa could not remember the daughter, but Kat proved to be a skinny girl in her twenties with an angular, freckled face, greasy red hair and greenish eyes.

'Father's a *gorgio*,' Alfie said offhandedly. 'Probably why she ain't been married afore; now 'er mother's gone off wi' er latest fancy man she's more alone than you'd credit. You might wonder why I looked further'n Sara, who's an 'andsome woman; truth is I 'ouldn't be easy with a pure traveller, not livin' in the coachman's flat.'

'You're half *gorgio* yourself, aren't you?' Questa said. 'Although your hair's not got any grey in it, and the gypsy men don't go grey much.'

'Oh ah, Dad was a farm labourer; that's why I'm good wi' stock,' Alfie said. 'We'll wed in church, me an' Kat. She'm agreeable.'

'Alfie, do you … does she … I mean you hardly know one another!'

'Aye, but there's more to it than knowin'; there's need, see, lovie. We needs one another.'

And since it was impossible to deny that Alfie needed a woman to manage his affairs and Kat, resented by the tribe, was clearly delighted to escape, Questa could only agree that they seemed to be doing the right thing. Ellen had not encouraged Alfie to lift a finger in the house and he had always handed his money straight to her, though she gave him pocket money to spend at the pub; now it meant that Alfie was completely lost without her. He needed someone, so why not a wife? Affection, love even, might follow, Questa could quite see that, so Alfie and his Kat stood as good a chance of happiness as any other couple. Italian peasants took an equally practical view of marriage and by and large their relationships worked out all right and stood the test of time. So Questa wished them luck, though she envied neither of them; the thought of physical intimacy still made her flesh creep.

Ellen's funeral took place on a Thursday morning; on the day

290

following, Questa got up and went downstairs, hating the lonely kitchen and the small tasks which she had once performed gladly, when Ellen had been alive and able to pop in and give her advice, or have a laugh over something she had done. She had barely riddled the Aga though, when there was a knock on the back door.

Gypsies wanting water, Questa thought, but it was Kat, with a brown paper parcel in her arms. She stared at Questa, anxiously gnawing her bottom lip with uneven, yellowy teeth. She had brushed her thick, greasy hair and then tied it back from her face with a piece of greyish string but her neck, Questa saw, could do with some attention and she was clearly very ill at ease.

'Marnin', Missus,' she said uncertainly. 'Alfie say I can't move into the flat till after the weddin' so I were wonderin' if I could use a room over 'ere? I said I'd doss under an 'edge but 'e got rare angry wi' me.'

'Yes, of course you can stay here,' Questa said at once. 'Goodness knows there are enough empty rooms, and we've spare beds, too. Have they made you move out, Kat?'

'Nah ... though I were glad to go. They've gone, all of 'em.'

There was a certain satisfaction in her tone. Presumably she realised that Alfie was unlikely to change his mind with her, friendless, living on his doorstep.

'Gone? *All* of 'em?' Questa stood on tiptoe and peered out of the kitchen doorway. 'Even the ones in the woods?'

'All of 'em,' Kat confirmed again. 'Can – can I come in, Missus?'

'Sorry, yes, of course you can,' Questa said, ushering the girl into the kitchen. As Kat passed her she became aware of a strong, eye-watering and rather unpleasant odour, similar to that given off by a vixen in the mating season. 'My name's Questa, by the way, so I'll call you Kat and you can call me Questa; all right?'

'Sure. But everyone else will call me Missus Rimmer; is that right?'

Questa smiled into the anxious, greeny-grey eyes. She could remember all too well feeling just the way Kat must be feeling now, and how marvellous Alfie and Ellen had been to her, how understanding over the small peculiarities which had soon disappeared under the influence of their quiet, friendly acceptance.

'Yes, lots of people will call you Mrs Rimmer,' she assured the

291

other girl, 'but friends will always call you Kat – unless you prefer Kathleen, of course? Now if you put your things on the chair we might as well have some breakfast together. You can sleep in the spare room, if you'd like to, or choose another room. Look, I'll show you round before we eat, shall I?'

'All over the 'ouse? I ain't never lived in an 'ouse.'

'Yes, if you like. In fact it would be better because then if I mention a room to you, you'll know where I mean. Now that little room, through there, is the scullery where in the old days they peeled potatoes and cleaned shoes, things like that. Today, of course, we just use it to keep sacks of potatoes in and dog-food. That door, there, leads into the butler's pantry where they used to do the flowers and prepare salads I believe, and the real pantry, which we use, is here.'

'Cor!' Kat said fervently. 'Ain't it all *big*?'

Questa laughed. 'Wait till you see the rest! Follow me.'

Downstairs the house was looking much better, though pretty empty still, but upstairs ...

'A bathroom!' Kat breathed. For the first time the green eyes shone with pleasure as she turned to Questa. 'I ain't never 'ad a bath.'

Questa, who had guessed as much, gestured her into the room.

'You'll like it, we all love having baths,' she said enthusiastically. 'The Aga, that's the stove downstairs in the kitchen, provides the hot water so you don't have to stint yourself. And Grace has some awfully nice scented soap which she'd be happy for you to use. Would you like to take a bath when you've seen your room?'

For the first time, a smile spread across Kat's face, completely transforming her. She's almost pretty, Questa thought as the thin mobile mouth tilted upwards and the long eyes slitted to show off her thick, tawny eyelashes.

'A bath, now? Ooh, that 'ud be grand – would Alfie mind?'

'He'll be delighted,' Questa said with real sincerity. She did not think that anyone who had lived with Ellen would care for life with a woman who stank like a polecat, or at least like an old vixen. There was no bathroom in the coachman's flat, but she had discovered that Ellen and Alfie bathed weekly in front of their kitchen fire in an old tin tub which they filled, laboriously, with kettles full of hot water. Once the house got organised Ellen sometimes took a bath there, but Alfie preferred his cosy spot before the fire. 'When we bath we put on clean clothes though – do you have any?'

Kat looked doubtfully at her small brown paper parcel. 'There's a skirt; it's thicker'n this one. It's me winter skirt.'

'I'll lend you something; or rather, I'll … here, let me start the bath running and whilst you undress I'll fetch something.'

Questa put the plug in and ran the water, then, leaving it running and Kat standing beside it with a dazed expression on her face, she hurried into Grace's room. She went through her wardrobe, selected a mustard-coloured cotton dress which Grace had once announced pettishly that she hated and a pair of cotton knickers, and returned to the bathroom. Kat, with a complete lack of modesty, was stripping off her shabby brown frock, revealing that she wore no underwear and that she had the very white skin common to redheads, though those parts of her skin which were in daily contact with the weather were a dirty fawn colour.

'Here we are; hop in the water,' Questa said. Kat tested the water with a toe, dabbled with one hand, then, holding her nose as though about to plunge into a fathomless sea, she stepped into the bath. Questa was not surprised to see a cloud of dirt float away from her body as she got in. 'There, isn't that lovely? Here's the soap.'

'Eh, it's grand,' Kat said. She leaned back and then, with a convulsive wriggle, ducked her entire body apart from her head beneath the warm water. She smiled up at Questa, looking like a mermaid with her hair fanning out in the water like seaweed. 'Who'd 'a thought it, eh? Me, Kat Swingler, in a proper bath in a real 'ouse!'

'And liking it,' confirmed Questa. 'You rub the soap all over you. Shall I do your back?'

'You can wash me 'air, if you'd be so good,' Kat said, blinking drowsily. 'Oo, ain't this loverly, though? You're ever so kind, gal … I bet me 'air could do wi' some soap.'

Washed, her hair proved to be a delicious mass of tiny curls, richly copper-coloured, setting off the very white skin to perfection. Alfie doesn't know what he's got, Questa thought rather apprehensively. With some flesh on her bones – lord, she's as thin as I was when I first came here – she's going to be really lovely. And Alfie's pushing sixty ... oh lor!

Questa left Kat to get dried and dressed in the mustard-yellow cotton and went back to the kitchen. She cooked porridge, boiled two eggs, sliced bread and spread margarine on it. Then, before Kat could see what she was doing, she dunked the brown dress in the hottest water she could bear, well laced with soap-flakes. It proved to have been a blue dress, or possibly green, but since it all but fell to bits in the water and would plainly never be worn again, the colour was really academic. Questa wrung it out and put it over the line, but she would have to tell Alfie that unless he wanted his wife-to-be to scandalise the neighbourhood by walking around naked, he had best find her some clothes.

'An egg!' Kat said when she saw the breakfast table. 'That's rare good of you, Questa. Wi' our fambly, the men gets the eggs, or the kids.'

'Well here everyone gets their fair share, and that includes you,' Questa said firmly. 'If the hens are laying well we have a couple of eggs each, so eat up, Kat; you could do with a bit more flesh on your bones.'

'That's what Ellen said,' Kat remarked, digging into her egg. 'The gal need feedin' up, she said. Leave 'er wi' us this comin' summer, she told Sara last spring, an' I'll see 'er fat as butter an' wed to me son by autumn at the latest.'

Questa, eating her egg, nodded and reflected that she might have known Ellen would have had a hand in it. She must have decided that if Alfie didn't marry soon he never would, and she loved her boy, she would want the best for him. Whether Kat turned out to be the best or not it was a bit early to say, but she seemed good-hearted and although gypsy men tended to be idle layabouts, the women worked hard from the moment they rose in the morning until they sought their beds at night.

Which will suit Eagles Court fine, Questa reflected. And Ellen would think of me and mine as well as of Alfie, bless her. But just wait until Grace gets home and finds we've an addition to our family! The loss of Ellen would grieve them all, but Kat, with her funny ways, would probably make that loss easier to bear.

Kat chose a tiny dressing room near the back stairs. When Questa queried her choice, she said simply that she was used to small places and felt awkward with a big room around her.

'I were born and bred in a caravan,' she explained. 'There ain't much room in one o' them. At night, you lies under your blanket, or if the weather's good you lies out, under the stars. I some'ow can't get used to bein' under a roof but wi' lots of space round me.'

'You'll tell me next you're going to sleep in Alfie's little room when you're married,' Questa teased her. 'And that you'll leave the bedroom with the brass bedstead for visitors.'

Kat looked down at her feet in the old boots which had belonged to Ellen and which fitted her pretty well.

'I ain't never been wi' a man,' she said. 'I dunno 'ow I'll tek to it. But I reckons wi' two of you in one bed, It'll feel powerful strange anyways.'

'That's true,' Questa said, 'but you're going to be very happy, Kat, because Alfie's the kindest man I know. Now I'm going to work in the garden when I've finished with the stock; Bert works full-time for us now, but even so he can use my help. What will you do?'

'Whatever 'elps most,' Kat said at once. 'Alfie told me to do Ellen's jobs, 'e said you'd show me 'ow they was done.'

A little to Questa's surprise, for she did not think gypsies ever owned cows and therefore had no need to milk one, Kat proved an apt pupil. Milk hissed into the bucket in no time, compared with Grace's slow progress, and Kat mucked out pigs, hunted for eggs – and found more than Questa would have done – and was generally amazingly helpful. She did not know a weed from a growing plant, but again she was quick to learn and was very soon hoeing between the bean rows as though she had been doing it all her life.

That evening, when Alfie hailed Kat off to cook him a meal, Ran came around to make sure, he said, that Questa was not too lonely.

'I've got a friend of Ellen's staying; Alfie's bride-to-be,' Questa said with a chuckle, and told Ran about Kat, including the news that the couple would not marry until the autumn since it was then that Ellen had planned the wedding, and then that the gypsies would be in the neighbourhood, helping with harvests, gleaning in the fields and generally earning their keep for the winter to come.

Having told him the story, Questa admitted how surprised she had been when Kat had taken so readily to certain tasks such as milking the cows.

'Because she can't have done it before, can she?' she ended. 'Yet she's most awfully good; Blossom let her take a full bucket right off, she made me wait ages.'

Ran, sitting in Ellen's old chair drinking a glass of elderberry wine, chuckled. 'My dear girl, she'll have been milking cows since she was no taller than a day-old calf, and in a meadow, what's more! Gypsies steal from the cows in the meadows, you'll see a brat of five fill herself a mug whilst the cow stands and chews the cud ... they're the experts, the young'uns. And she'll have nicked eggs from every farmer for miles around, so no wonder she knows better than you where the old hens hide their clutches.'

'Oh!' Questa said, feeling rather foolish. 'Well, Ellen must have known that, I daresay, but she still wanted her for Alfie.'

'She'll do well by all of you, my dear, regardless of how she learned to milk; loyalty is a gypsy virtue and you've taken her in. She won't ever forget that.' He drained his glass and stood up on the words, reaching for his sticks. 'Well, I'd best be going; Alfie's not going to have things all his own way for much longer, you know. My hand-controlled car should be here in eight or nine weeks.'

'Hand-controlled? I didn't know there was such a thing!'

'Oh yes; my order's been in a couple of years at least, but I got word a week back that I was next on the list. It'll be good to be independent and mobile again.'

'Gosh, that will be good, Ran. What will you do with the Lagonda, though? It's such a lovely car. If I could drive I'd save up and buy it off you. I wish I *could* drive.'

'I shan't be selling it. You know how ironical fate is though. I thought how good it was that the hand-controlled car would arrive before Christmas. when my son was supposed to come home, and the next day I had a letter from him – he's moving on, it'll be a year before he's back. So the Lagonda will be eating its head off in the stable, I suppose.'

Questa giggled. 'Oh, well, at least it won't be guzzling petrol. What changed your son's plans, Ran?'

'He wants to do a stint on a sheep-station in the Northern Territories. Says it's an unrivalled opportunity, which it is, I suppose. He might come home on his way through though, if he decides to sign on with a North American farm for a bit, so I could see him over the holiday.'

'Oh, well, that'll be nice for you,' Questa said hollowly. The more attached she got to Ran, the more she dreaded the return of his far from prodigal son. 'You can't possibly quarrel over a Christmas holiday, can you?'

'Unfortunately, my dear, we can! Last time he was home I behaved like an old fool and he behaved like a young one, but this time it'll be different. A lot of time has passed, he's had heaps of training in different farming methods, he's had plenty of experience of being told what to do by other people instead of shouting out the orders ... that will make a difference, I'm sure. And to tell you the truth, I've missed him hellishly. It hasn't been so bad since you've been here and have popped over more often, but it's lonely, evenings.'

'Well, if he doesn't come home for a year, then I'll be a lot more independent, too, by the time he gets back,' Questa said rather forlornly. 'I only met him once, but I rather got the impression that he would much prefer my land to my company.'

Ran tutted and shook his head.

'Young fool! But when you met him we'd quarrelled and he was on his way out and touchy as sin. Don't you dare turn away from me when the boy comes home, young woman! I'll be very hurt if you don't consult me from time to time.' Ran adjusted his sticks and limped across the kitchen flags. 'Just because I'll have a son, that doesn't mean I don't need my adopted daughter ... you didn't know you were my adopted daughter, did you? Well, that's how I look on you, so don't try to be too independent, Questa my dear.'

'Oh, I won't, I wouldn't, but your son ...'

'He'll very soon grow as fond of you as I am; he's probably always wanted a younger sister,' Ran assured her. He balanced on one stick and opened the back door. 'I don't want you to get swelled-headed, but you're strong, brave and very pretty! Look at that, Alfie's halfway across the yard, I swear that man's got second-sight.'

'Thank you, but your son was really rude and nasty to me last time we met,' Questa mumbled. 'I'm a bit ... a bit ...'

'Last time he was home he was a bombastic, self-opinionated young tank commander who thought he knew everything and spent a lot of time and energy trying to prove that his hearing hadn't been affected by the infernal machine he drove,' Ran said cheerfully, swinging across the threshold. 'He had horrendous nightmares: tanks are huge, unstoppable death-dealers, and when your nerves are shot to pieces sometimes you take it out on others. Forget that touchy young tank commander and get ready to welcome the real person, the man who's sorted himself out and come to terms with what he's lost and what he's gained.'

'A bit like me,' Questa said thoughtfully, wandering across to the car. 'I was touchy – I had nightmares, too.'

'Yes, a bit like you,' Ran said. Alfie opened the passenger door and ushered the older man tenderly inside. 'See you in a day or two, my dear. Sleep well!'

Questa waited, waving, until the car turned the corner and was out of sight, then she returned to the kitchen. She made herself a hot drink, took it through to her room, then sat on the edge of the bed and stared sightlessly before her.

Her enemy, the man who had beaten her, was coming back, but not as soon as she had dreaded. He might have changed, she supposed doubtfully, but she did not like him; he had been cruel, not a bit like his kindly, understanding father. It made her feel terribly alone to think back to that encounter on the river bank, but she would not be alone for long. Presently Kat would steal into the house and make her way up to the tiny bedroom she had chosen, though she would not do so until a good deal later.

She and Alfie would be sitting in the coachman's flat, getting to know one another. And here sat Questa Adamson with her hot drink, all alone as usual.

She began to undress, then sat down on the bed again. Oh, God, but she was lonely! Young Atherton was coming back for a few days at Christmas, and whilst he was here he would monopolise her friend Ran, her comfortable adviser. Alfie had Kat, Grace had Alan, Dickie had Roma. Even Ellen had gone – Ellen who understood her so well. On the thought she went to the drawer and pulled out the thyme pillow, holding it against her face. The strong, sweet smell of the wild thyme comforted. Ah, the glade in the woods where the thyme grew and the breeze carried the scent of it into the birch trees, stronger than the pale perfume of primroses, sweeter than the smell of crushed spring grass!

Slowly, she laid the pillow down on the bed. Slowly, she curled up, resting her cheek on it.

Slowly, she relaxed.

And slept.

Thirteen

She woke to the patter of raindrops on leaves. She was curled up in something warm. She opened her eyes and looked down and it was a sheepskin cloak worn with the fleece on the inside, and she was cuddled down amongst dry dead leaves. She knuckled her eyes and stretched, trying to understand what had happened, and realised she was in the hollowed-out centre of a tree and that, outside, it was raining heavily.

It would not do to jump up or move hastily until she had properly come to herself; sleep still blurred the outlines, her hands were clenched into warm, defenceless fists, her cheek was creased with lying on something ...

She sat up carefully so as not to bang her head against the tree. She peered out through the inverted vee of the split in the mighty trunk. Nothing but the rain, channelling down the trunks around, soaking into the thick beech mast underfoot, pattering on the abundant leaves overhead. Dark leaves; the leaves of high summer.

She shuffled nearer the entrance and looked up. The sky was overcast, grey with cloud. It looked as though the rain had set in and might continue for a week, but it was neither cold nor windy, which was one blessing. When – if – she left her shelter she might get wet but she would not be unduly chilled.

She heaved herself out of the hollow but stayed close to the trunk. It was drier under here, where the leaves and branches overhead were thickest. And now she could hear something other than the patter of the rain; it was an odd sort of sound, strange yet rhythmical. A bumping, beating noise, as though a heartbeat, many times magnified, was thumping away near at hand. She glanced to her left, where the sound seemed to be coming from; and froze.

300

Marcus knelt on the ground before a mighty beech. With his clenched fists raised he struck the trunk again and again as though he were trying to fell the tree with his bare hands. As she watched he moved his head slightly and she caught a glimpse of his face – that strong, familiar face. But it looked for a moment like a stranger's face, contorted as it was by grief and wet, not just with the steadily falling rain but with his tears, painfully shed.

She had meant to observe, to follow, to watch until she was sure, but she had only to see his grief and despair to forget everything but how she loved him. She scrambled to her feet and ran across the short distance which separated them. She flung her arms round him and pressed her face to his, cooing meaninglessly, intent only on showing him how much she cared, soothing his hurt.

'Marcus, ah don't, my darling, don't! I'm here, I'm back, now tell me what's gone wrong, what's happened to hurt you so?'

His eyes shot open. The whites were bloodshot, the lids swollen. He heaved a great, deep sigh, then turned and took her in his arms as naturally as though they had not been parted two minutes.

'Questa! Ah, prayers are answered, then! It's Gaius. He's dead.'

'Marcus, not the boy you told me about, not your brother?'

He nodded, pain etched on his face, robbing it of lightness, laughter.

'Yes. My brother Gaius, who wanted to be a soldier, like me. I said he was a child of the devil, a spoilt brat … Questa, I loved him, wanted only the best for him.'

'Oh, my dearest!' She rubbed his hands between her own; they were cold and as she rubbed she heard the hiss of his sharply indrawn breath. She looked down. The long, strong fingers were streaked with blood, the knuckles split and bruised. 'Oh God, who's done this?'

He looked down at his hands, indifferently. 'Me. Punching the tree. Railing against fate, you could say. Oh Questa, he was going to make a first-rate soldier, a leader of men, and now …' His voice broke.

'I know, love, I know. Marcus, d'you want to talk about it? Can you tell me what happened?'

301

'He was with a group of friends, young soldiers every one. They were being taken across the channel ... there was a storm ... two boys were drowned. One of them was Gaius.'

His voice trailed into silence. Questa was still holding both his hands. Hypnotically, she smoothed her thumbs round and round in his palms, avoiding the cuts and abrasions.

'Oh Marcus, I'm so sorry. Has his body been recovered?'

'No; there can be no burial rites. Questa, I feel worse because at one time I resented Gaius – birthing him killed my mother. She was in her mid-forties when he was born, too old for child-bearing. My father had slaves, I thought he could have used them, but I know better now. If a man has one love he cannot just turn from her at will. I didn't blame Gaius really, but I think my father did; he gave the lad everything because the one thing he couldn't give him was forgiveness. And Gaius knew it, it made him bold, too bold.'

He ground his teeth and fell silent. Another tear squeezed itself from under his lid and trickled slowly down his lean cheek.

'Gently, my love, gently! Tell me what happened.'

He sighed, shrugged. 'He and a couple of friends were on deck; they had been ordered below. They say a boy was washed overboard and Gaius dived in ... the sea was like a boiling cauldron, neither of them stood a chance.'

He paused again. This time, Questa stayed silent. Let him tell it at his pace and in his own way, she cautioned herself. This has hurt him deeply; perhaps in the quiet retelling he may find some measure of comfort.

'They sent a messenger with the news. Gaius was highly regarded; they will do all that's necessary. I can only wish I'd told him I was proud of him instead of calling him evil names.'

'It was a dreadful thing, a tragic accident. But Marcus, it was wholly an accident, no one could possibly be held responsible, not even the other child. When boys play ...'

'Aye. But if I'd not let him go, if I'd said he was my heir, must stay in Britain, he might still be alive!'

Questa hugged his hands gently, in silent sympathy, and presently he turned and looked at her. She looked steadily back, out of eyes which were big with tears.

'You're crying for him too,' Marcus said. 'Or is it for me that you weep?'

'I'm crying for your pain and for Gaius's untimely death,' Questa said steadily. 'But to lay blame on yourself is wrong, Marcus. Mourn Gaius, think of him often with love, but don't reproach yourself for what is not your fault. It's – it's self-centred to think that you had any part in his death just because you agreed to let him stay with the army. If you'd brought him home he might have been gored by a bull or thrown by one of your young horses. It's happened and you can do nothing. You must learn acceptance, as I've had to.'

She knew that it was easier on her, though. Accepting the death of a woman in her eighties was one thing; coming to terms with the loss of a loved younger brother was quite another.

But Marcus nodded, then stood up. He took her hands and pulled her up, too. She saw that he was soaked to the skin, his strong curls flattened and wet, his cloak running with water, but his eyes were peaceful, his mouth firm.

'Good. I know you're right. I'll raise a memorial to him so that his name will live on, and I'll call my first child after him. I loved him and will never forget him, but you're right, to spend my life mourning for what I cannot put right would be both foolish and useless. I'll put it in hand at once; will you come with me now? Back to my house? You won't leave me?'

The words *as well* hovered, unsaid but implicit.

'I can't stay, you know that. But one day, soon, I'll come to you again, I promise. I can promise now, knowing my way. You'll take good care of yourself? And trust me to return?'

He sighed, then pulled her to him. Wet, chilly, still sluiced with rain, their mouths met and the flame of their love leaped between them, burning its fiery course from their mouths to the core of their beings. Questa was the first to draw back and that with reluctance.

'Oh Marcus, I wish I could stay for good, be with you always! Perhaps one day … but it's early, there's no need for me to rush off at once and when I do go I'll be back, I swear it. Are the horses well?'

He laughed down at her, his eyes mocking, loving, the darkness of despair banished from them for now, at least.

'Come and see for yourself! It's raining and cold and horrible, but in the stable it will be warm and snug. We could lie in the hay ... I would trace your lips with my finger and plait your hair; I would feed you with cream and honey and bind you with hoops of gold. Questa, I love no other.'

She looked up at him and saw truth shining from his dark eyes. Whatever had happened between him and the golden-haired slave girl it had not been love, she knew that for certain now. She reached up and kissed his chin, letting her body lie against his for a second.

'All right, I'll come. Shall we look at the horses before we examine their stabling, though?'

Hand in hand, they began to walk beneath the dripping trees.

When she woke back in her bed, she was warmed through and through by the blissful knowledge that she had got back into the dream and found that Marcus really loved her, would never forget her no matter how long she stayed away. What was more she had been of help to him, had eased his pain and guilt over his brother's death at sea.

They had spent hours together, and whatever they did they had held hands or been close, touching constantly, like lovers, since neither could bear to break the physical closeness. But they were no such thing; still something held Questa back. But now, lying in her own bed, she felt her breasts with a sort of shy curiosity, trying to gauge the differences in her body which she had only recently begun to notice.

When she had first come to England she had been flat as a boy, with little to show her femininity. Even pubic hair, which quite young girls grew, she had been told, had hardly put in an appearance on her emaciated body. Dr Barnes had said that it was natural, in time of war, for a girl to stop menstruating and that her lack of development was also due to poor food and to her general condition. She had said that when Questa was less tense and better fed, she would begin to develop as a young woman should.

Well, dear Dr Barnes had been right. Questa knew that her

304

breasts were growing, rounding to a presentable, normal size. The tiny berries of her nipples were bigger, too, and a deep rose-pink. Sometimes when she was in the bath and washing herself they went red, hardened, and stood out. She did not know why, she just knew that it happened.

But though she had not consciously considered it before, she now realised that her womanliness, if you could call it that, had been there from the start in her dream. It was only in real life that she had had to wait, and wait again. She was almost sure that even her hair had been longer, thicker, right from the first time she had begun to dream, whereas in reality she knew she had still looked rather like a shaggy and unkempt boy. It had been a long time before people who did not know her stopped thinking her a boy, whereas Marcus had never shown the slightest doubt, because there had been no reason to doubt. In his time, she was completely feminine.

And earlier, lying in the stable-loft with Marcus's hands on her, she had been aware of her breasts as never before. When Marcus had touched them, at first caressingly, then demandingly, they had tingled, sending strange, exciting sensations arrowing through her. Under his fingers they had seemed to swell and engorge in a way which was part pain, part pleasure. Does this mean I am becoming a woman at last, Questa wondered now? Fully a woman, with the ability to conceive and bear a child?

Outside her window, the dawn light was strengthening, the birds beginning to wake. Sleepy chirrupings would soon turn into strident morning calls, Questa knew; if she were to get any sleep at all she had better stop thinking about Marcus and make her mind a blank.

'I wants us to 'ave a picnic up in them 'ills, so's I can pick the wild thyme and 'ave a little thyme piller, like the one Ellen gave you,' Kat said one morning, as she and Questa worked in the dairy. Questa was using the butter churn on the cream which had been skimmed off a gallon of Cowslip's rich milk, whilst Kat poured the skim into a bucket to feed Cowslip's new-born calf. They had two new cows now, Cowslip and Buttercup, since Questa had decided to build up their dairy herd with the money from selling eight of her young pedigree gilts.

'Why d'you want a thyme pillow?' Questa asked. 'Who told you about it, anyway?'

'Alfie, acourse. Alfie said as 'ow you'd been lookin' right poorly till 'is old lady got you that there piller. I don't sleep so good under a roof, but if I 'ad that piller ...'

'Oh, I see. Why not? We could get Patrick and Bert to do the work so that we could take Saturday off,' Questa agreed. 'After all, Ellen's been gone two weeks, and quite soon now the others will be back. It does seem strange that you've never met Grace or Dickie. Come to that, we could get Alfie to run us up in Mr Atherton's car I expect.'

But at this Kat shook her head with a quick, sly glance at Questa which made her look, for one horrible moment, just like her mother.

'Nah, that won't do. Jest us, Questa.'

Questa finished her churning and dipped a finger into the butter. 'More salt,' she muttered. 'Why just us, Kat? You do like Alfie, don't you? A lot, I mean.'

'Oh ah, but I's a bit skeered, like,' Kat said gruffly, picking up the bucketful of skimmed milk as though it weighed next to nothing. For all her thinness she was a strong young woman and Questa fancied that she was already putting on weight. 'I don't know nothin' about bein' wed.'

'Oh! Well, I can't tell you much, because I've never been wed either. But I should have thought you'd know more than me – I mean caravans aren't very big and ... well, not *private*, either.'

'Oh, you 'ears every mortal sound they makes,' Kat admitted. 'I used to shove me 'ead under me blanket an' try to stop me lugs up. But you couldn't see much, what wi' curtains an' the dark an' all.'

Questa killed an instinctive urge to say 'I should hope not!' and remarked, instead, that she had always supposed that bulls and boars and rams had quite a lot in common with men.

Kat looked baffled. 'You got that wrong, missus,' she said positively. 'Bulls an' boars an' rams don't lie down when they's at it, an' cows an' gilts an' ewes don't shriek out, neither.'

'Do women, then?' Questa asked, torn between fascination and abhorrence. She seldom allowed herself to consider such things and thought if Ellen only knew what her daughter-in-law was discussing with such freedom and frankness she would turn in her grave, then immediately realised that nothing was further from the truth. Ellen would have said, with a sniff, that whatever a man and a woman got up to it was natural, same as for animals, and Questa need have no fears because natural never hurt no one, and anyway one day, when her time came, she would find out the truth for herself.

Kat paused in the doorway however, the heavy bucket dangling from one thin, freckled hand.

'Do a woman joinin' wi' a man shout out? Wuss'n a vixen on heat,' she said decisively. 'I's skeered of doin' it wrong, see? That's why I axed you.'

'I wish Ellen had talked to you,' Questa said. She mixed some more salt with her butter, tasted it, nodded. 'This is about right, now. I'm selling this batch to Mr Atherton since his son's coming back any time now and his people don't make butter. But failing Ellen, Alfie's a good person to ask about things. He's very gentle, he'll put you right if you do something wrong. So stop worrying and leave it to him. And tomorrow we'll go to the hills and collect thyme for your pillow – if it's fine, that is. If it's raining we'll think again.'

It was not raining. In fact it was another cloudless blue day with swallows swooping low over the yard when Questa left her room and went through to the kitchen. Kat was there already, looking hollow-eyed.

'I ain't goin' to give in,' she said, when Questa asked her why she did not sleep out, if that was the only way she could get some rest. 'Anyroad, be tomorrer I'll 'ave that piller. This time tomorrer I'll 'ave slep' like a log all night!'

'And since the sun's shining, the quicker we get on with things the sooner we can leave,' Questa said. It was a long tramp to the hills of Wales; if they were to be there and back by nightfall, they had no time to waste. 'Come and help me with the milking, will you? You're quicker than I am.'

'It's 'cos of them fingers, the ones you cotched in suffin', so they was 'urt,' Kat said blithely. 'Alfie told me about 'em, said it slowed you down. Never mind, you're quicker'n me at most things.'

'Umm, yes,' Questa said. So Alfie had noticed how she fumbled with the teats at first, trying to keep her little fingers out of harm's way. But he was so nice, so understanding … he had never let her know that he'd noticed her poor, deformed hands. 'But my fingers are all right now, you know. They don't get in my way when I milk any more.'

On impulse, she stretched her hands out in front of her and looked at them; really looked, critically and not shrinkingly. She had to look hard and searchingly to see anything was wrong at all and wondered how they had managed to straighten themselves so well, to take on the same shade as the rest of her skin in place of the livid purple of scar tissue? She put her hands closer to her face; yes, her little fingers were not quite straight, but they weren't crooked and deformed, either. Just … well, just not quite straight!

'Well, I'm damned!' she said slowly. 'Kat, they look all right!'

Kat was in the pantry, getting the loaf out. It was no longer Ellen's baking, but Questa had done her best and thought the bread passable. Kat squinted across at her through the bright sunlight falling across the room.

'All right? 'Course they looks all right! You done it afore you come 'ere, Alfie said, and you've bin 'ere nigh on eighteen month. Are we 'aving breakfast or not?'

'Not. We'll take sandwiches and eat them when we arrive,' Questa said. 'Oh Kat, isn't it a marvellous day?'

It was a long way, longer than Questa had anticipated, though they cut across country, which saved them the very much longer journey by road. But despite the distance, she thoroughly enjoyed the tramp. Kat walked easily, with a long, swinging stride which Questa speedily copied, and of course they talked as they went. Kat's prurient interest in the ways of a man with a maid seemed to have dissipated after their talk, and instead they discussed farming, animals, gypsy lore, anything and everything that occurred to them.

Questa soon discovered that though Kat was ignorant in some ways – she could barely read, and then only the simplest of words, and could not add up, despite having spent two years, 'on and off', she said, in school – she was wiser than many older people in others. She knew about wild life, how to trap for food, when to leave well alone, how to recognise each animal from its spoor or excreta. She could name every wild flower, every herb, growing in hedge or pasture, could tell Questa which were edible, which were to be avoided.

Of the war she spoke little. Travellers, she said, had been hard hit by all the rules and regulations and found rationing strange and unnatural. But she managed to convey that, despite these things, the travellers had still gone very much their own way.

'Every man's hand is agin us,' she said with an indifference which Questa found truly astonishing. 'Tidn't mek much difference that they Germans were out to git ole England, folk still blamed us for owt and nowt. Ne'ertheless, what we couldn't buy we'd git, some'ow.'

'But everyone was going short,' Questa said. 'I mean even the king and queen and the little princesses had ration books.'

Kat snorted. 'Oh ah? din't they never tell you nothin' about the black market?'

They had not, but Kat soon put Questa right. The rich, as usual, had not gone short of anything which mattered. 'Money 'ud buy you anythin', jest about,' she said. 'There was gals, they'd sell their kewpongs an' points an' that for a few quid ... still goes on, I'd dare swear.'

'I wonder if that's why Grace has such nice clothes?' Questa mused, remembering the apparently unending supply. 'She said it was pre-war stuff, but I always did wonder. Just think, she and Dickie will be back in two or three days.'

'Aye. And you'll 'ave to tell 'em about Ellen – and about me,' Kat said with some relish. 'Wonder what they'll say about me, eh?'

'It's none of their business,' Questa said stoutly. 'It's my house, I can do what I like with it. Besides, in a few weeks you'll be living in the coachman's flat, with Alfie.'

'True. Ah, one more medder an' we're in the woods, gal!'

Questa looked across the sloping uphill meadow, fringed at the top with trees. Kat was right, they were nearly there. The hills, which had looked so distant, were suddenly upon them, the scent of the thyme they had come to pick was in their nostrils, the breeze blew cooler, here, than on the lower reaches of the hillside.

'Where's this thyme, then, gal? Right at the top?' Kat closed her eyes and shivered ecstatically. 'Eh, I do love goin' right up to the tops, where the silence is so loud you can 'ear it, an' the wind blows cold.'

'No, the thyme grows best about halfway up,' Questa told her. 'I'll show you.'

They could see the stream and followed it until they reached the little glade with the wild thyme, purple now with blossom, spread out like a carpet before them.

'There! Shall we have our food, now?'

Kat plonked herself down on the grass and unfastened the satchel slung around her shoulders. Questa followed suit. Because of the weight they had not brought a drink but the stream would be sufficient, and they had split the sandwiches so that she carried egg and ham and Kat had honey and bramble jelly. Each had brought an enamel mug and now Questa got to her feet and went and dipped them, one at a time, into the stream.

'Here,' she said, putting Kat's mug on the ground beside her. 'How does that taste?'

'Good,' Kat said after taking a deep drought. She wiped her mouth with the back of her hand. 'Gi's them sangwiches, I'm fair starved!'

They ate contentedly, drinking the cool, fresh, stream water, finishing up with an apple each.

'We'll 'ave a nap,' Kat announced when they'd eaten. 'Then we'll stuff the thyme into our satchels. Go on, gal, treat yourself to forty winks.'

Questa knew that she would never dare sleep here, not a second time. Even now, the memory of Marcus's brown hand sliding down that girl's stomach disturbed her, bringing back the pain she had suffered, the sharp, unbearable jealousy.

'I'm not tired,' she said. 'I'll go for a wander round.'

Kat grunted. She was already dozing, her tawny lashes on her cheeks, her hand beneath her head.

'Please yourself,' she said without opening her eyes. 'Wake me in an hour or so.'

'Right,' Questa said. She kicked off her shoes and went and paddled for a bit, gradually making her way upstream until she could paddle no further, since at that point the stream came from underground. It was still hot but the breeze was pleasant so she continued to climb. It would be nice to reach the top and to see what was on the other side.

The hill grew steeper, heather-covered, with the brash brassy yellow of gorse starring it at intervals. Grasshoppers chirped, small birds murmured and trilled, a stone-chat sat on a bramble and chattered his strange little cry at her, eyeing her all the while with a mixture of interest and alarm. Presently, she came upon something very like a road, made up of big, flat stones. The stones were overgrown and half-obscured with earth but you could still trace the road clearly enough because the heather and gorse had not flourished here the way they flourished elsewhere.

Questa followed the road to the summit, but the view was rather disappointing; more hills, stretching away into the blue distance, each one seeming higher than the last. And on the other side of her particular hill there were stands of fir trees leading down to a bracken-filled valley, buzzing with flies which swooped drunkenly above the curled fronds of the bracken and attacked anything that moved. Birds swooped on them, but apart from the birds the flies had things all their own way and Questa decided she had explored far enough in this direction. When she looked behind her she could see Eagles Court, tiny and toylike in its fields, with Atherton Hall looking just a stone's throw away. Both estates looked cared for and kempt, so there was a lot to be said for a distant view. Questa stared for a moment, then turned down the hill again, following the wide road, wondering where it would lead her.

She soon found that it was easier to follow the road upwards than down. As she got lower, so the undergrowth increased until she had quite a job to find the flat stones with her eyes, let alone with her feet. Finally, deciding that the road must just have petered out, she flung herself down in disgust, and immediately knew she was still on the road from the shape of the stones on which she sat.

Still. She dared not go back to the glade in case she fell asleep there, so if she was going to indulge in a nap she would do so here, beside the roughly paved road. She sat down in the long grass, then lay back – or would have lain back, but for one thing. There was an obstruction just here. She rubbed her shoulder ruefully where it had landed on a large rock rearing out of the ground. Curses, what was it? It looked a little like a milestone ... just where was this road halfway to – or from, for that matter? She rolled over on to her stomach and began to investigate.

It was not a milestone; when she examined it she realised that what she was seeing was just the tip of the iceberg; the rest of the stone was buried beneath the gorse and heather. She dug about with a piece of stick, then tore up some of the undergrowth, but apart from the fact that it was clearly man-made and had a line of what looked like writing chipped out on its surface, it was a mystery.

Curious, Questa heaved at the roots of the heather, but it was too tough and the gorse was too prickly, so she gave up, sitting back and glaring resentfully at the stone. Not a milestone – what on earth was it, then? Stuck up here beside the old Roman road ... desperately, she dug a bit more with her piece of stick and managed to confirm that the writing really was writing and not just faint marks. It was oddly angular writing ... heavens, it was in Latin!

For a moment she frowned at it, trying to concentrate, to stop her mind from going back and worrying at something Marcus had said – what did this stone have to do with Marcus, for goodness sake? Then she remembered: *I'll raise a memorial to him so that his name will live on* – Marcus had said he would do that for his brother Gaius, who had been drowned at sea.

With renewed interest she attacked the heather and gorse which had half-choked the stone, ripping it briskly, uprooting, destroying. Soon she had it half clear and sat back, sweat streaming down her back and making her shirt stick to her wet skin. That was better, she might not be able to read all of it, but she

312

should be able to see enough to know whether her guess was right.

She could not read it, but she thought she could see the name Gaius. She had seen other remembrance stones, similar to this one, but she could not remember much about them; probably her father had taken her to museums as a child. Alan said he had been fascinated by ancient civilisations so what more natural than to take his daughter to such places? She sat back on her heels, trying to remember the translation of the writing on those other stones. It was coming into her mind, word by word almost. It had read something like: *To the spirits of the departed, I beg that so-and-so, son of such-and-such, who died after only fifteen years of life, be remembered kindly, as I, so-and-so, son of such-and-such, shall remember him.*

This stone must say something very like that. It seemed odd that Marcus had set it up so far from the estate, but Questa recalled hearing somewhere that the Romans wanted their dead remembered, and who better to remember and say a prayer than the travellers along a well-used road?

She ran a hand over the roughness of the stone – poor Gaius, she could feel tears for him forming at the back of her eyes, even though he had been dead two thousand odd years, and she had never known him in life, nor even in her dream.

But the stones she crouched on her were hard and she still had a lot to do; they must pick the thyme and fill their satchels with it and then make the long walk back. It would seem twice as long, Questa knew from experience, as the walk out had seemed, but that would be because they had done what they set out to do and were tired after their day.

She rolled over and knelt up. Sadly, she touched the stone with her fingertips, trying to feel some kinship with Marcus, who had ordered the stone put there. But too many thick years lay between them; all she could feel was rough, lichened stone and a faint sadness because there had been loss here, and pain. As she knelt there a butterfly, blue as the sky overhead, fluttered past her and landed for a moment on the grey stone. It spread its wings, then trembled them and took off again, a tiny aeroplane tacking hither and thither across the sky, no doubt drunk on

313

heather honey and sunshine. Pretty little creature, it would probably make shorter work of the miles between these hills and Eagles Court than she! Reluctantly, Questa got to her feet. She gave the stone one last, valedictory glance, then set off for the glade. Poor Kat, you could tell how truly exhausted she must be if she were still sleeping soundly after their long walk and a couple of hours snoozing in the sun!

She reached the glade and called to Kat, still lying exactly as she had left her. The older girl woke and gazed around her, bewilderment in her face, then she saw Questa and smiled.

'Oh, Ques, I needed that!' she remarked, sitting up and knuckling her eyes, then stretching and yawning enormously, so that Questa could have seen her tonsils had she been so inclined. 'Well, let's git on, gal!'

They made short work of the thyme, picking enough for a pillow in ten minutes.

'We've left it rather late, we'll have to hurry,' Questa said to Kat as they began to walk down the hill once more, satchels bulging. 'It's more my fault than yours, I was dreaming away up the hill, but we really should have left an hour or more ago.'

'Why's it matter? If it gits dark, so what? We've eyes to see an' young legs to tek us 'ome,' Kat said sturdily. 'I likes a-walkin' in the dark, anyroad. Powerful good smells there are of a night-time.'

But they were saved the worst part of the walk. They had to cross the main road at one point and Kat gestured Questa back; car headlights were coming fast towards them.

'Wait on, gal, you don't wanter git yourself run down,' she observed. 'Let 'im pass!'

But as the headlights caught the two of them, the car slowed, then stopped a little past them and began to reverse. Immediately all Questa's doubts rose to the surface. She might have turned and run but for the fact that someone wound down the passenger window and a familiar voice called her name. 'Questa! What on earth are you doing? Who's your friend?'

Questa jumped, then ran forward, scarcely knowing whether to laugh or cry. She had missed Grace so much, but she was the bearer of such incredibly bad tidings.

'Oh, Grace, I'm so glad to see you, this is my friend Kathleen, she's staying with us for ... look, something terrible has happened, I don't know how to tell you ... is Dickie awake?'

'No, fast asleep. Do get in, Questa, you can talk as we go. We're both pretty tired, we caught an early ferry from Dun Laoghaire so we've been travelling most of the day.'

Alan leaned across Grace and the child sleeping on her lap. He opened the back door of the car, then gestured her inside. Even in the semi-darkness Questa fancied she could see concern in his face.

'Something's happened! I knew we ought to have kept in touch, but we were miles from civilisation and somehow the days just passed in a daze of sunshine and good food. Jump in, both of you, and tell us what's gone on.'

Questa got into the back and moved up so that Kat could follow.

'Look, I'm sorry to have to tell you this in such a blunt way, but Ellen died more than two weeks ago. We tried to contact you but we didn't have an address or anything ... the funeral's over and we're doing our best to get back to normal because that's what Ellen would have wanted. And Kat's moved into the house to give a hand ... she's been wonderful.'

'My God! Ellen, dead? What happened, my dear?'

Alan sounded shocked and upset, too. He had known Ellen when he was a lad; she must have been a sort of link with the young Charles, and Questa knew that Alan had liked her a good deal. He had teased her, laughed at her, but he had respected her common sense approach to life as well as her deep knowledge of the countryside.

'She got pneumonia and then had a fall. It was that and shock, the doctor said. She had a lovely funeral, her people, the travellers, came from miles around; they were really fond of her, as we all were. I don't know what we'll do without her, to tell the truth.'

'It's a terrible blow,' Alan said. He sounded shocked but thoughtful, too, almost abstracted. 'Look, let's get indoors; we'll talk then. I'm absolutely shattered; she was old I know, but she always seemed so healthy and in command. I don't think I've taken it in properly yet.'

The car drew up outside the kitchen door and for the next twenty minutes everyone was too busy to talk much. After the briefest of introductions Kat disappeared into her room with the satchels of thyme, Questa began to make a meal, Alan unpacked the car and Grace took Dickie, still sleeping soundly, up to bed. It was not until an hour later, when they had eaten a makeshift meal of cold pie and potatoes and Kat, who had scarcely opened her mouth all evening, had taken herself off to bed, that they really got down to talking about what had happened.

'I'm sorry I never even asked if you'd had a good time,' Questa said remorsefully, after she had re-lived, for Alan, the last few hours of Ellen's life. 'It's just been so terrible, losing Ellen, that I've scarcely thought about what you would be doing.'

'We enjoyed ourselves all right,' Grace said.

Grace had been remarkably low-key ever since her return, Questa thought, remarkably restrained and thoughtful. Even when Questa had divulged that Kat was half-traveller and was to marry Alfie in the autumn despite being less than half his age, she said nothing really unpleasant. She did not say sharply that she did not intend to share the house for a good few weeks with a gypsy, and Questa, who had rehearsed what she would say in defence of Kat, was quite taken aback.

'You did? Good; and how was Ireland?'

'I loved Ireland,' Grace said with real enthusiasm. 'It's as beautiful as the countryside around here. Alan's family used to have property in Donegal. You should see the colours, Questa, all pale blues and mauves and greens ... I loved it. I said I'd like to live there, one day.'

'And I said it wouldn't be for quite a while,' Alan said, smiling at Questa. 'My business needs me, but one day, when we've saved some money, I'd like to go back and become landed gentry where my forefathers once farmed.'

Questa stared from one to the other. 'Does this mean ...?'

Alan nodded, looking self-conscious. 'Yes, it means Grace has said she'll marry me.'

'That's wonderful!' Questa said. She meant every word. She was fond of Grace and liked Alan well enough, and besides, it would mean that she would not have to worry that Grace might want Eagles Court either for herself or for her son. She smiled from one to the other as they sat squeezed close in one of the big armchairs.

'I take it that Alan knows Dickie and I are half-brother and sister? So if I never have children, Dickie will probably inherit this place!'

There was a complete and utter silence. The fire in the stove settled, the flames hissed and overhead a board creaked. Alan sat as if turned to stone; Grace was frozen, opposite.

'Dickie's ... *what*?'

'He's m–my half-brother,' Questa stammered, staring from one to the other. 'You must have known, Alan! If Ellen could see the likeness, then surely you, who were so much closer to my father, must have seen it too? Didn't Grace tell you? Didn't she explain that ...'

Alan got to his feet. He was sickly white, his thin hands gripped into fists, a scowl beginning to form on his normally placid brow.

'Well, Grace?'

Grace was scarlet, her eyes darting daggers at Questa. 'Alan, I meant to tell you ...'

But she was talking to herself. Alan had left, shutting the door far too gently behind him.

Fourteen

Across the room, empty now save for themselves, the two girls stared at each other.

'You've finished me,' Grace said at last. Her voice was low, almost indifferent. 'When did Ellen tell you?'

'Just before she died. She seemed to think it was important. She seemed to think that you might use it in some way. Look, Grace, I really am very sorry, I had no idea that you'd agree to marry Alan and not tell him about Dickie and – and my father. He – he wouldn't have *minded*, for God's sake! Whatever possessed you to keep quiet about it?'

'Lots of reasons, but there are only two which need concern you. One was that Alan wanted to marry me ages ago, and I turned him down. I thought he was ... oh I don't know, boring, plain, that sort of thing. I told him, and it was true, that I still loved Charles no matter what he'd done to me and that made Alan jealous, made him very bitter against Charles, though clearly it didn't last; they were too close for that.'

'And the other reason?'

'I was ashamed of having come here hoping to be able to take over from you, with Dickie as the heir,' Grace said in a red-faced rush. 'It wasn't a nice thing to do, but I was so desperately unhappy, I really rather hated you. I even hated Cain, just for a moment or two.'

'Cain?'

'That's what I called Charles, because he was Adamson – Adam's son, get it? Cain was Adam's son, and the first murderer. Charles might just as well have murdered that little seventeen-year-old, because she died, Questa, when she found out he didn't ... had never ...'

'You mean he broke your heart,' Questa said sadly. 'But you

318

know very well that he did love you, because later he married you, didn't he? Men don't marry women they don't love, Grace!'

'Oh, but they do, of course they do! A man will marry a woman he almost loves, or nearly loves, when the love of his life has left him. Questa, you know nothing – nothing! Why do you think I said I'd marry Alan? Why do you think Alan's walked out of here looking like grim death? Why, because he knows he's not even second-best, he's the only one left, it wasn't just Cain, remember, there was Simon Syrett ... '

'I think, Grace, that you underestimate yourself as well as other people. If Alan's really not even second-best, if you accepted him simply because you feel he's the only one left, then he's right to walk out on you and you shouldn't be looking upset, because to lose someone you don't care about doesn't hurt, not much. If, on the other hand, you love Alan, then you ought to tell him so and not let him believe that he's been deceived deliberately for some obscure reason.'

Grace, who had been pacing the kitchen, collapsed into a chair and Questa sat down opposite her. They stared at each other.

'I ... I'm not sure how I feel,' Grace said at last. Her voice sounded neither sorry for itself nor sulky, but puzzled. 'I do like Alan a lot, I almost loved him in Ireland, when we were together, laughing at the same things, sharing the same jokes, fussing over Dickie. But then I think of Cain, who was so tall and blond, I remember how I felt when he touched me – when he looked at me, come to that – and I know it can't be love I feel for Alan. It's much tamer, much quieter altogether.'

'I know you say I know nothing, but wasn't what you felt for ... for Cain first love? Calf love, if you like? And isn't the feeling you have for Alan not so much quieter as deeper, more pro- found? Because you're both older and you aren't going to feel that fluttery, desperate sort of feeling which is – is so intense that it almost hurts, not twice in one lifetime. Is it possible, Grace, that you expect too much from your own feelings?'

'Oh Questa, you ...' Grace stopped short. She turned her eyes away from Questa's and gazed, instead, at her hands lying idle in her lap. She frowned down at them as though she had never seen hands before, but Questa felt that her thoughts were far away, that she was not seeing her hands or the kitchen or anything else, but was looking back, into the past.

'Yes? What do you want to say, Grace? That I know nothing?'

Grace continued to stare down at her hands, then she looked up at Questa and answered as though she had not heard the last sentence.

'What do you know about first love? You're a dark horse. No one could talk about first love who hadn't experienced it, yet you … well, you don't even know any men!'

'It doesn't matter what I know or what I don't know, it's what I understand that's important, and I believe I do understand about some feelings.' Questa got up from her chair and dropped to her knees in front of Grace, taking the older woman's hands in her own and gazing earnestly into the blue, bewildered eyes. Because they were bewildered, she could see that now, not just hurt and a trifle sulky but bewildered by what was happening to her. 'Grace, you'll never feel that total subjugation to one man again, not in quite that way at any rate. You can't, human beings can't live with such powerful, painful feelings. I think Ran would say that they were the prerogative of the young. You've got to settle down and fit your feelings to how you are now, not how you were. Oh dear, I'm not very good at explaining, but you're more experienced than I – can't you see how it has to be?'

'You mean I'm too old for love? Questa, that can't be true, people far older than me fall in love!'

Questa sat back on her heels and sighed. How on earth could she get it over to Grace that first love was just that, first love, and couldn't be re-tasted, not with the same degree of flavour, at any rate? Besides, she was not certain she was right, she just believed she was from watching others and from her own small experience.

'Of course you can fall in love, you can do that at any age! But I don't think the knife-edge intensity can be there any more, not after the first time. It – it's greedy to expect it, Grace. The first strawberries taste like something out of paradise, but by the end of the season strawberries are just commonplace. See what I mean?'

Oddly enough, the food analogy was one which clearly

touched a nerve in Grace. She nodded slowly, and for the first time the hands in Questa's no longer tried to pull away.

'Yes, I can see ... yes! Oh God, Questa, what have I done? You're absolutely right, I do love Alan, I want him to be a part of my life. I don't want him to walk out of here tonight and avoid me because he feels he's been cheated. What should I do?'

'Go to him,' Questa said. 'Tell him, not me.'

'Oh, but ... where's he gone?'

'I don't know. To his room, or out into the night. Follow him, Grace. If he's important to you, and I think he is, then find him and tell him so. Alan's a good man, he'll do his best to understand.'

'Ye-es, but suppose he isn't interested now? Suppose he thinks I'm just a gold-digger, after his money?'

'He won't. Go on, Grace, or I'll lose all patience with you.'

Grace stood up, patted the folds of her cream-coloured dress, put a hand to her hair, then headed for the door leading out into the hall.

'Right. See you in the morning.'

Questa watched the door close and began to clear up for the night. Oh Ellen, she thought, how did I handle it? Will they get together, after all? I hope they do, but if they don't, Grace will stay here, with me, and we'll both work at getting Eagles Court straightened out.

Only what would be the point, if Grace was doing it so that Dickie could inherit when Questa was dead and gone? And suppose Grace still thought that she and Dickie had the more rightful claim on the estate? It wouldn't make for an easy or comfortable working relationship. No, it was better for everyone that Grace and Alan should marry and leave her to manage here alone. And with Ran's help, and Kat and Alfie, she ought to be able to make a go of it, with or without Grace.

Alan was her man of business, though, the executor of her father's will. He would not let her down, even if he wouldn't have quite the same interest in Eagles Court with Grace no longer here. And Kat isn't going to run out on me, Questa told herself, suddenly tired and uncertain, longing for reassurance, wishing Ellen alive and here again with all her might. Kat and Alfie and me ... we'll manage, somehow.

Her tasks all done, she took herself off to the small parlour and bed. But before she went she tiptoed up the stairs and listened shamefacedly outside Alan's door, and then outside Grace's.

Nothing. Not a sound. Neither the heavy breathing of a sleeper nor the twanging springs of a lover. Only silence.

So she lay her head down on her ordinary feather pillow and slept soundly, and dreamlessly, until morning.

Next morning Questa got up as usual. She wondered whether to go upstairs and let Roma out, but when she was only three stairs up the dog came bounding down to meet her, wagging her plumy tail. Questa stroked her, glanced up at the stairs in case this meant that Dickie was on his way down, then headed for the kitchen with Roma bouncing at her knee.

Kat, looking bright-eyed, was already in the kitchen with the back door wide open and sunshine streaming in. She had filled the kettle and was putting it over the hob but she turned and grinned at Questa as she heard the door open.

'Slep' like a bloomin' log I did,' she announced. 'I jest shovelled the thyme into a pillercase and lay me 'ead on it and orf I went into the land o' dreams. Bes' night's kip I've 'ad for a while, I tells you.'

'Yes; Ellen knew a thing or two,' Questa admitted. 'I wonder if Grace is getting up to give a hand?'

'No need,' Kat said at once. 'Let's get on wi' it, you an' me.'

'Well, she's home now, perhaps if I take her a cup of tea ...'

'Leave 'er lie,' Kat said brusquely. 'She'll come down when she's ready.'

'Oh, Kat, d'you think she and Alan made it up? Oh, you don't know, but after you went to bed they had a row.'

Kat grinned at her and seized the kettle as it began to hiss. She tilted it above the brown teapot, then stirred the brew vigorously.

'Likely they did,' she said. 'Are you 'avin' a cup afore you start the milkin' or not?'

'Yes, please. I hope they did make it up, because in a way it was my fault that they argued ... if you could call it an argument. Alan just walked out after ... oh well, we'll know soon enough I daresay.'

The two girls drank their tea and went out to the meadow with Roma dancing at their heels. The cows were waiting by the gate and walked sedately along to the cowshed, quite happy to be led into the stalls to be milked. Questa and Kat, already slipping into a familiar routine, took a cow each, got their stools, and started work.

With the milk hissing into the metal pail, Questa had the leisure to consider once again just what was going to happen with Grace. If only I hadn't opened my big mouth – but how was I to know?

The milk began to slacken, the bursts grew shorter, more fitful. You did know though, Questa reminded herself. You knew quite well that Grace might not have told Alan; she's a devious person, you knew that too. So why did you come right out with it like that, when they were tired and still shocked by the news of Ellen's death? Were you jealous because they were planning to get married and you weren't? There won't be any wedding bells for you, Questa Adamson.

But her reiteration of her own name just reminded her once again of Grace's story, Grace's plight, and when she moved on to Daisy and then finished with her, too, she was anxious to return to the kitchen and find out if a remark which she should never have made had had the dire consequences which had seemed possible the previous evening.

'Can you deal with the milk?' Questa asked Kat when they had poured the buckets into the churns. 'The milk lorry comes to the end of the other side of the arch, the driver will hump them on to the lorry for you.'

'I'll do it, no bother,' Kat said breezily. 'Will you start grub?'

Now that they were settling down, Bert came and fed the stock and saw to things, and usually ate with them, though Patrick didn't start until later in the morning.

'Yes, of course, if Grace isn't down, that is.'

Questa went into the kitchen, kicking off her boots outside the back door and padding across the stone tiles in her socks. Dickie came into the room through the other doorway just as she entered.

'Hello, Ques! It's nice to be home, though we had a lovely

holiday! I don't 'member getting back last night ... did you know Mummy and Uncle Alan are going to get married? Mummy wants a house in the country and a flat in London ... she says I can take Roma and I can come and see you whenever she does ... she says I can have a pony of my own!'

'That sounds lovely, Dickie,' Questa said, but with a sinking heart. What had she done? It was bad enough to have hurt and embarrassed Grace – and Alan, too – but to have hurt poor Dickie would be worse. And if Grace had to tell her son that it was all off ...

Dickie sat down and leaned over to get a slice of bread just as the kitchen door opened again and Grace slouched into the room. Slouched was the only word. She was in her blue dressing gown, with her hair loose around her shoulders and no make-up on. She looked, Questa saw thankfully, extremely pleased with herself.

'Morning, Ques, morning Dickie, darling! Pour me a cup of tea, Ques, I'm so thirsty you wouldn't believe.' She looked self-conscious suddenly. 'Alan won't be long ... can I give you a hand with the brekker?'

'Please. Can you make the porridge? Make enough for six, because Bert comes in for breakfast now. He's full-time, or as good as.'

'All right. Did you bring some milk in? We could do with some; there's only half a jug left in the pantry.'

'Oh gosh, we shot all the milk into the churns,' Questa said guiltily. 'I never thought ... Dickie, be a pal! Go and tell Kat to rescue some and bring it in for breakfast, would you?'

'Which cat?' Dickie said, looking puzzled.

'Oh damn, you were asleep last night ... darling, there's a lady called Kat come to help us, she's got red hair, she's going to take the cows back up to the pasture when she's got the churns sorted out. Tell her to bring some in, there's a good boy.'

'Okey-dokey,' Dickie said jauntily. He slid off his chair and headed for the back door. 'Shan't be long.'

'Well, that was tactful of you, Ques,' Grace said approvingly as soon as Dickie had disappeared, with Roma so close her nose must have been touching the back of his leg. 'It's all right, Alan understands. We're going to be married, just as I said!'

'Oh Grace, I'm so glad! I was such a fool, but it doesn't matter now, all that matters is that you'll be happy, both of you. And Dickie of course.'

'Yes. I caught Alan up just outside his room and just flung myself into his arms, Questa, simply flung myself, and I told him how sorry I was and how I loved him, just like you said, and he sat me on the bed and talked to me very seriously, about truth and love and things like that. And then ... ' she looked arch, 'one thing led to another and next thing I knew it was morning.'

'And you were still in Alan's room?'

'In Alan's *bed*, my dear girl! After all, I had to prove I meant what I said and that seemed as good a way as any. And a man who's deeply in love has desires ... if I let him down now he'd almost certainly turn to someone else, someone he didn't think anything of, perhaps ... oh, but you wouldn't understand.'

'I do understand,' Questa said. She thought of Marcus's brown hand against the milky skin of the slave girl's stomach and swallowed hard. 'Oh, I do understand, Grace! So it's all settled, then? How soon will you get married? Alfie and Kat will be marrying in only just over a month; they'll have the banns read in church quite soon and you have to wait three weeks, apparently.'

'We're not going to rush a thing,' Grace said contentedly. She looked so lovely, warm and soft and pleased with life, that Questa felt almost jealous. If this was what making love did to a girl, then the sooner she, too, experienced it the better.

But that was wrong, stupid! It was different for Grace, she had been married before, she knew what she was missing. As for me, it really doesn't apply. I had better get down to being content with my lot and working hard, Questa thought rather dolefully. After all, heaps of people never marry.

'So when will it be, Grace? Your wedding, I mean.'

'Well, it's the end of August now, so probably some time in the spring or even early summer. I'd like April or May, myself, such a pretty time of year. Only Alan rather wants me to find a house and so on – we thought nearish to London – so I'll probably be leaving here in a couple of weeks. Before Kat and Alfie are married, I expect. There's so much to do, Ques, you've no idea!

I probably shan't have much of a trousseau but I'll need bits and pieces, and Dickie will be going to a new school so he'll want the uniform. Alan rather fancies Windsor, but I thought Tunbridge Wells would be nice, there's some beautiful countryside in Kent, we could have a cottage ... '

Love, Questa thought rather sourly, ladling porridge into dishes, seemed to have – temporarily at least – blinded Grace to certain facts. One was that if they lived in Tunbridge Wells and Alan had to commute to London every day, Grace would soon be just as lonely in Tunbridge Wells as out in the country somewhere. She was just thinking, rather unkindly, that this would just serve Grace right, when Grace remarked: 'We'll probably live in town during the week, of course, in Alan's house. Then Dickie can go to school in town, and come down to our country place with us at weekends and holidays.'

'Lovely,' Questa said glumly. 'I shan't be seeing much of you, then.'

'No, I shouldn't think so,' Grace said sunnily. 'You'll be able to get on here and do whatever you want without me nagging and Dickie tagging.' She giggled. 'Why, you can plant those vines and welcome. We'll come down and get sozzled like I said, but I shan't have to pick the things, or tread them or whatever.'

'I will plant grapevines,' Questa said shortly, 'when you've gone. Early winter's the right time, I believe. Ah, here's Dickie back.'

Dickie came in, accompanied by Kat lugging a large enamel jug.

'Here's your milk, gal,' she announced, thumping the jug down on the table. 'Nice an' 'ot from the cow.'

Grace gave a faint moan and averted her face. So she had not changed completely then, Questa thought with a wry smile. Alan would see the real Grace, as well as this smiling, gentle creature.

'Milk my porridge, Mummy,' Dickie commanded, taking his seat at the table once more. 'Where's Ellen?'

Questa opened her mouth to speak but Grace was before her.

'Ellen died whilst we were away; she was very old,' she said. 'Never mind, you won't miss her as much as you might have done, because we're going to live with Alan, remember.'

Dickie gave one horrified glance round the table, threw himself sideways off his chair on to the floor and burst into tears, rubbing his face into the rag rug and howling dolorously.

'Dickie, it's all right, don't cry, Ellen's gone to heaven, remember,' Questa said desperately. 'Grace, you really are the silliest ...'

'Darling, don't cry ... oh God, why don't I think? And I was so terribly happy!' Grace wailed. 'Dickie, Ellen's gone to Jesus, I didn't mean to say she'd died, exactly.'

Questa was about to tell Grace pretty sharply that she was an even worse idiot than she had at first supposed when Dickie raised a tear-blubbered face from the rug and climbed slowly back on to his chair.

'I don't want her to go to Jesus, I want her here,' he said slowly, rubbing a grubby fist across his eyes. 'When'll she be back?'

'Oh, later on,' Grace said vaguely. She mouthed something at Questa, then mouthed it again, slower and more clearly. 'Day of Judgement', mouthed Grace, adding waspishly, aloud, 'So don't you look at me with that righteous expression, Questa Adamson, unless you're prepared to deny the D of J, and put up with all the carry-on,' she added, jerking her head at the rag rug.

Kat was grinning from ear to ear; Grace, pink-faced, was clattering the pans in the sink and Questa was about to sit down and start her own porridge when the door opened again and Alan came in.

He looked ... different. Taller. Broader. Even his hair did not seem quite so sparse and his smile made him almost attractive. His eyes sought Grace's and his smile changed subtly, becoming possessive, proud.

'Darling!' Grace cooed. 'Come and have some breakfast. Questa, get Alan's porridge, would you?'

'You get it; I'm about to eat,' Questa said rather crossly. She had just noticed that Alan was not wearing his glasses and his shirt was open at the neck instead of neatly fastened and worn with a tie. Which was the real Alan, then? This relaxed, smiling, not-so-old man or the tense and anxious one, glancing quickly from face to face, wanting to please but not knowing quite how to do it?

327

'Morning, Gracie. Morning, Ques, Dickie ... Kat,' Alan said. 'Any tea? I think I'll have a bath if that's all right. Put the porridge on hold would you, sweetheart?'

'Oh, but darling ...'

'I'll go and run the bath; you bring me a cup up,' Alan said. He smiled meaningly at Grace. 'You can come and scrub my back if you like.'

'Alan! Really – we aren't married yet, you know ...' Grace began, to be put in her place immediately.

'Aren't we? Well, I'd never have guessed it. I feel very married indeed, and very happy as well.' He strode across the kitchen and kissed Grace possessively and positively, then put her away from him, smiling down into her flushed face. 'See you shortly, darling.'

He left, shutting the door with rather more exuberance than care.

'Shouldn't slam the door,' Dickie muttered through porridge. 'Uncle Alan's noisy today.'

'I expect it was a mistake,' Questa said soothingly. 'More porridge, Dickie?'

Alan stayed for three days, and when he left Grace went too, but she left Dickie at Eagles Court.

'Questa, are you sure you don't mind?' she asked anxiously as she and Alan, dressed for town, stood beside the car on the gravel sweep, no longer weedy and neglected. 'Only as you said you'd have him whilst we honeymoon, it seemed like a good idea to leave him here for a few days. We'll be house-hunting, shopping, doing all sorts of things that would bore him to tears. But we'll be back at the weekend, I promise.'

'He'll be fine with us,' Questa said. 'And it's Kat's wedding soon – you wouldn't miss that, would you, Grace?'

'No, of course not,' Grace said, looking shifty. Questa guessed that Grace considered the wedding of a farm labourer and a gypsy to be far beneath her, but she would probably come back and attend it rather than openly acknowledge herself to be a snob.

'Well, we'd best be off,' Alan said. He wasn't looking shifty, he was looking mighty pleased with himself, proud of the woman beside him, proud of his own cleverness in winning her. The shock of finding out that Grace had been married to his best friend had been totally forgotten, or at least discounted, in the thrill of possessing her. He no longer asked himself awkward, painful questions because he thought he knew the answers. Grace might have loved another long ago, but right now she had gone to bed with him, therefore she loved him, so he was prepared, Questa thought, to slay dragons and bring fortresses tumbling down for his fair lady.

Love is blind. Someone had said that, at some time, and now Questa could see for herself that it was true. Grace had no faults, not for Alan, or none that he could see. And even Grace was clearly seeing Alan through rose-coloured spectacles. She clung to his arm, gazed into his eyes, deferred to him. Does this happen to all lovers, Questa wondered, as she waved the travellers away. If I made love with someone, would I seem perfect to him and would he seem perfect to me? But it was useless to conjecture. I've got a farm to run and bedrooms to clean, Questa reminded herself. And turned back to the house.

Kat made a pretty bride. Not many girls were lucky enough to be married in white in these difficult days, but Questa and Grace had spent a good deal of time in the attics and had discovered trunks of old linen up there, and now Questa had a use for a cream damask tablecloth and some old lace curtains.

She took the material into the village on the carrier of Ellen's rusty old bicycle, with Kat striding alongside. Miss Eleanor Howe had been an expert dressmaker for years, she had made uniforms during the war and now, retired at last, she pottered about doing alterations and pining, she informed them, for a nice sewing job with plenty of material and no expense spared.

'Well, you're welcome to use the entire tablecloth, which is pretty big as you can see, and the lace might make a veil, but that isn't really unlimited material,' Questa said apologetically. 'It's the pattern; this tablecloth was the only one with lilies on, though they aren't terribly noticeable, I suppose. They're done in shiny whilst the rest of the cloth is dull, which is rather nice for a wedding dress, we thought. And it is to be my wedding present to Kat, so I'm paying for it to be made, out of my egg money. It's nice strong material and it's got no marks or stains on.'

She and Kat were in Miss Eleanor's front room, which smelled rather strongly of cabbage and cat and faced the village street so that Miss Eleanor did not get bored as she worked. She scorned net curtains, so was as much observed as observer, but it seemed to suit her for she waved with unabashed friendliness at everyone who glanced in, and kept tabs on all the passers-by.

'It'll mek up into somethin' lovely,' she declared now, eyeing the gleaming mass of material with real pleasure. 'I'll 'ave it done in a coupla days, what's more. Ah, there goes Mrs Ellis – did you know 'er daughter Betty's gone an' got 'erself in the family way? The young feller's in the army ... young Betty's dad don't know yet and when he do he ain't goin' to be over-pleased for all that 'e got Mavis into trouble hisself twenty odd year ago.' She raised a hand and her voice at the same time. 'Mornin', Mrs Ellis, lovely day for a stroll!'

'We don't hear much about what's happening in the village, so I'm afraid I don't know Betty or her mother,' Questa said almost apologetically. 'We're too far out, I suppose.'

'Ah, true. Not that I 'old wi' gossip,' Miss Eleanor said, causing Kat and Questa to exchange a swift, astonished glance. 'Never 'ave nor never will. Was you thinkin' to 'ave the skirt full, or straight, or sorta swathed? No, you won't want it swathed, or they'd likely talk ... straight would be nice seein' as you're so slim, Miss.'

Kat frowned over the problem but Questa solved it.

'Full at the back, straight at the front,' she said. 'I saw a picture of a bride in a copy of *Illustrated* – shall I draw it for you?'

'No need; what number? You don't know, I suppose. 'ere, 'ave a look at these.' Miss Eleanor handed the girls a pile of old patterns and it was not long before Questa saw what she had in mind.

'Golly, I'd look like a princess in that,' Kat gasped, and Miss Eleanor, eyeing first the picture, then the material and lastly Kat, agreed that the gown would suit Miss ideal.

'Lucky you've got a stringy sorta figure,' she said, patting the material. 'You'll get your weddin' gown, Miss, an' some material over for a train ... you'd like a train, I dessay?'

Upon being informed what a train was, Kat, with shining eyes, agreed she would like one – and a veil, yes a veil would be nice as well.

'I can't believe it,' Kat said breathlessly as they returned to Eagles Court later in the morning. 'Will she really mek it like the picture, Questa?'

'She will. You'll look really nice, really fashionable,' Questa assured her. 'Alfie will be astonished!'

He was. And so were the villagers. Kat's mass of fiery curls were taken in hand by Grace, who came back as promised and became fascinated by the entire wedding as soon as she was allowed to see The Dress.

'The village dressmaker made it? Out of a tablecloth? My God, Ques, it's the loveliest thing I've ever seen. Oh, I'd give my eye-teeth to get married in a gown like that! Kat, you are a lucky girl ... who's taking the photographs?'

'Photys? No one,' Kat said derisively. 'What'ud Alfie an' me want wi' photys when we're got each other?'

'Look, Alan's got a camera, I'll tell him he must take a couple of photographs. Can I buy the dress off you, Kat, for my wedding? I'll pay a fair price.'

'It wouldn't fit you, Grace,' Questa said gently. 'Kat's a different shape from you – she's slimmer, though you're much of a height.'

'I'll lose weight,' Grace vowed. 'What do you say, Kat? I mean you could do with the money, couldn't you? How are you doing your hair?'

'My hair? Oh, I'll tie it back, or shall I leave it loose?' Kat shrugged. 'Loose, I dessay.'

'It would look marvellous done up into a sort of coronet on top of your head, with just a few wisps coming down, and some sort of lilies in a wreath around it. I'll do it for you if you like.'

So it was that Kat floated down the aisle on Alan's arm, he being the only male she knew who could give her away, looking so lovely that Alfie did not recognise his forthright, hardworking fiancée. The fiery hair subdued into a soft pompadour, the lilies, the veil, and her tall, straight figure made regal by cream damask, were almost too much for Alfie. Questa, sitting in the pew opposite with Ran and Grace, saw the fright in his eyes as this strange and glorious woman came to a halt beside him. He

331

turned, took a panicky step away from her ... and Kat's hand shot out. She grabbed him and held him tight until the service started and Alfie, no doubt recognising the fingers of iron digging into his arm, relaxed a trifle.

'Don't she look a treat, though?' Miss Eleanor said to Questa outside the church. 'I were fair proud ... eh, she looks a picture!'

'She looks lovely,' Questa agreed. 'The dress is just perfect – did you know that Mrs Syrett wants to borrow it for her own wedding next April?'

'No! Well, I can't say as I'm surprised. Would she like me to alter it for her?' She chuckled. 'Or does she think she'll lose some weight afore then?'

'Yes, I think she'd like you to alter it,' Questa said. 'I don't think she'll ever be as slim as Kat, do you? Why don't you come up to the Court in a couple of days and ask Mrs Syrett about the alterations yourself?'

'I'll do that,' Miss Eleanor said. 'I might mention as I'm a dab 'and at mekin' something real nice outer a few scraps of material. Anyroad, 'ere comes the bride, git ready wi' that rice!'

Grace and Alan had come down only for a couple of days, it transpired, and intended to leave after the wedding and return to town, taking Dickie with them.

'There's a good infant school not four doors away from Alan's place,' Grace said. 'He'll be happy there, and I can keep an eye on him. There's a beautiful square garden that the school has the key to, and they do nice lunches, or he can come home if I'm around. Alan's got me into a small hotel a couple of hundred yards away,' she added hastily, 'So it's all perfectly proper.'

'All right, if you're sure you wouldn't rather leave Dickie for a week or two? No, it's all right, I do understand, and it's been difficult sometimes finding someone to take him into the village and fetch him again when school's over,' Questa admitted. 'Let me know when the wedding date's been fixed.'

'Darling, of course!' Grace trilled. 'If there's one person who simply must be there or I wouldn't feel properly married, it's you.'

The two were chatting in the kitchen over preparations for an evening meal whilst Alan helped Dickie to pack.

'And you'll fix something with Miss Eleanor? Kat said you could borrow the dress, incidentally, only she wants it back. For her daughter, she said, believe it or not.'

'Tonight's the night she'll discover what it's all about, then,' Grace said. 'Unless they jumped the gun, of course.'

'They didn't,' Questa said, trying not to stress the first word too obviously. 'Alfie's quite strict in his way, and Kat just wants to please him.'

'Hmm. Well, he's in his fifties, if you ask me it's a rum do to marry a girl less than half your age when you've had no previous experience of marriage. If you ask me, Kat may never find out what it's all about, let alone produce a daughter; not fathered by Alfie, at any rate.'

'Fortunately, however, no one's going to ask you,' Questa pointed out. 'Kat and Alfie will manage very well I think you'll find. Have you finished those potatoes?'

Grace nodded and began to drop peeled potatoes into a pan of cold water. 'Yes, there's enough here to feed an army, I should think. Are they going away for a day or two, or are they in the flat?'

'They're in the flat.'

'Not in that dreadful old bed of Ellen's?'

'It's not dreadful,' Questa said shortly. She could see Ellen's exhausted, yellowish face against the pillows, the patchwork quilt pulled up to her chin, the weariness in those bright, dark eyes. 'Chuck the spuds over, I'll put them on the hob.'

'Well, I wouldn't want to have my wedding night in the bed someone had just died in …' Grace began, to be firmly cut short by Questa.

'Ellen didn't die in it, Grace. She died somewhere else. Now for goodness' sake stop getting at poor Kat, who never did you any harm, and let's get this meal on the go!'

That night, after Grace, Dickie and Alan had gone and the lights in the coachman's flat had been extinguished, Questa put herself to bed, then sat up with the thyme pillow lying across her knees and thought.

She was so lonely! She wanted desperately to be able to

dream of Marcus, to regain the sense of purpose which her dreams seemed to give her. Things had changed so much since Ellen's death, her whole future, which had seemed secure and sunny, was suddenly just one enormous question mark. It seemed silly to think that a dream could make you more content with your lot, more positive in your attitude, but that was how she felt.

She lay down and was about to pick up the thyme pillow from its place under the bed when, from outside, she heard a shriek so loud and startling that the hair on her head prickled erect.

What on earth was it? She was out of bed almost before she had thought and halfway across the room, heading for the door. She wrenched it open, crossed the hall, burst into the kitchen. The Aga clicked and settled, the cold tap dripped. Blot, the young cat, raised an enquiring, triangular face. From outside, suddenly, came another shriek, another, another, ending in a long, gurgling moan.

In the spring, vixens screamed like that, but this wasn't spring and it wasn't a vixen, it was ... Good God, it must be Kat, she must be in some dreadful trouble, suppose Alfie had had a stroke or some such thing?

Questa was out of the kitchen door and halfway across the cobbled yard when she remembered, belatedly, what Kat had said to her on the subject of gypsies and lovemaking.

'*Do a woman joinin' wi' a man shout out? Wuss'n a vixen on heat,*' she had said.

Feeling remarkably stupid, Questa turned back towards the small parlour. What a good thing she had remembered – how awful if she had burst into Kat's marriage chamber to rescue her from ... well, to rescue her! How Ellen must be chuckling right now, wherever she was!

The thought that Ellen was somewhere – for her first reaction to Ellen's death had been the dreadful, hollow realisation that Ellen was nowhere, that she had no sensation of an Ellen who had moved on to enjoy an after-life – seemed so cheerful, so natural, that she actually laughed as she re-entered the small parlour. She got back into bed and put the thyme pillow in position, then laid her head on it.

334

Why not? she thought defiantly. Why not? She was not at all sure that the thyme pillow made the slightest difference to her dreams, but she did think that perhaps intent had something to do with it. At least she was actively trying to dream of Marcus. And Ellen had believed in the pillow, dear Ellen, who had meant her nothing but good, had understood her loneliness, her fears.

She closed her eyes, sniffed contentedly at the scent of the dried thyme, and waited for sleep to claim her.

Fifteen

She dreamed she was standing by a gate, leaning over it, looking into the rolling meadow beyond. Tall summer grasses ripe for cutting seemed to indicate that the month was May or June. She looked out, across the meadowland to the woods, and beyond them to the blue of the hills. Where was he? She closed her eyes, enjoying the warmth of the sun on her lids, and immediately her ears took over the search. Voices, faint but clear, someone laughing, a rhythmic shushing sound ...

She opened her eyes and looked to her left. In the next meadow, stripped to the waist and with iron sickles in their hands, a number of men were cutting the grass. Girls with wooden rakes followed them, spreading the cut grass so that the sun could dry it into hay. She recognised one of the girls at once: the golden-haired slave girl, her hair glossier, her whole body rounder, more mature. Lovelier, if that were possible.

Immediately, doubt stabbed Questa like a knife; should she have stayed away? had things changed? But someone came up behind her and a hand slid round her waist and all her doubts fled.

'Hello, little stranger! Come to watch us cut the hay? It's a good crop, isn't it? How quietly you stole up today, one minute the gate just hung there and the day was grey, the next you leaned upon it and the sun came out.'

'The sun's been out all day, by the looks of things,' Questa said, twisting round to smile up at Marcus. 'There's not a cloud in the sky.'

'And you have no soul,' Marcus informed her, his mouth so near her ear that his breath tickled. 'I know the sun's shone all day, why else did I order the hay to be cut? But all my days are grey until you come; that's poetic licence.'

'How pretty, even if it isn't true,' Questa said. 'Are you feeling happier, dear Marcus?'

'Yes, dear Questa; time heals. And you?'

'The same. I suppose erecting the memorial stone helped; why did you put it so high in the hills, though?'

They had been wandering down the lane which led back to the house. On either side of them, on top of the banks, hazels spread their branches, making a dappled shade through which they wandered. But now Marcus pulled her to a halt and turned her so that he could look down into her face. He was frowning slightly.

'You saw it? You read it? What did it say?'

Immediately, she realised she had jumped to conclusions. The stone she had found had not been the memorial, or if it had ... but it was pointless to follow that path. She looked up at him, loving his face even when it frowned at her.

'Sorry, stupid of me. I couldn't read it, I barely caught a glimpse of it as I passed, I don't know why I thought it might be Gaius's memorial. It wasn't, obviously.'

'No.' He shook his head. 'No, I've still not decided on the exact wording. I want you to see my home, I've meant to invite you in often enough, but today, with most of the servants haymaking, we can have it to ourselves.'

He put his arm round her, giving her a hug, then he let his glance warm and soften, his lips twitch into a wicked, conspiratorial smile.

'Well, all right, but I bet the house isn't empty. Won't they, the servants, wonder why you're bringing a strange female into your home?'

He snorted, taking her elbow firmly, cupping it in one strong, brown hand. 'Wonder? They aren't paid to wonder. Come along.'

Meekly, she went with him. Down the lane, casting sideways glances at the high banks, seeing the wild strawberries, the snail with its cream and brown shell striped like a humbug hiding under a leaf, the heavy masses of what looked like cobweb in which caterpillars spun and ate. Little wild flowers, mosses, a jutting rock, a tiny hollow with a thread of water tinkling down, a blackbird's nest at eye-level, the feathered fledglings, beaks agape, waiting for their next meal.

They went under the arch and into the main courtyard. As Marcus had said, there were fewer people about today because most were in the fields. He had told her before that he did not believe in house slaves and field slaves, on his estate everyone pulled their weight, helping with the crops when they were needed or working in the house, the dairy, the granary.

The house was all she could have imagined and more. The kitchens were magnificent. The chief cook worked in an all-enveloping apron, a cloth tied around his head. He made pastry just as Questa had seen Ellen doing, though the flour came out of a great sack and the fat out of a wooden cask. There was a bath-house with beautiful mosaic tiles on the floors and Marcus explained the heating to her, though at this time of year, he assured her, it was not needed for warming the house but simply supplied hot water for the baths and for general domestic use.

All the rooms on the ground floor were tiled, some plainly, some with beautiful and elaborate patterns. The bath-house tiles sported dolphins, Neptunes with tridents, flying fish and odd-looking ships with a great many oarsmen and tiny, stunted sails. In the dining hall men and women hunted a deer, all on foot and armed with bows or spears, and in another room a huge bowl of fruit surrounded by rather stilted flowers dominated the floor.

But it was in the central reception hall that the mosaic was most stunning. Questa simply stood and stared.

The tiles depicted a young Roman centurion in his full regalia: the plumed helmet, the body armour, the leather kilt, with a dog to one side of him and a great black stallion on the other. And the face of the young man was Marcus's face.

'Marcus – that's *you*! What a clever picture. Tell me about it.'

'My father had it done when I got my first posting, along with my first battle wounds,' Marcus said. He stroked a forefinger along his brow where the three-inch scar creased his flesh. 'See? But the artist wouldn't put the scar in, said it spoiled his picture, so my father drew it in with paint. Old fool!' But he spoke with deep affection and a reminiscent smile twitched at his lips. 'When I came home we always seemed to rub each other up the wrong way so that I went back to my regiment in high dudgeon. Yet I loved him, and he me.'

'He was proud that you got your wound in defence of the empire, I expect,' Questa said. 'The artist must have been very good, it's just like you.'

'Hmm, I was younger, then,' Marcus said, but Questa could see he was pleased. 'Come and look at the rest of the house.'

It was an elaborate and beautiful dwelling. In addition to the mosaic floor tiles there were wall tiles too, and long tables, stools and benches, some elaborately upholstered, others merely of polished wood or marble. The main bedroom boasted a carved wooden bed with many richly embroidered coverings; it had been his father's couch, Marcus explained; he had never slept in it himself, preferring a smaller, plainer bed in a smaller room. 'For a single man it is ideal; snug and much easier to keep warm,' he explained. 'But when I marry I shall lie here, with my wife. Do you like the hangings? They can be drawn over the windows at night, ensuring complete privacy – and warmth, in winter. See the mirror? And the little bottles for your scent, your paint? They were my mother's. She was a good woman; you would have liked her.'

'I'm sure I would,' Questa said gently. She had not failed to notice how he had subtly told her that the scent and paint bottles were for her. 'Oh, Marcus, let's go outside again now. I want to see your dairy and the cellars where you store your wine.'

At breakfast the next day Kat and Alfie couldn't catch each other's eyes without giggling. Knowing full well what they were laughing about did not make it any easier for Questa to treat them naturally, but she did her best. Nevertheless she was glad when Alfie took himself off to the Hall, leaving her and Kat to their usual tasks.

'I thought you'd give Alfie his breakfast in your flat, the same as Ellen used to,' Questa said as the two of them headed for the cowshed. 'Won't he be late, eating with us?'

'Won't matter, not today,' Kat said, looking smug. 'Mr Atherton's gone up to London to see 'is solicitor. Seems 'is son's comin' back 'ome an' 'e wants to mek arrangements.'

'Arrangements? What sort of arrangements?'

They reached the cowshed and went inside. The four dairy cows were already in their stalls; Bert had brought them in earlier. Moving automatically, both girls got their buckets and stools and started on their first cow. Not until the milk was hissing into the bucket did Kat answer Questa's question.

'Oh, things like who'll 'ave the final say over what, I guess. Last time 'e was 'ome, seems they fell out 'cos they both wanted to rule the roost. This time Mr Atherton says 'e wants to mek sure it works out. Seems 'e's rare fond o' the lad despite the argy-bargy.'

Thinking of the ferret-faced one, Questa sniffed disparagingly. 'I can't imagine why! I thought he was thoroughly unpleasant. Still, I suppose I'll have to be polite for Ran's sake. But it'll spoil things, I'm sure of it.'

'You'll git accustomed,' Kat said, finishing with Blossom and standing the full pail over by the door, where an unwary kick by cow or girl would be unlikely to reach it. 'Poor Questa, you've 'ad a lot of changes lately, one way an' t'other.'

'Yes, I know what you mean.' Questa stripped the teats one by one, then pushed back her own stool and picked up the bucket. 'But it's the place that matters, though I'll miss Ellen for the rest of my life, I shouldn't wonder. She taught me – oh, everything, just about.'

'Yes, she were a good woman,' Kat said. 'She wouldn't let the travellers come near nor by, you know, once you come 'ere to live. Said you'd got nightmares enough, wi'out adding to 'em. Afore then, travellers wouldn't miss out on the Court, came 'ere to 'elp with 'arvest in th'old days, then to git fresh vegetables an' a bit of 'elp, like, when the war were over, but they did what she said, acos they knew she were a wise woman with their interests at 'eart.'

'I wonder why she thought they'd upset me?' Questa said, sitting down and resting her forehead against Buttercup's side. 'I don't see why I should mind gyp – I mean travellers coming in from time to time.'

'You would've,' Kat said. 'You was a nervy thing in them early days, Ellen told me.'

'You mean you came here? Before Ellen died? And she never said anything and I never saw you? Well I'm blessed!'

'Ad to come, din't I? To see Alfie. Old Ellen made the 'rangement years agone, when I were just a bit of a thing. So Sara brung me 'ere twice or three times every year an' Ellen telled me what I were to do when she passed over. But 'twas only I, not t'others.'

'How did I miss you?' marvelled Questa. 'I'd have sworn I saw everyone who came on to the estate.'

'I come after dark, or fust thing of a mornin', or when you was over at the 'all,' Kat explained. 'You saw me once, I were in the wood, but I slipped away when you come near. An' once in the village, but you din't know who I was, acourse.'

'Well, I wish I'd known you before, when Ellen was alive,' Questa said. 'But having you here, Kat ... it's been more of a help than you'll ever know. I still get lonely, of course, and now that you're in the coachman's flat with Alfie I'll feel lonelier in the long winter evenings I daresay, but it won't be anywhere near as bad as it would have been without you.'

'Next winter? Ho, by then you won't be alone,' Kat said bracingly. 'Shall I tell the cards, arter we've done in 'ere?'

'Tell the cards what?'

'No, stupid – tell 'em! Go through 'em for you, tell you what's comin' for you in the nex' few months.'

'Oh, tell my fortune, you mean! I didn't know you could. If you like, but not until we've finished work. Only ... suppose it's something nasty that I'd rather not know about?'

'Well, if it's comin' to me, reckon I'd rather know than not. Or I could read the tea-leaves if you'd rather.'

'Why? Are there nicer fortunes in tea-leaves? Honestly, Kat, you do say daft things sometimes! Do it at elevenses time then – you can do Bert's at the same time.'

Kat snorted. 'Bert! He'm commonplace, Questa. I'll git me pack an' bring it over at 'leven, then.'

For the rest of the morning the girls worked in companionable silence. Questa's thoughts kept straying to Marcus though, and how impossible the situation was. She was in love with a dream, there could be no future in it. Yet she was happiest when she was

341

with him, because when she dreamed that was reality and all the worries which beset her when she was awake were as nothing beside her happiness with Marcus.

But what about the Court and her plans for it, the vines she wanted to plant on the hill, her flock of sheep, the dairy herd she intended to build up? Grace had bowed out, Dickie might inherit after Questa's death if she did not have a family of her own, but there was still the Court itself to consider. After all, if she spent all her time and energy trying to dream of Marcus, what would happen to it? She knew, really, that it would deteriorate quite fast without her keenness and the money she had raised from the sale of furniture, her stock and the tiny amounts which Alan was uncovering.

Elevenses time came at last. Questa was in the kitchen baking when the back door opened and Bert stepped out of his boots and shuffled across to the table in his socks.

'Mornin', miss,' he said, sitting down heavily on a ladderback chair. 'Kettle's on the go, I see.'

'And I've got some rock cakes in the oven,' Questa told him. 'We'll try them when they come out ... help, do I smell burning?'

She didn't, but the rock cakes were cooked and presently, when they had cooled on a wire tray, she and Bert took one each.

'They'm grand, miss,' Bert said through a mouthful. 'Where's Kat got to, then?'

'She's searching for her tarot cards, to read my fortune,' Questa said, grinning. 'She'll do yours as well if you want, Bert.'

Bert, still chewing, shook his head vigorously. 'That don't do to meddle wi' things to come,' he muttered. 'Don't you let 'er start none of 'er wizardry on you, Miss. Ellen 'ud be right angry if she knew.'

'Ellen could tell fortunes, I bet,' Questa protested. 'What makes you think she couldn't, Bert?'

'Oh, I in't sayin' she *couldn't*, miss, but did she ever offer? No, that she didn't, acos she knewed it were wrong. Young Kat, she don't know right from wrong an' that's a kindly way o' puttin' it.'

'Well, I don't see any harm in it. I don't believe she really can foretell the future though, which is why I'm going to let her do the cards or the tea-leaves or whatever she wants. But tell her to leave you out of it, Bert, if that's how you feel.'

'That's 'ow I feel,' Bert said. He reached for the rock buns. 'They in't bad, Miss Questa; you'll mek up into a grand little cook yet!'

Questa made the coffee and agreed that the rock buns weren't too bad, considering they were made with dried egg. They were luckier than most and had a fair number of eggs from the hens but the buns were an austerity recipe of Ellen's and she had stuck to it, dried egg and all.

'But when I make scones with Ellen's recipe ... ' she was beginning when the back door opened and Kat came in complete with a pack of large and extremely dirty cards.

'Gi's a bun,' she said, thumping herself down at the table. 'I found up the pack.'

She reached for a rock cake whilst Questa, standing by the Aga, poured coffee into the mugs. Bert, still sitting foursquare at the table, sniffed.

'Them's Ellen's,' he said accusingly. 'What are you doin' with 'er pack? If you tell fortunes you oughter 'ave your own pack.'

'Tarot cards is 'ard to come by these days,' Kat said indignantly. 'Cost an arm an' a leg, an' all. Jest you shut your face, Bert Barnard.'

'Tarot cards? Them wi' death an' that in?' Bert's weathered country face definitely paled, Questa thought. 'I'm orf if you'm meddlin' wi' that sorta thing. Now Miss Questa, why don't you come along of I, tek a look at the weaners?'

'Later, Bert. I'm going to have my coffee first,' Questa said demurely, and then, seeing the expression on his face, 'Look, it's just a game, that's all, I shan't take it seriously.'

'If you feel like that ... ' Kat snatched the cards up again and shoved them in the pocket of her full cotton skirt. 'No, don't you bother to ask me, Questa Adamson, acos these aren't no game an' I won't set 'em out for anyone who don't tek 'em serious.'

'Good,' Bert said, heading for the door. 'Best thing I 'eard all bloomin' day.'

As soon as he had gone, Kat brought the cards out of her pocket and began to shuffle them.

'Sit down and do's I say,' she said. 'Oh, pass over me coffee first, I'm desperate thirsty.'

'I thought you wouldn't do it if I didn't take it seriously,' Questa said, obediently bringing two mugs of coffee over to the table. 'Or was that just for Bert's benefit?'

'Oh ah. Because you'll tek it serious enough, once I gits agoin'. Ellen thought I 'ad a gift for it.'

'How can anyone have a gift for shuffling cards and then dealing them out?' Questa said, as they took up their positions. She eyed the cards in Kat's hands uneasily. 'Gosh, I see what Bert meant – what unpleasant looking characters.'

'Oh ah. Cut!'

Questa cut the cards, there was more shuffling, then she cut them again and Kat began to deal them on to the table. After a long look at them she leaned back in her chair.

'There's a long journey ... that's a good start,' she said with considerable satisfaction. 'We know that's true, see? So we'm on the right track, like.'

Questa, who suspected this was Kat's first foray into fortune-telling, muttered something noncommittal.

'Ah, now that's a feller, or is it jest a stranger ... I'm not quite clear on that. Le's 'ave another go.'

She dealt again. Questa, who had been watching, demanded, 'Where's the death card? I know there is one, Ellen mentioned it once.'

'Still in me 'and, I dessay,' Kat said. She looked shifty. 'What d'you want to know about death, gal? You're in the prime o' life, like me!'

'You never know. I knew a little boy once who fell out of a hayloft and broke his neck. He wasn't quite seven.'

'Oh. Well, I don't know as ... hey, 'ands off me pack!'

'You've taken the death card out,' Questa said as the cards splayed out from their hands and fell all over the table. 'You've only got half the pack here, by the looks.'

'Well, I'm only 'alf trained, like,' Kat grumbled, trying to get the cards back into a pile and knocking two or three to the floor as she did so. 'Let me read your palm then, eh? I'm good at that.'

'Or the tea-leaves, why don't you try the tea-leaves?' Questa

344

said mockingly. Now that Kat had given up pretending, she realised that she had been almost dreading what the cards might say. But having cut the tarot pack down to size with her own secret disbelief in Kat's powers and Kat's admission that she was not the expert she had pretended, a sort of lightness had come over her, a willingness to play.

'Nah, not the tea-leaves. Sides, we've jus 'ad coffee, 'aven't we? I'm never sure if I've jest drank tea or coffee when it's you what made it,' Kat said, getting a bit of her own back. 'Right then, show me your dirty little 'and.'

'My hands are lovely and clean,' Questa said, holding them out, palm uppermost. Kat carefully turned them over and stared at the knuckles. Questa giggled. 'The lines are on the other half, silly! Get on or I'll read your bumps and you won't like that a bit.'

'Why 'ouldn't I like it?' Kat said, still studying Questa's knuckles.

'Because I'd have to make them first, and I'd do it with relish after the way you've mucked me about. Come on, get a move on, I mean it.'

'You're bloomin' jolly all of a sudden,' Kat grumbled. 'Ellen said you looks at the fist first, acos it tells you if someone's doin' a labourin' job or if they're aggressive – scars on the knuckles, see – an' a bit about their past. Then you goes over and sees the future.'

She turned Questa's hands palm uppermost as she spoke and hunched over them, staring first at one and then the other.

'Ever bin real ill ... I mean stay-in-bed ill?' she demanded after a moment. 'Tell you what, you're goin' to meet someone ... no you aren't, you've met 'im already. Tall, dark an' 'andsome, I shouldn't wonder.'

'That is the oldest line in the world,' Questa said. 'How many children will we have, then, me and this handsome man? What's his name? Is he rich enough to help rebuild the Court?'

The news that the roof would cost over a thousand pounds to mend had depressed her deeply at the time and even now it kept coming back into her mind like a shadow of ill-fortune.

'I can't see names nor fortunes,' Kat said indignantly. 'What d'you think I am? If I 'ad a crystal ball, now ... '

Questa giggled. 'I bet I could tell a fortune as good as you can,' she said. 'What about ink puddles? Have you ever tried ink?'

'Ink puddles? You're 'avin' me on!'

'I'm not, in fact. Stay here.'

She ran from the room, to return with a large bottle of Quink. She went over to the dresser, poured the ink, or some of it, into a saucer and then returned to the table.

'Pull the curtains,' she said. 'And we'll both stare at the ink and concentrate and we'll see pictures of our future. Really, it's just as likely to work as palms and cards and tea-leaves. Besides, we've tried your ways, now try mine.'

'Yeah, but I never 'eard of usin' ink,' Kat protested, 'That sounds rare daft to me.' But she went over and pulled the curtains across, then walked back to the table. 'I say, that mek a difference, I'll give you that!'

It did. The saucer of ink, which had just looked like a saucer of ink in the sunny kitchen, looked quite different in the dimness. For a start, it looked rounder, like a dark crystal, and the reflections showed up better: a tiny Kat walked across the kitchen and sat carefully down in her chair, a tinier Questa leaned forward on her elbows to stare into the saucer before her.

'I think you mustn't jiggle it,' Questa said. 'I think it has to be quite still, then you can ask it questions. It won't answer, of course, but it'll show you what you want to know.'

'It do keep movin', though,' Kat said presently. Her voice was low, drowsy. 'There are ripples, like. Ah, now it's settlin'.'

Before Questa, her own earnest, wide-eyed face stared back at her. I look prettier in the ink, she thought. My eyes are bigger, my hair longer and thicker – what's that?

A face, behind her own. Smiling at her through the mirror of the ink. Just for a moment, a blink of a second, then gone, and the ink was steadying as the ripple caused, she supposed, by her jump of surprise, eddied and settled.

'Did you see that?' Kat's whisper was awed.

'Hush. Yes. Don't spoil it.'

Because it was coming clear now, in the ink. Questa could see grass, a circle of trees, a glint of water beyond them and a man

346

standing there, smiling across at someone. The someone was a girl and she was walking towards him. The girl came right into the clearing; she was looking down at her feet, dreaming along, completely unaware, Questa thought, that she was not alone. Then the man moved and the girl looked up and saw him. She took two hasty steps towards him, hesitated, stopped. Then she glanced back and it was Questa, looking prettier than Questa had ever seen herself look. She turned back to the man and he smiled at her. He held out his hands. The expression on his face was so full of love and hunger that Questa could have wept for him, and then the girl put her hands into his and he drew her close, so close that they blended into one almost, in the dappled sunshine and shadow of that little glade.

The sudden opening of the back door with the resultant stream of sunshine frightened both girls half to death. Kat actually gave a shriek, but it was only Alfie, nipping back, he explained, to borrow some pig-meal since Atherton's hadn't been delivered and so he thought as he was here, he might as well have his elevenses with them.

Questa sat very still, a hand over her pounding heart. What did it mean? What on earth had she seen? Past, present, future? What was more, who had she seen? Had it really been herself? And that man, had it been Marcus? Only there had been something different, something which somehow hadn't fitted … She tried to reconstruct the scene in her mind's eye but already it was fading, becoming an imagining and not a seeing. She stood up. The ink blinked at her in the sunshine, innocent, a bit of girl's foolishness, but she had a splitting headache, and she had felt fine before they drew the curtains.

'Kat?' Questa said urgently, pitching her voice low. Kat had got up and swished the curtains back as soon as the door opened, and Alfie was over at the Aga, making himself a cup of coffee, talking about weaners and about Ran Atherton, who would be coming over later to tell them about his prodigal son's return. 'Kat, what did you see?'

Kat came over and sat down again in the chair she had just vacated, frowning and screwing up her eyes.

'A coupla kids,' she said in a low, puzzled voice. 'An' me an' you, holdin' them between us. Mine 'ad red 'air, but yours were dark. Yours were a gal, mine a boy. Well, I reckon you know, acos you was lookin' in too. My, who knows what we'd 'a seen if that Alfie 'adn't come in! Nobbut I'm fair glad, I've got the wust 'eadache I ever did 'ave; come outer nowhere, too.'

'And me,' Questa said. Kat hadn't seen what she'd seen, so presumably it was your own fortune you saw in the ink puddle and not someone else's. But had she really seen anything? A glade in a wood, a man and woman, a hungry embrace. Was it the past she had watched, or the future? It could have been anything, or nothing. Anyway, it was fading already, becoming more difficult to believe in, easier to dismiss. And she might have done just that but for Alfie. He carried his coffee over to the table, sat down and reached across for a rock cake ... then his hand froze over the dish. Questa saw that he was staring at the saucer of ink as a rabbit stares at a snake.

'So that's what you was up to, with the curtains closed,' he said at last. 'Kat, I oughter tan your arse, teachin' Questa tricks like that.'

'It wasn't her, it was me,' Questa said. 'Someone told me about it once, so I thought we might try it. It's all right, Alfie, no harm done.'

'It weren't me mother what told you about it,' Alfie said. He sounded aggressive, definitely not like himself at all. 'She wouldn't meddle wi' that, not unless ...'

'It wasn't her, it was someone in Italy,' Questa said soothingly. 'It's all right, Alfie, it was just a bit of fun.'

Alfie snorted and picked up the saucer as though it might bite him. He took it over to the sink and poured the ink away and watched as it swirled round the stone sink and out of the plughole in a surprisingly blue stream considering how black it had looked in the saucer.

'Fun! Well, don't go meddlin' like that again, either of you, or I'll have suffin' to say that you won't much like. What did you see, anyroad?'

'Oh, just our faces,' Questa said vaguely. 'I thought I saw someone looking over my shoulder ... ' a shudder shook her. She remembered the face, but now, in her mind's eye, it looked different, both sinister and sad. 'But it wasn't anything, you came in too soon.'

'Oh ah. Kat?'

'Nothin'. Well, a kid, that's all. Ourn, Alfie.'

Alfie grinned reluctantly. 'Go on wi' you, Kat Rimmer, you know 'ow to git round a bloke! Come on then, no more ink. Swear it.'

'I'm not swearing ... oh, all right,' Questa said with some reluctance, whilst Kat agreed, with alacrity, that she wouldn't try ink magic again.

Presently Alfie went back to the Hall, riding on the tractor with two bags of borrowed pig-meal in the trailer, and Kat and Questa returned to their work, both rather quieter than usual.

When they went indoors for their midday meal however, Questa could not resist raising the subject once more. 'Kat, if the ink doesn't show the truth then why did Alfie get so cross?'

Kat, slicing bread, shrugged. 'Dunno. That's men for you! Mind, my 'ead's only just stopped 'urtin'. 'Ow about you?'

'The pain eased about an hour ago. But inside, my mind's all churned up. I feel as if I'll never be satisfied unless I do it again and – and *prove* that there's nothing in it. But we swore we wouldn't.'

'And we won't,' Kat said stoutly. 'Alfie wouldn't say "don't" without good reason. You'll just 'ave to wait for that little gal, Questa, same's I will for me lad.'

'But you believe in the lad and the girl, don't you?' Questa said shrewdly, after some thought. 'You saw them, you don't have any doubts.'

'You saw them as well, you must 'a been as convinced as what I was. The little gal was ever so like you, 'cep' she 'ad curly 'air.'

'Mm, hmm ... but suppose it was me when I was little? I mean suppose it was showing the past? Your mum with a lad and my mum with me as a toddler. Perhaps that's what Alfie meant when he said what was truth.'

This had clearly never occurred to Kat. She looked surprised, then annoyed, then she shook her head, her brow clearing.

'No use, Questa, my mum, Sara, ain't a bit like me to look at and she never 'ad no boy! An' it was you wi' the kid, I dunno 'ow I know but I does. An' I don't want to do it again after all, not even if Alfie said we could. Best not to know what's comin', by and large. Best to be there when it does an' tek it as it comes. Chuck over the corned dickie an' I'll mek sangwiches while you mash the tea.'

'I'll slice some onions,' Questa said. 'I love corned beef with onion; it gives it more bite, somehow. And I stewed some plums last night, we could have them with custard if there's any milk left.'

Later that week, perhaps because she was feeling more secure in her new, lonelier life, Questa slept on the thyme pillow again and dreamed that she and Marcus rode to the hills with food and a skin of Marcus's best wine in their saddlebags. Once there, they played like two children, paddling in the streams, chasing butterflies across the purple heather of the high moors, watching a small, dark and surly-looking mountain-man bring a herd of goats down to water them before nightfall.

'Your house and your servants frighten me,' Questa told Marcus as they lay on the soft and mossy turf when their meal was finished. 'You live in such style, compared to me.'

'We'll camp out in a shelter and raise sheep and horses and make love every night,' Marcus said, caressing her smooth bare arms. 'I need no pomp or style, but I need you.'

'I need you as well,' Questa said honestly. 'But I want ... oh, I don't know what I want!'

'Where do you live, from here?' Marcus asked lazily, rising on one elbow and gesturing around them. 'Is it far? Might we visit today? If I knew your home I would know better how to make mine right for you.'

It was a lovely thought; concern shone from him, she could feel it every time he laid a hand on her. But she could not, of course, tell him the truth.

'No, it's too far,' she said vaguely. 'It's a lot farther on.'

'Then I suppose you'll want to leave me here, and go your ways,' he said as the sun began to sink in the sky. 'No point in you trailing down into the valley only to climb the hills again.'

'I'll come back with you; I go home a different way,' Questa said, and was relieved when he accepted this without further questioning.

With the sun setting in the west, therefore, they rode gently along the wide new road, then turned off it into the winding little lanes with their high banks and rampant summer growth.

'This has been the happiest day of my life,' Questa said when they were rubbing down the horses in the field, using wisps of hay, their tack piled up against the gate. 'If I live to be a thousand, I'll never forget today.'

Marcus finished rubbing down, ran a hand along his mare's gleaming neck, then turned to her.

'Oh no, sweetheart, there will be other, better days,' he said softly. 'Days which don't end with you going off in one direction and I in another. Days which end in sweet content, our bodies one, our minds in tune.'

Questa dropped her hank of hay and ran into his arms. She clung, suddenly urgent, suddenly afraid, though she did not know what she feared.

'Marcus? I love you so! I'll never, never leave you!'

False, false, a tiny voice in her mind said tauntingly. You can't make a promise like that, knowing what you know! Tell him the truth, why don't you? Make him face facts, as you will have to face them, one day.

'I know, sweetheart, I know. Let me hold you.'

Together, sweetly, they clung in the deepening dusk.

Sixteen

Christmas 1948 came and went; young Atherton came home, but Questa did not see him – she made sure of it. She kept well out of the way and though she rang Ran on Christmas morning she did not visit again until the holiday was over.

In February, Kipper had another litter of puppies and Questa, who had missed Roma almost as much as she had missed Grace and Dickie, decided she must have a dog of her own. Loneliness was something she might have to learn to live with, but there was no law which said she might not find companionship where she could. So she waited until the pups were six weeks old and then went round to the Hall one bright morning in early April, when the sun was shining and the birds were shouting their delight that winter was finally done.

She dragged a not unwilling Ran out of the house into the spring sunshine, and over to the stable block. Then, together, they went into the loose-box just as she had done when she chose Roma, and leaned over the partition.

'Which shall I have, Ran? They won't be old enough to leave their mother before Grace's and Alan's wedding, I know, but I'd like to choose now, and come over and see it quite often so that it knows me well by the time I take it home.'

Questa contemplated the puppies wriggling about in the straw with as much interest and attention as though she had not gone through this ritual before. But she did not intend to be cheated out of this puppy, which would not be the runt of the litter but the best, because she wanted a working dog this time.

'Roma was only young but she helped to get the cattle in, mornings and evenings, and she was getting good with the sheep, too,' she had told Ran when she arrived that morning. 'I can't

352

cope without some more help, Ran, and a dog is a lot cheaper than another farm labourer!'

Kipper's new litter was just as enchanting as the earlier one. Fat, blunt-nosed puppies with squeaky barks and bright eyes stared up at her, then forgot her in play, pouncing on each other, squabbling over their mother's teats, charging from one side of the loose-box to the other, growling with mock ferocity as they seized ears and tails.

'Go for a bitch,' Ran advised, now. He leaned on the door beside her, examining the pups critically. 'They're a grand bunch; same parentage as Roma of course.'

'I'll have ... the one with the black patch over her eye. No, I won't, I'd rather have the one with the all-white head and the brown patch on her shoulder. Or do you think the speckled one is the best, perhaps?'

'Make up your own mind,' Ran said, refusing to be drawn. 'It won't make any difference, every one's a winner.'

'I don't see how you can say that; you can't with people,' Questa told him. 'The nicest mothers and fathers sometimes have stinking children and sometimes stinking mothers and fathers have lovely kids. So what's different about dogs?'

'Selective breeding,' Ran said, grinning at her. 'People don't go in for that much, Questa! How are things up at the Court?'

'Well, we haven't had much rain lately, so I can tell myself that the repairs to the roof have worked, which is good. And everything's organised for the weekend, so that Kat and I can go up to London for the wedding. Dickie's being a pageboy – Alan said he's spitting feathers with fury; he thinks only cissies wear pale blue satin knee breeches and frilly shirts.'

'He's got a point,' Ran said drily. 'How long do you plan to be away? A couple of days? A week?'

'Gosh, no, just overnight. We're going up to London on the Friday evening, me and Kat, and staying at Alan's house overnight. I'm not exactly a bridesmaid because I didn't want to be, I'd feel foolish in a frilly dress and dancing pumps, but since it's Grace's second marriage ... or is it her third? Well, anyway, it's not her first, so she's settled for Dickie as a pageboy and me as friend of the bride. I'll help her to do her hair and so on.'

Ran grinned again and reach out a long arm to rumple Questa's short, dark hair. She had grown it longer and then, in a moment of annoyance, had hacked it off short once more.

'You'll help do her hair? Look what you've done to your own!'

'It saves time,' Questa said, ducking to avoid his hand. 'Besides, Kat took me into the village and the barber styled it so it's better than it was. And short hair's going to be all the rage now that film-star person has had hers cut off.'

'In fact it suits you,' Ran admitted. 'But even so, I wouldn't have thought you could have done the sort of styles Grace would want on her wedding day.'

'She's going to have it loose and flowing,' Questa said. 'All I have to do is pin her veil in place with a wreath of white roses on top. And check that she looks all right from the back, I gather, since that's what people stare at during the ceremony.'

'That shouldn't be beyond you,' Ran agreed. 'What are you wearing?'

'A suit! Grace got it specially for me, wasn't that nice of her? It's a lovely lime-green colour and it's made of some sort of silky stuff. I felt really smart when I tried it on. It was too big, but Grace and a friend of hers altered it and now it's just right.'

'Wish I could see you parading around London in it! Tell you what, why don't you come straight from the station to the Hall, and have dinner with me after the wedding? Then you can tell me all the gossip and I can see you in all your splendour. What's Kat wearing?'

'Oh, the most marvellous creation, wait till you see it! Alfie bought it off a spiv in town; it's most unusual, a sort of blue-grey slate colour, and its flowing and full. Kat looks like a duchess, or the queen or something.'

'I shall look forward to it. You will come to dine?'

'Well, of course! Will you meet the train with the car? And take us home afterwards?'

'And you used to be such a nice, meek little thing, who never asked anyone for anything,' Ran mourned, with a twinkle in his eye. 'Yes I'll meet you off the train and either Alfie or I will drive you home afterwards. Which would you prefer, my common-place Austin or the luxuries of the Lagonda?'

'I don't mind since I adore the Lagonda but prefer your driving to Alfie's. Not that there's anything wrong with his driving, but he doesn't have much flair, does he? Oh, I never asked you; what did your son say when he was here at Christmas about coming home in the summer?'

'He'd better come soon, or I shan't know him,' Ran grumbled. 'A two-day visit at Christmas, then a letter every twelve weeks and a phone call on my birthday. That's not what I want. Actually though, he's doing another month or two in Scotland, learning how to rear beef cattle. I wonder if there's some girl up there, myself – can't think why else he should stay.'

'Perhaps to learn about rearing beef cattle?'

Ran grinned. 'Oh, perhaps. Certainly that's a line I know almost nothing about. Not that Scottish cattle are the same as our fat beasts, but you learn something new every day in farming. And he'll be home quite soon now; he actually unbent enough to say that he'd make a real effort to get back before we cut the hay ... wonders will never cease! And I bet he'll come up the drive and saunter into the kitchen as if he's never been away, and will look very askance if I try to celebrate his homecoming.'

'Well, it will be nice to meet him properly at last,' Questa murmured diplomatically. Her recollections of young Atherton were such that even thinking about his return made her heart sink, but she was prepared to take Ran's word for it that he had changed. 'So which puppy shall I have? Go on, Ran, make up my mind for me.'

'Right. The one with the black patch.'

'Oh! But ... '

Ran chuckled and straightened up. He manoeuvred himself neatly around on his sticks and set off, out of the stables.

'You've made up your mind, you contrary young woman! Which one do you want? Speak now or forever hold your peace.'

'The one with the little brown freckles, then,' Questa said, hurrying after him. 'I'll call her Pepper because she's peppered with freckles.'

'Excellent. Well, you may have her in six weeks, because I like the pups to be three months old before they leave Kipper. And in the meantime feel free to come over whenever you have a spare moment. No need to come into the house, go straight to the stable. Unless you've time to spare for an old fellow like me.'

'Huh! You don't fool me that you feel like an old fellow, or think of yourself as one, either,' Questa said, hurrying across the stableyard in Ran's wake. 'I wish you were coming to the wedding, though. Grace will look stunning and I bet the food will be awfully good.'

'Wasn't asked. No reason why I should be, come to that. I always had reservations about young Grace, even as a kid. However, she seems to have turned out all right; Alan will see she sticks to the straight and narrow. Now come in and have some tea; Mrs Clovelly would be most upset if she knew you'd been and gone without a word.'

On the day before the wedding Questa and Kat, dressed in their best, set off at an early hour with one case between them and two dozen eggs, a pot of cream and a side of bacon in a covered basket which Kat carried over one arm. They had a taxi to the station at Craven Arms, took a packet of marmalade sandwiches and two apples for their breakfast, and hopped off the train at Shrewsbury and bought cardboard cups of coffee to wash the food down.

As an old hand in London, Questa took a loudly marvelling Kat on the underground, by bus and finally on foot, across the metropolis and right to Alan's front door.

Questa and Kat were impressed by the house. It was a four-bedroomed semi-detached, with quite a sizeable garden by London standards. There was a large drawing room, a smaller dining room, a pleasant kitchen and a study with a big desk and a couple of comfortable chairs. The guest room was decorated in cream and green with twin beds, a large dressing-table mirror, wall-to-wall carpeting, a phenomenon which Kat thought unbelievably luxurious, and a handbasin in one corner with running hot and cold water.

Kat would have been happy to spend the evening in the room trying out the beds, peering from the window and running the hot tap, but Questa told her that food would be served downstairs and thus persuaded her back to the drawing room and her host.

Grace was there to welcome them, as were Dickie and Roma, but they left soon after the guests' arrival, since Dickie had to be bathed and put to bed in Grace's rented flatlet down the road, and Grace still had quite a lot to do in preparation for the following day.

'Don't forget to send Questa down to me by nine at the latest, Alan,' she said, standing in the hallway with Roma's lead in one hand and Dickie's small paw in the other. 'We've a lot to do!'

'London is no place for either Dickie or Roma, though,' Alan said as he closed the door on his fiancée and turned to lead his guests back into the drawing room. 'Dickie's a good lad, he likes his school, but he's spent long enough in the country to know what he's missing. The flat is tiny of course, but even here he's too restricted, and there are no animals, no meadows for him to roam. But we've got the cottage for weekends and once we're married we'll be able to use it regularly, I hope ... and I like to think he may come to you, Questa, from time to time, especially in the summer holidays.'

'Like my father did with Uncle Joshua? Sure, why not? If we manage to find enough money to have the roof replaced, that is,' Questa said. 'We've patched it up, but the men say it won't last because the wood's rotted; it really needs re-tiling. Still, it'll do for now and with only me there it's not so important.'

'No, I suppose not,' Alan said vaguely. 'I'm sure you'll manage. How's married life, Kat?'

'Grand, but you'll know all about it for yourself soon enough,' Kat said. 'Alfie sends you 'is best, and says to tell you to tek good care of 'er.'

'You may be sure I will,' Alan said. 'I hope you both enjoy yourselves tomorrow. We've done our best with the buffet and despite the shortages it should be quite a spread. Incidentally, you know we've deferred the honeymoon until the autumn? Well, we've decided to go to Paris next September, so if you could possibly have Dickie then we'd both be most grateful.'

'Yes, of course,' Questa said readily. 'He's welcome any time.'

'Good, good. Now there's an amusing comedy play on the wireless presently, Kat, so if we may leave you for a moment, I'd like a word with Questa about her affairs.'

'Suits me,' Kat said. She was curled up in one of the big, soft armchairs, shoes off, eyes fixed on the wireless set. 'See you in a bit, if I don't jest fall asleep!'

'Very well. We shan't be long.'

Alan led Questa from the room, across the hall and into his study. It was a cool evening but he must have turned the gas fire on earlier for the room was pleasantly warm. Alan gestured Questa to sit down in one of the armchairs, then took the other himself.

'Ah ... now my dear, I'd just like to clear up one or two things. They are painful things to Grace, otherwise it would have been her place to tell you, but I said I'd do it, and I will.'

'Dickie said he didn't want to be a pageboy because of the costume,' Questa said, assuming that Alan was going to ask her to keep an eye on the little boy. 'But he'll be all right, I'm sure.'

'Ah, Dickie! Well, it isn't precisely ... look, Questa, this is just between ourselves, all right? What I'm about to tell you isn't for anyone else's ears. Agreed?'

'Yes, of course.'

'Right. Well, the truth is, I don't think Grace and your father were ever married.'

'*Not* married? Then Ellen was wrong?'

'Hmm, no, Ellen was right. I'm afraid Grace was fibbing. Charles *was* Dickie's father, but he never got round to marrying Grace.'

'So he's still my brother?'

'Your half-brother. Yes. But when Grace discovered she was expecting a baby, and the father was dead, she had to do something quickly, so she married Simon Syrett. Dickie's name really is Syrett, because though Grace knew very well that she was going to have a child she didn't tell Simon and ... well, in short, she lied to save Dickie from the stigma of illegitimacy. Which isn't a bad thing to do, after all.'

'No-oo. So what about her claim on the estate?'

Alan cleared his throat uncomfortably and stared at the yellow flames hissing up and down the porcelain backing of the fire.

'She has none and nor does Dickie since he's officially Simon Syrett's son. Very foolishly, she thought that since she knew he was Charles's boy, and since she also knew that the house which Charles rented had been destroyed by enemy action, she might get away with saying they had married. I must stress, Questa, that at the time she was at her wits' end, almost penniless, desperate to give her son a future ... you won't hold it against her? She's very fond of you, dear, she never would have prosecuted her claim, I'm sure of it.'

'Oh, it's all right,' Questa said. 'Who knows, in her circumstances I might have done the same.'

'Yes, that's true, you might ...' Alan stopped short and Questa saw a painful flush burn up his face and across his high, balding forehead. 'No. No, my dear, I can't let you think that for one moment. You would never take advantage ... behave in such a way. You have been reared in a hard school; Grace, I'm afraid, was brought up to believe that the world owed her a living and that anything she wanted she could take. However, she is truly sorry and intends to behave honourably in future.' He sighed and stood up, taking his spectacles off and polishing them, then putting them back on and walking over to the door.

Shall we join Kat and listen to the play until bedtime?'

The wedding went off beautifully, marred only by Dickies expression, which was one of deep outrage. He felt a fool in his frilly white shirt and blue satin knee breeches and scowled throughout the ceremony, the photographs and the reception, though he got considerable satisfaction, Questa thought, from spilling a variety of foodstuffs all over himself, to such an extent that Grace insisted he change before the speeches.

Once in grey shirt, grey shorts and black boots he was a model of good humour, sitting between Questa and Kat and enjoying everything, not least the food. His small pockets bulged with titbits saved for Roma, and he chattered away merrily, reminding them every few sentences that he was to come to the Court in September, when Mummy and Uncle Alan were in Paris, and might very possibly come down next Christmas, too. He saw them off with a trembling lip, but was partly reconciled to his loss by the fact that he was being taken to the cottage, thus missing a whole week of school.

'I did the poor little boy no favour when I said he and Grace could move in with me,' Questa said, as she and Kat waved to the small figure on the platform clinging to his new step-father's hand. 'Before, he never knew what he was missing.'

'He's got the dawg; 'e wouldn't 'ave ole Roma but for you,' Kat pointed out. 'Don't worrit over 'im; 'e'll do okay. Nice kid.'

They both snoozed in the train after their exciting day, but Ran met them as arranged and drove them first to the Court, where they dropped Kat off with Alfie, and then back to the Hall where Mrs Clovelly clucked delightedly over Questa's green suit and served each of them with half a grapefruit soaked in rum and brown sugar followed by a curry, with fresh fruit and junket as dessert.

'That was really delicious,' Questa said as they drank their after-dinner coffee in the study before a roaring log fire, for the early May evening was chilly. 'Mrs Clovelly is a pearl past price, Ran. I do my best with the cooking, and Kat tries too, but we'll never reach her standard.'

'She's wonderful Ran agreed. 'So you enjoyed your trip to London. Sorry to leave? Wish you'd never fallen under the spell of the Court?'

'I love this place more than anywhere else on earth,' Questa said solemnly. 'I couldn't live anywhere else – and as for London, I think I'd die in a month there now that I know what it's like to live somewhere like this.'

'Well, that's good to hear. So you'll struggle on, then?'

'I'll struggle on,' Questa confirmed. 'And struggle's the word. Did I tell you Bert fell through the stairs coming down from the attic with that big chiffonier? He says the stair was eaten up with dry rot and needs treatment, so heaven knows where we'll find the money for that.'

'Marry a millionaire,' Ran said idly. 'It's the only answer.'

'Oh, right. Mr Atherton, will you marry me?'

Ran threw back his head and roared with laughter, then wiped his eyes and got to his feet.

'I suppose I'm the nearest thing to a millionaire you've met, but I'm afraid running a place like the Hall keeps me very nearly as poor as the Court keeps you! Come on, I'll drive you home, your eyelids are drooping, if I don't take you now you'll fall asleep on me.'

Together they walked round to the stableyard, where the car waited for them. Ran helped Questa into the passenger seat of the Austin, then got behind the wheel, throwing his sticks on to the back seat. They drove through the windy darkness, with rain beating now and again on the windscreen. The sunny afternoon had been followed by a chilly evening and now that night had fallen it was a wild one, the wind lashing at the branches and the rain beating down on them.

'I'll drive round the back, as close to the door as I can get; you dive in, check that everything's all right and give me a wave,' Ran instructed her as the car made its way up the long, tunnel-like drive. 'An able-bodied man would go in with you, but you'd curse me if I tried it. It takes me so long to get in and out of this sardine tin, you see.'

'It's all right, I'll be fine,' Questa said , and when the car drew up she hopped out happily enough. The back door was unlocked, the Aga closed down for the night. She lit the lamp that always stood ready by the back door, then raised it in salute to Ran, who waved back, engaged first gear and drove slowly under the arch and away.

Alone, Questa sighed, chucked her coat across a chair, and glanced around her. What was there to do? But Kat must have been in and cleared through, guessing she would be worn out by the time she got back. The kettle was still hot, but she wasn't thirsty, though a bottle in the bed would be nice … comforting. She picked up the lamp, pushed the kitchen door open, crossed the hall and went into the parlour. Her bed looked small and lonely – cold, too. She found the rubber hotwater bottle hanging on the back of the washstand and carried it back to the kitchen and filled it with the kettle. Then she returned to the small parlour.

She should wash, but she did not bother, just stripped off the silk suit, dropped it on the floor and climbed into bed in her undies, the bottle clasped in her arms. She was terribly tired and somehow deeply depressed, though she had no idea why. But at least she was warm, and fed, and did not have to get up specially early since the next day was Sunday, when Bert and Patrick came over early and did all the chores so that Questa and Kat got at least one day's lie-in.

Still, summer was almost here; soon they would be cutting hay and picking soft fruit ... she guessed that she would have to work extremely hard and very probably sell most of her stock to make the money necessary to pay for the roof repairs and begin on the dry rot. Right now the Court needed her full attention.

But it would not always be so. Once she had sorted things out ... she fell asleep at last with a smile on her lips.

The trouble was, having discovered by default so to speak that there was dry-rot damage to the attic stairs, Questa felt honour bound to investigate further. With considerable trepidation she called in a firm who promised a free investigation and free estimates. Questa was too sensible to hope for free repairs as well, but it did occur to her that people so generous might be willing to let the recipient of their estimates pay a lesser cost than they would normally have asked, or might even let them pay over a long period rather than have to borrow once more from the long-suffering bank.

This did not prove to be the case. The firm came. They spent the better part of two days poking and prying, and came down with long faces. The ticking which she had noticed in the attic was death-watch beetle. It wasn't incurable, but it would cost, the man said, shaking his head. And the dry rot would have to be cut out and replaced with sound wood unless she wanted the place to fall quite literally about her ears – he listed the places he had found traces, and most of the attic seemed to have suffered – whilst woodworm, though treatable, was quite a costly business to clear.

'But the roof's sound in several places,' he said at last, as though awarding her at least some small accolade. 'A bit of flashing round the chimneys, some new tiles, and it'll be watertight for a few years yet.'

So one bright June day, armed with these facts, Questa set out to visit Ran. She found him in the kitchen having coffee with Mrs Clovelly and talking about what sort of food they would be able to provide for the haymakers, but he heard her story, read the estimates and then scowled down at the figures on the page before him.

'This isn't good,' he said at last. 'Look, Questa, come into the study. I've something to say to you.'

Comfortably ensconced in an armchair, with a delightful breeze blowing in through the open window and lifting her hair from her warm forehead, Questa was inclined to think that her troubles, though bad, were not insoluble. But Ran tossed the papers on to his desk and sat down opposite her, looking worried.

'Questa, my dear, a talk between us is long over-due. Before Ellen died she warned me ... but of course I've kept putting it off, hoping something would turn up for you, a hidden bank account, or some stocks and shares which Alan might sell ... anything, really.

'But Ellen knew it was a pretty vain hope. She told me all about you long before you ever turned up here, you know. She was very fond of you, dear, and wanted the best for you. That was why she worried about Dickie and Grace; she couldn't bear the thought that you might work your heart out for someone else.

'She told me how she'd tried to stop you buying too much stock, because she realised that you would diversify too widely and get yourself into financial trouble. She was right, wasn't she? You don't have enough sheep to make money from them, you've invested in pigs, but not in a big enough way to call yourself a pig farmer, you bought a tractor and a pony but you don't have the workers to bring all your land under cultivation, perhaps not for many years, perhaps never.'

'I could get by if it wasn't for the house,' Questa muttered. 'Ran, I could almost hate the house, really I could! It eats money. I sell pigs or lambs and it buys me a few tiles to keep the worst of the wet out of the back attic rooms and provides the money to pay a man to fix them. The money we make from the milk feeds us, just about, but it doesn't feed the sheep as well, not in wintertime. So I sell furniture and scrap around and sell the eggs ... Ran, what am I really doing wrong? Whilst Ellen was alive there was the kitchen garden but it hasn't done as well since her death and I don't seem able to keep up with everything, though Kat's marvellous and Bert is nearly full-time now.'

'You've spread your net so wide that you're catching almost nothing in it,' Ran told her. 'Retrench, my dear. You didn't sell the windfalls to the cider people last year either, did you? You were too busy with other things. Well, stop worrying about putting the rooms back in order, spread tarpaulins over the attic floors so that at least the rain doesn't go any further and decide which of your stock pays and which doesn't. The dairy herd means a lot of work for you, it ties you to certain hours, it means you have to employ Bert on a Sunday, and Patrick too. Why not shed them?'

'My cows? Oh Ran, I do like them and we can sell the milk without any trouble at all. But the pigs are the most awful bind, really they are. They aren't healthy by nature, like the cows are, they keep getting various ailments and they need a great deal of looking after. I know Alfie's marvellous with them, but he isn't here all day and ... well, if I've got to get rid of anything it will be the pigs.'

'And how often do you use Scamper? I know you used her in the cart to bring the hay back to the stackyard, but you hardly ever ride her.'

'No, but I can't sell her, I'd never manage the hay without her. And I really do need the tractor, how else would I plough, or rather how would Patrick plough? I got an astonishingly large amount of money for the corn, you know.'

'There was a long silence. Ran stared at Questa, Questa stared at the fire. Finally, Ran spoke.

'Yes, you were well paid for the corn. But you had to hire the combine, my dear. What did that cost?'

'O-oh Ran, I wish you weren't so clever! It ... it cost quite a lot. If only I'd had two fields down to corn – or three – then it would have been more economical but as it was ... '

'And the hay; how much did you cut?'

'A whole meadow; just one large one, because the mower had to be hired, but we had enough hay to last the cows and Scamper through the winter, with some over for the sheep.'

'It might have paid you better to cut several meadows and sell what hay you didn't need,' Ran said thoughtfully. 'Questa, you

364

listened hard when Alan was ill and I talked to you both about farming; what went wrong?'

'I wanted to try everything,' Questa wailed. 'Oh Ran, I even wanted to grow grapes! Up on the hill behind the house, where they used to grow ...'

She stopped short.

Ran smiled at her. 'So you took your father's idea seriously? I think he had a point, and old Joshua believed him in the end, otherwise he'd never have consented to Charlies going off to Italy the way he did. You once told me Ellen always reckoned the hill wasn't terraced at all, it was sheep-paths, but I'm inclined to think it had been terraced, long ago. And why not for grapes? Far in the past the weather was very much warmer in Britain than it is now, so it's perfectly possible. But grapes are for some day when you've got the time and the money to experiment. Not for now, when you're heading fast for financial trouble. Do you want me to help you to get out of it, my dear, or would you rather I minded my own business and left you to struggle?'

Questa did not answer at once. In her mind, she had already given up the pigs. But the sheep? The cows? Her dear little black and white pony, and the goats who uncomplainingly ate their way across her worst and most thistly pastures? And it would mean letting Patrick go and only having Bert on a part-time basis again. She tried to imagine the cowshed empty, the sloping field next to the lane no longer dotted with grazing sheep, and her eyes filled with tears. Why was life so cruel? With only a little more money she might have made it a success – or with a house which wasn't falling down round her ears, of course.

'Don't leave me,' she said at last, unconscious of the pathos both in the words and her tone. 'Help me to do *something* right at least.'

Ran got up and limped across to her. He put his arms round her shoulders and gave her a hug.

'My dear child, you do almost everything right, but you've bitten off more than you can chew; the house is falling down and with the best will in the world, Kat and Alfie together can't make up for Ellen. Now here's a nice big sheet of paper. Come over to the desk and we'll draw up a rescue plan.'

He spread out the paper, wrote in big, firm capitals QUESTA'S PLAN, and then beckoned her over.

'You'll sell the pigs, then? Because your heart isn't really in them. Alfie's is, but he's my pigman so he won't shed too many tears. And I think you should sell the flock because although you make money from the lambs you have to pay someone else to shear which makes them not particularly profitable. And sheep have to be dipped and checked for ticks and disease, and when they go to the ram there's all the uncertainty over whether they're in lamb or not; they're quite labour intensive, sheep. So if I were you I'd cut Patrick out altogether because he's got another job anyway, and tell Bert that I'm offering four days a week so he can do two for you as well, which should be sufficient. He's a good worker is Bert.'

'But can I keep the cows? And the goats? And Scamper?'

'Yes, if you intend to build up a dairy herd and concentrate on them. Don't let the kitchen garden go again though, because it's high yield and high returns. Bert will be just as happy digging and planting early potatoes in a garden as beet in a field, and you might hire the tractor out for ploughing when you aren't using it yourself. There are smallholders around here who'd be glad of a plot ploughed by an expert like Bert.'

'What about the corn?'

'Forget it for a year or two.' Ran advised. 'You haven't the manpower. Cut the grass for hay instead – have you ever heard of silage?'

'Yes, but I don't know what it is.'

'For a quarter of an hour Ran lectured Questa on silage and the making of it, its food value for cattle, the ease with which she might construct a small silage pit so that, during a very wet season, she might put green hay down to cook until it formed the dark brown, tobacco scented silage which cows found irresistible.

'And the house, Ran? The woodworm and beetle and dry rot? What do I do about that?'

'Have it done bit by bit,' Ran advised. 'Make haste slowly, love. And because you won't be using your acres, rent them out to others. Agricultural land can yield quite decent rents, you know.'

'Who would want more land?' Questa asked. 'People around here seem to have more than enough.'

'I'll rent it,' Ran said. 'I'll need extra land now that I'm expanding my flock.'

'Expanding your flock? You said last spring that you had more than enough; you sold off lambs, Alfie said so.'

Ran looked self-conscious. 'If I buy your flock I'll need more land. They're good ewes, sturdy yearlings, I could do worse. So I'll leave them where they are for the time being ... we'll arrange a price between us. When the boy gets back he'll need something to grumble about, he can grumble that I keep too many sheep.'

'Oh Ran, you are so good! I'll repay you one day, I promise. And now I'd better get back and tell Kat what we're going to do. She and Alfie have worried for days, ever since the man said 'Death-watch beetle' in fact.'

'And keep your eyes skinned for buried treasure,' Ran called after her as she crossed the hall. 'I was bitterly disappointed when you told me the army had found Joshua's secret cellar, but it isn't only wine that can make you unexpectedly large sums of money. Keep your eyes peeled and you never know what you may come across. Good luck, my dear, let me know how you go on.'

During the next few weeks Questa was so busy trying to live up to Ran's expectations of her that she hardly stopped work at all except to fall into an exhausted sleep.

She sold the pigs – Ran bought quite a lot of them – and the sheep, and, after some heart-searching, she got a good price for the sturdy little tractor. She kept Scamper and the cows, but she hardened her heart and sold four of the goats, though she kept two nannies because, as she had told Ran, they throve on the very worst pasture and now that she could milk them, were very little trouble.

She missed Bert's help sadly, but she and Kat found that, with no sheep or pigs and only two mild nanny goats to look after, they managed quite well between them. This year the windfalls would be gathered, bagged up and sent off to Bulmer's to be made into cider, and the kitchen garden was meticulously weeded and planted out. Most of the soft fruit was sold and Kat proved to have green fingers; what she planted lived and thrived and they found there was a ready market for the asparagus which they had planted despite the fact that it would be a year before any of the crowns produced spears for cutting. A big shop told Questa they would take any local asparagus she offered them, and she and Kat, fired with enthusiasm, hastily built another bed, layering it liberally with Scamper's rich, straw-cut dung.

Every Saturday morning now she and Kat went off to the market in the pony-cart and sold flowers, homemade cakes – the bees had been told of Ellen's death and continued to provide them with plenty of honey – and all the fruit they could lay their hands on. Soft fruit of all sorts sold well, and their early potatoes, planted when Ellen advised, were on their stall at least ten days before anyone else had lifted a tuber.

Ran Atherton's son, who had promised to be home for haymaking, now changed it to a promise to be back for harvest. Even the thought of his return made her nervous, but she tried for the most part to ignore the threat, or simply to remind herself that Ran would always stand her friend.

With the money from the sale of her stock she had started the attack on the death-watch beetles, woodworm and dry rot and felt that she was getting somewhere at last. But she did not try to dream of Marcus. Dreams, she was beginning to realise, could make you supremely unsatisfied with your own life, could point up your loneliness, your inadequacies. She wanted to dream of Marcus because he was the perfect companion, the lover who demanded nothing, yet she loved the Court deeply and if dreams endangered it, they would have to wait.

July came, and with it Grace, Alan and Dickie. It was fun to have them back, fun to spend a fortnight the way they had spent most of that first year, companionably. Alan was down only for weekends but Grace laughed and joked and told stories about her new life, and Dickie tore about with Roma and the new puppy, Pepper, close at his heels.

They missed Ellen, of course, and talked of her often, but nevertheless it was a happy time. They re-lived the months they had spent together, that first Christmas when Alan had been so ill, when only Ran's offer of a chicken to roast had saved their

Christmas dinner from being vegetarian, the way they had all worked together to make that holiday a success.

Questa was glad of Grace's company in another way, too. Alfie took Kat off to visit relatives who were staying nearby and Ran's son came home for a few days. It was only a few days at the end of Grace's fortnight, but even so it meant that Questa could not see Ran, and she had grown very dependent on him for company as well as advice. But when Grace left and Ran's son had gone as well, Questa went to the Hall to give a progress report and to ask Ran how his own particular visit had gone.

'We had an argument,' Ran said, looking gloomy. 'Still, it wasn't much. Alfie says you can't have two cocks on one dunghill and I suspect he's right. But we'll settle down once he's home for good, in a month. He won't put it off again, he promised. How did Grace's visit go?'

'We had a lot of fun. We played charades and hide and seek and sardines,' Questa said. It was her first visit since the holiday and she sat on the edge of Ran's kitchen table, chattering happily away, glad to be with her old friend again. She dreaded young Atherton's arrival mainly because she feared it would cut her off still further from ordinary human contact. 'We were out of doors a lot, and Grace was very sweet, she's desperately in love with Alan, you know. I never thought she could love someone so much and it's good to see that she really does. But Dickie missed Ellen, and though Kat did her best she couldn't take Ellen's place for him. We missed you, as well. Alan could have done with another man around when he came down at the weekend, he said so several times.'

'I should have sent the lad over,' Ran said, still looking gloomy. 'It would have given him something to do – other than criticising everything I've done on the farm since he was home last, of course.'

'Oh, poor Ran! No wonder you look tired!'

'Oh, I'll survive, I'm a tough old blighter. You look worn out yourself though, Questa,' Ran said, looking critically at her pale face. 'Still worrying about the roof and the dry rot?'

'A bit. But now that I'm alone again I'll come to terms with it. Your buying the flock was a tremendous help; I really started the work with that money and every time I can afford it I'll be getting a bit more done.'

'Good. One of these days you'll look round and realise there's nothing more left to do, and then you'll feel quite flat and strange.'

'Agreeing, Questa thought ruefully that she wouldn't mind feeling a bit flat and strange, if it also meant feeling a bit less worried. Sometimes she felt as though the house was dragging her down, its weight actually resting on her shoulders so heavily that she could scarcely stand upright. The farm work was nothing compared with the dreaded tick of the death-watch beetle, the soundless munching of the woodworm, the stealthy encroachment of dry rot. And though tonight was hot and breathless the summer had not been a particularly good one; they had had torrential rain in late June and it had managed to prove the roof repairer a liar since the mended portion had let the water through almost as badly as the untreated tiles.

Still. Life could be a lot worse.

'You were right about the pigs as well as the sheep, by the way,' she said before she left. 'We'd never have coped with them all, but by saving on Bert's wages and having smaller feed bills, we should pull through this coming winter without having to embarrass Alan by asking him to borrow more money. And we're making a nice bit of profit from Ellen's market garden. Next summer we'll be selling asparagus spears for lots of lovely money, so I really do think that, one day, we'll get on top of it.'

Ran laughed and heaved himself out of his chair.

'You'll do,' he said, smiling at her. He walked over to the door and peered out. 'I wouldn't be surprised if we have a storm. At least it would clear the air; it's so humid that even breathing is difficult. Don't leave it too long before you come visiting again!'

It reminded her, of course. In her dream Marcus always pleaded with her to come back soon, and this lapse must be the longest yet. But so much had happened, so many things had needed her undivided attention, she had not dared even to try to dream. But haymaking was over, harvest had not yet started, her bank account still had some money in it, and she was settling down to what was becoming a lonely yet satisfying life. So perhaps she might start to dream again soon, now that she had a quiet mind and was more relaxed.

Questa turned to give Ran a last wave and set off resolutely for the Court. It was not yet completely dark, though the sky was heavily overcast and midges danced around her head in a way which seemed to indicate that Ran might be right about a storm. She would go the back way, she decided, taking the short-cut across the pastures and fields and over the bridge which was really three treetrunks laid across a narrow bend of the small river.

She had barely started out, though, when she became aware that her conscience was nagging her. It was as though she had left something undone, or done something wrong, and someone, somewhere, was telling her to remember, to think. She stopped halfway across the first meadow, listening. She heard the far-off rumble of thunder, but not the voice she was half-expecting. Had Ran called out to her, because he had thought of some other means of helping her to keep her head above water? Did he want her to go back? But no, it was not that. It was an uneasiness deep within her, as thought she had just remembered a pan left over a hot fire or a bath-tap still running. Hurry, hurry, her subconscious seemed to be telling her; don't you remember what you did? Then hurry, girl, you're needed!

She set off again; she would take the short-cut, since she felt so strongly that she should get on. She would skirt the bog, bright with kingcups and ladysmock at this time of year, go through the wood and emerge into the field where Scamper would be grazing. She could clamber on to his back and ride home, though he was not always easy to catch. Perhaps it might be better to walk, or run, rather; she was trotting already.

Had it not been for her feeling of urgency, she might have enjoyed hurrying along in the gathering dusk. Looking up, though, she realised that it was not really dusk, it was the clouds massing thunderously above her head. She hoped they would not decide to send torrential rain down and soak her to the skin. If that happened, she might easily find it best to ride Scamper since he could get through mud quicker than she.

She hurried along in the increasing gloom. She crossed the

371

river, slipping on the log-bridge in her haste but managing to get across without wetting her feet, and went round the bog, twice sinking in anyway so that her boots had to be tugged wrathfully out with a disgusting squelching sound. She was halfway across Scamper's field and calling the pony to her when she heard, once more, the crash of thunder and felt rather than saw a jagged flash of lightning flare across the dark sky. Even as she stopped and stared she heard, from behind her, the sound of hooves on turf. Scamper was in front of her, small ears pricked, eyes staring at something over Questa's shoulder. Questa half-turned, saw a tall, riderless horse bearing down on her ... and tried to dodge at the last minute.

She felt a numbing blow on her shoulder just as the thunder pealed again, and saw the grass of the pasture rush to meet her. She heard, faintly, Scamper's shrill whinny and a deeper, answering neigh ... and then darkness devoured her, dragging her down, stealing her senses.

Seventeen

She knew at once that she was on foreign soil, that this was not some remote part of Marcus's estate. She was lying on turf, soft, thyme-smelling, but there was a freshness in the breeze and a certain something in the air which spoke of high and open country.

She sat up. She was quite near the top of a hill, well above the tree-line. She could see wiry heather, gorse, bracken. It was a summer's day ... she looked around her ... and it was very early. The sun was only just up and the breeze of morning was stirring the heather, making the curled bracken fronds sway.

Marcus was near; she knew it, it went without saying. She could sense his nearness, though even when she rose to her feet and looked around her she could not see him. Then, abruptly, horribly, she heard his voice, but not with her ears; his voice was in her head. He was saying her name, faintly, urgently, and she knew he needed her badly, that he was in some sort of trouble, that she must get to him at once.

Panic was near but she controlled it. Look around you, she ordered herself fiercely. Where are you? Where is he?

Her eyes scanned the scene. A hilltop, vaguely familiar. She glanced behind her, then remembered. The Roman road! She had found it in her own time and now she must find it again; it would lead down to Marcus's villa and Marcus, for some reason best known to himself, must have travelled up it. He must be nearby, he must!

She set off downhill, and immediately saw the road. The big, flat stones of it, the grass just beginning to encroach between those stones, and something ... something ...

She ran, bouncing downhill, never letting herself slow, her mind afire with terror. It was he! She knew it was he, a crumpled figure lying across the road not moving ... dear God, don't let him be dead, don't let him be dead, let me get to him before ...

She reached him, knelt down. He was lying on his back, eyes closed, his face ... ah God, his face! Sheet-white beneath the tan, the heavy lids down over those dark, expressive eyes, the humorous mouth closed.

He groaned. Desperately, Questa laid a hand on his broad forehead.

'Marcus! Oh my love, what happened?'

His eyes opened, slowly, painfully. They roamed vaguely over her face then sharpened, focused. He smiled with his eyes, lovingly, trustingly.

'Questa, I was searching ... for you. I wanted to tell you ... but I disturbed a raiding party; they'd taken cattle. I was on them before I realised. They tried to steal my horse but he broke free and galloped off. Little men, dark and wild. I tried to turn away ... there was a thud as though someone had punched me in the stomach. I was on the ground, weak, faint ...'

He moved his hand in a vague gesture and Questa looked down – and gasped, a hand flying to her mouth. The hilt of a spear stuck out of his side. The weapon must have spitted him to the earth as he lay. She heard a cry and a long, pain-racked moan and did not realise for a moment that it was she who had made the sounds.

'Marcus! Oh my love, my love!'

'Hold me, Questa. I've ... a long ... journey.'

His voice was fainter already; weaker. She lay down beside him on the round, flat cobbles of the road and put her arms gently around him. He said again, 'Hold me', and one hand groped slowly across his chest, seeking, seeking.

She took his hand and held it to her face. Her tears ran down, wetting his brown fingers, dappling his shirt, already blood-dappled.

'Ques? What will you do when ... I'm gone?'

She looked down at him, at the strong face, the loving eyes. Her man. Lost to her.

'Do? I'll live out my life alone. I want no one but you, my love.'

He sighed and his fingers tightened on hers for a second.

'I also.' He breathed shallowly; she could see it hurt him to talk. 'I wish things ... had been ...'

'Yes. Me, too. But we've had a lot, Marcus, so much loving and trusting! So much laughter and hope.'

He nodded and his eyes closed, then his fingers tightened on hers and his eyes flew open.

'Questa? Where are you? Don't go, don't leave me!'

She bent down over him, close, close, holding tightly to his hand. 'I'll never leave you again,' she murmured. 'I wish the spear was – was through me, not you.'

'Pull it forth.' His voice was firm suddenly, commanding. 'Pull long and firm and it will come forth. Don't fear for me; there will be no pain, only relief.'

'I couldn't! It might hurt you.'

He actually laughed, though he grimaced with pain at the same time.

'My love, I could linger like this for hours. I can barely see you, I can scarcely feel your touch. Let me go, sweetheart, let me go clean and quick.'

His eyes were on her face and suddenly she could feel his pain, the anguish he must be suffering as the light around him dimmed despite the strengthening sun, as he became unable to feel her hand in his as his once-strong, once-proud life ebbed.

'All right, my love. I'll try.' She disengaged her hand gently and watched his own fall back on to his broad, blood-splattered chest.

She took hold of the spear; a shudder shook him and she shook to the same spasm as she began to pull with all her might.

It came, then caught. He gave a terrible, hoarse cry which echoed round the hills, 'Questa! Questaaa ...'

She gritted her teeth and heaved desperately, and the spear jerked forth, followed by bright blood which streamed from his body and then slowed, stopped, but not before it had splattered her legs, the road, Marcus's still face.

His head fell back. Her name still echoed around them as though only in those particular syllables could he find release from his pain. She tossed the blood-boltered spear into the dust and laid her fingers gently on his sweat-damp brow, feeling it cool already beneath her touch. She wanted to rail at fate, to find and punish the thieves who had taken his life so needlessly, but she could do nothing. She could only kneel in the dust and let her tears fall on to that strong, dead face.

Kat woke in the night when the thunder started to rumble. She had never liked storms, but right now she felt snug and safe, cuddled down in the big brass bedstead with Alfie's back warm against her stomach. And it was so oppressively hot and unpleasant that they needed a storm to clear the air. Besides, chances were it wouldn't be much, just a bit of thunder and some lightning and then some nice gentle rain, very likely. They could do with rain, the land was parched, they'd been watering in the kitchen garden for ten days now and very tired of it she was.

But she was wrong. The electric storm fell on them like a pack of wolves on a solitary lamb. The thunder cracked and rumbled, at first far off and then nearer and nearer, until it was right overhead, and the lightning stabbed at the earth and lit up great sheets of sky so that even in the snugness of their small bedroom over the stables, Kat found she could not just roll over and ignore the violence outside.

After one particularly loud clap, Kat leaned over and shook Alfie's shoulder.

'Alfie, I's skeered … can you 'ear that din? 'Appen we'll be struck and roast in our bed. Let's get outside!'

Alfie moaned and rolled over.

'Outside? You must be mad, gal, outside's rare dangerous in a storm like this. 'Sides, there's a lightning conductor on the 'ouse, that'll bear the brunt if anything's goin' to git struck. Hey, I saw that right through the curtings!'

'That' was a livid fork of lightning, plunging to earth and accompanied by the most vicious crack of thunder so far.

'I doesn't like it at all,' Kat said, trying to sit up, put the pillow over her head and stare at the window all at the same time. 'Gi's a cuddle, Alfie!'

'In a minute.' Alfie got out of bed and drew back the curtains. He peered out. 'Cor, look at that! That's a rare 'un – the 'ole sky

376

was lit up, reckon you could see from 'ere to the village clear as daylight if you was in the Court!'

'Oh, oh, pull them curtings acrost agin!' Kat said fearfully. 'That do skeer me, Alfie. Is Questa frit of storms?'

'Dunno. Got more sense, likely,' Alfie said. He got back into bed. 'My, but I've never sin a worse one … ah, that shook the 'ole place!'

Kat twined her arms round Alfie's neck and hugged him fiercely.

'Be kind to me, Alfie,' she said coaxingly. 'Be kind to your Kat, cos she's mortal 'fraid o' thunder an' lightnin'.'

'What, now? Wi' that goin' on? Oh well, a bit o' kindness will tek your mind off of the storm, I dessay.'

Kat giggled and cuddled close, her strong, bare body already aroused by fear and by the thought of him.

'Oh Alfie, I's skeered, I's skeered,' she murmured against his mouth. 'Tek me mind off it, there's a good feller.'

Half an hour later, Alfie rolled on to his back and examined the ceiling above his head.

'Dawn's comin' up,' he announced drowsily. 'You're a gal you are, Kat Rimmer! What 'ope of some shut-eye before it's time to go to work, eh?'

Kat, lying on her back and eyeing the ceiling equally drowsily, said, 'Storm's grumblin' off. Be a nice mornin', I 'spect.' Is that sunrise, reflectin' on the ceilin'?'

'Can't be, come to think. Oh, my Gawd!'

Alfie was out of bed and stripping the curtains back on the words. For a moment he just stood there, both arms outstretched, silhouetted against the brightness, then he turned.

'It's on fire … the Court's on fire! Git up, Kat, git up, Miss Questa's in there!'

It had been a rough night, Ran reflected, filling the kettle at the sink and carrying it carefully over to the stove. He had gone to bed as soon as Questa left and had woken just before the storm started, uneasy because of the electricity in the air, he supposed. He had sat bolt upright, sweat channelling down his back, all the hairs on his head prickling erect, and as he did so he had heard, faint and far, the first rumblings of thunder.

His mind had gone straight to Questa, of course. Would she be home yet? Ought he to telephone her, make sure she was all right? But a glance at the watch on his bedside table told him what he already knew; that she would have been home and in bed a good while ago. He lay down again, but as the storm worsened so his worries increased. Were the beasts all right? Would the boy forgive him for their latest row and come home later in the month as he had promised? How sad it was that you could love someone wholeheartedly and even understand him pretty well, yet you had no power to see in advance how he would take things, and precious little self-control either, when harsh words were said.

The last row, the one that had had been over Questa really, had quite shaken Ran. That the son he truly loved, all that he had left of Janet, his beloved wife, could have turned on him just because he'd bought a few sheep from a neighbour, seemed almost unbelievable. It still hurt him to remember the scene.

'You've almost doubled the size of the flock? You've bought more sheep, when you spent a whole day last time I was home telling me that the land would support so many sheep and no more ...'

'But my dear boy, I've rented sufficient pasture from the Court to graze twice that number of sheep. You've always approved of acquiring more land, and anyway, it was to help a neighbour. The poor girl has no one to advise her, she diversified too much and now the house ...'

His son had interrupted, his dark eyes cold with rage. It seemed to Ran that the boy was always angry, always finding fault.

'What's the matter with you, Dad? You're not in love with some silly little girl who reminds you of her mother, are you? Because that's the only reason I can imagine to make you part with good money on what amounts to a pretext ...'

Ran had got angry then, in his turn.

'In love? And what the devil would it matter if she was like her mother – I scarcely knew the woman. How dare you, boy!

She's young enough to be my grand-daughter and a nicer, more hardworking little lass you'd have to go a long way to find! You'd better watch that sharp tongue of yours ... in love, indeed! You're jealous!'

'Me, jealous? Of some greasy little Italian from the back-streets of Naples? Though I'm not here much, people talk ... they say she's a real Italian peasant despite her birth, she's stingy, land-hungry ... Oh, I'm going back to Scotland before I say something I'll regret; at least there's sanity there, not a besotted old man wedded to the old ways!'

It had been a bitter row, not the argument he had called it, but thinking about it now, he realised that in a way his son had been right; he did love Questa, but only as he might have loved a daughter, had he been lucky enough to have one. And the only daughter-in-law he looked like getting was a big, raw-boned Scots lass with red hair and freckles, whose father owned a distillery as well as a great many black Angus cattle.

'I thought about bringing Diana home this time,' his son had said, whilst they were still speaking civilly, before the argument over the sheep. 'But there's a deal of work to do at this time of year on any farm, and she has a good job in the city, too. She works in her father's distillery, but she's not just a figurehead, she's a valued member of staff. So she has to make sure her job's covered before she's away even for a few days.'

'Are you going to marry her, then?' Ran had asked, to receive another of those cold, dark-eyed looks and a shrug.

'Don't know. Haven't asked her, yet.'

But right now he must start thinking of his son with affection, seeing the boy's problems, trying to make sure that friction did not again arise. The trouble always came down to the same thing anyway, in the end. They both wanted to run the farm and neither was prepared to be subservient to the other's wishes.

But it is my responsibility as well as my property, Ran told himself now, making tea in the small brown pot and getting a mug down from the dresser. The boy feels ... dispossessed ... that's the trouble. He was a good captain, he loved his horrible tank and his crew, he enjoyed the war, or quite a lot of it anyway.

Then he came back to find me still in charge, proud of having managed without him for six years, and he couldn't take it. He loves me, I do know that, but he resents me too. How can he do both? But he does, and I should understand perfectly, since it's exactly the same for me. I love him but I resent his strength, his abilities, even the ease with which he can do things which take me far too long because of my legs.

The tea made, he took it over to the sink and drank it, looking out over the yard. The thunder was grumbling away into the distance but there were still occasional claps and now and then a shaft of lightning speared to earth, lighting up the sky. In the distance, in fact, he could see what he might have taken for the first sign of sunrise, except that it was not in the east. Something might have been struck, he supposed. And then the phone rang, sharply, making him jump before he put the mug of tea down on the draining board and set off at his best speed for the instrument, which stood in the hallway, just inside the front door.

He snatched at the receiver; who could be ringing him at this hour? It was very early still, though day had dawned perhaps half an hour since.

'Hello? Ran Atherton speaking.'

'Mr Atherton, it's Alfie. Can you come, sir? The Court's on fire, it went up like a tinder-box, all them old beams ... I'm in the box at the end of the lane and ...' Alfie's voice cracked, then strengthened again, '... and Miss Questa 'asn't come out yet. I rang the fire brigade, they'm comin' as fast as they can, but I doubt they'll be in time. Oh sir, can you come?'

Ran said he would get there as soon as possible and slammed the receiver back on to its rest, then leaped for the door. The car was tucked away in its garage and it took him so long to get it out, so long to get himself into it! He would go across country, for ten days there had been no rain to fill the river or make the ground slippery and treacherous, he was capable enough on his sticks.

His coat hung on the back of the door, his boots stood beneath. He donned both, grabbed his sticks and set off. So far as he could recall there were no particular setbacks if he went cross-country. He would go round the bog and open all the gates, not attempt anything stupid like climbing over them. Dear God, that poor kid, he hadn't stopped to ask Alfie any pertinent questions about where the fire had started or whether it had spread to the small parlour, and now he had no time for questioning.

He followed the same route that Questa had taken the previous evening. He waded the river, not daring to try the log-bridge, not with two sticks. He avoided the bog since he knew that it would be decidedly tricky if his sticks sank in too deep, and that lost him a few minutes, then he was across and entering the field in which Scamper was placidly grazing.

He went straight across the long dry grass, his heart pounding, his legs beginning to protest at the treatment he was handing out. But Ran ignored physical weariness. What a fool, what an old fool he had been, to let the lass go home alone last night! But what else could he have done, he had no foreknowledge that the storm would be so fierce, let alone that lightning would strike, endangering her life. He would not let himself think anything worse than that ... hurry Atherton, you old fool, he scolded himself, trying to increase his pace yet further; the sooner you arrive the sooner you'll know the score.

He swung himself briskly across the pasture, with the pony trotting across to him, eager for company. Drat the little mare, if only she had worn a head-stall he might have ridden her ... if only he could have mounted, burdened as he was with his sticks and his crippled legs!

In the stableyard the firemen had arrived and had worked unceasingly, but you could see, Kat thought, that the fire had had too long to take a hold. She and Alfie had done their best with buckets of water and with a long bass broom from the stable, but they might as well have saved themselves the trouble. The place was ablaze and the rain, curse it, held off. The roof had caved in shortly after she and Alfie had burst out of the stable, and very soon she had known that no one in there could possibly have survived. Even now, with the hose turned on the conflagration at last, with firemen everywhere, hacking away with their axes, aiming the water first on this section, then on that, you could see that there was not going to be much left of the upper storey of Eagles Court.

'There be no one in th'ouse,' Alfie had shouted to her at one point. 'Dunno where she be, but she bain't 'ere.'

He had battled through to the small parlour as soon as he could, and now pronounced it empty, though he told Kat breathlessly that had she been there she'd likely be dead.

'Damn gurt beam right down acrost the bed, a-smoulderin' still,' he declared. 'She – she must've teken a walk when the storm started. Mebbe she'm like you, Kat, an' don't care for all that noise.'

Kat should have been relieved, but in her secret heart she feared that Questa had probably decided to sleep upstairs, in the room she kept prepared for guests. She had told Kat only a couple of nights ago that she really must sleep up there from time to time, to keep the room aired. If so ... Kat shuddered and turned away from the scene of devastation, the stink of burning. If so, then there was nothing anyone could do, but even to think it brought the hot tears to Kat's stinging, fire-reddened eyes. She loved that girl, they were closer than sisters. What would she do if Questa, her best, her only friend, had been killed?

She was staring blankly across the stableyard to the arch without really seeing anything when she noticed a movement. She focused her eyes sharply and saw a man approaching the house, heading for the arch. The light was strengthening with every minute that passed so she could also see that he walked with two sticks ... and he was leading a pony with something draped across its back. A lamb? Too big. A long coat, perhaps?

With a ridiculous, unspecified hope suddenly blooming in her heart, Kat ran across the yard and out under the arch.

'Oh, Mr Atherton sir, I ain't 'alf glad to see you ... what've you got there?'

'It's Questa,' Mr Atherton said breathlessly. 'Give us a hand, Kat. She's not a great weight, but she seems heavy when you've heaved her on to a pony's back and led the beast for the best part of half a mile. She had a fall last night after she left me, or so I suppose. She might have been startled by the thunder or lightning and missed her footing. She's still not regained consciousness, so I couldn't ask her. Is there a doctor here?'

Kat put out her arms and took Questa's weight. She hugged the other girl's slight form whilst tears spilled out of her eyes and down her cheeks.

'Oh, Mr Atherton, I thought she were dead,' she blurted out at last. 'She weren't in the small parlour, but she've been talkin' about airin' the guest room ... I thought ... I thought ...'

'She's safe, my dear, but she needs a doctor,' Mr Atherton said. 'Is there any chance of someone going down to the box and telephoning for Dr Speed? Where's Alfie? I came over on foot, because its quicker than getting the car out, I never dreamed we might need the car!'

A fireman approached them. He sketched a salute, then turned to Ran. His face was blackened, his eyes red-rimmed and streaming.

'Need any 'elp wi' the young lady, sir? We're all trained in first aid ... fainted, did she, when she saw the 'ouse?'

'I don't think she's seen the house; she must have had a fall on her way home last night. I found her lying halfway across her pony's pasture as I was crossing the fields on my way here. She's freezing cold and still unconscious,' Ran said, indicating Questa. Kat had sat down on the mounting block and still held the younger girl in her arms. 'I'd like her to see a doctor.'

'We'll whistle one up, sir,' the fireman said. 'But if she's that cold perhaps she'd be best in bed.'

Kat stood up. She filled her lungs and bellowed.

'Alfie!'

After a few moments Alfie appeared from around the corner of the house. He was filthy, weary, unhappy. But he took one look at Questa and a tremulous grin broke out on his face before he turned away to blow his nose into a large, sooty handkerchief.

'Well, I'm damned, so the littl'un got out, somehow,' he said thickly, 'Gawd, tha's bin quite a night! We've bin that worried, me an' the old lady, thinkin' she musta bin in there ...' He gestured to the ruin behind him. 'Passed out, did she? Well, who could blame 'er, with 'er 'ome set afire? Give 'er 'ere, Kat, I'll tek 'er up to the flat. She'll come round quick enough in a soft bed, wi' friends standin' by.'

'She never reached home last night, Alf,' Ran said. 'And thank God for it – whatever tripped her up and knocked her unconscious saved her life, because if she'd gone home and gone to bed ... well, it doesn't bear thinking about. But one of the firemen has gone for a doctor, so we'll soon have her right.'

Alfie nodded, taking Questa tenderly in his arms.

'You wait 'ere, sir, an' tell the doctor where to come.'

Kat and Alfie disappeared into the stable and Ran stood and waited whilst the fireman 'whistled up' the doctor he promised. Ran could not climb the ladder-like stairs up to the coachman's flat, so having directed Dr Speed he hung around the yard, waiting for the doctor's verdict. The man came down at last, frowning.

'She's still not regained consciousness,' he said briefly. 'She isn't actually my patient, though I visited the Court several times when the child and Miss Adamson's companion were ill with 'flu. What a tragedy, eh? A fine old house like that ... the lightning, was it?'

'Yes, that's right. Doctor, is she badly hurt? I expect Mrs er ... Mrs Rimmer told you that I found her, lying in a field halfway between the Hall and here?'

'Yes, she mentioned it. Is Miss Adamson a relative of yours, sir?'

'Umm, yes,' Ran lied. 'Is she concussed? When I stumbled on her – almost literally, I might add – it looked as though she'd called the pony and then slipped and knocked herself out trying to get out of his way. The ground on which she lay was well cut up with hoofprints anyway.'

'I see. There are no signs of a bump on the head, but they'll examine her far better than I could in hospital, so I've sent for an ambulance. We'll have her in the General, I think, until we find out just what happened. The red-haired girl ...' he jerked his head behind him, towards the coachman's flat, 'says she'll look out a nightgown and so on. It's probably no more than shock and a touch of hypothermia but I'd be happier to have her under my eye. Can you go with her, see her admitted to the ward and so on? Or the red-head?'

'Mrs Rimmer had better go,' Ran said, indicating his sticks. 'I might be more trouble than I'm worth. But when Questa – Miss Adamson – can leave hospital she must come to me, I've plenty of spare rooms and spare time, too. She'll be well looked after.'

'We'll talk about that later,' the doctor said. 'She's only a youngster, but I've been told that Eagles Court is her property, though there's some fellow – he isn't a guardian, but some sort of a trustee ...'

'That's right, her solicitor is Alan Patterson, a friend of her father's. I'll send for him presently.'

'And she doesn't know about the fire?'

Ran shook his head. 'She couldn't. She was with me last evening, we were discussing her plans for the coming year. She must have fallen on her way home, she couldn't possibly have known about the fire.'

The doctor pulled a face.

'Rotten news someone will have to break,' he murmured. 'Still, let's not worry about that until we've got her straightened out. Alf Rimmer's gone off to find me a door; we'll bring her down on that.'

'But Alfie carried her up,' Ran protested. 'Can't he carry her down?'

The doctor shook his head. 'Better not. I don't think she's broken anything but we can't be sure until she's been X-rayed. You'll come and see me later? When we've done some tests and so on?'

'Naturally. I'll ring the hospital. Or could you ring me? The number's Appersley 207.'

'I'll ring you,' the doctor said readily. 'Ah, Alf's found me a door. Speak to you later then, Mr Atherton.'

Questa wandered in a strange land. Marcus was dead, and she was alone. The hills were foreign to her, but not unfriendly, only she was so unhappy that she scarcely noticed her surroundings.

Once, she went down from the hills and into the soft and fertile valley where Marcus's villa stood. After she had revisited all the places she had once loved around the villa and found them empty of the presence she sought, she went and picked a few half-ripe apples from Marcus's young orchard and took them to the horse field. Marcus's horse, the one he had ridden on that fateful day, was back with his herd. She shuddered. She called the stallion over and he came, delicate stepping, wide-eyed, blowing softly through his arched nostrils as she held out a palm with an apple on it.

When she had searched the villa and its environs and found nothing, she climbed up into the blue and distant hills again, and sought the spot where his body had lain.

It had gone. Not even the blood remained, the stones were clean and dusty, the grass flourished between them.

She sat down on the rough paving and listened. She could hear a stone-chat clicking away and a robin's liquid note. She waited for an echo, the echo of her name called out in agony and love, bouncing off the distant hills. Nothing. Only the warm sun and the little breeze and the birdsong. Marcus had left this place as totally as he had left the villa. Only Questa remained.

'Questa? Wake up, my dear! My goodness, you should see how nice the weather is today, and I've brought you the last of the raspberries from your own garden so you can enjoy them before they're over for the year. Look at the sunshine, doesn't it make you want to be outdoors?'

The small white face on the pillow did not stir, the eyelids did not so much as flicker, the lashes remained demurely on the pale cheeks. Ran sat back in his chair and sighed.

How long was it going on? It had been three whole days since the fire, they had done every test imaginable and were satisfied that there was nothing physically wrong with her, yet she did not wake up! Kat had spent hours at her bedside, chatting; Alfie popped in whenever he had a moment; the hospital staff were kindness itself. He had telephoned Alan, who had rushed down with Grace and Dickie and Roma; Sister had allowed Roma to sit on the bed; Grace had wept and clutched Questa's hands and begged for forgiveness, though for what apocryphal sins Ran could not imagine. Yet so far, nothing had had any effect.

'She's in shock,' the doctor had said. 'It may take her a while to pull round but she'll come back to us; don't worry.'

But he was worried, Ran could tell. He came too often to the bedside, looking down at his patient with an anxious frown, taking her pulse, talking to her.

'Ellen 'ud know what to do,' Kat said later, as the three of them left the hospital and headed for home once more. 'She allus knew what were best for Questa – an' for me. Why she taught me ...'

She stopped short.

'Taught you what?' Ran said. He was sitting beside Alfie, not driving, because he knew Alf loved to handle the big old car and besides, it was a strain to drive too often. 'Go on, don't tell us half a story.'

'She taught me to tell the cards an' to read palms,' Kat said slowly. 'But 'twas Questa who showed me the ink magic.'

The car jerked; Alfie had let the clutch out too fast.

'Ink magic? What on earth's that when it's at home?' Ran tried to sound joking, pleasant, but he felt annoyed with Kat. Why couldn't the woman be helpful, instead of rambling on about Ellen, who wasn't here, and fortune-telling, which could scarcely aid them now!

'Oh, you pours ink into a saucer and you draws the curtings ...'

'That's jest a woman's thing,' Alfie said, cutting across his wife's words. He sounded partly apologetic and partly annoyed; Ran assumed that the annoyance was aimed at Kat. 'Don't tek no notice, Mr Atherton.'

'No, but when we did the ink magic, we saw Questa with a babby. Honest, we did, both on us. So she'll come outer this awright, or there woun't 'a bin no babby, would there?'

'No,' Ran said obediently. What on earth was the girl on about? 'Well, now that we've cleared that up ...'

'You'm right, old gal!' Alfie said. He swivelled round in his seat and grinned widely at his wife. 'By golly, you'm right! She'll come outer this!'

'Well, of course she will, given time,' Ran said impatiently. 'But it can't be doing her any good, all this intravenous feeding ...'

'Ellen would 'a thought o' somethin',' Kat said. 'Like that thyme piller. Why, she give Questa a thyme piller ...'

'That's it! That's it, old gal! Well, if you ain't a bright'un! We'll tek that bloomin' piller in tomorrer, see what it can do!'

She had wandered a long way, right down the hillside and as far as the little glade where she had been, once, in her own time, with Grace, Ellen and Dickie. It was just the same. The stream tinkled over its rocky bed, the grass was soft and sweet, the ferns by the water's edge uncurled their fronds in the shade of the trees.

Suddenly, she wanted to sleep. She lay down on the grass. She could not remember when she had last slept, it was so long ago. She looked across at the glade and saw again in her imagination that brown hand moving over that smooth whiteness and wished with all her heart that she and Marcus had been lovers so that she would have had something warmer than mere kisses to remember.

'Marcus, where have you gone? Are you still here, somewhere?'

She spoke aloud, her voice full of loneliness and despair, but no one answered, and the silence settled back again, smoothing the ripples of her unhappiness as a pond smooths the ripples of a thrown stone.

She pillowed her head on the softness of the grass and smelt again the scent of crushed thyme ... so like before, so like before!

She slept.

She knew she was dreaming, now. The scene had a haziness, a blurring of the edges, which did not speak of reality. Marcus sat beside her, his skin sun-tanned, the breeze lifting the dark hair from his forehead. He was throwing stones at a small target he had set up, a cairn of stones, just by the little brook. He looked down at her and his eyes warmed in the way she knew and loved.

Questa looked up at him.

'Are ... are you a ghost, Marcus?'

Her own words frightened her, brought to mind flapping sheets, clanking chains. But Marcus just looked down at her and smiled his tender, mocking smile.

388

'You must go back. You must be brave, too. But you don't have to forget me; in fact you mustn't ever do that. Promise me?'

She still knew she was dreaming, that was the funny thing, knew it with every fibre of her being, and it wasn't what Ellen had called a true dream. Marcus looped an arm around her shoulders and it was a dream-arm, even the air she breathed, unscented by the blossoms around, was dream-air. But that did not stop her meeting his gaze with her own, putting all her love into her glance.

'I promise.'

'Good. Be brave and loving and you'll find what you seek. The past lies buried deep.'

It didn't make sense. She started to say it didn't make sense but the whole scene was slipping away, the stream was tiny, a thread, the glade so small she could have held it in the palm of her hand. Only the scent of thyme grew stronger, more definite … she stirred, put out a hand and felt smooth linen.

'Marcus, don't go!' she whispered. 'I promise I'll never forget you … don't go!'

But she knew he had gone and, beneath her cheek, the crisply starched pillow rustled as she woke.

'You're coming home with me, Questa, to the Hall. The authorities here all think it best.'

Ran sat on the visitor's chair, Kat sat on the end of the bed. Questa, enthroned by pillows, looked from one to the other.

'That's kind Ran, but I don't think I could be a good guest. I still feel strange, I'll be better at home.'

She looked at Kat. Kat looked at her hands.

'I can take care of you, with Mrs Clovelly's help, twenty-four hours a day,' Ran said. 'Don't deny me the pleasure of being of use, Questa.'

'Kat?'

'It's for the best, gal,' Kat said. 'Come back when you're stronger, eh?'

'What's happened?' Questa said feebly. 'What's happened to the house? Has the roof fallen in or something?'

Kat and Ran exchanged desperate glances. If Questa had felt better, she would have smiled to herself, but she felt too weak, too indifferent as well, to do more than raise her eyebrows and wait for the truth to emerge.

'We tried to keep it from you until you could see for yourself, until you were stronger,' Ran said gruffly at last. 'There was a fire on the night of the storm, my dear. The house was struck by lightning and there's a good deal of damage.'

'Oh. Is my room ruined, then?'

'It's not so much your room as the upstairs,' Kat said, timidly for her. 'But it smells pretty bad, Ques, and everywhere's a turrble mess. There's all sorts down ... the firemen chopped and sluiced and did a deal o' damage. Truth to tell, it'll need an army to put it right.'

'Oh,' Questa said. 'Then I can't come home?'

'Not yet. So you'll go wi' Mr Atherton won't you, love? You know 'e'll tek good care of you.'

'All right.'

'That's settled then,' Ran said briskly. He stood up and began to put on his coat. 'I'll drive over for you tomorrow at about noon, my dear. That's when they're going to release you.'

'Thank you,' Questa said politely.

Kat leaned over the bed and gave her a kiss. 'Nice that you're lookin' a bit better,' she said. 'We'll come an' see you often whiles you're at the 'all. Don't you worry about nothin'.'

'Thank you,' Questa repeated. It would have been nice to return Kat's kiss or to ask where she would be sleeping whilst at the Hall, but the numbing indifference which had swept over her as soon as she came round, to find herself in hospital, could not be so easily dismissed. Nothing really mattered; this life which she found herself living had no roots in reality, it was just a weird extension of the weird dream she had dreamed about Marcus.

'Bye for now, then, Questa. See you in the morning.'

'Cheerio, me old love. Keep your pecker up!'

Questa leaned against her pillows and had to force herself to glance over to the doorway, to conjure up the travesty of a smile which was all, it seemed, she could manage right now.

The door closed behind her friends. Questa sat. Some time later, she had no idea how long, a nurse came in with a meal on a tray. She set it out before her patient, chatted, asked which drink Questa would prefer, fetched it from the trolley.

Questa sat. The nurse told her to eat, so she ate. The nurse popped back later and voiced disapproval because her patient had not drunk the nice cup of tea. Questa drank. At ten o'clock the nurse came again and told Questa it was time she went to sleep.

Questa lay down, staring sightlessly before her. Perhaps she slept, but if she did so it was with her eyes fixed unblinkingly on the ceiling above her.

'She gives me the willies, honest! She just sits there you know, until you tell her to move or lie down or whatever, and then she does it. I went in last night to check that she was all right, it must have been about two o'clock in the morning, and she was still lying there with her eyes open. I asked if she couldn't sleep and she just thanked me very politely and went on lying there. It's uncanny.'

Nurse Crimmond pursed her lips disapprovingly; she disliked patients who neither chatted nor gossiped and never handed out chocolates or biscuits to hungry night staff.

'I know, she's like a little zombie,' Nurse Andrews volunteered. She thought the patient a pretty thing, though far too thin. The nurses were washing and drying up the cups used for the patients' late night drinks, a companionable task when undertaken in the ward kitchen with a couple of friends. 'She doesn't have many visitors either, and there doesn't seem to be a boyfriend, but the visitors she does have are awfully nice.'

'She wants to go home,' the probationer volunteered shyly. 'I reckon she's just so homesick there's no bearin' it.' She knew what she was talking about, sometimes she was so homesick she thought seriously about running away.

'Oh, Evans, what makes you say that? She doesn't look at photographs of home or talk about it or anything.'

'No-oo, but when she was first beginning to come round she was talking to someone called Marcus. She thought he was

391

wonderful, you could tell just by what she said … and the other night when I went into her room …'

'What was she doing? Dancing a tango?'

Little Lucy Evans glared at big, brassy Staff Nurse Crimmond. 'No, Staff. She was crying.'

Eighteen

'The poor child! My goodness, Mr Atherton, what a change in a person – I can scarcely credit it's the same girl! But we'll soon have her smiling again, soon find up her appetite. Why the food they give 'em in hospital these days ... well, it's a wonder to me that more don't simply turn their toes up and that's the truth!'

Mrs Clovelly was making an apple pie from the cookers stored in the apple loft, using illicit butter and a precious egg to make the pastry richer. She would serve it with clotted cream and brown sugar – also illicit – and she just hoped no one would blame her for trying to tempt the poor little thing's appetite before she faded away entirely.

Ran, leaning on the edge of the kitchen table pinching the off-cuts of pastry and eating them raw, pulled a face.

'They meant well at the hospital and did their best, but nevertheless I'm glad we've got her under our roof, Mrs C. I thought she was doing so well, pulling back after the terrible things that happened to her during the war, but of course Ellen's death hit her hard and the accident seems to have almost finished her off. But she's got lots of courage and determination; now she's home she'll begin to improve with each day that passes, you mark my words.'

'Home, sir? If it isn't just like you ... with her own home gone up in smoke, good as. But she'll want to go back there I don't doubt, one of these days.'

'Oh yes, of course, and so she should, but until the place has had the most tremendous amount of work done, it simply isn't safe to live in, not even the downstairs rooms which are the least affected. To tell you the truth, Mrs C, I'm extremely worried about her future. The Court is little more than a shell at present; when she sees it she's going to be heart-broken.'

393

'Well, she won't be seein' it for a bit, sir, so we'd best try to prepare her, gradual like. When can she get up, do you suppose? Because she's too active to want to lie there for weeks at a time … besides, she was always fond of the animals. I believe it would do her a power of good to see those precious cows and goats of hers. No harm come to them, did it?'

'No, her beasts were all safe and I think you're right, Mrs C. She loves her stock far more than bricks and mortar so we'll let her have a couple of days in bed to get used to us, and then I'll suggest she tries a morning up.'

Questa looked cautiously around the pretty bedroom in which she found herself. Strange things seemed to have happened to her inner mind and spirit. First, it was as though the wall she had painfully built up between her present life and the past had been torn down and what she could see there was not what she expected. As yet she could only force herself to take tiny, quick glances, but one day, she knew, she was going to have to examine what had gone before and face up to it.

When she came round after dreaming Marcus had died and found herself in hospital she had, quite simply, cocooned herself in numbness, a refusal to think at all. And now she found removing her snail-shell of indifference was a painful business; every time she came out a little way the cruel cold of the world forced her to retreat once more, but she knew she must keep trying, come out a little further each time. Even in hospital she had done her best to smile, to thank, but now she needed to do more than that. She must come fully back, begin to live again … and goodness knew she had plenty of problems to keep her occupied, with the Court burnt and her future so insecure.

And Ran was so good, so kind! This lovely bedroom, with flowers in the empty grate and a tall jug of iced lemonade by the bed, was his way of making her welcome, and a tin full of mint lumps (his sweet ration for a month at least) made her realise that she was not just liked but loved. And when you were loved, she reasoned, you must show love in return. So she would do her very best to come out of her shell and stay out, for Ran's sake as much as for her own.

Besides, she had work to do. She must, for her own peace of mind, try to push Marcus to the back of her thoughts. She knew she would never walk his acres again, admire his villa, his vineyard, the herd of horses grazing on the hill fields. Only the line of the blue and distant hills would always be the same, a constant reminder of him. But she knew she had dreamed her dreams for a reason, and that reason was – had to be – deeper and more profound that a mere need to fall in love, important though that had been.

So when Ran came upstairs to tell her that her supper was nearly ready he found her sitting up and taking notice, apologising for her lack of attention when he had visited her in hospital.

'I couldn't somehow come back,' she said, knowing her words must seem meaningless, yet hoping that Ran would see the truth beneath them. 'I was caught in a sort of dream – it was horrid. But I'm getting back now, more and more.'

'That's grand,' Ran said heartily. 'Now we thought you'd best stay in bed tomorrow, but the day after ...'

'Stay in *bed*? Me? Now that I'm home, or as good as? Oh Ran, don't expect me to be an invalid, when all I want is to get up and see to things again! I'll take it quietly tomorrow if I must, but I need to potter around, get used to being at home and on my feet ... and the day after I must go to the Court. I've no idea how bad things are there, but I ought to find out, you know I ought. Alan said I might be able to claim on the insurance for some things. I shall have to go up to London and have a talk to him.'

'My goodness, you are feeling better,' Ran said, his brow lightening. 'Look, I think you're right as it happens, you'll be best doing, better than lying in bed dreading what you'll find when you go home. But take my advice and make haste slowly. It'll pay you in the long run.'

'You sound like Ellen; she was always saying that,' Questa said. 'I suppose I'll always miss her, but at least I have only happy memories of her, and she was very old.'

'True. Ah, here comes Mrs Clovelly with your tray; it takes me all my time to get myself up the stairs, I doubt if I could manage a cup of tea, let alone a whole meal on a tray, but I'm having a lift installed in a few weeks and then I'll be able to whizz up and down in no time.'

'You do hate to feel there's anything you can't do,' Questa observed. 'First you get a car with hand controls so you can drive that, then you have a lift put in ... oh, Mrs Clovelly, that looks wonderful and smells like sheer paradise!'

'If it brings the roses back to your cheeks, love, then I'll make a chicken supreme every blessed day, and bake an apple pie an' all,' Mrs Clovelly said, placing the tray tenderly on Questa's knees. 'Well, it just goes to show what an hour or two in a decent bed will do – you're twice the girl the men carried up them stairs this morning.'

'Ambulances are hell,' Questa said. 'I was so upset when they made Mr Atherton drive behind and insisted that I travel by ambulance because I knew it would be a bumpy, hard ride, and it was. But I'm recovering fast, as you can see – lunch helped.'

'Oh, that was just a scraped together snack,' Mrs Clovelly declared, dismissing homemade vegetable soup, poached eggs on toast and baked custard as a mere nothing. 'You didn't mek much inroad, either.'

'I was still too shaken up,' Questa said. She remembered enjoying the food at first and then going into a sort of daze in which eating no longer seemed important or even possible. But that, she told herself firmly now, was a thing of the past. Now she had work to do and she could only do it if she was fed, fit and on her feet.

'Well, you eat up now. Mr Atherton, if you'd like to stay here, I'll send Lily up with your meal and you can keep each other company.'

Ran raised his eyebrows at Questa. 'Well? What do you say?'

'It would be very nice to dine with you, sir,' Questa said demurely. 'Only don't expect scintillating conversation, because I'm going to concentrate on the food!'

Her first sight of the Court shocked her, but by then she was partially prepared. From the front it didn't look too bad if you didn't stare closely, but around the back ...

'All those gaping windows, and my lovely kitchen swimming

in water and ash, though the fire only really gutted the top floors,' she said sadly to Ran, who had driven her round in the car. 'Whatever shall I do? Where shall I start?'

'Personally, I think you'll have to forget the Court as it was and start thinking in terms of another, smaller house. It would cost the earth to get the repairs done and, in my opinion, as it stands at the moment, it's extremely dangerous. If times were less hard you could repair most of the ground floor, but you'd have to tackle the rest eventually and I don't see that it's possible, not yet. But if you built a cottage at the back of the stable, facing out towards the hills, you could cannibalise existing stone and perhaps do it quite cheaply. Look, even if you marry and have half-a-dozen kids you'd never fill that house. What you need is four bedrooms, a couple of reception rooms and all the usual offices as they say. The Court was far too big for you, just as the Hall is far too big for me.'

'Oh, but it was so old ... it had stood here for centuries ... it was my family home!'

'It was only three hundred years old, and there's been a house on this site for far longer than that,' Ran said, smiling slightly. 'Look at it like this, my dear; the lightning did you a favour. The house has been so badly damaged that you can't live in it, it's virtually demolished, in time you can completely demolish it, but until you can afford to do so just turn your back on the existing house and rebuild. And Questa, even if you could rebuild, would it be sensible? Think of the rambling old passageways and still-rooms and sculleries, to say nothing of studies and libraries and games rooms and music rooms. They'll never be practical in this post-war world, when no one can afford dozens of servants and gardeners and so on, so just dispense with them and be grateful.'

'You're right. And since I never intend to marry I suppose I might as well make it just a couple of bedrooms and a huge big kitchen,' Questa said thoughtfully. 'Yes, there's a good deal of sense in that. And of course I knew there had been a house here for far longer than three hundred years,' she gave him a quick, sly glance. 'A couple of thousand years, more like.'

'Well, probably for six or seven hundred years. So shall I come up to London with you and we'll get down to business? See what money is available, what you can do and what you can't? And before we do that we'll go all over the house with a reliable building contractor and see how much can be used again and how much is a dead loss.'

'That would be marvellous, if you really wouldn't mind,' Questa said gratefully. 'When you think, Ran, of how I used to like to tackle things myself, I feel really ashamed of the way I'm leaning on you. But the truth is, since my – my illness, I don't want to do things alone. I need someone to tell me if I'm doing right. And Kat, dear though she is to me, isn't quite enough.'

'No, I don't imagine she knows very much about finances, or building, for that matter,' Ran agreed. 'But she's hot on human nature and she's becoming a fine gardener. You'll be able to keep the kitchen garden under cultivation, even if you have to let the cows and goats go for the time being.'

'Let my animals go? Oh, but why?'

'Because until you've built your cottage you've got nowhere nearby to live,' Ran explained. 'I suppose Kat might manage the four cows you've got at present, and even the goats aren't that much work, but you had planned to expand your dairy herd and that, I fear, will be impossible whilst things are still at sixes and sevens. You were very lucky, you know, that thanks to Alfie and Kat and the fire service, the fire never reached the stable block, but of course the cart-shed went and the dairy, which means it won't be as easy to make your goat-milk cheese.'

'I'm just so grateful the stable block and the coachman's flat are all right,' Questa said fervently. 'But with Ellen gone and Kat and I with our hands full, we don't really need the dairy. We'll just go on keeping some milk back for ourselves and sending the rest to the Milk Marketing Board. And since the cart was burnt to ashes I suppose a cart-shed isn't that important.'

'Good girl. And you'll stay with me, until you can move back in? You've no idea what a difference it's made having someone young about the place.'

'When does your son come home?' Questa asked, carefully casual. She had no intention of being caught on the premises by that most objectionable of young men. 'I wouldn't want him to think I was encroaching on his preserves.'

'He'll take to you when you meet,' Ran said. He sounded doubtful, though. 'He's all right, it's just that war does strange things to young men. We'll sort it out though, once he's home for good.'

'Yes, I'm sure you will. Only wasn't he coming back again this month? It'll be August in less than a week.'

'That's right. He's got some hare-brained scheme in his head though and he's gone shooting in France, just for a couple of weeks. He'll be back in early August ... that is if he doesn't change his mind yet again. Sometimes I wonder if he'll ever come home.'

Questa's heart lifted, then she scolded herself. How could she rejoice over something which would give Ran such pain? And anyway, she would go back to her own home when she was able to do so and once there, it wouldn't be so quick and easy to apply to Ran for help, or to spend the evenings chatting, learning, becoming easier and easier with each other. No, she should want his son to come back as quickly as possible.

'He'll come home,' she said bracingly, therefore, 'and when he does, I'm sure we'll all learn to get along. As for the house, well, as I told you, it was beginning to get me down. I don't think I'd ever have got it back into a decent condition so, if you don't mind coming with me, I'll go down to the telephone box and ring Mr Clarkson and see what it'll cost to have a tiny cottage built, in the orchard I think.'

'You don't fancy the view? If you build alongside the existing house you'd be able to see right across to the hills of Wales. I've always envied you that view.'

Questa swallowed. Ah, those hills! Of all the things that had changed here, they alone had remained inviolate, their humped shoulders, misty with distance, unaltered for two thousand years.

'No, I can manage without the view,' she said quietly. 'The orchard will be lovely, especially in spring.'

The trip to London began badly. Alan was forced to tell them that though the furniture was covered by insurance, he had been unable to find any company willing to insure the great old barn of a house against Acts of God.

'I seem to spend my time telling Questa that there will be a little money, but never quite enough,' he said ruefully to Ran as they sat in his office and drank coffee. 'And it's the same story now, I'm afraid. Even the most helpful of builders needs money to build a place, and it's the sort of money Questa just can't afford.'

'But it won't cost the earth to build a cottage,' Ran said impatiently. 'She doesn't want a castle, man, just a cottage! Good lord, I've cottages on my estate that she could have and welcome, only they aren't conveniently situated for her own property.'

'We-ell, what sort of cottage? I'd imagined a house ...'

'Two bedrooms and a big kitchen,' Questa cut in. 'I'd like a bathroom, but if it isn't possible with the money available ...'

'Ah, if you'll be content with something that small then you'd definitely be able to afford it,' Alan said. 'Mind, if you rented out the land we could probably get planning permission to build a proper house, not necessarily for you but for whoever rented the land. Then you could live very comfortably on the proceeds in your cottage and just keep the kitchen garden so that you had something to cultivate. Or if you didn't like that idea then perhaps the best thing to do would be to move away, get a little place in a village somewhere ...'

'No!' Questa said at once. 'No, I won't! I want the land myself, I want to see it with my cattle on, my sheep!'

'What about a loan?' Ran said, seeing that Alan was about to tell Questa that she was crying for the moon. 'A bank loan I mean, so that she can begin to re-stock? Surely a bank would lend Questa enough money when they know she's got such a potentially excellent property?'

'Not a minor they won't,' Alan said gloomily. 'And she won't come of age for another year. Still, that can be got round.'

'A cottage would cost about £500,' Ran said deliberately. 'Don't tell me she won't have that much, old boy!'

'Oh! Well, yes, of course, but she'll still have to furnish it and keep herself. And I thought you wanted the Court demolished so that the ruins were made safe?'

'No,' Ran said, 'not if it's going to cost the earth. Besides, what's unsafe about them? The walls are sturdy old stone, the ground floor is in a mess and the upper floor is badly damaged, but provided she doesn't try to live there it should be all right. It's just the roof, the attics and a good part of the bedrooms which were destroyed.'

'And a good job too,' Questa said crossly. 'The attic was riddled with woodworm and dry rot and death-watch beetle, I'd never have cured it and made it sound in a thousand years, so why not accept what's happened and be glad of it? I've got to be,' she added beneath her breath.

'Oh, in that case ... will you put the work in hand?'

'Certainly,' Ran said. He got to his feet. 'Thanks for your time, old chap.'

They had come up by train and went home the same way. Once they were safely ensconced in a carriage, Questa leaned close to Ran and lowered her voice.

'Ran, why does Alan want me to rent the place? Even with the house burned out, all he thought about, really, was renting. I don't understand it.'

'He wants you to make money, not just spend it,' Ran said gently. 'His legal mind wants to see you settled and, in a way, off his conscience. Whilst you're struggling along in a cottage, trying to farm, he'll feel honour bound to do what he can for you, but if you were living off a fat rent he'd be able to wash his hands of you. I think, my dear, that it's partly because of the ... the relationship between your father and Grace that he feels like that. When Charles made him his executor he had no idea that Alan and Grace would ever get together. I'm sure he thought they were poles apart or he would never have appointed Alan to a position of trust concerning his beloved daughter.'

'But I've always got on well with Alan,' Questa protested. 'I've always thought of him as very much my friend.'

'Yes, and you were right to do so most of the time. But you are, I believe, very like your mother?'

'Yes, I believe I am. Certainly in the photographs Alan found for me she's dark haired, like me, with a similar shaped face.'

'Grace was terribly, painfully jealous of your mother. You know that now, I take it?'

'Yes. But I don't know how *you* know,' Questa admitted. 'I never said a word about all that business.'

'No, you didn't. But Alan did. He came over and had a heart-to-heart after he'd made – various discoveries. About Dickie being Charles's son and so on.'

'Oh! I wonder why he told you?'

'Because he's a serious young man who wants to do the right thing, and he was madly in love with Grace. He wanted to do what was right, and he needed advice, so he came to the only older man he felt knew both parties well enough to voice an opinion.'

'And you told him to go ahead and marry Grace?'

'I told him that she was selfish and thoughtless, but she was also desperate for love and a man of her own. And I told him that she was sorry for what she'd done, and with him to guide her ...'

Questa laughed delightedly. 'Oh aren't you clever, Ran? That would be just the sort of thing Alan was longing to hear. Is that why you gave him that particular advice though, or did you mean it?'

'I meant it, more or less, but what's the good of giving someone advice which they patently don't want and won't follow? And I also said that Dickie needed a father, and who better than his real father's best and closest friend?'

'Dear Dickie,' Questa said softly. 'So you sorted Alan and Grace out; now do the same for me. What am I to do, Ran?'

'The same as them. Find yourself a nice young man, marry him, and you'll have someone to live in your cottage with you, someone to give you a hand with all your crazy schemes.'

'I won't ever marry,' Questa said. 'I – I did know someone, but he – he died. There won't be anyone else. I'm happy alone.'

'I'm sorry; I didn't know,' Ran said. 'But you're so young, Questa, you must give life a chance! There's someone for you, waiting in the wings.'

'Perhaps. And now let's talk about my cottage!'

'Phew, isn't it hot?' Questa was picking spinach for market and straightened her aching back for a moment. 'I'd love some iced lemonade.'

Kat, picking the next row, turned and grinned, then straightened up in her turn.

402

'The only place round 'ere with ice is the 'all,' she said. 'I thought you was stayin' away whilst young Atherton and 'is dad get to know one another. What did Mr Atherton say when you told 'im you was movin' out?'

Ran's son was home. He had come, as promised, only a couple of days earlier, and as soon as the telegram arrived with the date and time when he would expect to be picked up at the station, Questa had packed a bag and gone back to the Court.

But not to the house, of course. She had seen an advertisement for a caravan in the local newspaper, had rushed to Ran, borrowed the money and had the caravan parked in the orchard that very same day. It had been in a good state of repair and the kitchen at the Court, though filthy and smelling of destruction and with ash on every surface, still had running water in the sink and a paraffin stove borrowed from the Hall. Furthermore, the downstairs cloakroom still operated, so with some of the facilities of the Court to fall back on, the caravan, Questa insisted, suited her fine.

'How d'you mean, what did he say? Oh, about me living in the caravan, d'you mean? He said was it watertight, did it have a good lock on the door and what was the bed like, so far as I can remember. He didn't ask if it had ice-making facilities, if that's what you mean.'

Kat giggled. 'Don't be daft, Ques! It were common knowledge he din't want you to move out. An' a caravan, when all's said an' done, ain't quite the same as a cottage! Didn't 'e try to mek you change your mind?'

'Well, not really,' Questa admitted. She bent once more to her task and addressed Kat again, her voice muffled by her position. 'I might have been quite hurt, except that I know he's as worried over his son coming home again as I am. Was, I mean.'

'Why was you worried? If 'is old man is nice, which Mr Atherton most certainly is, then why shoun't the son be nice as well?'

'I've met young Atherton once. He hit me. I don't want to meet him again,' Questa said positively. 'I don't think he'd try to hit me a second time, mind you, he'd not dare, but I can't forget last time, you see.'

'Ho, 'it you, did 'e? And 'ow old was you then?'

This time it was Questa's turn to laugh.

'It wasn't a childhood fight, it was two years ago! It's rather complicated; he thought I was trespassing – well, I was, but I wasn't doing any damage – and he held me up at gun-point. That's not the way to behave to someone who's had guns pointed at them in earnest. Anyway, I try not to think about it. He was very unhappy then, so Ran says.'

'Held you up at gun-point? What does Ran say about that?'

'Nothing, because I never told him. How did we get on to this subject, anyway? I thought we were talking about iced lemonade.'

'We were, and there ain't none, 'cept at the 'all. But the water from the tap's nice an' cold. Want me to fetch us some of that lemonade we made last week?'

The precious lemons had yielded an excellent supply of juice, the bees had not been mean with their honey, and the result was a delicious, thirst-quenching drink which was stored at present in the cool, stone-shelved pantry to the right of the sink. Because the caravan was so small and cramped, quite a lot of Questa's possessions were scattered about the kitchen still, though her bed had been gutted and all her clothing had gone up in flames.

'No, you keep on picking, I'll go,' Questa said. 'I'll fill a bottle and we can have alternate swigs. Are you sure you can sell this much spinach tomorrow, though? We've picked a sackful already.'

'It cooks down,' Kat said briefly, picking fast. 'Don't be long.'

'Lightning's my middle name,' Questa said. She put her basket on the ground rather thankfully and set off for the house. It still made her feel sad to go in there, but she consoled herself with the recollection that she had never known the Court in its heyday and that she would be far happier housekeeping for herself in a cottage, without the responsibilities and worries of what was virtually a mansion.

Once in the kitchen she filled a jug with cold water from the tap, then went across the room and into the pantry. The big earthenware jar of lemonade stood on the cool floor under the marble slab, stoppered with an enormous cork. Questa removed the cork, tilted

404

sufficient lemonade into her water to flavour it, replaced the cork, then made her way back into the kitchen. Once there, she looked thoughtfully at the jug. It would soon get warm outside, and the lemonade would get full of swimming garden pests unless she found a cover for it. She remembered a jug with a lid ... but where had it gone? So much had been destroyed, but surely a large enamel jug might have escaped the worst of the damage?

She could see nothing suitable in the kitchen, but remembered that in the big old dining room a sideboard had escaped damage. Would there be covered jugs in there which she might use?

She crossed the hallway, not without difficulty because a great beam lay across it, and went into the dining room. Kat, Alfie and Bert had piled up rescued articles in there so she found the jug she wanted and walked back across the hall, glancing at the cellar door as she did so. Odd, how she had once dreaded the very thought of going into the cellars, yet for a few days she had been telling herself that she really ought to explore, and the thought had filled her not with creeping horror but a sort of anticipation. Suppose she found old Joshua's secret cellar, just for a start? She was ashamed, now, of having told Ran that the cellar was empty when she had no idea which was the secret cellar or even if the ones Alan and Grace had stared around by torchlight included Uncle Joshua's one-time hoard. To find that hoard would be fun, and Ran would be most awfully pleased. Old liquor was worth a lot of money, he said. She might sell it and buy cows, or another cart ... she would have to borrow a cart next haymaking, that would go against the grain ... or she might even buy some labouring time, for she had been forced to let Bert go once the Court had been destroyed.

Right now she really should be returning to the garden and poor, hot Kat. But she stood the jug down on a cleanish bit of floor and went over to the cellar door. She pushed it; it did not yield. She remembered that it was always locked, in case Dickie fell down the stairs, she supposed, and looked around her for the key. So far as she could remember it had hung just beside the banister, but the nail was empty now; the key, if it hadn't been chucked away or burnt, was probably lying somewhere in the rubble and ash beneath her feet.

Oh well, so that was that, then. It might have been rather fun to explore those cellars with a bright light and Kat to keep her company – they could clutch each other and shriek over spiders or anything horrible they might find – and it would ease her conscience over telling Ran that unnecessary lie. She remembered standing at the top of the steps whilst Grace and Alan went below, waiting for their return with a hammering heart, and then, when they came up, slamming the door shut again on the darkness beneath and turning the big old key decisively in the lock.

There were three cellars, Alan had said, the farthest one clearly a wine cellar; but empty. And that, at the time, had been enough for her. All she had wanted was to shut the door and forget cellars, wine and all.

Now she turned and crossed the hall again, picking up the lemonade as she went. Right then, she was beginning to see that she must forget the bad things about the war and remember the good: the kindness of the peasants, the bravery of the partisans. And in order to do that she would face her dread of dark underground places and explore the cellars. She would not have it said that fear of the unknown had forced her to leave any part of her inheritance unexamined.

Outside, the sun shone and Kat greeted the lemonade with real enthusiasm. Working away, picking the long dark leaves of spinach, Questa was able to contemplate cellars with scarcely a qualm. She would get a couple of strong torches from somewhere and they would sally forth!

'It's lucky, in a way, that the rain didn't start yesterday instead of today. Imagine picking spinach in this!' Questa, helping Kat to pile several sacks of spinach, a couple of trays of eggs and some rather good Victoria plums into the back of the old Atherton jeep, indicated the lowering sky from which a constant, steady rain was falling. 'Are you sure you can manage without me?'

'Yeah, course I can! 'Sides, Alfie's goin' to treat me to dinner at The Arms, an' anyroad, I'm wi' Mrs Breckenridge today and 'er stall's one of they wi' a right good striped canvas cover, so the weather don't mek much difference. What'll you do whiles we're gorn?'

'Dunno. Pick some more plums, make some butter – I put the milk into the separator – and fiddle around generally. I had thought I'd get the kitchen at the house cleared out, but it's such a depressing job, so I'll leave it for a sunny day I think.'

'Oh, right. Cheerio, then.'

Kat got into the passenger seat of the jeep and waved to Questa, but Alfie rolled his window down and stuck his head out.

'Why don't you go up to the 'all?' he said persuasively. 'Young Atherton's not so bad, an' the boss would be rare glad to see you. You don't want to mek 'im un'appy, do you?'

'Well ... but not today, perhaps later in the week,' Questa said quickly. 'Bye, Alfie, have a nice day!'

The jeep splashed out of the courtyard and Questa, with a sack over her head and another round her shoulders to ward off the rain, dived into the kitchen and looked dispiritedly around her.

It had been such a pleasant room, once ... but that had been Before. So many things had changed since Marcus's death, as though her luck had run out with his life. Even her home had gone, though as a result of that loss she had grown closer to Ran – and now she had lost him, too.

Not for ever, though, she comforted herself as she walked across the detritus left from the fire. When his son has settled down a bit perhaps Ran will feel able to visit me here, or perhaps when his son goes away for a day I might go back there. It did seem hard to be disinherited by the wretched young Atherton, but she did not see herself fraternising with that cruel and weasly person.

She got a bass broom out of the cupboard and began, desultorily, to brush the kitchen floor. They did this a couple of times a week and the place was beginning to look a bit better; eventually they would have to tackle it properly, get rid of all the burnt stuff, but as yet, with only herself and Kat working on the place, it was impossible. Every hour they had they needed for the beasts and the garden, and even so they went to bed every night and slept like logs, exhausted by their labours.

After she had cleared a bit more rubbish she considered her morning. There was a great deal to do, there always was, but somehow she didn't feel in the mood today. She and Kat had done the milking, even the goats had been persuaded to give up their strong, pungent milk. She ought to hoe between the vegetable rows or pick some runner beans, but it really wasn't the day for it. A nice indoor job would suit me today, Questa thought, and decided, to punish herself for even considering it, that she would go and cart the dung from Scamper's field over to the muck-heap at the back of the stable block.

She set off grimly, pushing the wheelbarrow with the fork balanced across it. At the field she gave Scamper an apple, loving the feel of the soft lips nuzzling her palm, promised the pony that she would ride her just as soon as she had a spare moment, then began tracking down and shovelling up the conical piles of dung.

When the barrow was full she pushed it back to the yard, emptied it and returned to the field. Blast Scamper's abilities in the dung-producing line, she thought petulantly, filling the barrow for a second time. She and Kat had meant to move the pony to a field nearer home, but they'd put it off, and this was the result. Thank God cow-dung doesn't have to be carted, she thought, shovelling away, and of course if we'd changed the pony's field instead of leaving her here for so long this wouldn't have been necessary, either. But worms were endemic in horses anyway and if you left a horse in a field full of dung, what could you expect?

It took her until lunchtime to clear the field. The rain continued to fall steadily, a grey curtain between herself and the August countryside. Taking a break once the field was clear, Questa went into the kitchen and washed her filthy hands and face, discovering a crop of small blisters at the base of her fingers and treating them with caution. Then she went back to the caravan. It was small, untidy and cluttered with a quantity of most peculiar things. A drench for the cows, Questa's small stock of clothing, two pairs of rubber boots, some sandals and some slippers, various pans and some crockery and cutlery and, in an untidy heap on the table and by the tiny sink, vegetables of every shape and size.

'Food, food,' Questa muttered when she had dried her hair on a thin roller towel, changed her green cotton shirt and faded grey trousers for a grey cotton shirt and patched black trousers. 'What can I eat, I'm starving!'

She found half a loaf, some cheese and a handful of radishes. Then she put the kettle on the primus and sat down and got out one of her farming books. Opening it at random, she cast herself down on the narrow seats which would, later that day, become her bed, and began to read and eat simultaneously. When the kettle boiled she made herself a cup of cocoa which she drank between bites of her food. Only when she had finished her meal did she put down her book, rub her hair with one hand until it stood up spikily at the back, and glance at the chaos around her.

Well, it was so small, that was the trouble. She was used to a bit of space around her but she would grow accustomed to this and, besides, any day now the builder would be coming along to mark out the footings for her cottage. It wasn't as if she would be in the caravan for ever ... and then to her annoyance tears filled her eyes and she felt her loneliness, her misery, like a physical burden, bearing her down.

She scolded herself fiercely and scrubbed her eyes dry with the backs of her hands. Then she told herself not to be a self-pitying fool, and set off into the rainy afternoon. She had cleaned Scamper's field, but there was always work in the orchard ... she could pick the rest of the plums for a start.

She fetched a basket from the tackroom and went along to the orchard. The plum trees grew right along the back of it, where the grass was deepest – and wettest. Wasps and bees buzzed indiscriminately around the fruit, making it plain that they considered plums their own particular treat, but Questa began to pick, waving them away when they flew at her face, ignoring them the rest of the time. When her basket was half-full she was soaked and more than a little cross. Why on earth hadn't she let Ran take her into town and buy her a waterproof as he had wanted to do? Both her sacks were drenched and smelled of the fertiliser they had held before she emptied it out ... bone-meal and something worse, she guessed, sniffing disgustedly at them as she threw them ungratefully on to the grass. They might have sheltered her from the worst of the weather, but she hated them anyway, she would rather get soaked, and she was wet already since the sacking was scarcely waterproof.

When the basket was full she picked it up from the grass, and, leaning heavily to starboard, began to trek back between the trees. The crop would not be as good as last year's because at the height of the terrible storm it had hailed violently and the hail had knocked down some of the tiny unripe fruit. Still, it could have been worse – had the storm occurred earlier, Alfie pointed out, they might have lost the entire crop.

She went across the puddled paving in the yard, wondering rather drearily when Kat would return from the market. Despite the fact that it was high summer, she was chilly as well as wet. She wondered whether Kat would light a fire when she got back ... if so, she would gratefully accept an invitation to spend the evening at the coachman's flat. The caravan had only the tiny primus stove for heating.

In the kitchen she set the plums down carefully on a faded towel – dry fruit kept longer than wet – and then spread a clean tea-towel over them. That done, she wandered through into the small parlour, wondering for the hundredth time whether it would be possible to make this room and the kitchen habitable, just until her cottage was built. But Alan had said it would be a waste of money and even Ran had advised her not to spend money needlessly but to return to the Hall until the cottage was complete.

The small parlour was a bit of a mess; even Questa's preju-diced eyes could see that. They had moved the beam which had lain across her bed into the hall, but the ceiling was filthy, the paintwork sooty, and the window-frame blackened and blis-tered, the glass long gone. The window-seat, where she had liked to sit, was still there though. Hard wood, someone had said when she'd remarked on it. And polished, not painted. It had somehow managed to be merely blistered and scorched, not burnt up.

Outside, the rain drove almost horizontally across the park. It had puddled the gravel and the big lawn, now grazed flat and relatively respectable by the goats, was spongy with rain. Where the goats were tethered, in fact, it was getting quite poached ... I'll have to move them in an hour or so, Questa told herself resignedly. One of these days that grass will be a lawn again; I mustn't let it go completely to rack and ruin.

She was about to turn around and leave the small parlour and the house, when, faintly on the breeze, she heard the sound of trumpets. A fragile and silvery sound, it floated across the rain-sodden countryside, and sounded as though it were coming from the wood. Immediately alert, she shot across to the parlour window; she would not have time to go round by the kitchen now. She sat on the sill and wriggled herself through the empty sash and dropped on to the gravel. She ran across the lawn, the grass as she neared the wood so tall that it wet her to the knee, and into the trees.

For a moment, as she entered the wood, she thought she saw the gleam of a road, the movement of marching men, but then she looked again and it was nothing, only the steady drip, drip of rain from the branches overhead, only the patter of raindrops on the leaves. Underfoot, the thick beech mast steamed slightly, and on all sides of her the great trunks loomed, cathedral-like in the steadily falling rain. Questa heaved a sigh and sat down under the nearest beech tree. She was so wet it scarcely mattered if she got wetter, but what was the point? She had thought she heard trumpets, imagined a movement ... now she knew both had been wishful thinking and she had best get back to the kitchen, pick up her basket, and get on with picking the plums.

She stood up, stretched – and saw him.

A man, just coming around the great bole of the nearest tree. He saw her very nearly as soon as she saw him, and stopped short.

'By Jupiter, you startled me!'

It was he! Dark hair slicked to his head by the rain, the curls flattened. Dark eyes, narrowed against the drops which ran down his broad forehead, spangled the thick, dark eyebrows. Broad shoulders, a spare, strong body, and that lean, laughing, danger-ous face!

'Marcus! Oh Marcus, I never thought ... I never dreamed ...'

She ran at him, went to throw herself against his chest ... and stopped short, cringing back, hands flying to her mouth.

It was like the worst nightmare, the very worst. For she looked into the face she loved more than any other, smiled into those dark, remembered eyes – and saw only bewilderment and a sort of distaste mirrored there.

He did not know her! He had forgotten! She was nothing to him – worse, he thought her mad, or forward, or both.

With a moan, she turned from him and ran as fast as she could, dodging through the trees, slipping, feeling branches catch at her hair, but indifferent to everything except escape. He did not know her! Perhaps she was mad, perhaps it had all been too much for her, but she had recognised him at once. Ah, the pain of that speechless rejection would be with her always, overshadowing the comfort that he had once brought.

She skidded across the stableyard and burst into the empty kitchen. There were the plums, tiny spheres beneath the tea-cloth, and there was her basket, with leaves and twigs and water in it.

She snatched it up. She heard footsteps coming hastily across the yard, then a figure darkened the doorway.

The man with Marcus's face had followed her. He gave her a crooked, hesitant grin.

'I'm most awfully sorry I scared you – you thought I was someone else, didn't you? And I'd no business to be in the wood, of course, except that I was coming to visit you.' He held out a thin, bronzed hand, then dropped it to his side once more as she made no move but stood, like a deer at bay, backed against the dead Aga, the basket held protectively in front of her.

'Who ... who are you?' Her voice came out very thin and scared sounding.

'I'm Martin Atherton, Ran Atherton's son.'

'Martin *Atherton*? Oh, but you can't possibly be young Atherton – I met him once, a couple of years ago. He had a thin, ferrety sort of face and he ... well, he ...'

'You probably mean Fred Atherton, my cousin,' the man with Marcus's face said. 'He came to give my father a hand for a bit after I left, but he didn't fit in. I take it that you're Questa Adamson, the owner of all this somewhat battered splendour?'

'Yes,' Questa said flatly. Now that she looked properly, she could see that although young Atherton looked exactly like Marcus, he did not have his scars and he most certainly was not wearing his clothes. A waterproof cape and dark trousers tucked into wellington boots were not what Questa usually saw on Marcus's lean, athletic body.

'Well, I came to ask you to supper ... my father's invitation of course.'

He looked across the kitchen at her and suddenly she hated him, hated him with a force and vigour which surprised her. How dare he come here, looking just like Marcus, and try to patronise her, to hand out invitations from Ran, who was quite capable of coming round himself, would have come round in the normal course of things. She did not want to have to sit opposite a pair of dark eyes which looked at her with indifference bordering on dislike ... he could keep his supper.

She said as much. 'No, thanks. I'm having a meal with friends tonight.'

The man raised his thick brows; he looked taken aback, as though he had expected her to leap at his invitation like a trout at a fly, Questa thought savagely. Well right now all she wanted was for him to leave, and the quicker the better. Then and only then could she think about what had happened: his sudden appearance, whether or not she had made a fool of herself (she suspected that she had), how she would manage to live cheek by jowl with someone who looked like Marcus but who was patently not the man she loved.

'I see. Tomorrow night?'

'I'm out tomorrow night as well.'

He heaved an exaggerated sigh. 'What about the night after that? Or the one after that? My father told me not to take no for an answer, you see.'

'I can't. I'm too busy,' Questa said wildly. 'Tell Ran ... oh, tell him I'll come over some time.'

The man stared at her hard. He came a step closer. Questa, dismayed, shrank even further back.

'You thought I was someone else,' Martin said. 'Not Fred – we aren't alike at all. Someone you dislike?'

Questa said nothing, but tightened her lips. He saw and grinned lopsidedly again.

'Look, I may look like him, whoever he is, but I'm *not* him; savvy? It's been years since I ate a little girl.'

413

There he went, patronising her again! Questa gripped the basket handle tightly with both hands and took a step towards him, chin up, eyes reflecting her strong annoyance.

'And it's been years since anyone mistook me for a little girl,' she said coldly. 'Good afternoon, Mr Atherton.'

She went to blast past him but he put out a hand and grasped the door-post, effectively blocking her path. He was no longer smiling.

'You've the bad manners of a little girl,' he said coldly. 'Don't think I'm longing for your company, because nothing is further from the truth. I'm just the messenger. I'll tell Dad you'll arrive tomorrow evening at eight.'

And before she could say any of the things which burned on her tongue he had dropped his arm, turned on his heel and crossed the yard in half-a-dozen swift strides, vanishing under the arch.

Nineteen

The day after her encounter with Ran's son, Questa caught the bus into Ludlow, having decided that she must buy herself something new to wear. I'll have to have supper with them, I can't possibly snub Ran by refusing, she told herself, and if I had something decent to wear at least young Atherton wouldn't be able to despise my appearance, so I'll buy a dress – why not? And maybe some shoes, too, pretty ones. It was not Ran's fault that his son had Marcus's face, and she could not envisage life without Ran close by to consult and laugh with; they must all three be friends, otherwise life would rapidly become impossible.

So, having made the decision, she was walking past the Butter Cross on King Street, wishing she could have persuaded Kat to accompany her, when someone crossed over the road in front of her and she found herself almost nose to nose with Ran Atherton.

And coming face to face with Ran when she was not expecting to see him proved to be a revelation. They had been meeting on and off most weeks for over two years, yet she thought she had never really looked at him before. Now she was looking, and she could see how very like his son he was. To be sure his hair was white as snow, his brows grizzled, but he must, she realised, have been the image of Martin when he was a young man, and it went without saying, therefore, very like Marcus. Odd that she had never noticed the likeness before, but then she had scarcely looked for it, with no reason to do so.

'Good morning; I didn't expect to see you in town! What are you up to?' Ran said. He drew her to a halt. 'I understand you're coming to supper tonight; what do you think of Martin? We're very wary of each other, but so far, touch wood, we've managed

415

to see eye to eye over quite a lot of things and we've scarcely had a cross word.'

'He's very like you to look at,' Questa said guardedly. 'Only not so nice. I'm buying a dress. You wouldn't like to come with me, would you?'

Ran grinned, his mouth tilting appreciatively. 'After that kind compliment, young lady, nothing would give me greater pleasure – and afterwards I'll take you to Greys on Broad Street and buy you a coffee and a cream cake, and then I'll drive you home; the car's parked up by the castle.'

'Thank you, but ... who's with you?' Questa asked rather apprehensively. She did not want to share a vehicle with Martin when she was wearing her worn tweed skirt and a blouse with patched sleeves.

'No one; are you insinuating I'm not safe to roam abroad without a keeper? Because if so, I shall take umbrage! But I suspect you're worried about Martin's whereabouts – don't be. He's gone into Craven Arms to see the feed merchants. Now where will you try for this dress? Ellcot's? Bodenham's?'

'Well, I did think it might be better if Martin and I met again over supper with me looking smart,' Questa admitted. 'As to where I'm going for my dress, I'll go anywhere – everywhere. I might like to look around, take my time.'

Questa blinked as she spoke, hearing her words with astonishment. Could that be Questa Adamson talking? She had really despised Grace's predilection for shopping; it would be very strange if, in her turn, she was going to get interested in such things. But she was not destined to find out on this occasion at least, since they walked into Bodenham's and there, on a model, was the sort of dress she knew at once she would feel at home in. It was a honey-gold colour with a softly draped bodice and a flared skirt which would, she thought hopefully, hide her thin brown legs.

'Look at that!' she and Ran exclaimed in chorus, then laughed at each other. 'Try it on,' he urged. 'It looks a just like a Questa Adamson creation to me.'

The saleslady got the dress off the model and despatched it, and Questa, to the nearest changing room. Questa emerged, barefoot,

416

with the skirt swirling satisfactorily around her calves as she came dancing towards her friend.

'I say!' Ran exclaimed. 'You could look for a year and not find anything prettier.'

'Yes, it is nice,' Questa agreed. 'I think I'll have it.'

So, having cast an indifferent eye over the rest of the stock, she paid for the dress, watched the assistant fold it carefully into a brown paper bag, and tucked it under her arm.

'Now shall we have that coffee?' she said, 'I won't bother with shoes.'

'No coffee until the shoes are chosen,' Ran told her. 'Come on, there's a good shop just up the road.'

The shoes were high-heeled ones; she felt silly in them but Ran, who seemed to have divined, in an uncanny way, that she was trying to look sophisticated, insisted that she should buy them since, he said, they looked just right with the dress.

'I always knew you were my type of girl,' he said as they took their places at a round window table in the tea-shop of his choice. 'Any female who can buy the first dress and the first pair of shoes she tries on is worth her weight in gold.'

'Well, I don't like shopping much,' Questa admitted. She looked in awe at the cakes displayed on the trolley which a frilly-capped waitress was pushing past their table. 'Gosh, are those eclairs?'

'They are. Want one?'

'Ooh ... but what will you have?'

'I'll get a selection and then we can both choose,' Ran said tactfully. 'Waitress!'

An hour and most of the cake selection later, they left the tea-shop, with Questa admitting to Ran that the dress had been bought so that she would not disgrace him over supper that evening.

'I think I was a bit rude to your son,' she said diffidently. 'But I don't think he liked me much and ... oh well, I thought I'd get a nice dress and behave politely so that he would like me a little better.'

'He may be a touch jealous,' Ran said as the two of them began to make their way up High Street, heading for the castle high on its mound above them. 'I suppose I do talk about you, and the Court, rather a lot.'

As they emerged into the market square, Questa stood stock still for a moment, gazing round-eyed at her companion.

'*Do* you? Why, Ran?'

'Because you're fighting like a little tiger to get the place together, and I admire that. What's more, I think you'll succeed one day, given help and the right sort of advice. So I talk about you ... see?'

'Yes. It seems understandable to me; after all, I've been here and your son hasn't. If he wanted you to talk about him, he should have come back ages ago.'

'Yes, you're right, but perhaps I didn't encourage him to come back. Jealousy can work both ways, and ... but let's not talk about it. Here's the car, now I'll show you how adept I am at backing it out of a very small space. The fellow who came in after me parked rather close, as you can see.'

The two of them travelled home in the best of tempers with one another. Ran dropped Questa off in the stableyard and said when he got home he would ring the builder again.

'But they're up to their eyes in work, and they have to have permits for every brick they lay and more for timber, and there's a questionnaire they have to fill in now with ninety questions on it,' he said gloomily. 'I've been talking to Rogers in the village. He's in a smaller way than Mr Clarkson but, I think, more likely to have the time and patience to discuss your plans and see what can be done. Though he did admit that, right now, building anything is a nightmare. But the Court is stone-built, and if you aren't going to rebuild the dairy he could use those stones for the cottage, and if he thinks repairs to the Court are feasible we may only be talking about timber, piping, tiles and so on. Anyway, they'll get going as soon as its humanly possible to do so. Too much red tape is there, I told Rogers, to be cut.'

'And what did Rogers say?' Questa asked, getting nimbly out of the car and scooping her parcels up in her arms.

'Oh, he agreed, said he'd like to take a horsewhip to some of the people who glory in it. Shall I call for you, my dear? It's no trouble, and you won't want to walk far in those high heels.'

'I could come over in my wellingtons and change in your downstairs cloakroom,' Questa suggested, but, though Ran laughed, he shook his head.

'Play it my way for once, my dear. Be Cinderella in her coach, let me transport you in your pretty dress, feed you, and take you home again. I'll be here at seven.'

'You, not ... not anyone else. Promise?'

He grinned and looked, for a moment, very like Martin.

'I promise. Until seven, then.'

'Well, I 'opes as 'ow you enjoys yourself, Ques ... show us the dress before you goes off, eh?'

The two girls were in the kitchen, carefully drying their latest picking of plums. The big old table hadn't survived the fire but they had carted in what Alfie called a harvest table out of the barn, and were using this to sort and clean their produce.

Questa, thinking lovingly of the golden dress, nodded vigorously. 'Yes, of course I will. I shall feel very odd going over to the Hall and having to meet someone other than Ran and Mrs C., but we are all neighbours and it would be silly to keep up a stupid feud just because his cousin was nasty to me. It wasn't Ran's boy who hit me that time, by the way. It was his cousin, Fred Atherton, or so he said yesterday. But I'm nervous, I don't mind admitting it, because Martin Atherton wasn't very nice to me ... well, he was sarcastic and sneering, not really nasty, but not nice either.'

'Oh, 'e was, was 'e? But you'll be fine an' dandy wi' Ran there to keep an eye, you know that. An' it weren't 'im what cracked you over the 'ead and that's a good job. Alfie thought it din't sound like the son. What'll me and Alfie 'ave to eat, later though, eh? Any ideas?'

Kat's many talents had not included an ability to cook, but she was a fast learner and could make most things now, given time. However, after a day working hard in the garden, during which she and Questa had picked many pounds of runner beans as well as the remainder of the plums, she clearly did not relish the thought of having to provide Alfie with a cooked meal.

419

'I made vegetable soup earlier, and there's the rest of the cold rabbit,' Questa said. 'And there are some lovely little new potatoes; I dug a few before I came in.'

'Cor! We'll save the soup for tomorrer an' just 'ave the rabbit an' a few runners an' the spuds,' Kat said. 'Is it awright to eat mint sauce wi' rabbit? I loves mint sauce.'

'Of course it is; look, I'll go and pick the mint and you can scrub the little potatoes. Then we can take everything up to your flat to cook. I do wonder about lighting the Aga, I'm sure it's all right, but Alfie won't let me in case the boiler bursts, though I don't see why it should.'

'Alfie know a thing or three,' Kat said. 'It ain't really fair for us to eat what you've cooked when you're goin' out tonight, but ... go on then, get some o' that lovely mint!'

Questa scurried across the yard and into the garden, picked a large bunch of mint and scurried back. It had been a fine, warm day and was dry still, though judging by the way the midges were dancing over the waterbutt it might rain again later.

'Here we are,' Questa said breathlessly. 'Come on, if you've finished the spuds let's take the stuff up to the flat. Oh, I forgot to ask you, how did the market go yesterday?'

'Sold every blessed thing, din't I?' Kat said triumphantly. 'That spinach went like 'ot cakes, could'a sold twice as much. Made nigh on a fiver for you.'

'Marvellous! Because the dress and shoes cost a pretty penny ... oh, can I change at your place, Kat, rather than have to struggle in the caravan?'

Kat nodded and the two girls dived across the yard, scattering the hens as they went.

'I'll feed you later,' Questa shrieked to them as she passed. 'Bless you, every single one of you, for all those eggs!'

'Oh ah, the eggs sold well, I 'ad orders for more,' Kat said from behind her. 'Townies like farm eggs.'

'What other sort of eggs are there?' Questa said rather scornfully. 'I do miss potato peelings when I'm feeding them, though. They made the poultry-meal go much further.'

'Won't git no more peelings till late autumn,' Kat said as they

420

burst into the flat. 'Lemme put a match to the fire. You go an' put that there dress on, so's I can see. I think I'll mebbe git an extry frock, meself.'

'What d'you care about clothes?' Questa said mockingly. 'When you first came here, Kat, you had a summer skirt and a winter one, that was all. An extra frock, indeed!'

'Oh ah. Well, I's changed,' Kat announced. 'Gettin' *gorgio* ideas in me old age. Still, 'avin' jest a coupla skirts never did me no 'arm. You'm right there.' She struck a match and held it to the kindling and the fire crackled up at once. Gypsies, even half-gypsies, had a way with fires, Questa thought. Give Kat damp wood, old leaves and a match and she would coax a few flames out of them in minutes. Now, with dry wood and coal and a crumpled-up newspaper, she could boil a kettle on her fire shortly after it was lit.

'You chopped the mint yet?' Kat asked presently, knowing full well that Questa was still staring at the blue and gold of the new flames. 'If not, I'll do it. I love the smell.'

'I love the crunch,' Questa said.

She rummaged in the drawer of the dresser and got out an old knife which Ellen used to swear by, though its blade was dark with age and thinned down to a sliver of its former self by constant use. She began to crunch through the tightly held bunch, keeping the knife as close to her fingers as she could, then turning it to thump bruisingly on the cut mint, crushing it until the sweet smell filled the small room. 'There! Where's the sugar and vinegar?'

'Where it's always kept,' Kat said. She balanced the pan on the side of the fire and shook some salt into the water. 'So you are goin' up to the 'all, despite what you said.'

'Well, yes. If you remember, when I said I wouldn't have anything to do with young Atherton, it was because I thought it was he who'd pulled a gun on me, but now I know it was his cousin ... '

'The Marquis of Carabas,' Kat said, and giggled. Alfie was teaching her to read, a real labour of love since, bright though she was, Kat's reading was extremely limited and her writing consisted of making her mark when it was absolutely necessary.

421

Ellen had been shocked by this lack, and had told Alfie that his bride must learn to read properly and to write as well.

'The Marquis of Carabas – that's 'Puss in Boots,' isn't it?' Questa said now, sprinkling a tiny amount of sugar on to the crushed mint and then judiciously adding vinegar. 'What do you think of it?'

Why Alfie had chosen fairy-tales as a method of teaching his wife to read she had no idea, but it was surprising how quickly Kat was learning. She seemed to enjoy the stories too, and often retold them to Questa whilst they milked the cows or worked in the garden.

'What, Puss? Oh, it's good. I like the end, where the giant turns into a mouse an' Puss pounces and flattens im',' Kat said artlessly. 'Splat blat, one up to the cat!'

'Yes, I remember, then he tells the princess his master is the Marquis of Carabas ... can't remember *why*, though,' Questa said. 'When you start talking about fairy-tales and nursery rhymes all sorts of things come back, bit by bit. It's as though all my baby memories were just waiting to be woken up. The other day I remembered a song someone used to sing to me, probably my father, because I expect my mother would have sung in Italian.'

'Oh? How'd it go?'

> I'm looking for the ogo pogo,
> The funny little ogo pogo,
> His mother was an earwig,
> His father was a whale,
> And I want to put a little bit of salt on his tail.

Kat turned round from dealing with the fire and the potato pan and grinned.

'High-class stuff,' she observed. 'Can't imagine them two gettin' into bed, can you?'

'You're awful; it's just a nonsense song,' Questa said, giggling. 'It's annoying, though, that I can't remember the rest of it. Or does everyone remember like that? In dribs and drabs?'

'Dunno. No one ever sang to me, exactly, but they all sung round the fire of an evenin', so I know a few songs. One I allus liked was …' she looked around self-consciously, 'but you don't want to 'ear me caterwaulin'!'

'Yes I do! Not caterwauling, I mean singing,' Questa said. 'Go on, give us a song – I gave you one.'

'Huh! Call that ogo pogo thing singin'? Still, 'ere goes.'

Kat sang tenderly, with a clearness and fervour which was entirely missing from her speaking voice.

> Every time we say goodbye I die a little,
> Every time we say goodbye I wonder why, a little,
> Why the gods above me, who must be in the know,
> Think so little of me, they allow you to go.

'That's nice,' Questa said slowly. 'I like songs, Kat. In some ways they can say what you mean and how you feel better than words.'

'You're a crazy gal, that don't make no sorta sense,' Kat said. But she spoke indulgently, and with affection. 'Let's git this dinner on the go, or Alfie will come in an' find us still a-doin'.'

'Right,' Questa said cheerily. How fortunate it was that a chance joke about Puss in Boots had taken Kat's mind completely off the entire Atherton family, and before she had had to explain about the muddle, too. But she had reckoned without Kat's tenacity.

'Questa, if young Atherton weren't the feller what slapped you about, why wasn't 'e very nice to you? I mean 'e didn't even know you!'

'Umm … well, I suppose I wasn't very nice to him, to be truthful. But I really hate being patronised, even if people don't mean it like that.'

'Oh! Well, mebbe 'e'll improve on acquaintance, as they say.'

'Maybe. And maybe if I don't start the rest of the meal soon, Alfie won't get his dinner till breakfast time!'

As he had promised, Ran came on the dot of seven o'clock. He drove into the yard in his Austin, looking urbane and handsome in a black jacket. Questa, hurrying self-consciously down from the flat in her new dress and shoes, stared at him as she opened the passenger door.

'Gracious, Ran! You look *terribly* smart, like a film star.'

'This is my pre-war dinner jacket. It's too tight across my stomach so I can't do it up and the shirt has gone yellowy. But since you were going to dress up, the least I could do was follow suit. Glad you like it, and now hop in, Cinders, or we'll be late for the ball.'

Questa hopped in and chatted spasmodically throughout the short drive, for in truth she was very nervous. It was all very well to say she had been rude, would behave better and would make friends with Martin Atherton, but it was not as simple as that. She had made an almighty fool of herself, all but flinging herself into the chap's arms, and he had shown her that he did not think much of such behaviour. How could they be at ease with each other after such an unfortunate beginning to their relationship?

'Well, here we are. For goodness' sake don't be so nervous, pet – Martin isn't going to eat either of us!'

And Martin, obviously primed, Questa thought resentfully, was the soul of politeness, a model of decorum. He smiled at her, said he was glad to meet her officially at last, asked how the plum harvesting had gone, admired her new dress ... and all the while he looked at her, stared really, as though trying to fathom what made her tick.

Supper, however, was a delight. Fresh green pea soup with a thick curl of cream on the top of each dish, young roast chicken with all the trimmings, a lemon mousse so light it could have taken wing had they not eaten it up so quickly, and some very creamy cheese with Mrs Clovelly's homemade oatcakes to follow.

Questa ate wholeheartedly, as she always did, then dusted oat-crumbs off her fingers and leaned back in her chair, replete.

'That was all absolutely delicious,' she said contentedly. 'Thank you for asking me, Ran. It was cold rabbit at home, and home-made vegetable soup. I like soup all right, but I've never really cared for rabbit.'

'No, but it was unrationed during the war and we got into the habit of eating it fairly regularly, I suppose. However, now that food rationing is beginning to ease off a bit, perhaps we'll be able to start replacing rabbit with lamb or beef.'

'It's economics with us at the moment,' Questa admitted. 'Do you know, if we lived on what we grow and catch for a year, we might easily be able to afford to buy a little car? And that would mean we could take our own garden produce to market instead of having to beg lifts all the time.'

'I don't mind taking you and your produce into town occasionally, or even quite often,' Ran said. 'I usually go in myself on market day. It doesn't make much difference whether I take you and a great many bunches of carrots too.'

As he spoke he shot a quick glance at Martin, and Questa thought it was rather a defiant look, as though he was daring Martin to voice an objection to his neighbourliness.

Martin, however, who had listened to the conversation placidly enough, raised a dark brow. 'Didn't you have a pony and cart? What happened to it?'

'The cart was burned in the fire,' Questa said, turning to him almost naturally. 'But I suppose it would be more sensible to get another cart, especially since neither Kat nor I can drive.'

'And a cart is very much cheaper and uses almost no petrol,' Martin said gravely.

Questa gave him a hard stare, then looked demurely down at the tablecloth, collecting crumbs with a wetted forefinger as she did so. 'You're right, but a horse uses hay!'

'Yes, but you grow hay. None of us get very good petrol crops!'

It surprised a snort of amusement out of Questa and she shot a quick glance at Martin, then gave him the benefit of her three-cornered smile. She was rewarded immediately by a warming of those dark eyes and a crooked grin.

'And since we've all finished this delightful meal, why don't we go into the drawing room? I think poor Mrs C deserves the rest of her evening to herself, but I'll be happy to bring the trolley with coffee and biscuits through there.'

When he had gone, striding through the doorway, Ran stood up and gestured for Questa to go ahead of him. 'Trot along, my dear,' he said. 'You know the way to the drawing room just as well as I, and I need to gather myself together after sitting for so long.'

But Questa waited and the two of them left the dining room

425

together and progressed into the drawing room where Ran took the chair nearest the fire and Questa collapsed bonelessly on a small stool at his feet. Martin brought the trolley rattling through with coffee set out on it and looked a little tightlipped when he saw them, relaxed and dreamy, not even bothering to talk. He served the coffee in silence, apart from a certain clattering of cups, and Questa, who really had relaxed, began to feel edgy and uncomfortable once more.

'Shall we play cards?' Ran asked when they had drunk their coffee and eaten the tiny dark chocolate biscuits Mrs Clovelly had conjured up from somewhere. 'If we start talking farming we'll be here until tomorrow!'

'Oh, I really should go,' Questa said uneasily, scrambling to her feet. 'I can get home perfectly all right, Ran, no need to get the car out.'

'As if I'd let you walk all that way in the dark,' Ran said at once. 'Why, I'll never forget what happened on the night of the storm. If I'd driven you home ...'

'If you'd driven her home she'd have been burned in her bed from what Alfie was telling me,' Martin interrupted, his voice hard. 'As for walking, Questa, you'll do no such thing. I'll run you back, the Lagonda's right outside the door.'

Questa looked uneasily from one to the other. There it was again, that thinly veiled antagonism, and for what reason? Ran was looking very hard at Martin, Martin was staring back. You could almost see his dark curls standing on end; if he had been a dog he would have been growling, circling his father stiff-legged.

'Martin, I said I'd take her home and ...'

'Father, for God's sake be sensible! You brought her over, let me run her back.'

Ran began to heave himself out of his chair and Questa wanted to scream at him to stop being so silly, to remember all the things he had said to her about the hostility between them being as much his fault as his son's. And then, as though he had heard her thoughts if not her words, Ran leaned back in his chair. He looked tired suddenly, and old.

'All right. Come and see us again soon, my dear. And Martin, if you'd be good enough to pour me a whisky, I'll make my way up to bed and wish you both a very good night.'

Martin went silently over to a side-table with some bottles on it. He poured amber liquid from a bottle, then turned to his father, the glass held out.

'Water? Or are you taking it neat?'

'Half and half, please Martin. Do you want one? Questa? I'm so sorry, my dear, I should have asked you before, but I've never known you accept a drink yet, so ...'

'No, thanks,' Questa said firmly. 'Look, it's a warm night and still quite light; I'm serious when I say I'd just as soon walk. You two stay here and have your drink; I'll enjoy a moonlight stroll.'

She was halfway to the door when Martin reached out and put a hand on her arm. His touch was light, there was no compulsion in it, yet it stopped her in her tracks.

'Very well, Questa, I'll walk with you if you prefer. Dad, let me carry your drink upstairs for you, then you can have it in your room.'

'I'll drink it down here, thanks, old man.' Ran took the drink and sipped it, holding it out to the fire, then raising it in a salute to Questa. He smiled at her, his eyes glittering in the firelight. 'Better let him walk you home, my dear. Even independent young women shouldn't be out in the fields after dark, you'll be safer with Martin. I'll come over and see you in a day or so, take a look at the orchard – the house isn't pegged out yet, I suppose?'

'No, not yet. In fact Mr Rogers hasn't been near or by. But if you've had a word with him ...'

'I'll have another, don't fret. We'll get him moving, you see if we don't. Goodnight, now.'

'Goodnight, Ran. And thanks for a lovely evening,' Questa said as Martin ushered her through the doorway and across the hall. As he opened the front door she turned to him in a last desperate attempt to get him to change his mind. 'Look, I'm often out alone at night, I don't mind at all, I'm not nervous or ...'

'Would you rather drive or walk? My dear girl, I told my father I'd take you home and I will. The sooner we set out the sooner you'll be home and on your own again, so why not give in gracefully? And why not smile whilst you're about it? Has anyone ever told you that when you smile you're quite blindingly pretty?'

'No, they haven't,' Questa said, astonished. He had paid her a compliment – had he meant to do so or was he being sarcastic? She looked up at him and he smiled mockingly, and she realised she could not read his expression at all, far less understand what had made him call her pretty. 'But we were talking about my going home, and I'd rather walk than ride on such a fine evening,' she finished, making a lightning decision.

Martin was an enigma; sometimes he seemed relaxed and amusing, good company, friendly. But at other times he was sour and tight-lipped with a sarcastic gleam in his dark eyes. Because he worried her and she did not know what to make of him, she decided that they would be better striding out in the open air rather than sitting in the close confines of the Lagonda.

'You'd get rid of me quicker by car.' He said it gravely, without the hint of a smile, but she could sense the amusement behind his words. 'Imagine, two minutes in my company or twenty ... don't say you're going to opt for twenty?'

Put like that, it would sound really rude if she changed her mind and went by car. The hall was dim, but she could just about make out his face and she was sure he was amused by her dilemma.

'I'll walk.' She looked up at him, as straightfaced as he. 'But we can cut the time down a bit if we run. I daresay we could do it in as little as ten minutes if we ran really fast.'

She was still looking at him and saw the lopsided grin break out, a flash of white teeth in the dusk. He flung up a hand in a fencer's salute.

'Touché! We'll walk at a nice, steady pace and perhaps we'll get to know each other better. May I give you my arm, Miss Adamson?'

It was quite dark by the time they reached the river and the bridge, and Martin stopped on the bank, staring with some dismay at the three stout logs spanning the water.

'Oh lor, I forgot how it rained yesterday! And you in those high heels, too. I'd better carry you.'

'No you won't,' Questa said at once. 'A fine fool I'd look if you slipped and we both fell in. Besides, I cross that bridge a couple of times most weeks, winter and summer, and I've never seen the water actually over the logs.' She slipped her shoes off as she spoke and held them in one hand. 'See? Simple … bare feet grip better than the best footwear, if you ask me.' She looked pointedly at his smart black leather shoes. 'Should I carry you, perhaps?'

'It's good of you, but it won't be necessary.' Martin unlaced his shoes and took them off, then grinned down at her. 'What a little thing you are without high heels … why, your head barely reaches my shoulder.'

'Height isn't everything,' Questa said. She walked out on to the log bridge, turning in mid-stream. The outside log was a little lower than the other two and it occurred to her that Martin would not know this and might easily come a cropper. 'Mind the outside log, it's sunk a bit lower than the others, it's a bit tricky.'

The river was noisy, the water splashing up on to the logs in places, but there was no danger. Martin grinned, walking steadily out across the bridge to join her.

'What did you say? Keep moving or we'll bump!'

'I said don't tread on the outside log or you may … watch out, Martin!'

Still walking steadily he came closer, but even as she watched his foot descended on to the outer log, and he lost his balance. He lurched, skidded, toppled … and went sideways, an arm, flung out, knocking Questa off-balance. For a moment she strove to remain upright, tottered, took a wild step backwards … and they were both in the river.

It wasn't deep but the shock of the cold water had them both gasping. Questa had landed on top of Martin and they rolled apart, their laughter and curses mingling, one minute above the water, the next below it, until they managed to struggle into a semi-sitting position with just their heads above water.

'Questa, are you all right? Oh your lovely dress!'

'I dropped a *shoe*,' Questa wailed between giggles. 'The water's running so fast … hang on a minute.'

429

She ducked under the flow, fumbling around, then emerged, streaming.

'No use ... oh, I'll try nearer the bank.'

'You won't. Leave it, it's all my fault, I'll buy you a new pair, and a dress. Let me give you a hand ...'

He knelt up, held out his arms to her, and the next moment she was being held hard against his chest as he struggled to his feet, lifting her clear of the water for a second, then standing her down on the flat stones. And kissing her.

How they kissed! Questa thought afterwards that all her misery over the loss of Marcus went into that kiss, because Martin looked like Marcus, and felt like Marcus, and kissed ... oh, but he kissed wonderfully, like no one else, first with little kisses all over her cheeks and nose and chin, then homing in on her mouth with a splendid heat and savagery which made her cling to him, breathless with delight, almost swooning with the pleasure he brought her.

But the water was chilly and a little wind caught at the hem of her wet dress and wrapped it clammily round her legs. Questa gave a sigh and moved back, albeit with some reluctance.

'Martin, I think I must have gone mad, or is it you? We've only met twice in our lives!'

He looked down at her, his eyes dancing, trying to make his mouth prim and failing miserably. 'Once met never forgotten; I've known you before.'

As he said it he took her waist in his hands and lifted her up on to the bank, then scrambled up after her and shook himself violently as a dog would. Water flew from his hair in a fine arc and Questa put her hands flat to her own hair, squeezing water from it.

'When? When did you meet me before?'

On dry ground, though they were still dripping, he put both arms leisurely around her hips, linking his hands just under the swell of her bottom and swaying her gently from side to side.

'If I say *in my dreams* you'll think me a real idiot. Seriously, though, I believe we must have met before, perhaps when we were a good deal younger – kids, probably. From the first moment

I set eyes on you, in the wood, it was like seeing an old friend. And it was the same for you, wasn't it?'

'Yes, it was,' Questa said. She leaned against him, tilting her chin so that she could look into his face. 'Ran's talked so much about you, but he's never said anything which helped me to make a picture of you. Yet ... I *knew* you, or thought I did.'

'It was the same for me, though I didn't want to admit it. ' He turned her so that his arm was around her and, thus entwined, they began to walk towards the Court. 'We'd better get back to your place before you die of cold. Never mind your shoe, if it doesn't turn up I'll buy you some more. It was my fault that you fell, after all. And now tell me just what you hope to do with the Court and the grounds and everything.'

In perfect amity, wet, draggled and happy, they walked on through the dusk, one minute Questa jabbering away as though she had known him all her life, the next Martin giving his opinion, suggesting, approving.

When they reached the Court she led him round the side, to the orchard, and up to her caravan. It looked dark and unwelcoming in the thin moonlight and, despite herself, Questa sighed and hesitated.

'What's the matter? Not very welcoming, is it – but I'm coming in with you. I hereby invite myself in to get dried out and to make sure you get dried out too.'

Suddenly, the caravan was an adventure again, something to laugh about, something to test ingenuity. Happily Questa led him into the tiny shacklike room, lit the primus and the oil-lamp, put cocoa in two mugs, added the hot water and a splash of milk, ferreted for biscuits and finally sank down on the padded bench, setting the drinks and biscuits on the table between them.

'There! Oh, towels! Hold on a moment.' She rooted out a couple of thin towels and began to rub her hair with one of them, handing the other to Martin. Martin took the towel but shook his head reproachfully, laying his towel on the bench as he did so. Then he took her towel from her, his eyes very bright in the lamplight.

'That's not the way – I'll dry you, then you can dry me.'

'I can't … you can't … we hardly know …' Questa began, to find him shaking his head at her once more, with loving reproach and more than a hint of teasing in his dark eyes.

'Aren't we old friends? Didn't we play together in our youth? Old friends aren't afraid to touch. Come here, nothing dreadful will happen to you, I promise you.'

She went and sat by him, feeling her heart beating so hard that she was shaken by its rhythm. He put his arm around her, gentling her until she relaxed, then he began to dry her. First her hair was gently rubbed, then her face, her neck …

'Take off your dress.'

'No! You'll have to do the best you can with my dress on, Martin Atherton!'

'Don't be a little silly. Slip it off and I'll put my towel round you so you're just as respectable as a girl on the beach. Come on, it'll be lovely, just you try it.'

He must have unbuttoned the dress at the back whilst drying her neck for he didn't wait for her agreement but slid her neatly out of the dress as though he had spent many years undressing young women – which he probably had, Questa thought, trying to feel cross about it – and wrapping the second towel around her in the same movement. He rubbed and cuddled and soothed and the primus roared and the little room got warmer and warmer and Questa grew more and more relaxed. Presently Martin stopped rubbing her and simply cuddled her and then he kissed her, the sort of kisses they had shared in the river but even better, because now she was warm and drowsy and as content as a cat who's had the cream, and because the padded bench was soft beneath her shoulders and Martin's body was hard and demanding and exciting and …

'Martin! Oh, I don't think we should, stop it! Get off me!'

Martin got off with surprising alacrity. He slithered on to the floor, but retained a hold on her wrist, his fingers firm on her warm skin.

'Little Questa, you shouldn't make love so prettily and then change your mind just when I'm beginning to think … however, no harm done. Except, possibly, to your towel.'

Questa looked down. The thin towel had parted under the

strain and, whilst still perfectly respectable, she could see strips of bare Questa in the gaps.

'O – oh! Where's my dressing gown?'

It hung on the back of the door. She took the dressing gown down and turned her back on Martin, letting the towel drop only when the garment was safely across her shoulders. Fastening it round the waist with a vicious tug she turned back to him, feeling her cheeks hot with embarrassment. That she could have behaved like … well, like a slut with a man she scarcely knew had shocked her to the core, and telling herself that he looked like Marcus was no excuse. She had never behaved so wantonly with Marcus, and had berated herself for not doing so, for not giving herself as generously as she had given her love. Yet this man, a virtual stranger, had kissed her, cuddled her, and she had been willing to let him go considerably further than she had even dreamed of going with the man she loved.

Except Marcus had been a dream, hadn't he? Just an odd dream which had come to mean as much to her as reality. She had known she must leave the dream and had done so, but she hadn't been happy, truly happy, since. Now perhaps, because of Martin, she could recapture that delightful sense of adventure, of belonging, which had been so precious to her when she first came to Eagles Court.

Whilst she put on her dressing gown Martin had been sitting on the padded bench, long legs stretched out, eyes half closed, watching her with a kind of lazy pleasure, but something in her expression must have made it clear to him how she felt. He sat up and reached for her, taking her hands in a warm, safe clasp.

'Look, I think we both behaved out of character and I can see you feel bad about it. Don't! There's nothing wrong with a bit of gentle lovemaking when two people find they have a strong mutual attraction. Neither of us have done anything to be ashamed of – in fact I've seldom felt such a sense of rightness, of naturalness, when I've held a girl in my arms. I've only known you a couple of days, but already you're important to me and I want to see more of you. Is that so wrong?'

'You've seen more of me than most people have,' Questa said ruefully, glancing down at her dressing gown. But she did not pull her hands away, and she sat down beside him in a comfortable, easy way for she was sure of him now, as sure as she had been with Marcus. This man meant her no harm, he meant well by her. If they became lovers it would be by her will as well as his.

'Don't turn it into a joke; I'm trying to say that ... oh damn it, I can't believe we've only just met. I feel as if I've known you for a thousand years.'

On the words, he let go her hands and pulled her into his arms and she went there as naturally as though he had held her thus many, many times.

'Perhaps you have,' she murmured, just before their lips met again. 'Oh Martin, perhaps you have.'

Twenty

Next morning Questa was singing at the top of her voice as she went out to the cowshed. Kat, getting the stools out, turned and stared at her friend.

> Oh, what a beautiful morning,
> Oh, what a beautiful day,
> I've got a beautiful feeling,
> Everything's going my way-ay,
> Everything's going my way.

'You sound rare 'appy, Ques,' she remarked as the younger girl came bouncing across the brick floor towards her. 'Lorst a tanner an' found a shillin', 'ave you?'

'No. I don't need shillings to be happy – though I daresay they might help. I'm happy because ... because the sun's shining and I had a lovely time with the Athertons last night and because he's coming over again today to talk to the builder with me. And I'm happy because he thinks I'm pretty and no one's ever said that to me before and Martin, me and Ran are going to be the best of friends, the best of neighbours!'

'He? Ran, d'you mean?'

'Ran? No, not Ran, I meant Martin. His son. You know, the one ...'

'The one you didn't like? The one who was sarky an' rude to you, so's you was rude back? Is that the Martin you means, gal?'

Questa seized her stool and took it over to the patient Buttercup, who was chewing the cud in her stall as though she had all the time in the world to stand and wait to be milked. She sat down, adjusted the bucket and leaned her head against Buttercup's smoothly rounded side. Then she began to milk and talk at the same time, raising her voice above the zing of the milk hitting the galvanised bucket.

'Yes I do mean that Martin, only I was wrong, Kat. He's, oh, *so* nice! Easily the nicest man I've ever met, except for one, and he – he died. And he likes me, can you believe? Really likes me, I mean. Do you know we fell in the river, he slipped on the logs as he was crossing the river and knocked me in as he went down – we both went right under – I lost one of my shoes and banged my knee. Martin pulled me out and then he came back to the caravan with me to dry off and we had cocoa and talked and talked ... He didn't leave until two a.m., and – and we kissed a goodnight kiss!'

'Good lor,' Kat said, her eyes rounding. 'What's this Martin feller got that the rest 'aven't? I ain't never seen you tek no notice of a bloke before, Ques!'

'What blokes have I met to take notice of, though, Kat? Everyone's always saying I don't meet people, and you go and say that!'

'You meet plenty. There's the feed merchant's son, the one with the little sports car, 'e's axed you out, don't deny it. An' there's the feller what 'as the local buses, an' the young man who comes round an' fetches the milk away each mornin', an' the one who come up to you in the market an' said 'e'd bin looking for a gal like you all 'is life ... What's this Martin got that they 'aven't, eh?'

'Oh, Martin's different, he's special. He says we must have met when we were kids, before the war, and I think he may be right. I thought I knew him the first time we met, even though he was cross and I was a bit scared, so probably we were quite friendly back in the old days. And he's coming over this morning to talk to me about the cottage in the orchard. Oh Kat, I'm so happy I could burst!'

'Don't go a-doin' that,' Kat advised, busily milking Daisy. 'There's enough of a muddle, what wi' the fire an' all, 'thout you sprayin' yourself all over the yard. Why do 'e want to talk about the cottage in the orchard, any road?'

'Don't take me so literally,' Questa said with a giggle. 'As for what Martin intends to do about the house, I don't know. But I

436

hers, not only muffling any remark she might have been about to make but also having the effect of taking her mind completely off conversation.

Kat, clanking across the yard with the sterilised buckets, brought the pair of them down to earth. Martin moved reluctantly away from her and Questa seized the yard broom and began to brush along the channel, every now and then sloshing water from another bucket to help her clear the muck.

'Here, I'll fill that,' Martin said, taking the empty bucket from her. 'Where do you get the water from? House or trough?'

'House, please,' Questa said, with heightened colour and shortened breathing. 'Oh hello, Kat … come and be introduced. This is Ran Atherton's son Martin … Martin, Alfie's wife, Kathleen Rimmer.'

'Nice to meet you,' Kat said, grinning. 'I'd 'a knowed you anywhere, mind, after what Questa said this mornin'.'

'Oh? What was that?'

'Never you mind! But she's right, any road. Ques, I put the kettle on, it's nigh on time for 'levenses. You comin'?'

Martin set off for the house, his empty bucket clanking by his side, and Questa tore her eyes and attention from him for a moment to to answer her friend. She could tell from the smirk on Kat's face that it must have been painfully obvious she and Martin had been in each other's arms seconds earlier. Still, there was nothing wrong with that, it was not as though either of them had any other attachment. Besides, already she was beginning to accept Martin as the arbiter of her actions, and if he saw no wrong in it …

'Oh yes, we'll both come. Mr Rogers won't be here for a bit and anyway, he'll drive into the yard, we'll see him from your flat, Kat.'

'It's pretty 'ot up there. I thought we'd bring the jug down, same's we done yesterday,' Kat said. 'There's gingerbread, too. I've 'ad it in the tin three days, so it should be sticky enough.'

'Sounds marvellous,' Martin said, overhearing as he arrived back, water sloshing over the lip of the bucket with every step he took. 'I take it I'm invited, particularly to share the sticky gingerbread? Here you go – mind yourself!'

think he realised that I didn't much want to tackle Mr Rogers alone … anyway, he's coming over in time for elevenses, he said. Oh Kat, he's *so* nice, you'll like him awfully, just you wait and see.'

'Oh ah? What do 'e look like?'

'Imagine the nicest face you can, with nearly black hair, a bit curly, and very dark eyes. And put it on a strong, lean sort of body, and make the face kind of dangerous looking, with a smile that doesn't quite show, only you know it's there, and that's Martin.'

'Oh ah?' Kat said again, sounding unimpressed. 'Sounds alwright … but I likes dark-'aired men, me, so I'm bound to like 'im, if 'e's dark.'

'He is dark,' Questa confirmed. 'As dark as … ' She stopped short, then went on in a sort of mumble, 'as dark as Ran must have been, once. I've finished Buttercup; shall I start on Blossom next?'

'Might as well. What do Ran think about you an' 'is son, eh?'

'Think? What is there to think? Besides, we didn't know we liked each other whilst we were at the Hall; it was later, after we'd fallen in the river.'

'Aye, I can imagine,' Kat said, and gave a sort of snort, then tried to turn it into a cough. 'There ain't nothin' like findin' yourself up to your eyes in cold water to bring out passion between a feller an' a wench. Well-known fact.'

'Oh, is it? I fell right on top of him, too,' Questa said with relish. 'Almost drowned him, I shouldn't wonder. Some people might have been very annoyed, but he's ever so strong, he only laughed – we both laughed, even after I realised I'd lost my shoe – it was one of my new ones, Kat, which is pretty serious, only Martin says he'll buy me another pair because it was his fault.'

'Oh, Mr Money-bags, flashin' 'is gelt around,' Kat said. 'Goin' to buy you a new dress an' all, is 'e? Cos the water won't 'a done that lovely dress no good, lovie.'

'The dress is fine, actually. I wrung it out and hung it over the cupboard door and when I woke up this morning it was just like new. Well, there was some mud on it, but I'll put it through the wash and it'll be grand, I'm sure. I'll always like it anyway, because it as what I was wearing when Martin told me I was pretty.'

Kat finished squirting the last of the milk into her bucket, then stood up and looked over at the younger girl with affection and exasperation mingling in her expression.

'Questa, for the lord's sake stop puttin' yourself down,' she commanded. 'You're turble pretty, me an' Alfie was noticin' only last week 'ow pretty you'd growed. You shouldn't need young Atherton to tell you what's plain as the nose on your face!'

'Well, I do,' Questa said. She began to milk her second cow, her fingers quick and firm on the long, rubbery teats. 'Didn't you like it when Alfie said you were pretty, Kat?'

There was a long silence. Questa, stealing a look at Kat, settling down on her stool to start on her second cow, saw that her friend was blushing and had a faraway look in her eye.

'Kat? I bet Alfie often says you're pretty!'

Kat jumped. 'Yes, 'e do mention it from time to time,' she said guardedly. 'Alfie likes me white skin.'

'You see? Well, you probably knew you were pretty, but I didn't. So of course when Martin said what he said, it meant more to me than it would mean to someone else, perhaps. What do you think?'

'I din't know I were pretty,' Kat objected. 'Alfie say so, but I aren't sure if 'e's just bein' polite, like. Still, I do get a kinda glow when 'e say nice things.'

'There you are, then,' Questa said, triumphantly if obscurely. 'I wonder if I ought to put on my new dress when I've mucked out? Only Martin's got to see me some time as I really am, and I really ought to wash the dress before I wear it again.'

'You looks fine,' Kat said hastily. 'Did you 'ave breakfuss before you come out?'

'No. Why, have you had yours already?'

'No, not yet. Then we'll talk about it again over our porridge, or we ain't never goin' to git the work finished!'

At ten-forty five, when Questa, with her hair tied up in a duster and faded dungarees on, was finishing off the mucking out of the cowshed, Martin strolled into the yard. She saw him before he

438

saw her and was able to admire him for a moment before she called out. He was wearing a thin white shirt, open at the neck which set off his warmly tanned skin, and what looked like – and in fact proved to be – a very elderly pair of ex-army trousers, the ends tucked into the inevitable rubber boots. His hair curled across his forehead and he narrowed his eyes against the sun as he came out from the shaded arch and into the paved yard, glancing round curiously as he did so. Questa realised with a pang that he must remember the house in its prime since he had often visited here before the war – did he think her a careless mistress to have let it get into such a state? But she could scarcely have helped the fire damage and apart from that the yard was no worse than any other farm property.

'Martin, I'm just finishing mucking out. Shan't be long.'

Martin's face lit up and he came towards her. 'Good morning! I'm a bit early, but ...'

He reached the cowshed, ducked to look inside, then swept her up in his arms, yard broom and all. Questa dropped the broom and flung her arms round his neck, kissing him soundly on one thin, slightly bristly cheek.

'You haven't shaved,' she observed, as his mouth sought hers. 'Hey, don't, someone might see!'

'I shaved in a hurry,' Martin admitted. 'And I don't care who sees – when I kiss my girl I'm happy for anyone to see!'

'Your girl? How can I be your girl? We've only known each other ...'

' ... Two days,' he finished before she could get the words out. 'Silly little dope, I knew the first time I set eyes on you that you were going to be my girl, it was just a matter of how long it would take to get you to drop your guard, admit you fancied me.'

'Fancied you? Me? I thought you were horrid, the nastiest person I'd ever met.' She leaned back in his arms the better to frown up into his face. 'In fact I can't understand myself at all, behaving the way I have. It's as though I've gone slightly mad.'

'That doesn't matter, and anyway lovers are always mad, they say, so why should we be different?' She started to protest, but he gathered her close again, clasping her so tightly that air whuffed out of her lungs and in mid-protest his mouth found

439

He grabbed the bucket by its rim and its base, swung it in a leisurely arc and aimed for the brick channel. The water rushed along like a river in spate, carrying the rest of the cow muck with it. Questa nimbly jumped out of the way and brushed frantically, pushing the rich smelling mix of muck and water along the channel and out through the round hole which gave straight on to the muck heap.

'There you are, another job finished,' Martin said, as though he had personally cleaned the cowshed. 'Where's the ginger-bread? I could drink the well dry, too.'

'D'you want a beer?' Kat said, turning back halfway across the yard. 'Alfie's partial to a beer of a night, so we've got some.'

'Not for me, Kat. I'd like a coffee though, if that's what you and Questa are about to have.'

'Fancy her offering you beer,' Questa said in a low voice when Kat had clattered up the stairs to the coachman's flat. 'She never hands it out as a rule, it's Alfie's treat, she says. She must have taken quite a fancy to you.'

'Sensible woman,' Martin said. 'Look, I want Rogers to take a look at the house; I still think it might prove cheaper and less trouble to renovate a few rooms and then gradually do the rest, rather than build something new from scratch.'

'You still like the house, don't you?' Questa said shyly as the two of them settled themselves on the mounting block. It was a huge hunk of stone, as old as the hills, Ran said, and a favourite perching spot for the girls when the weather was fine. 'I love the Court very much, Martin, though I've not known it as long as you have, but I'm determined to be practical. I can't afford to keep the place up as it should be kept, I hate housework to tell you the truth, so I've told myself to settle for a cottage in the orchard and that's what I'm prepared to do.'

'Very sensible, if it's the better option,' Martin agreed. 'Dad was telling me how you'd been gradually emptying the attics and selling off the furniture. It seemed a shame, but what a blessing you did, otherwise it would all have gone up in flames.'

'Yes. Or been ruined, like most of the downstairs furniture was,' Questa said, leaning against him. 'Isn't it odd, Martin? I really dreaded you coming home ... now I can't think of anything

441

which has made me happier. Is Ran pleased that you like me?'

She was looking at Martin as she spoke and she saw, without fully understanding it, the chill which swept over his expressive face. She felt him stiffen slightly, withdraw a little.

'Dad? I don't know, I haven't said much to him.'

'Why ever not? He'll be really pleased, he wants us all to be friends.'

Martin shrugged. 'I don't know – it seemed too soon. Anyway, I'll have to break it to him in a week or so that I want the family sapphire, so ...'

'Family sapphire? Oh Martin, you aren't going to sell it, are you?'

Martin laughed and the chilly look fled completely. 'Sell my mother's sapphire? No, indeed. It's a betrothal ring, Questa, given to their intended brides by the men in our family. I believe I'll have a use for it in a week or two ... or perhaps tomorrow. Here!'

He took her left hand and made little circling motions around her ring finger with his own index finger.

'O – oh,' Questa breathed. 'Are you asking me to ...'

'Well, 'ere we are at last. Tek the tray, that's rare 'eavy. Shove up, Questa, let me climb aboard!'

Kat, her curls catching the bright rays of the sun so that she looked like a burning bush, held the tray out beseechingly. Martin took it from her and put it down in the centre of the mounting block, then took her hand and heaved her up beside him. Kat immediately twisted round and began to pour the coffee from the tall jug into three mugs. The gingerbread, smelling delicious, was already cut into chunks, standing ready on a pink and gold plate which Questa had only seen decorating Kat's sideboard before. Evidently it was brought out for use on special occasions, and this was one of them!

'There we are, everyone's got a mug; 'elp yourselves to gingerbread,' Kat said, very much the hostess. 'It's 'ot in the sun, but I likes it. 'Ow about you two?'

'We like it as well,' Martin said without consulting Questa. 'We'd better drink up though; old Rogers should be along any minute.'

'You're right there, I can 'ear a car,' Kat said, through a

442

mouthful. 'Ye – es, that's up on the main road but I reckon it's 'im.'

Questa, listening in the sudden hush, could hear a car too, probably on the main road, chugging along, turning the corner into their lane, slowing at the sight of the tall stone gateposts with the stone eagles perched on top.

She picked up her mug and drank thirstily, then took a chunk of gingerbread in one hand and slid off the mounting block. Her dungarees snagged on the rough stone but she ignored them and headed for the archway.

'I'll tell Mr Rogers to park in the shade,' she called back. 'Better than bringing the car through here. Shan't be long.'

No sooner had she disappeared than Kat turned to Martin.

'Well, you've bin gettin' your legs under the table an' no mistake,' she said with what Martin guessed was her usual formidable directness. 'What's it all about, eh? From what I 'eard you wasn't exac'ly keen on the idea of young Questa livin' 'ere and trying to run th'old place. Said all manner o' things about 'er – called 'er a graspin' peasant once when your dad said she was doin' 'er best for the place. Got your eye on the Court, 'ave you, is that why you've took up with 'er? Not what it was, but still there's a tidy bit o' land, I'd say.'

'I didn't know Questa when I called her names,' Martin said stiffly. He could feel a flush warming his cheekbones. 'Alfie shouldn't have eavesdropped, not on a thoughtless remark made in anger, and he shouldn't have repeated it, not even to his wife. I was hitting out at Dad, I thought he was making a fool of himself over a bit of a girl, that was all.'

'And now you think you'll put 'er out of 'is reach, I suppose?' Kat said shrewdly. 'If you make the poor lass fall in love wi' you then she ain't likely to end up as your mother-in-law – right? But the Athertons would still 'ave the Court, like you allus wanted.'

'No! most definitely not right,' Martin said with furious emphasis. 'What would be the point of courting a girl I didn't love, answer me that! A life of misery, that's what I'd get, and no burnt-out old ruin of a house could make up for that. As for the

443

land, Dad already rents quite a lot of it, and Questa can't sell – you've evidently not heard of the entail – so I'm not hoping to get the land away from her. Besides which, we've got plenty for what we need and if it hadn't been for Dad being half in love …'

He stopped short.

'That's it, let's 'ave the truth,' Kat said, encouragingly. 'No 'arm in the truth between us two, Mr Atherton. So your Dad's 'alf in love wi' young Questa … what makes you say that?'

Martin took a deep breath. 'It was what I thought,' he said broodingly. 'Since we're being truthful, Kathleen, I thought she'd hooked *him* and not the other way about. A land-hungry girl …'

'Peasant, you means,' Kat said.

'No! Oh, I said it, but I didn't know her then, had never met her in fact, unless we met when she was just a child. Let me tell my story my own way, please, or we'll not get through before Questa comes back.'

'Right. Sorry. On you goes.'

'I thought she was desperate for stability, a land-hungry girl with no roots, no real background. At one time I doubted that she was Questa Adamson, to tell you the truth. I thought probably Questa had died or been killed out in Italy and some other young woman had taken her place and was keen to get what she could.'

'But you don't believe that no more?'

'Good lord, no! My father wondered, but apparently she's so like her mother that from the moment he clapped eyes on her his doubts disappeared. No, but even accepting she was who she said she was, I didn't trust her. All she had was a great barn of a house, a lot of land which she had no money to exploit but couldn't sell, and a pretty face. I knew she must be pretty because her mother was a great beauty, you see.'

'Questa weren't pretty, not when she fust come 'ere. I've 'ad it from Alfie that she were a starveling, all bone and no flesh,' Kat said frankly, and Martin shivered involuntarily. The thought of Questa knowing hunger and want hurt him worse than a blow, but Kat talked on, apparently regardless. 'Seventeen she may 'ave been, pushin' eighteen, but she looked more like twelve, Alfie say.'

'Yes, but can't you *see*, Kat, I couldn't possibly have known that? I thought she would take one look at the Court, then another at the Hall, and see where her advantage lay. If she could persuade my father to marry her she would have it all, the money to do the Court up or the Hall as her home. It wouldn't have mattered which way she played it.'

'Oh ah? Then why stay away? Why not come 'ome and look after your property, your inheritance? You still aren't mekin' much sense, young Atherton.'

'I did come home, didn't I? And every time, we quarrelled. Not always about Questa, but about the place, the way it should be run. To tell you the truth, Dad and I would have quarrelled over how many angels could dance on the point of a needle if the question had ever arisen. And we're still pretty bad. One or other of us is always having to bite his tongue, snap off a remark in mid-sentence. There are all sorts of things I'd like to do, but Dad still thinks he can run the place as though it was the thirties. Mechanisation is a red rag to a bull, so I thought if I went away and got myself the sort of experience the place needs ...'

'You could come back an' tek over?'

'No! Good God, woman, you're as bad as my old man! I thought I could maybe persuade Dad to change his ways or as a last resort I would have taken a job as estate manager somewhere nearby. That would show him I was serious, wanted to have at least some say in the running of the place. But I knew he wouldn't want me to take over; he's in his sixties, capable still. I wanted to share the place, the way a father and son should share.'

'And Questa? Where did she come in?' Kat's greenish eyes were hard, her gaze piercing. 'Go on, Mr Atherton, convince me you aren't bein' sweet to 'er for your own ends!'

'I can't. If you don't want to believe me you won't,' Martin said bluntly. 'All I can tell you, say to you, is for God's sake use your eyes! She's not just beautiful, she's got a sweetness, an appeal, which I can neither understand nor resist. At first all I could see was a pretty child who might have won my father's love where I myself had so blatantly failed. Then it was as though I'd always known her, always wanted her. I touched her, kissed her ... there won't ever be anyone else, Kat. Not for me. And I hope and believe she's the same. Though one odd thing did happen the first time we met.'

'What were that?' The green eyes were warmer now, the smile encouraging.

Martin scowled down at his hands for a moment, trying to get things sorted out in his mind. 'Well, I'd come over to invite Questa for supper; I was walking through the wood when we met totally unexpectedly. I came around the bole of a tree, it was pouring with rain so I was walking with my head down, not really looking where I was going, concentrating on what I would say when I reached the house ... and there she was, with a sack around her shoulders and another over her head. We both stared for a moment, and then she ran towards me. She called something, a name ... I thought at first she'd said *Martin*, but later I thought not. And she was about to throw herself into my arms, I'm sure of it, when suddenly she sort of drew back. I tell you she looked at me with real fear in those great dark eyes of hers, her mouth was trembling, and she suddenly whisked around and ran.'

'You followed?'

'I most certainly did. We met again in the kitchen and when I asked, she admitted that she'd thought, just for a moment, that I was someone else.'

'She didn't say who?'

'No.' Martin gnawed his lip. 'But it was someone she cared about, I'd stake my life on it. The look on her face, when she thought she recognised me ... well, it was like a kid on Christmas morning, when the puppy she thinks she'll never own jumps out of a parcel.'

'She ain't never 'ad a man,' Kat said positively. 'Not a lover, any road. So 'ow d'you feel about 'er now?'

'Look, we met for the first time two days ago ... she's special to me already, I don't deny it, but you can't expect ... ' He met the stare of a pair of green basilisk eyes and threw up a hand in a gesture of defeat. 'All right, all right, I want her. I mean I want to marry her,' Martin said quickly, irritably. 'It's too soon, it's madness, but there's no one else for me; I swear it.'

Kat patted his shoulder. It occurred to Martin that she was

probably several years younger than he, yet she had behaved throughout their encounter like the older and more mature of the two. But gypsies were, in one sense, old beyond their years. She'd lived rough, fought for her very existence, knew a thing or two. And she loved Questa. You could never doubt it, having seen the two of them together.

'Okay, I believe you. But she ain't got nobody, nobody 'cep' me an' Alfie. Someone's got to look out for 'er. No 'ard feelings?'

'Not if I've passed muster,' Martin said, grinning. He felt as relieved as though he had just passed some incredibly hard and important examination. 'I'm glad she's got you, Kat. She's really fond of you – Alfie too. And I think she's fond of my father ... and she's getting used to me as well.'

Kat chuckled. 'Oh ah. Here she comes now though, with Mr Rogers an' all. Best say nowt to 'er; she might tek it wrong.'

Martin grinned. 'A fat lot you'd care! Very well, then, mum's the word.'

They had gone solemnly round the Court, with Mr Rogers stopping in each room and making notes on a little bit of a pad which he produced from his pocket. Every now and then he shook his head sadly, or turned to tap panelling, kick at a skirting board, peer doubtfully up a chimney. But at last, back in the kitchen once more, he took a deep breath and began to summarise how he felt about rebuilding the Court. Questa had been patient, but there had been several moments when she had longed to scream at the old man that she had not got all day even if he had, and would he please get on with it, so she was relieved that he had decided to give tongue at last.

'Well, Miss, the truth is the old place is in a bad state, a very bad state. The building stone is good, that's true, but you'd need a mort o' timber to replace the roof. The ground floor ain't too bad, the fire mainly hit the bedrooms and the attics, but putting it right ...' Mr Rogers sucked his breath in doubtfully, 'Well, it ain't only that it 'ud cost you. It's the paperwork, the licences an' permits ... you'd need such a deal o' stuff, you see. Why the rule is, no more'n a hundred pun' to be spent without a licence and even when you've got the licence, a place mustn't cost more'n fourteen hundred pun' and you can't build up to more than a thousand square feet anyway. To tell the truth, Miss, they'd never give you permission to rebuild, not if it were ever so. There's a turble shortage o' timber, it's nearly all imported 'ardwood, and believe it or not you need a deal of influence to lay your 'ands on cement powder, to name but one item. What's more, permits for this sort of work are like hen's teeth unless you know someone what know someone, if you understand me.'

'Then it's out of the question to repair the house?' Questa said patiently. 'Is that what you're trying to say, Mr Rogers? But you could undertake to build me a cottage in the orchard?'

'Ah well now, that 'ud be another thing altogether. Take a look, shall us?'

Questa and Martin led the way to the orchard, careful neither to touch each other nor to catch each other's eye. Mr Rogers, with his watery blue eyes, the dewdrop which kept forming on the end of his long, quivering nose, and his air of hapless pessimism, had to be treated as a joke rather than the harbinger of gloom and despondency which he seemed to consider himself, but it would have been rude and hurtful had they laughed. They walked soberly to the orchard therefore, and Questa pointed out the spot where she considered a cottage might be built.

'Hmm,' Mr Rogers said thoughtfully, eyeing the spot. 'Hmm. We could mek use of the back of the stables; that 'ud save brick.'

'Couldn't you build it out of the stones from the burnt-out dairy?' Questa asked hopefully. 'They wouldn't cost anything.'

More teeth sucking and head shaking; Questa and Martin continued to avoid each other's eyes.

'Well, I dunno as I might manage something,' Mr Rogers said at last, in a tone so lugubrious that he might have been giving them the worst possible news. 'Not that we've much summer left, mind ... but my men could make a start in a week or so.'

'What's wrong with next week?' Martin said briskly. He clearly felt he had been silent long enough. 'Miss Adamson will need a roof over her head by the summer's end, man! She's living in a caravan, you know.'

'Oh ah, but folk have lived in worse and for longer,' Mr Rogers pointed out. 'During the war folk lived in th'underground up in

London for weeks at a time. I'll do me best, but I can't work miracles, nor I can't make no promises. Still, we might start next week … just wi' the footings, mind.'

'Right. Miss Adamson will expect you then,' Martin said. 'Thanks very much, Mr Rogers – is there anything else you need to do?'

'Not for now, Mr Atherton. Reckon we've sorted out all we need to sort for now.' Mr Rogers tugged at his old grey cap and turned away. 'If you need me afore, you can always ring the offices.'

'Some offices,' Martin said when they heard Mr Rogers's old van start up and go chugging down the drive. 'His front room, and that all covered in dust-sheets which have to be taken off each evening so his missus can sit there in style and listen to the wireless. Still, no doubt he'll do his best.' He turned and put an arm around Questa, giving her a quick squeeze. 'Do you know how hard it was for me to keep my hands off you whilst old Rogers was huffing and puffing?'

Questa beamed at him.

'What did you and Kat talk about whilst I was trying to get old Rogers to park that van in the shade?'

'Oh, this and that … you and me, mainly,' Martin admitted. 'She wanted to know whether my intentions were honourable; that sort of thing. Which brings me to my next question; who do I remind you of?'

'Trick question; not fair,' Questa said. 'Does it matter?'

'Yes,' Martin said baldly. He was no longer smiling. He pulled her to a halt a hand on each of her upper arms. 'Please, Questa.'

She stood between his hands, frowning down at her bare feet in their dusty, open sandals. She could scarcely tell Martin about Marcus, he would never believe her, would think her mad. And because of him, she was no longer sure, herself, about Marcus. Had he been so like Martin, or was it just that they were both dark? To her horror, she realised that in the short time she had known him, Martin's face had somehow grown clearer in her mind's eye than Marcus's, so that she might never know, in the future, which was which, or even whether she could remember Marcus at all.

It seemed a poor return for love, and for a moment she struggled with herself; to tell or to lie? Ah, but why not tell the truth without actually committing herself to an explanation? That was perfectly possible and would be safer for them all, in the long run.

'Questa? Who was it?'

She looked up at him at last, trying to keep her eyes clear and candid, praying he would not see through her small subterfuge.

'Well, you're supposed to look awfully like your father when he was young, but of course I didn't know him then ...'

He actually pushed her away, pushed her hard. She looked up into his face, astonished, and saw pain there, raw, undisguised.

'You little slut! So *that* was it, that was why you came running – you thought I was Dad, you thought you could trap him into a liaison, and then when that little trick failed you thought you might as well have me!'

'Martin? What are you saying? What do you mean? I only said you were supposed to look ...'

He rounded on her at once, his eyes still hot with anger. 'Don't tell me what you said, I heard all right, I heard! And I'm off. Tell Kat ... tell her she can keep you, tell her ... oh God, what's the use? What's the bloody use?'

He was actually crying, there were tears running down his face. She could have wept for him, for the anguish he was going through so needlessly. She ran after him, tugging at his arm, trying to get him to look at her.

'Martin, you misheard! Martin, what I said was ...'

He snatched his arm away, then elbowed back viciously. His elbow caught her in the chest, painfully hard. It winded her so that she fell to her knees, both hands flying to her aching ribs whilst she fought to get the air back into her lungs. She knelt there for maybe half a minute, then recovered and staggered to her feet just in time to see him striding across the meadow where Scamper was cropping the long, summer-faded grass.

Should she run after him, try again to explain? But it was useless, pointless. He might listen to her this time – but next time, and the next? Whilst he was so riven with jealousy of his father that he could not even hear his name without exploding into a

450

violent physical rage, there was no way she could be comfortable with him. Yet she loved him. She knew it now, knew it by the tearing pain inside at the thought of never seeing him again. They would part because she had been afraid to tell the truth, afraid he would think her mad. Well, it would have been better had he thought her mad rather than bad, because now he believed her to be the sort of girl who would encourage an elderly man to fall in love with her for the sake of his money and property. A gold-digger, perhaps something worse.

She was still standing under the arch, gazing sightlessly across the meadows, when Kat came and found her.

'Hello-ello-ello, what's up wi' you?' she said cheerfully. 'Don't say old Rogers give you bad news, gal!'

Old Rogers? The interview with the builder seemed a lifetime away, as though it had happened to a different person on a different planet. Questa turned slowly and tried to smile at Kat. It was a poor effort, she knew it, and it did not fool her friend for one moment.

'Oh, Kat, he's going to build in the orchard; repairing would be too costly and he wouldn't get the permits.'

Kat came quickly across the short distance which separated them and put her arm round Questa's shoulders.

'Come on, back wi' me, we'll get ourselves some food,' she said. 'What's the matter, lovie? You look real miserable.'

'Yes, I am.'

'What 'appened? Where's Martin?'

'Gone.'

'Gone? What, 'ome for 'is dinner, do you mean?'

'Just gone. For good I think. Kat, he asked me wh – who I thought he was, the first time we met, and I didn't want to tell him, I really didn't, so I said ... I said folk told me he's like his father, and he just flew at me! He gave me a shove, called me all sorts of names, said I was after their money, and then he went. I tried to go after him, explain, but he hit out again and when I could follow he'd gone too far, right across Scamper's field. And anyway, what's the point, if he feels like that?'

'No point,' Kat said slowly. 'Only Questa, he's mortal fond of you, he told me so himself. And turble jealous of 'is dad, no one

451

'as to tell you that, you can see it, plain as plain. He must 'a misunderstood, thought you said ... oh, I dunno, only he *do* like you, I can't think ... '

'Nor me,' Questa said drearily. 'Look, perhaps it's for the best, probably we'd never have been happy, he's got an ungovernable temper and I get scared when people shout, let alone hit! Anyway, I didn't know him very well, it isn't as if ... oh, what's the use? Kat, when he turned away from me, he was crying!'

'Oh ah? Men do, lovie, when things get too much for 'em. I reckon the pair of you 'ave lived too high these past couple o' days. Ride out the storm, Ques; it'll all come right in the end, I'll put money on it.'

'No point. It was all a mistake and it's best treated as such,' Questa said with unexpected firmness. 'We were fools – people don't fall in love at first sight, Kat, except in a fairy story. Now I've come down to earth and I'm staying there. I'll get that cottage built and live in it and never even think about bloody Martin Atherton or any other bloody men – never, never, never!'

She pushed past Kat and went at a ragged run towards the kitchen.

Kat, left standing staring after her, shook her head slowly.

'Love! Cor, that's a rare painful business if you asks me. An' Martin weren't the only one what was crying either. Poor ole Ques, 'asn't she suffered enough?'

Twenty-one

The rest of the day passed, for Questa, in a daze. The two girls worked side by side and Questa did her best to act naturally; perhaps she succeeded, for Kat said nothing more about the quarrel. But that night, in the privacy of her cramped little caravan, Questa cried herself to sleep.

Perhaps because of her unhappiness her dreams were confused, miserable, but at one moment she found herself dreaming of Marcus. He smiled down at her tenderly, and she saw that though he was superficially very like Martin, they did not have quite the same face. She had forgotten the deep scar across Marcus's brow as well as the fact that his expression was more patient, and the lines which experience had drawn on his face cut a little deeper.

'You're unhappy; don't be,' Marcus said. 'There's always a reason behind what a man does or says, but sometimes you have to look beneath the words themselves to the hurt under them before you can understand. And understanding brings acceptance.' And then he was gone and she was alone again, wandering across an Italian landscape as she had done once, watching everything that went on with the heightened awareness which extreme danger brings. And all the while she thought about what Marcus had said, and how true it was, and even in her dream she was comforted by what he had told her.

She woke when dawn stole through the thin curtains by her head, and lay there, luxuriating in the warmth that comes from sharing a trouble, as though Marcus really had advised her, really did know what was happening between her and Martin. And even when she had told herself that it was a dream, just a dream, and that she was still alone, she only half-believed.

It was another rainy day. The clouds overhead looked sullen, unrelenting, as though they could happily continue to pound the long stair-rods of rain down on the land for a month. As Questa dressed she could see through the caravan's tiny window the long orchard grass bending beneath the onslaught, the tree branches drooping. The fact that it was August, Questa thought ruefully, meant nothing so far as the clerk of the weather was concerned. What a good job she hadn't planted her vines yet; mildew was a real killer even in Italy, where they had a lot more sun than they had here. She would have to take that into consideration when – if – she planted her vines.

She always left the caravan immediately she had dressed, made her way to the kitchen and lit the primus stove beneath the kettle. Alfie was going to check out the Aga when he had time, and she hoped that would be before winter set in. Today she hurried into the kitchen, lit the primus stove, put the kettle on, got out two mugs, and then went over to the cowshed where Kat was already tying the cows into their stalls in preparation for milking.

'Morning, Questa! Sleep all right?'

Kat looked concerned, but Questa just smiled.

'So so. Will you take Buttercup first?'

Whilst they milked the cows, almost silently for once, Questa mulled over what Marcus had said. Even allowing for the fact that the words had come from her subconscious and not from any outside source, she decided they were true. Martin would not have been so horrible to her had he understood that she was simply saying he was like his father; he had somehow interpreted the remark to mean more than its face value.

She finished Blossom, her second cow this morning, and stood up, bucket in one hand, milking stool in the other. 'Kat, you know the row Martin and I had yesterday? You haven't said much ... is there any reason?'

Kat, finishing her second cow at the same time, stood up too. She looked indecisively at Questa for a moment, then nodded slowly.

'Aye, there is. I feels a trifle to blame. See, I'd been askin' Martin about 'is intentions, like, towards you ... well, you don't 'ave a dad or a mum to ask them sort o' questions so I thought I better, an' one thing led to another. 'e was talkin' about 'is father as though they were enemies.'

'Enemies? Kat, you can't be serious.'

'Well, perhaps rivals is a better word. So a kind of jealousy of 'is dad were at the top of 'is mind, like, because of what I'd bin a-sayin'. Ran's a fine-lookin' man for 'is age … I think Martin sees that so far as steppin' into 'is father's shoes goes, 'e'd best not 'old 'is breath.'

'No, but why shouldn't they work together? It happens a lot, on farms.'

'Oh aye, but I reckon it's different when a bloke's bin away, like what Martin 'as. All over the world 'e went, ain't that so? It ain't as if 'e came out o' the army straight away, either, when the war ended. Alfie was tellin' me 'e signed on for to train young fellers, went to Germany, saw all sorts. Then when 'e come 'ome, 'e found Ran managin' perfectly well without 'im. Bit of a facer, that.'

'Ye-es, I can see that,' Questa said slowly. 'But that's no reason to take it out on me, Kat.'

'No? When 'e thought you was tellin' 'im you was fond of 'is father, the very feller 'e already sees as competition? Perhaps 'e *wanted* to 'ear you say suffin' else. Ques, old love, *did* Martin remind you of 'is Dad? Cos if so, you've never mentioned it afore.'

'No. I thought, just for a moment, that he was someone else. A – a friend. A man.'

'And you din't want to mek Martin jealous by tellin' 'im? That would 'ave been understandable, kind even, but wrong-'eaded, in this instance. You tell 'im the truth, flower. You won't never regret it.'

'I'm never going to speak to him again,' Questa said mulishly. 'If he was to walk in here this minute … '

'Good morning, Questa, Kat. Questa, could I have a word?'

Questa must have jumped a foot; even Kat blinked and the bucket in her hand rattled. But she held a hand out and took the other bucket from Questa's nerveless fingers, giving Martin, for it was he, a quick, friendly grin.

'Go on, gal,' she advised. 'I'll deal wi' this. Get yourselves a cup of tea an' 'ave a talk, like.'

'I'm not sure … '

Martin took a step towards her, then a step back. She registered that he was soaked to the skin without really thinking how he had got in such a state, assuming he had driven over, since farmers, she knew from experience, would never walk if they could ride.

'Ques? Please? I was abominable yesterday ... I just want to tell you how sorry I am.'

'You've told me,' Questa said gruffly. How could she possibly go off with him when she had just said she'd never speak to him again? And besides, she had made up her mind hadn't she, that they were best apart? Only the sight of him standing there looking so hangdog did strange things to her, turned her knees to water and the rest of her to a raging inferno of longing. 'It's all right, you don't have to say it again.'

Kat left, with the full buckets hanging heavily from each hand. Martin moved into the cowshed. He looked wild and pale and in his eyes she saw the same pain she had seen in them the previous day.

'Ques, don't send me away – I've spent the entire time since we parted yesterday walking – we must talk, I need to explain.'

'No wonder you're soaked!' The words burst from her and, having said them, it seemed only natural to go to him, to touch his cold face and the hair which was flattened to his skull with the wet. 'Why on earth didn't you go home? I thought you had.'

'Couldn't. Couldn't face Dad, for a start, knowing ... thinking ... '

Questa stiffened and moved a little away from him. 'Knowing what? Look, if we're to talk, does that mean you'll listen? To what I'm actually saying rather than what you think I'm going to say?'

He bent his head. Water droplets ran down from his hair and dripped off the end of his nose. He looked beaten, exhausted. 'Of course. Can we go to your caravan?'

It would not have been a good idea; he had come dangerously close to making love to her in that very caravan; she acknowledged it now, together with the fact that she had wanted him as badly as he had wanted her – worse, perhaps, since she could admit to it even after their short but violent quarrel.

'No, not the caravan. Come into the kitchen. The kettle's on in there.'

He nodded and followed her meekly as she swept across the yard.

In the kitchen the kettle was boiling, steam lifting the lid so that it rattled. Without looking at him, Questa indicated the roller towel hanging on the back of the door.

'Take it off the door and rub yourself dry,' she said in a small voice. 'I'll make the tea.'

'Right.' She heard him fiddling around with the roller and as she poured the water into the pot, she saw him begin to rub his hair rather half-heartedly, with the towel still attached to the door. In spite of herself, she giggled.

'You take it off the door ... oh, let me!'

She took the roller down, untangled the towel and handed it to Martin. He thanked her and began towelling his hair vigorously, then he took off his jacket. It dripped on to the floor, the water running from it.

'Hang it on the door,' Questa said. 'There are pegs.'

The pegs had not suffered in the fire. Once, she had hung her coat there every night, taken it down again every morning. Once there had been a clothes-horse in front of the Aga on washdays, and a clothes-rack up by the ceiling which let down on a system of ropes and pulleys so that you could load it with wet linen and then haul it up above your head once more – out of sight, out of mind.

'There. Why isn't the Aga lit?'

'Because Alfie thinks the tank might blow up if it isn't holding water. I don't really understand it. Anyway, what's the point?'

She looked at him directly for the first time. He shrugged. He had stripped down to shirt and trousers; he looked better now, no longer ill at ease.

'Well, this room isn't too bad, in fact it's quite respectable. It must be or you and Kat wouldn't use it the way you do. So why not go the rest of the way and make it decent again?'

Questa poured milk into two mugs, then poured tea from the round china pot. She carried the mugs over to the long harvest table. She sat down in one of the ladderback kitchen chairs and, after a moment, Martin took the seat opposite her.

Questa looked steadily at him across the table. 'Why should I make it decent? Mr Rogers said it wouldn't be possible to repair even a small part of the house – you heard him.'

'Mr Rogers is a hidebound old fool,' Martin said. 'Let him build the cottage, if and when he can get all the permits and licences and supplies, but in the meantime, why don't we get a couple of rooms in order again, so you can at least camp out in some sort of comfort?'

'I'll think about it,' Questa said guardedly. 'Is that what you wanted to talk to me about?'

He heaved a huge sigh and put both elbows on the table, staring steadily across it at her. 'No. I wanted to tell you that I was sorry for the way I behaved, and to say … well, that if it's my father … only when I started to think, I couldn't believe you'd … not that there would be anything wrong in loving him, only you … you and me … '

'I'm very fond of him, but only as a father-figure,' Questa said stonily. 'Martin, why did you fly at me the way you did? What did you think I said?'

'Why, that you had thought I was my father the first time we met, in the woods. Only even if you did … even if the look you gave me was meant for him … since then … oh my God, Questa!'

He reached across the table for her, the hunger in him plain for anyone to see.

Questa, however, evaded his seeking hands.

'No, Martin, just listen to me for a change, and listen properly, will you? I said, and these are my exact words, *You're supposed to look awfully like your father when he was young* … Martin, that was all I said. Surely you can't have misunderstood that?'

He grinned suddenly, joyously, then sobered, reaching again for her hands. She frowned, shook her head, put her clasped hands below the table, in her lap.

'Well? That was what I said, wasn't it?'

Martin looked down at his hands for a moment, still stretched out, supplicating. Then he heaved a sigh.

'I don't know what it was you said, not exactly. Questa, my

father has crippled legs, which is very sad, but at least when you look at him you know he's crippled. I'm rather deaf; tanks do that to some people. Sometimes I hear everything perfectly, but at other times, when I'm agitated, or when there's other, extraneous noise in the background, I have – great difficulty. I asked you who you thought I was, that day in the wood, and you just looked down at your toes, oh, for ages. I suppose the nagging suspicion was born then, that perhaps there was someone else, and when you looked up, your eyes so clear, as though you'd made up your mind to tell me the truth ... all I heard was *like your father*. And the rest you know.'

'Oh, Martin!' Questa's hands shot out and took his, but though he clasped them for a brief instant he pulled away, to lean across the table, taking her shoulders gently between his hands and bringing his face close to hers.

'Sweetheart? I love you so much, without rhyme or reason, without cause or impediment ... say you love me, too!'

'Oh, Martin!'

He kissed her, with the table still between them, and Questa felt her happy heart banging against her ribs whilst all her stern resolves to teach him a lesson, to steer clear of him, to make him sorry, vanished unregretted into limbo.

At last they sat back, starry-eyed.

'Come and sit on my lap; I can't bear you to be over there and me here,' urged Martin. 'Come on, we've got a lot to talk about.'

'More than you know,' Questa said. 'Is that why you didn't take any notice when I warned you that the outer log was slippery on the bridge? Because you didn't hear me? Why on earth didn't you say?'

'Oh, did you warn me? I don't tell people I'm deaf because it sounds ... oh, you know, old men with ear-trumpets sort of thing, and Tom Dutton in Billy Bunter. All the cruel old jokes everyone laughs at aren't funny when it's you they're pointing at. And of course it isn't just the deafness. A lot of things happened in the war – to you as well, I know – which changed me. My tank killed men, you could say I killed them. There was a woman ... I still see her face in my dreams, sometimes. And there were other things I can't think of without getting nightmares or the horrors.

Sometimes I think my mind is more crippled than my father's legs, and he's much braver than I. He's accepted my mother's death, though they adored each other; you never hear him talk about it. Nor about the hunting accident which deprived him of so much, and he's very even-tempered, suffers fools gladly ... all the things I can't do, in fact.'

Questa went around the end of the table and perched rather uncomfortably on Martin's knee. But she would not have refused him closeness at such a time, particularly as she, too, yearned to have him near.

'It's odd you should say that, because I said it once, to Ellen I think it was. I said my mind was crippled even more than my fingers and she said not to worry, it would be as strong as ever once time had healed me by its passing. Something like that, anyway.'

Martin laughed softly, picking up her hands and carrying them to his mouth. He kissed each finger tenderly, then turned to her.

'There's nothing wrong with any of your fingers, they're as pretty as the rest of you. So are we friends again? Can I ask you to marry me without fear of interruption this time?'

'You can ask, only perhaps we shouldn't rush into things,' Questa said. 'We really *don't* know each other well enough yet, Martin. We're going to have to get to know one another a good deal better. I'm a great coward, you know, and your rage terrified me. I expect I'm annoying, and I still have quite bad nightmares sometimes, and anyway I do want to see my land as productive and healthy as I can make it. We'd argue about how I did things, and where I spent my money, and about the stock, and you wouldn't like it if I asked your father for advice but I always have and I suppose I always shall. So you see it won't be plain sailing by a long chalk. Martin, I like you more than anyone else I know, I may even love you, but I'm scared of marriage and responsibility and living with someone else.'

'You're right. We don't need symbols to tie each other down,' Martin said contentedly, stroking her arm. 'We'll get to know each other better if we don't have people interfering all the time, congratulating us and wondering about us. Tell you what, why don't we work on these two rooms together, see what we can do? Dad manages very well without me; I can give you and Kat a hand with the chores and then you and I can get down to tackling the renovation of part of the house. There's nothing like working together to bring out the worst in one's nature; I'll probably discover you're mean as hell and kick kittens.'

'I'd like that,' Questa said, smiling at the thought of kicking anything, let alone a kitten. 'And shall we promise to tell each other things, and not try to keep them dark? And to try very hard not to lose our tempers?'

'Done.' He shook her hand solemnly, not an easy thing to do with the other person lolling comfortably in your arms. 'Let's start right now ... we'll take a look around and you can tell me what you think we ought to do first.'

'Right. Oh, we'd better go and tell Kat right away, though. Poor thing, she's taking all the milk out to the churn by herself. I mucked out yesterday so it's her turn today, but we usually take two buckets each up to the churn.'

'Oh? Where is it?'

'Just the other side of the arch, so the driver of the milk lorry doesn't have to bring his big wagon right in, and doesn't have to lug it either. And don't say it wouldn't hurt him to lug it – I can see the words longing to come out, Mart – because what if everyone said that?'

Martin, who had filled his lungs preparatory to saying something very similar, let the breath out in a long whistle instead.

'You say we need time to get to know one another and yet you read my mind with uncanny accuracy! Oh well, you're the boss. Let's go and talk to Kat.'

Later that day, because of the relentless downpour, they decided to start an inventory of what was left in the house which could be used in Martin's planned renovation.

'But we did suggest using some of it to Mr Rogers,' Questa began, only to be told very firmly to shut up and count lengths of usable timber and unbent nails.

'I thought I was going to be the boss,' Questa grumbled, hauling a long, well-polished plank out of a miscellaneous pile of singed and blackened wood. 'I thought I was going to tell *you* what to do!'

461

Martin, heaving a joist out of the same pile, said smugly that if Questa wished to boss him she had only to say so, and added, 'Don't throw a plank back because it's dirty and burnt round the edges, girl, a bit of work with a plane and it will be as good as new!' which rather gave the lie to his first remark.

'All right, all right! Oh look, here's a really good cupboard door!' Questa waved it at him and got a sooty kiss, which seemed like a fair exchange to her. 'What next? I wish the kitchen table hadn't gone up in smoke, I loved that table.'

'We'll buy you another, or I'll get old Arthur Bradstock to make you one,' Martin promised recklessly. 'And a couple of upholstered chairs would be nice. Let's move into the dining room and see just how much of your furniture is still usable.'

'We had some decent chairs ... oh!'

'Why do you say that?'

'Because Alan said the furniture was insured, but not the house. Might it be better to throw all this lot out and claim for them?'

'That's fraud. But my guess is they'll only pay out a certain sum, and that'll be pretty well regardless of anything we manage to salvage. No, we'll get anything worth having and then we'll start on the actual fabric of the house itself.'

'Today?' Questa almost wailed. 'Oh, my hands are filthy and I've split my nails and there isn't a bath any more. Well, there is, but the stairs aren't safe and anyway I don't think there's any water ...'

'Stop moaning,' Martin said lovingly. 'You shall come back to the Hall and I'll bath you myself, with delicious rose-scented soap and beautifully hot water! How's that for a bribe?'

'I can hardly wait ... especially for what Ran would say,' Questa said scornfully. 'You have stupid ideas, Martin Atherton, and if you think I'm going to dig out those great squares of stone with my bare hands you've got another think coming. And I saw you eyeing those rafters and things when we went upstairs with old Rogers, but I *won't* help you lug them out from under all that rubble so that we can use them again, I really won't.'

'We'll do it tomorrow,' Martin said soothingly. 'When you're fresh. Now don't throw things, that tile would have done me no good at all if you hadn't missed by half-a-dozen feet.'

'I missed on purpose,' Questa snarled, staggering across the room with her latest find, a filthy oil-painting with its gilded frame blackened almost beyond recognition. 'I just hope I don't die of exhaustion, that's all.'

'You won't; you're a tough little creature,' Martin said cheerfully. He put down a hallstand which he had just rescued and took her in his arms. 'Poor kid, I'm a wicked slave-driver. Go and clean up and I'll take you down to The Passing Soldier and buy you a pie and a pint.'

'I don't want a pie and a pint, I want a bath,' Questa wheedled. 'Why don't you climb the dangerous stairs, cross the dangerous floor and see if the bath is still usable?'

Mr Rogers, asked for his opinion, had merely reiterated the dangers of fire, which could eat insidiously halfway through stairs and floors without, he assured them, any outward sign whatsoever.

'You're sick of me already; you want me to plunge fifteen feet and end up crippled for life,' Martin said. 'Anyway, it's getting too dark to see properly. Come on, wench, back to the Hall. My father, who has many faults, many *many* faults, has some good points, too. One is that he never grudges a pretty girl the use of his bathroom, another is he has the best cook in the entire county of Shropshire. We'll go and bath and dine there, and you will gracefully accept the offer of a bed for the night, and tomorrow we'll start all over again.'

'It does sound tempting,' a filthy, exhausted Questa admitted, tightening her grasp round his neck. 'And I thought farming was hard work – demolition is far worse! Only I'm not sure I can walk as far as the Hall without collapsing. And, does Ran know we quarrelled? He must wonder where you were last night. I don't think I want a lot of questions, do you, Martin?'

'No problem. I haven't been home so he knows nothing, but in any case he wouldn't ask questions. I am twenty-eight, Questa, and I've lived away from home for so long that Dad simply accepts whatever hour I turn up as the right one. As for walking, you won't have to do that. No, it's all right, I shan't suggest carrying you, I'm pretty damn tired myself. We'll go down to the box at the end of the drive and ring Dad. When I tell him he's got a guest he'll come like a shot.'

'He'll come like a shot because he wants to be useful to you,' Questa said as they left the Court behind them and headed across the yard. 'He really longs for your good opinion, Martin.'

'Oh, hell, I know it. I'm a surly blighter, or I was, rather. But from now on, with you beside me, I'll be different. You wait and see.'

Despite her tiredness, Questa really enjoyed her evening at the Hall. She was offered her old bedroom and gladly accepted, looking with positive longing at the neat single bed with its crisp white sheets and the counterpane covered with yellow roses. Before they ate she undressed and slid into the big, deep bath in the guest bathroom and almost fell asleep in the lovely hot water, relaxing in the rose-scented suds that Martin had promised her and drying herself afterwards on a huge white towel.

Dinner was a feast, despite Mrs Clovelly having had no idea that she was to have a visitor.

'One more, and one who enjoys her food, is never a problem,' she declared when Questa went guiltily into the kitchen to admit she was staying for dinner. 'There's a lovely melon, it'll cut up into half-a-dozen it's so big and fat, and Mr Atherton had a fancy for pork so there's a nice piece of that sizzling in the oven ... Oh, don't worry my dear, you're always welcome here. There's pears in port wine for pudding. With homemade ice-cream.'

After the meal – 'Cheese and biscuits in your honour, my dear, and some of Mrs C's delicious peppermint creams,' Ran told her – they sat over their coffee and talked about the Court and its problems.

'Though he's my son, so I probably shouldn't say it, if he says you can renovate then I'd back his judgement against old Rogers any day,' Ran said decisively when Questa explained the plan. 'Mr Rogers has grown lazy and he hates paperwork. Though I've no doubt he'll start building that cottage as soon as he's able – I do have some influence – he won't put himself out to go through all the complications of a renovation. No, you do what you can yourselves, I only wish I could lend a hand.'

'You can,' Martin said at once. 'You could tell us what's usable and what we might as well throw away. You can come over in the car ... it would all help.'

'Well, I'll do my best,' Ran said. He looked gratified, Questa saw. 'I don't know much about actual building, mind, but I can tell a sound floor from a rotten one and a sound stretch of plastering too.'

'And you could stop your son from working me to death, perhaps,' Questa said tartly. 'He started out saying he'd help me and within five minutes he was handing out orders like a sergeant-major and barking at me if I didn't jump to it.'

'No, like a tank captain,' Ran said, though his mouth curled at the corners. 'Tank captains are renowned for bossiness; probably they can't help it and you just have to put up with it. Still, I can but try to curb his urge to give orders. What time in the morning do you intend to start?'

'After milking,' Questa said at the same moment that Martin said, 'At the crack of dawn.'

Ran raised his eyebrows. 'A disagreement between master and man already, I see. We milk mechanically, of course, but I see no reason why Martin shouldn't start on the house by himself whilst you and Kat do your farm work. I'll pop over from time to time, and make a point of being around when you're having your midday break. I'll bring a picnic tomorrow, we can all share it, Kat too.'

'That would be lovely,' Questa said, whilst Martin made asserting noises and looked rather glum. 'And thanks so much for letting me use your lovely bath, you don't know how wonderful it is to be clean all over. The caravan's very nice but there isn't much room, and a bath is out of the question, of course.'

'You should have stayed here before,' Ran said remorsefully. 'I would have suggested it, only I knew you wanted to be on the spot, near your place. But now that you've agreed to stay here for one night, surely I can persuade you to stay until you've somewhere to live at the Court, whether it's in the renovation that you're planning or in Mr Rogers's orchard cottage?'

Questa laughed but shook her head. 'Tonight is lovely, a real

465

treat,' she said. 'But it wouldn't be fair on Kat or Alfie if I did it on a regular basis. No, tomorrow night I'll be back in my caravan.'

'But not when it gets cold,' Martin put in. 'No way will I let my girl sleep in a tin-can in an orchard whilst I'm in a decent house with a proper roof over my head.'

Ran raised his brows slightly at the possessive note in Martin's voice, but made no direct comment. He was trying hard to get it right, Questa saw.

'Quite right, Martin. Now if you'll excuse me I'll get off to bed. If you want to be home in time for the milking, my dear, you'll be up before Mrs C puts in an appearance, but I'm an early riser so there will be tea in the kitchen from about six o'clock on.'

'I'll be up then, too,' Martin said. 'Shall I give you a real treat, bring you a cup of tea in bed?'

Ran shot them another quick glance. He's been told almost nothing, Questa thought rather unhappily. Oh dear, I do hope this doesn't mean more friction. But what could Martin tell him, after all? That they liked each other, had quarrelled, made it up? No, as Martin said, it was too soon in their young and struggling relationship to have to take on board the opinion of others. Besides, Ran knew them both; he must be as aware as Questa of the strong currents running between them, so that when they brushed hands unexpectedly electricity crackled and her blood raced.

'Questa, don't dream – shall I bring you tea in bed?'

To Questa, at any rate, his intimate tone spoke volumes. She felt her face grow hot and turned away, suddenly sure that Ran would know what such an innocent-seeming remark implied. She could imagine it all too well, that was the trouble: Martin leaning over the bed to kiss her awake, a hand sliding down under the covers, touching, caressing.

'No, it's all right, Martin, thanks, I'll be up and dressed before you, I daresay. Goodnight, Ran. Sweet dreams.'

Martin waited until Ran could be heard slowly mounting the stairs and then came across and took Questa in his arms.

'I thought the old man would never go,' he said roughly. 'How am I going to wait? How long will it take until you're sure? You don't know what it's like to want someone the way I want you.'

'Do I not? You might be surprised,' Questa said with her

'There, why don't you say it? We'll get married; yes, I know we will. But we'll need money, sweetheart, and one of us will have to get out and earn it until the Court begins to pay its way. I'm certainly not going to hang on your sleeve, any more than I'll hang on my father's.'

'I see.' Questa jumped to her feet. 'Well, I don't intend to think about it, far less worry myself over it, until it happens. We'd better get on. Can I start whitewashing the kitchen walls yet?'

'Have you got all the black off them, that's the question? Because if not, the whitewash won't stick. Oh by the way, I keep meaning to ask you and then forgetting. What's behind that door over there, under the stairs? I thought it was a cupboard, but it's locked.'

'That? Oh, it leads to the cellars.'

'Cellars?' Martin said, his eyes gleaming. 'Now they won't have been touched by the fire – what was down there?'

'No idea. Nothing, I think. They're just musty old cellars,' Questa said hastily. She felt she had quite enough on her plate right now without discussing the cellars. Indeed, her resolve to explore them had been completely forgotten since Martin's arrival and it now seemed supremely unimportant. 'Come and look at the kitchen, see if you think I've scrubbed the walls clean enough.'

'In a minute. Where's the key?'

'To the cellars, d'you mean? I've no idea. Lost, probably. It used to hang by the banister, but it must have got burned up. Do come on, Martin, I want to get going with the whitewash.'

'No, hang on a minute. Let's just see if we can find the key.'

'Martin, there's absolutely no point!' Questa said crossly. So far as she was concerned, the less likelihood there was of getting into the cellars the better. There was so much to do, they couldn't waste their valuable time poking about underground! 'We'd have found the key if it had been in any handy spot, we've probably thrown it out with the rest of the rubbish.'

'True. Then this calls for brute force, and I'm the brute to force it,' Martin said gleefully. 'Stand back!'

He roared across the hall and crashed heavily into the cellar door, then stepped back, clutching his shoulder.

'Ouch! I don't think that bloody door is a door, I think it's a brick wall painted to look like a door. It didn't give an inch ... well, it didn't even give a fraction of an inch.' He kicked the door resentfully with a booted foot. 'I'll have to get an axe, I suppose, which will probably get me nowhere, but I'll have to try, we can't let a locked door beat us, can we?'

'Yes we can, willingly,' Questa said. 'I'm not fracturing my collar bones bouncing off a locked door, so don't expect it. There's nothing in there, I'll take a bet on it.'

'Well, unless I can get in ... hold on, how about that beam?'

'It's far too heavy. Look, if you're determined to try I'll fetch a hammer,' Questa was beginning when Martin raised his foot and kicked as hard as he could in the region of the door handle. To her very real astonishment the door cracked and, after a second vicious kick, gave. It swung eerily for a second, back and forth, back and forth, then slowly opened inwards to its fullest extent, showing the gaping black descent behind it.

'There we are, then,' Martin said, looking pleased with himself. 'All it needed was a bit of muscle. Who goes first?'

'You can go first, only get a torch,' Questa said. 'I'm not going down into that blackness without a torch!'

'There used to be electricity down here,' Martin said, already half-a-dozen steps down. 'I distinctly remember someone saying that old Joshua cared more about his cellars ... oh, but that was before the army; at any rate there's no light here now.'

'So I see. Wait, Martin, don't go any further ... there's a torch in the kitchen drawer.'

Questa ran into the kitchen and fumbled in the drawer beside the sink. The torch had been useful in the winter but she hadn't used it since the lighter days started. Was it still there and if so, would it still be working? It was there. She pushed the switch and a pale circle of illumination sprang up. That was a relief, anyway. She didn't want to go down into the cellars but would not have dreamed of letting Martin go alone and, besides, it was silly to be afraid – darkness, after all, was not an enemy. Many a time during the war she had welcomed darkness because it meant she could begin to move across country again, unobserved by friend and foe alike.

She reached the top of the steps. Martin had disappeared but as she began a fumbling descent, with one hand sliding uncertainly along the wall, he reappeared again.

'Got the torch? Chuck it over, then.'

Rather unwisely Questa obeyed and found herself alone, with Martin striding ahead, the beam of the torch lighting his way. Questa shouted, 'Oy! Wait for me!'

'Oh!' The torch beam wavered, then turned back. 'Sorry, I thought you were right behind me. There's a whole series of cellars, you know ... I can't believe old Joshua didn't use them for something.'

'Whatever it was, the army will have stolen it,' Questa said bitterly. 'Or destroyed it, anyway. They won't have left me any treasure-chests to discover on a rainy afternoon, you know.'

'Oh no, they would have been far too busy ... here, give me your hand, this next one is quite a lot lower.'

The first two cellars had been empty, with no sign that anyone had so much as visited them. The third was different. Mounted against the walls were what looked like a great many small boxes, all sloping slightly.

'What on earth ... ?'

'Wine racks,' Martin said briefly. 'Well, wouldn't you know!'

'What? What, Martin?'

'Not a single bottle,' Martin said disgustedly. 'If this was your uncle's secret cellar it wasn't secret enough for the army. And I was quite looking forward to sampling fine old port.'

'What a shame,' Questa said absently. 'And this is the last cellar, by the looks of it. Never mind; now we can go upstairs and try to mend the door so that we can lock it again. I wish you hadn't burst it open like that; I won't sleep easy in my bed with the door open.'

'You don't sleep at the Court,' Martin pointed out. 'Besides, what harm can possibly come from down here? Unless you believe in ghosts?'

'Shut up,' Questa said crossly. 'Of course I don't believe in ghosts, and if there are any listening, I'm only kidding. Can we go back yet?'

'No, not until we've found the other cellars,' Martin said

obstinately. 'Think of the ground floor of the Court, Ques – there have to be more cellars hidden away somewhere.'

'Why? Why on earth should anyone build cellars? It isn't as if they were particularly useful.'

'But they were! Secret hiding places, store rooms, the place everyone kept their contraband liquor ... I'm sure I read somewhere that cellars always follow the ground-plan of the house above.'

'Well, these don't,' Questa said. 'Come on, Martin, it's cold down here and I want my tea. Besides, Kat will be looking for me; it must be time we brought the cows in for milking.'

'You're scared ... wooo-oooh!' Martin said. He shone the torch below his face and made vague motions in the air with one hand. 'I am the ghost of Eagles Court, my bones lie in the furthermost corner of the cellar, I command you, find them!'

'Don't be a bloody fool, Martin,' Questa said. But she jumped back automatically when he moved towards her, landing heavily against one of the wine racks. 'Ouch, those things hurt ... oh look what you've made me do!'

Straightening, she had pulled on the rack for support and it had swung away from the wall, revealing a dusty archway in which was set a small and even dustier door.

'You clever girl!' Martin said, peering. 'There is another cellar – I told you there was. Come on.'

The door opened under his hand but it was so low that he had to bend almost double to get through. But get through he did, the torch wavering unsteadily before him. Questa followed hastily, she had no desire to find herself in an empty wine cellar in the pitch dark.

'Ah-ha!'

'What?' Questa collided with Martin's straightening figure and clutched him nervously. He grunted and turned to put his arm comfortingly round her.

'Sorry I mucked about; I expect you've got a good reason for not much liking underground places,' he said gruffly. 'But look, sweetheart!'

He swung the torch around the small, smelly room. The air here seemed older and earthier than the air in the outer cellars, but also more pungent, with a sharp vinegary scent which was not entirely unpleasant. Questa, leaning gratefully against him, frowned.

'What?' she said again. 'I can't see anything except ... what are those bundles?'

'It's Uncle Joshua's secret cellar,' Martin said with hushed reverence. 'Look at all the booze – and thank God the army didn't find it, my love, or they'd have been too drunk to wage a war.'

'I don't suppose the ones stationed here waged much of a war,' Questa said. 'Is it *all* drink, Martin?'

'Bound to be. I can't think what else would be down here! No small, heavy chests of gold, I don't think.'

'No-oo, I suppose not,' Questa said wistfully. 'But wouldn't it be nice if there were?'

'Oh, this stuff will do,' Martin said. He was examining the shelves nearest him. 'I say, some of these bottles are really old. Dad said it would be worth a small fortune, but with post-war prices being what they are, I'd say it's worth quite a large fortune.'

'Really? Martin, are we talking about ... well, a dairy herd?'

Martin gave a shout of laughter which echoed eerily round the small room and hugged her hard. 'Oh, at least ... and the cost of a builder to give us a hand upstairs, I wouldn't be surprised. Well, that really is a find, wait till I tell Dad!'

'Your father said there was a secret cellar,' Questa said remorsefully. 'He asked me if I'd found it and I ... well, I said it was empty, I didn't say I'd never been down here. Don't tell him, let him think I found the first cellars and thought they were the extent of it.'

'Sure, sure,' Martin said. He took a bottle, dark with dirt, out of the rack. 'Better take a couple of these up to the daylight, though, just to make sure of what we've got. Coming?'

'Yes ... but Martin, when you said there were more cellars, did you mean just one more? Shouldn't there be several more?'

Martin, carefully piling a couple more bottles into his arms, shook his head.

'What does it matter, sweetheart? We've found the one that matters. And I thought you didn't like it much down here?'

'I didn't, but now I'm getting used to it, I'm wondering why

473

this cellar sort of sticks out to one side. What's up above? And why aren't there more, to the side?'

'The cellars only followed the main part of the house, and I was only interested in further cellars in case we could find old Joshua's secret hoard,' Martin explained ingenuously. 'I suppose there might be other cellars, but I don't think they matter much, and I want to get this lot upstairs before ... what are you going over there for?'

'There *is* a little chest,' Questa said. 'Do bring the torch over here a minute, and I'll see ... wait, perhaps if I lift it ... '

She heaved the small chest up in her arms but it was unexpectedly heavy and she swayed, then set it down hastily with a clank.

'Gosh, I can't even get it off the ground!'

'It's probably got bricks in,' Martin observed. 'Why did it tinkle, though? Gold bars, do you suppose?'

Questa heaved on the lid and it opened suddenly, all but coming off in her hand. She peered inside as Martin shone the torch downward.

'It's a great big old book,' she said disappointedly. 'A family Bible ... and an eagle, made of brass or something. Not gold I don't think ... does gold go green?'

'No, unfortunately. Do you want to bring the book up with us so that we can take a look in daylight? I don't think we can manage the bottles and the brass eagle as well, but you could carry the book I daresay.'

'Yes, I could. Martin, is this cellar floor made of metal, do you suppose?'

'No, it's just an ordinary dirt floor; can't you see it is?'

'Yes, but the little chest clanked when I dropped it.'

'The eagle must have knocked against something,' Martin said. 'Come on, love, let's get back upstairs.'

'In a minute. I just want to take a look under the chest.'

Martin muttered impatiently but waited whilst Questa heaved the small chest to one side, then sat back on her heels and stared down at the floor.

'Well? Any gold pieces?'

'No. But there's a metal ring set into the floor just here; the

474

edge of the chest must have caught it when I put it down,' Questa said, frowning down at her feet. 'Do you know, I think this floor must be flagged, only it's covered by about an inch of dirt, except for the ring.'

'I believe you're right, the floor is flagged,' Martin said, having scraped at the packed earth with a penknife which he produced from his pocket. 'And why would a flagstone have an iron ring set in it – unless it was meant to be tugged so that the stone could move? Here, stand back a moment while I have a go.'

Martin heaved on the ring, grunting as his muscles cracked with the strain. Suddenly the stone moved and began to rise whilst packed earth, dry as tinder, clouded out from it. And beneath the flagstone Questa could see total blackness by the torch's faint glow. She dropped to her knees and leaned over, shining the torch down into the hole.

'Nothing ... well, it just seems to be a very low cellar, probably not even six feet deep,' she said in a disappointed voice. 'I wonder why it's there, Martin? It doesn't seem logical to go down deeper still.'

The past lies buried deep.

The words seemed to echo around her head, making her wonder where on earth she'd heard them before.

'Martin? Can we go down?'

'No point,' Martin said briefly. 'There's nothing down there. It must be a cellar from an earlier building on this site. Sweep the torch around a bit, you'll find it's empty, I'm sure.'

Questa obediently shone the torch as far as its beam would reach and Martin was right. So far as she could see, the room, if you could call it a room, was empty. But on the other hand, it was large – it didn't seem to have any walls that she could reach with the torchlight, which seemed rather odd.

'Yes, it does look empty,' she said slowly at last, kneeling back. 'Only I can't see how far it goes – it's ever so big, Martin, at least as big as the cellars we've come through, and it doesn't seem to have any walls.'

'It must have limits; but it sounds as though it isn't a cellar at all, just a space left by the builders for some reason. No point in going down there obviously, so move over, sweetheart, and I'll replace the flag,' Martin said. He had leaned it against the wall and was moving his precious bottles back nearer the doorway. 'You can see there are no steps or stairs or anything leading downward, which must mean, I imagine, that it's just part of the foundations, put in to keep these cellars dry – they are nice and dry actually, did you notice?'

'Ye-es ... but I'd still like to go down and take a look. I *must* go down,' Questa said, hearing what amounted to a whine in her own voice with some horror. 'Martin, wait ... I shan't be long.'

She sat down, dangled her legs over the space and held a hand out for the torch, which Martin had taken from her the better to choose which bottles he considered worthy of being taken up-stairs.

'Oh Ques, you'll get absolutely filthy, but if you must you must, I suppose,' Martin said, handing over the torch. 'Don't be long, though, will you? Remember Kat and the milking.'

'I won't be long,' Questa promised. 'I just have the strongest feeling that I ought to take a look.'

And with that Questa, who was afraid of the dark and under-ground places, dropped, feet first, into the gaping black hole.

Twenty-two

Despite being with Martin, despite telling herself that darkness was a friend, Questa had not liked the cellars very much, not even the wine cellar with its shelves full of liquid gold. But in this odd place, with the ceiling only inches above her head and an echoing space around, she felt for some strange reason almost at home.

'You all right?'

Martin's head, upside-down, appeared in the hole. Since she had the torch, her light must be going up to him but nothing came down to her. Only the light of the torch in her hand illumined, with increasing dimness, the space about her.

'Yes, I'm fine. I think you're right, it's just an air-space.'

'I'm sure I'm right. Are you coming up now?'

'Not ... not quite yet. Let me take a look around. I'm curious.'

'Oh. Well, in that case ... ' a brief scrabbling ensued, then Martin, a smear of dirt on one cheek and his hair on end, joined her. 'Give me your hand, sweetheart. We'll explore together. By Jupiter, isn't it big?'

'Yes; I still can't see the walls. Why did you say *By Jupiter* just then? I've only heard you say it once before, and that was when I startled you in the wood that first time.'

'Did I say that?' Martin chuckled. 'It's better than swearing in front of a lady, I suppose. What's that on the floor ahead?'

Together, their fingers entwined, they walked towards whatever it was on the floor. First Questa thought it was coils of ropes, then perhaps pieces of wood, then markings in the earth. But whatever it was, it was difficult to see through the layer of velvety dust which covered the entire floor. Questa was wearing a cloth tied round her head to keep her hair clean. She untied it and began systematically sweeping at the floor as smoothly as possible, but even so dust-clouds arose.

'Phew! Dust of ages,' Martin said, sneezing. 'What is it? Some kind of linoleum?'

'No, it's ... oh Martin, look!'

Appearing slowly, as Questa's duster cleared it, was a face. A man's dark face, the eyes staring at them as though he could actually see the two people who had brought light back to him after so long. A strong face beneath the plumed helmet, with dark, thick eyebrows, steady eyes, a straight nose and a humorous mouth.

'It's ... it's ...'

'A centurion,' Martin breathed. He dropped to his knees, producing a linen handkerchief from his trouser pocket and beginning to clear the floor alongside Questa. 'A Roman soldier, sweetheart – this is a mosaic pavement, a very fine one, too. See, there's his dog ... there are his servants, his home, all depicted in tiny coloured tiles. Dear God, and Joshua kept his wine almost on top of it and never thought to look further!'

'It's Marcus,' Questa breathed. 'It *is* him. Oh, Martin, isn't he like you? But how come it's still here, when everything else has gone, the villa, the grounds, the grapevines up on the hill ... I don't understand.'

'I don't know what you're talking about, sweetheart, but I do know that this is a work of art,' Martin said. 'And I was raving about the contents of Joshua's wine cellar – this is a major archaeological find – oh, how Charles would have rejoiced, how he would have loved this!'

'Yes, I suppose ... ' Questa was on her knees, gently clearing the dust from the horse, when the torch light suddenly vanished. 'Damn! Do turn it on again, Martin, it's black as pitch in here.'

There was a pause, then Martin reached out and took Questa's hand across the space between them. 'Questa, I didn't turn it off, it went, it died. It was rather dim before, I expect you noticed; I suppose the batteries were pretty near finished. What a fool I was, not to tell you to bring a lamp! We'd best start making our way back, I think.'

'Oh, right,' Questa said, cheerfully but with a thumping heart. 'Which way is out?'

There was another pause. Then the hand in hers squeezed her fingers reassuringly. 'Which way do you think?'

'Umm ... well, the thing is, I can't see anything at all, so I suppose out might be in any direction. What should we do? Just start walking?'

'Or shouting,' Martin said rather grimly. 'We don't know how far this air-space extends, sweetheart, and has it occurred to you that we could walk right under the trap-door and never know it? Because there's no more light up there than there is down here. I think we should just sit down quietly, hold hands and let our eyes get accustomed to the dark. And if we still can't see any glimmer of light in five or ten minutes, then we'll start shouting.'

'But who is there to hear us?' Questa said, unable to keep a quiver out of her voice. 'Kat knows we were decorating, she'll just think we finished early and went off together. They'll never dream we're down here.'

'Of course they will, sweetheart! Oh, not immediately, perhaps, but when I don't go home for a meal Dad will raise the alarm ... well, no, not at once, because he'll assume I've taken you out ... but if I'm not back by bedtime ... if you aren't around tomorrow morning, when Kat gets up to do the milking, then they'll start to search.'

'Tomorrow morning!' Questa's voice rose. 'Martin, if we aren't out of here well before then I'll probably go mad! I – I don't like the dark very much, not when it's this dark.'

'Hush. Just look around you and listen too.'

In the dark, the two of them cuddled close, finding comfort in each other's nearness. Questa, eyes straining into the total, velvety black, was sure there was no light, not even the faintest glimmer. But she knew now that they were in Marcus's villa, and there had been doors, steps, passageways. Now all there seemed to be was this vast space. Perhaps if they set off straight before them, they would find something, some means of escape?

It was hard not to start chattering just to stop the fear mounting within her, but somehow she managed it, staying totally quiet and listening and looking with all her concentration. Looking got her nowhere; indeed, she found the total darkness so frightening that after a few moments she simply closed her eyes. Better to tell herself she was deliberately seeing nothing than begin to suspect she was blind! And listening did very little, either: at first the muffling silence seemed unbroken, then she heard Martin's quiet, even breathing, the tick of his wristwatch, the tiny movements which clothing makes as your body moves infinitesimally within it to the rhythm of your breath.

'Martin, is your watch one of those with fingers you can see in the dark?'

Martin chuckled and tightened his grip on her fingers for a moment, then put up his other hand and stroked her cheek. 'Watches have hands, not fingers. And yes, I believe ... can you read it?'

He rustled and Questa felt his hand gently clasp one of her drawn-up knees. She stared into the darkness and then, suddenly, she could see a tiny, tiny glow – two tiny pinpricks in the infinite dark.

'Yes, I can see the hands!' she exclaimed. 'It's either four o'clock or five, I'm not quite sure which.'

'Four,' Martin said, obviously taking a look himself. 'Well, at least we can keep our eyes on the time, it's not as though we won't know how the hours are passing. Now I'll let my sleeve down over it again, so it doesn't distract me. Any luck with seeing? Or hearing?'

'I think we're down too deep to hear much,' Questa said at last. 'And the same with seeing. But shouldn't we try feeling, Martin? If we hold hands and try to feel where the trap-door is ... wouldn't that work?'

'Yes, it might,' Martin agreed. 'Only we must keep hold of each other. Because the ceiling's so low sound does odd things ... I don't want to have you in one half of this space going slowly crazy and me in the other. So don't let go – savvy?'

'I won't,' Questa assured him. 'I'm far too afraid. Oh, how I wish we'd never found that wretched secret cellar! Suppose they come down, Kat and Alfie and your dad, and don't realise the secret cellar's there? Because the wine racks were on the door, weren't they, and it swung shut, I'm almost sure. How will they find us then? Suppose they don't bump against the wine racks?'

'They will. And as soon as we hear them we'll holler … want to practise?'

'Not particularly.'

'Want to sing, then? How about a nice sing-song?'

'I'd rather walk around and trawl for the trap-door,' Questa said. 'I'll hold you very tight, really I will. I'm a bit short so there isn't much point in me putting my arm up, I doubt I'd reach the ceiling, but you can … oh do let's have a go, Martin! Surely it's worth a try?'

'Yes, of course it is. And if we find it, then we're sure to think of a way of getting up there.'

'Oh, my God! when I jumped down I thought you'd haul me up, only then of course you jumped down. Martin, if we find the trap, will we be able to get through it?'

'Yes, we shall,' Martin said stoutly. 'Once I've got a grip on the edge I can pull myself up, then lean over and haul you out too. And then, in the secret cellar, we'll find the doorway easily enough.'

'Yes. Of course.' Questa said in a small voice. 'Hold on to me … don't let me go. Shall we walk straight ahead?'

'We'll do our best. If we really are walking straight ahead, then we'll bump into a wall at some stage or other. Come on.'

They walked cautiously forward. It was stupid, Questa realised, but once they started walking what chiefly concerned her was the absolute, unshakeable conviction that she was about to bang into a wall, hard and painfully. She guessed that Martin, with one hand held above his head, fingers trailing on the ceiling, would be even more conscious of it than she.

'Martin, look, I'm going to hold on to you with one hand and point the other one straight ahead, so when we get near the wall we shan't bump. All right?'

'Excellent. Ah, wait a minute … no, it's just an uneven bit of ceiling.'

'The floor's uneven too,' Questa said. 'Oh Martin, stop!'

'Sure. Why?'

'Suppose … suppose there's a big hole, leading down into a lower cellar yet, and one of us falls through it?' Questa quavered. 'Oh Martin, let's sit down again. I just stepped into a small dip and I got an awful jolt. I could have broken my back if it had been a bit deeper.'

'Right,' Martin agreed at once. 'Both together, sit.'

They collapsed. Questa, feeling around, could tell that they had somehow strayed off the mosaic paving; beneath her fingers now was what felt like large, uneven flagstones.

'Martin?'

'What, sweetheart?'

'Did you … did you think of a hole in the ground? Was that why you weren't all that keen on trying to find the trap-door?'

'Yes,' Martin said briefly. 'Want to sing?'

'Umm … not for a minute. I mean suppose Kat's up there and we don't hear because we're singing so loudly? But actually, I'm trying to think, trying to see in my head … well, have you noticed that we're not on the mosaic floor any more?'

'No, I hadn't noticed, but you're right. We've moved on to …' he still held Questa's hand but she could feel him leaning away from her. ' … big paving stones of some sort.'

'Yes. I should think we've moved out of the main hallway and into the courtyard. The courtyard would be more or less where our stableyard is now, with the hill rising up behind the outbuild-ings, so I suppose we're under the kitchen, probably.'

'I see,' Martin said. 'I forgot what an expert you must have become, being lectured by Charles half the time and dragged round his digs and excavations the other half. So you're basing your guess on the usual plan of a Roman villa, I take it? Well, if you're right we're probably likelier to hear Kat from where we are now than from any other position. So we'll stay here for a bit, shall we?'

'All right,' Questa whispered. 'I'm awfully tired, Martin. Shall we just snooze for a little while?'

'Yes, that's sensible, sweetheart,' Martin said gently. 'Here, lean on me.'

He gathered her warmly into his arms and Questa, with a little sigh, laid her head on the comfortable hollow in his shoulder and tried to forget their predicament, striving to remember in more detail what she had seen in Marcus's villa in those dreams which had grown misty of late.

'Martin?'

'Yes, love?'

'What time is it?'

Martin laughed and gave her another little hug.

'It's not quite five o'clock. I thought you were going to try to have a sleep?'

'I was, but I can't. I think Kat will have come in to look for me by now, to help with the milking. We didn't hear anything, did we?'

'No, but I don't suppose she did much more than poke her head around the door and shout. She won't have gone through into the hall. But tomorrow, or perhaps later tonight when she sees you aren't in the caravan, she's bound to search.'

'We'll be awfully thirsty by tomorrow morning,' Questa said pensively. 'Let's play a game ... how about twenty questions?'

'I'm not feeling terribly intellectual right now,' Martin said. 'Tell you what, you tell me a story, then I'll tell you one. Or better still, tell me half a story, stop in the middle, and I have to finish it. Okay? Right then, you kick off.'

'Once upon a time there was a boy called Jack,' Questa started. 'He lived with his mother in a little hut in a forest clearing, and the only thing of value they possessed was a cow ... '

By the time Martin's watch showed midnight they were sick of stories, they had sung all the songs they knew, and an icy, miserable exhaustion was setting in.

'I don't want to die down here,' Questa said at one point, burrowing into Martin's arms. 'It's awful, like being buried alive ... entombed!'

'You aren't going to be here for very much longer, a few hours at the outside,' Martin told her. 'We'll be rescued by morning all right. Look, do you want to move again? Have another go at finding that trap-door? You'll have to put up with me going very, very slowly, and you'll have to go slowly too, as we test each foot in front of us before we step, but at least we'd be doing something.'

'No; it's too dangerous,' Questa said obstinately. 'I'm almost sure that the big kitchen would have been underground, and you

483

reached it across the hallway. If I'm right then somewhere around here, either to the right or left of the mosaic floor, there's a really big drop.'

Martin said nothing for a moment. Questa thought she could almost *hear* him thinking. Anyway, in the fix they were in, why didn't she just tell him what she meant? Dream or no dream, Marcus had lived here once, in the very villa they had got themselves entombed in, and she had been shown around it. Surely she could use that knowledge to help them out of here?

'Martin, can I tell you something? It's something quite odd and probably difficult to believe, but I would like to tell you. Especially now, and here.'

'Don't tell me anything unless you want to, and not if it upsets you,' Martin said softly. 'I can live with you having a past which … which is past and which shouldn't concern me.'

'I want to tell you. Besides, if you like you can think of it as another story to pass the time. Only … oh well, here goes.'

She started stumblingly, badly, with the story of that first night at Eagles Court when she had walked up in the dark and heard the trumpet, seen the marching men. But Martin listened without comment, save occasionally to touch her cheek or squeeze her shoulders, so she grew bolder, more positive. She told him about the vines, about the dream friendship which had turned into something warmer and more precious, about the strong physical likeness between Marcus and himself.

'So I fell in Scamper's pasture and knocked myself out, and when I came round I was back in the dream and Marcus, Marcus was … he was dying,' she ended. 'At least I was with him, Martin, though I couldn't do much. At least he didn't die alone.'

The hand which had been around her shoulders moved, to smooth down over her hair, her neck, her wet cheek. Martin sighed and stirred.

'You poor kid – to dream so constantly and vividly,' he said. 'As if you hadn't suffered enough!'

'Oh, but I loved the dreams, if they were dreams,' Questa said quickly. 'Marcus was real to me; far more real than anyone had ever been before. When he died it was as if a part of my life had died with him, in fact until you came along I didn't care very much what happened to me. I – I loved Marcus, you see. He was kind and good, and I fell in love with him even though I knew I couldn't stay with him, couldn't give him the son he longed for.'

'Well, no, you couldn't,' Martin agreed. 'Sweetheart, you didn't truly believe in that chap, did you? Because all that stuff about time being like a river … it doesn't wash, you know. Time moves on, and we move with it. Understand me? You had extraordinarily vivid and realistic dreams, but that's all they were.'

'True dreams, Ellen called them,' Questa said.

'And just what did Ellen say she meant by *true dreams*?'

'She didn't say. But Martin, we're in Marcus's villa, really we are. That man with his dog and his horse in the mosaic … it's them, really it is. I'd know Marcus's face anywhere, in any time.'

'I believe you, sweetheart. But don't forget, you've seen a good many Roman villas in your time. Your father ate and slept Roman villas, Alan told me he was a bore on the subject, and Grace said Charles used to lug you to digs when he couldn't get anyone to keep an eye on you. I know you couldn't remember any of it, but subconsciously it was all there, waiting to be used, dug out.'

'But that can't be so, because I couldn't remember anything about my life before the war. It's only begun to come back to me, in dribs and drabs, since Marcus died. So how could I use past experience to imagine everything, when I remembered nothing? How could I invent Marcus? Dear Martin, I saw that mosaic when it was shiny and new, two thousand odd years ago! I asked Marcus whether he was really the man in the tiles and he said he was, his father had commissioned it when Marcus got his first command. Don't tell me I imagined all that because I couldn't have done, I'm not nearly clever enough.'

'The mind is capable of a great deal, especially when it's been injured in some way. I've never asked you what happened to you during the war, sweetheart, and I never will, because I believe it's best forgotten. God knows, I'm trying to forget my own experiences hard enough. But you had a bad time, didn't you?'

'Yes,' Questa admitted in a small voice. 'But some of the time it was lovely, and people were so good … the peasants saved my life a dozen times over, Martin.'

'Yes, I realise that. But your faith in human nature must have been very shaken. Certainly your attitude to men was – a little unusual, to say the least. I remember some story going round the village that you didn't like being touched, you didn't even like shaking hands.'

'I didn't, because it was my fingers – they broke my fingers. It was ages before I could let anyone touch my hands.'

'Quite. Yet Marcus could touch you; right?'

'Yes; he was different.'

'Well, there you are then. Your subconscious had to persuade you that men weren't all bad, that the relationship between a man and a woman could be beautiful and enjoyable. So your dreams came up with the perfect man, one whom you could love without any risk of physical intimacy.'

'That's not right! Oh, Martin, how can I make you see? He was so *real*, no one could have made him up. And there was the memorial stone ... I didn't tell you about that. I found it, in the hills, when I was with Kat one day. A memorial stone which Marcus had set up to commemorate his young brother, Gaius, who was drowned at sea.'

'I suspect, sweetheart, that you dreamed the memorial stone too. These things happen, one muddles fact and fiction, we all do it. And Marcus himself was probably an amalgam of all the people you loved and trusted, your father, people who had helped you ... and your subconscious got to work on all of them and produced Marcus. Look, let me tell you about the two sides of the brain and the consequences of their differences, which bring about the condition we call *déjà vu*, just for a start.'

He told her; in a gentle, persuasive murmur he explained the inexplicable. And Questa listened, and murmured agreement, and did not believe a word of it. Marcus was real! She had dreamed him, but that did not make him less real. And the memorial stone existed, she was sure of it. But they were in danger, lost and alone. She would say no more but take what comfort she could from his closeness, and try very hard to pass the time whilst praying with every fibre of her being that they would soon be rescued.

Oddly enough, considering their position, Questa slept deeply once she dropped off. She may have dreamed, she did not know, but she had no recollection of it when she woke, only a thought firm and strong in her head. She moved in the circle of Martin's arms and realised that they were actually lying down and cuddled close; she could feel the stone of the paving stones beneath her hip and smell the velvety dust mingling with the warm, masculine smell of Martin's body so near her own, and she could hear the tiny, curling snores coming from his half-open mouth.

She pulled a little away from him, then shook him. He groaned and half sat up; she had her hands on him so she could feel every movement.

'Martin, wake up! Where's the torch?'

'Wha-what? Oh, Questa, I thought ... the torch? My God, where is it, did it go out ... oh!'

There was a world of meaning in that last syllable. Clearly, Martin had forgotten their troubles in dreams and had abruptly been reminded of them.

'Don't do anything rash, Martin, just find the torch,' Questa said impatiently. 'And when you find it, give it to me, don't do anything else with it. Do hurry, though. If my idea's no good then we'll want to start shouting soon.'

'Start shouting?' Rustling, which meant, Questa thought, that Martin was sitting up, yawning, knuckling his eyes and consulting his wristwatch. 'What's the time?' My dear girl, it's only four o'clock, scarcely time to start shouting, not if we want to be heard anyway.'

'Yes, but what I thought was ... oh, give me the torch!'

'Here, but it won't work you know, it died, remember? Flat battery, I guess.'

'Or batteries, if I'm right,' Questa muttered. 'Don't move away from me, dear Martin, only I do need both hands for a second ... oh damn, oh, thank God!'

'What was all that about?'

'I lost the screw-on end,' Questa said. 'It's all right though, I found it again, it had dropped into my lap. Ah, now just let me ...'

In the darkness, she had unscrewed the end of the torch and shaken the contents on to her lap. Had there been only one battery in the torch she would have been horribly disappointed, but her vague recollection of it was right; there were two. She felt the first one slip into her hand, then the second. With great care she tucked one under each armpit to warm them for a few minutes. Then she replaced them in the torch, with the spring and the screw-on end and very slowly and carefully stood up.

'Martin, can you stand up too?' she said in a wobbly whisper. 'Because we may not have long ...'

Martin stood up; she felt him do so.

'Here goes then – oh, I pray it works!'

She pressed the switch on the torch and immediately a pale beam of light illumined the air-space. Just for a moment Questa could even see, before her, the vague outline of some walls ... good thing they had not moved any farther, then, because to fall over something like that, in the total darkness, would have been to court a broken leg at least.

'Hooray! Quick, turn it on the ceiling. There it is – come on, sweetheart!'

Martin seized her hand and Questa, still clutching the torch, ran with him across to where they could now see, clearly enough, the blacker gap where the flagstone was still missing.

'Don't move ... I'll turn around and grab you in thirty seconds flat,' Martin said. He jumped, hung for a second, kicking wildly with his legs, then drew himself up and out on to the floor above, his biceps cracking with the strain. Immediately he turned and lay on his stomach, arms invitingly extended.

'Jump, Ques!'

Questa jumped and was caught just as the torch dimmed, wavered and went out for the second time in twelve hours.

It did not matter. They rolled away from the hole in the floor which they could no longer see, giggling with the sudden release of tension, bumping into the racking, knocking over one of the bottles Martin had put out ready to take back to the daylight with them.

'Mind ... don't forget that trap-door's still there, still dangerous,' Martin said, suddenly anxious. 'Where are you? My God, but it's as dark here as it was down in the dungeons. Hold still, my love ... yes, there's the hole ... here's the flag ... Keep still, don't move, I'm going to lower it slowly into place. Once it's down we can afford to try to find the doorway, which shouldn't be too difficult.'

It was not difficult at all, not once the flagstone was safely closed and they could move around the secret cellar, admittedly in the pitch dark but at least without the fear of plunging back down into their recent prison. Martin found the door, fumbled it open and still there was only darkness, without so much as a tiny gleam of light.

'It's all right now, Questa, we're almost home and dry,' Martin said, taking her hand and pulling her through into the next, empty cellar. 'Is that light I see?'

It was. Pale and faint, so faint that only eyes long accustomed to total darkness could have made it out, a tiny thread of light from the upper world was making its way towards them, coming down from the hallway, across the first cellar, because they had left both intervening doors open.

'Now the stairs, and we're back in the house,' Martin said exuberantly. 'Here, you go first ... upsadaisy!'

They lurched into the hallway. Their coffee mugs sat on the beam, the kitchen door was open, showing more pale dawn light spilling across the quarry tiles. It all looked so – so ordinary, so commonplace!

'Who would have thought that we had been lost underground, buried alive, given up by our nearest and dearest, and found, all in less than a night?' Martin demanded, as they staggered into the kitchen. 'Oh lor, the fire's out. Want a drink?'

'Yes please, but water will do,' Questa said. 'I know I slept down there, but I'm terribly tired still. You'd better go home, I suppose, and I'll go back to the caravan.'

'We'll go together,' Martin said. 'I could sleep on a clothes-line, though I found it impossible to sleep down there.'

'You snored,' Questa said indignantly. 'You slept like a log, really you did. It was me who woke first.'

'Well, we won't argue. Come on.'

In the pearly dawn light they stole across the stableyard, around the side of the walled garden and into the orchard. The caravan stood there, secretive, smug, the long grass heavy and grey with dew. Questa pushed the door open and went inside, closely followed by Martin. She smiled at the tiny, unloved room which was suddenly where she most wanted to be.

'Dear caravan,' she murmured, 'how nice and light and warm you are. Put the kettle on, Martin.'

Martin lit the primus into hissing life and perched the kettle on top whilst Questa put cocoa into two mugs. 'There's no milk and I'm not going back to the dairy for any,' she said as the kettle began to steam. 'Want a biscuit?'

'No, thanks, the drink will do,' Martin said. 'How did we get so filthy – I take it I'm as filthy as you?'

Questa glanced across at him and giggled.

'Your face is black, and your hands are too,' she said. 'We stirred up quite a dust, one way and another. Are you cold? I am, a bit.'

'Yes, I am. It's odd, because it was chilly down there, you'd think we'd feel beautifully snug up here with the primus going and everything, but I imagine it's reaction. Come and sit here and put the blankets round you whilst I pour your cocoa.'

Questa perched on her bunk and wrapped herself in the blankets, then when Martin brought the mugs of cocoa over she spread the blankets over him too and they sat in companionable silence, drinking and staring at the blue and hissing primus ring.

'All done,' Questa said at last in sleep-drugged tones, standing her mug on the floor. 'Got to sleep now. G'night.'

'Goodnight, sweetheart,' Martin said. 'Move over a bit, you're hogging all the mattress.'

'Sorry,' Questa murmured. She obediently moved over and felt Martin's strong body cuddle down beside her and his arms enfold her. Her last thought was that Kat would have to manage the milking unaided for the second time in twelve hours.

Then she dived into sleep with the eagerness of a thirsty man draining his glass.

Waking was difficult. Questa came up groggily from the depths, because someone was banging something awfully loudly. She whimpered a protest and tried to cuddle down, but there was someone in her bed – wretched person – with elbows and knees which seemed determined to get in her way and prevent her from shutting out the horrible noise with a nice handful of blanket.

'She must be there, or she wouldn't 'ave locked the bloody door! Wake up, gal, you've got a visitor!'

It was Kat – what on earth was Kat doing making so much din in the middle of the night when she, Questa, had barely gone to bed? She opened her eyes. Through the thin curtains by her head daylight blazed … and the person slumbering close beside her was Martin Atherton, dark lashes lying on lean brown cheeks, dark brows beetling into a protesting frown as she gently shook him.

'Martin!' Questa hissed. 'Do wake up, it's morning, we've got a visitor … oh *do* wake up!'

Martin stirred and groaned. It was a very masculine groan, not at all the sort of sound Questa would have made. But she got out of bed, climbing over his still-recumbent body, and went to the door, opening it a crack.

Kat stood outside, and Ran. They both looked extremely worried, as did the young woman standing beside them. She was tall and well-built, with chestnut-coloured hair and a creamy complexion and she was wearing an expensive looking biscuit-coloured gabardine coat with tan lapels and a tie belt.

'Oh dear, I'm most awfully sorry, I'm afraid I overslept,' Questa said 'But after what happened last night I suppose I was so exhausted that I just couldn't wake up at the proper time. Look, just give me a tick … Kat, be a dear and take Mr Atherton and his – his friend over to the kitchen, make them a coffee. I'll be as quick as I can, then I'll join you.'

'What's going on, my dear?' Ran looked worried. 'Have you seen Martin? When neither of you came back last night we were very anxious, we thought … well, I don't know what we thought! At first, just that Martin had taken you out to supper, but when it got later and later … Have you seen Martin, Questa?'

'Martin's fine,' Questa said. All of a sudden she realised she did not want to admit that the two of them had spent the night sharing a very narrow bunk bed in the caravan and that Martin was still drowsily stirring in that very same bed just behind her left shoulder. 'I'll explain … just give me a minute …'

491

'Oh, all right, we'll see you presently. By the way, I can scarcely introduce you properly right now but this is Diana McClintock, she's come all the way down from Scotland to see Martin. Diana, this is Questa Adamson, but we'll go away now and let you tidy up and – and so on. See you in a bit.'

Questa was turning away when Martin fell out of the bunk. He crashed heavily on to the floor and cursed drowsily and uninhibitedly. Questa tried frantically to shush him with a finger to her lips but he took no notice, sitting up on the floor and giving a huge yawn whilst stretching both arms as high as he could.

'Wha's going on?' he demanded loudly. 'Who tipped me out of bed?'

Ran had been turning away, Miss McClintock had been following, but at the sound of the crash they both froze in their tracks. Kat was staring at the caravan doorway; the beginnings of a grin twitched her mobile mouth.

Questa slammed the door and shot the bolt across, then leaned against it, her heart beating like a trip-hammer. Martin, sitting on the floor and rubbing his elbow in slow, ruminative fashion, turned a wicked eye on her. His mouth was not smiling, Questa saw resentfully, but his eyes were.

'Sorry, sweetheart, was that Dad? I wonder what he thought?'

'The worst, I imagine,' Questa said acidly. 'Martin, did you fall out of bed on purpose? What a wretch you are!'

'On purpose? Certainly not – my elbow's probably cracked, and one knee, too.' He grinned winningly at Questa over his shoulder, then heaved himself upright. 'I bet Dad's spitting feathers,' he said. 'And all for nothing, if he did but know.'

'And Diana McClintock,' Questa reminded him. 'What about her?'

'Diana *who*?'

'You heard,' Questa said. Ignoring him but keeping her back turned, she pulled her worn checked shirt over her head and got a clean blue one off the small pile of clothes in the top dresser drawer. She slipped it on, then contemplated her trousers, which were a sight.

'Diana McClintock is *here*?'

'Yes,' Questa said baldly.

492

'Outside, just now? She heard me falling out of bed? She knows we both spent the night … oh well, at least it solves one complication.' Martin got slowly off the floor and rubbed a hand through his short, black hair, then pulled a face. 'I'd love a cup of tea,' he said plaintively. 'Do we have time to put the kettle on?'

'What complication does it solve?' Questa asked. But she reached for the milk churn full of water which she kept by the door and tipped a judicious quantity into the kettle. She set the kettle on the primus and indicated that Martin should light it which he did whilst she put on her clean blue cotton skirt and removed her filthy trousers under cover of the skirt's fullness.

Martin sighed and pumped the primus. 'I rather think she thought that she and I might make a go of it, if I took the job her father kept shoving at me,' Martin said. 'But she's not my type; I like small, dark girls with wide, innocent eyes and hair all full of builders' dust.'

'My eyes are certainly not innocent,' Questa said crossly. 'Of all the insipid descriptions, that's about the worst I've ever heard. And I'm not particularly small either.' But she picked up a brush and attacked her hair. Dust flew. 'You stay here and drink the tea; I'm going to do my best to explain to your father.'

'We'll both go,' Martin said. 'Just what will you say? That it was all completely inn-o-cent, dear Ran; bad, lecherous Martin simply happened to fall asleep in my bed, that's all!'

'Have you forgotten what we found last night? Have you forgotten being buried alive and scared half out of our wits?' Questa asked him, splashing water out of the churn straight into her face. 'When we show him, tell him, do you think he'll care where you spent the night?'

Martin stared at her, then frowned. 'Show him what? The secret cellar?'

'No, stupid, though that will give him a big thrill; the other cellar, the dungeon … and the painted pavement.'

Martin stared harder than ever, then he smote his brow with his hand. 'Did it really happen? Do you know, sweetheart, I've been thinking it must have been some horrible sort of nightmare … but you say it's all there, still? Just waiting for us to show people?'

'Yes of course it is,' Questa said impatiently. 'Unless we both had an identical nightmare, of course. That will take your father's mind most effectively off where we spent the night.'

'No, it won't,' Martin said. He reached for the brush and began to tidy his own hair, then he dipped the end of the towel into the milk churn and washed his face. 'But he'll have to be civilised. And Diana will have to go back to Scotland.'

'Good,' Questa said, not mincing matters. 'She's awfully nice looking, I'd rather she was in Scotland than here.'

Martin threw the towel on to the bed and took her in his arms. He bent his head and kissed her, lingeringly. Questa sighed and trembled into a response, then tugged herself free.

'Really, Martin, your father's waiting! Skip the tea and let's go right over there.'

No matter how thoroughly one knows one is right, no matter how innocent one's actions, walking into a room which contains three people who think one has been doing something wrong is never easy, as Questa discovered when she and Martin entered the kitchen.

Kat had served coffee and biscuits and the three of them had, judging by their faces, been indulging in some sort of recriminations. At least Diana was pink and Ran's cheekbones were flushed, whilst Kat looked downright angry.

'Ah, Martin. My dear boy, I'm glad to see you unharmed, but I do think that some sort of explanation is due. Mr McClintock was coming down south on business and he dropped Diana off last night at The Passing Soldier. She rang the Hall, hoping to be able to speak to you if not see you. I explained you were late back but got into the car and came here, tried the caravan, tried the Court itself, got Kat and Alfie to help me search ... we couldn't find a trace of you. It was weird: two mugs of coffee, only half-drunk, your working things thrown down anyhow – and worst of all, the Lagonda still parked out on the gravel sweep. I couldn't think where the two of you could have gone on foot. I've had a very worrying night of it.'

'Of course, I forgot the car,' Martin said. 'Hello, Diana, nice to see you, though I'm sorry you've walked into such a drama. But you were the last person I expected to see.'

'You wouldn't be seeing me now, except that your father asked me to wait,' Diana said. 'And now if you don't mind I'll be on my way. I just thought it would be nice to see you again, Martin. I – I wanted to ask you whether you'd be coming back to Scotland. I didn't realise you had ... reasons to stay here, in England.'

'I did tell you it was unlikely I'd be back,' Martin said gently. 'Look, just let me have a few words with my father and then I'll run you into the village ... the car's still outside I suppose.'

'It's no' necessary,' Diana said rather woodenly. 'If someone would just ring for a taxi I'll be on my way. Thank you for your hospitality, Mr Atherton. Goodbye, Martin, Miss Adamson.'

'Oh ... goodbye,' Questa said lamely. She felt she should ask the older girl to stay, but what would be the point? Martin had made his feelings clear enough. 'I'm sorry we worried you, but it wasn't our fault, really it wasn't.'

'I was not worried, it just seemed an opportunity to see Martin,' Diana McClintock said stiffly. 'Where's the telephone?'

'At the bottom of the drive,' Kat said quickly. 'I'll tek you down there, shall I?' To the others she added, 'Shan't be a tick.'

'It's good of you, Kat, because I think I'd like a word with these two,' Ran said rather grimly. 'Come back when you've seen Miss McClintock into her taxi, would you?'

Kat grinned cheerfully round the room. 'Wouldn't miss it for the world,' she said. 'See you presently, then.'

The two girls left the kitchen, closing the door carefully behind them. Martin, who had stood up when they left, sat down again and glanced across at Ran, a slight, sardonic smile on his face.

'Sorry about that added complication, Dad, but I had no idea she'd follow me down south. I told her I'd not be going back ... anyway, that aside, you said you'd searched for us; where, precisely?'

'All over the Court; Kat did the upstairs, Alfie and I the rest. We even went down into the cellars, though I was pretty sure you wouldn't have stayed down there long. I know Questa doesn't much like underground places.'

'We were down there,' Martin said grimly. 'You didn't search far enough. My God, Ques, do you realise that if they tried to find us down there last night and failed, they might well not have bothered with the cellars again? But all's well that ends well, as the poet says.'

'You were in the cellars?' Ran looked angrily at his son. 'I knew you'd been down there, you'd had to break the lock on the cellar door, but you most certainly weren't still there when we searched, so don't lie to me, please, Martin. You're a grown man, you've a perfect right to behave in any way you see fit, but Questa's a minor, I feel her to be very much my responsibility, you had no right to – to –'

'No right to do what, Dad? To take Questa down to her own cellars?'

Ran shrugged. He looked tired as well as angry, now. 'I just told you, we searched the cellars! And what's more to the point ... ' he looked uncomfortably across at Questa, sitting perched on the harvest table, quietly listening, 'I recognised your voice coming from the caravan. You'd no right to take advantage of a trusting young girl, to – to –'

Martin straightened his shoulders and Questa could see he was enjoying both Ran's embarrassment and the pit his father was about to dig for himself. Hastily, she slithered off the table and faced Ran.

'It's all right ... we did spend the night in the cellars, we'd not been back in the caravan long, but come with us please, Ran.' She turned to Martin. 'Light the lamp would you? And perhaps it might be best if you got another torch as well. In the caravan I've got a decent little torch with a new battery in the drawer in the middle of the table. Then we needn't try to convince anyone, we can show them.'

Martin nodded. He went unhurriedly into the hall and fetched the oil-lamp, lit it, turned to the back door, then looked over his shoulder at Questa, his glance commanding.

'You aren't to take Dad anywhere until I get back,' he said. 'But you wouldn't, would you? It's a dangerous place.'

'I won't say a word until you get back,' Questa promised, reading the anxiety in his eyes. 'And we'll wait for Kat, too.'

As soon as his son had gone, closing the door behind him, Ran limped across the room and put an affectionate hand round Questa's neck, shaking her gently.

496

'My dear child, I didn't realise how fond I'd grown of you until I thought you'd disappeared, you and Martin. Oh, I was angry with him – I still am – for treating you in so cavalier a fashion, but if I were twenty years younger I'd probably do the same. So let's not quarrel, because I want both of you here, near me.'

'You'll get both of us,' Questa said. 'Dear Ran, it's not what you think, honestly. Wait until you see!'

'Well, we searched those cellars, including the secret one with not a wine bottle in sight,' Ran said obstinately. 'I can't imagine where you could have hidden yourselves. Look, I know men have appetites – women too, for that matter – but there is an institution which caters for such things; it's called marriage. If you and Martin …'

'Ran, don't! Don't say things you'll regret later,' Questa said, dismayed at the pain and embarrassment mingling on her old friend's face. 'Martin and Kat will be back presently and … ah!'

They came into the kitchen together, Martin flourishing the torch, Kat with her small, triangular face alight with curiosity.

'Martin tells me we're a-goin' down into that cellar,' she said briskly. 'So I nipped up to the flat an' got me own torch. Don't trust that little one e's brung with 'im.'

'Right. The expedition will now commence,' Martin said, handing the oil-lamp to Questa and giving his father the torch. 'We'll use the lamp at present, save the torches for later. Dad, the stairs are steep and there's no hand-rail – besides, you'll need your sticks once we get on to level ground, so give me your arm.'

'I got down perfectly well yesterday, thank you very much,' Ran said stiffly, but Kat, prancing ahead, turned and winked at Martin.

'Alfie give you 'is arm yesterday,' she reminded him. 'An' you very near measured your length in the second cellar, so let the lad give you an 'and.'

Ran looked taken aback, then laughed. 'Pride, that's all it is. Pride in abilities I had once but don't have any more. And I don't just mean the ability to descend cellar steps unaided, either.'

Questa, following behind, saw Martin's hand tighten for a moment on his father's arm, saw Ran lean a little towards his son, smiling, saying something beneath his breath. They both

497

laughed and suddenly she saw that they were at ease, if only temporarily, that Ran's admission of his hated dependence, Martin's sympathy for that dependence, had broken down a barrier of misunderstanding which had begun to loom over-large in their lives.

'Here we are, the first cellar. Carefully down the steps, girls.'

Martin and Ran got down without any trouble, but Questa saw the care with which Martin helped his father and was glad. It would be so good if the two men she loved could begin, at last, to love each other.

'Next cellar – duck, Dad, it's lower than you think.'

They traversed the second cellar, came to the blank wall with the tiny door set well back so that it looked like a shadow amongst shadows.

'Into the secret cellar,' Ran said jovially. 'A shame the army got there first ... I always hoped they'd not found the door, but no such luck.' He got through the low doorway, not without difficulty, then stood up, supported partly by his stick and partly by Martin's strong arm. 'Well? Where do we go from here?'

'Pull on that racking ... go on, Dad, give it a real heave. Questa fell against it, that did the trick, but it will pull out if you put some muscle into it.'

Ran heaved and the racking pulled away from the wall, the hinges creaking, bringing with it a section of false wall and revealing the small, low door set down two steps. Ran and Kat both gasped. Questa laughed.

'Wait till you see! I'll go first, I've got the lamp, and it *is* low and difficult.'

'And you were in here all the time?' Ran asked in honest amazement when at last all four of them stood in the secret cellar. 'All these bottles ... there's a fortune here!'

'Yup. But we weren't in here, otherwise we'd probably have heard you. And anyway, we could have got out easily enough. Look around you.'

But even with the light of the lamp, no one spotted the ring set in the flagstone; Questa had to go over and point it out and then Martin had to heave on it, before the other two would believe.

498

'My God, a deeper cellar,' Ran exclaimed when at last the flagstone was laid flat on the cellar floor. 'You went down?'

'Of course. Anyone would have,' Martin said impatiently. 'Just kneel and look, Dad, for now at any rate. It's a good drop.'

'Ye-es ... I can't see any walls, either, it must be huge,' Ran said, his voice echoing round the big, bare chamber. 'So you went down – can we follow suit or is there nothing to see?'

'We'll go down. Girls first, then I'll get you down somehow.'

Ran watched as Questa swung by her arms and dropped, then Kat did the same with Questa steadying her.

'My arm muscles are the strongest thing about me,' Ran pointed out when Martin began to discuss methods of getting him into the lower cellar. 'You go first, Martin, and catch me as I drop.'

Two minutes later all four began to make their way slowly across the great open space.

'It's an air-space, left by the builders of Eagles Court, or perhaps an even older house,' Martin explained. 'Seen it yet, Questa?'

'No, not yet. It's odd, we were here only a few hours ago, longing to get out, yet I'm not a bit afraid or ... here!'

She could see, through the dust, the faint colours of the painted floor.

'It's a different one,' Martin said after a moment, during which he industriously cleared an area of mosaic for his father and Kat to see. This time the picture showed an elderly man with elaborate curls, a forked stick in one hand.

'It must be the bath-house,' Questa exclaimed. 'Yes, that's Neptune, and there's a big shark with enormous teeth, and an octopus ...'

Questa, acutely conscious of Martin's dark eyes fixed on her, though she was not looking towards him, blushed and let her voice fade into silence.

'And there are more of these mosaics?'

'At least one ... ' Martin was beginning when Questa interrupted.

'There will be several,' she said eagerly, 'and because of the state of preservation there will be other things too, once we can bring lights down here and really look. Ran, it is special, isn't it? The other mosaic, the one we found yesterday, is ... oh, most beautiful.'

'It's like a miracle,' Ran said. With some difficulty he laid his sticks down and knelt, running his hands reverently over the little coloured tiles. 'This isn't just special, my dear, it's a rare find, probably unique. And it's been there all those years, all those years!'

'Almost two thousand years,' Questa said, but so softly that she thought only Martin heard. 'Hidden away safely for two thousand years, to make sure the Court lived on, despite everything.'

Martin had heard. He squeezed her hand; then, in the comforting dark, with the other two intent on the gradual revelation of the mosaic as their blackened handkerchiefs tenderly swept, he kissed her. And Questa kissed him back, and remembered kissing Marcus right here, in the bath-house, with only a passing slave to notice, and his favourite hound, Abacus, watching them with a question in his big, mild eye.

Yet the lips which had kissed her so often in her dreams had been no sweeter than the lips which claimed hers now, the love she felt for him no stronger than the love which flowed through her at the mere sight of Martin.

They're the same yet they're different, she thought as Martin's mouth moved on hers. Marcus said we'd meet again because we were made for each other, so don't question, just be thankful. And love him. Love them. Love Martin-Marcus.

Twenty-three

'So you went down with just a torch, found the secret cellar, then discovered the trap-door, the moving flagstone. And went below, and moved back in time a couple of thousand years.' Ran smiled from face to face, sitting in Kat's flat, to which they had repaired to drink coffee and talk over their find. 'And then what? Why didn't you answer when we called? Why stay so long in the lowest part? Why didn't you come right out, for that matter?'

'The torch went out and we had no means of making a light,' Questa said briefly. 'It was very frightening. Darkness like that is like blindness; without Martin I'd have gone mad. We tried to feel for the trap-door but we couldn't find it, probably we were walking in circles and anyway, it's ever so big. We didn't see the walls when we were down there just now, except in the far distance, did we?'

'True,' Ran said. 'So you were in the pitch dark, with no means of producing a light and no possibility of finding your way out without one. You must have been terrified – anyone would have been. How did you pass the time?'

'We talked, and told stories, and sang songs. And every now and then we looked at Martin's wristwatch, because it has little luminous dots on the hands so you can tell the time even in the dark, more or less.'

'And then?'

'Then we fell asleep,' Martin said, taking up the story. 'We were tired as well as pretty scared. It's so deep, you see, I couldn't help wondering what would happen to us if no one thought to come hunting. After all, the lower cellars must have been lost for centuries, we found them entirely by chance. If Questa hadn't found a little chest with a bible and a brass eagle in it – good heavens, it's down there still, we never gave it another thought,

501

did we, Ques? If she hadn't put the chest down and heard it chink on the iron ring set into the flagstone, if she hadn't bothered to dig around to find out what had made the noise, we probably never would have found the villa ourselves.'

'And when you woke?' prompted Ran, when Martin's voice faded into silence. 'What happened when you woke?'

'I remembered during the war that the partisans used to warm up their batteries just to get a few minutes more light when the batteries seemed to be finished,' Questa said. 'And I remembered Turos telling me once that if you leave a battery and don't try to switch it on again, it can sort of gather the last little remains of its strength after a few hours and give you just a tiny flash more light. So I opened our torch and tucked the batteries under my arms for a few minutes. And we saw for long enough to find the trap-door and get out.'

'Thank God for that,' Ran said, with great feeling in his voice. 'I can't bear to think ... so I won't. You are both very dear to me.'

'And to each other,' Kat remarked brightly. 'You gets on like an 'ouse afire, the pair of you. Gonna mek a go of it, then?'

'Kat!' Ran said reprovingly, then smiled at her. 'But fools rush in ... sorry, Kat, I don't mean that as rudely as it sounded. Well, you two? Don't sit there grinning, tell me if I may congratulate you both and give my new daughter a kiss?'

Questa felt the heat rush into her cheeks. She looked uncertainly from Martin to his father and back again. She and Martin had agreed that it was too soon to discuss marriage and she remembered her strong feeling that they did not know each other well enough for such an important commitment, but that was before they had spent that night together in the lowest cellar.

'Would you kindly let me propose for myself?' Martin said indignantly. 'Damn it, Dad, all I can offer Questa right now is a share of my share in the Hall; I don't even have a job of my own.'

'Look, you've told me your story and I accept it completely, even to the almost unbelievable fact that the pair of you went to sleep in the caravan in the early hours of the morning with never a thought for what other people would say – or worse, think. But have either of you any idea of the bally-hoo that will start the moment Questa tells the authorities what's buried beneath the cellars of Eagles Court? If you intend to get married, then I strongly advise you to marry first and tell people about the mosaics second. God knows what they'll suggest: turning the place into a museum probably, or opening it to the public at the very least, but you must see that the Court is rebuilt first, at someone else's expense. Enough of it so that you can act as caretakers for what lies below. You've heard of Egyptian tomb-robbers? Well, the English underworld is never slow to latch on to an idea … this place will have to be surrounded by security people night and day I shouldn't wonder, once it gets out that it's built on top of an ancient Roman villa.'

'So I'm to propose marriage so as to be able to act as a security guard?' Martin said incredulously. 'And Questa is to accept so as to have someone to force the authorities to rebuild Eagles Court? If we marry, Dad – and it's still if, because neither of us would want to marry just to quieten wagging tongues – we'll do it in our own time and for far better reasons.'

'Like love?' Questa said softly, smiling into Martin's dark and angry face. 'Isn't love the only good reason for marrying?'

'Yes of course it is, only …'

'And do you love me?'

'Dammit, girl, you know full well I do, but I don't want …'

Questa had been sitting on the one of the chintz chairs by the fire whilst Martin and his father occupied the narrow couch. Now she stood up and went over to Martin, holding out her hands and, when he put his own into them, pulling him to his feet. She leaned against him shamelessly, her face tilted up so that she could still hold his eyes.

'I think I know what you do want, and since it's exactly what I want as well, why can't you say so? If you want to marry someone it's the done thing to say so, you know.'

'In front of witnesses? With Dad and Kat watching?'

'What better way of ensuring that you go through with it? Speak now, Martin Atherton, or forever hold your peace.'

Martin heaved a big sigh and his arms went round Questa and tightened in a hug.

'Will you marry me please, Questa?'

'Yes, I will. Where's my engagement ring, then?'

'It's the big sapphire, in the bank,' Ran said from behind them. There was a smile in his voice and when Questa pulled herself out of Martin's arms, she saw he had a smile on his face too. It did not take much imagination to see that he was really delighted. He stood up, grabbed a stick, and held out his hand to his son.

'Martin, many congratulations! You've won yourself a rare prize, and I'm *not* referring to the Court or the villa or anything but this little girl here. She's worth more than the lot of them put together, I just wish your mother could have known her.'

'Let's 'ave a toast, coffee ain't good enough,' Kat bubbled, jumping to her feet. 'I got a bottle of Ellen's sloe gin 'ere ... that'll bring the colour to our cheeks!' She produced the bottle, then came over and gave Questa a hug. 'You won't never regret this day,' she announced, with tears standing in her eyes. 'Me an' Alfie's ever so 'appy, bein' married is the best thing what ever could 'appen to a gal.'

'It's not so bad for a bloke either,' Martin supplied, carefully pouring the sloe gin into four glasses. 'Well, that changes things. I'd been going to suggest that Questa approach the authorities right away, but as things stand we'll go and see the vicar first, and get the banns organised. How does three weeks today suit you?'

'It would be lovely,' Questa said with what Ran afterwards told her was absolutely no maidenly shrinking whatsoever. 'Let's all swear not to say anything about the villa yet, though. Time enough for that.'

'Time enough,' Kat echoed raising her glass. 'To the bride and groom, when they is wed. You can wear my weddin' dress, Ques,' she added, 'since that Grace let me 'ave it back once she were spliced, though it'll be too big for you, no danger.'

'I'm going to buy her a dress,' Ran said firmly however. 'Something lacy, I think, with a long train.'

'And a nice, thick veil, so I can't see her face and change my mind,' Martin said. He pinched Questa's cheek. 'Three weeks, eh? How about Scotland for a honeymoon?'

'How about staying right here?' Questa countered. 'Once we're married, remember, we're going to tell everyone about the villa. We shan't be able to leave, and I'm sure I shan't want to. The only thing is, will we have to live at the Court? Because, if so, you're going to have to get used to that bunk, and it is most awfully narrow.'

'I don't mind,' Martin said, treating her to a lecherous leer. 'Anyway, perhaps in three weeks we'll have got the small parlour ready for use.'

'Or you could come to the Hall ...' Ran began eagerly, then shook his head. 'Sorry; not the answer, of course. Look, everyone should have a honeymoon; don't say anything about the villa until you come back. Where would you like to go, Questa my dear?'

'Cromer; to the house Daddy and I went to years ago,' Questa said promptly. 'Only of course Daddy only came to leave me there and then, later, to pick me up. When I first remembered the place it struck me as a bit odd that I could remember Mr and Mrs Carter so clearly, but still couldn't really remember Daddy, but it was because he used to go off on his digs and things, wasn't it, and thought I'd only be bored or get in the way? And of course I hated being left, so I sort of washed things like that out of my mind completely. Only unfortunately a lot of other things went as well.'

'That's right, my dear,' Ran said gently. 'Charles was a good father, but ancient civilisations were an obsession with him.'

'And he liked women too, didn't he?' Questa said quietly, almost sadly. 'I thought Grace must have behaved badly, I couldn't believe it of my father, but now I'm almost sure that he left me with people so that he could have weekends and holidays and things with his lady-friends.'

'No one wanted you to know that,' Ran said. 'You'd forgotten, or put it out of your head, so Alan thought, and I agreed when he put it to me, that it would be best left that way. But since you've remembered, yes, Charles was a great one for the ladies.'

'Did you know, Martin?' Questa asked, turning her head. 'Now that we've talked about it, I'd rather know.'

'Yes, I knew,' Martin admitted. 'But I didn't think it was terribly important to keep it from you; Charles was human. What's wrong with that?'

'Oh, I suppose I thought he was perfect and couldn't bear to admit that I wasn't the be-all and end-all of his life,' Questa said. 'Still, now that I do know, I love him just as much. I wish he hadn't been unkind to Grace, of course, but otherwise ... well, I love him the way I loved him when I was little.'

'Uncomplainingly, undemandingly. I remember it well,' Ran said. 'His little shadow he used to call you, when you were just a tiny tot. He brought you to stay in the village two or three times, but you were too small to remember that. And you've grown up very nicely, my dear. Your father would have been proud of you.'

'He'd have loved the villa, too, wouldn't he?' Questa said wistfully. 'But we'll love it just as well, in our way. And now, Martin, if we're going to call on the vicar ...'

It was harder work planning a wedding than Questa had realised and it took all of her time, to say nothing of her energy. Besides, they had decided they could not bear to start married life in the caravan, so the work of getting four rooms or so ready for occupation went on.

But at last, as the day neared, they began to feel they were ready. At Ran's insistence Martin had made wooden steps which led down into the lowest cellar of all, and set up a number of boxes, each of which would have a primed oil-lamp upon it. They had explored as far as they could by lamplight, and now knew that there were indeed obstacles in the shape of the outer walls and even some broken-down internal ones; that there were steps down, leading to a place of pipes and aqueducts and gurgling, tiled channels, and that this was where the hot water for the central heating and the baths had come from.

'Hypocausts,' Ran said. 'The man who decided to build the first manor house on the ruins of the Roman villa may well not have known anything about such things, obviously he wouldn't have known about the Romans' heating system; that knowledge was lost for many centuries. He thought the ruins were useless, but the site was perfect for the house he had in mind, so he just levelled the outer walls down to six feet or so to act as his foundations and left the rest, undiscovered, below.'

'But why not go right down to ground level? When you look at the Court it looks as though it's on ground level,' Questa pointed out. 'It isn't higher than the surrounding countryside, for example.'

'No, because over many hundreds of years the Roman villa would have sunk, or the surrounding countryside would have built up. Anyway, the ground levels must have changed. Just think how many years, Questa! Time for most things to alter beyond recognition.'

'Yes,' said Questa, but in her mind she thought that the changes had not been that huge, that obvious. Trees were still trees, flowers still bloomed, and men and women still fell in love. Now and then, although she did her best to prevent it, a face swam into the forefront of her mind; a dark, beautiful face, very like Martin's yet not Martin. But Marcus no longer existed, even if he once had. She could not completely forget him, nor did she want to do so, but he must belong to her past, he must be like an old photograph brought out occasionally and smiled over, then put away again. If she could not entirely forget, at least she could put it behind her. A beautiful episode, a warmth in her heart, it was like a blanket between her and the war, her and the reality of her pre-war life. And once I'm married to Martin, properly married, I'll forget Marcus's smile, his touch, the way we were together, she told herself, and knew that even if she never actually forgot, at least the memory would grow faded and tender, a pleasant first love instead of the painful, agony-racked loss of those early days.

Sometimes, as they toiled together, she caught Martin looking at her strangely though. Sometimes he would start a question, break off, change the subject, come over and kiss her quickly, or passionately, holding her as though he was loath to let her go even for a moment.

Was he aware of it, then, did he know that at times she still suffered from divided loyalties? Could a young and virile man, with his life in front of him, feel jealous of a dream lover long-dead though not forgotten? Was she being fair when she sought likenesses between them instead of differences?

If only she could have talked it over with someone, but that would scarcely have been fair. So instead she lay in the caravan telling herself that she simply must forget Marcus, cast his

507

memory from her once and for all, whilst knowing it to be impossible.

Things came to a head the very day before the wedding, when everyone, it seemed to a bewildered Questa, was in a horrible mood. Grace, Alan and Dickie, all putting up at The Passing Soldier, came and bewailed the fate of the house and moaned about how sad it was to see a beautiful old place in ruins. Questa had intended to take them below, to the cellars, but she immediately decided not to do so; if they blamed her for the lightning strike, God knew what they would do when they saw the mosaic pavings.

Ran was grumpy as well, which was unusual. The reception was being held at the Hall, with his full and enthusiastic backing, but the firm who were catering had changed the colour scheme at the last minute, and when Questa went over to tell Ran how annoying the Patterson contingent were being, he could hardly sympathise for his own annoyance over the chief caterer's insistence on pink tablecloths, which Ran thought vulgar.

Kat helped milk the cows first thing, then went off with Alfie to buy herself something to wear. Why does she need something special, when it's me that's getting married, Questa thought peevishly. No one will look twice at Kat, not tomorrow.

So when she ran Martin to earth, actually underneath the tractor, which had developed trouble in its gear-box, she was desperate for sympathy and understanding.

'Martin, I don't want to take Alan down to the lower cellar after all. Do you know, he's moaning about the mess the fire made as if I did it myself, with my own little box of matches? I'm so annoyed with him … and besides, you know what Grace is like, she'll start talking about it at the wedding reception and we shan't be able to go to Norfolk after all, we'll have to stay here, on guard.'

'Then don't take either of them down to the cellars to see our painted pavements,' Martin said. He wriggled out from under the tractor and grinned at her out of a dirty, grease-smeared face. 'What's he done to deserve a treat like that, anyway? Let him suffer!'

'Well, it seems rather mean, because he and my father were

both keen on ancient civilisations at one stage,' Questa muttered. 'And though he lost interest once he was in his twenties, I suppose, for old times' sake, I ought to show him.'

'No indeed, why should you? Of course it may well restore your family fortunes, but why should that matter to Alan? His stepson might have inherited once, but with you and me getting married and me so young and virile, you'll have half-a-dozen kids tugging at your skirt before you know it ... heirs and heiresses by the score. So he can forget all thoughts of personal advantage, and might not be interested anyway in the circumstances. No, don't show them our finds, let them stew.'

At once, Questa began to feel that perhaps she should take them down to the cellars, after all. Alan was her father's executor and best friend, the find would have thrilled Charles beyond belief, would not the next best thing to showing her father the mosaics be showing Alan?

She said as much.

'Okay, if that's how you feel, d'you want me to clean myself up and come with you?'

'Yes ... no ... oh, everyone's in such a horrible *mood*,' Questa said petulantly. 'I bet it rains tomorrow too. And all the rest of the week.'

'I like a rainy day; it's good for the crops,' Martin said.

'Oh, the crops! But happy is the bride that the sun shines on, you know; what about *that*?'

'I like a sunny day, too,' Martin said promptly. 'Do you want me out from under here or can I get on with the gear-box?'

'I don't care what you do; if you don't want to help me, don't.' Questa swung on her heel. 'The tractor's far more important than me, I do know that!'

She was halfway across the yard when an arm encircled her waist and lifted her off her feet. Martin's other hand caressed her cheek. 'Who's in a worse mood than all the others put together?' he whispered. 'Come on, let's leave them to stew – we'll go out, just you and me.'

'I bet there's oil on my face now,' Questa said, but her mood had lifted. The sunshine, which had streamed down unregarded all morning, suddenly warmed her through her thin cotton shirt.

'Oh Martin, you do understand me so well! I'm not sure if I like it, but in a way it's a comfort. Am I being as horrid as everyone else, is that what you mean?'

'Well, you're certainly affected by their moods,' Martin said with rare tact. 'Now how about it? We could saddle up a couple of nags, Cloud for me and Scamper for you if you want her particularly, and go for a good gallop ... or take a picnic – ever been up to the hills in September? The colours are amazing and somehow the sunshine's all the sweeter for being chancy, rose-gold rather than platinum.'

'That's very poetic,' Questa said approvingly. 'Where will we go then, on our mettlesome steeds?'

'Oh, up to the hills, if you'd like that. The Welsh hills ... see them, dreaming in the sun? It'll be nice up there on a day like today, we won't take a meal, we'll stop at a pub somewhere and I'll treat you to a thumping good lunch.' He kissed the top of her head. 'Your last lunch as a free woman, come to think of it.' He twirled her around to face him. 'Well? Are you going to have lunch with me, li'l lady?'

'The hills! Oh, Martin, I love them ... hills never change, do they? But wouldn't it be really rude to leave Alan and Grace out of it? Only if we don't leave immediately there won't be any day left to enjoy.'

'The Pattersons are doing their own thing today, and don't need us to amuse them. Right? Off we go then. Good thing you've got trousers on ... tell you what, why don't you ride Chip? She's Dad's new strawberry roan, she's got a lovely temperament, and it'll save us trailing back and forth with Scamper. You can come home with me in the car and we can tack up together.'

'I really would like that,' Questa said eagerly. 'All right, just let me shout Kat.'

Kat was sensible and understanding, as always. 'You're doin' the best thing, Mr Martin,' she said. 'Tek 'er out of 'erself, give 'er suffin' else to think about. She'll calm down lovely up in them there 'ills, be all ready to face tomorrer.'

So Questa and Martin tacked up the horses, told Ran they were going for a ride and set off after a hasty elevenses in the kitchen with Mrs Clovelly, who was just as nice as Kat had been and told Questa that every bride suffered from pre-wedding nerves but not every bride had a feller as thoughtful as Martin.

'He does want you to be happy,' she said, her eyes moistening. 'Over and over he says it: *just so long as she's happy, Mrs C,* he says. He was always a good lad, heart in the right place ... just like his father. And they're better friends now they aren't in one another's pockets, too.'

'I know, I'm lucky,' Questa agreed. 'We may not be back until quite late though, Mrs C, because it's getting on towards lunch-time now. Don't worry, and don't let Ran worry either.'

'Worry we shall if you're out after dark, and dark falls early in September,' Mrs C said at once. 'Come in be dusk, there's a good girl.'

'Well, I expect we will ... only all of a sudden I wish we hadn't said we'd get married and have a wedding and things, I wish we could just run off to Norfolk without any fuss and come back and say we were married. Then if we're making a mistake it wouldn't matter so much.'

'A mistake? Nonsense, child, you're doing the most sensible thing either of you has ever done! And as for pretending to be married, who do you think that would fool? No, we all have to go through with it, and mostly we have a lovely day, like you will. Now get off with you ... and remember it's apple and almond pudding for dessert tonight.'

'Oh! We'll be home, then. Can't miss my favourite pud! And thanks, Mrs C.'

'Thanks?' Mrs C's grey eyebrows arched. 'Thanks for what, may I ask?'

'Thanks for loving Martin as much as I do, and saying so! What time's dinner? Eight o'clock? Right, see you then.'

Horse-riding is good exercise and fun, but it isn't relaxing, or not when you don't do it regularly. After a couple of hours of alternately trotting and cantering along country lanes, with the ground gradually beginning to slope upwards, Questa was glad to dismount, tie Chip to a tethering post, and go into a white-washed inn.

'I don't know whether my idea was such a bright one now,' Martin said ruefully as he carried two half-pints over to the table where Questa was lowering herself on to an old oak settle. 'A saddlesore bride who walks up the aisle bow-legged could give rise to all sorts of untrue rumours.'

Questa, sipping cautiously at her drink, snorted and blew foam off the top, then mopped frantically as it meandered down the side of the glass.

'What a dreadful thing to say,' she said reproachfully. 'You're no gentleman, Martin Atherton!'

'Am I not? Well, a real lady wouldn't have known what I was talking about, Miss Adamson! Would you like a cornish pastie and salad, or a ploughman's?'

'A ploughman's what?' Questa said, setting her beer down on the table in front of her. 'Is it a drink?'

'No, idiot, it's what pubs call bread and cheese and pickles. It's homemade bread and very good cheese, as a rule.'

'Oh. What will you have, Martin?'

'Ploughman's. More filling. But you choose whatever you want. You can have sandwiches if you'd rather. They do a corned beef one, or cheese, or ham ... they put a bit of salad at the side, too.'

'I'll have a ploughman's as well, I'm really hungry,' Questa said, in the surprised tone of one who has never admitted to hunger before. 'Could I have a lemonade with it? This stuff is bitter!'

'Right. I'll order it in a tick. Anything else? Something to rub on your war-wounds, by which I mean your saddlesores.'

'Certainly not. I'm not saddlesore, just ... just a little tired. But this rest will set me up for the remainder of the ride.'

Martin, about to set off for the bar once again, reached over and rumpled her hair. 'Poor darling! Never mind, it's not far now. When we get right up into the hills we'll look down on Eagles Court and the Hall and feel like king and queen of the universe, see if we don't!'

'Isn't this beautiful? Shall we dismount, turn the horses out into that meadow, and go the rest of the way on foot? Then we can

sit down quietly and contemplate the view and eat the sandwiches the landlady sold me and drink the fizzy lemonade.'

'Bless you, Martin,' Questa said, swinging wearily down from
her saddle. 'I love riding, but it is tiring, it would be nice to sit by
the stream and rest for a bit. Only I'd like to walk a little farther
along the track if you don't mind.'

The clearing was near here, the clearing where she had spied
on Marcus and Lucilla; she could never forget it, not in a million
years, but she had no need to remind herself more sharply than
necessary.

'Fine by me.' Martin took her mare's reins and tied them up
so that Chip could graze, then turned both horses out into the
meadow, shutting the gate firmly behind them. 'A bit of a walk
won't do us any harm and I do love to look back when we get
above the tree-line and see the Court and the Hall looking so tiny
and perfect.'

'It's only from a distance that the Court looks perfect,' Questa
said ruefully. 'Come on then, let's get going. Come to think of it,
if we go on along this track, doesn't it turn into the old Roman
road?'

'Yes, I believe it does – so you do know the area? You've been
here before?'

'Yes, several times. It was here I found, or I thought I had …'
she hesitated, shooting a quick sideways glance at his profile, 'the
stone Marcus had set up in memory of his young brother, Gaius.
Do you remember me telling you about it, in the cellar? And you
telling me that it was a dream, all of it? Well, that may be, but I
didn't dream the stone. I'll show it to you if you like.'

'I'd like to see it,' Martin said politely. 'As for dreaming it, what
usually happens, sweetheart, is that you find something like the
stone and you fit it into your dream, and afterwards you're
muddled about which came first, the stone or the dream. Do you
see what I mean?'

'Yes. But I don't *think* it was that way round. Honestly.'

'Sweetheart, if it makes you happy …'

'Don't humour me,' Questa said warningly. 'I tell you things
I've never told anyone else, you're undoubtedly right and it is –
was – just a dream, but the stone … well, wait and see.'

513

They walked on, silent beneath branches heavy with late summer leaves, already turning gold as the year faded. Sunshine slanted through the branches and fewer birds sang, Questa thought, than she had heard here before. As they walked, the character of the track and the surrounding countryside changed. The trees became smaller, stunted, their branches all bent at the wind's will. Hedges petered out, and soon they were walking through short, sweet-smelling foliage – heathers, rushes, wiry grasses – with gorse bushes heavy with yellow blossom replacing the trees.

'The blasted heath,' Martin said, but Questa just nodded and walked on. She knew this so well! Very soon they would come across the first signs of the Roman road, the big flat stones still, after two thousand years, only half-hidden by the low-growing, wiry grass, then farther up the track they would see the memorial stone, and even if Martin could not altogether believe her, he would have to admit that it was some sort of a monument.

She was walking along, a hand in his, when suddenly she was stopped in her tracks just as though she had hit a brick wall face on. Martin noticed nothing, would have continued to walk, only her hand clung to his, pulling him back. It was ... oh, it was unmistakable! This was the spot where, two thousand years earlier, Marcus, spitted with a spear, had died calling her name. These were the very hillsides which had echoed to his warrior's shout!

'Yes? What is it, sweetheart?'

'It – it was here ...'

'Oh, the stone, the memorial stone. I can't see ... ah yes, there it is.'

She had not realised it was so close, but she followed him anyway, still handfasted, glad perhaps to be able to pass off that intimate moment of acute recollection and loss as no more than that of recognition of the memorial tablet, which she could just about make out between the close-growing heaths.

'Here we are, love. But of course it's half-buried. A lot of heathers have died since it was erected, that's plain at any rate.'

'Yes. Like the old villa under the Court, it's sunken ... there, can you see it? The name?'

Martin studied it for a moment, eyes half-closed. Then he began to heave and tug at the heathers.

'This may be quite a find,' he said breathlessly. 'I can't read all of it though, not until I've dug down. Fortunately the soil is very friable and loose, it's mainly peat I suppose. Are you going to give me a hand in the interests of science?'

'Yes, of course, but can you read Latin, Martin? I can't, unfortunately, but I did think I recognised a couple of names.'

Martin, digging with a bit of wood, grunted. 'I wasn't at public school for nothing, you know. Can you help me to clear the rubbish? Don't dig, it's hard work, just clear.'

'Well, I will ... good gracious, I never realised it was so *big* – it's got a great deal of writing on it, too.'

Martin grunted again. Sweat was pouring down his face, making him blink and rub his eyes with a filthy fist. Questa reflected that they seemed doomed to have dirty faces one way and another, every time Marcus or his villa came into their lives.

'Have some lemonade, Martin. Go on, you're dreadfully hot – are you sure you should be working so hard in this sunshine? You teased me about being tired out tomorrow, but the same applies to you, you know!'

'What? Oh yes, I'd like a drink. Then, when I've cleared it all, I'll read you what it says. So long as you won't be disappointed.'

'Oh? Was I wrong, then? Well, it doesn't matter,' Questa said. Indeed, it did not matter, because she was realising more and more, with every day that passed, that it was Martin who mattered to her now. She loved Marcus, would always love him, but he was just an episode in her life. Martin was her life, her hope, her future. She could no more forget Marcus than she could forget her father, but he would not, in future, have any real part in her life. With her marriage tomorrow, she would become a part of Martin, bone of his bone, flesh of his flesh, and that was right and proper and as it should be.

They sat down, drank some lemonade, and ate a sandwich each. Then Martin spat on his hands and got down to it whilst Questa cleared away the torn-up heather, the roots, the grasses, the small, rough rocks. At last Martin sat back on his heels and wiped his filthy hands across his sweaty face and began, silently, to read the stone, his lips moving as he sorted and translated into English the Latin words he saw before him.

'Right,' he said at last. 'It *is* a memorial stone. But it's got nothing to do with anyone being lost at sea. It's in memory of the son of Tiberius – the chap's first name is worn away – who was killed on this spot by brigands. That's the nearest I can get to it. And it was set up by his son, Gaius, whose mother was ... I'm not sure of the finer meanings, but a servant perhaps.' He stood up and walked over to where Questa was sitting, then sank down beside her and put his arm round her. 'Poor darling, are you very disappointed?'

'No. It's still a find, isn't it, Martin?' She sighed and leaned against him, then reached up and kissed his cheek, a feather-light touch. 'Shall we go home, now?'

They rode home gently, in the deepening dusk. Oddly, Questa chattered but Martin was rather quiet. He insisted on rubbing down both horses whilst Questa went indoors and cleaned herself up for dinner; consequently he was late and got a telling-off from Ran.

'It wasn't his fault, he got in an awful state digging out an old tombstone so that he could translate the writing on it for me,' Questa said. 'Then we re-buried it; it was awfully well preserved, so Martin thought it ought to be buried again, didn't you, darling?'

Darling! She had never called him that before. He touched her hand lightly, to show he had noticed, all the while aware that there was a significance about the memorial stone which he had missed. When he had read it for her he'd looked at her once, then quickly averted his eyes. Just for a moment Questa had looked stricken, vulnerable ... yet it was not the stone she had expected, so why should it affect her so?

Later that night, alone in his bed for the last time, he pictured her alone in hers. She was spending this last night in her caravan, sleeping – he hoped – on that incredibly hard little bunk. Not dreaming. He found himself almost praying that she was not dreaming.

In her narrow bed in the caravan, Questa slept. But when the moonlight came through a crack in the curtains and fell across her eyes she woke, and sighed, and wondered why she had not told Martin that they had dug up Marcus's tombstone. She hadn't understood at first, but gradually, as she thought about it, she worked it out. The slave girl, looking rounder, prettier – she had been pregnant, of course. Marcus saying he would name his first son after his brother Gaius, searching for Questa in the hills ... perhaps he had wanted to tell her he had a son. Even the family likeness which had come down through the years so that Martin was heartbreakingly like Marcus to look at made sense, now she had seen the stone.

But it wasn't important. Martin was a proud and loving man and she had to understand that he could neither accept what had happened to her – she was beginning to doubt it herself – nor the fact that she had once loved another.

She wondered about the tombstone, wished she could have read the exact wording so that she would have known a little more. But she loved Martin deeply and you do not give pain, deliberately, to those you love. It should be enough for her that Marcus lived again in Martin, though only as we all live on, in our children and our children's children.

She lay in the moonlight for a little longer, remembering all the mysteries: Dickie's shadow-people on the lawn, the pictures she had seen in the ink pool, the accident which had resulted in her being with Marcus when he needed her most. How much had really happened, and how much was just her wounded mind, seeing what others could not, fearing what others feared not, imagining whatever she needed to make life bearable? Even Dickie's shadow-people could so easily have been the result of the strange life he led at that time, with Grace using him, leaning on him, but denying him the normal life of a five-year-old boy.

A man to love without fear, that was how she had seen Marcus. A man who was all man, yet took nothing from her save a few kisses. A man who had prepared her for Martin and the love which would presently take over her whole life.

But it would never do to go to her wedding haggard and worn after a sleepless night. So she reached up and pulled the curtain across and, presently, slept. She woke when the dawn chorus started, when the first pale light of the new day tapped at the caravan window. She sat up and ran her fingers through her hair and looked across to the white gown, hanging across the narrow wardrobe, ghostly in the half-light.

Today was the day! Today was the start of it! Across the years, across the greatest divide of all, she sent a loving farewell winging to Marcus, letting him know that it was over, that she was letting him go at last.

Then she got out of bed and began to prepare herself for her wedding.